# CROCODILE CREEK:
# 24-HOUR RESCUE

### A cutting-edge medical centre
### at the heart of a community.
### Fully equipped for saving lives and loves!

**Crocodile Creek's state-of-the-art Medical
Centre and Rescue Response Unit is home to a
team of expertly trained medical professionals.
These dedicated men and women face the
challenges of life, love and medicine every day!**

### Two weddings!
Crocodile Creek is playing host to two weddings
this year, and love is definitely in the air! But…

### A cyclone is brewing!
As a severe weather front moves in,
the rescue team are poised for action—
this time with some new recruits.

### Two missing children!
As the cyclone wreaks its devastation, it soon
becomes clear that there are two little ones missing.
Now the team has to pull together like never before
to find them…before it's too late!

**Alison Roberts's
THE PLAYBOY DOCTOR'S PROPOSAL
is the first of four continuing stories revisiting
*Crocodile Creek*. Look out for books from
Meredith Webber, Marion Lennox and
Lilian Darcy. Join them every month in
Mills & Boon® Medical Romance™**

**With her arms full of the white silk train of Emily's dress and the soft tulle of her veil, Hannah was walking very slowly, her arm touching Ryan's as he held the silk ribbons joining the wreaths on the heads of the bridal couple. They got a little tangled at the last corner and there was a momentary pause.**

And Ryan looked at her.

There could be no mistaking the sensation of free-fall. The feeling that all the cells in her body were charged with some kind of static electricity and were desperately seeking a focus for their energy.

Or that the focus was to be found in the depths of the dark eyes that were so close to her own. This was a connection that transcended anything remotely physical. The caress of that eye contact lasted only a heartbeat, but Hannah knew it would haunt her for life.

It was a moment of truth.

A truth she hadn't expected.

One she most certainly didn't want.

She was in love with Ryan Fisher.

# THE PLAYBOY DOCTOR'S PROPOSAL

BY
ALISON ROBERTS

**MILLS & BOON**
*Pure reading pleasure*

First published in Great Britain 2007
Harlequin Mills & Boon Limited,
Eton House, 18-24 Paradise Road, Richmond, Surrey TW9 1SR

© Alison Roberts 2007

ISBN-13: 978 0 263 85261 5

Set in Times Roman 10½ on 12½ pt
03-0907-40306

Printed and bound in Spain
by Litografia Rosés, S.A., Barcelona

**Alison Roberts** lives in Christchurch, New Zealand. She began her working career as a primary school teacher, but now juggles available working hours between writing and active duty as an ambulance officer. Throwing in a large dose of parenting, housework, gardening and pet-minding keeps life busy, and teenage daughter Becky is responsible for an increasing number of days spent on equestrian pursuits. Finding time for everything can be a challenge, but the rewards make the effort more than worthwhile.

**Dear Reader**

How lucky am I?

To have colleagues who are also my friends, whose skills I have the utmost respect for, and who share a love of the genre and a dedication to making each story the best yet.

To work together and have the challenge of a scope broad enough to link several books and the sheer fun of intertwining the stories of each other's characters is an enriching experience.

So here we are, back in *Crocodile Creek,* and we're throwing a cyclone at our own bit of Northern Australia. Scary stuff!

I'm more likely to experience a bad earthquake or maybe a tsunami where I am in New Zealand, but it's a good idea to be prepared for whatever dramatic turns nature can take, and we can get some bad storms at times.

Here's what you can do if a strong wind warning is issued:

Bring your pets inside and move stock to shelter
Secure outdoor furniture
Tape across large windows to prevent shattering.
Stay inside during storm.
Partially open a window on the sheltered side
  of the house.
Stay away from doors and windows.
If you have to go outside, watch out for dangling
  and broken power lines.

Is a cyclone enough of a link for our stories? We didn't think so. There's also a little boy called Felixx…

Happy reading

Love

*Alison*

# PROLOGUE

'SHH, now, Felixx!'

'Hush, OK?'

'Silence. We have to have silence for Alanya to get well.'

For days this was all he'd heard, it seemed to Felixx. He crept around on the edge of Alanya's illness, too scared to ask how bad she was, shut away from seeing her except for one or two short visits to the wellness shelter each day, during which he knew he had to be silent or she wouldn't get better fast enough.

Sometimes he asked people, 'How's Mummy?' He liked to call her Mummy because that's who she was. She always wanted him to call her Alanya, because that was her spirit name, but as she couldn't hear him right now, he said 'Mummy' and it helped a little bit.

The silence helped, too. He had to stay as quiet as anything, or she might not get well. He knew that, but it was so hard. The fish on his sneaker helped. Mummy had drawn it with his felt pens. Mostly the bright orange one. She'd done it the day he'd showed her the hole.

'We can't afford a new shoe just yet,' she'd said. 'So let's make it special. The hole can be his eye, see?'

He could poke his finger in the hole. In and out. It was tight at first but now it was easy. His finger went in and out.

In and out.

It helped him to stay quiet. To stop the questions he so badly wanted to ask, like, 'Mummy...Alanya...are you feeling better? Do you need more medicine?'

She didn't seem to be eating very much. They gave her carrot juice to drink, to drain the toxins from her system. How long did toxins take to drain?

Where did they come out?

He was too scared to ask any of these questions, but he listened more than the healing sisters thought. He heard words like 'worried' and 'taking too long' and after this he stayed even quieter, stopped even asking, 'How's Mummy?' in case his talking, even outside the healing shelter, was the thing stopping her from getting well.

Late one night...he couldn't remember, maybe the sixth or seventh night of her illness...he couldn't sleep, and crept over to the healing shelter because there was light coming from its windows. It was cold and his feet were bare and he didn't dare go inside, but he listened underneath the window and heard more words. 'Getting worse' and 'I don't know' and 'ambulance'.

After this, everything got so confusing, when he thought about it he couldn't think the way it had gone. He fell asleep on the couch on the veranda of the healing shelter, and a big car came with red lights. He hid under the blanket in case he got in trouble for being there. He heard men's voices. 'Too late' and 'useless' and 'bloody quack treatments'. Someone found him—Raina, one of the healing sisters—and he pretended to be asleep and she carried him gently in her arms to his bed, and by the time he got there he must have really been asleep because he didn't remember anything else until morning.

Then there were more words—'very peaceful' and 'gone away on the most wonderful journey'—but he was so good, he didn't say anything himself in case it made Mummy…better call her Alanya…in case it made her worse. A lot of boring time went by. He wasn't allowed to see her at all. He had some meals, breakfast and lunch. Were they saying it was Alanya who had gone on the wonderful journey? When was she coming back? He didn't want to ask because that would not have been hushing and staying silent.

Raina sat him down and hugged him and kissed his forehead and told him, 'Your auntie Janey is going to come and get you, sweetheart.'

He didn't know he had an auntie Janey. He wanted to ask who she was and when she was coming but he was so, so good, he stayed quiet and silent and hushed and didn't say a word.

# CHAPTER ONE

'YOU'RE *not!*'

'Yes, I am. What's the big deal? It's only a few days off work.'

'You never take days off work. In all the time I've known you, Hannah, and that's, what—three years? You've never missed a shift.'

Senior Nurse Jennifer Bradley collected the paper emerging from the twelve-lead ECG machine and Dr Hannah Jackson cast an experienced eye over the results.

'Bit of right heart failure—there's notching on the P waves but everything else looks pretty good for an eighty-six-year-old. No sign of infarct.'

The elderly patient, who had been sound asleep while the recording was being taken, suddenly opened her eyes.

'Give it back,' she said loudly. 'You're a *naughty* girl!'

The complaint was loud enough to attract the attention of several staff members near the central desk. Heads turned in astonishment and Hannah sighed inwardly. One of them would be her fellow senior registrar, Ryan Fisher, wouldn't it? And, of course, he had a grin from ear to ear on overhearing the accusation.

Jennifer was stifling a smile with difficulty. 'What's the matter, Mrs Matheson?'

'She's stolen my handbag! I've got a lot of money in my purse and she's taken it, the little blonde trollop!'

Hannah heard a snigger from the small audience by the central desk. It would have been a good idea to pull the curtain of this cubicle but in the early hours of a Monday morning, with the emergency department virtually empty, it hadn't seemed a priority.

'Your handbag's quite safe, Mrs Matheson,' she said soothingly. 'It's in the bag with your other belongings.'

'Show me!'

Hannah fished in the large, brown paper bag printed with the label PATIENT PROPERTY and withdrew a cavernous black handbag that must have been purchased at least forty years ago.

'Give it to me!'

Hands gnarled with arthritis fumbled with the clasp. The bag was tipped upside down and several items fell onto Doris Matheson's lap. The contents of the opened packet of peppermints rolled off to bounce on the floor and a number of used, screwed-up handkerchiefs were thrown after them.

'There, I told you! There was a *thousand* dollars in here and it's *gone!*' A shaky finger pointed at Hannah. '*She's* taken it! Call the police!'

Ryan wasn't content to observe now. He was standing at the end of the bed. Faded blue eyes peered suspiciously at the tall, broad masculine figure.

'Are *you* the police?'

Ryan flashed the ghost of a wink at both Jennifer and Hannah. 'I've had some experience with handcuffs, if that's any help.'

Hannah shut her eyes briefly. How did Ryan get away with this sort of behaviour? Sometimes, if he was any more laid back, he'd be asleep. What a shame Doris hadn't stayed asleep. She was sniffing imperiously now.

'Arrest that woman,' she commanded.

'Dr Jackson?' Ryan eyed Hannah with great interest. She couldn't help the way the corners of her mouth twitched. This *was* pretty funny. It was just a shame it was going to give Ryan ammunition he wouldn't hesitate to use.

'She's stolen my money.'

Ryan stepped closer. He leaned down and smiled at Doris. One of those killer smiles he usually reserved for the women he was flirting with. Which was just about every female member of staff.

Except Hannah.

His voice was a deep, sexy rumble. *'Really?'*

Doris Matheson stared back. Her mouth opened and then closed. Hannah could swear she fluttered her eye-lashes and stifled another sigh at the typical feminine reaction to being the centre of this man's attention. The coy smile Ryan received was only surprising because of the age of their patient.

'What's your name, young man?'

'Ryan Fisher, ma'am.'

'And you're a policeman?'

'Not really.' Ryan's tone was that of a conspirator re-vealing a secret. 'I'm a doctor.'

The charm he was exuding was palpable. Totally fake but, for once, Hannah could appreciate the talent. It wasn't being directed at her, was it? She didn't need to arm herself with the memories of the misery men like Ryan could cause the women who trusted them. It was certainly defusing a potentially aggravating situation here.

'Ooh,' Doris said. 'Are you going to look after me?'

'You're about to go to X-Ray, Mrs Matheson,' Hannah said.

'What for?'

'We think you've broken your hip.'

'How did I do that?'

'You fell over.'

*'Did I?'* The question, like the others, was directed at Ryan despite it being Hannah who was supplying the answers.

'Yes.' Hannah looped her stethoscope back around her neck. 'And we can't find any medical reason why you might have fallen.' The cause had been obvious as soon as Hannah had been within sniffing distance of her patient. She hadn't needed the ambulance officer's report of an astonishing number of empty whisky bottles lined up on window-sills.

Ryan was smiling again but with mock severity this time. 'Have you had something to drink tonight, Mrs Matheson?'

She actually giggled. 'Call me Doris, dear. And, yes, I do like a wee dram. Helps me sleep, you know.'

'I'm sure it does, Doris.' Ryan's tone was understanding. He raised an eyebrow. 'But it can make it difficult to remember some things, too, can't it?'

'Ooh, yes.' Doris was looking coy again. 'Do you know, I almost forgot where the bathroom was one night?'

'Did you forget how much money you might have had in your purse, too?'

'I *never* keep money in my purse, dear! It might get stolen.'

'It might, indeed.' Hannah got a 'there you go, all sorted' kind of glance from Ryan. She tried hard to look suitably grateful.

'I keep it in the fridge,' Doris continued happily. 'In the margarine tub.'

'Good thinking.' Ryan stepped back as an orderly

entered the cubicle. 'Maybe I'll see you when you get back from X-Ray, Doris.'

'Oh, I hope so, dear.'

Hannah held up her hand as her patient's bed was pushed away. 'Don't say it,' she warned.

'Say what?' Ryan asked innocently.

'Anything about naughty girls,' Jennifer supplied helpfully. 'Or arresting them. And especially nothing about handcuffs.'

'Not even fluffy ones?'

Jennifer gave him a shove. 'Go away. Try and find something useful to do.'

They were both laughing as Ryan walked away. Relaxed. Enjoying the diversion of an amusing incident. But Jennifer could afford to enjoy Ryan's company, couldn't she? Happily married with two adorable small children at home, she was in no danger of being led astray.

Neither was Hannah, of course. She knew too much about men like Ryan Fisher. Great-looking, *fun* men like the ones who'd made her mother's life a misery after her dad died, not to mention the guy who'd broken her sister's heart not so long ago.

Hannah only ever let herself get involved with nice, trustworthy, serious men like her father had been. She'd believed herself to be totally immune to men of Ryan's ilk.

Until three months ago.

Until she'd met Ryan Fisher.

Jennifer was still smiling as she tidied the ECG leads away. 'I still can't believe you're taking time off,' she told Hannah. 'I've never even known you to be sick. You're the one who always fills in for other people like Ryan when *they* take days off work.'

Hannah glanced towards the central desk. Ryan—the

king of holidays and all other good things life had to offer—was now leaning casually on the counter, talking to a tired-looking receptionist. Probably telling her one of his inexhaustible supply of dumb blonde jokes. Sure enough, a smile was starting to edge the lines of weariness from Maureen's face.

'I'm going to check the trauma room while it's quiet,' Hannah told Jennifer.

'I'll help you.' Hannah's news of taking time off had clearly intrigued her friend, who didn't consider their conversation finished. 'And there I was thinking that, if *I* didn't drag you out occasionally, you'd spend all your time off studying or something.'

Hannah picked up the laryngoscope on top of the airway trolley and pulled the blade open to check that the battery for the light was still functional. 'Are you saying I have no life?'

'I'm saying your career takes the prize as your raison d'etre.'

'I always wanted to be a doctor.' Hannah snapped the blade back in line with its handle, switching off the light. 'Now that I *am* one, I intend to be a very good one.'

'You *are* a very good one. The best.'

'We'll see.' The glance between the two women acknowledged the growing speculation within the department over who was going to win the new consultant position. She had been the only serious contender until Ryan had thrown his hat into the ring today. Was that why she was so aware of his presence in the department tonight? Why everything about him seemed to be rubbing her up the wrong way even more than usual?

'Anyway…' The wind had been taken out of Jenny's sails, but not by much. She opened a box of syringes to restock the IV trolley. 'You don't need to prove how good you are by living and breathing emergency medicine.'

'So you're saying I'm an emergency department geek?' Hannah tilted the ceiling-mounted, operating-theatre light so it was in a neutral position. It would be fair enough if she was. Hannah loved this space. Fabulous lighting, X-ray and ultrasound facilities, every piece of equipment they could possibly need to cover the basics of resuscitation and stabilisation of a critically ill patient. Airway, breathing, circulation. To be faced with a life-threatening emergency and succeed in saving that life was all the excitement Hannah needed in her life.

Jenny caught her expression and clicked her tongue with mock exasperation. 'I'm just saying you could do with more in your life than work.'

'And that's precisely why I'm taking a few days off.'

'Touché.' Jenny grinned, magnanimous in defeat. 'OK.' She shoved the syringes into their allocated slot and then used her forefinger to stir the supply of luer plugs and IV connectors, pretending to count. 'So where the hell is Crocodile Creek, anyway?'

'Australia. Far north Queensland.'

'Oh! Has this got something to do with your sister?'

'Yes. I've been invited to a wedding.'

'Susie's getting *married?*'

'No, though I'm sure she'd be over the moon if it *was* her wedding. She's being a bridesmaid to her best friend, Emily.'

'Do you know Emily?'

'No.'

'So why have you been invited to her wedding?'

'Well…' Hannah leaned against the bed for a moment. It wasn't often they got a quiet spell, even at 2 a.m. on a Monday morning and the break hadn't gone on long enough to get boring yet. 'Susie didn't have a partner to invite and we haven't seen each other since she jumped the ditch and came to New Zealand for Christmas. I'm starting to feel guilty about how long it's been.'

'It's only March and it's a hell of a long way to go to ease a guilty conscience. Auckland to Cairns is about a six-hour flight, isn't it?'

'It sure is.' Hannah groaned. 'And then there's the little plane from Cairns to Crocodile Creek, which will take another couple of hours, I guess.'

'It must be a long way north.'

'About as far as you can get. The hospital there is the rescue base for the whole of far north Queensland. That's why I need the Friday on top of the weekend. I have to get right into the heartland of sugar and cane toads.'

'Eew!'

'Actually, it's right on the coast. It sounds gorgeous.'

'You've never been there before?'

'No, and Susie's been living there for as long as I've been working here. It's high time I checked out what my little sister is up to.'

'I thought you were twins.'

By tacit consent, the doctor and nurse were leaving the trauma room, satisfied it was ready for a new emergency. Hopefully, they'd be back in there soon with some real work to do.

'She's four minutes younger than me.'

'And she's a physiotherapist, right?'

'Yeah. She started medical school with me but she hated it. Too much pressure.'

'You must be quite different.'

'Personality-wise, definitely. To look at, no. We're identical.'

'Wow! Do you have, like, that twin thing?'

'Which "twin thing" is that?' They were near the central desk now. Ryan had disappeared, presumably into the only cubicle with a drawn curtain. The nurse on triage duty, Wayne, was sitting, drumming his fingers on the counter.

'You know, when one twin sprains her ankle, say, here in Auckland and the other twin falls over in a supermarket in central London.'

Hannah laughed, dismissing the suggestion with a shake of her sleek head. But was it so ridiculous? Was it just that she was missing a sister who had always also been her best friend or did those niggling doubts about how happy Susie was have a basis in some form of telepathic communication? Was the urge to travel thousands of miles at a very inconvenient time to attend the wedding of two people she only knew through Susie's emails just an excuse?

'Apparently this wedding is going to be great fun.' Hannah tried to find a more rational explanation for the urge she hadn't been able to resist. 'The groom, Mike, is Greek and his parents own a boutique hotel right in the cove. Susie reckons it'll be the biggest party the Creek has ever seen.'

Jennifer's peal of laughter made several heads turn.

'What's so funny?' Hannah's eye was caught by the light on the radio receiver that linked the department with the ambulance service. It was blinking.

Jennifer could hardly get the words out clearly. 'You're going to *My Big Fat Creek Wedding*!'

Grinning, Hannah still managed to beat Wayne to the microphone. 'Emergency Department.'

'Auckland four eight here. How do you receive?'

'Loud and clear,' Hannah responded, her grin fading rapidly. 'Go ahead.'

'We're coming to you from the scene of a high-speed

multiple MVA. The chopper's just landing to collect a second seriously injured patient who's currently trapped, but we're coming to you with a status-one seven-year-old boy.'

The grin had long gone. Status one was as serious as it could get. Under CPR, not breathing or uncontrollable haemorrhage were all possibilities for the priority designation. This ambulance would be coming towards the hospital under lights and sirens.

'Injuries?'

'Head and facial trauma. Partially unrestrained front-seat passenger—the safety belt wasn't latched securely.'

This wasn't the time to feel angry at someone failing to strap a child into a car seat properly. Or to wonder why they were travelling at 2 a.m. in the first place.

'Vital signs?'

'GCS of 3.'

The child was profoundly unconscious. Quite possibly due to bleeding around his brain.

'Airway?'

'Unsecured.' The paramedic raised his voice as the siren came on in the background. The vehicle must be in heavier traffic now. At night, just having the beacons flashing could be enough warning of the urgency of their mission. 'There's severe facial trauma and swelling. We've got an OP airway in but that's all.'

The boy needed intubation. Securing an airway and optimising oxygen levels were a priority in a head injury. Especially in a child because they had a greater chance of neurological recovery than an adult after a head injury and therefore warranted aggressive treatment in the early stages. If the paramedics had been unable to intubate due to the level of trauma, it could mean that this was going to be a challenging case.

Hannah could feel her adrenaline levels rising and the tension was spreading. Nearby staff were all listening avidly and the curtain on cubicle 4 flicked back to reveal that Ryan was also aware of what was happening. Hannah's heightened awareness registered the interest and at some subconscious level something like satisfaction was added to the emotional mix. She was taking this call.

This would be her case, not Ryan's. Just the kind of case she needed to showcase the skills that would be a major consideration in choosing the new consultant for the department.

'What's the oxygen saturation level?' she queried briskly.

'Ninety-four percent.'

Too low. 'Blood pressure?'

'One-thirty over sixty-five. Up from one-twenty five minutes ago.'

Too high for a seven-year-old. And rising. It could well be a sign of increasing intracranial pressure.

'Heart rate?'

'One hundred. Down from about one-thirty.'

Too slow for Hannah's peace of mind. And dropping. It could also be a worrying sign. 'What's your ETA?'

'Approximately five minutes.'

'We'll be ready for you.' Casting a glance over her shoulder, Hannah could see Ryan moving towards the resuscitation area she and Jennifer had just checked. Not that she was about to decline any assistance for dealing with the incoming case but she didn't want Ryan taking over. It wasn't as though there was only one victim arriving, was it? She pushed the button on the microphone again.

'Do you know the ETA for the chopper?'

'Negative. Fire service is on scene, though.'

It shouldn't take them long to cut the second victim clear of the wreckage, then. 'And that's also a status-one patient?'

'Affirmative. Chest trauma. It's the mother of our patient.'

Ryan would be able to lead the team on that case. In resus 2. Or they could share the main trauma room if necessary. Hannah's plan of action was forming rapidly as she replaced the microphone.

'Put out a call for an anaesthetist, please, Wayne,' she directed. 'And let's get a neurosurgical consult down here. Sounds like we might need someone from Plastics, too. Jenny, you're on the trauma team tonight, aren't you?'

'Yes.'

'And you, Wayne?'

'Yes. Resus 1?'

Hannah nodded, already moving towards the area. She pulled one of the protective plastic aprons from the large box on the wall. Ryan was already tying his behind his back.

'Could be a tricky airway management,' he said.

'Mmm. I've called for some anaesthetic back-up but I'll see how I go.' The direct look Hannah gave Ryan could leave him in no doubt that she intended to lead this resuscitation effort. The subtle twitch of an eyebrow let her know the message had been received and understood. It also hinted at amusement rather than intimidation.

'I'll stay until the mother gets here,' he said calmly. 'In case you need a hand.'

'Thanks.' The acknowledgement was perfectly sincere. There was a child's life at stake here and Hannah would never let any personal considerations affect her performance. She would stand back in a flash if she thought Ryan's skills would improve the management. Never mind that he would get the credit for managing a difficult case.

It was just annoying that people that mattered were keeping a count of those credits at present. And disappointing that a competitive edge of any kind had crept into

Hannah's working environment when one of the things she loved best about her work was the way a team of people could work together and the only kudos that really mattered was a successful outcome to that work.

The decision on the consultant's position was only a week or two away. A position that represented everything Hannah was striving towards in a career she was passionate about. Why had Ryan decided to compete at the last minute like this? It wasn't as if he really *needed* the position. He didn't have a massive student loan, the repayments of which would benefit enormously from an increase in salary. He didn't need to prove himself in a field that was still dominated by males in senior positions. He was an Australian. Auckland wasn't even his home town.

She couldn't help flicking a glance towards the tall man who had now donned protective eyewear and a pair of gloves and was lounging at the head end of the bed. Why hadn't Ryan Fisher just stayed on his side of the ditch? In that Sydney emergency department where he'd honed his not inconsiderable skills? Life would be so much easier if he had. And it wasn't just due to that professional competition.

Jenny pushed the IV trolley into an easily accessible position and then stood on tiptoe to check that the tubes attached to the overhead suction and oxygen supplies were firmly in place. It was still a stretch for her short stature and Ryan was quick to step forward.

Without a word, he saved Jenny the awkward task and then gave her one of those killer smiles in response to her thanks. The senior nurse turned back to the IV trolley but Hannah noticed the extra glance that went in Ryan's direction.

Not that he had noticed. The registrar was lounging again, his keen glance taking in the mill of the gathering trauma team and registering the growing tension.

The few minutes before the arrival of a serious case was a strange time. A calm before a storm of unknown proportions. Equipment was primed and ready. Staff were wearing protective gear and waiting. Wayne stood behind a kind of lectern that had the paperwork necessary to document every moment of the resuscitation effort and he was fiddling with a pen.

Hannah had pulled on gloves and was unrolling the airway pack on the top of a stainless-steel trolley. Others were simply standing. Waiting. There was nothing to do until their patient came rolling through those double doors. Nobody liked to speculate in too much detail on what was about to arrive because that could give them tunnel vision. A conversation that required distraction of mental focus was just as unwanted. What usually happened was a bit of gossip or a joke. Light-hearted banter that could relieve tension before it achieved destructive proportions. Something that could be abandoned as easily as begun.

And Ryan could always be counted on to provide a joke that would make everybody laugh.

Everybody except Hannah. She made a point of never laughing at Ryan's jokes because the vast majority of them were at the expense of women with blonde hair. Like hers.

Sure enough, he was telling one now.

'So this blonde—Cindy—is in desperate financial straights and she prays for help. "Please, God, let me win the lottery or I'll have to sell my car." But she doesn't win so she prays again, "Please, God, let me win the lottery. I'm going to have to sell my car *and* my house."'

Everybody was listening. Or half listening. Waiting for the distant wail of the siren that would advertise that the calm was over. Hannah kept her gaze on the trolley, checking that there was a range of paediatric-sized tubes and that the laryngoscope was still working.

She didn't have to look at Ryan to know exactly what the image would be. He would be standing completely at ease with just a hint of a smile and a twinkle in those dark eyes that advertised an upcoming punchline. It might be a terrible joke but everybody would be listening and would be prepared to laugh because Ryan commanded that sort of attention. And popularity. Without even trying.

Hannah lips pressed themselves into a thinner line as she made sure that the more serious gear that might be needed for a surgical airway was at hand. No, it wasn't just the professional competition that irked her. It was the fact that she had been as attracted to Ryan as every other woman who'd set eyes on him from the moment he'd arrived in this department three months ago.

It had been so unexpected. He was the epitome of the type of man she had always steered very well clear of. Despised, even, thanks to the collateral damage she had seen them produce in the lives of women she cared about. One of life's golden people. She had probably been the first woman ever to freeze out an advance from him. Was that why he was persevering for so long? Did she represent some kind of challenge?

'She *still* didn't win,' Ryan was continuing. 'She's down on her knees, pleading and this time God speaks to her.' His voice dropped to a deep rumble that Hannah could actually feel in her bones. 'And he says, "Work with me here, Cindy. *Buy a ticket!*"'

Sure enough, there was a wave of laughter. A wave that faded with dramatic swiftness, drowned out by the faint wail of a siren. Then the sound of the approaching siren died as it sped onto the hospital grounds with just its beacons flashing. Seconds later, the stretcher appeared. A third crew member was moving rapidly beside the stretcher, a bag-mask unit over the face of the child, trying to keep oxygen levels up on the short journey between the ambulance and the trauma bay.

The team went into action as a unit. The transfer of the small body was smooth—made easier by the fact he was strapped to a backboard with a collar to protect his neck. And although this team was well used to seeing victims of major trauma, it was a shock to get their first close-up view of this little boy.

Waiting at the head of the bed to manage the airway, Hannah sucked in a quick breath that was almost a gasp. No wonder he hadn't been intubated and it would have been far too dangerous to attempt a nasopharyngeal airway. His nose and mouth were almost lost beneath swollen and lacerated tissue. There were obvious facial fractures and the eyelids were so swollen it was impossible to open them enough to assess the pupils with a torch.

'Do we know his name?'

'Brendon,' one of the paramedics supplied. 'His mother was initially conscious enough to be calling for him.'

He was wearing pyjamas, Hannah noticed as she leaned forward. Bright red racing cars on a blue background. 'Brendon, can you hear me?' She reached over his shoulder. Why had he been in a car in pyjamas instead of safely asleep in his bed? 'Squeeze my hand if you can hear me, sweetheart.'

A response hadn't really been expected and Hannah moved swiftly to take the tip of the suction unit Jennifer was holding. The child was moving air but there was a nasty bubbling sound and the probe on his finger revealed an oxygen saturation level that was far too low to be acceptable.

'Rapid sequence intubation?'

'If it's possible.' Hannah's gaze flicked up, relieved to find one of the senior anaesthetic registrars now standing right beside her.

Ryan was on the other side of the bed and farther down, moving in to assess IV access and flow and to look for other potential injuries as the pyjamas were cut clear of the small body.

ECG electrodes were being attached. Jennifer was using a bag mask to assist the delivery of oxygen. Hannah suctioned as much blood as she could from Brendon's mouth and nose.

'I can't see anything that clearly looks like CSF,' she said. Not that that discounted the possibility of skull fractures or spinal damage.

'Saturation's down to ninety per cent. Let's go for the intubation,' the anaesthetist advised. He took the bag mask from Jennifer and began to squeeze it rapidly, increasing the amount of oxygen reserves to cover the down time for trying to get a tube into Brendon's throat. He was clearly prepared to provide back-up rather than taking over the procedure.

Hannah drew in a slow breath to dispel any nerves. She heard herself issue instructions for the drugs needed, like suxamethonium to relax muscles and atropine to prevent the heart slowing dangerously. The formula for determining the size of the endotracheal tube was there instantly—the diameter equalled the age of the child divided by four, plus four.

'I'll need a 6 millimetre, uncuffed tube,' she informed Jennifer. 'And I want you to hold his head while we ease this collar off.'

It was a challenge, easing the blade of the laryngoscope past the swollen lips, broken teeth and a badly lacerated tongue, and Hannah had to use the suction unit more than once. It was an unexpectedly easy victory to visualise the vocal cords and slip the tube into place.

'I'm in.' The tone was one of satisfaction rather than triumph, however. There was still a long way to go but at least they were on the way to stabilising a critically ill patient.

'Well done.'

With her stethoscope now on Brendon's chest to check for correct tube placement and equal air entry, the quiet words of praise were muted and, for a moment, Hannah thought they might have come from Ryan.

But he was no longer standing beside Brendon. Hannah had been concentrating so hard on her task she had managed to block the sounds of the second patient's arrival and the stretcher was now being swiftly manoeuvred to the other side of the trauma room.

'Blunt chest trauma with tachycardia and hypotension. No sign of a tension pneumothorax.' she heard Ryan stating. 'We could be dealing with an acute pericardial tamponade.'

Would Ryan attempt a procedure to drain off the fluid inhibiting the function of the young mother's heart? It would be a very impressive coup as far as patient treatment if it was successful. Hannah couldn't help casting frequent glances towards his side of the room as she worked with the anaesthetist to get Brendon's ventilator setting right, supervised the amount of IV fluid that was being administered, started an infusion of mannitol, which could help reduce intracranial pressure, and arranged transfer for an urgent CT scan of the boy's head and neck.

Sure enough, Ryan was preparing to intubate his patient, cardiac monitoring was established and kits requested for both pericardiocentesis and chest drainage. Ryan looked determined and confident but less than happy about the challenge he was about to face. And no wonder. From what Hannah could see, the woman's condition was deteriorating rapidly.

Ominous extra beats were disrupting the line of the ECG trace on the screen of the monitor.

There was time for one more, rapid secondary survey on Brendon before he was taken to the CT suite.

'Some of these bruises look old,' she commented.

'Maybe he plays rugby,' Jennifer suggested.

'You reckon his mother does as well?' Wayne had been helping Ryan's team in the initial preparation of his patient. 'She's covered in bruises as well.'

Hannah eyed the clothing remnants Wayne was putting into a patient property bag. 'Dressing-gown?' she queried.

He nodded. 'I don't think their trip was planned.'

A police officer was standing well to one side of the now crowded area. 'Have any relatives been contacted?' Hannah asked him.

'We didn't need to. The car she was driving had just been reported stolen.' The police officer's face was grim. 'By her husband.'

Hannah absorbed the information like a kind of physical blow. Was her patient an innocent young victim caught up in a situation involving domestic violence? Had his mother's desperate bid to protect him ended in a disaster he might never recover from? Would he even still have a mother?

It seemed unlikely. Ryan was sounding uncharacteristically tense as Brendon's stretcher was taken through the double doors on the way to CT.

'We've got VF. She's arrested. Charging to 200 joules. Stand clear!' He looked up as he recharged the paddles. 'Hannah, are you free?'

Hannah's hesitation was only momentary. She had been

planning to follow protocol and accompany Brendon but he already had an expert medical escort in the anaesthetic registrar. She knew what Ryan would do if the roles were reversed and *she* asked for assistance. Hannah turned back.

'I'm free,' she said quietly. 'What do you need?'

# CHAPTER TWO

'WE'VE got sinus rhythm.'

Ryan dropped the defibrillator paddles with relief. The same kind of relief he'd noted when Hannah had turned back to help before he'd delivered that last shock. Not that he'd doubted he could count on her in a professional capacity. He could see her pulling on gloves and positioning herself beside the tray containing the pericardiocentesis and chest drain kits as he reached to check his patient's pulse.

'Carotid is barely palpable,' he reported grimly.

'Systolic pressure is fifty-nine,' Wayne confirmed.

'Let's shut down the IV. Just run it enough to keep the vein open,' Ryan ordered. 'There's been no response to a fluid challenge and if we're dealing with thoracic haemorrhage it'll only be making things worse.'

'Ventricular ectopics starting again.' Hannah had an eye on the monitor screen. 'And the systolic pressure is dropping. Down to fifty-five.'

The patient was threatening to arrest again. Ryan reached for a scalpel and Hannah had the forceps ready to hand him a moment later. Then the cannula for the chest drain. In less than a minute, blood was draining freely into the bottle. Too freely. All too soon, the bottle was almost full.

'Have we got someone from Cardiothoracic on the way?'

'No.' Jennifer shook her head at Ryan's terse query. 'Sorry. They're unavailable for fifteen to twenty minutes. They're tied up in Theatre with a post-bypass complication.'

'Have we got a thoracotomy kit?' He could almost hear a collective intake of breath. 'She's exsanguinating from a chest injury and about to go into cardiac arrest again. A thoracotomy might be a long shot but it's the only hope we've got.' Ryan knew the statistics were not on his side but at least they would be doing something other than watching this woman bleed to death.

Hannah nodded once, as though she had gone through the same thought processes and was in agreement with him. 'Want me to scrub as well?'

'Yes. Thanks.'

Wayne was sent to find the rarely used sterile kit. Jennifer took over the task of manually ventilating their patient. Ryan scrubbed fast. Ideally he should have the chest opened in less than two minutes. Faster, if there was another cardiac arrest.

'Have you done this before?' Hannah squeezed soap into her hands beside him.

'Yes. You?'

'Never even seen it.'

'Know the indications?'

'Penetrating thoracic injury with traumatic arrest or unresponsive hypotension or blunt injury with unresponsive hypotension or exsanguination from the chest tube. Overall survival is between four and thirty-three per cent but higher for penetrating injury.'

'We've got VF again,' Jennifer warned. 'No…it's asystole.'

Speed was now critical. A flat-line ECG meant that the heart couldn't be shocked into producing a rhythm again. Chest compressions on someone with blunt trauma were also contraindicated because it could worsen the injury. Opening the chest was the only option with any hope at all now.

It was good that Hannah had never seen the technique. Explaining things as he started this incredibly invasive procedure somehow eased the tension of a desperate measure to save a life.

'We'll make bilateral thoracotomies in the fifth intercostal space, mid-axillary line—same as for a chest drain.' Ryan worked swiftly with a scalpel and then a heavy pair of scissors. 'I'll be ready for the Gigli saw in a sec.'

He showed her how to use the serrated wire saw, drawing a handle under the sternum with a pair of forceps and then joining the handles and using smooth, long strokes to cut through the sternum from the inside out.

Hannah was ready with the rib spreaders. For someone who hadn't done this before, her calmness and ability to follow direction was a huge bonus.

'You can see why this is called a "clam shell" thoracotomy,' he said as he spread the ribs away from the anterior incisions. 'Suction, thanks.' Ryan sucked out blood and clots from the chest cavity, hoping it would be enough for the heart to start beating again spontaneously.

It wasn't.

'Where's she bleeding from?'

'Haven't found it yet.' Ryan placed both hands around the heart. 'I'm starting internal cardiac massage. Can you find and compress the aorta against the spine, Hannah? We want to maximise coronary and cerebral perfusion. I'll clamp it in a minute.'

* * *

She was totally out of her depth here. It was a huge relief when back-up from the cardiothoracic surgeons finally arrived. They were impressed with Ryan's management of the case so far, which was hardly surprising. Hannah wouldn't have had the confidence or skill to go further than the chest drain insertion.

The thought that Ryan might deserve the consultant's position more than she did was not a pleasant one.

Edged out as people with far more experience than she had took over, Hannah could only watch. It was hard, feeling the tension and increasing frustration as they failed to get the young woman's heart started again, having controlled the haemorrhage from the damaged aorta.

Maureen's signal, with the message that Brendon was now in the paediatric ICU and an invitation to discuss the results of the CT scan with the consultant, was welcome. Hannah slipped, unnoticed, from the resuscitation area.

She couldn't afford to stand around admiring Ryan's skill and thinking how easily he might win the position she'd wanted for so long. Or to share his disappointment at the inevitable failure he was facing. Empathy would create a connection that was too personal. Even worse than laughing at one of his stupid jokes. It would only make it that much harder to maintain the necessary distance between them.

Any reduction in that distance could only make her vulnerable.

And Hannah Jackson did not do vulnerable.

She'd always been the strong one. Ever since she was ten years old and her father's sudden death had made her small family almost fall apart. Hannah had been strong for her mother. For Susie. For herself.

The lesson had been hard but valuable. Strength was

protection. The only way to get through life without being scarred too deeply.

Being too tired didn't help when it came to being strong.

When Hannah entered the staffroom nearly an hour later, she could feel Ryan's dejection all too easily. He had his back to her as he made coffee but his body language said it all. Slumped shoulders. Bent head. The way he was stirring his mug so slowly. If it had been any other colleague she wouldn't have hesitated in offering commiseration. A comforting touch or even a hug. But this was Ryan. Distance was obligatory.

'No go, huh?'

'Nah.' Ryan straightened his back. 'Didn't really expect to win that one but it was worth a try. Want coffee?'

'Sure, but I'll make it.'

Ryan was already spooning coffee into a second mug. 'You take sugar?'

'No.'

'Milk?'

'No.'

He'd been in the department for three months and didn't know how she took her coffee but she was willing to bet he'd know the preferences of all the female staff who responded to his flirting. And that was every one of them.

Except her.

'So how's your little guy, then?'

'Not flash. He's in paediatric ICU but the scan was horrible. Multi-focal bleeds. If he does survive, he'll be badly brain damaged.'

'Might be better if he doesn't, then. You saw the father?'

'Yeah.' There was no need for further comment. The glance Ryan gave Hannah as he handed her the mug of black coffee told her he shared her opinion that the man she'd had to talk to about the serious condition of his child was an uncaring brute. Responsible for the death of his wife and quite likely his son, not to mention the admittedly less serious injuries sustained by the other drivers involved, and he hadn't given the impression of being overly perturbed about any of it. 'And they can't even charge him for anything.'

'No.' Ryan went and sat down on one of the comfortable armchairs dotted around the edge of the room.

The silence was heavy. Too heavy.

Ryan cleared his throat. 'Hey, have you heard the one about the blonde who didn't like blonde jokes?'

Hannah sighed. She sat down at the central table, deliberately putting Ryan out of sight behind her right shoulder. Maybe it wasn't good to sit in a depressed silence but this was going a bit too far in the other direction, wasn't it? She sipped her coffee without saying anything but Ryan clearly ignored the signals of disinterest.

'She went to this show where a ventriloquist was using his dummy to tell blonde jokes. You know, like, how do you change a blonde's mind?' He raised his voice and sounded as though he was trying to speak without moving his lips. "Blow in her ear!" And what do you do if a blonde throws a pin at you? "Run, she's still holding the grenade."'

'Yeah, yeah.' Hannah allowed herself to sound annoyed. 'I know.'

'Well, so did this blonde in the audience. She was furious. She jumps to her feet. "I've had enough of this", she shouts. "How dare you stereotype women this way? What does the colour of someone's hair have to do with her worth as a human being? It's people like you that keep women like me from reaching my full potential. You and your kind continue to perpetrate discrimination against not only blondes but women in general and it's *not* funny!"'

'Mmm.' Despite herself, Hannah was listening to the joke. So Ryan was actually aware of why someone like herself might take offence at his humour? Interesting. Did that mean he was intentionally trying to get under her skin? That his charm with her was as fake as it had been with Doris Matheson and he actually disliked her type as much as she did his?

Ryan's tone was deadpan. 'The ventriloquist was highly embarrassed. He goes red and starts apologising profusely but the blonde yells at him again. "Stay out of this, mister. I'm talking to that little jerk on your knee!"'

Hannah snorted. Somehow she managed to disguise the reluctant laughter as a sound more like derision. She didn't want to laugh, dammit! Not at one of Ryan's jokes and not when she'd just been through a gruelling, heart-breaking and probably fruitless couple of hours' work. She knew exactly why he was trying to make her laugh. It had to be the quickest way of defusing an overly emotional reaction to a case. But if she let him make her feel better, it would be worse than empathising with *him*. She could feel the connection there, waiting to happen. It needed dealing with. She had to push Ryan as far away as possible.

'You just can't help yourself, can you?'

'I thought you might appreciate that one.'

'What makes you think I'm in the mood for jokes right now?' Hannah swivelled so that she could give Ryan a direct look. 'Doesn't anything dent your warped sense of humour? Even a battered wife who died trying to get her child to a safe place?'

'That's precisely why I thought a joke might be a good idea,' Ryan said wearily. 'Sorry, maybe I should have left you to wallow in how awful it was. Maybe question your abilities and wonder endlessly what you might have been able to do better.'

'It might be more appropriate than telling jokes.'

'Really? What if another major case comes in in the next five minutes, Hannah? You going to be in a fit state to give that person the best you can?'

'Of course I am.'

'Well, lucky you. Some of us need to distract ourselves. Lift our spirits a bit. There's always time for wallowing later.'

'I don't believe you ever wallow,' Hannah snapped. She wasn't going to admit that even that stifled snort of laughter *had* done something to ease the emotional downside of this job. She'd rather believe that it was being able to channel her frustration and anger into a confrontation that had been building for some time. 'And you distract yourself often enough to be a liability in this department. You've been here, what, three months? And how many times have you taken time off to flit back to Australia? Four, five times? I should know—it's usually me that does extra shifts to cover the gaps.'

This distraction was working wonderfully well. Hannah was really hitting her stride.

'You know your problem, Ryan? You're shallow. You're so intent on having a fun life you can't even spare the time to think about someone else.'

'Oh?' Ryan was staring at Hannah and she'd never heard him use such an icy tone. 'Shallow, am I?'

'You might find it more beneficial to your career to review cases like we've just had. You never know. Try having a professional discussion with a colleague next time instead of telling *stupid* jokes. You might learn something.'

'From you?' Ryan snorted. 'I doubt it.'

'Why?' Hannah's tone was waspish. 'Because I'm blonde?'

'No.' Ryan stood up, abandoning his cup of coffee. 'Because you're less experienced professionally and far less competent when it comes to relationships between people. You're judgmental, Dr Jackson, and you don't even bother finding out the facts before you make those judgments.'

He stalked behind Hannah and she had to swivel her head to keep glaring at him as he made his parting shot. 'And when I'm consultant, it might be nice if you made *me* coffee, babe. Not the other way round.'

'Dream on, mate!' What a pathetic rejoinder. Hannah could only hope Ryan would take it as she meant it—referring to the consultancy position and not the coffee-making.

Jennifer came in a few seconds after Ryan had left. Her eyebrows had disappeared under her fringe.

'What on earth's wrong with Ryan? I've never seen him look so grumpy!'

'He's a grumpy man.'

Jennifer laughed. 'He is not and you know it. He's a lovely man and if you weren't trying so hard not to like him you would have realised that by now.'

'I'm not trying hard,' Hannah protested. 'It's easy. Besides, it was your friend in Sydney that told you what a reputation he had for breaking hearts. The man needs an emotional health warning attached.'

Jennifer shook her head, smiling. 'Yeah…right.' She took another glance at Hannah. 'You look pretty grumpy yourself.'

'It's been a bad night. I hate cases like that—especially when they shouldn't have happened in the first place.' She sighed again. 'And I'm tired. Roll on 7 a.m.'

'Roll on Friday more like. Isn't that when you leave for a few days' R & R in the sun?'

'Sure is.' Hannah's spirits finally lifted—a lot more than Ryan's joke had achieved. 'You know, I'm finally really looking forward to this trip.'

'I could do with some time away from this place myself. Could be just what the doctor ordered. For both of us.'

'Mmm.' Hannah's agreement was wholehearted. But it wasn't the place she needed the break from. A few days away from Ryan Fisher was definitely what this doctor was ordering.

Hannah Jackson could go to hell in a hand basket.

The glimpse of a woman with sleek blonde hair disappearing into the melee of economy class was enough of a reminder to sink Ryan Fisher's spirits with a nasty jolt.

He slid his cabin baggage into the overhead locker with the same ease he slid his long body into the comfortable window seat at the rear of the business class section of the plane. Seconds later, he returned the smile of a very pretty young air hostess.

'Orange juice would be lovely,' he agreed. 'Exactly what I need.'

The frosted glass was presented while economy-class passengers were still filing past, but Ryan killed the faintly embarrassed reaction to the envious glances. Why shouldn't he travel in comfort? He had to do it often enough to make it a boring inconvenience and he'd decided he may as well make the travel as enjoyable as possible when the destination usually wasn't.

At least this time he could look forward to what lay at the other end of his journey.

'Is there anything else you need, sir?'

Ryan suppressed a wry smile along with the temptation to ask the crew member for a thousand things. How about a miraculous cure for a little girl in Brisbane that he had far more than just a bond of family with? Or perhaps freedom from the ridiculously powerful attraction he had felt for Hannah Jackson ever since he'd first laid eyes on her three months ago?

No. He was over that. As of last Monday night when she'd told him exactly what she thought of him. She hated him. He was shallow—telling jokes when he should be taking on board the misery of others. Lazy—taking time off to flit back to Australia to have fun at regular intervals. Out to win the job she felt was rightfully hers.

Ironic that he'd actually set out to catch Hannah's attention by demonstrating his clinical ability. He hadn't expected the head of department to twist his arm and put his name forward for the upcoming consultancy position but then he'd thought, Why not? The anchor of a permanent job could be just what he needed to sort out his life. And at least that way Hannah would see him as an equal.

Would really *see* him.

How idiotic would it be to waste any more time or emotional energy hankering after someone who didn't even have any respect, let alone liking, for him?

'No, thanks.' He smiled. 'I'm fine.'

Ryan sipped his chilled juice, stretching his legs into the generous space in front of him and enjoying the fact that the seat beside him was empty. So were both the seats on the opposite side of the aisle. There was, in fact, only one other occupant of business class and Ryan found himself listening to the well-dressed man with an American accent telling the air hostess that all he wanted was to go to sleep and could he have one of those eye covers? Apparently he hadn't expected a diversion to Auckland or a night in an airport hotel and he'd had more than enough of travelling for now.

'It should have been a straightforward trip to Sydney and then Cairns,' he was saying. 'Instead, I'm bunny-hopping through the south Pacific. Inefficient, that's what it is.'

'There's been a few disruptions due to some bad weather,' the hostess responded. 'Hopefully we'll be able to bypass it on this trip.'

Ryan didn't care if they hit a few bumps. Despite what Hannah thought of him, he didn't often get a smooth ride through life. OK, so maybe he didn't wear his heart on his sleeve and go around telling everyone his problems, but it was just as well, wasn't it? Imagine how low he'd be feeling right now if he'd made it obvious just how attracted he'd been to Hannah and had been squashed like the bug she clearly thought he was?

Well, she wouldn't get the opportunity now. No way. He wouldn't have her if she threw herself at him. Wrapped up in a ribbon and nothing else.

A soft sound like a strangled groan escaped. That short flight into fantasy wasn't likely to help anything. He drained his glass and handed it back as part of the preparation for take-off. Then he closed his eyes as the big jet rolled towards the end of the runway. Maybe he should follow the example of the other occupant of business class and escape into a few hours of peaceful oblivion.

The trip promised to be anything but restful. Hannah had an aisle seat, for which she was becoming increasingly grateful. It meant she could lean outwards.

She had to lean outwards because the man beside her was one of the fattest people Hannah had ever seen. He could easily have used up two seats all by himself but somehow he had squeezed in. Apart from the parts of his body that oozed through the gaps above and below the armrests and encroached considerably on Hannah's space. Any sympathy for his obvious discomfort had been replaced by a more selfish concern about her own when the personality of her travelling companion began to reveal itself.

'Name's Blair,' he boomed at her. 'How's it going?' He certainly wasn't shy. 'They make these seats a bit bloody small these days, eh? Just want to pack us in like sardines so they make a profit.'

'Mmm.' And they were allocated the same amount of baggage weight, Hannah thought crossly. What would happen if every passenger was Blair's size? Could the plane flip over because the baggage compartment was too light? Use twice as much fuel? Drop out of the sky?

Hannah wasn't a great fan of flying. She leaned further into the aisle and gripped the armrest on that side as the plane gathered speed.

'Not keen on flying, huh?' Blair was leaning, too. 'Wanna hold my hand?'

'Ah…no, thanks.' Hannah screwed her eyes shut. 'I'm just fine.'

'It's OK. ' Blair was laughing as the wheels left the tarmac. 'I'm single.'

There was no point pretending to be asleep because Blair didn't seem to notice. He obviously liked to think aloud and kept himself amused by a running commentary on the choice of movies available, the tourist attractions of Cairns showcased in the airline magazine and the length of time it was taking for the cabin crew to start serving refreshments.

The reason for any delay was revealed when the captain's voice sounded in the cabin.

'G'day, folks. Welcome aboard this Air New Zealand flight to Cairns. We're expecting a bit of turbulence due to strong westerly winds courtesy of a tropical cyclone in the Coral Sea region going by the name of Willie. I'm going to keep the crew seated until we get through this next layer of cloud.'

Blair made a grumbling sound.

'Once we're cruising at around thirty-five thousand feet, things should get a bit smoother,' the captain continued. 'You'll be free to move around the cabin at that point but I would suggest that while you're in your seats you do keep your seat belts firmly fastened.'

Sure enough, the flight became smoother and the cabin crew began to serve drinks and meals. The steward that stopped beside Hannah cast a second glance at her companion, listened to him patiently while he complained about the delay in being fed and then winked at Hannah.

'I'll be back in a tick,' he said.

When he returned, he bent down and whispered in Hannah's ear. Then he opened the overhead locker and removed the bag she specified. Hannah unclipped her seat belt and stood up with a sigh of relief.

'Hey!' Blair was watching the removal of the bag with concern. 'Where're you going, darling?'

'We've got a bit of room up front,' the steward informed him. 'I'm just juggling passengers a bit. If you lift the armrest there, Sir, I'm sure you'll find the journey a lot more comfortable.'

Much to Hannah's astonishment, 'up front' turned out to be an upgrade to business class. Her eyes widened as she realised she was going to have a window seat—no, both the seats—all to herself.

'You're an angel of mercy,' she told the steward. 'Wow! I've never flown business class before.'

'Enjoy!' The steward grinned. 'I'll make sure they bring

you something to drink while you settle in and have a look at the breakfast menu.'

Hannah sank into the soft seat, unable to contain her smile. She stretched out her legs and wiggled her toes. Not much chance of developing a DVT here. There was any amount of elbow room, as well. She tested it, sticking her arms out like wings. She even flapped them up and down a little. Just as well there was no one to see her doing a duck impression.

Or was there? Hannah hadn't yet considered the possibility of a passenger on the other side of the aisle. She turned her head swiftly, aware of a blush starting. And then she recognised the solitary figure by the window and she actually gasped aloud.

Glaring was probably the only description she could have used for the way Ryan Fisher was looking at her.

'Oh, my God!' Hannah said. 'What are *you* doing here?'

# CHAPTER THREE

'I WAS about to ask you the same thing.'

'I got upgraded.' Hannah hadn't intended to sound defensive. Why did this man always bring out the worst in her? 'Things were a bit crowded down the back.'

'Here you go, Dr Jackson.' A pretty, redheaded hostess held out a tray with a fluted glass on it. 'And here's the menu. I'll come back in a minute to see what you'd like for breakfast.'

'Thank you.' Hannah took a sip of her juice and pretended to study the menu, which gave a surprisingly wide choice for the first meal of the day. There were hours of this flight left. Was she going to have to make conversation with Ryan the whole way?

It was some sort of divine retribution. Hannah had been feeling guilty ever since Monday night when she'd let fly and been so rude to a colleague. She couldn't blame him for either the retaliation or the way he'd been avoiding her for the last few days. The personal attack had been unprofessional and probably undeserved. He couldn't know where the motivation had come from and Hannah certainly couldn't tell him but…maybe she ought to apologise?

She flicked a quick glance from the menu towards Ryan.

He was still glaring. He wasn't about to use their first meeting away from work to try building any bridges, was he?

Hannah wished she hadn't looked. Hadn't caught those dark eyes. She couldn't open her mouth to say anything because goodness only knew what might shoot out, given the peculiar situation of being in this man's company away from a professional setting. Imagine if she started and then couldn't stop?

If she told him her whole life history? About the man her mother had really fallen in love with—finally happy after years of getting over her husband's tragic death. Of the way she'd been used and then abandoned. Hannah had known not to trust the next one that had come along. Why hadn't her mother been able to see through him that easily? Perhaps the attraction to men like that was genetic and too powerful to resist. It might explain why Susie had made the same mistake. Fortunately, Hannah was stronger. She might *want* Ryan Fisher but there was no way she would allow herself to *have* him.

Oddly, the satisfying effect of pushing him firmly out of her emotional orbit the other night was wearing off. Here she was contemplating an apology. An attempt at establishing some kind of friendship even.

Ryan hadn't blinked.

Hannah realised this in the same instant she realised she could only have noticed because she hadn't looked away. The eye contact had continued for too long and…Oh, *God!* What if Ryan had seen even a fraction of what she'd been thinking?

Attack was the best form of defence, wasn't it?

'Why are you staring at me?'

'I'm still waiting for you to answer my question.'

'What question?'

'What you're doing here.'

'I told you, I got upgraded.'

'You know perfectly well that wasn't what I meant. What the hell are you doing on this flight?'

'Going to Cairns.' Hannah didn't need the change in Ryan's expression to remind her how immature it was to be so deliberately obtuse. She gave in. 'I've got a connecting flight at Cairns to go to a small town further north in Queensland. Crocodile Creek.'

Lips that were usually in some kind of motion, either talking or smiling, went curiously slack. The tone of Ryan's voice was also stunned.

'You're going to *Crocodile Creek?*'

'Yes.'

'So am I.'

'Did you decide what you'd like for breakfast, Dr Jackson?'

'What?' Hannah hadn't even noticed the approach of the redheaded stewardess. 'Oh, sorry. Um… Anything's fine. I'm starving!'

The stewardess smiled. 'I'll see what I can surprise you with.' She turned to the other side of the aisle. 'And you, Dr Fisher? Have you decided?'

'I'll have the fresh fruit salad and a mushroom omelette, thanks.'

Ryan didn't want to be surprised by his breakfast. Maybe he'd just had enough of a surprise. As had Hannah. She waited only a heartbeat after the stewardess had moved away.

'Is there a particular reason why you're going to Crocodile Creek at this particular time?'

'Sure is. I'm best man at my best mate's wedding.'

'Oh…' Hannah swallowed carefully. 'That would be…Mike?'

Ryan actually closed his eyes. 'And you know that because you're also invited to the wedding?'

'Yes.'

Ryan made a sound like a chuckle but it was so unlike the laughter Hannah would have recognised she wasn't sure it had anything to do with amusement. 'Don't tell me you're lined up to be the bridesmaid.'

'No, of course I'm not. I don't know Emily that well.'

'Thank God for that.'

'My sister's the bridesmaid.'

Ryan's eyes opened smartly. Hannah could have sworn she saw something like a flash of fear. Far more likely to be horror, she decided. He disliked her so much that the prospect of being a partner to her sister was appalling? That hurt. Hannah couldn't resist retaliating.

'My twin sister,' she said. She smiled at Ryan. 'We're identical.'

Ryan shook his head. 'I don't believe this.'

'It is a bit of a coincidence,' Hannah agreed, more cheerfully. Ryan was so disconcerted that she actually felt like she had control of this situation—an emotional upper hand—and that had to be a first for any time she had spent in Ryan's company, with the exception of Monday night. Maybe this wouldn't be so bad after all. 'So, how come you know Mike so well?'

But Ryan didn't appear to be listening. 'There are two of you,' he muttered. 'Unbelievable!'

Their conversation was interrupted by the arrival of their food. Hannah was hungry enough to get stuck into the delicious hot croissants and jam she was served. Ryan was only halfway through his fruit salad by the time she had cleaned her plate and he didn't look as though he was particularly enjoying the start of his meal.

Hannah had to feel sorry for him but she couldn't resist teasing just a little. She adopted the same, slightly aggrieved tone he had been using only a short time ago.

'You didn't answer my question.'

'What question?' Ryan wasn't being deliberately obtuse. He looked genuinely bewildered.

'How do you know Mike? The groom at this wedding we're both going to.'

'Oh… I was involved in training paramedics in the armed forces for a while, years ago. Mike was keen to add medical training to his qualifications as a helicopter pilot, having been in a few dodgy situations. We hit it off and have stayed in touch ever since.' Ryan stirred the contents of his bowl with the spoon. 'I was really looking forward to seeing him again,' he added sadly. 'The last real time we had together was a surfing holiday in Bali nearly three years ago. After he got out of the army but before he took himself off to the back of beyond.'

'Crocodile Creek does seem a bit out of the way,' Hannah had to agree. Besides, thinking about geography was a good way to distract herself from feeling offended that Ryan seemed to think all the pleasure might have been sucked from the upcoming weekend. 'It was easy enough to hop on a plane to Brisbane to spend a day or two with Susie.'

'I got the impression you never took time off.'

'I don't take rostered time off.'

'Unlike me.' Ryan said it for her. ''Cos you're not lazy.'

Hannah wasn't going to let this conversation degenerate into a personality clash. Here was the opportunity she had needed. 'I never said you were lazy, Ryan. You work as hard as I do. You're just more inclined to take time off.'

'For the purposes of having fun.'

'Well…yes…' Hannah shrugged. 'And why not?'

Would this count as an apology, perhaps? 'All work and no play, etcetera.'

'Makes Jack a dull boy,' Ryan finished. 'And Jill a very dull girl.'

Was he telling Hannah she was dull? Just a more pointed comment than Jennifer telling her she was an ED geek? If he saw her as being more *fun*—say at a wedding reception—would he find her more attractive?

Hannah stomped on the wayward thought. She didn't want Ryan to find her attractive. She didn't want to find *him* attractive, for heaven's sake! It was something that had just happened. Like a lightning bolt. A bit of freak weather—like the cyclone currently brewing in the Coral Sea, which was again causing a bit of turbulence for the jet heading for Cairns.

The two cabin-crew members pushing a meal trolley through to economy class exchanged a doubtful glance.

'Should we wait a bit before serving the back section?'

'No.' The steward who had been responsible for Hannah's upgrade shook his head. 'Let's get it done, then we can clear up. If we're going to hit any really rough stuff, it'll be when we're north of Brisbane.'

Hannah tightened her seat belt a little.

'Nervous?' Ryan must have been watching her quite closely to observe the action.

'I'm not that keen on turbulence.'

'Doesn't bother me.' Ryan smiled at Hannah. Or had that smile been intended for the approaching stewardess? 'I quite like a bumpy ride.'

Hannah and Ryan both chose coffee rather than tea. Of course the smile had been for the pretty redhead. Likewise the comment that could easily have been taken as blatant flirting.

'I don't know Emily,' Ryan said. 'Maybe you can fill me in. She's a doctor, yes?'

'Yes. She's Susie's best friend.'

'Susie?'

'My sister.'

'The clone. Right. So how long has she been in Crocodile Creek?'

'About three years. She went to Brisbane to get some post-grad training after she finished her physiotherapy degree and she liked it so much she decided to stay.'

'I thought she was a doctor.'

'No. She started medical school with me but it wasn't what she wanted.'

'How come she lives in that doctors' house that used to be the old hospital, then?'

'She doesn't.'

'That's not what Mike told me.'

'Why would Mike be telling you about my sister?'

'He wasn't. He was telling me about his fiancée. Emily.' Ryan groaned. 'We're not on the same page here, are we?'

'No.' And they never would be. 'Sorry. I don't know much about Emily either, except that she's a really nice person and totally in love with Mike and his parents are thrilled and hoping for lots of grandchildren.'

Ryan was still frowning. 'If you don't know Emily and you don't know Mike, why have you been invited to their wedding?'

'As Susie's partner, kind of. We haven't seen each other since Christmas.'

'That's not so long ago.'

Hannah shrugged. 'It seems a long time. We're close, I guess.'

'Hmm.'

Ryan's thoughts may as well have been in a bubble over his head. As best man, he would have to partner Hannah's clone. Another woman who wouldn't be on the same page. Someone else who would think he was shallow and lazy and a liability.

Hannah opened her mouth to offer some reassurance. To finally apologise for losing it on Monday night in such an unprofessional manner. To suggest that they would both be able to have a good time at the wedding despite having each other's company enforced.

She didn't get the chance.

Her mouth opened far more widely than needed for speech as the plane hit an air pocket and seemed to drop like a rock. The fall continued long enough for someone further down the plane in economy to scream, and then they got to the bottom with a crunch and all hell broke loose.

The big jet slewed sideways into severe turbulence. The pitch of its engine roar increased. The water glass and cutlery on Hannah's tray slithered sideways to clatter to the floor. The seat-belt sign on the overhead panel flashed on and off repeatedly with a loud dinging noise. Oxygen masks were deployed and swung like bizarre, short pendulums. Children were shrieking and someone was calling for help. The stewardess who had been pushing the meal trolley staggered through the curtain dividing business class from the rest of the cabin, her face covered in blood. She fell into the seat beside Hannah.

'I can't see anything!'

Hannah was still clutching her linen napkin in her hand. She pushed the tray table up and latched it, giving her space to turn to the woman beside her, who was trying to wipe the blood from her eyes.

'Hold still!' Hannah instructed. She folded the napkin

into a rough pad. If her years of training and practice in emergency departments had done nothing else, Hannah would always bless the ability to focus on an emergency without going to pieces herself. 'You've got a nasty cut on your forehead.' She pressed the pad against the wound as best she could, with the plane continuing to pitch and roll.

'I came down on the corner of the trolley.'

'What's happening?' Ryan was out of his seat, hanging onto an armrest for support.

By way of answer, calmly overriding the noise of the engines and distressed passengers, came the voice from the flight deck.

'Sorry about this, folks. Bit of unexpected rough stuff. We should be through this pretty fast. Please, return to your seats and keep your belts firmly fastened for the moment.'

Ryan ignored the direction. 'Anyone else hurt back there?'

'I don't know.' The stewardess was leaning back in the seat, her face pale beneath smeared blood. 'We were still serving breakfast. It'll be a mess. I should go and help.'

Ryan held back the curtain to look into the main body of the cabin. Clearly, he was trying to see where he might be needed most urgently. Forgetting one's own fear and helping someone who'd happened to land in the seat beside her was nothing compared to the courage it would need to take command of the kind of chaos Hannah could imagine Ryan assessing.

Mixed in with her admiration of his intention was a desire to prove she could also rise to the occasion. Ryan's courage was contagious.

'Hold this.' Hannah took the hand of the stewardess and placed it over the pad. 'Keep firm pressure on it and the bleeding will stop soon. I'll come back and check on you in a bit.' She unclipped her seat belt and stood up. The oxygen mask bumped her head but Hannah ignored it. The jolt from the air pocket must have caused their deployment because she wasn't at all short of breath so the oxygen level had to be OK. Lurching sideways to get past the knees of the stewardess, Hannah found her arm firmly gripped by Ryan.

'What *do* you think you're doing, Hannah? Sit down and belt up.'

'Help!' A male voice was yelling loudly. 'We need a doctor!'

'Stay here,' Ryan ordered crisply. 'I'll go.'

But Hannah knew that her own courage was coming from the confidence Ryan was displaying. If he left, she might be tempted to strap herself safely back into her seat and wait for the turbulence to end.

People needed help.

'No,' she said. 'I'm coming with you.'

Something unusual showed in Ryan's eyes. Did he know how terrified she was? What an effort trying to match his bravery was?

Maybe he did. The glance felt curiously like applause. He let go of her arm and took her hand instead, to lead her through the curtain. Hannah found herself gripping his fingers. He'd only done it to save her falling if there was more turbulence, but she was going to allow herself to take whatever she needed from this physical connection. What did it matter, when it felt like they might all be going to plunge to their deaths at any moment?

She followed Ryan through the curtain to become the new focus for dozens of terrified passengers as they moved down the aisle. Some were wearing their oxygen masks, others trying to get them on. She saw a young woman with her face in her hands, sobbing. A much older woman, nursing what looked like a fractured wrist. A nun, clutching her crucifix, her lips moving in silent prayer. The steward was waving at them from the rear of the aircraft.

'Here! Help!' he shouted. 'I think this man's choking.'

'It's Blair!' Hannah exclaimed.

Her former seat neighbour was standing, blocking the aisle. His hand was around his neck in the universal signal of distress from choking and his face was a dreadful, mottled purple.

Ryan was moving fast. He let go of Hannah's hand to climb over the empty seat that had initially been hers to get behind Blair.

'I've tried banging him on the back,' the steward said unhappily.

Ryan put his arms around Blair but couldn't grasp his fist with his other hand to perform an effective Heimlich manoeuvre. There was just too much of Blair to encompass and there was no time. The huge man was rapidly losing consciousness and there was no way Ryan could support his weight unaided.

Blair slumped onto his back, blocking the aisle even more effectively. There was no way for anyone to move. Ryan looked up and Hannah could see he was aware of how impossible it was going to be to try and manage this emergency. She could also see that he had no intention of admitting defeat. It was a very momentary impression, however, because the plane hit another bump and Hannah went hurtling forward to land in a most undignified fashion directly on top of Blair.

She landed hard and then used her hands on his chest to push herself upright. Blair gave a convulsive movement beneath her and Hannah slid her legs in front of her old empty seat to try and slide clear. Ryan grabbed Blair's shoulder and heaved and suddenly Blair was on his side, coughing and spluttering. Ryan thumped him hard between his shoulder blades for good measure and the crisis was over, probably as quickly as it had begun, as Blair forcibly spat out what looked like a large section of a sausage.

'Let's sit you up,' Ryan said firmly.

Blair was still gasping for air and had tears streaming down his face but somehow, with the help of the steward and another passenger, they got him back into his seat. Hannah jerked the oxygen mask down to start the flow. At least one person was going to benefit from their unnecessary deployment.

'We're through the worst of it now, folks. Should be plain sailing from now on.'

The timing of the captain's message was enough to make Hannah smile wryly. Catching Ryan's gaze, her smile widened.

'He doesn't know how right he is, does he?'

Ryan grinned right back at her, with the kind of killer smile he gave to so many women. The kind that old Doris Matheson had received the other night. But it was the first time Hannah had felt the full force of it and for just a fraction of a second it felt like they had connected.

Really connected. More than that imaginary connection Hannah had taken from the hand-holding.

And it felt astonishingly good.

Good enough to carry Hannah through the next hour of helping to treat the minor injuries sustained. Splinting the Colles' fracture on the old woman's wrist, bandaging lacerations and examining bruises.

The other occupant of business class had been woken by the turbulence and offered his services.

'I'm a neurosurgeon,' he said. 'Name's Alistair Carmichael. What can I do to help?'

'We've got a stewardess with a forehead laceration,' Hannah told him. 'You're the perfect person to check and make sure she's not showing any signs of concussion—or worse. Mostly, I think it's going to be a matter of reassuring people.'

Hannah made more than one stop to check that Blair wasn't suffering any lingering respiratory distress.

Ryan worked just as hard. The first-aid supplies on the plane were rapidly depleted but it didn't matter. The plane was making a smooth descent into Cairns and Blair, who had been the closest to a fatal injury, was beaming.

'You saved my life, darling,' he told Hannah when he was helped from the plane at Cairns by paramedics who would take him to hospital for a thorough check-up.

'Yes.' Ryan's voice seemed to be coming from somewhere very close to Hannah's ear and she gave an involuntary shiver. 'Interesting technique, that. You should write it up for a medical journal.'

Hannah turned her head. Was he making fun of her?

'The "Jackson manoeuvre",' Ryan said with a grin.

Hannah was too tired to care whether he was laughing at her. And the incident *had* had a very funny side. 'Yeah,' she said. 'Or maybe the "Blonde's Heimlich"?'

Much to Ryan's disappointment, they weren't sitting anywhere near each other on the connecting flight to Crocodile Creek, despite the much smaller size of the aircraft. It seemed to have been taken over by a large contingent of rather excited Greek people who had to be part of Mike's family. They were too busy talking and arguing with each other to take notice of strangers, and that suited Ryan just fine. He was tired and felt like he had too much to think about anyway.

Fancy Hannah being able to laugh at herself like that! Or had it been some kind of dig at him? Ryan knew perfectly well how his blonde jokes got up her nose. They had become a kind of defence mechanism so that no one would guess how disappointed he was when Hannah took no notice of him. He might get a negative reaction to the jokes but at least she knew he existed.

And what about the way she hadn't hesitated to go and help others when she had clearly been terrified herself by the turbulence. That had taken a lot of courage. She obviously didn't like flying. Ryan had seen the way she'd looked at the size of their connecting aircraft. He hoped she was as reassured as he had been by the information that the tropical storm was now moving out to sea and their next journey would be much smoother. They were even forecasting relatively fine weather for the rest of the day.

'But make the most of it,' the captain warned. 'It could turn nasty again tomorrow.'

That caused the volume of conversation around him to increase dramatically as the Greek wedding guests discussed the ramifications of bad weather. Ryan tuned out of what sounded like superstitious babble of how to overcome such a bad omen.

Hannah was sitting as far away as it was possible to be down the back of the cabin. Had she arranged that somehow? She was beside the American neurosurgeon, Alistair, who had proved himself to be a very pleasant and competent man during the aftermath of the turbulence. Distinctive looking, too, with those silver streaks in his dark hair. He had put the jacket of his pinstriped suit back on but he was asleep again.

There was an odd relief in noticing that. Surely any other man would find Hannah as attractive as he did? And he hadn't known the half of it, had he? No wonder he hadn't recognised her from behind on the larger plane. He'd only seen her with her sleek blonde hair wound up in a kind of knot thing and baggy scrubs covering her body. The tight-fitting jeans and soft white shirt she was wearing today revealed a shape as perfect as her face.

Impossible to resist the urge to crane his neck once more and check that the American was still asleep. He was. So was Hannah, which was just as well. Ryan wouldn't want her to know he'd stolen another glance. He settled back and dozed himself and it seemed no time until the wheels touched down on a much smaller runway than the last one.

He was here. At the back of beyond, in Crocodile Creek. For three whole days. With Hannah Jackson. What had happened to that fierce resolve with which he had started this journey? That Hannah could go to hell because he was no longer interested? That he was completely over that insane attraction?

It had been shaken by that turbulence, that's what. It had gone out the window when he'd taken hold of her hand and she hadn't pulled away. Had—amazingly—held his hand right back.

Ryan sighed deeply and muttered inaudibly.

'Let the fun begin.'

# CHAPTER FOUR

HEAT hit her like a blast from a furnace door swinging open.

Thanks to the early departure from Auckland and the time difference between Australia and New Zealand, it was the hottest part of the day when they arrived in Crocodile Creek.

The bad weather that had made the first leg of the journey so memorable seemed to have been left well behind. The sky was an intense, cobalt blue and there were no clouds to filter the strength of the sun beating down. It was hot.

Very hot.

Descending the steps from the back of the small plane onto the shimmering tarmac, Hannah realised what a mistake it had been to travel in jeans.

'I'm cooking!' She told Susie by way of a greeting as she entered the small terminal building. 'How hot *is* it?'

'Must be nearly forty degrees.' Susie was hugging Hannah hard. 'What on earth possessed you to wear jeans?' She was far more sensibly dressed, in shorts, a singlet top and flip-flop sandals.

'It was cold when I got up at stupid o'clock. Our flight left at 6 a.m.' Hannah pulled back from the hug. 'You've let your hair grow. It looks fabulous.'

Susie dragged her fingers through her almost shoulder-length golden curls. 'It'd be as long as yours now, if I bothered straightening it.'

'Don't!' Hannah said in mock alarm. 'If you did that, nobody would be able to tell us apart and it would be school all over again.'

'Yeah…' Susie was grinning. 'With you getting into trouble for the things I did.'

The noise in the small building increased markedly as the main group of passengers entered, to be greeted ecstatically by the people waiting to meet them. The loud voices, tears and laughter and exuberant hugging made Susie widen her eyes.

'That's *another* Poulos contingent arriving. Look at that! This wedding is a circus.'

Why did Hannah's gaze seek Ryan out in the crowd so instantly? As though the smallest excuse made it permissible? She turned back to Susie.

'What's your bridesmaid's dress like?'

'Pink.'

'Oh, my God, you're *kidding!*'

'Yeah. It's peach but it's still over the top. Sort of a semi-meringue. Kind of like you'd expect some finalist in a ballroom dancing competition to be wearing. I could keep it to get married in myself eventually—except for the lack of originality. Five other girls will have the same outfit at home.'

'*Six* bridesmaids?'

'Yes, but I'm the most important one. Poor Emily doesn't have any family and she only wanted two bridesmaids—me and Mike's sister, Maria, but there were all these cousins who would have been mortally offended if they hadn't been included and, besides, Mike's mum, Sophia, is determined to have the wedding of the century. I think she only stopped at six because it was getting hard to find the male counterparts. Funnily enough, they weren't so keen.'

'How's Emily holding up?'

'She's loving every minute of it but going absolutely mad. And she'll need a lot of make-up tomorrow to cover red cheeks from all the affectionate pinching she's getting.' Susie's head was still turning as she scanned the rest of the arrivals. 'Let's go and find your bag before we get swamped. If Sophia starts introducing me as the chief bridesmaid, I'll probably get *my* cheeks pinched as well. Oh, my God!' Susie did a double take as she lowered her voice. 'Who is *that?*'

There were two men standing a little to one side of the crowd, their attention on the signs directing them to the baggage collection area. One of them was Ryan. His head started to turn as though he sensed Hannah's gaze so she transferred it quickly to the other man. It was easy to recognise the person who had been dozing in the seat beside her on the last leg of her long journey. In that suit, he had to be even hotter than Hannah was in her jeans.

'He's an American,' she told Susie. 'A neurosurgeon. Alistair…someone. He's here for the wedding but he didn't say much about it. I got the impression he wasn't that thrilled to be coming.'

'That's Gina's cousin, then. Gorgeous, isn't he?'

'I guess.' Hannah hadn't taken much notice. Who would, when someone that looked like Ryan Fisher was nearby? 'Gina?'

'Also American. A cardiologist. She's getting married to Cal next weekend. I told you all about her at Christmas. She arrived with her little boy, who turned out to be Cal's son. Cal's one of our surgeons.'

'Right. Whew! *Two* weddings in two weeks?'

'Wedding city,' Susie agreed. She was leading the way past where the men were standing. Hannah could feel the odd prickle on the back of her neck that came when you knew someone was watching you. She didn't turn around because it was unlikely that she'd feel the stare of someone she didn't know with such spine-tingling clarity.

'Some people are going to both weddings,' Susie continued, ' and they've had to travel to get here so everybody thought they might like to just stay and have a bit of a holiday in between.'

'He won't have much of a holiday if he stays in that suit. And I thought I was overdressed!'

'Oh! The guy in the suit is the American?' Susie threw a glance over her shoulder. 'So who's the really gorgeous one who's staring at you?'

Hannah sighed. 'That'll be Ryan.'

'Ryan Fisher? The best man?'

'Yes.'

'Wow!' Susie's grin widened. 'My day's looking up! Mike told me what a fabulous guy he is but he forgot to mention he was also fabulous looking.'

'Don't get too excited,' Hannah warned.

'Why? Is he married?'

'No, but he might not be too friendly.'

Susie's eyebrows vanished under the curls on her forehead. 'Why not?'

Hannah sighed inwardly, feeling far too hot and weary to start explaining why her sister could well have to deal with unreasonable antipathy from someone because he disliked her mirror image.

'I'll fill you in later.' It was much easier to change the subject. Very easy, in fact. 'Good grief!'

'What?' Susie's head turned to follow the direction of

Hannah's astonished stare at the small, dark woman wearing black leather pants, a top that showed an amazing cleavage and…red stiletto shoes. 'That's Georgie.' She smiled. 'You'll meet her later.'

As though that explained everything! 'She must be as hot as hell in those clothes.'

'She's got super air-con for travel. She rides a Harley.'

'In *stilettos?*' Hannah's peripheral vision caught the way Ryan was also staring at the woman. There was no mistaking the appreciative grin on his face. 'Good *grief*,' she muttered again.

'I guess Georgie's here to meet Alistair. Georgie's Gina's bridesmaid and Alistair's here to give Gina away. He was supposed to arrive yesterday but his flight from the US was delayed by bad weather, and Gina and Cal are on one of the outer islands today, doing a clinic. So wow! Georgie and Alistair…' Susie shook her head. 'Leathers and pinstripes. They look a perfect couple. Not! Is that your bag?'

'Yes. Coming off first for a change.'

'Let's go, then.'

While it was a relief to escape the terminal building— and Ryan—it was a shock to step back out into the heat. And the wind. Huge fronds on the palm trees were bowing under its strength and Hannah had to catch her hair as it whipped into her face.

'Hurry up, Hannah! My car's over here and we're going to run out of time if we don't get going.'

'But the wedding's not till 4 p.m. tomorrow.' It was too hot to move any faster. 'What's the rush?' Hannah climbed reluctantly into the interior of a small hatchback car that felt more like an oven and immediately rolled down her window.

Susie started the engine and fiddled with the air-conditioning controls. 'It's all a bit frantic. I'm sorry. There's a rehearsal later this afternoon and I've got a couple more patients I just have to see before then.' She turned onto the main road and the car picked up speed rapidly. 'If you roll up your window, the air-con will work a lot better.'

Hannah complied and a welcome trickle of cool air came from the vents.

'Are you seeing your patients at your rooms?'

'No, I've finished the private stuff for today. These are hospital cases. Old Mrs Trengrove has had a hip replacement and absolutely refuses to get out of bed unless I'm there to hold her hand, and Wally's been admitted—he's one of my arthritis patients and it's his birthday today so I'll have to go and say hello.'

'Do you want to just drop me off at your place? I'm sure I could find my way to the beach and have a swim or something.'

'No, you can't swim at the beach. The water's all horrible because of the awful weather we've had in the last few days and it's stinger season. With the big waves we've been getting, the nets might not be working too well. Besides, I want to show you around the hospital. If you take your bathing suit, you could have a dip in the hospital pool.'

'Sounds good.' Hannah tried to summon enthusiasm for the busman's holiday delight of visiting the hospital.

'It's fabulous. You'd love it, Hannah. Hey…' Susie turned to look at her sister. 'They're always short of doctors. You could come and live with me for a while.'

'I couldn't stand working in heat like this.'

'It's not always like this.'

'It *is* beautiful.' Hannah was looking past sugar-cane plantations and the river towards rainforest-covered mountains in the distance.

'Wait till you see the cove. You'll fall in love with it just like I did.'

'The roads are quieter than I expected.'

'Bit quieter than usual today. I expect it's got something to do with the big fishing competition that's on.'

They crossed the river that gave Crocodile Creek township its name, drove through the main part of town and then rattled over an old wooden bridge to cross the river again. Rounding the bend on a gentle downhill slope, Hannah got the postcard view. The picture-perfect little cove with the white sandy beach and the intriguing, smudged outlines of islands further out to sea.

'The sea's the wrong colour at the moment,' Susie said apologetically. 'It's usually as blue as the sky. That's the Athina.' She pointed at the sprawling white building with Greek-style lettering on its sign that advertised its function as a boutique hotel. 'That's where the reception is being held tomorrow. And that rambling, huge house on the other side of the cove is the doctors' house.'

'Ah! The original hospital which is now the hotbed of romance.'

'Don't knock it!' Susie grinned at her sister. 'You could live there if you didn't want to squeeze into my wee cottage. Who knows? You might just find the man of your dreams in residence.'

'Doubt it.'

'Yeah.' Susie chuckled. 'The man of *your* dreams is probably buried in a laboratory somewhere. Or a library. Or an accountant's office.'

'Dad was an accountant,' Hannah reminded her. 'It didn't stop him being a lot of fun.'

'True.' Susie was silent for a moment. 'And Trevor was a brain surgeon and had to be the most boring man I'd ever met.'

'Hey, you're talking about the man I was engaged to for three years.'

'And why did you break it off?'

Hannah laughed. 'Because I was bored to tears. OK, I agree. There should be a happy medium but I haven't found it yet.'

'Me neither,' Susie said sadly. 'There always turns out to be something wrong with them. Or, worse, they find something wrong with me.' She screwed up her nose as she turned towards her sister. 'What *is* wrong with me, Hannah?'

'Absolutely nothing,' Hannah said stoutly. 'The guys are just idiots and don't deserve you. You're gorgeous.'

'That makes you gorgeous as well, you realise.'

'Of course.' Hannah grinned.

This was what she missed most about not having Susie living nearby any more. The comfort of absolute trust. Knowing you could say anything—even blow your own trumpet—without having it taken the wrong way. Not that they didn't have the occasional row but nothing could damage the underlying bond. And nothing else ever came close to the kind of strength a bond like this could impart.

'We're both gorgeous,' she said. 'Smart, too.'

'I'm not as smart as you. You're a brilliant doctor, soon-to-be emergency medicine specialist. I'm only a physiotherapist.'

'You could have easily been a doctor if you'd wanted, as you well know, Susan Jackson. You're doing what you want to do and you're doing it brilliantly. Anyway, being seen as clever isn't an advantage when it comes to men. It intimidates them.'

Although Hannah had a feeling that Ryan Fisher would be stimulated rather than intimidated by an intelligent woman if he ever bothered trying to find out.

'Look!' Susie was distracted from the conversation now. 'That's the Black Cockatoo, our local. And that's Kylie's Klipz. Kylie's amazing—looks like Dolly Parton. She's our hairdresser and she'll be doing all the hair and make-up for tomorrow. That's the Grubbs' place with that rusty old truck parked on the lawn and…here's my place.'

Susie parked outside a tiny cottage with two front windows in the shade of a veranda that was almost invisible beneath bougainvillea.

'Cute!'

'Speaking of cute.' Susie was unlocking her front door as Hannah carried her bag from the car. 'What's wrong with Ryan Fisher? Was he rude to you on the plane or something?'

'Not exactly. I just happen to know he's a player.'

'How do you know that? Do you know someone that works with him in Sydney?'

'He doesn't work in Sydney any more. He works in Auckland.'

'As in the same place you work?' Susie had opened the door but hadn't made any move to go inside.

'Exactly.'

'He's in your ED?'

'He's the guy who's after my job. I told you about him.'

Susie's jaw dropped. '*Ryan's* the holiday king? The Aussie playboy who's been driving you nuts with all those blonde jokes?'

'That's him.'

'The one who's out to date every nurse in the department in record time?'

'Yep.'

'So why have you been calling him Richard the third in your emails?'

'Because he reminds me of that bastard that Mum fell in love with when she'd finally got over Dad's death. *And* the creep who dumped you just before you went to Brisbane. He's a certain type. Skitters through life having a good time and not worrying about hurting anyone along the way. A flirt.'

'I'll bet he doesn't have any trouble getting a response.'

'He drives a flashy car. A BMW Roadster or something.'

'Nice. Soft top?'

Hannah ignored the teasing. 'He knows I can see right through the image. He hates *me,* too.'

Susie finally moved, leading the way into one of the bedrooms at the front of the cottage. 'I didn't get that impression from the way he was staring at you at the airport.'

'He was probably staring at you. At *us.* Wondering how he could be unlucky enough to be partnered with my clone.'

'That bad, huh?'

'Yep.' Hannah threw her suitcase onto the bed and snapped it open. 'No time for a shower, I don't suppose?'

'Not really. Sorry. Put your togs on under your clothes and take a towel. You can swim while I do my patient visits.' Susie made for the door. 'I'd better throw a shirt over this top so I look more respectable to go to work. It's lucky we don't stand on ceremony much around this place.'

It was blissful, pulling off the denim and leaving Hannah's legs bare beneath the pretty, ruffled skirt that she chose. The lacy camisole top was perfectly decent seeing as she was wearing her bikini top instead of a bra. Hannah emerged from the room a minute later to find Susie looking thoughtful.

'I just can't believe that the guy Emily was telling me about is the same guy you've been describing. As far as Mike's concerned, he's a hero. Practically a saint.'

Hannah dampened the image she had of Ryan when he was about to ignore the captain's direction to stay safely seated during severe turbulence to go and help where he was needed. He certainly had the courage that provided hero material. But a saint? No saint could get away with emitting that kind of sexual energy.

'Mike's not a woman,' she said firmly. 'I doubt there's a saintly bone in that body.'

'You could be right.' Susie's forget-me-not blue eyes, the exact match of Hannah's, were still dreamy. 'He's got that "bad boy" sort of edge, hasn't he?'

'I wouldn't say it like it's a compliment.'

Susie closed the front door behind them. 'Shall we walk? It's only a few minutes if you don't mind being blown about.'

'Yes, let's blow the cobwebs away. I could do with stretching my legs after all the sitting in planes.'

With a bit of luck, the wind might blow the current topic of conversation away as well.

No such luck.

'You have to admit, it's attractive.'

'What is?'

'That "bad boy" stuff. The idea that some guy could give you the best sex you've ever had in your life because he's had enough practice to be bloody good at it.'

Hannah laughed, catching her skirt as it billowed up to reveal her long legs. A car tooted appreciatively as it shot past. Thank goodness she was wearing a respectable bikini bottom instead of a lacy number or a thong and that her summer tan hadn't begun to fade yet. Despite being blonde and blue-eyed, she and Susie both tanned easily without burning.

'I don't do one-night stands or even flings,' Hannah reminded Susie. 'You know perfectly well the kind of trouble they lead to.'

'Yeah.' But Susie seemed to have finally got over her last heartbreak. 'But you always think you might just be the one who's going to make them want to change. And they're such *fun* at the time. To begin with, anyway.'

They walked in silence for a minute and Hannah looked down the grassy slope dotted with rocks and yellow flowers that led to the beach. A quite impressive surf from the murky sea was sending foamy scum to outline the distance up the beach the waves were reaching.

'You've never done it, have you?' Susie asked finally. 'Let your hair down and gone with sheer physical attraction? Slept with someone on a first date or fallen in love just because of the way some guy *looks* at you.'

'Never.' If she said it firmly enough she could convince herself as well, couldn't she? She couldn't admit, even to Susie, how often Ryan infiltrated her thoughts in the small hours of the night. It was lust she felt for the man. Nothing more.

Or should that be *less?*

'Sometimes I wish I were as strong as you,' Susie said wistfully.

'Someone had to be, in our family. The voice of reason, that's what I was. The devil's advocate.'

'You were always good at picking out what was wrong with the men Mum brought home.'

'Just a pity she never listened to me. She lost the house because she went ahead and married that slimeball, Richard the first.'

'Yeah. At least she's happy now. Or seems to be. Jim adores her.'

'And he's comfortably off and perfectly sensible. I'm sure Mum's learned to love fishing.'

'Hmm.'

Hannah couldn't blame Susie for sounding dubious. She made a mental note to ring her mother as soon as she got home.

'Come this way.' Susie pointed away from the signs directing people to the emergency and other departments of Crocodile Creek Base Hospital. 'We'll cut through the garden to the doctors' house and I can show you the pool and then shoot off and see those patients. Might be better if we leave the hospital tour until Sunday. Your flight doesn't leave till the afternoon, does it?'

'3 p.m.'

'Bags of time. I'll be able to introduce you properly to every hungover staff member we come across instead of confusing you with too many names.'

'I'll meet them at the wedding in any case.'

'You'll meet a few of them tonight. We're hoping to whisk Emily away after the rehearsal and take her out to dinner to give her a kind of hens' night. Which reminds me, I need to pop into the house and see who's going to be around. Gina might be there and Georgie should be back by now.'

'Is the dinner going to be at the Athina?'

'Heavens, no! Sophia already has the tables set up and about three thousand white bows tied to everything. She'll be making the family eat in the kitchens tonight, I expect— or they'll be roasting a lamb on a spit down on the beach. Such a shame about this weather.'

The lush tropical garden they were entering provided surprisingly good shelter from the wind thanks to the thick hibiscus hedges, and Hannah found she was too hot and sticky again. Her head was starting to throb as well, probably due to dehydration.

'Any chance of a glass of water?'

'Sure. Come up to the house with me.'

Skirting a sundial in the centre of the garden, Hannah could hear the sound of laughter and splashing water. An irresistibly cool, swimming pool sort of sound. The pool was behind a fenced area, screened by bright-flowered shrubs that smelt gorgeous, but Hannah didn't get time for a proper look because Susie was already half way up a set of steps that led to the wide veranda of a huge old two-storey building. Following her, Hannah found herself in a large kitchen and gratefully drank a large glass of water while Susie dashed off to see who was at home.

'There's nobody here,' she announced on her return. 'Come on, I'll bet they're all in the pool as it's still lunchtime.'

The air of too much to get done in the available time was contagious and Hannah hurriedly rinsed her glass and left it upside down on the bench amongst plates that held the remains of what looked like some of Mrs Grubb's legendary chicken salad sandwiches. Susie was a woman on a mission as she sped out of the house and she was only momentarily distracted by the bumbling shape of a large, strangely spotty dog that bounded up the steps to greet her.

'Rudolf!' Susie put her arm out as though she intended to pat the dog, and Hannah had no idea what happened. A split second later, Susie was tumbling down the steps with a cry that was far from the delighted recognition of the dog and then—there she was—a crumpled heap at the bottom.

'*Susie!* Oh, my God! Are you all right?'

Hannah wasn't the only one to rush to her sister's rescue. More than one dripping figure emerged through the open gate in the swimming-pool fence.

Two men were there almost instantly. And one of them was Ryan.

'What's happened?'

'She fell down the steps. There was this dog.'

'Damn, who left the gate open?' Another dark-haired man with a towel wrapped around his waist appeared behind the others. 'CJ, you were supposed to be watching Rudolf.'

'I was being a *shark!*' A small wet boy wriggled past the legs of the adults to stare, wide-eyed, at Susie. 'I had to be underwater,' he continued excitedly. 'With my fin on top—like this.' He stuck a hand behind his neck but no one was watching.

'It wasn't Rudolf's fault.' Susie was struggling into a sitting position. 'It's all right. I'm all right.'

'Are you sure?' A man with black curly hair and a gorgeous smile was squatting in front of Susie. 'You didn't hit your head, did you?'

'No. I don't know what happened, Mike. I just… Oh-h-h!'

'What's wrong?' Ryan moved closer. 'What's hurting?'

'My ankle,' Susie groaned. 'I think it's broken.'

'Just as well Luke's here, then,' Mike said, turning to another man who had approached the group. 'And they say you can't find an orthopaedic surgeon when you need one?'

'I *don't* need a surgeon,' Susie gulped. 'I hope.'

'I'll just be on standby,' Luke assured her. 'I am on babysitting duties after all.'

'*I'm* not a baby,' CJ stated. His hand crept into Luke's. 'You said I was your *buddy.*'

'You are, mate. You are…'

'Let *me* have a look.' Ryan's hands were on Susie's ankle. He eased off her sandal before palpating it carefully. 'I can't feel anything broken.'

'Ouch!'

'Sorry. Sore in there, is it? Can you wiggle your toes?'

There was a small movement. 'Ouch,' Susie said again. She looked close to tears and Hannah crouched beside her, putting an arm around her shoulders. 'I don't believe this. How could I have done something this stupid?'

'Accidents happen,' Ryan said calmly. He laid his hand on top of Susie's foot. 'Can you stop me pushing your foot down?'

'No. Oh, that *really* hurts.'

'It's starting to swell already.' Hannah peered anxiously at Susie's ankle. She might not have been very impressed if this injury was in front of her in the emergency department, but this was no professional environment and this was her sister. And Ryan looked nothing like he did in the ED. Hannah's gaze swung back to her colleague for a moment. He was practically naked, for heaven's sake. Tanned and dripping and...gorgeous. And giving Susie that killer smile.

'I think it's just a bad sprain but we'll need an X-ray to be sure. At least you chose the right place. I believe there's an X-ray department not far away.'

'It's not funny,' Susie wailed. 'I've got to wear high heels tomorrow. Little white ones with a rose on the toe. My dress is nowhere long enough to cover an ankle the size of an elephant's. I need some ice. Fast.' Susie leaned down to poke at the side of her ankle. 'What if it's broken and I need a cast? Oh, Mike, I'm so sorry! This is a *disaster!*'

'Forget it,' the curly haired man told her. 'The only thing that matters right now is making sure you're all right. Let's get you over to A and E.'

'I'll take her,' Ryan offered. 'Isn't Emily expecting you back at the Athina?'

Mike glanced at his watch and groaned. 'Ten minutes ago. And I'm supposed to have all the latest printouts from the met bureau. The women are all petrified that Willie's going to turn back and ruin the wedding.'

'As if!' Luke was grinning. 'There's no way Sophia's going to let a bit of weather undermine a Poulos wedding.'

Hannah could feel an increasing level of tension curling inside her. This was no time to be discussing the weather. Or a wedding. Susie needed attention. Her sister's face was crumpling ominously.

'*I'm* ruining the wedding,' she wailed forlornly. 'How could I have been so *stupid?*'

Hannah glared at Ryan. If he made even one crack about anything blonde, he would have to die!

Ryan's eyebrows shot up as he caught the force of the warning. Then he looked away from Hannah with a tiny, bemused shake of his head.

'Nothing else hurting?' he asked Susie. 'Like your neck?'

She shook her head.

'Right. Let's get this sorted, then.'

With an ease that took Hannah's breath away, Ryan took charge. He scooped Susie into his arms as though she weighed no more than the little boy, CJ. 'Emergency's that way, yes?'

'Yes,' Luke confirmed. 'Through the memorial garden.'

'Can I go, too?' CJ begged. ' I want to watch.'

'No,' Luke said. 'We told Mom we'd be waiting here when she got back.'

Mike was grinning broadly. 'You sure you want to go in like that, mate?'

'No time to waste.' Ryan was already moving in the direction Hannah had approached earlier. 'We need ice. And an X-ray.'

Hannah was only too pleased to trot behind Ryan. This was exactly the action that was required and there was no way she could have carried Susie herself.

'I'll bring your clothes over,' Mike called after them. 'I'll just call Emily and let her know what's happening.'

* * *

What was happening was a badly sprained ankle.

Despite ice and elevation and firm bandaging, Susie's ankle was continuing to swell impressively and was far too painful to put any weight on at all.

'Crutches.' An older and clearly senior nurse appeared in the cubicle Susie was occupying nearly an hour later. 'At least I won't need to give you a rundown on how to use them, Susie.'

'Thanks, Jill.' But Susie took one look at the sturdy, wooden, underarm crutches and then covered her face with her hands as though struggling not to burst into tears.

There was a moment's heavy silence. The cubicle was quite crowded what with Hannah standing by the head of Susie's bed, Ryan—now dressed, thankfully—and Mike leaning on the wall and Jill at the foot of the bed, holding the horrible accessories Susie was not going to be able to manage without.

Then the silence was broken.

'What are you saying?' came a loud, horrified, female voice. 'She can't *walk?* How can we have a bridesmaid who can't *walk?*'

'Oh, no!' Susie groaned. 'Sophia!'

'I was wondering how she'd take the news,' Mike said gloomily. 'Em didn't sound too thrilled either.'

A young woman with honey-blonde hair and rather serious grey-blue eyes rushed into the cubicle.

'Susie, are you all right? Is it broken?' She leaned over the bed to hug her friend. 'You poor thing!'

Hannah's eyes widened as the curtain was flicked back decisively. It wasn't just Mike's mother who had accompanied Emily. There were at least half a dozen women and they were all talking at once. Loudly. Anxiously.

'Susie! Darling!' The small, plump woman at the forefront of the small crowd sailed into the cubicle and stared at Hannah. 'What *have* you done to your hair?'

'I'm not Susie,' Hannah said weakly, as her sister emerged from Emily's hug. 'I'm her twin, Hannah.'

'Oh, my God!' The young, dark-haired woman beside Sophia was also staring. 'You *are* identical. Look at that, Ma! You wouldn't be able to tell them apart.'

An excited babble and an inward flow of women made Hannah back into the corner a little further. Alarmed, she looked for an escape route, only to catch the highly amused faces of both Mike and Ryan. There was nothing for it but to hold her breath and submit to the squash of people both wanting to pat and comfort Susie and to touch Hannah and see if she was actually real.

Jill looked as though she knew even her seniority would be no help in trying to evict this unruly mob from her emergency department and was taking the crutches out of the way for the moment, but the movement attracted Sophia's attention.

'What are those?'

'Susie's crutches.' Jill picked up speed as she backed away.

'She needs *crutches?*' Sophia crossed herself, an action that was instantly copied by all the other relatives. 'But we can't have crutches! The photographs!'

'It's all right, Ma.' The woman who had to be Mike's sister, Maria, was grinning. 'It doesn't matter if Susie can't walk.'

'It doesn't matter? Of course it matters!' Sophia's arms were waving wildly and Hannah pressed herself further into the corner. 'There are six dresses. We have to have six bridesmaids and Susie is Emily's best friend. She has to be in the photographs. In the ceremony.' A lacy handkerchief appeared from someone's hand and Sophia dabbed it to her eyes. 'But with crutches? Oh, no, no, no…' The sympathetic headshakes from all directions confirmed that this event was cataclysmic.

'Never mind Willie,' Mike murmured audibly to Ryan. 'This is going to be worse than any cyclone, believe me.'

'Ma, listen!' Sophia's shoulders were firmly grasped by Maria. 'We can use Hannah instead.'

*'What?'* The word was wrenched from Hannah and everybody was listening now. And staring. And then talking, all at once.

'No, her hair's all wrong.'

'She's the same size. She'll fit the dress.'

'Nothing that curling tongs couldn't fix.'

'No crutches!'

'Nobody will know the difference.'

'I'll know,' Emily said emphatically. 'And so will Susie.' She still had her arms protectively around her friend.

'Would it matter?' Susie spoke only to Emily. 'I'd rather it was Hannah than me in the photos, Em. I'd just spoil them.'

'No, you wouldn't.'

'Yes, I would. It would be the first thing anyone would notice when they looked at the pictures. Or when they're sitting in the church. Instead of saying, "Look at that gorgeous bride," they'd be saying, "Why is that girl on crutches? What's wrong with her?"'

The chorus of assent from the avid audience was unanimous. Emily looked appealingly at Mike but he just shrugged sympathetically and then grinned.

'Up to you, babe,' he said, 'but it does seem fortuitous that you chose a chief bridesmaid that's got a spare copy of herself available.'

Hannah looked at Ryan. If this crazy solution was going

to make everybody happy then of course she would have to go along with it. But would Ryan?

Clearly, it *was* going to make everybody happy. Especially Susie.

'I'll still be there,' she was telling Emily. 'And Hannah's like part of me anyway.'

'Hannah? Are you OK with this?'

'Sure.' Hannah smiled warmly at Emily. 'I'd be honoured.'

'Hannah! Darling!' Sophia was reaching to squeeze Hannah's cheeks between her hands. 'Thank you! Thank you!'

Nobody asked Ryan if he was OK with the plan. Hannah caught his gaze and for a moment they just stared at each other. Another moment of connection. They were the two outsiders. Caught up in a circus over which they had no hope of exerting the slightest control.

It was a bit like dealing with the turbulence on that plane trip really. Had that been only this morning? Fate seemed determined to hurl them together. As closely as possible.

Ryan's expression probably mirrored her own. There was nothing they could do about it so they may as well just go with the flow.

There was something else mixed in with the resignation. Maybe it was due to the almost joyous atmosphere in the cubicle at having solved a potentially impossible hitch to the perfect wedding. Or maybe, for Hannah, it was due to something she didn't want to analyse.

It was more than satisfaction.

Curiously, it felt more like excitement.

# CHAPTER FIVE

CLOUDS were rolling in towards the North Queensland coast by 5 p.m.

Stained-glass windows in the small, Greek Orthodox church in the main township of Crocodile Creek were rattled with increasing force by the sharp wind gusts.

'Did you hear that?' Emily tugged on Mike's arm. 'It's getting worse.'

'Last report was that Willie's heading further out to sea. Stop fretting, babe. Spit for luck instead.'

'I've given up spitting, I told you that.' The smile Emily shared with her fiancé spoke of a private joke and Hannah found herself smiling as well. Emily and Mike had the kind of bond she had only ever found with her sister. One where an unspoken language said so much and just a look or a touch could convey a lot more than words.

If she was ever going to get married herself, Hannah would want that kind of a bond with the man she was going to spend the rest of her life with. She had known it wouldn't be easy to find a man she could trust to that extent. No, that wasn't quite true. Trevor had been as reliable and trustworthy as it was possible to be—perhaps because he was so hard working and scientific and couldn't tolerate anything that required imagination or spontaneity.

The relationship had gone from one of comfort to one of predictability. And then boredom had set in. In the end, Hannah had been quietly suffocating. The opportunity that moving to Auckland to take up her first registrar position had afforded had been too good to miss. Much to poor Trevor's unhappy bewilderment, she had also moved on from their relationship.

She hadn't been in another relationship since. Hurting another nice, kind, trustworthy man was not on the agenda. Risking personal disaster by trying the kind of man who was fascinating was also a place Hannah had no intention of going. Of course Susie was right. That 'bad boy' edge was attractive. It would be all too easy to think like most women—that *they* would be the one to make the difference—but it never happened like that. Not in real life.

Emily tore her eyes away from Mike to smile apologetically at Hannah. 'I must sound like a real worry wart,' she said, 'but I've got a long veil. Can you imagine what it's going to be like in gale-force winds?'

'There are six of us.' Hannah glanced at the lively group of young women milling behind her that included Mike's sister, Maria. 'I'm sure we'll be able to keep your veil under control.'

Sophia put the finishing touches to yet another of the large, alternating peach and white bows she was tying to the ends of the pews and then clapped her hands.

'Another practice!' she ordered. 'Michael! What are you doing? Go back up to the front with the others. Ryan! You're supposed to be making my son behave.'

'That'll be the day,' Ryan muttered. 'Come on, mate. Let's get this over with and then we can hit the bright lights of Crocodile Creek for a stag party, yes?'

'That really *would* be the day,' Mike responded with a grimace. 'There's a lamb on a spit turning as we speak and every member of the family has about six jobs to do later. I think you're down for potato-peeling duties. Or possibly painting the last of the damn chicken bones.'

'Chicken bones?'

'Quickly!' Sophia's tone suggested that there would be trouble if co-operation did not take place forthwith.

The two men shared a grin and then ambled up the red carpet of the aisle, and the rear view made Hannah realise how similar they were. Both tall and dark and handsome. They were wearing shorts and T-shirts at the moment but Hannah could well imagine what they'd look like tomorrow in their dark suits, crisp white shirts and bow ties. Just…irresistible.

Emily was watching the men as well and she sighed happily. 'I can't believe this is really going to happen,' she whispered. 'It's just too good to be true.'

Her eyes were shining and Hannah could feel the glow. What would it be like, she wondered, to be *that* happy? To be so sure you'd chosen the right person and that that kind of love had a good chance of lasting for ever? Mike looked like Ryan in more than an outward physical sense. They both had that laid-back, mischievous gleam that advertised the ability to get the most enjoyment possible out of life. And that did not generally include settling down with one woman and raising a family. Had Emily been the one to change Mike? Did being Greek make the difference? Or was she heading for unimaginable heartbreak?

No. Hannah didn't believe that for a moment. She had seen the way Mike and Emily had looked at each other.

They had found the real thing, all right. Standing in this pretty church, about to rehearse the steps for a ceremony to join two lovers in matrimony, Hannah couldn't help a flash of envy. It was a bit like winning the lottery, wasn't it? Only it was a human lottery and you couldn't buy tickets. And even if you were lucky enough to find one, you might forget to read the small print and think you'd won, only to have the prize snatched away. It had happened to both her mother and to Susie, and Hannah knew why. Because 'the Richards' had had that hint of a 'bad boy' edge. They had been playboys. Fun-seekers. Like Ryan.

The pageboys and flower girls were being rounded up from their game of chase between the empty pews. They were holding plastic beach buckets as a prop to represent the baskets of petals they would hold tomorrow. Sophia herded them into place and repeated instructions they had apparently misheard on the first rehearsal.

'Gently!' she insisted. 'You are throwing rose petals, CJ, not sticks for Rudolf!'

Maria was examining her nails. 'They're full of silver paint,' she complained. 'I never want to see another chicken bone in my life.'

'What's with the chicken bones?' Hannah queried. 'I heard Mike saying something about them as well.'

'Wishbones.' Emily was moving to take her place in the foyer. 'Painted silver. Sophia's planning to attach them to the little bags of almonds the guests will be given. Not that anyone's found time to put the almonds in the bags yet, let alone attach the wishbones.'

'They're for fertility,' Maria added. 'The almonds, that is. And boy, do I wish they hadn't been scattered around at my wedding. Watch out for the ones in your bed, Em. I'd sweep them out if I were you or you might end up like me, with four little monsters under five.' She was peering anxiously past Hannah to see if her small children were doing what they were supposed to on reaching the end of the petal-throwing procession.

'Uncle Mike!' one of them shrieked. 'Did you see me pretending to throw petals?'

Mike swept the small girl into his arms and kissed her. Ryan held out his hands and got high-fives from two small boys—a gesture that was clearly well practised. Then he pulled them in, one on each side of his body, for a one-armed hug.

'Good job, guys,' Hannah heard him say.

When did Ryan get to spend enough time with young children to be that at ease with them? Did he have a big family with lots of nieces and nephews? Maybe he'd been married already and had his own children. The notion was quite feasible. It would explain his frequent trips back to Sydney. Not that it mattered to Hannah. She was just aware of how little she knew about her colleague. Aware of a curiosity she had no intention of satisfying.

'I hope the aisle's going to be wide enough.' Emily had come back to her cluster of bridesmaids. 'My dress is *huge*. A giant meringue. Do you think there'll be room for a wheelchair beside me?'

'A wheelchair?' Hannah was glad she'd paid attention to Susie's emails. 'Is Charles Wetherby giving you away?'

'Yes. He's the closest thing to a father figure I've got.'

Reading between the lines of those emails, Hannah had the impression that Charles was a father figure to more than just Emily. With an ability to know more about what was happening within the walls of the hospital he directed than his staff were always comfortable with. A man with a quiet strength and wisdom that provided the cement for a remarkable small community of professional medics. A community that her sister was very much a part of now.

'I'm sure there'll be room,' she said confidently.

'Susie!' Sophia was sounding flustered. She was waving frantically from the altar end of the aisle. 'Pay attention, darling!'

'It's Hannah, Ma, not Susie,' Maria shouted.

'I knew that. You know what I mean. Come on, girls. In your pairs.'

Hannah and Maria were first. They walked along the red carpet beneath the elaborate chandelier, the gilt frame of which had miniature copies of the paintings of various saints that decorated the walls of this church between the stained-glass windows. The tiny crystals tinkled musically overhead as another gust of wind managed to shake the solid brick building.

Maria glanced up at the chandelier and muttered something under her breath that could have been either a curse or a prayer. Maybe a bit of both, Hannah decided, as Mike's sister flashed a grin at her.

'It's going to be a wild wedding at this rate!'

Hannah nodded agreement but found herself swallowing a little nervously. Even if Willie was out to sea and moving in a safe direction, this was still as close to a tropical cyclone as she felt comfortable with.

The first rehearsal made it easy to remember what to do this time. Hannah and Maria climbed to the top of the three steps and then waited until the other pairs of bridesmaids were on the lower steps before they all turned gracefully in unison to watch the bride's entrance.

Hannah felt a complete fraud. If only Emily and Susie weren't so set on her standing in. She couldn't even follow someone else's lead. She was the chief bridesmaid. It was up to her to make sure all the others did the right thing at the right time. There was a point when she would actually be a closer part of this ceremony, too. When the bride and groom were wearing the matching orange-blossom wreaths on their heads that were joined by satin ribbons, they would take their first steps as man and wife with a tour three times around the altar. It would be Hannah's job to hold up the train of Emily's dress and keep her veil in order. As best man, Ryan would be right beside her, holding up the ribbons joining the wreaths.

He would be wearing his tuxedo and Hannah would be so dressed up and groomed she wouldn't even feel like herself. She would have to be Ryan's partner in this ceremony and probably at the reception. She might even have to dance with him, and she was going to feel so uncomfortable she would be hating every minute of it.

And you'll look miserable, a small voice at the back of her mind warned. You'll make Susie miserable and probably Emily and definitely Ryan, and they'll all wish you'd never been invited to this wedding. Hannah noticed the nudge that Mike gave his best man by bumping shoulders. There was a whispered comment and then a frankly admiring stare from both men as the girls behind Hannah proudly arranged themselves on the steps. The men grinned approvingly. The girls giggled. They were all enjoying every moment of this circus.

And why not? It was going to be a huge party. The wild weather would probably only enhance the enjoyment of those safely tucked away inside. It was play time, not work time. Why couldn't she just relax and have fun, like they were?

Everybody thought she was boring. Too focussed on her career. Too ready to troubleshoot problems before they even occurred. It should, and probably did, make her a very good doctor, but too many people had criticised that ability in the last few days. Jennifer thought she had no life of her own outside work. Ryan thought she was dull. Even her own sister had commented on her lack of spontaneity or willingness to reap the rewards of taking a personal risk.

Hannah had never allowed sheer physical attraction to be the deciding factor when it came to men. Or slept with someone on a first date. Not that she intended to jump Ryan's bones, of course. Or fall in love with him because of a look, or, in his case, more likely due to the kind of smile she'd experienced in the plane that morning. The kind her junior bridesmaids were enjoying right now.

She could, however, throw caution to the winds for once, couldn't she? Given the current weather conditions in Crocodile Creek, it would be highly likely to be blown a very long way away, but would that be so terrible?

For the next twenty-four hours or so, she was going to have to pretend to be Susie. Someone with a rather different perspective on life and taking risks. This could be the perfect opportunity to step outside her own comfort zone. To really let her guard down and simply enjoy the moment, without trying to see down the track to locate potential hazards.

What did she have to lose? On Sunday she would get on a plane again to go home. Back to being herself. Back to working hard enough to ensure the success she craved. Hopefully, back to a new position as an emergency department consultant. And how much time would she get to have fun after that? This weekend could be seen as a kind of hens' party really. A final fling before Hannah became wedded to a new and intense phase of her career.

And it wouldn't hurt to show Ryan Fisher that she *did* know how to enjoy herself. That she wasn't all work and no play and as dull as ditchwater.

*Yes!*

Hannah hunched her shoulders and then let them drop to release any unconscious tension.

And then she smiled at Ryan. Really smiled. Here we are, then, her smile said. Let's have fun!

Good grief!

What had he done to deserve a smile like that? One that actually touched Hannah's eyes instead of just being a polite curve of her lips.

Ryan had to fight the urge to glance over his shoulder to see whether the real recipient of the smile was standing nearby.

Hell, she was gorgeous. It was going to be more than rather difficult to stick to his resolution if she was going to do things like smile at him like that. Almost as bad as discovering it had been Hannah and not Susie wearing that frilly skirt. The one that the wind had whipped up to reveal a pair of extremely enticing legs as he and Mike had driven up to the hospital earlier that afternoon. He'd never be able to see her wearing scrubs trousers in the ED again without knowing what lay beneath the shapeless fabric.

Mind you, that hadn't been half as disconcerting as what had happened later. Ryan had been entertaining hopes of finding Susie's company perfectly enjoyable. Of maybe being able to learn why his attractive colleague was so uptight and had taken such an instant dislike to him.

To have Susie incapacitated and Hannah stepping in to fill the breach had been a cruel twist of fate. Not that he'd allowed his disappointment to show, of course. Not when Emily had looked so happy. When Emily looked that happy, Mike was happy. And if his best buddy was happy, Ryan certainly wasn't going to do anything to tarnish the glow.

He'd go through with this and he'd look as if he was enjoying every moment of it. It would be hard *not* to enjoy it, in fact, and if he could only make sure his resolution regarding Hannah Jackson didn't go out the window, he could be sure he wouldn't spoil that enjoyment by getting some kind of personal putdown.

But it would help—a lot—if she didn't smile at him like that. As though she had put aside her preconceived and unflattering opinions. Opened a window in that wall of indifference to him and was seeing him—*really* seeing him—for the first time.

She did look a bit taken aback when he offered to take her home after the rehearsal but she rallied.

'Sure. I guess it's on your way, seeing as you're staying in the doctors' house. I might even go as far as the hospital and check on Susie.'

'It's good that she decided she would stay in overnight and get that intensive RICE treatment. It should help a lot.'

'Mmm.' Hannah's tone suggested that nothing would help enough unless, by some miracle, Susie awoke after a night of compression bandages and ice and elevation to find her foot small enough to wear her shoe and the ability to stand and walk unaided, which was highly unlikely. 'I need to stop at her house and collect a few things she might need, if you're not in too much of a hurry.'

'Not at all.' Ryan lowered his voice. 'With a bit of luck, I'll arrive at the Athina *after* all the potatoes are peeled.'

Hannah made no response to that and Ryan kicked himself mentally. What was he trying to do here? Prove how shallow and lazy he was?

'Tell Susie I'll be up to see her later,' Emily said as they left the church. 'If she can't come to the hens' party, we'll just have to take the party to her.'

'I think Jill might have something to say about that,' Mike warned. 'She's not big on parties happening in her wards.'

'Yeah.' Emily nodded sadly. 'She'd say that I should know the R in RICE stands for rest. Tell Susie I'll come and get her later in the morning, then, so she can come and supervise. Kylie can still do her hair and make-up.'

To Ryan's disappointment, Hannah was ready for the wind when they stepped outside. She had wrapped her skirt firmly around those long brown legs and was holding it in place. On the positive side, the action affected her balance and a good gust sent her sideways a few moments later to bump into Ryan. She could have fallen right over, in fact, if he hadn't caught her arms.

Bare arms.

Soft skin.

Enough momentum in the movement for Ryan to feel the press of her breasts against his hands. It wasn't the first time he had touched her skin but the tension of that incident in the plane hadn't really afforded an opportunity to analyse the effect. It was, quite simply, electrifying. Or was that because this contact had come about so unexpectedly?

No. He'd known, all along, that there would be something very different about touching this woman.

Something very special.

He didn't want to let go. The urge to pull her even closer and kiss her senseless was as powerful as what felt like hurricane-force winds funnelling through the church car park, whipping their hair and buffeting their bodies.

Simply irresistible.

Oh…*God!*

The strength of the grip Ryan had on her arms was

sending shock waves through Hannah, not to mention the delicious tingle of what had to be that latent lust kicking in.

And he looked…as though he wanted to *kiss* her!

Even more shocking was the realisation that she *wanted* him to.

Letting her hair down and being prepared to enjoy this weekend was one thing. Making out with Ryan Fisher in a church car park was quite another. And quite unacceptable.

Hannah wrenched herself free. 'You've got Mike's car?'

'Yes. That Jeep over there.'

The vehicle was vaguely familiar. Hadn't that been the one that had hooted when her skirt had blown up around her neck on that walk around the cove? Had it been Ryan getting a close-up view of her legs?

The tingle became a shaft of something much stronger that was centred deep in Hannah's abdomen but sent spirals all the way to the tips of her fingers and toes. Battling with the door of the Jeep so it didn't catch in the wind and fly outwards was a welcome diversion. Why was she feeling like this? Had she somehow flicked a mental switch back there in the church that could lead her rather too far into temptation?

How inappropriate.

But intriguing.

Ryan wouldn't think twice about following his inclinations, would he? Sleeping with someone on a first date or having a little weekend fling? Hannah couldn't help casting a speculative glance at her companion as he started the Jeep and they moved off. His hands gripped the steering-wheel with enough strength to keep the vehicle straight despite the strong winds but they didn't look tense. Strength and a capacity to be gentle. What had Susie said about bad boys and getting the best sex you ever had?

Maybe her thoughts were too powerful. Something made Ryan turn his head. He held her gaze for only a heartbeat and then gave her one of those smiles.

Oh…help! Hannah spent the next few minutes until they were driving over that rickety bridge wondering if Ryan was discreet. Whether what happened on camp would stay on camp. Seeing as she'd never actually heard any firsthand gossip about his previous conquests, it seemed likely that the answer was yes. The added bonus of dealing with that distracting attraction as well as proving she could be fun might well mean that her working relationship with Ryan could be vastly improved. Even when she got the consultancy position and, effectively, became his boss.

It was quite difficult to rein in her thoughts and focus on her immediate intentions.

'I might change my clothes before I go and visit Susie.' Thinking out loud was partly to ensure Ryan didn't know what she'd really been thinking about. 'I've still got my bikini on under this and it's not as if I'm going to get a chance to swim.'

'That's a shame. The pool's great. Very refreshing.'

'It has been a long day, hasn't it?' Hannah agreed. 'Feels like for ever since we left Auckland.' A different time. A different place. Different rules were definitely allowable.

'You could have a swim after you've been visiting.'

'I'd still need a change of clothes and, besides, it gets dark early here, doesn't it?'

'About eight, I think. But there are lights around the pool. People often swim at night over summer from what Mike was telling me.'

'Tempting. I might just do that. This heat is really getting to me.' It wasn't the first time that day that Hannah had lifted the weight of hair off her neck to try and cool down a fraction. 'I don't think I've ever felt this hot in my life.'

'Mmm. You look pretty hot.' Ryan's grin suggested that he was commenting on her sexual appeal rather than her body temperature but, for once, Hannah wasn't put off. Was that because the flirtatious comment was acceptable under the new rules that seemed to be forming?

She laughed. 'You're hopeless, Ryan.' Then she pointed ahead. 'Stop here—that's Susie's cottage.'

Ryan followed her as far as the veranda. When Hannah emerged a few minutes later, wearing light cargo pants and a shirt over her bikini and with a towel and underwear and things for Susie in a carry bag, he was lounging against one of the posts framing the steps. Strands of bougainvillea snapped in the wind and a shower of dark red petals had left blooms caught in the dark waves of his hair.

'Why am I hopeless?'

Had he been stewing over the casual reprimand the whole time he had been waiting for her?

'Because you're an incorrigible flirt,' Hannah informed him. 'You can't talk to women without…' She had to leave the sentence unfinished. 'Without making them feel like you're attracted to them' had been the words on the tip of her tongue but what would happen if he responded by saying he *was* attracted to her? In theory, letting her hair down was great, but this was actually quite scary. What if he said she had nothing to worry about because there was no way he could be attracted to her? Hannah's mouth felt oddly dry.

'Most women appreciate a compliment,' Ryan was saying. 'I try to be nice. To establish a good rapport with the people I work with.'

'Hmm.' Hannah didn't have to try and make the sound

less than understanding. Professional rapport had boundaries that Ryan clearly took no notice of.

He hadn't moved from the support of the post. To get to the car, Hannah had to go down the steps, which meant moving closer to the stationary figure.

'I work with you, Dr Jackson.'

'You do, Dr Fisher.' Hannah gripped the handles of her carry bag more firmly and made the move to the top of the steps.

'I'd like *us* to establish a good rapport. I don't think we've really got one yet, have we?'

'No.' She was close to Ryan now. She could almost have reached out and plucked petals from his hair.

'Why is that, Hannah?'

'I…ah…' It had been a mistake to make eye contact at this proximity. Words totally failed Hannah.

'Maybe we could try again,' Ryan suggested softly. 'We're in a new place that has nothing to do with work. We could make this weekend a new start.'

'Ah…' Something had already started. Hannah watched the way Ryan's gaze slid from her eyes to her mouth. The way his head was tilting slightly. She had to close her eyes as a wave of desire threatened to make her knees wobble and send her down the steps in an undignified stagger.

Had she mirrored that tilt of his face? Leaned closer to Ryan? Or had he just closed the gap of his own accord so that he could kiss her?

Not that it mattered. The instant his lips touched hers, *nothing* else mattered.

Yes, it was the start of something new, for sure. Something Hannah had never experienced. The first brush of paint on a totally new canvas.

Soft lips. A gentle pressure. Long enough to be intensely arousing but not nearly long enough. Hannah wanted more.

A *lot* more.

She wanted to taste this man. To touch him. To have him touch her. To fill in more of that canvas because she had no idea what colours and textures it would encompass or what the finished picture might be like. What that brief kiss *had* told her, however, was that the picture would be bigger and more exciting than any she'd ever seen.

It was Ryan who bent to pick up the carry bag, which had slipped, unnoticed, from Hannah's fingers.

'This way, Dr Jackson,' he murmured. 'Your chariot awaits.'

Hannah didn't want to move. Unless it was to go back into the cottage and take Ryan with her. It was disappointing that he hadn't suggested it himself. Surely he would normally follow through on a kiss like that?

Perhaps he intended to. He smiled at Hannah.

'Maybe,' he said lazily, 'we can do something else about establishing that rapport later.'

'Rapport, huh? That's a new word for it.' Susie lay on her hospital bed with her leg elevated on pillows, bandaged and packed in ice. 'So what was it like, then?'

'The kiss?' Hannah chewed the inside of her cheek. 'Not bad, I guess.'

Susie pulled a pillow from behind her back to throw at her sister.

'OK, it was great. Best kiss I've ever had. Satisfied?'

'No. Are you?'

Hannah smiled wryly. 'No.'

'So what are you going to do about it?'

'What can I do? OK, he might have been tempted to kiss

me for some reason but I can't see it going any further. He doesn't even like me. I don't like him. I'm just…attracted to him physically.'

'Maybe he's pretending not to like you because he's really attracted to you and you haven't given him any encouragement.'

'I kissed him! What more encouragement could he need?'

'Maybe he likes to take things slowly.'

'Ha!'

'Yeah.' Susie grinned. 'He doesn't look the type to take things slowly. Never mind, you've got the whole weekend in a tropical paradise. Something's bound to happen.'

'Forty-eight hours isn't that long.'

'But weddings are very romantic. And it's not as if you won't be seeing each other after you go home.'

'We won't be "seeing" each other when we go home. This is purely physical, Susie. An opportunity to get it out of my system. I mean, what if I'm sitting in a rest home when I'm ninety-five and I regret never trying a one-night stand? Doubt that I'd have the opportunity then.'

'So Ryan's not a long-term prospect, then?'

'Are you kidding? Would you take up with Richard the second with the benefit of hindsight?'

'No… Yes… Maybe…' Susie sighed. 'But Ryan might be different. He might not take off as soon as he spots greener pastures.'

'*Ha!*' Hannah put even more feeling into the dismissive response this time.

'Will you be seeing him again tonight?'

'No. I'm going to finish watching this movie with you, go and have a quick dip in the pool and then go home to sleep. I'm stuffed.'

'Why don't you skip the movie and see if you can find

him over at the doctors' house? I've got some stuff about Emily I was going to tell him so he could put it in his best man's speech.'

Hannah groaned. 'He's probably got it written already. One long string of blonde jokes.'

'It's a good excuse to talk to him.'

'He'll be at the Athina. Peeling potatoes or something.'

'He might be back by now. He got up as early as you did so he's probably equally stuffed.'

'I could go and have a swim.'

'What's the weather like out there now?'

'Horribly windy but still hot. It's not raining.'

'The pool's nice and sheltered. You probably won't be the only one there. Lots of people like to cool off before they go to bed. You sleep a lot better that way.'

Hannah wasn't the only one in the pool.

Ryan was there.

'I've done my potato-peeling bit,' he told Hannah. He was watching her shed her outer clothing. 'I really needed to cool off.'

Hannah slid into the water with a sigh of pleasure. The pool area was sheltered but it was still windy enough to make the water slightly choppy and the wind on wet skin pulled the heat out quickly enough to raise goose-bumps when Hannah stood up at the shallower end of the pool. She ducked down and swam breaststroke into deeper water. 'This is gorgeous.'

'Isn't it?' Ryan was swimming towards her. Only his head was showing but, thanks to Susie's accident, Hannah was only too well aware of what the rest of Ryan looked like. She took a determined breath.

'Susie's been telling me things about Emily that might

be useful for your best man's speech. Or have you finished writing it?'

Ryan grinned. 'No. Haven't started. Thought I might just wing it.'

'Well, there's a funny story about her spitting on Mike's helicopter.'

'Why did she do that?'

Hannah trod water, edging further away from Ryan. 'She was terrified of flying in helicopters and there's this Greek thing of spitting for luck. Only when the Greeks do it, it's kind of a token spit.' Hannah turned and swam a few strokes before shaking wet strands of hair from her eyes and taking another breath. 'When Emily did it, Mike had to clean the helicopter and there's a long-standing joke between them now about the paintwork getting corroded.' Hannah trod water again and turned. She should be a safe distance away from Ryan now.

She wasn't. He had kept pace with her.

'Interesting,' he said. 'I did know that Em hated helicopters. The night Mike proposed to her, they'd been sent on a mission that got cancelled and he landed them on a secluded beach. She thought they were crashing so she was really angry but Mike said that emergency measures had been necessary because he really needed to talk to her.'

'It all worked out, then.'

'Mmm. They have a very good rapport.' Ryan twisted his body in the water so that he was floating on his back. 'How's our rapport coming along, Dr Jackson?'

'Pretty good, I think.' Was it a feeling of insecurity that made it a relief to find her feet could touch the bottom of the pool here?

'Could be better, though, couldn't it?' With a fishlike movement, Ryan turned again, moving sideways at the same time so that he was within touching distance of Hannah. He caught her shoulders and Hannah seemed to simply float into his arms.

Not that she tried to swim away. She could have. Her feet were secure on the tiles at the bottom of the pool as she stood up and it would have been possible to get enough momentum to escape.

But she had no intention of escaping. This was it. She just had to get over the fear of doing something so out of character. Falling into what looked like a matching desire in Ryan's dark eyes, it became possible to step over that boundary.

'Yes,' she managed to whisper.

And then he was kissing her again and it was totally different to that kiss on the veranda. This one had a licence to continue. This one rapidly deepened so that Hannah had to wind her arms around Ryan's neck to keep her head above water. She could feel his hands on her bare skin, along with ripples from the disturbed water that seemed to magnify the sensation. His fingers trailed from her neck down her back, held her waist and then stroked their way up to cup her breasts.

At the same time, his lips and tongue were doing things that were arousing Hannah more than she would have believed possible. His face and lips were cool, thanks to the relentless wind, but the inside of his mouth was far from cool. It was hot enough to fuel an already burning desire. Hannah kissed him back, sucked headlong into that desire until she totally forgot herself. When he held her closer, Hannah found herself winding her legs around Ryan so that she couldn't float away.

Ryan groaned. 'God,' he murmured, pulling her hips even closer with an urgent strength to his grip. 'I want you, Hannah. You know that, don't you?'

Hannah tried to swallow, but couldn't. 'I want you, too.'

'Not here. Somewhere dry.'

Hannah had all the incentive she needed to throw caution to the winds for at least one night of her life. She even managed to sound as though she was quite used to being carried away by physical passion.

'Your place or mine?' she asked with a smile.

'Mine's closer. Just up those steps. It's Mike's old room. You can get in through a door on the veranda so nobody will see us.' Ryan bent to kiss her again and then he took her hand in his to lead her from the pool. 'You sure about this, Hannah?'

'What's not to be sure of? As you said, it's important to establish a good rapport with the people you work with.' She tightened her fingers around his, shivering as she climbed the steps of the pool and the wind caught at more of her exposed skin. Or was it the thought of where she was going and what she knew they would do that caused that shiver? Not that she had any intention of backing out. No way.

'Lead on, Dr Fisher.'

# CHAPTER SIX

IT WAS the curious howling sound that woke Ryan.

The first fingers of light were stretching under the roof of the wide veranda to enter his room and he could just make out the smooth hump of the feminine shoulder beside him.

Without thinking, Ryan touched the skin with his lips. A butterfly kiss that was as gentle as the way he traced the delicious curve of Hannah's hip with his hand, loving that dip to her waist that was accentuated by her lying on her side.

Loving everything about this woman. This new version of Hannah Jackson.

Her intensity. Softness. Suppleness. The way she accepted everything he had to offer and had responded in kind.

Thank God he hadn't stuck to that resolution to stay well away from her.

If he had, he would have missed out discovering just how good it was possible for sex to get. His experience last night had been the best he'd ever had in his life.

And Ryan knew what had made the difference. It was knowing he'd been right the moment he'd first laid eyes on Hannah. That there was a reason why the attraction had been so powerful. It was just possible he had found what he desperately needed in his life.

More of an anchor than a permanent job represented. The haven of a relationship that could be trusted. Could grow into something strong enough to last a lifetime. Could become a whole family even.

Something *good*. Love that wasn't darkened by the grim side of life. He was so tired of being strong for the people he loved. Not that he'd ever stop, but he badly needed something that would let the sunshine back into his own soul.

Someone he could be totally honest with. Someone that he could actually allow to see that things ripped him apart sometimes. He was fed up with hiding. Being flippant because he couldn't afford to share how he really felt. Making other people laugh because he'd discovered that was the best way to escape his own fear or misery.

Not that he'd ever made Hannah really laugh and, in a way, that was scary. Could she see through him? Despise him for being less than honest with himself and others? Had she been hurt in the past by a man who hadn't been able to connect on an emotional level and was that why that prickly barrier had been between them since that first meeting? If so, he could understand. Forgive and forget any of the putdowns.

Ryan pressed another soft kiss to Hannah's shoulder. Then he lifted her hair to kiss the side of her neck. She'd dropped that barrier last night, hadn't she?

One night.

A perfect night.

Ryan let his breath out in a contented sigh. Never mind that dawn was breaking. Last night had been just the beginning. The connection had been established and it could be the foundation for something that was going to last for ever.

Right now, Ryan had no doubt that it was entirely possible he could spend the rest of his life loving Hannah— in bed and out of it.

* * *

The dream took on colours that were so beautiful they took Hannah's breath away. She could actually *feel* them and the building excitement was something she remembered from childhood, waking up to a longed-for day that was going to bring something very special.

She was flying in her dream. Soaring over some incredible tropical landscape towards the place she most wanted to be. But she wasn't going to reach her destination because the edges of reality were pushing the dream away. The sense of loss was only momentary, however, because the reality was the touch of Ryan's lips. They were on the side of her neck, delivering a kiss so gentle it made her want to cry. Instinctively, she turned towards him, seeking the comfort of being held, only to find his lips tracing a line from her neck all the way to her breast. Stopping when they reached the apex and the cool flick of his tongue on her nipple took Hannah's breath away for real.

There was still a dreamlike quality to this, though, and Hannah kept her eyes closed even as her hands moved to find and touch Ryan where she now knew he most liked to be touched. The whole night had been a dream—the stuff of erotic fantasy—so why not keep it going just a little longer?

Thank God she had given in to that urge to experience something new. To find out if Susie was right and she'd discover the best sex of her life. Even in her wildest dreams until now, she hadn't had any idea what it could be like. Hannah could understand perfectly what had drawn her mother and her sister and probably countless other women into relationships that could only end in heartbreak.

Not that she was going to allow this to go that far. This was just a perfect ending to a perfect night. A one-night stand that Hannah could treasure the memory of for the rest of her life.

With a small sound of absolute pleasure, she slid her arms completely around Ryan to draw him closer.

It was raining when they woke again. Rain driven sideways by a wind that hadn't abated at all during the night. If anything, it was worse.

'What's the time?'

Ryan reached to collect the wristwatch he'd dropped by the side of the bed. 'Nearly nine.'

'Oh, my God, I can't believe we've slept in!' Hannah slid out from the tangled sheets, covering her bare breasts with her hands while she looked for her clothes. 'I've got to get back to Susie's place and get sorted. We're supposed to be at Kylie's salon by nine-thirty. It's probably chaos out there by now.'

'It would be chaos whatever time it is.' Ryan put his arms behind his head, clearly intending to watch Hannah getting dressed. 'Don't worry about it.'

'Where's my phone?' Hannah felt more in control now that she had her underwear on. 'Susie's probably been trying to text me. I put it on silent mode at the rehearsal yesterday and I completely forgot to reset it.'

'You got distracted,' Ryan said with satisfaction. 'The wedding's not till 4 p.m. Don't stress.'

Hannah pulled on crumpled cargo pants. Impossible not to feel stressed with the sound of rapid footsteps on the wooden boards of the veranda behind the thin curtain and then the excited bark of a dog.

'I need to get out of here without anyone seeing me.'

'Why?'

'It would be embarrassing if everyone knew I'd spent the night here.'

'Why?' Ryan repeated. 'It's nothing to be ashamed of. We're both single, consenting adults, aren't we?'

'Yes…' But there was an element of shame as far as Hannah was concerned. She'd never done anything like this in her life. This kind of selfish physical indulgence might be normal for Ryan and the women he chose, but it couldn't be more out of character for her. She'd always made sure she was ready to commit to an exclusive relationship before going to bed with someone.

'And it was fun, yes?' Ryan wriggled his eyebrows suggestively. 'I certainly enjoyed it.'

'Mmm.' Hannah tore her eyes away from the sight of Ryan getting out of bed. He obviously felt no need to cover himself. This was a man who was quite comfortable in his own skin. An enviable confidence that Hannah could only aspire to. She did her best. 'Me, too,' she added with a smile.

Ryan covered the floor space between them with an easy couple of strides. He drew Hannah into his arms and kissed her. 'I *really* enjoyed it,' he murmured. 'You're amazing.'

'Mmm.' The sound was a little strangled this time. Hannah wasn't so sure about daylight kisses. Sexual fantasy needed the cover of dark. She drew away. 'Could you keep an eye out and tell me when the coast is clear on the veranda? I can go down the other end, away from the kitchen, can't I?'

'Yeah.' Ryan turned away and picked up his shorts. 'I'll come with you.'

'No need. It'll only take me a few minutes to walk and I could do with the fresh air.'

'It'll be fresh all right. Might feel quite cold after yesterday with this rain. Did you bring a jacket?'

'No.'

'Then why don't you let me drive you home? I've got to take Mike's Jeep back up to the Athina, anyway. I'd better check in and see what my best-man duties involve. I suspect I'll have to stick with Mike for the rest of the day.'

And Hannah would need to be with Emily. She probably wouldn't see Ryan again till later that afternoon. No more daylight kisses to contend with. The odd sensation in her stomach had to be relief, rather than disappointment, surely?

'A ride would be good,' she said. 'That way I can get sorted faster.'

The veranda was deserted and no one interrupted their journey through the garden to the car park. As they scrambled from the end of the veranda, Ryan took hold of Hannah's hand and it felt so natural it would have been rude to pull hers away. As they left the gardens behind them, Hannah glanced at the hospital buildings but there had been no message from Susie yet and she would be back here in no time. Would she tell her sister about last night?

Maybe not. Not yet, anyway. The experience was still too fresh. Private and...precious?

Would Ryan say anything?

Maybe not. The way his hand still held hers was comforting. As though he shared a reluctance to break the illusion of a bond they'd created last night. Hannah was even more confident he could be discreet when he dropped her hand at the sight of someone running towards them.

Wet curls of black hair were plastered around Mike's face. 'I was just coming to find you, mate. Hi, Hannah.'

'What's up?' Ryan wasn't smiling. Neither was Mike.

'There's been an accident up at Wygera. Harry called me to see if I can do a first response with the Jeep. I've got a good paramedic kit in the back.' Mike was still moving and both Ryan and Hannah followed. 'I was on the way to the house to find a doc to come with me, but you'll do just fine.'

'Do you want me to come as well?' Hannah queried.

'Please.' Mike caught the keys Ryan threw and unlocked the doors of the Jeep. 'Sounds like there are at least three casualties. All teenagers.' He opened the back of the vehicle and pulled out a light, which he stuck to his roof. A cord snaked in through his window and he plugged the end into the cigarette lighter. A bright orange light started flashing as he turned on the engine.

'Where's Wygera?' Ryan pulled his safety belt on as Hannah climbed into the backseat.

'It's an aboriginal settlement about fifty miles from here. We'd normally get the chopper out for something like this but there's no way anyone's going to be flying today.' Gears crunched and the Jeep jerked backwards as Mike turned with speed and they took off. Hannah clicked her safety belt into its catch.

'What's happened?' she queried. 'And don't you have an ambulance available?'

'They're all busy on other calls right now and it'll take time to get a vehicle on the road. There's been trouble with the bloody bulls, by the sound of it—thanks to this weather.'

They were on the main road now, and Hannah could feel how difficult it was going to be, driving fast in the kind of wind gusts they were being subjected to. The windscreen wipers were on high speed but the rain appeared to be easing a little. Hannah shivered. She was damp and still hadn't had the opportunity to get any warmer clothing. Wrapping her arms around herself for warmth, she listened as Mike continued filling them in.

'There's a guy up at Wygera by the name of Rob Wingererra. They've acquired a few rodeo bulls. Long story, but they're a project for the teenagers up there. Huge animals with wicked horns. Apparently the wind caused some damage last night and brought a fence down and damaged a shed. The kids went out to try and get the bulls rounded up and into shelter and they got out of hand. Some kid's been cut by corrugated iron, one's been gored by a bull and another sounds like he might have a crush injury of some kind after getting caught between a bull and a gate.'

'How long will it take us to get there?'

'It's an hour's drive on a good day but I'm hoping to get there sooner than that. Hang on tight back there, Hannah, but don't worry. I know this road like the back of my hand. We'll just need to watch out for slips or rubbish on the road.'

He certainly knew the road. Having gone over the bridge and through the township, Mike headed towards the foothills of the mountains that divided the coastal plain from the cattle country Hannah knew was further inland. At the speed they were going, they would arrive there as fast as any ambulance was capable of. As they rounded one corner, Ryan threw a glance over his shoulder.

'You OK, Hannah?'

The tone was caring. How long had it been since a man had been this concerned for her well-being? It was dangerous to allow it to matter.

'I'm fine,' she said hurriedly.

'No, you're not—you're freezing!' Ryan twisted his body beneath the safety belt, pulling off the lightweight jacket he was wearing. 'Here. Put this on. '

'Thanks.' Hannah slid her arms into sleeves that were still warm from Ryan's skin. 'Are you sure you don't need it?'

But Ryan wasn't listening. 'What information have you been given about these kids so far?'

'There's a health worker at the settlement, Millie, who's

very good. Rob called her after he found the kids and they've got them inside at his place. She's controlled the bleeding on the boy that got cut but it sounds like he might have lost quite a bit of blood. The one who got poked by a horn isn't feeling too good. He's been vomiting but Millie thinks that might have something to do with a heavy night on the turps. The other one has sore ribs, maybe a fracture, so he's finding it painful to breathe.'

'Sounds like a mess.'

'I'm glad I've got you two along.' Mike flashed a grin over his shoulder at Hannah. 'Not the chief bridesmaid duties you were expecting this morning, eh? Sorry about that.'

Hannah smiled back. 'Actually, this is probably more within my comfort zone.'

'We'll have back-up pretty fast. There'll be an ambulance not far behind us and they'll send another one as soon as they're clear. We just need to do the initial triage and make sure they're stable for transport. Couldn't ask for more than two ED specialists on my team.'

'Let's hope it's not as bad as it sounds,' Ryan said. 'At least the rain's slowing down.'

'I've put in a good word to try and get some sunshine for Em this afternoon.'

Ryan laughed. 'You think the big guy's going to listen to you?'

'Hey, I've collected a few brownie points in my time. At least as many as you. Or maybe not.' Mike glanced at his friend. 'How's your dad doing?'

'Not so great. It's hard on Mum.'

'She must be delighted to have you in Auckland now.'

'Yeah.'

'Few trips to Brisbane still on the agenda, though, I guess? How's Michaela?'

Ryan shrugged. 'You know how it is,' was all he said.

'Yeah, buddy.' Mike's response was almost too quiet for Hannah to catch. 'I know.'

What was wrong with Ryan's father? And who was Michaela? An ex-wife? Hannah slumped back a little in her seat. How ridiculous to feel jealous. A timely reminder that this was just one weekend of her life; she didn't need to get caught up in Ryan Fisher's personal business. That was the road to the kind of emotional disaster Hannah had carefully avoided in her life thus far.

Caught up in her own thoughts and then a text conversation with Susie, who had heard about the drama at Wygera and was happy to wait for Emily to collect her, it seemed only a short time later that a tall water tower came into view. The cluster of houses nearby had a sad, tired air to them, with the rusting car bodies on the sparse greenery of surrounding land adding to an impression of poverty.

The eucalyptus trees were huge. They had been here far longer than the housing and would no doubt outlast most of these dwellings. Right now, the majestic trees were dipping and swaying in the strong wind, participating enthusiastically in a form of elemental ballet. Small branches were breaking free, swirling through the air to join the tumble of leaves and other debris on the bare ground. A larger branch caught Ryan's attention as it landed on the steep roof of the tidiest building they'd seen so far.

'It's the local hall,' Mike told him. 'Built to withstand snow, from what I've heard.' He grinned. 'Really useful, huh? It should manage the odd branch or two, anyway. We've got a turn-off up here and then we should almost be at Rob's place.'

A young woman could be seen waving frantically as they turned onto a rough, unsealed road.

'Target sighted,' Mike said. 'One windmill!'

Hannah was amazed he could sound so relaxed. And that Ryan could share a moment of amusement. She felt completely out of her depth here. They had one paramedic kit between the three of them and three potentially seriously injured teenagers. Hannah had never worked outside a well-equipped emergency department before.

'Hell, you took a long time,' the young woman told them. 'The boys are hurt bad, you know.' She led the way into the house. 'Stupid bulls,' she added with feeling.

'They weren't being nasty,' an older woman said. 'They were scared by the wind and that flapping metal on the shed. Hi, Mike!'

'Hi, Millie.' Mike smiled at the health worker and then at a man who was holding bloodstained towels to the leg of a boy on the couch. 'G'day, Rob. How's it going?'

'I'll let you tell me,' Rob said. His weathered face was creased with anxiety. 'I think I've finally managed to stop the bleeding in Jimmy's leg now, anyway. I've been sitting on the damn thing for an hour.'

Mike had set his backpack-style kit down on the floor and was unzipping it to pull out a stethoscope. 'This is Ryan,' he said, 'and that's Hannah. They're both doctors.' He glanced at the two other boys, who were sitting on the floor, leaning against the wall. They both had a rug over their legs and they both looked miserable. One had a plastic basin beside him. He shifted his gaze to Millie questioningly.

'Hal's got the sore ribs and Shane's got the puncture wound.' She smiled at Hannah and Ryan. 'Guess you've all got one patient each. Who wants who?'

Hannah swallowed a little nervously. An abdominal goring from a long bull's horn could have resulted in nasty internal injuries that would be impossible to treat in the field. Broken ribs could result in a tension pneumothorax and there were no X-ray facilities to help with diagnosis. A cut leg seemed the safest option. Even if Jimmy had lost enough blood to be going into shock, the treatment was easy. Stop the bleeding, replace fluid and supply oxygen.

'I'll have a look at Jimmy,' she said quickly. 'Have you got a sphygmomanometer in that kit, Mike?'

'Yep.' Mike pulled it out. 'You want to check Shane, Ryan?'

'Sure.'

'Mary?' Mike spoke to the girl who'd shown them inside. 'Could you go back to the road, please? There should be an ambulance arriving before too long and it was really helpful to have you show us where to stop.'

'But I wanted to watch,' Mary protested. 'Are you going to sew Jimmy's leg up?'

'Probably not,' Hannah responded. 'Not until we get him to hospital anyway.'

'Do as you're told,' Millie added firmly.

Hannah moved towards Jimmy, who looked to be about fourteen. 'Hi.'

The youth stared back silently for just a second before averting his eyes, which gave Hannah the impression he'd taken an instant dislike to her.

'I'm going to be looking after you for a bit, Jimmy,' she said. 'Have you ever had your blood pressure taken?'

He shook his head, still avoiding eye contact.

'It doesn't hurt. I'm going to wrap this cuff around your arm. It'll get a bit tight in a minute.'

Ryan had gone to Shane who looked younger than the other two. He was holding a teatowel to his side and it, too, was blood soaked.

Hannah unwound the blood-pressure cuff from Jimmy's

arm. His baseline recording for blood pressure was within normal limits but he was young enough to be compensating well for blood loss. She would need to keep monitoring it at regular intervals.

'I'm going to put a small needle in the back of your hand,' she warned Jimmy. 'OK?'

'Why?'

'You've lost a fair bit of blood. We need to give you some fluid to get the volume back up. Blood doesn't work as well as it should if there isn't enough of it going round. Is your leg hurting?'

'Yeah, course it is. It's bloody near chopped off.'

'Can you wiggle your toes?'

'Yeah.' The tone was grudging and Jimmy still wouldn't make eye contact. Was it just her or were all strangers not welcomed by these teens?

'I don't think it's in too much danger of dropping off, Jimmy, ' she said calmly. 'I'll check it properly in a minute. When I've got this needle in your hand, I'll be able to give you something to stop it hurting so much.'

Ryan seemed to be getting a similar suspicious response for being a stranger. Shane didn't look too happy when he put his hand out to touch the teatowel.

'Mind if I have a look, buddy?'

'Are yous really a doctor?'

'Sure am. Just visiting from New Zealand.'

'He's a mate of mine,' Mike told the boys. 'He's going to be the best man at my wedding.'

'Oh, that's right!' Millie exclaimed. 'You're getting married today, Mike. Crikey, I hope you're not going to be late for your own wedding. Dr Emily would be a bit cheesed off.'

'We'll get sorted here in no time,' Mike said calmly.

'Hal, I'm just going to listen to your chest while you take a few breaths, OK?'

'But it hurts.'

'I know, mate. I want to make sure those ribs haven't done any damage to your lung, though. Try to lean forward a bit.'

Hannah had the IV line secured and a bag of fluids attached and running. She got Rob to hold the bag. Having been given the kudos of being Mike's best friend, Ryan now had a more co-operative patient.

'Does it hurt if you take a deep breath?'

'Yeah.'

'Can I have a look at it?'

'I guess.'

'Wow, that's a pretty impressive hole! These bulls must be big fellas.'

'Yeah.'

'Does it hurt if I touch here?'

'Nah. Not much.'

For the next few minutes a rather tense silence fell as they all worked on assessing and treating their patients. Hannah didn't want to disturb the makeshift dressing on Jimmy's leg in case the bleeding started again, but she made a careful examination of his lower leg and foot to check for any serious damage to blood supply and nerves.

Mike was worried about a possible pneumothorax from Hal's broken ribs and got Ryan to double-check his evaluation.

'I think you're right,' Ryan said. 'Breath sounds are definitely down on the left side but it's not showing any signs of tensioning. One of us should travel with him in the ambulance, though.'

The need for constant monitoring and the potential for serious complications from the injury went unspoken, but

Hannah could feel the level of tension in the room creep up several notches.

Ryan glanced around him. 'Anyone heard the one about the blonde and the bulls with big horns?'

Hannah almost groaned aloud. Just when she'd been impressed by the professional, *serious* manner in which Ryan was approaching a job that should have been as much out of his comfort zone as it was for her, he was about to revert to type and tell one of his stupid jokes. Make light of a serious situation.

And then she caught Ryan's gaze.

This was deliberate. He knew exactly what he was doing. This was a ploy—as much of a skill as applying pressure to stop heavy bleeding, only it was intended to work in the opposite direction. A safety valve to relieve pressure. A way of defusing an atmosphere that could be detrimental if it was allowed to continue.

What if Hal picked up on how dangerous a pneumothorax could be and got frightened? He would start to breathe faster, which would not only hurt but interfere with his oxygen uptake. Shane might start vomiting again and exacerbate an internal injury. Jimmy might get restless and open the wound on his leg, with further blood loss.

They were all listening already.

'So, she tells him exactly how many bulls there are in this huge paddock and demands that he honours his side of the bargain and gives her the cute baby one.'

If this was a practised skill, as that almost defensive glance had suggested, what did that tell her about the man Ryan *really* was? Was the fun-loving, laid-back image simply a veneer?

'And the farmer says, "If I can tell you the real colour of your hair, will you give me back my baby bull?"'

Maybe the times Hannah saw Ryan so focussed on his patients—as he had been with Brendon's mother on Monday night and with Shane only minutes ago—said more about who he really was. Or the concern she'd heard in his voice when he'd asked if she was OK on the trip up here. Or…that incredible ability to be so gentle she'd discovered in his touch last night.

No. Hannah couldn't afford to believe in the serious side Ryan was capable of presenting. That was the short cut to disaster that her mother and sister had followed so willingly. She was stronger than that. She could push it away. It was easy, really. All she had to do was remember the way he flirted. The way women flocked to queue up for a chance to go out with him.

He might have the ability to be serious but it couldn't be trusted to last. Serious stuff couldn't be allowed to continue for too long. It just had to be broken by the injection of fun.

"'Now…give me back my dog!'"

Even though she'd only been half listening, Hannah found herself smiling. Shane and Jimmy were giggling. Hal groaned because it hurt, trying to laugh, but he still managed a big grin. Rob and Millie were still laughing when two ambulance officers came through the door with Mary. Eyebrows shot up.

'We heard there was an accident here,' one of them said, 'not a party!'

How many doctors would be able to achieve that? Hannah wondered. Then her own smile broadened. How many doctors had such a supply of awful jokes that could seemingly be adapted to suit the situation? As a demonstration of how useful it could be to be so laid back, this had been an eye-opener. The tension that had filled this room when Hannah had arrived and had threatened to get worse later had gone. Much of the anxiety had left the faces of Rob and Millie and even the boys were all still grinning, even when faced with imminent transport to hospital.

It didn't take long to sort out the transport arrangements. Mike would travel in the ambulance with Hal and Jimmy. Shane demanded to travel with Ryan in the Jeep.

'You can't do that,' Millie said. 'You'd better wait for the other ambulance. You've got a hole in your guts.'

'It's pretty superficial, luckily,' Ryan told her. 'It's going to need a good clean-out and examination under local, but I don't see any harm in Shane riding in the Jeep to start with, anyway. We can meet the other ambulance on the road and transfer him then.'

'Guess that'll be quicker.' Millie waved at Mike as he climbed into the back of the ambulance. 'You'd better get back in time to get your glad rags on, eh?'

Hannah was in the backseat of the Jeep again and Ryan kept up an easy conversation with Shane, interspersed with the occasional query and frequent glance that let Hannah know how closely he was monitoring the lad's condition.

They got back to Crocodile Creek before a rendezvous with the second ambulance. Hannah gave herself a mental shake when she realised that she was disappointed. It wouldn't do to be shut in the confines of a vehicle with no company other than Ryan's, she told herself firmly. It would make it impossible not to feel the strength of the connection that daylight and even a semi-professional working environment had failed to dent.

Disturbingly, it seemed to have become stronger. Hannah stood back in the emergency department of Crocodile Creek Hospital after doing a handover for Jimmy. When Ryan finished transferring the care of Shane to the hospital staff, he turned to look for her. When he spotted her, standing near the water cooler, he smiled.

A different sort of smile. It went with a questioning expression that suggested he really cared about whether she was OK. Like his tone had been when he'd given her his jacket to keep her warm. It touched something deep inside Hannah and made it impossible not to feel happy.

Dangerous, dangerous territory.

She wasn't going to fall in love with Ryan Fisher.

Hannah simply wasn't going to allow it to happen.

# CHAPTER SEVEN

WHEN had it happened?

*How* had it happened?

It wasn't just the atmosphere. The way Mike and Emily were looking at each other as they walked around the altar, taking their first steps as man and wife. Or the chanting of the priest as he gave them his blessing. Or the collective sigh of approval coming from the packed church pews.

There was no question it *had* happened, however.

With her arms full of the white silk train of Emily's dress and the soft tulle of her veil, Hannah was walking very slowly, her arm touching Ryan's as he held the silk ribbons joining the wreaths on the heads of the bridal couple. They got a little tangled at the last corner and there was a momentary pause.

And Ryan looked at her.

There could be no mistaking that sensation of free-fall. The feeling that all the cells in her body were charged with some kind of static electricity and were desperately seeking a focus for their energy.

Or that the focus was to be found in the depths of the dark eyes that were so close to her own. This was a connection that transcended anything remotely physical. The caress of that eye contact lasted only a heartbeat but Hannah knew it would haunt her for life.

It was a moment of truth.

A truth she hadn't expected.

One she most certainly didn't want.

She was in love with Ryan Fisher. She could... incredibly...imagine that this was a ceremony to join *them* in matrimony, not Mike and Emily and the notion only increased that delicious sensation.

Fortunately, Hannah had a huge armful of fabric she could clutch. It brought back memories of the cuddly blanket Susie had dragged around with her for years as a small child, much to Hannah's disgust. The fleecy square had become smaller and smaller over the years and was finally abandoned but somehow the last piece had emerged just after their father had died and Susie had slept with it under her pillow and had genuinely seemed to derive comfort from the limp rag.

Hannah had never needed an inanimate object for comfort.

Until now.

How stupid had it been to go to bed with Ryan?

She *knew* she didn't do one-night stands. She had always believed that that kind of intimacy should be reserved for a relationship that meant something because it was too hard to separate physical and emotional involvement.

Had her subconscious tricked her into believing that, for once, she could do just that? Or had she known all along that her attraction to Ryan had only needed a push to become something far deeper and she had been drawn towards it as inevitably as her mother and sister had been drawn to involvement with the Richards? Had she despised his flirting because, deep down, she had been jealous?

Stupid, stupid, stupid!

How horrified would Ryan be if he guessed how she was feeling? Or, worse, would he take advantage of it, in the Richards style, making the most of having some female fall at his feet—just until he got bored and moved on to a more exciting playground?

Any of those wayward thoughts, generated by the chaos and excitement of the afternoon's preparation for this ceremony, of allowing her one-night stand to become a one-weekend stand had to be squashed.

This had all the makings of a painful ending already. If even a tiny bit more was added to the way Hannah was feeling, it could be just as disastrous as spending weeks or months in a relationship, only to have it end. She might have had no intention of making an emotional investment but something had been automatically deducted from her account without her realising.

Hannah liked that analogy. It wasn't possible to withdraw the sum but she could, at least, stop throwing good money after bad and pull the plug.

Firmly enough to break the chain so she could throw it away.

Facing the congregation as they made their final circuit, Hannah looked up, finally confident she had control again. There was a woman in the second row in the most extraordinary hat she had ever seen. A vast purple creation with bright pink artificial flowers, like giant gerberas, around its brim.

In front of the hat sat Mike's mother, a handkerchief pressed to her face to mop up her tears of joy. His father was using his sleeve to wipe his. Beside them sat a little row of children—the pageboys and flower girls who had done a wonderful job of petal-strewing and had had to sit quietly for the more serious part of the proceedings.

As a sensible insurance policy, Susie sat at the end of

the pew, hemming the children in, her crutches propped in front of her, and beside her, in the aisle, was Charles in his wheelchair with one of the flower girls sitting on his lap. The adults were both smiling happily but there was an almost wistful element in both their expressions.

It *had* been a gorgeous service. Sophia must be thrilled that everything had gone so perfectly despite the worry that the worsening weather that afternoon had caused.

Not that any of the bridal party had had time to fret. Kylie, the gum-chewing, self-confessed gossip queen, had worked like a Trojan to make them all as beautiful as possible. Hannah had been startled by how she looked with her soft, natural curls bouncing on her shoulders and more make-up than she would normally have worn. By the time she was encased in her peach silk, sheath dress with the big flower at the base of a plunging halter neckline that matched the explosion of froth at knee level and the sleeveless, silver bolero jacket, Hannah felt almost as gorgeous as Emily looked in her cloud of white lace and flowers.

The men had peach silk bow ties to match the bridesmaids' dresses and silver waistcoats to match their jackets. Hannah hadn't been wrong in thinking they would look irresistibly handsome in their dark suits and white dress shirts. And Ryan, of course, was the best looking of the lot, with his long, lean frame encased in tailored elegance and his dark hair groomed to keep the waves in place. Even a very recent shave hadn't been enough to remove the dark shadow, however, and Hannah couldn't help remembering the scratch of his face that morning on some very tender areas of her skin.

With some difficulty, she dragged her thoughts back to the present. Yes. It had been an over-the-top, fairy-tale wedding ceremony for two people who were obviously very deeply in love and that had the potential to make any single person like Susie or Charles Wetherby reflect on what was missing from their own lives.

It had to be contributing a lot to Hannah's own heightened emotional state. With a bit of luck, she would see things quite differently once they were away from the church.

It was nearly time for the bridal procession. Hannah could see Charles moving his wheelchair and Susie whispering to the children to give them their instructions. They would come at the end of the procession after each pair of bridesmaids and their male counterparts had moved into the aisle. Hannah's partner was, of course, Ryan. She would have to take his arm at least until they got to the foyer, where she would need both hands to help Emily with her veil.

It might take all twelve available bridesmaids' hands, judging by the howl of the wind that could now be heard over the trumpet music. The blast of air inside that came as someone opened the main door of the church was enough to catch Emily's veil and threaten to tear it from her head. The chandelier overhead rattled alarmingly and a crashing sound brought a gasp from everybody standing to watch the procession.

People were craning their necks to see what had happened but they were staring in different directions.

'It was the flowers!' someone near Hannah exclaimed. 'Look!'

Hannah looked. She could see the huge vase of exquisitely arranged peach and white blooms that had toppled from its pedestal near the altar. A large puddle was spreading out from the mound of scattered blooms amongst the shards of broken china.

'No, it came from outside,' someone else shouted. 'Everybody, sit down!'

The priest was looking as alarmed as his congregation. Hannah caught a glimpse of Sophia crossing herself as the priest hurried down the side aisle. Another loud splintering noise was heard as he reached the foyer and his robes were whipping around his legs.

'Close the door,' they heard him order. He came back to where Emily and Mike had halted a few seconds later. 'There are slates coming off the roof,' he reported. 'You can't go out that way.'

A buzz of consternation rippled through the crowded pews. What was happening? Was this a bad omen for the bridal couple? The noise level continued to increase as the priest spoke to Mike and Emily, pointing towards another door at one side of the church.

'You'll have to go out through the vestry. It's not safe this way.'

'No, no, no!' Sophia was powering down the side aisle, gesticulating wildly. Hannah saw a pretty young woman in a dark blue dress with a matching ribbon in her curly hair get up hurriedly to follow her. 'They can't go backwards,' Sophia cried. 'It's bad luck!'

A chorus of assent came from the congregation nearby. The priest was looking deeply concerned and even Mike and Emily exchanged worried glances.

'How about "take two"?' Ryan suggested calmly. 'We'll push rewind. You guys go back to the altar, have another snog and then go down the side and out the vestry door. That way, you won't be going backwards before you leave the church.'

'How about it, Ma?'

'It's a great idea,' the young woman beside Sophia said firmly. 'Isn't it, Mrs P.?'

'I don't know. I really don't know. This is bad....'

'Don't cry, Ma,' Mike ordered. 'Have you got a spare hanky there, Grace?'

The sound of more slates crashing into the courtyard decided the matter. As one body, the bridal party turned and moved swiftly back towards the altar. The sound of spitting for luck from everybody at the end of the pews was clearly audible despite continuing, excited conversation.

'Hey!' Ryan leaned towards Hannah. 'Aren't you supposed to be hanging on my arm?'

'I don't think we rehearsed this bit.' But Hannah obligingly took the arm being offered.

'I haven't had a chance to tell you but you look fabulous in pink.'

'It's peach, not pink.'

The second kiss that Mike and Emily shared in front of the altar was a little more hurried than the first. They were all aware of the priest now standing by the vestry door, virtually wringing his hands with anxiety. He wanted his church emptied, preferably without anyone being decapitated by flying slates.

Sophia looked as though she would benefit from smelling salts. Unplanned happenings were threatening to disrupt the most carefully orchestrated wedding that Crocodile Creek was likely to experience.

The loose slates weren't the only surprise. Hannah was close behind the bride and groom as the priest opened the vestry door and there, in front of them, was a couple locked in a rather passionate embrace.

It had to be that girl, Georgie, she had seen at the airport. Hannah would have recognised those red stiletto shoes anywhere.

Ryan nudged her. 'Isn't that Alistair—that American neurosurgeon?'

'Yes, I think so.'

'Seems like they've been having their own little ceremony.'

'Mmm.' What was it about this place? Something in the tropical air? Romance seemed to be around every corner.

Maybe *that* was the problem. She'd get over Ryan in a flash once she was breathing nice clean, sensible New Zealand air again. Not that there was time to think even that far into the future. Some of the male guests had braved the front entrance to make sure it was safe to leave the church from this side. Vehicles were being brought right to the door and the mammoth task of shifting the whole congregation to the Athina for the reception was under way.

Any hint of blue patches between the boiling clouds had long gone. It looked as though another heavy, squally rain shower was imminent.

'Quickly, quickly,' Sophia said to everyone passing her at the door. She had clearly abandoned her carefully thought-out transport arrangements and was planning to move everybody as fast as possible. 'We must get home!'

She made Emily, Mike, Ryan, Hannah and Susie squeeze into the first of the limousines. 'The bride mustn't get wet!' she warned. 'It's bad luck!'

Sophia spat three times as Emily and Mike climbed into the spacious rear of the car. What with the huge wedding dress and then Susie's crutches, there wasn't much room left for Ryan and Hannah. They ended up on the same side as Susie with Hannah in the middle. A crutch pressed against her thigh on one side but that discomfort paled in comparison to the disturbing effect of having such close contact with Ryan's thigh on the other side.

'Well, that was fun.' Mike had a huge grin on his face. Then he turned to Emily and his smile faded before he kissed her tenderly.

'Don't mind us,' Ryan drawled.

Mike surfaced reluctantly. 'You should try this some time, mate. It's not that bad.'

'Mmm.' Ryan's sidelong glance at Hannah involved a subtle quirk of an eyebrow. *I know,* the glance said. *I've enjoyed that particular pastime quite recently myself.*

'Hey!' Mike was grinning again. 'If you got around to it soon enough, we could give these suits another airing. I'll return the favour and be *your* best man.'

'I'll keep that in mind.'

Why did Ryan choose that moment to slide his hand under the peachy froth of Hannah's skirt to find her hand? To hold it and give a conspiratorial kind of squeeze?

Had he got some crazy notion himself during that ceremony—as she had? Was Hannah going to be tricked into believing she was a candidate for his bride?

*No!*

She pulled her hand free but the gesture lost any significance because the driver of the limousine chose precisely that moment to slam on his brakes and she, Ryan and Susie tumbled forward.

'Ouch!' Susie cried.

'Are you all right?' Ryan helped her back onto the leather seat.

Mike slid the glass partition behind his head open. 'What's going on?'

'Rubbish bag flying around in this wind,' the driver told him. 'Sorry—but it landed on the windscreen and I couldn't see a thing. You guys OK back there?'

'Fine,' they all chorused.

Including Hannah. She *was* fine now that Ryan wasn't holding her hand. Now that they'd all been shaken out of the romantic stupor emanating from the bridal couple.

'Crikey!' The car slowed again as it crossed the old wooden bridge into the cove. 'If that water comes up any more, this'll get washed out to sea.'

The creek was more like a raging torrent and the wind was whipping up small waves on its swift-moving surface. The strings of fairy-lights adorning the exterior of the Athina were seriously challenging the staples holding them in place and Mike heroically gathered Emily's dress together to scoop his bride into his arms and carry her the short distance from the car to the restaurant doors.

Huge, fat drops of rain were starting to fall but Mike moved fast enough to prevent Emily's dress getting damp.

'Thank goodness for that.' She laughed. 'Sophia will be feeling my dress the moment she walks in.'

'Let me check.' Mike ran his hands down the embroidered bodice of the dress and then yanked Emily close. Laughing again, she wrapped her arms around his neck and lifted her face for a kiss.

Ryan's voice was close to Hannah's ear. Too close.

'They have a good rapport, don't they? Just like us.'

Hannah swallowed hard. Even his voice was enough to stir desire. A sharp yearning that was painful because she couldn't allow herself to respond.

'Later,' Ryan murmured. The word was spoken too softly for anyone else to overhear.

'*No!*'

She hadn't expected her response to come out with such vehemence but the promise Ryan's word had contained was too much. *Pull the plug,* her brain was screaming. *Now!*

The momentary freezing on Ryan's part was strong enough for Hannah to sense his shock at the rebuttal but there was no time to try and soften the rejection with any kind of explanation or excuse. The second and third cars from the church had pulled up and Mike's parents spilled out, along with several more clouds of peach-tulled women and dark-suited men.

'Your dress!' Sophia wailed. 'Let me feel your dress, darling! Is it wet?'

'No, it's completely dry. See?' Emily did a twirl in front of the mass of wedding presents piled up in the restaurant entrance.

Mike's father, George Poulos, beamed happily. 'Inside. Everybody inside. Our guests are arriving. It's time to eat, drink and be merry!'

The next hour was a blur of posing for the photographer and then introductions amongst a loud, happy crowd who were determined to ignore the shocking conditions outside. The howl of the wind, the intermittent thunder of rain on the roof and the crash of huge waves on the beach below the restaurant windows were largely drowned out by the enthusiastic live band and even more enthusiastic guests.

Hannah did her best to ignore the rather dark glances that were coming her way from Ryan. It was easy to avoid him by talking to other people. Like Grace, the young nurse with the blue ribbon in her hair.

'It's been my job to try and keep Mrs P. calm,' she told Hannah. Blue eyes that matched her ribbon rolled in mock exasperation. 'As if! Don't be at all surprised if there are a few doves flying around in here later.'

'Plates!' Mike's father carried a stack past them, weaving through a circle of dancers. 'For later,' he threw over his shoulder at Hannah and Grace. 'Don't tell Sophia.'

'I'd better distract her. Excuse me.' Grace hurried away.

'*Opa!*' someone shouted.

A chorus of echoes rippled through the room and Hannah saw a lot of small glasses being raised to lips.

'Ouzo?' A waiter had a tray of the small glasses, as well as the more traditional champagne flutes.

'Maybe later.' Hannah was having trouble trying to keep her head clear enough to remember all the names and she knew she would have to keep it clear to deal with the conversation that was bound to occur with Ryan.

He was right behind the waiter. 'What did you mean, "No"? "No", what?'

'I meant "no" to later,' she said with a resigned sigh.

'But I thought…is something wrong, Hannah?'

'Not at all.' Hannah smiled—reassuringly, she hoped. She would have to work with Ryan. She didn't want to offend him. 'Last night was lovely. Great fun.'

*'Fun?'* Ryan was staring at her. He had no right to look so shocked. Surely *he* did this kind of thing all the time? A bit of fun. Move on.

'This is Harry.' Grace had returned to where Hannah was standing, staring dumbly back at Ryan. 'He's our local policeman here in the cove. Hi.' She smiled at Ryan. 'You did a good job as best man.'

'I do an even better job at dancing.' Ryan's killer smile flashed as he extended his hand. 'Come on, let me show you.'

It was a snub, Hannah realised as Ryan turned away with Grace on his arm without a backwards glance. He *was* offended for some reason.

Harry was staring after the couple as though he didn't approve any more than Hannah did, but then they managed to smile at each other. In fact, it wasn't that difficult for Hannah to smile. A glow of something like pleasure curled within her. He had liked being with her, then. It had been good enough for him to want more.

If she wasn't so weak, she would have wanted it herself. How wonderful would it be to sink into a relationship with someone like Ryan and enjoy it for what it was? An interlude. One that would set the standard for the best that sex and probably companionship could offer. But to do it without losing too much of her heart and soul?

Impossible.

He would wreck her life eventually.

She would end up like her mother, settling for something that was better than nothing. Learning to enjoy fishing.

Or alone, like Susie, unable to find anyone that excited her as much as the first man who had really stolen her heart.

Harry was telling her something. Hannah made an effort to focus on the tall, good-looking man with a flop of black hair and a worried expression.

'I'm trying to keep tabs on what's happening with Willie,' he told her. 'They're making noises about upgrading it from a category 3 to a 4.'

'Is that serious?'

Harry nodded. 'Cyclones are all dangerous. 'Specially Aussie ones—they're known for exhibiting a more erratic path than cyclones in other parts of the world. The higher the number, the more danger they represent. A category 3 is a severe tropical cyclone. You can get wind gusts up to 224 kilometres per hour and can expect roof and structural damage, and a likely power failure.'

'The slates were certainly flying off the church.'

'There's a few people with tarps on their roofs already. They'll lose them if things get any worse.'

'And they're expected to?'

'It's been upgraded to a 4. It's running parallel to the coast at the moment but if it turns west we'll be in trouble.

A 4 has winds up to 279 kilometres per hour. You'll get significant structural damage, dangerous airborne debris and widespread power failures.'

As though to underline Harry's sombre tone, the lights inside the Athina flickered, but there was still enough daylight for it not to matter and they came back on almost immediately.

'I'm with the SES—State Emergency Services,' Harry finished. 'In fact, if you'll excuse me, I should make a call and see what's happening.'

Just as Harry disappeared, Ryan emerged from an animated group of Greek women nearby.

'*Fun?*' he queried with quiet menace. 'Is that all it was for you, Hannah? *Fun?*'

This was disconcerting. She would have expected a shrugged response from Ryan by now. A 'there's plenty more fish in the sea' kind of attitude.

'It *was* fun.' She tried to smile. To break the tension. 'But we both know it could never be any more than that.'

'*Do* we?' Ryan held her gaze. Challenging her. 'Why is that?'

'Oh, come on, Ryan.' Hannah looked for an escape. Someone to talk to. A new introduction. Where was Susie when she needed her? Nothing seemed readily available. They were marooned. A little island of hostility that was keeping all the happy people away with an invisible force field. 'We're not on the same page, remember?'

'Obviously not,' Ryan snapped. 'There I was thinking that we had made a fresh start. The start of something that could actually be meaningful.'

Meaningful? Oh, help! It would be so easy to believe that. Hannah so *wanted* to believe it. To believe *she* could be the one to tame this particular 'bad boy'. To have him love her so much he would be content to settle down and never get bored.

The wheelchair arrived beside them so smoothly neither had noticed.

'I'm Charles Wetherby,' the man said unnecessarily. 'I must apologise for this awful weather Crocodile Creek is turning on for you. I hope you're still managing to enjoy yourselves.'

Hannah had the weird feeling that Charles had known exactly how much they were enjoying themselves and was there to do something to defuse the atmosphere.

Ryan controlled the flash of an ironic smile and managed to introduce both himself and Hannah to Charles without missing a beat.

And then he excused himself, as though he couldn't stand being in Hannah's company any longer.

He was hurt, she realised. She hadn't expected that at all. It was confusing. Why would he be hurt...unless he was being honest. Unless he really had thought there was something meaningful going on.

No. He might think that—for now. He might even believe it long enough for Hannah to trust it, but he was a type, wasn't he? He was, what, in his mid-thirties? At least a couple of years older than she was, given his professional experience. If he was into commitment he wouldn't still be playing the field. And what about Michaela? Was she someone who had believed in him and had now been discarded?

Hannah had to paste a smile onto her face to talk to Charles.

'You look so like Susie,' he was saying. 'It's a real treat. Must be wonderful to have a sibling that you're so close to.'

'It is.'

'Uncle Charles! Look at me! I'm dancing!'

The small blonde flower girl who had been sitting on Charles's knee during the ceremony was part of a circle of dancers, between two adults. She wasn't watching the steps any more because her head was twisted in Hannah's direction and she had a huge smile on her face.

'This way, Lily.' Mike's sister, Maria, had hold of one of Lily's hands. 'We go this way now.'

'*Opa!*' The cry to signal a new round of toasting the bridal couple rang out.

'Ouzo?'

'No, thanks.' Hannah shook her head at the attentive waiter. Lily had given her an excuse to watch the dancers and Ryan was now part of the circle. So was Mike. And then the circle disintegrated as Sophia bustled through.

'Eat! Eat! The food will be getting cold.'

Ryan and Mike took no notice. With an arm around each other's shoulders and their other arms extended, they were stepping in a dance of their own. Happy. Relaxed. The bond of a deep friendship was obvious to everyone and they all approved. They were clapping and stamping their feet in time with the music and calling encouragement.

And then George was on the dance floor, a plate in each hand.

'No!' Sophia cried.

But the sound of smashing crockery only brought a roar of approval and more people back to the dance floor.

Hannah turned away. She spotted Susie sitting with a very pregnant woman. They had plates of food from the buffet.

Not that Hannah felt hungry. Watching Mike and Ryan dance had left her with a curious sense of loss. How long had Ryan known his best friend? Ten years? More? Their bond appeared unshakable. Mike trusted him completely.

But Mike wasn't a woman. The ending of a friendship, however close, could never destroy someone as much as the ending of the most intimate relationship it was possible to have.

It was really quite straightforward so why was her heart winning the battle with her head right now?

Why did she feel this sense of loss? As though she had just made a terrible mistake?

Because it was already too late. She was in love with this man.

She was already prepared to believe in him.

And if he gave her another chance, she would take it.

Take the risk.

Do whatever it took to spend as much time as possible with him. In bed and out of it.

The rest of her life, even.

# CHAPTER EIGHT

This had to be the ultimate putdown.

And he had only himself to blame.

It had only been one night. Hannah Jackson was only one of hundreds of women Ryan had met since he'd grown up enough to be interested in the opposite sex. Thousands, even, and he'd dated a fair few in those early years. Slept with enough to know how rare it was to find a woman who could be both intellectually and physically stimulating.

He could have dealt with that attraction, however powerful it had been, when that was all it was. Moved on with maybe just a shrug of regret. But Hannah had taken down that barrier. Taken him by the hand and shown him a place he had never been to before. A place he didn't want to leave.

And now she was shoving him out. Had put that barrier back up and….it *hurt,* dammit! Nobody had ever treated him like this before—and she'd accused *him* of being shallow? What reason did she have? She might have been hurt in the past, he reminded himself. Some bastard might have treated her badly enough to leave scars that hadn't healed yet.

No. It didn't matter how good the reason might be. Or how fresh the scars. Why the hell would he set himself up for another kick in the guts like the one she'd just delivered? With a smile, no less. A damning with faint praise.

*Fun?* Like a night out? A party? A game of tennis?

'What's up, mate?' Mike's fingers dug into his shoulder. 'You look like you're at a funeral, not a wedding.'

'Sorry. Miles away.'

'Not in a happy place, by the look of that scowl. Forget it. Come and eat. The lamb's wonderful and Ma will be force-feeding you soon if she doesn't see you holding a plate.'

'Good idea. And I think a drink or two is overdue as well.'

'Just don't get trollied before you have to make that speech and tell everyone how wonderful I am.'

Ryan laughed. 'More like seeing how many stories of your disreputable past I can dredge up. What time am I on?'

'Just before the cake-cutting. I think Ma's got it down for about 8:30 p.m.'

'Cool. Gives me half an hour to see how much I can remember. What was the name of that girl in Bali? The one with all the tattoos?'

'Don't you dare! You might get Em worried I haven't settled down.'

'And have you?'

'No question, mate. I'll never look at another woman. I've found the one for me. Oh, great—a slow song! Catch you later. Go and eat. I'm hanging out for a waltz with my wife.'

Lucky man, Ryan thought, watching Emily's face light up as Mike reached her and the way she seemed to float dreamily in his arms as they found a space on the dance floor.

Lucky, lucky man.

The lights had flickered more than once in the last hour but this time they went out and stayed out.

Hannah, sitting with Susie, the very pregnant doctor

called Christina and her gorgeous, dark-skinned husband Joe, who had turned out to be a fellow New Zealander, had also been watching the bridal couple dance. And Harry and Grace, who were dancing towards the edge of the crowd. And the woman who hadn't taken off that extraordinary purple hat with the huge flowers.

'That's Dora for you,' Susie was saying. 'She's so proud of that hat she'll probably wear it when she's polishing floors at the hospital for the next week or—'

She stopped as the room plunged into semi-darkness. The candles on tables provided only a dim light that would take a few moments to adjust to. People were just shadowy figures. The dancing had stopped and there was an uncertain kind of milling about, both on the dance floor and around the tables. The couple who were not moving at all in the corner caught more than Hannah's attention.

'Who *is* that?' Susie whispered loudly. 'I can't see in this light.'

'Whoever they are, they seem to like each other.' Joe grinned.

Susie winked at Hannah. 'Yeah. I'd say they've got a pretty good rapport all right.'

Hannah elbowed her sister. A reminder of what had started this small life crisis she was experiencing was not welcome.

They found out who the male of the pair was almost immediately, as Charles Wetherby rolled past their table accompanied by a young police officer who was holding a candelabrum. The flames on several candles were being dragged backwards to leave little smoke trails due to the speed with which the men were moving.

'Harry Blake!' The tone was urgent enough for conversation to die amongst everyone within earshot and the reaction to it spread rapidly. A lot of people could hear what

Charles had to say as Harry seemed to attempt to shield the woman he'd been kissing so passionately by steering her further into the dark corner and then striding forward to meet the hospital's medical director.

'Bus accident up on the mountain road,' Hannah heard him say.

'I think it was *Grace* he was kissing,' Susie whispered. 'Woo-hoo!'

'Shh!' Hannah warned. 'This sounds serious.'

Joe's chair scraped as he got up and moved towards the knot of men. Christina's bottom lip was caught between her teeth and she laid a protective hand, instinctively, on her swollen belly. Tension and urgency were radiating strongly from their centre of focus.

Everybody who could hear was listening avidly. Others were trying to find out what was being said.

'What's going on?' someone called.

'Why are the police here?'

'Why haven't the lights come back on?'

'The hospital's four-wheel drive is on its way here to pick up whatever hospital staff you think you might need on site. Have you seen Grace? If we've got to set up a triage post and then get people off the side of the mountain, we'll probably need an SES crew up there, as well....'

Mike was heading towards the expanding knot of male figures. So was Ryan. Hannah got to her feet. If this was a major incident, they would need all the medical expertise available.

Charles would be magnificent in any crisis, Hannah decided. So calm. So in touch with what was happening everywhere in his domain.

'We've been on standby to activate a full code black disaster response, thanks to the cyclone watch on Willie,' he told the cluster of medics now around him. 'I'm going to go ahead and push the button. We have no idea how many casualties we might get from this bus but it looks likely we're in for trouble from Willie so it'll give us a few hours' head start. A dry run, if you like.'

'What's happening?' Sophia pushed her way towards Charles. Dora Grubb was not far behind her, the pink flowers on her hat wobbling nervously.

'There's been an accident, Sophia,' Charles said. 'A bus full of people has vanished off the road near Dan Macker's place. Big landslide, thanks to all the rain we've had this week.'

'Oh… *Oh!*' Sophia crossed herself, her face horrified. 'This is bad!'

'I'm going to have to call in all available medical staff, starting with everyone here. Including Mike and Emily. I'm sorry, Sophia.'

'*Oh!*' Sophia looked stricken now. 'But the cake! The speeches!' Then she rallied, visibly pulling herself together. She stood as tall as possible for a short, plump person. 'Of course you need my boy,' she said proudly. 'And our Emily. Who else can look after those poor people if they need an operation? Emily! Darling! Let me help you find something else to wear.'

Hannah looked down at the froth of peach tulle around her knees and on to the flimsy white shoes with the flowers on the toes.

Mike noticed the direction of her glance. 'I've got spare flight suits in our room and Em's probably got a spare set of boots. Ryan? You'd better come and grab a suit, too.'

'Thanks, mate.'

'At least you won't have to roll up the sleeves and legs. Come with me, you guys. Let's get kitted up.'

It was Susie's turn to look stricken. 'I want to help but I'm useless with these crutches!'

'Not at all,' Charles said. 'You can stay with me and Jill. There's a lot of admin we'll need to do at the hospital. Code black means we've got to empty as many beds as we can. Set up a receiving ward. Mobilise stores. Reorganise ED...'

The list was still continuing as Hannah hurried in the wake of Mike and Ryan. She could also hear Dora Grubb talking excitedly to Sophia.

'They'll need food, all these rescue people.'

'We *have* food. Too much food. All this lamb! I'll tell the chef to start making sandwiches.'

It took less than ten minutes for the four young medics to encase themselves in the helicopter service issue overalls.

Emily sighed as she took a glance over her shoulder at the mound of white lace and silk on the bed. 'It was nice while it lasted,' she said, 'being a princess.'

'You'll always be a princess, babe,' Mike assured her. 'And I reckon you know how sexy I think you look in those overalls.'

Hannah carefully avoided looking anywhere close to Ryan's direction. She could understand the look that passed between Mike and Emily because she had stolen a glance at Ryan moments before, when he'd bent to lace up the spare pair of Mike's heavy steel-capped boots, and there had been no danger of him catching her glance.

It was a completely different look to civvies. Or scrubs. Or the white coat that doctors never seemed to bother with any more. He looked taller, somehow. Braver. Ready to get out there and save lives. And there was a very determined tilt to his chin that she hadn't seen before. Tension that visibly knotted the muscles in his jaw.

Was he anticipating a tough job at the scene of the bus crash or was it controlled anger? Directed at her?

Whatever.

Sexy didn't begin to cover how he looked.

Hannah scraped back her carefully combed curls and wound an elastic band to form a ponytail. Would Ryan see *her* as looking adventurous and exciting in these overalls with the huge rolled-up cuffs on the arms and legs?

Not likely.

Especially as he appeared determined not to actually look directly at her at all.

Even in the back of an ambulance a commendably short time later, when they had collected gear and co-ordinated with other personnel at the hospital, he was avoiding anything as personal as direct eye contact.

Mike was with them. Emily had ended up staying behind at the hospital to oversee the set-up and preparation of Theatres. Because of the weather conditions, with injured people exposed to the rain and wind, she needed to organise fluid warming devices and forced-air warmers on top of making sure she was ready to administer a general anaesthetic at short notice.

A second ambulance was following with another crew and all Crocodile Creek's available fire appliances had gone on ahead. Police had been first on scene, and by the time Hannah arrived, the road was lined with vehicles—a chain of flashing lights they had glimpsed from miles away as they'd sped up the sometimes tortuous curves of the mountain road. Lights that had haloes around them right now thanks to the heavy curtain of rain.

A portable triage tent was erected on the road to one side of the massive obstacle of mud, rocks and vegetation. Guy ropes had it anchored but the inflatable structure was looking alarmingly precarious in the high wind and its sides were being sucked in and then ballooning out almost instantly with a loud snapping sound.

The generators used to fill the outlines of the tent with compressed air were still running, powering lights, including some that were being directed downhill from the point where large skid marks were visible. There was more noise from the fire engines whose crews were rolling out winch cables from the front of the heavy vehicles. Pneumatic tools like the Jaws of Life were being primed and tested. As a background they were already tuning out, the wind howled through the treetops of the dark rainforest around them.

Harry Blake, wearing a fluorescent jacket that designated him as scene commander, met the ambulance, framed by the back doors Mike pushed open and latched.

'Who's in charge?' he queried briskly.

'I'm liaising with the medical director at the ED.' Mike clipped his radio to his belt. 'What frequency are we using on site?'

'Channel 8.'

Mike nodded. 'Channel 6 is the hospital link.' He leapt out of the back of the ambulance. 'I'll go down and triage with these two doctors and then we'll deploy all the other medical crews we get. What's it looking like down there?'

'It's a bloody mess,' Harry said grimly. 'The bus must have come off the road at speed and it rolled on the way down. The windows have popped out and we've got people and belongings all over the place. Some of the seats have come adrift inside and there's people trapped, but we can't get inside until the fire boys get a line or two onto the bus.'

'It's not stable?' Mike was sliding his arms into the straps of his backpack containing medical supplies.

'Hell, no. It could slide farther, especially if it keeps raining like this.'

Hannah and Ryan were out of the ambulance now, standing beside Mike. 'Don't forget your helmets,' he reminded them. Then his attention was back on Harry. 'Any fatalities?'

'At least one.' Harry raised his voice to a shout to be heard as they started walking and got closer to the generators. 'There's a guy who's been thrown clear and then caught under the bus. He's at the front and we think he's probably the driver. We won't be able to shift him until we can jack up the front corner somehow.'

'The fire guys going to be able to use their cutting gear down there? Is it safe to have them clambering around?'

'We've got nets anchored on the slope. It's not too bad for climbing. There's an SES crew down there at the moment, trying to clear the scene of everybody who's able to move.'

'How many are we dealing with?' Ryan had jammed his hard hat on and was pulling the strap tight.

Harry shook his head. 'Haven't been able to do a head count yet. There's injured people over quite a wide area. We think there's two or three still trapped in the bus, from what we can see. One of the passengers who's not hurt thinks the bus was quite full. There's about ten people we can bring up now. Could be fifteen or twenty still down there needing attention.'

Mike and Ryan shared a glance. This was huge. It was going to stretch their resources and everybody's skills.

'Let's do it.' Ryan pulled on latex examination gloves and then heavier ones for climbing. He gave Mike a thumbs-up and Mike responded with a terse nod and another shared glance. They had faced difficult situations before. They were more than ready to tackle this one. Together.

Hannah felt oddly excluded. Even when Mike put her after Ryan and before himself to protect her as she climbed down the steep, slippery slope, she didn't really feel a part of this small team.

Ryan hated her. He didn't want her there.

Within the first few metres of their climb, however, any thoughts of personality clashes or anything else that could affect a working relationship were forgotten.

A woman lay, moaning. 'My leg,' she groaned. 'I can't get any further. Help...'

This was an initial triage. No more than thirty seconds could be allocated for any patient to check for life-threatening injuries like uncontrolled haemorrhage or a blocked airway. Mike had triage tags in his pocket. Big, brightly coloured labels with an elastic loop that would alert all other personnel to the priority the victims had for medical attention. This woman was conscious and talking. It took less than thirty seconds for Ryan to examine her.

'Fractured femur. Closed. No external bleeding. Airway's clear.'

Mike produced a yellow label. Attention needed but second priority. 'Someone will be with you as soon as possible,' he reassured the woman as they moved on. 'We've got to check everybody else first and then we'll be back.'

'But it *hurts*...Oh-h-h....'

It was hard, leaving her to keep descending the slope. A huddle of people near the base of the nets were bypassed. They were all mobile and being looked after by SES people. Grace was there, organising the clearance of the less injured from the scene. Mike gave her a handful of green triage tags that designated the lowest priority. Hannah saw a young Asian couple clinging to each other, looking terrified, and she could hear someone talking in a foreign language that sounded European. Had the bus been full of tourists? It could make their job more difficult if they couldn't communicate with their patients.

A young woman lay, unconscious, against the base of a huge eucalyptus tree.

'Hello, can you hear me?' Hannah pinched the woman's ear lobe. 'Non-responsive,' she told Mike. She laid a hand on the woman's neck and another on her belly. 'She's breathing. Good carotid pulse. Tachy.'

The elastic of a pink triage label went over her wrist. Highest priority. This case was urgent, with the potential to be saved and the likelihood of rapid deterioration if left. They moved on.

'There's one over here,' a fire officer yelled at them. 'He's making a weird noise.'

'Occluded airway.' Mike repositioned the man's head and the gurgling sound ceased. Another pink tag.

Winch hooks were being attached to the bus. There were no big lights down here and the rescue workers had to make do with the lamps on their helmets. A curious strobe effect to viewing the disaster was evident as lights intersected and inspected different areas. It made it easier to deal with, Hannah decided, because you could only see a patch at a time. A single patient, a broken window, dented metal, broken tree branches, strewn belongings and luggage.

Just the top half of the unfortunate man who had been caught beneath the front wheel of the bus. It took only a moment to confirm the extinction of life and give the man a white tag to signify a fatality so that nobody would waste time by checking him again.

'Don't go downhill from the bus.' A fire officer with a winch hook in his hand shouted the warning. 'We haven't got this thing stable yet.'

The doors of the bus were blocked because it was lying, tilted, on that side. The emergency hatch at the back was open, however, and must have been how some of the less injured had escaped the wreckage.

Mike saw Ryan assessing the access. 'Not yet, buddy,' he said firmly. 'You can just wait until it's safer.'

*Safer,* Hannah noted. Not *safe.* It could never be really safe to do something like this, could it? And yet Ryan was clearly frustrated by having to hold back.

Hannah shook her head to clear the water streaming down her face from looking up at the hatch. She was soaked now and the wind was chilling. She flexed increasingly stiff fingers and cast a glance at her colleagues.

There was certainly no doubting Ryan's commitment to his work and the people he cared for. How many ED specialists would be prepared to work in conditions like this? To risk their own lives without a moment's hesitation to try and save others?

Mike might have been off the mark in making people think Ryan was some kind of saint, but he hadn't been wrong in advertising him as a hero. They both were. The way these two men worked together suggested they had been in situations before that had not been dissimilar. There was a calm confidence about the way they worked that was contagious.

Like Ryan's courage in that plane turbulence had been.

What if she couldn't redress the antipathy Ryan now held towards her and the one who didn't win that consultancy position in ED felt obliged to go and work elsewhere? If she never had the chance to work with him again?

The sense of loss she had experienced watching him dance with Mike came back strongly enough to distract Hannah for several seconds. Was it always going to haunt

her? Did she have to be ruthlessly squashed at frequent intervals in order for her to perform to her best ability? Like now?

Hannah continued the triage exercise with grim determination. They found another five people with fractures
and lacerations who needed yellow tags. One more pink
tag for a partially amputated arm and severe bleeding. An
SES worker had been doing a great job of keeping pressure
on the wound. Then they were given the all-clear to check
out the bus.

'Not you, Hannah,' Mike stated. 'You can check in with
the SES guys. Make sure we haven't missed anyone. Get
someone to check further afield as well. We've got debris
over a wide area and injured people could have moved or
even fallen further down the slope.'

Hannah moved to find someone to talk to but she
couldn't help stopping for a moment. Turning back to
watch as the two men climbed into the bus.

Turning back again a moment later, when alarmed
shouting heralded a noticeable shift in the position of the bus.

'Oh, my God…' Was the bus going to move with the
extra weight? Slide and possibly roll again down the side
of this mountain?

Remove any possibility of repairing the rift she'd
created with Ryan?

Remove Ryan from her life with the ultimate finality of
death?

'No-o-o!'

It was a quiet, desperate sound, snatched away and disguised by the howl of the wind. If it was a prayer, it was
answered. Having taken up some slack from one of the
winch cables, the movement stopped. Mike actually leaned
out a broken window with his thumb and forefinger
forming the 'O' of a signal that they were OK.

It was only then that Hannah realised she had been holding her breath. A couple of minutes later and Ryan and Mike emerged from the bus.

'One pink, one yellow, one white,' Mike reported. 'One's unconscious and another's trapped by a seat.' He reached for his radio. Medical crews could now be co-ordinated, specific tasks allocated, patients treated and evacuated. The most seriously injured patients would be assigned a doctor who would stabilise and then escort them to hospital.

Hannah was joined by a paramedic by the name of Mario, issued a pack of gear and assigned the case of the woman who had been pink-ticketed at the base of the eucalyptus tree. Mike and Ryan were going to work on the pink-ticket patient inside the bus. Hannah watched them climb inside again. A scoop stretcher was passed in along with the pack of resuscitation gear by firemen who then waited, knowing their muscle would be needed to assist with extrication.

Once again Hannah felt that sense of loss as Ryan vanished from view and this time she couldn't quite shake it off.

She *needed* him, dammit! This was so far out of her comfort zone, it wasn't funny. The rain might be easing but she was still soaked and cold and her fingers felt uselessly stiff and clumsy.

The effort to concentrate seemed harder than it had ever been. Hannah was trying to recall the workshop she'd attended at a conference once, on the practice of emergency medicine in a hostile environment. Control of the airway was the first priority, of course, with cervical spine control if appropriate.

It was appropriate in this case. Hannah's gloved hand came away streaked with blood after touching the back of the young woman's head. Had she been thrown clear of the bus and hit the tree she now lay beside? If the blow had been enough to cause her loss of consciousness, it had potentially caused a neck injury as well.

'I need a collar,' she told Mario. She placed her hand, side on, on the woman's shoulder, making a quick estimate of the distance to her jaw line. 'A short neck, please. And a dressing for this head wound.'

It was difficult, trying to assess how well their patient was breathing. Hard to see, given the narrow focus of the beam of light from her helmet. Hard to feel with her cold hands and impossible to hear with the shouting and noise of machinery. And over it all, the savage wind still howled. Large tree branches cracked ominously and small pieces of debris like broken branches flew through the air, occasionally striking Hannah in the back or hitting the hard helmet she wore with a bang, magnified enough to make her jump more than once.

'I don't think we can assess her for equal air entry until we get her into an ambulance, at least,' she said. 'She's certainly breathing on her own without any respiratory distress I can pick up.'

Which was a huge relief. While this woman was probably unconscious enough to be able to be intubated without a drug regime, the lecturer at that conference had discussed the difficulties of intubation in a situation like this. Often, the technique of cricothyroidotomy was more appropriate and that wasn't something Hannah wanted to attempt with limited light and frozen fingers.

IV access was more manageable. Hannah placed a large-bore cannula in the woman's forearm and started fluids. She remembered to use extra tape to secure both the cannula and the IV fluid lines. The lecturer's jocular warning was what she'd remembered most clearly about that workshop. "If it can fall out," he'd said, 'it *will* fall out.'

Mario had the expertise and strength to move the woman onto a backboard and strap her securely onto it. And then the firemen took over, inching their way up the mountainside with the help of ropes and the net.

Moving to follow them, the beam of Hannah's light caught something that made her stoop. She picked the object up. It was a shoe. A rather well-worn sneaker with a hole in the top and what looked like a picture of a bright orange fish done in felt pen or something similar. What startled her was its size. It was small.

Very small.

A child's shoe.

But they hadn't come across any children in their triage, had they? Hannah had the awful thought that it could be the fatality inside the bus. But maybe the owner of this shoe was uninjured? Not seen amongst that huddle of frightened people who had been waiting for help up the slope? Hannah certainly hoped so. And if they were, they might have one bare foot and be grateful to see that shoe. Hannah stuffed it into the large pocket on the front of her overalls.

It wouldn't have been easy for a child to climb, even with the hand- and footholds the net provided. They were wet now and very muddy. Hannah slipped, more than once, and had to save herself by grabbing the netting or a tree root or branch.

How could fifty metres seem such a long way? And how long had they been on scene? Certainly no more than an hour, but she felt as though she had just completed a full night shift in the ED and a busy one at that.

The third time she slipped, Hannah might well have fallen but she was caught by her arm in a vice-like grip.

'Are you OK?' Ryan asked.

It had to be her imagination that she could hear the

same kind of caring in the query that she had heard in the car on the way to Wygera that morning. An aeon ago. In her current state it was enough to bring the sting of tears to her eyes. She blinked them away.

'Yeah…thanks…'

'Not easy, this stuff, is it?' Ryan was climbing beside her. Just below them, the scoop stretcher containing his patient was making slow progress upwards. 'How's your woman?'

'Still unconscious but breathing. A head injury but I have no idea how bad it is yet.'

'You'll be able to do a more thorough assessment in the ambulance. We won't be far behind you if you run into trouble. Mike says they're going to stage departures so we arrive at the ED at about six-minute intervals. Just pull over and keep your lights on and we'll stop to help.'

'Thanks,' Hannah said again. Professional assistance but at least he was talking to her. She was almost at the top of the slope now. A fire officer had his hand out to help her onto the road and the noise level increased markedly. She could still hear Ryan's call, though.

'Hey, Hannah?'

'Yeah?'

'You're doing a fantastic job. Well done.'

Those tears were even closer all of a sudden. They couldn't be allowed to spill. Hannah clenched her fists as she got to her feet on the road and her hand struck her bulky pocket. She peered down at Ryan.

'Hey, did you come across any children in the bus?'

'No. Why?'

'I found a shoe. A kid's size shoe.' She pulled it from her pocket. 'See?'

'Could have come from anywhere,' Ryan said. 'Maybe there's a kid amongst the green tickets.'

'Yes, I thought of that. I'll check with Grace later.'

'It could have come from spilled luggage as well. Or even been thrown away. Looks pretty old.'

'Hannah?' Mario, the paramedic, was calling. She could see the backboard supporting her patient being lifted into the back of an ambulance. 'We're nearly ready to roll.'

'On my way.' Hannah turned to give Ryan a smile of thanks for his help but he wasn't watching. He had already turned back to his patient.

'I'll take over the ventilations there, Mike. You've done a fantastic job up the hill.'

A fantastic job. Like her. So the praise hadn't really been personal, had it? The doors of the ambulance slammed shut behind her and someone thumped on the back to give the officer driving the signal to go. Hannah took a deep breath.

'Let's get some oxygen on, Mario. A non-rebreather mask at ten litres a minute. And I want a slight head tilt on the stretcher. Can we do that with a backboard in the way?'

'Sure, we'll just use a pillow under this end.'

'Let's get some definitive baseline measurements, too. Blood pressure, heart rate and rhythm, oxygen saturation.' She pulled a stethoscope from the kit. 'I'm going to check her breathing again.'

It felt good to be on the move towards a fully equipped emergency department and hospital. Hannah would feel far more in control then. Far less likely to be thrown off balance by overly emotional reactions to someone else's words or the way they looked at her. Or *didn't* look at her.

It helped to know that Ryan would be on the road within minutes, though. Travelling in the same direction she was. Sharing the same experiences and goals that had arrived in their lives so unexpectedly. To get through this ordeal and help as many people as possible.

They were on the same page now, weren't they?

What a shame it was just too late.

# CHAPTER NINE

THE contrast couldn't have been greater.

The Poulos wedding had been a happy circus. Crocodile Creek Base Hospital was hosting a miserable one.

Injured, bewildered people filled the cubicles and sat on chairs. A moving sea of professional staff was doing everything necessary. Doctors, nurses, clerks, radiographers and orderlies were doing their jobs. And more. The fact that it was late at night and the majority of people here were not rostered on duty meant nothing. A disaster response had been activated and there was nobody associated with this medical community who wasn't prepared to do whatever they could to help.

There was a lot to be done. Hannah's case was the first serious one to arrive so she had the initial advantage of all the staff she could possibly need to assist.

Luke hadn't yet gone to the receiving ward where he would be available on the surgical team, along with Cal and Alistair. Emily was still in the department as well, because minor cases needing surgery were going to have to wait until all the majors had been dealt with. They both came to assist Hannah. Charles wasn't far behind.

'You should get changed out of those wet overalls,' he

told Hannah. 'There's plenty of people here to take over. Susie can show you where the scrubs are kept.'

'Soon,' Hannah promised. 'I just want to make sure she's stable.' Having come this far with the injured woman, Hannah was reluctant to hand over. 'If that's OK with you, Dr Wetherby?'

Ryan might be registered to work in Australia but Hannah wasn't. It was Charles who could give her permission. It was up to him whether he trusted that she was competent enough not to cause problems he would have to take ultimate responsibility for.

The look she received was assessing but Charles had obviously seen enough to make a decision.

'Go ahead,' he said.

Mario and a male nurse had moved the woman, still strapped to her backboard, onto the bed.

'Right.' Hannah nodded, tucking away the pleasure that someone like Charles Wetherby was prepared to trust her. 'This woman was apparently thrown clear of the bus and was found unconscious. There's been some response on the way in but nothing coherent. I'd put her GCS at seven. She was initially tachycardic at 120 but that's dropped in the last fifteen minutes to a rate of 90, respirations are shallow but air entry is equal and the oxygen saturation has been steady on 97 per cent on 10 litres.'

Standard monitoring equipment was being attached to the woman, like ECG leads, a blood-pressure cuff and an oxygen saturation monitor. Someone was hanging the fluids from a ceiling hook and another nurse was taking the woman's temperature.

'Thirty-five point six degrees centigrade,' she reported.

'Not hypothermic, then,' Emily commented.

'Blood pressure was initially one-twenty on eighty. Last measurement was one-thirty on seventy.'

'Widening pulse pressure,' Luke said. 'Rising intracranial pressure?'

'Quite possible. She has an abrasion and haematoma in the occipital area. No obvious skull fracture. Pupils were equal and reactive.'

'They're not now.' Emily was at the head end of the bed, shining a bright torch into the woman's eyes. 'Right pupil is two millimetres larger and sluggish.'

'Do we know her name?' Luke asked.

'No.' Hannah glanced at one of the nurses. 'Perhaps you could check her pockets? She may have some ID.'

'We need some radiography,' Luke said. 'Preferably a CT scan. And where's Alistair? If we've got a neurosurgeon available, this is where he should be.'

Charles pivoted his wheelchair. 'I'll find him.'

The movement of the woman on the bed was unexpected. Restrained, due to the straps still holding her to the backboard, but unmistakable.

'She's going to vomit,' Emily warned.

'Let's turn her side on,' Hannah ordered. 'I'll need suction.'

It was easy to turn the woman onto her side and keep her spine protected, thanks to the backboard, but it was another sign that the pressure could be building dangerously inside her head.

The nurse checking her pockets had easier access with the patient tipped to one side. 'I've found something,' she said. 'It's a passport. An Australian one.'

'Great. At least she'll understand the language. And we'll be able to use her name.' Hannah glanced up at the monitor, to see what was happening with the blood pressure. 'What is it?'

'Janey Stafford.'

'*What?*' The startled query came from Luke. 'Did you say *Janey Stafford?*'

'Do you know her?' Hannah asked. It could be helpful for an unconscious person to hear the voice of someone she knew.

'I… I'm not sure.' Luke was looking stunned. He reached over and lifted the oxygen mask the woman had on. Was he looking for a feature he might recognise? Hannah wondered. Like that small mole at the corner of her top lip?

Luke was backing away. Shaking his head.

'You don't know her, then?'

'Not really. It was her sister I knew.' The tone was dismissive. An 'I don't want to talk about this' sort of tone. 'It was a long time ago.'

Emily was staring at Luke. Then she blinked and refocussed. 'Do you want me to intubate?' she asked Hannah.

Alistair walked into the resus bay at that moment.

'I'll hand over to an expert,' Hannah said. Having given Alistair a rundown on their findings so far, she found herself stepping back. Luke did more than step back. He left the resus bay completely.

But then a new emergency was coming in. Luke hadn't pulled the curtain closed behind him and Hannah could see Ryan arriving with his multi-trauma case from the interior of the bus. They were still using a bag mask to ventilate this patient. There were two IV lines in place and Ryan looked worried.

'Bilateral fractured femurs,' Hannah heard him tell Charles. 'Rib fractures and a flail chest. GCS of nine.'

Charles directed them to resus 2 and Luke disappeared behind the curtain along with them.

The picture of Ryan's face was not so quick to disappear for Hannah. She had seen him work under duress before. Seen him tired and even not a hundred per cent well himself, but she had never seen an expression like the one he had walked in with.

So grim. Determined. So…lacking in humour.

Instinct told her that it wasn't just the grim situation that was making Ryan look like that. He was the one who always made an effort to defuse just such an atmosphere. He seemed like a different person. Gone completely was that sparkle. The laid-back, golden-boy aura that had always seemed to cling enough to be easily resurrected.

It didn't look like Ryan intended smiling for a long time to come and Hannah didn't like it. He was being professional and she knew he would have the skills to match anything he had to face, but something was wrong. Something big was missing. The real Ryan seemed shut off. Distant.

Was it sheer arrogance to wonder if his anger at her had something to do with his demeanour?

Hannah shivered and wasn't even surprised to hear Charles's voice from close by.

'Go and get out of those overalls. Get some dry scrubs on and get a hot drink. I don't want to see you back in here for at least ten minutes.'

It did feel better, being in dry clothes. And the hot chocolate and a sandwich she found in the staffroom were wonderful.

'At least you're getting a bit of the wedding breakfast.'

Hannah smiled back at the plump woman. Susie would be surprised to see that Dora had taken off her hat. 'It's delicious,' she said. 'Thank you so much.'

'You're all doing such a wonderful job. Those poor people out there. There are a lot that are badly hurt, aren't there?'

Hannah nodded, her mouth full of the first food she had eaten since a hurried lunch too many hours ago. She had taken a moment to check on Janey's progress, to find she'd gone for a CT scan and that Alistair was planning to take her to Theatre immediately afterwards, if necessary, to relieve any pressure building from a bleed inside her skull. Emily had gone to get ready to administer an anaesthetic.

Ryan was still busy stabilising his patient, ready for the surgery Luke would have to perform to deal with the major fractures sustained.

More cases were coming in, prearranged to arrive at a steady but not overwhelming rate. Susie had hopped past on her crutches, a sheaf of papers scrunched in one hand.

'I've got to locate a new supply of O-negative blood,' she told Hannah. 'And there's so many other things to do. We're still trying to discharge people to one of the rest homes and find accommodation for everyone from the bus. You OK?'

She was, surprisingly, more than OK, thanks to the food and hot drink.

In the corner of the staffroom sat two tired-looking children. Lily was still in her flower girl's dress and CJ hadn't changed out of his small suit.

'Can we go now?' CJ asked Dora.

'We're supposed to stay here,' she replied. 'You know what they said about my house. It's not fit to be in when the cyclone comes.'

'Is it definitely coming, then?' Hannah's appetite faded and she swallowed with difficulty.

'They reckon it's going to hit us by morning. Susie's arranged some beds for the children to stay in here overnight. Dr Wetherby and CJ's parents are going to be busy all night by the look of things.'

'But you said—' CJ's lip wobbled ominously '—you *said* we could go and see if the puppies have arrived before we have to go to bed.'

'My dog's due to whelp again,' Dora explained to Hannah. 'Goodness knows why Grubby keeps letting her get in pup. It's me who ends up doing all the work.'

*'Ple-ease?'* begged CJ.

Dora looked at the clock. 'I guess we've got a fair few hours before the weather gets dangerous. If we went home quick and then came back again, I guess Dr Wetherby won't notice we've gone.'

'Don't tell,' CJ ordered Hannah. 'Will you?'

'I'm sure nobody will ask me,' Hannah responded. She watched as Dora took a small hand in each of hers and led the children away. A very capable woman, Dora. Hannah was sure no harm would come to the children.

And that reminded her of the shoe.

Over the next hour, as Hannah assisted in the treatment of several people, she had two things on her mind. One of them was watching for glimpses of Ryan, to see whether he was still looking so distant and miserable.

He was. More than once he passed Hannah with barely more than a glance. Never a smile. Or a comment that might have lifted her spirits. To imagine him telling a joke seemed ridiculous. He had changed into scrubs as well so he looked like the Ryan she had always known.

She just wished she could see a flash of him behaving the way he always had.

The other thing on her mind was the shoe. At every opportunity she asked different members of the staff whether they had come across a small child amongst the patients. Someone advised her to check with one of the clerks and, sure enough, when she did, she struck gold.

'There *was* a kid. A little blonde girl,' she was told. 'Chloe, I think her name was. She had a broken arm.'

'How old was she?'

'I can't remember. Four or five.'

The right sort of age to fit a shoe the size of the one Hannah had found.

'Where would she be now?'

'I have no idea, sorry. Maybe the plaster room? It was ages ago, though. She might have been sent home.'

Except that she had no home to go to, did she?

The thoughtful frown on Hannah's face must have looked like fatigue to Charles. He rolled towards her.

'You've been on duty for more than four hours,' he said. 'It's time you took a break. At least two hours' standdown before I see you back in here, please. It's going to be a long night and it might be just the beginning of what we need you for with the way Willie's decided to behave.'

Hannah nodded. A break was exactly what she needed right now, wasn't it?

The soaked pair of overalls lay where she had left them, in the corner of the women's locker room. Nobody had had time to tidy yet. Hannah fished the shoe out of the pocket and went looking for the child she now knew existed.

Jill Shaw, the nursing director, passed her in the corridor, with her arms full of a fresh supply of IV fluids.

'Have you seen a little girl?' Hannah asked. 'About five? With blonde hair?'

'You mean Lily? I think Mrs Grubb's looking after her. She should be in the hospital somewhere.'

'No, not Lily. A child from the bus crash. I need to know if this is her shoe.' Hannah showed Jill the worn sneaker with the faded fish picture on the toe.

Jill shook her head. 'Sorry.'

Ryan emerged from the door to the toilet just behind where Jill and Hannah stood.

He still looked grim. Distant. Lines of weariness were etched deeply into his face. He looked so…serious.

*Too* serious for Ryan Fisher under any circumstances. It just didn't fit. Hannah could feel her heart squeeze into a painful ball. She wanted to touch him. To say something that could raise just a hint of smile or bring back just a touch of life into those dark eyes.

But she couldn't. Partly because Jill was there and mostly because Ryan wasn't even looking at her. He was looking at the object in her hand.

'For God's sake, Hannah. There are more important things to be worrying about right now than a bloody *shoe!*'

Jill raised an eyebrow as she watched him stride away. 'It's time he had a break, I think.' She turned back to Hannah. 'They're collecting all the unclaimed property in Reception. Why don't you leave it there?'

Reception was crowded. People with minor injuries from the bus crash that had been treated were waiting for transport to the emergency shelters. Other accidents attributable to the awful weather conditions were coming in in a steady stream. And there were still the people that would normally present to Emergency with the kind of injuries and illnesses they could have taken to their GP in working hours. Many of these people had been bumped well down any waiting list. Some were giving up and going home. Others were still waiting—bored, miserable and increasingly impatient.

'I don't give a stuff about bloody tourists off a bus,' an irate man was shouting at the receptionist. 'I pay my bloody taxes and I want to be seen by a doctor. *Now!* I've been waiting hours. Is this a *hospital* or what?'

Hannah gave the receptionist a sympathetic smile. Near her desk was a sad-looking pile of wet luggage, some back-packs and other personal items like handbags, hats and sunglasses.

The angry man stormed back to his seat. Then he jumped to his feet. 'I've had enough of this,' he shouted. 'I'm bloody going home.'

Casting a glance around the waiting room, Hannah could tell nobody was sorry to see him go. She doubted there had been much wrong with him in the first place. He should see the kind of injuries that were having to wait for attention inside the department.

Hannah didn't really need a two-hour break. Maybe she should go back and help. She could leave the shoe on the pile because it probably did belong to the little girl and she might come looking for it.

Something made her turn back before she reached the pile, however. Something niggling at the back of her mind since her gaze had skimmed the more patient people still waiting for attention.

And there she was. A drowsy little blonde-headed girl, almost hidden with her mother's arms around her. She had a pink cast on her arm.

Hannah walked over to them, absurdly hopeful.

'Is this Chloe?'

The mother nodded, a worried frown creasing her fore-head. 'Is there a problem? I thought we were all finished. We were just waiting for a ride to the shelter.'

'No problem,' Hannah assured her. 'I just wondered if this could be Chloe's shoe?' She held the small sneaker out but the hope that she might have solved this small mystery bothering her was fading rapidly.

Chloe was wearing some white Roman sandals. Two of them.

The little girl opened her eyes. 'That's not my shoe,' she said. 'It's the boy with the funny name's shoe.'

Hannah caught her breath. 'What boy?'

'The boy on the bus.'

'I didn't see a boy,' her mother said.

'That's because he was hiding in the back of the bus. With his friend.'

'A friend?' Hannah blinked. Surely the searchers couldn't have missed *two* children? And where were the parents? They would be frantic. Everybody would know by now if they had missing children.

'He had a dog called Scruffy,' Chloe added. 'They were hiding so the driver wouldn't see Scruffy.'

So the friend was a dog? There had been no reports of a dog at the accident site that Hannah was aware of and that would be something people would talk about, surely? Chloe's story was beginning to seem unlikely.

'Chloe has a very good imagination,' her mother said fondly. 'Don't you, darling?' Her smile at Hannah was apologetic. 'It was a pretty long, boring bus ride.'

'I can imagine.'

'I *did* see them,' Chloe insisted. 'I went down the back of the bus when you were asleep, Mummy. His name was F-F-*Felixx*,' she said triumphantly. 'Like the cat.'

'I don't think so, darling. I've never heard of a little boy being called Felixx.'

'But it's *true*, Mummy.' Chloe was indignant. She wriggled away from the supporting arm and twisted her head sharply up to glare at her mother.

And then the small girl's eyes widened in surprise.

A split second later she went completely limp, slumped against her mother.

For a stunned moment, Hannah couldn't move. This was unreal. Talking one moment and apparently unconscious the next? Automatically she reached out to feel for a pulse in Chloe's neck.

Chloe's mother was frozen. 'What's happening?' she whispered hoarsely.

Hannah's fingers pressed deeper on the tiny neck.

Moved and pressed again.

'I don't know,' Hannah said, 'but for some reason it seems that Chloe's heart might have stopped.'

Another split second of indecision. Start CPR here in the waiting room and yell for help or get Chloe to the kind of lifesaving equipment, like a defibrillator, that she might desperately need? There was no question of what could give a better outcome.

She scooped the child into her arms. 'Come with me,' she told Chloe's mother as she ran towards the working end of the department.

'I need help,' she called as soon as she was through the door. *'Stat!'*

Ryan looked up from where he was squatting, talking to a man in a chair who had a bloodstained bandage on his hand. He took one look at Hannah's face and with a fluid movement he rose swiftly and came towards her.

'What's happened?'

'I have no idea. She just collapsed. I can't find a pulse.'

'Resus 2 is clear at the moment.' Charles was rolling beside them. 'I'll find help.'

Hannah laid Chloe on the bed. It had been well under a minute since the child had collapsed but, horribly, her instincts were screaming that they were too late. There had been something about the feel of the child in her arms.

Something completely empty.

Her fingers trembled as they reached for the ECG electrodes and stuck them in place on a tiny, frail-looking chest.

Ryan was reassessing her for a pulse and respirations. 'Nothing,' he said tersely. He reached for a bag-mask unit. 'What the hell is going on here?'

'Could it be a drug reaction? Anaphylaxis? What analgesia has she had for her arm?'

'Do you know if there were any prior symptoms?' Ryan had the mask over Chloe's face and was delivering enough air to make the small chest rise and then fall.

The normal-looking movement of breathing gave Hannah a ray of hope. Maybe they *weren't* too late. But then she looked up at the monitor screen to see a flat ECG trace. Not even a fibrillation they could have shocked back into a normal rhythm. She moved, automatically, to start chest compressions.

'She was fine,' she told Ryan. 'A bit drowsy but fine. She was talking to me. Telling me about the shoe and a boy who was on the bus.'

Any worries about a potentially missing child were simply not part of the picture right now.

More staff were crowding into the resus area to assist. One of the doctors, Cal, was inserting an IV line. One nurse was rolling the drugs trolley closer, the airway kit open on top of the trolley.

Charles was there. A solid presence. Beside him, Chloe's mother was standing, white faced, a nurse close by to look after her.

'An undiagnosed head injury?' Charles wondered aloud.

'A lucid period before total collapse?' He shook his head. 'Couldn't have been that dramatic.'

Ryan looked over to Chloe's mother. 'Does she have any medical conditions that you know of? Heart problems?'

'No-o-o.' The word was torn from the woman in the form of a sob. The nurse put her arms around the distraught mother. As awful as this was, it was better for a parent to see that everything possible was being done, in case they had to deal with the worst possible outcome.

Hannah kept up the chest compressions. It wasn't physically hard on someone this small. One handed. Rapid. It didn't take much pressure at all.

'Stop for a second, Hannah.'

They all looked at the screen. The disruption to the trace that the movement of CPR was causing settled.

To a flat line.

'I'm going to intubate,' Ryan decided. 'Someone hold her head for me, please?'

'I'll take over compressions.' Cal stepped up to the bed and Hannah nodded. She moved to take hold of Chloe's head and keep it in the position Ryan required.

'Oh, my God,' she murmured a moment later.

'What?' Ryan snapped. His gaze caught hers as though challenging her to say something he didn't want to hear. She had never seen anyone that determined. Ever.

'It's her neck,' Hannah said quietly. 'The way it moved. It's…' She was feeling the top of Chole's spine now, her fingers pressing carefully. Moving and pressing again. 'There's something very wrong.'

It was hardly a professional evaluation but she couldn't bring herself to say what she thought.

It fitted. Chloe must have had a fracture that had been undisplaced. She might have had a sore neck but that could have been masked by the pain relief administered for her fractured arm.

A time bomb waiting to go off. That sharp, twisting movement when she'd looked up at her mother could have displaced the broken bones. Allowed a sharp edge to sever the spinal cord.

Death would have been instantaneous.

And there was absolutely nothing any of them could do about it.

In the end, she didn't have to say anything. Her face must have said it all. Cal's hand slowed and then stopped. He stepped back from the bed.

Chloe's mother let out an agonised cry and rushed from the room. The nurse followed swiftly.

Everybody else stood silent.

Shocked.

Except for Ryan. He moved to where Cal had been standing and started chest compressions again.

And Charles rolled silently to the head of the bed where he could reach out and feel Chloe's neck for himself.

'We don't *know* her neck's broken,' Ryan said between gritted teeth. 'Not without an X-ray or CT scan. We can't just give up on her. Cal, take over again. Hannah, I want an ET tube. Five millimetre. Uncuffed.'

Nobody moved. Only Ryan, his face a frozen mask, his movements quietly desperate.

Charles dropped his hand from Chloe's neck. 'Ryan?'

The word wasn't spoken loudly but it carried the weight of an authority it would be impossible to ignore. So did the next word. *'Stop!'*

For a few seconds it looked as though Ryan might ignore the command. Keep fighting to save a life when there was absolutely no chance of success. Hannah could feel his pain. She reached out to touch his shoulder.

Ryan jerked away as though he'd been burnt. Without a glance at anyone, he turned and strode away. Long, angry strides that didn't slow as he flicked the curtain aside.

'Everybody take a break,' Charles ordered. 'Jill and I will deal with what needs to be done here.'

The shock was dreadful. Hannah could understand why Ryan hadn't been prepared to give up. If there was anything that could have been done, she would have done it herself.

*Anything.*

They all faced terrible things like this, working in any emergency department. That it was part of the job didn't make it easy. Somehow they had to find a way to cope or they couldn't be doing this as a career.

What was making it worse than normal for Hannah was the feeling that Ryan *couldn't* cope with this particular case. There had been something in his body language as he virtually fled from the room that spoke of real desperation. Of reaching the end of a personal, if not professional, tether.

There was no way Hannah could leave him to deal with that on his own.

She had to try and help. Or at least *be* with him. To show him that she cared. That she understood.

An ironic smile vied with the tears she was holding back. To wallow with him, even?

# CHAPTER TEN

HE WAS disappearing through the doors to the ambulance bay.

Going outside into the storm.

As scary as that was, Hannah didn't hesitate to go after him. An ambulance was unloading another patient by the time she got there and Hannah had to wait a moment as the stretcher was wheeled through the doors. Mario had done the round trip again. He was holding a bag of IV fluid aloft with one hand, steering the stretcher with the other.

'How's it going, Hannah? OK?'

Hannah could only give him a tight smile and a brief nod, unable to think of anything but her personal and urgent mission. She skirted the end of the stretcher to dash outside before the automatic doors slid shut again.

The wind caught the baggy scrub suit she was wearing and made it billow. It teased her hair out of the band holding it back and whipped strands across her face. Her eyes stung and watered but Hannah barely registered any discomfort. It was too dark out here. The powerful hospital generators were being used for the vital power needed inside. Energy was not being wasted on outside lighting.

Where was Ryan?

Where would *she* go if she was in some kind of personal crisis and couldn't cope?

Just anywhere? Was Ryan even aware of the wild storm raging around him? Would he be thinking of his personal safety? Not likely. What if he went towards the beach? That surf had been wild and couldn't you get things like storm surges with an approaching cyclone? Like tidal waves?

If he had gone somewhere that dangerous, Hannah would still follow him. She *had* to. The bond she felt was simply too strong. If ever there was a case for following her heart, this was it.

Ryan *was* her heart.

Maybe he was heading for a safer personal space, Hannah thought as her gaze raked the swirl of leaves in the darkness and picked out the looming shapes of vehicles in the car park. He only had one space that could qualify in Crocodile Creek. His room in the doctors' house.

The room she had spent the most magical night of her life in.

Headlights from another incoming rescue vehicle sent a beam of light across the path Hannah was taking. Strong enough to show she was heading in the right direction to take her to either the beach or the house. The faded sign designating the area as the AGNES WETHERBY MEMORIAL GARDEN was tilted. Had it always been like that or was it giving up the struggle to stay upright under the duress of this storm?

Hannah wasn't about to give up.

She had to pause in the centre of the garden, just beside the sundial. She needed to catch her breath and gather her courage. The crack of a tree branch breaking free somewhere close was frightening. She would wait a few seconds in case the branch was about to fall on the path she intended to take.

It must have been instinct that alerted her to Ryan's presence in the garden. Why else would she have taken a second and much longer look at the dark shape in the corner which anyone could have taken as part of the thick hibiscus hedge behind it? Or was it because that shadow was immobile whilst the hedge was in constant motion, fuelled by relentless wind gusts?

He was sitting on a bench seat, his hands on his knees, staring blankly into the dark space in front of him.

Hannah licked lips that were dry from more than the wind.

'Ryan?'

'Go away, Hannah. Leave me alone.'

'No. I can't *do* that.' With her heart hammering, Hannah sat down beside him. Close enough to touch but she knew not to. Not yet. Ryan was too fragile. Precious. A single touch might shatter him.

So she just sat.

Very still.

They were two frozen shapes as the storm surged and howled above them.

A minute went past.

And then another.

Hannah wanted to cry. She had no idea how to help. What would Ryan do if the situation were reversed? When had she ever been this upset over a bad case at work? The closest she could think of was that little boy, Brendon, with the head injury and the dead mother and the abusive father who hadn't given a damn.

And what had Ryan done?

Told a joke. A stupid blonde joke. His way of coping or helping others to cope. Trying to make them laugh and thereby defusing an atmosphere that could be destructive.

No atmosphere could be worse than this. The pain of

loving someone and being totally unable to connect. To offer comfort.

Hannah chewed the inside of her cheek as she desperately searched her memory. Had she even *heard* a blonde joke that Ryan wouldn't already know?

Maybe.

'Hey…' Surprisingly, she didn't have to shout to be heard. The wind seemed to have dropped fractionally and the hedge was were offering a small amount of protection. 'Have…have you heard the one about the blonde who went to pick up her car from the mechanic who'd been fixing it?'

There was no response from Ryan. Not a flicker. But he'd never been put off by Hannah's deliberate indifference, had he? It took courage to continue, all the same. More courage than heading out into a potentially dangerous storm.

'She asked, "Was there much wrong with it?" and the mechanic said, "Nah, just crap in the carburettor."' Hannah had to swallow. This was so hard. How could anything be funny at a time like this? The punchline might fall like a lead balloon and she would seem shallow. Flippant. Uncaring. The things she had once accused Ryan of being. The *last* things she wanted to be seen as right now.

'And…and the blonde thought about that for a minute and then she nodded and she said, "OK…how often do I have to do that?"'

For a heartbeat, and then another, Hannah thought her fears were proving correct. The stone statue that was Ryan was still silent. Unmoving.

But then a sound escaped. A strangled kind of laughter. To Hannah's horror, however, it morphed into something else.

Ryan was *crying*.

Ghastly, racking sobs as though he had no idea *how* to cry but the sounds were being ripped from his soul.

Hannah felt tears sliding down her own face and there was no way she could prevent herself touching him now. She wrapped both her arms around him as tightly as she could, her face pressed against the back of his shoulder.

Holding him.

Trying to absorb some of the terrible grief that he seemed to be letting go.

Maybe it was Chloe's case that had caused it or maybe she'd been the straw to break the camel's back. The reason didn't matter. Ryan was hurting and if Hannah hadn't known before just how deep her love for this man went, there was no escaping that knowledge now.

She would never know how long they stayed like that. Time had no relevance. At some point, however, Ryan moved. He took Hannah's arm and pushed her away.

He couldn't bear it if Hannah felt *sorry* for him.

Adding weakness to the list of faults she already considered him to have.

He had to push her away. However comforting her touch had been, he didn't want her pity.

Searching her face in the darkness didn't reveal what he'd been afraid to find. The shine of tears on Hannah's face was unexpected.

'Why are *you* crying?'

'Because…' Hannah gulped. 'Because *you're* crying.'

Why would she do that? There was only one reason that occurred to Ryan. She cared about him. Cared enough to be moved by his grief, even if she didn't know where it was coming from.

A very new sensation was born for Ryan right then. Wonderment. He had revealed the rawest of emotions. Exposed a part of himself he'd never shared with another living soul and Hannah had not only witnessed it, she had accepted it.

Was *sharing* it even.

Oh, man! This was huge. As big as the storm currently raging over their heads.

Bigger even.

Ryan sniffed and scrubbed his nose with the palm of his hand. He made an embarrassed kind of sound.

'First time for everything, I guess.'

'You mean this is the *first* time you've ever cried?'

'Yeah.' Ryan sniffed again and almost managed a smile. The grief had drained away and left a curious sort of peace. Had the crying done that? Or Hannah's touch? A combination of both maybe. 'Well, since I was about five or six anyway.'

'Oh…' And Hannah was smiling back at him. A gentle smile that was totally without any kind of judgement. 'I'm glad I was here.'

'Yeah…' It was still difficult to swallow but the lump in his throat seemed different. A happy lump rather than an agonised one. How could that be? 'Me, too.'

They listened to the wind for a moment. Felt the fat drops of rain ping against their bare arms.

'I'm sorry, Ryan,' Hannah said.

'What for?'

'Lots of things.'

'Like what?'

'Like that we couldn't save Chloe.'

'We could have, if we'd only known.' Ryan felt the weight of sadness pulling him down again but he knew he wouldn't go as far as he had. Never again. Hannah had stopped his fall. Made something right in the world again. 'It shouldn't have happened.'

'No, of course it shouldn't, but I can see why it did. If there hadn't been so many injuries it would have been standard protocol to check her out a lot more carefully. To collar and backboard her until X-rays were done, given the mechanism of injury. But she was part of the walking wounded group. She only complained about her sore arm.'

'Tunnel vision.'

'Not entirely. With so many to care for, you don't have time to think outside the square. Tick the boxes that don't seem urgent. Anyway, it happened and it's dreadful and I know how you must feel.' A tentative smile curved Hannah's lips. 'I'm available for a spot of wallowing.'

Ryan shook his head. 'I don't do wallowing, you know that.' He snorted softly. 'Hell, if I went down that track with the kind of material I've got to keep me going, I'd end up like a character in some gloomy Russian novel. Chloe *did* get to me more than usual, though. Too close to home.'

'I don't understand.'

Of course she didn't. Why had Ryan thought that keeping his private life private would make things easier?

'I've got a niece,' he told her. 'Michaela. She's six and blonde and it could have been her in there instead of Chloe. Not that there's anything that could save Mikki so to have another little girl that didn't *have* to die and still did seemed just too unfair to be acceptable.'

'Mikki *has* to die?'

'It's inevitable. She's got neuroaxonal dystrophy. It's an autosomal recessive genetic disease and it's incredibly cruel. They seem perfectly normal at birth and even for the first year or two, and then there's a steady deterioration until they die a few years later. Mikki can't move any more.

She can't see or talk. She can still hear and she can smile. She's got the most gorgeous smile.'

When had Hannah's hand slipped into his like that? Ryan returned the squeeze.

'I love that kid,' he said quietly. 'She's got a couple of older brothers but she was special right from day one.'

'And she lives here, in Australia?'

'Brisbane. She's my older brother's child. He's taking it hard and it's putting a big strain on the marriage. He's a bit like me, I guess—not good at sharing the hard stuff in life. Easier to bottle it up and have a laugh about something meaningless.'

'Like a joke.' Hannah was nodding.

'Yeah. Shallow, isn't it?'

'You're not shallow, Ryan. You care more than anyone I've ever met. You've just been good at hiding it.' She cleared her throat. 'So Mikki's the reason you come back to Australia so often?'

'Yeah. I try to be there whenever things get really tough or when she has a hospital appointment. I can explain things again to her parents later.'

'It's a huge commitment.'

'I would have moved there to make it easier to be supportive but my parents live in Auckland. Dad had a stroke a couple of years ago. Quite a bad one and Mum's finding it harder to cope. So there I was in Sydney, commuting one way and then another. The travel time was playing havoc with my career so I had to choose one city and the job in Auckland happened to come up first. It doesn't seem to take any longer to get to Brisbane from Auckland than it did from Sydney and I'm only doing half the travelling I used to do.'

Hannah's smile was rueful. 'And I was thinking that Michaela was a girlfriend. Or an ex-wife.'

Ryan snorted. 'For one thing, any wife of mine would never become an "ex". For another, I haven't had time in my life for a relationship for years. Who would, with the kind of family commitments I've got?'

'But you go out with everyone. You never miss a party.'

'I'm in a new city. I need to find friends. Sometimes I just need to escape and do normal, social things. I still feel lonely but if you can't find some fun somewhere in life, it takes all the sense out of struggling along with the bad bits.'

'I can't believe I accused you of being shallow, Ryan. I'm really, really sorry.'

'Don't be. I can see why you did. I've never told anyone at work what goes on in my private life. I had a feeling that if I started I'd never be able to stop and it would be too hard. I'd end up a mess and people would just feel sorry for me. I've got too much pride to take that on board.'

'*I* don't feel sorry for you.'

'You don't?'

'No.'

'What *do* you feel, Han?'

'I...feel a lot.' Hannah was looking down, avoiding his gaze. 'I'm...in love with you, Ryan.'

There.

She'd said it.

Opened her heart right up.

Made herself as vulnerable as it was possible to get, but what choice had she had? There was no escaping the truth and she couldn't live a lie.

And hadn't Ryan made himself just as vulnerable? He hadn't cried in front of anyone in his adult life. He could have hidden it from her. Stormed off and shut her out before he let himself go. He'd been exercising control over his emotions for year after year. He could have done the same for a minute or two longer.

But he hadn't. At some level he had trusted her enough to show her who he really was.

An utterly amazing, caring, committed man.

How could she have been so wrong about him?

Ryan deserved nothing less than the absolute truth from her, no matter how painful the repercussions.

She was too afraid to look at him. It was too dark to be able to interpret expressions accurately enough in any case.

She didn't need to be able to see, though. She could feel the touch under her chin as Ryan tilted her face up to meet his.

Could feel the touch of his lips on her own, the rain-slicked smoothness of her skin against the grating stubble of a jaw that hadn't been near a razor since what was now yesterday.

The kiss was as gentle as it was powerful.

It told Hannah she didn't need to be afraid. Ryan understood that vulnerability and he wasn't going to break her trust if he could help it.

The first words he spoke when he drew away had to be the most important Hannah would ever hear.

She wasn't disappointed.

'I love you, too, Hannah Jackson.'

The rain was pelting down now. Ryan smoothed damp strands of hair back from Hannah's forehead.

'We need to find somewhere dry,' he said.

Hannah laughed. Incredible as it seemed, in the wake of what they had just been through and with the prospect of more gruelling hours of work ahead, there was joy to be found in life. In each other.

'Where have I heard that before?'

'We're on a break. We've got two hours to escape. To

forget about the world and be dry. And warm. And safe.' Ryan kissed her again. 'You'll always be safe with me, Hannah. I promise you that.'

She took his face between both her hands. 'And so will you be,' she vowed. 'With me.'

She let Ryan pull her to her feet and she smiled. 'I'd like to go somewhere dry with you. Very much.' Her smile broadened. 'Even though I already know how good our rapport is.'

'Yeah…' Ryan growled. 'I'm *fun*.'

'I didn't mean that, you know. It was so much more than that. I was just trying to protect myself.'

'From *me?*' Ryan sounded baffled.

'Yes. I thought it was far too dangerous to fall for someone like you.'

'Who, exactly, is someone like me?'

'Oh, you know. Someone fun. Clever. Exciting. Great looking. Too good to be true.'

'I'm someone like that?' Now he sounded very pleasantly surprised.

'Someone exactly like that. A bit too much like the man my mother fell head over heels in love with. And the one that Susie fell in love with. And they both got bored or hadn't been genuine in the first place, and it was me who had to pick up all the pieces. Do you know how many pieces you can get out of *two* broken hearts?'

'No. How many?'

'Heaps,' Hannah said firmly. 'Way *too* many.'

Ryan pulled her to a stop. Pulled her into his arms. 'Your heart's going to stay in one piece if I have anything to do with it,' he said seriously. 'I'm going to make it my mission in life.'

The promise was too big. Hannah didn't want anything

to make her cry again. She had to smile and try to lighten the emotional overload. 'Could be a full-time job.'

'I intend to make sure it is.'

'It might be a lifetime career.'

'I certainly hope so.'

'Of course, there's always the prospect of promotion.'

'Really? What kind of promotion?'

Why had she started this? Suddenly it didn't seem like a joke. 'Oh, maybe being an emergency department consultant?'

'I might not get that job. I've heard that I've got some pretty stiff competition.'

Hannah's heart was doing some curious flip-flops. 'I might not mind very much if I don't get that job.'

'Why not?'

'I might have more important things in my life than my career.'

Ryan was smiling. 'Such as?' He raised a hopeful eyebrow. 'You mean *me?*'

Hannah nodded shyly. 'Maybe even... How would you feel about a promotion to being a father?'

'Dr Jackson! Is that a proposal?'

'I don't know.' Hannah caught her bottom lip between her teeth. 'Would you like it to be?'

'No.'

Hannah's heart plummeted. But then she saw the gleam of Ryan's teeth.

'I'm old-fashioned,' he announced. 'If there's to be any proposing going on around here, *I'll* do it.'

And that's exactly what he did. In the heart of a tropical storm, in the middle of a garden, just beside a sundial, Ryan got down on one knee, holding both of Hannah's hands in his own.

'I love you.' He had to shout because the wind had risen again to snatch his words away and the rain was thundering down and the wail of a siren close by rose and fell.

'I love you, Hannah. You are the only person in existence that I can really be myself with. The only time in my life I felt no hint of being alone was when I had you in my bed. You make me whole. I don't ever want to live without having you by my side. Will you—please—marry me?'

'Oh, I think so.' Hannah sank to her knees on the wet flagstones of the path. 'I love you, too, Ryan.' It was easier to hear now that their heads were close together again. 'You are the only person in existence that I've ever…had such a good rapport with.' They were grinning at each other now, at the absurdity of choosing this particular place and time to make such declarations. Then Hannah's smile faded. It had just happened this way and because it had, it was perfect. 'Yes,' she said slowly. 'I would love to marry you.'

Ryan shook the raindrops from his hair after giving Hannah a lingering, wonderful kiss.

'Can we go somewhere dry now?'

Hannah nodded but the wail of the siren was still going and she hesitated when Ryan helped her up and then tugged on her hand.

'What's up, babe?'

'I can't stop thinking about it.'

'The bus crash? The cyclone that's on its way that we'd better find some shelter from pretty damn quick?'

'No…the shoe.'

'Did Chloe really tell you there was a boy on the bus?'

'Yes.'

'And you believe her?'

'Yes.'

'We'd better find Harry or someone, then, and let them know.'

Hannah nodded. 'I'd feel a lot better if we did. Do you mind?'

'Why should I mind?'

'It'll take a bit longer to find somewhere dry. To have that break.'

'Babe, we've got all the time in the world to work on our rapport.' Ryan had his arm around Hannah, sheltering her from some of the wind and rain. They had to bend forward to move against the force of the elements and get themselves back towards Crocodile Creek Base Hospital's emergency department.

But it felt so different than when Hannah had been going in the opposite direction on her search for Ryan. With his strength added to her own, she knew there was nothing she wouldn't be prepared to face.

Ryan paused once more as they reached the relative shelter of the ambulance bay. 'It *is* real, isn't it?'

'What, the cyclone? Sure feels like it.'

'No, I mean, how we feel about each other. The love.'

'As real as this storm,' Hannah assured him. 'And just as powerful.'

'What happens when the sun comes out?'

'We'll be in a dry place.' Hannah smiled. 'Having fun.'

Ryan looked over her shoulder through the doors into the emergency department. 'I don't think fun's on the agenda for a while yet.'

'No.' Hannah followed the direction of his gaze. Chloe was still somewhere in there. So were a lot of other people who needed attention. And when the aftermath of the bus crash had been mopped up, they could be on standby for the first casualties from a cyclone.

'It's not going to be easy.'

'No.'

'Are you up for it?'

'With you here as well? Of course I am. We can do this, Ryan. We'll be doing it together.'

'Together is good. Oh, and, Han?'

'Yes?'

'Can I have that blonde joke? The one about the carburettor? It was great.'

'You can have anything and everything I have to give,' Hannah told him. 'Always.'

Ryan took hold of her hand once more and they both turned towards the automatic doors. Ready to step back into a place that needed them both almost as much as they needed each other.

'Same,' Ryan said softly. 'For ever.'

0907/03a

# LOVE IN THE
# TIME OF BERTIE

# WISH YOU WERE HERE

## MIKE GAYLE

HODDER

First published in Great Britain in 2007 by Hodder & Stoughton
An Hachette Livre UK company

First published in paperback in 2008

3

A CIP catalogue record for this title is available from the British Library

ISBN 978 0 340 89566 5 (A format)
ISBN 978 0 340 82542 6 (B format)

Typeset in Benguiat by Hewer Text UK Ltd, Edinburgh
Printed and bound by Clays Ltd, St Ives plc

Hodder Headline's policy is to use papers that are natural, renewable
and recyclable products and made from wood grown in sustainable forests.
The logging and manufacturing processes are expected to conform
to the environmental regulations of the country of origin.

Hodder & Stoughton Ltd
A division of Hodder Headline
338 Euston Road
London NW1 3BH

www.hodder.co.uk

'Whatever happens in Las Vegas stays in Las Vegas.'

– Well known maxim attributed to holidays in Las Vegas
aka 'The Entertainment capital of the world'

For Mr and Mrs O'Reilly (Jnr)
who met on holiday.

It was nice you like a hell of initiation. I'm talking about the kind of change that lasts a lifetime. I can still barely believe it. But it's the truth: a chic in booking, package changed my life completely. So take it from me, if, change isn't exactly what you're looking for in life just beware your local travel agent's

## Beware your local travel agent's

When you're sitting at home flicking through the bunch of holiday brochures you picked up from your local high street travel agent, you never really think to yourself: 'This will be the holiday that will change my life', do you? Granted you might think: 'This will be the holiday that will leave me broke for the rest of the year.' Or: 'This will be the holiday that I finally learn to speak the local lingo.' Or even: 'This will be the holiday where I won't snog random strangers.' But I doubt very strongly that you'll be thinking: 'This will be the holiday that will change my life.'

But last year this was exactly what happened to me: a cheap last-minute seven-night package holiday changed my life in a way I never could have imagined. And I don't mean change like making the decision to re-decorate the hallway when you get back, or to give up smoking (again), or even changing careers. I'm talking about a big change. A life change. A change that might not seem huge if you're prime minister of England but if you're say, a thirty-five-year-old man working for Brighton and Hove city council, and you've just split up with your girlfriend after ten years together, it will seem huge.

I'm talking about a change that spins you round one-hundred-and-eighty degrees. I'm talking about a change

1

## In the beginning

It all started, as these things do, with the end of something big: me and Sarah. Ten years we were together. And then one day she just packed some of her stuff and left. It was difficult to work out how we'd managed to travel from the one state to the other but somehow we had. Then three weeks later on a warm and sunny August morning she called by to collect a few more things and tell me when she was going to move out the rest of her possessions.

'This time next week,' she said as we stood in the hallway. 'Is that okay?'

'Fine,' I replied choosing to stare intently at the pattern on the carpet by her feet rather than at her directly. 'Whatever you want – although I'm pretty sure that you're not going to get it all into the back of your Micra.'

I'd meant it as a joke not a dig. (Although in the time that had elapsed since she had left I had made many jokes that were actually digs, and many digs that were nowhere near to being jokes, and a few digs that were virtually indistinguishable from being verbal assaults, such was their subtlety.) Anyway, I could tell from her face that she had taken my joke about her car as a dig at her. For a few moments I thought about explaining to her that I was over her and that normal service had been resumed but I didn't of course because that would've shown that I

3

was sensitive to her feelings. Being sensitive, at least in her presence, seemed a tad too close to being vulnerable, which was a definite no-no with a vampire like Sarah. So instead of doing the joke explanation thing, I just stood there like an idiot and carried on staring at the carpet.

'Oliver's brother's got a van,' she explained, mentioning the 'O' word to me for the first time that day. 'He's agreed to help me move the rest of my stuff to the new place.'

Oliver was Sarah's work friend. I'd never liked him and I'm pretty sure he'd never liked me either. Unlike him, however, I was justified in my feelings on the grounds that he had clearly always fancied Sarah. I could tell from the moment she first dropped him into a conversation when he started working with her (Sarah was a senior case worker for Brighton Social Services) that he was bad news. When she came home from work her conversation was always 'Oliver said this . . .' and 'Oliver said that . . .' and then it was only a matter of time before it became, 'Oliver was telling me over lunch . . .' I couldn't say anything, however, because it was supposedly obvious that Oliver wasn't interested in her because he had a girlfriend. She came round to ours for dinner once but I never saw her again, because soon after that they split because things weren't 'working'.

I saw plenty more of Oliver though. Sarah became his shoulder to cry on. He'd come round for dinner at least once a week, and when friends came round to see us she'd invite him too. I once made the mistake of pointing out to her that as she spent every single second with him at work there was a strong chance that he saw more of her than I did. She didn't like that at all. 'He's just come out of the biggest relationship of his life,' she said. 'Can't

you show even a hint of sympathy?' I couldn't of course because I didn't like Oliver. I found him insufferable, and overly conscientious and a bit too pleased with himself but I didn't say any of that. Instead I said that I would try my best and give him a second chance.

'Nothing's going on with Oliver, you know,' said Sarah, now.

'Even if it was,' I replied, 'it's not exactly any of my business any more.'

'I know,' she said. 'I just wanted to make it clear, that's all.'

Sarah's 'I know' comment, rather than being bitter and twisted, was, I think, meant to be comforting. She wasn't having a go at me. Rather she was stating a simple fact of life. Still, I wasn't comforted in the least.

'What time do you want to come?' I asked.

'Around ten?'

'That's fine.'

'Will you be in?'

'Do you want me to be?'

Sarah didn't reply.

I sighed heavily. 'Don't worry, I won't be here.'

Sarah looked visibly relieved. 'I'll leave the keys in the hallway for you when I go.'

Another long silence signalled the end of business. This was going to be the last time we would ever see each other. Though Sarah had moved less than twenty minutes away she had managed to separate our lives so well that there was little chance of overlap. She had switched supermarkets so that we wouldn't accidentally bump into each other in the cereal aisle; she no longer took early evening walks in 'our' local park; our local pub, The George, was

5

now (at least for Sarah) a no-go zone; and as for mutual friends they all knew the score so there was no chance of an embarrassing encounter at a dinner party.

'Well, that's everything then,' she said. She glanced at the front door and then back at me and pressed her lips tightly together. 'Take care of yourself, Charlie.'

'You too,' I replied and then I offered a half-smile to signal that I appreciated this moment of warmth. She smiled back and in that instant I took a snapshot of her in my head. Brown hair tied back in a ponytail. Pale grey/green eyes. Fresh-faced features. Small silver hoop earrings. Mint-coloured pinstriped jacket. Green vest top. Tight blue jeans with huge black belt with silver buckle. Flat black shoes that looked like ballet pumps. A summer outfit.

Sarah then reached down to the floor by her feet and picked up the H&M carrier bags crammed full with stuff plundered from what used to be our bedroom. Without saying another word she opened the door, stepped into the communal hallway and closed the door behind her. Though I hated myself for it I found myself staring at the front door long after she'd gone, hoping and praying that there might be a sudden rattle of the letterbox signalling a last-minute change of heart. But it never came. She had gone. For good. And probably for ever.

At a loss what to do next I retired to the living room, collapsed on the sofa and turned on the TV. As I randomly channel-hopped, the phone rang. I couldn't help it but once again the first thought that leapt into my head was, 'It's her. She's changed her mind and she's standing on the front door step ringing me from her mobile.'

'Charlie, mate,' said the male voice at the end of the phone. 'What are you doing a week next Sunday?'

'What?' I stammered, battling with my disappointment. 'What are you on about now, Andy?'

'I'm asking you what you're doing a week from Sunday. That's what I'm on about.'

I projected myself into the future. All I could see was a lot of moping around the flat trying to make myself feel even worse than I already felt.

'Nothing much,' I replied eventually. 'Why?'

'Because you . . .' he paused to give himself a silent drum roll '. . . are coming on holiday with me.'

'Holiday?'

'Yeah.'

'With you?'

'Yeah.'

I went completely silent. This was typical of Andy. And I knew that if I was going to prevent him from talking me into something I didn't want to be talked into I was going to have to be firm.

'I can't.'

'Why not?'

'Because . . . because I can't.'

Andy wasn't fazed for a second by my sub-standard debating skills. 'You do know that I'm doing this for you, don't you?' he began. 'I was sitting here at home thinking about you and . . . everything that's going on and it just came to me – what Charlie needs is a holiday. Think about it. You, me and a nice beach somewhere hot. We can chill out for a week, sink a few beers and have a laugh – it'll be great. And you won't have to do any of the legwork either, mate. I went to a travel agent this afternoon and checked it all out for you. All you need to do is write me a cheque for roughly four hundred quid and in exchange

I'll give you the holiday of a lifetime.' He paused as if waiting for a round of applause. 'So what do you say?'

I had many reservations about my old college friend's suggestion, but they had less to do with the idea of going on holiday than with the idea of going on holiday with him. Despite his long preamble, I knew Andy well enough to know that this holiday wasn't about him wanting to help me out at all. It was about him wanting to go on holiday without his fiancée and using me as an excuse. He'd probably told Lisa that he wanted to take me away to help me 'get over Sarah' and while there might be a modicum of truth in that statement I strongly suspected a far more self-interested motive. I could just feel in my bones that Andy was going to use this holiday as a week-long practice run for his eventual stag-night, meaning he would inevitably end up dragging me to a lot of places that I wouldn't want to go to, persuade me to do things that I wouldn't want to do and generally force me to act in a way that wasn't really me at all.

And yet he was right. I did need a holiday. I did need a break from my usual routine. Sarah's leaving had completely kicked the stuffing out of me. And other than the option of going solo (which given my state of mind wasn't really an option at all) Andy's was the only firm holiday offer on the table. Fortunately for me I had one last trick up my sleeve – the perfect way to ensure that should he persuade me to go with him the balance of power wouldn't always be in his favour.

'What about Tom?' I asked.

There was a brief but telling silence.

'What about Tom?' he replied, faking indifference.

'Well, aren't you going to ask him too?'

'Of course not. Why would I conceivably invite a born-again Christian on holiday? It's not like they're particularly renowned for being the life and soul of the party.'

'But he's our mate.'

Andy sighed. 'To be fair to Tom, mate, even at university he was always more your mate than mine.'

'Well I'm not going without him,' I replied. 'So if you want me to go you'd better get dialling now because you're really going to have your work cut out for you.'

After that I didn't expect to hear from Andy on the subject of holidays again because I was absolutely confident that Tom would turn him down before he even managed to finish his first sentence. As I was getting into bed, however, just before midnight, the phone rang.

'You'd better start packing,' said Andy, 'because bible-bashing Tom is coming on holiday with us.'

'Yeah right,' I replied laughing. 'Do you think I'm going to hand over a cheque just like that so by the time I realise Tom's not coming you'll have cashed it and it'll be too late to back out? Give me a little bit of credit, Andy, I'm not that stupid. There's no way that Tom's agreed to come on holiday with us. In fact given the sort of thing I suspect you've got in mind for this holiday I'd say that you'd have more chance of persuading the pope to come with us.'

'Oh-two-four—' began Andy.

'What are you doing?' I interrupted.

'Encouraging you to call him.'

'Do you think I won't do it?'

'I'm telling you to be my guest. But just so that you know, Tom was actually much less work than you. All I

9

said was: "Do you fancy coming on holiday next week?" And straight away he replied that August is always pretty quiet in his office and that chances are it should be no problem for him to get the time off.'

'You're telling me he said, "Yes," just like that?'

'My powers of persuasion must work well on the God fearing.'

I paused and mulled over the situation. This didn't sound like Tom at all. There had to be something else going on. 'You know I will phone him, don't you?' I warned Andy. 'And I'll well and truly kick your arse if you're winding me up.'

'Like I said,' replied Andy boldly. 'Be my guest. And when you do, just remind him that we're going on holiday to have . . . fun.'

The following Monday, Andy called me at work to tell me he had booked the holiday. When I asked where we were going he refused to say, on the grounds that he wanted it to be a 'surprise'. The idea of being surprised by Andy made me feel very uncomfortable indeed: he was the sort of person whose surprises tended to be genuinely surprising. For example, once when we were at college Andy announced that he was nipping out to get a paper. Seventeen hours later, he called me from Belgium to ask if I could electronically wire him enough money to fly home. He's that sort of bloke.

Regardless of my concern, I was actually so relieved to have a date fixed when I would be free of the four walls of my flat that I actually didn't care where we went. All I knew was that once Sarah moved out of the flat for good my life would be as empty as my home. And so the idea

of being somewhere in the sun – if only for a week – seemed tailor-made for the peculiarities of my situation. I could escape day-to-day reality and recharge my batteries at the same time. And whether Andy had booked us in for a week in the Canaries or at a Butlin's in Minehead, it didn't matter. All that mattered was being somewhere else.

During that week Andy set a plan of action in motion. Tom (who was based in Coventry) would get the train down to Brighton on the Saturday night before the flight and stay over at my flat. Andy (who lived with his girlfriend Lisa in Hove) would come round to mine on the Saturday evening and stay over too. Following a leisurely Sunday morning breakfast we would make our way to Gatwick and catch the plane to our mystery destination. It felt good having a plan. For the first time in a long while, it felt as though I was moving forwards.

# SATURDAY

## Born again

It was just after three o'clock on the Saturday afternoon and I was standing in my bedroom staring at the empty suitcase in front of me. In terms of symbolism (always useful when you're looking for new and inventive ways to make yourself feel that little bit more unhappy) it was hard to find an object more fitting than an empty suitcase because my heart was empty and the flat itself was pretty empty too. Sarah and Oliver had been and gone while I'd been last-minute shopping for holiday stuff in town. In the time that elapsed between the two events they had managed to remove everything she owned. Now, given that when I'd bought the flat twelve years ago my furniture had consisted of a decrepit wardrobe, a musty-smelling chest of drawers and a sofa that I'd rescued from a skip; and given that the deal when Sarah had moved in two years later was that she would (with my blessing) systematically eradicate the flat of every single item of furniture and replace it with things that worked and looked nice (and hadn't come from skips) the flat was now, inevitably, empty. Oh, she'd left a desk in the spare room (I'm guessing because the front of one of the drawers has come off), a bookshelf in the living room and a few other items as well but these were all things that, like me, either no longer worked or were no longer needed.

Back to the suitcase. I had always hated packing. Always. This was mainly because I don't understand how it all worked. How was a person supposed to guess what they might need for every single occasion that might come up when visiting a foreign land? For instance, I have a band T-shirt that I bought when I was at college that says 'Death To The Pixies' on the front of it. Back in my college days I used to wear it all the time but now I don't wear it that often. That said, however, there are still times when I wake up at the weekend and think to myself, 'I really want to wear my "Death To The Pixies" T-shirt,' and I'll rummage through all the clothes in the ironing pile until I find it. And even though it's now grey (where it once was black and is now much tighter than it used to be), frayed on the neck and with loose stitching underneath one armpit, I'll put it on and wear it all day. And I'll be happy. And at the end of the day when it has fulfilled its function, I'll take it off and throw it in the dirty laundry basket where it will slowly make its way through the decommissioning process (dark wash clothes pile on kitchen floor to washing machine to tumble dryer to ironing pile in spare bedroom – where it will remain unironed until the next time I need it). Now, multiply the problem I have with my 'Death To The Pixies' T-shirt with a pair of favoured jeans, a white shirt that I think I look good in, trainers that are good for walking in (but not necessarily all that good to look at) and various assorted other clothes and accessories for which I feel various degrees of attachment and it becomes easy to imagine the problems I had with packing to go on holiday.

So how did I manage in the past? The quick answer is Sarah. She always did it. She'd get sick of me standing there slack-jawed with a 'Death To The Pixies' T-shirt in

one hand and a pair of threadbare-in-the-crotch faded Levi's in the other and she'd kick me out of the bedroom and sort it out herself. And the funny thing is, even though I hadn't had anything to do with the packing of my suitcase, once we'd reached our holiday destination I would always (without fail) find absolutely everything that I needed for every occasion. The right shoes for the right kind of bar. The right shirt for the right kind of restaurant. The right shorts for the right kind of beach. Everything. And on the one occasion (a holiday to Turkey in year five of our relationship) when I needed the right T-shirt for a day of wandering round a local market I opened the case and there it was: 'Death To The Pixies' in all its faded glory, neatly ironed and folded right in front of me. Right there and then I took off my hat to her (she had packed that too). No one could pack a suitcase like Sarah. No one. I can't really remember what I did about packing suitcases before Sarah came into my life. I suppose that back in those days I had a lot less stuff so it was an awful lot easier just to pile everything I owned into one suitcase and close the lid.

As the afternoon began to slip away from me and the suitcase remained empty I came to the conclusion that the best thing I could do would be to leave packing until later in the day. Retiring to my now sofa-less living room I sat down on one of two old dining chairs Sarah had left behind and turned on the TV. An old episode of *Murder She Wrote* was on one of the cable channels but despite being drawn into the plot I switched it off after ten minutes because I was unable to adopt my usual slouching position. As I debated in my head whether it was too late to drive into

17

town and order a new sofa from Argos (possibly something in black leather?) the phone rang. It was Tom. He was at the station and needed me to pick him up. As I put down the phone, picked up my car keys, grabbed my coat and locked the front door I remember quite clearly feeling happy for the first time in a long while. Tom's arrival meant that my holiday plans were in motion. There was now an implied momentum to my life. I was no longer stationary. Instead I was hurtling towards the unknown.

At the station I spotted Tom instantly amongst the crowd of recently arrived travellers. Though we were roughly the same age, Tom had always looked a good few years older than me. It was his lack of hair that did it. Tom had begun losing his hair in his early twenties and now that he was in his thirties I barely registered his lack of hair. There's something about men whose hair loss comes earlier in life that makes them cooler than the rest of us. It's as if they've had an entire decade to come round to the idea that their hair has gone for good and so by the time they reach their third decade it's quite clear that they patently don't give a toss about what's going on on top of their skulls. Possessing a full head of hair is no longer linked to their masculine identity. It's just the way things are. And when women say that they find bald guys sexy (and there are quite a few out there) it's this lot that they're talking about and not the late arrivals who are always too panicked by their hair loss to do anything other than look mortified.

'How long do you think we're going for?' I asked, staring at Tom's hulking suitcase and marginally smaller rucksack as I helped him load his luggage into the back of my car. 'We're going for seven nights. Not seven years.'

'And I bet you haven't even packed yet,' laughed Tom.

'You know me too well. How are you, mate?'

'Good,' he replied. 'Really good. And you?'

'Me?' I paused and thought about it for a few moments. Tom didn't know that Sarah had gone because I hadn't told him, although I reasoned that the situation would be pretty much self-explanatory once he saw the absence of furniture in the flat. 'All the better for seeing you,' I concluded.

In the past few years I must have seen Tom only a handful of times at best. This had more to do with conflicting timetables than a lack of desire. As far as I was concerned, even if I didn't see him for an entire decade he would remain, along with Andy, one of my closest friends in the whole world.

One Saturday afternoon about six years ago, when we had both managed to get our schedules straightened out, we finally managed to set up a weekend to see each other. Sarah had gone away to see her parents in Norfolk so I'd driven up the M40 to Coventry to stay with Tom for the weekend. It had been a while since we'd had a proper chat on the phone and even longer since we'd seen each other in the flesh, so this trip was in a lot of ways long overdue. It was great to see him. We spent the afternoon visiting hi-fi shops because Tom was in the market for a new system and in the evening we'd gone for a drink at what I assumed was his local pub. Anyway, we'd been doing the catching-up thing over a couple of pints of bitter in front of a roaring log fire when Tom suddenly gave me this oddly solemn look and told me he had some important news.

'I've become a born-again Christian,' he told me sombrely. 'I just thought you ought to know.'

He then took a sip of his bitter and looked at me expectantly, as though this was my cue to tell him my reaction. And if I'm honest I really didn't know what to say. I couldn't help thinking that it would've been easier if he'd told me he was gay, because at least then I could've given him a great big hug and thanked him for confiding in me. I could've shown him how accepting I was of this new 'side' to his personality by conjuring up a list of men that I reasoned I might be attracted to if I were that way inclined and had fun gauging whether there was any common ground in our 'types'. But of course Tom wasn't gay. He was a Christian, which though I tried hard not to, I admit I found disappointing.

I'd always found born-again Christian types to be little more than a walking cliché. I didn't really much care about what they got up to in the privacy of their own churches but it bothered me greatly when it all came out into the open. I didn't like them in the news trying to affect the laws of what is essentially a secular nation; I didn't like them handing me leaflets proclaiming that the Kingdom of God was nigh; and I especially didn't like them knocking on my front door trying to palm off their literature on me. In short if I were going to choose a group of people with whom I would genuinely like to have no contact at all, it would be born-again Christians. And now, much to my dismay, Tom was one of them.

Part of my surprise at Tom's revelation was based on a key factor that I was sure excluded him from potential born-again Christianisation: at university he had been pretty much the king of casual sex and though I hadn't kept track with his private life of late I was reasonably confident that little had changed. Over the course of the evening Tom

proceeded to tell me how it had all happened. One evening a few months earlier he'd been out with a bunch of work colleagues when he'd got chatting to a woman sitting with her friends at the next table. He told me that much of what happened next was a blur of alcohol and sexual tension but the next thing he recalled was waking up the next morning in this woman's bed. And although this sort of thing had been a semi-regular occurrence in his life what made this encounter distinct was that he didn't know this woman's name and never learned it. The guilt of the experience stayed with him for a long time. He told me that he realised that ever since his dad had died when he was nineteen, he'd felt he had a huge void in his life that he had desperately been trying to fill. A few weeks went by and then a chance conversation with a female colleague at work resulted in his accepting her invitation to attend an Easter service at her church. For the first time in his life, he'd found what he had been looking for.

My reaction was puzzlement. I was convinced that Tom was just going through a weird phase which he would eventually come out of. (Weird phases that had affected various college friends and associates in recent years had included interests in: militant veganism, druidism, Krishnaism, agoraphobia, burglary and suicide.) And so when he commented: 'You think I've gone a bit mental don't you?' my reply, I have to admit, was: 'Yes.'

Subsequently every time I saw Tom, I half expected him to have taken up dressing badly or I waited with bated breath for him to start trotting out stuff about God and Jesus in the middle of a conversation about transfer rumours at Chelsea. But he didn't do any of these things. Instead, he was just the same as ever, only he seemed

21

less, well, . . . restless . . . I suppose. Definitely less restless than me . . . or Andy . . . or any of the people I knew my age. He seemed as though he knew where he was going and why. As if everything was going to always be all right for him. And he didn't start spouting bible verses, singing hymns or being weird. He was simply less agitated.

A few months later Tom and Anne (the woman who had taken him to the Easter service) got together. A year after that they got engaged and the year after their wedding, Callum, their first kid, arrived swiftly followed by Katie, sixteen months later. And although I found it difficult over the years to stop thinking of him as being the victim of some sort of brainwashing conspiracy, over time that sort of stuff seemed less and less important and eventually I just went back to thinking of him as my friend Tom.

## Every single day

Back at the flat Tom followed me inside and I offered to make him coffee. He asked if he could sit down and I said, 'Yes, of course, make yourself at home,' which was missing the point because I think what he was actually saying was, 'Mate, why haven't you got a sofa any more?' I decided that it still wasn't the right time to go into the Sarah thing and so disappeared to make his coffee. He didn't follow me into the kitchen and instead sat down on one of the uncomfortable dining chairs to wait for me.

'So how are tricks?' I asked, handing over his coffee on my return to the living room. It was a repeat of my greeting at the station but I was hoping that this time it would elicit slightly deeper answers that might shed light on why he had agreed to come on holiday.

'Good, thanks,' replied Tom.

'And Anne and the kids?'

'Anne's great . . . and the kids . . . as always they're that odd combination of complete brilliance and nail-biting frustration. Katie's three now, and Callum's four and actually starts school in September – which really freaks me out. I mean, once they start school that's it, they're almost off your hands.' Tom paused and looked pointedly around the room. 'So is this what you trendy Brighton types call minimalist living?'

'Do you like it?' I replied. 'My interior designer did it. She's very good. I'd recommend her to anyone although I do think that living with her for ten years is part of the bargain.'

Tom sighed. 'Has she gone for good?'

I nodded.

'When did she go?'

'A while ago but she only took the last of her stuff this morning.'

Tom shook his head sadly. 'I'm sorry to hear that. I thought Sarah was really good for you.'

'Me too,' I replied.

'I suppose there's no way you two could sort your problems out?'

I shrugged half-heartedly. 'Not really. It's not like it was a mutual decision.'

'Oh.' He paused and then asked: 'But you're all right?'

'Me?' I replied. 'I'm a bit down obviously but it's nothing that can't be cured by a week in the sun.'

Tom nodded again and sighed as though drawing a line underneath the subject and then launched into a conversation about the flat which led to other conversations about mortgages, work promotions, getting older and getting fatter, old friends who seemed to have dropped off the face of the planet and policemen getting younger by the minute. The one thing we didn't talk about was the one thing I wanted to know most of all. So in the end, rather than wait for him to bring up the subject, I just came out with it.

'So, mate,' I began carefully. 'Not that I'm not glad you're here but what made you agree to this holiday jaunt of Andy's?'

'I can always go home if you don't want me cramping your style,' replied Tom mockingly.

24

'Of course I want you to come,' I replied. 'It's just that . . . well when Andy came up with the idea I was pretty sure that you wouldn't be into it, that's all.'

'Because?'

I shrugged awkwardly. 'Because . . . you know . . .'

Tom laughed. 'Ladies and gentlemen,' he said with a theatrical flourish, 'presenting for your delight and delectation that world-renowned born-again Christian stereotype.'

'Come on though,' I said trying to dig myself out of the hole I'd just dug, 'you must know what I mean – a week in wherever Andy has booked us – well it's not exactly going to be bible friendly is it? I mean, I was pretty wary the second Andy called and my moral standards are pretty lax. I'm just wondering how he talked you round?'

'He didn't,' replied Tom. 'I wanted to come. The week before I'd been thinking to myself that I could do with a bit of a break and then Andy called and I thought, "Right, well that's that sorted".'

'So you're saying that Andy's phone call was a message from God?'

Tom smiled. 'All I know is that thanks to you guys I get a kid-free week off work in the sun . . . which is exactly what I need right now . . .' He paused and looked around my empty living room, '. . . and I'm guessing it's probably what you need too.'

'You're not wrong there,' I conceded amiably. 'Well, it's good to have you on board because there's absolutely no way I'd go on this holiday with just Andy.'

'Nor me,' he replied. 'Although I'm guessing that it wasn't his idea to invite me.'

'That's not exactly true,' I replied, as I attempted to

25

fudge the truth. 'You and Andy are mates; it's just the whole religion thing he's not into.'

'Maybe,' replied Tom, 'but I wouldn't call us mates. I mean, even at college Andy was always more your friend than mine.' Tom paused and smiled. 'Is he still the same?'

'Could he ever be any different?'

'Hasn't he even mellowed a little bit with age?'

'I think getting older has actually made things worse,' I replied. 'Opportunities to let loose aren't quite as forthcoming as they used to be when we were younger. And now it's like he's constantly this huge ball of pent-up energy waiting for the chance to be released. Say he calls you for a drink, you can't just have one, it'll be six or seven and then he'll drag you to a club. Say you fancy some company while you watch a couple of DVDs. The DVDs won't get watched and your home will be turned over for an impromptu party. In between he's as right as rain, but I feel as though he's always looking for his next opportunity for excess.'

'Is he still doing the painting and decorating thing?'

'Yeah.'

'I wonder if the people who pay him to paint their houses realise that he's got a first in Applied Maths?'

'I shouldn't think even Andy remembers that sort of information. The good news though is that he and Lisa are finally going to get hitched.'

Tom raised his eyebrows in surprise. 'They're still together?'

'She's what you might call long suffering. You know, sometimes I look at Andy and I can't help but feel as if the whole of his life is really fragile . . . actually forget that. What am I talking about? The whole of all our lives

is fragile. Like the only thing holding us together is Sello-tape.'

'I think you're right,' said Tom. 'But with Andy it always seems more obviously so. But he's always been a bit like that hasn't he? Even at college.'

'But that's just it. We're not at college and we haven't been for a very long time. We've all moved on.'

'Apart from Andy.'

'Yeah. Apart from Andy.'

'Anyway,' said Tom finally. 'What about you?'

'What about me?'

'I know you probably don't want to talk about it. But, really, how are you coping? I mean with Sarah gone after ten years together you must find yourself really missing her.'

'Every day,' I replied. 'I miss her every single day.'

## Milk, two cans of Boddingtons and half a tin of beans

When the doorbell rang at about a quarter past eight that evening I knew it would be Andy. So when I made my way downstairs to open the door I was somewhat surprised to see his girlfriend Lisa with him. There was an air about Lisa, not of someone dropping off her boyfriend and then immediately going, but rather of someone who was coming in, possibly having a cup of tea and a general nose around and maybe a chat too. Childish as it might seem, I had been in a bit of a 'no girls allowed' frame of mind for some time (they're all unhinged/don't know what they want/all on the same side – delete as inapplicable). Of course women had their place in the world but, I reasoned, at this particular point in time their place wasn't my flat, with my friends, spoiling our pre-holiday enjoyment.

There was no doubt that Andy had done very well in getting (and even more so in keeping) a woman like Lisa. Though he was reasonably good looking (slightly less so than Tom but slightly more so than me) there was no arguing that Lisa was in her own quiet way the more attractive of the two. Her long brown hair was so dark that in certain lights it looked black and it framed the delicate features of her face perfectly. In contrast Andy had light brown hair with flecks of grey at the temples. His features

were dark and craggy, as though he had lived a hard life working in a coal mine and his eyebrows were so heavy that they cast a shadow over his entire face. But what lifted his looks were his eyes. They were an immediately striking shade of green mixed with grey.

Andy had met Lisa in a bar in Brighton one evening seven years ago when the two of us were out for a drink. Lisa was Canadian and had been working for a food marketing company for a year but had only just managed to get an extension on her visa. When she and Andy first got together I used to joke that Lisa was only after him for a British passport. What other reason could there be for someone that attractive to be with someone as useless as Andy? Actually I was well aware why someone like Lisa would be with someone like Andy. He had charm. By the bucket load. And not cheesy smarmy charm either. But the good type that makes girls fancy you and boys want to be your best friend.

I'd met Andy through Pippa, a girl I'd just started seeing in my first year at college. One night when Pippa and I were out drinking in Brighton, Pippa's friend Lara brought Andy along to join us. After the pub a whole gang of us walked back to Lara's house in Coombe Road and Andy and I ended up talking. It was friendship at first conversation . . . a few notches down from love at first sight. Andy told me about a party that was going on in Kemptown that we'd be mad to miss. Though I knew that Pippa would be upset if I went to the party without her, Andy presented such a persuasive argument ('There'll be girls, and loads of booze and really good music') and was so steadfast in his refusal to accept no for an answer that in the end it was easier to say yes. And though my actions resulted in me getting

dumped by Pippa the following day, the demise of my relationship led me to later pulling Holly, a mind-blowingly beautiful third-year fashion student who'd been at the party.

The downside of being Andy's friend was that there were times when he was no more and no less than a right pain in the backside. Back in college if I had an essay to hand in for the following morning, I would literally have to hide myself away from Andy because I knew if he found me I'd end up at a bar or a club or a party and then I'd wake up the following morning with a raging hangover and the essay still not done. And it would be me that would have to face the consequences of the big night out. It would be me that would have to sort out all the trouble that he'd get the two of us in. It was always me that had to clean up after him. I think that at the heart of the problem back then was the fact that Andy didn't want to grow up and did everything he could to delay the inevitable arrival of full adulthood. Once he left college he didn't want a career (hence his chosen diversion into painting and decorating). He didn't want the responsibilities of a mortgage (preferring instead to pay long-suffering Lisa rent).

The fact that he had finally relented to Lisa's suggestion that they get engaged said less about any supposed change of heart on the subject of matrimony and far more about the fact that even he was coming to realise that he couldn't stay twenty-one for ever. This was why I was sure that this holiday was more about him than – as he'd pitched it – about me. With his own wedding less than a year away, I could see that the holiday represented an opportunity for him to be young and stupid again. And I got a huge feeling of discomfort in the pit of my stomach that he was going to go all out to enjoy it.

'All right you two?' I said breezily greeting Andy and Lisa in a bid to cover my initial surprise.

'Yeah fine,' replied Andy. 'Are you going to let us in then or what?'

I suddenly realised that I was standing on the doorstep as though I had no intention of letting either of them past the door and quickly ushered them upstairs. At the front door to the flat I stopped and issued a sort of catch-all world-weary disclaimer: 'Sarah's taken her stuff. Yes, it is difficult to watch TV when a dining room chair is your only comfort. Yes, I will be buying some more furniture when I get round to it. No, I'm not interested in any furniture that you're trying to get rid of but I do appreciate the thought.'

Andy laughed and patted me on the back while Lisa rolled her eyes, kissed me on the cheek and followed Andy into the flat.

'Oi, Bullock!' yelled Andy in Tom's direction. 'Are you still in the God squad?'

'Just ignore him, Tom,' countered Lisa, digging Andy sharply in the ribs with her fingers. 'My boyfriend is a pig and he knows it.'

Tom seemed more amused than upset by Andy and as he hugged Lisa she commented on how long it had been since she'd last seen him. (Two years to be precise when Tom, Anne and the kids had come to stay with Sarah and me.) As Lisa released him from her embrace he turned to face Andy and the two men stood staring at each other for an uncomfortably long time and then they both burst out laughing.

'It's good to see you again,' grinned Tom.

'You too,' replied Andy. 'You too.'

As the two men fell into conversation I asked Lisa if she fancied a drink; this was the most subtle way I could think of to find out how long she was staying for.

'What time are you guys going out?' she asked, gazing around my empty living room.

'There's no rush,' I lied. I doubted whether my honest answer: 'The second you leave,' would've been appreciated.

'I'll stay for a cup of tea then,' she replied, 'but you can stop with the cold sweats, Charlie, I only came round because Andy needed a lift. I think in his ideal world he would've hurled himself from the car and had me drive by without stopping.' She leaned forward and ruffled Andy's hair affectionately. 'Isn't that right, sweetie? I'm cramping your style aren't I?'

'Massively,' said Andy with his eyes still fixed on the TV. 'I'll have a coffee while you're up there, babe.'

'Hang on,' she replied, 'it was Charlie that—' she stopped and sighed, something which I guessed she did an awful lot living with Andy. She looked at Tom. 'Since I've been nominated designated maker-of-hot-drinks for the evening would you like one too?'

'I'm fine thanks,' said Tom warily.

'No really,' said Lisa, 'I don't mind.'

'Okay then,' he replied. 'I'll have a coffee too if that's okay. White, no sugar. Thanks.'

'Right, you,' said Lisa addressing me in a tone that didn't invite any form of debate. 'Come and help me in the kitchen.'

As I stood at the tap refilling the kettle, Lisa rummaged through the various jars and tins that lived on top of the microwave looking for the coffee and the tea.

'So, how are you keeping?' she asked as she located

the tin that held the tea bags and fished one out ready on the counter.

'I'm fine.'

'Really?'

'Yeah, really.'

Lisa opened the fridge door and peered inside. 'Milk, two cans of Boddingtons and half a tin of beans,' she said woefully. She closed the door and rested the open milk carton on the counter in front of me. 'You're not fine at all, Charlie. At least that's not what this fridge says.'

'Well it's wrong.'

'And it's not what Andy says either. He says that you're still really cut up about . . . well, you know.'

I picked up a dirty teaspoon off the counter and ran it underneath the tap for a few seconds. 'Have you seen her at all lately?' I asked, avoiding eye contact. 'I know you two still see each other.'

'I spoke to her on the phone at the beginning of this week,' said Lisa after a few moments. 'It was nothing special. Just a catch-up call. We've been trying to come up with a date to have a proper meet-up somewhere in town.'

'How did she seem?'

'All things considered, she seemed okay.'

'Did she ask about me?'

'Don't, Charlie,' sighed Lisa. 'Please.'

I shrugged and stared at the kettle as it heated up in front of me. 'I've got some post for her.' I nodded at a pile of letters jammed in next to the tea bags on the microwave. 'It's mostly junk mail. I should've left it out for her to take with the furniture. I don't know whether she's that desperate for another credit card but if you're seeing her . . .'

Lisa declined the offer with an awkward smile.

'Fine,' I replied. 'I'll just bang them back in the post then.'

As the kettle finally came to the boil and switched itself off, I reached across to the wall cupboard, pulled out the first mug I could find and handed it to Lisa. It was only when it was in her hand that I realised that emblazoned across it was the inscription: 'The World's Greatest Lover.' Lisa just laughed and rested it on the counter while I stood there squirming with embarrassment.

Whenever Lisa came to my flat, she always made a big deal about the fact that she was quite fussy about the way that she liked her tea made and so usually made her own. Today was no different, and for some reason I found myself carefully studying her tea-making process. It didn't seem any different from my own.

'I need a favour,' said Lisa as she stirred the milk into her tea.

'What?'

She paused and looked at me. 'It's to do with Andy. I want you to make sure that he doesn't cheat on me.'

How was I supposed to react to a request like that? My gut instinct was to laugh it off but there was a look in her eyes that made me realise that this was no laughing matter.

'I'm not stupid, Charlie,' continued Lisa. 'I don't believe for a second that Andy came up with the idea of this holiday just for your benefit.'

'Well actually—'

'You don't have to deny it. You can still have the brownie points for being loyal to your friend, if that's what you're after.'

'Look,' I began, 'Andy might be a lot of things but he's not that much of an idiot.'

'Maybe not,' said Lisa. 'But he's not above trying anything once is he? Look, Charlie, I've got three brothers back in Montreal. I know what guys are like when they go on vacation.'

'I think you're forgetting that he's going away with an emotional cripple and a born-again Christian,' I replied. 'He'll be lucky to get anywhere near a girl with me and Tom in tow.'

She didn't seem convinced.

'All I'm asking is that you at least try to stop him doing anything he might regret.' Lisa paused and took a sip of her tea. 'You know he's going to ask you to be his best man,' she continued.

'No, I didn't,' I replied. 'He hasn't mentioned it at all. What about his kid brother?'

Lisa shook her head. 'You're his first and only choice.'

'That's really nice to hear and . . . well . . . I appreciate you coming to me like this but you know . . . I'm probably not the best—'

'You're his friend,' she interrupted. 'Nothing else matters does it? Surely you want what's best for him? Because I'm telling you now that if he's unfaithful I'll leave him. And I will not change my mind. Ever.'

'Have you told him that?'

'Not in so many words.'

'Maybe you should spell it out.'

'I told him that I didn't want him to go on this holiday and he's still going. I know what he's like, Charlie. And I know what girls on vacation are like too. And it scares me. This whole thing feels like some sort of mid-life crisis come

35

a decade too soon. I know he'll get over it and then he'll feel like he's ticked it off his list of things to do before he gets married but if I try to stop him he'll just resent me. You know as well as I do that he can't always be trusted to use his best judgement . . . at least not without some encouragement.'

'Fine, I'll try,' I conceded.

'Do you promise?'

'I don't need to. I'm sure he won't do anything, anyway.'

'I hope you're right. But at least this way I'll feel better if I know you're looking out for him.'

Putting down her tea, Lisa walked over to me, put her arms around me and hugged me tightly. I bristled immediately. Andy's girlfriend was putting her arms around me, and we were in the kitchen out of sight of the others and though there was nothing going on I didn't like the possibility of this situation being even slightly misinterpreted. At the same time I suddenly recognised in Lisa the same desperate loneliness that had dogged me during my last days with Sarah. I couldn't help myself. I put my arms round her.

'He loves you, you know,' I whispered in her ear as she clung to me.

'That's nice of you to say,' she said quietly. 'But I don't think it's true.'

You do remember we've been to Crete before, don't you, said Tom, barely able to fill his incredulity.

Of course I do, said Andy defensively.

And so why do remember what happened there?

Of course, he replied. Which is why we're not only going

Male, except it outraged disbelief. Mat...

me that of all the places in the world you could have chosen you had to choose the one place you know I would

obvious that I won't do this right...

## He really must be having some sort of early mid-life crisis

'Right, then,' said Tom as Andy returned from the bar carrying three pints of Hoegaarden. 'I know you've been enjoying keeping us in the dark over this holiday but enough is enough. Where exactly is it we're supposed to be going to tomorrow?'

It was now just after nine and the three of us were sitting in my local pub, The George. The George was nothing special. Just another one of those light and airy refurbished pubs with stripped floors, overstuffed leather sofas, a food menu that leaned towards the Mediterranean and a bar that featured a larger selection of bottled wines and imported beers than most. Its chief selling point was its clientele. Too lacking in loud music to attract the needlessly young but too trendy to attract the needlessly old, The George was the kind of place where a man of thirty-five could still feel at ease.

'Drum roll please, maestro,' said Andy as he set the beers down on the table. 'Prepare yourself to be shocked and amazed as once again your favourite uncle Andy delivers the goods because tomorrow, my friends, we are flying to . . . Crete.'

I stared at Andy in horror.

'I know,' said Andy, presumably mistaking the look on my face for delight. 'Genius, isn't it?'

37

'You do remember we've been to Crete before don't you?' said Tom, barely able to hide his incredulity.

'Of course I do,' said Andy defensively.

'And so you do remember what happened there?'

'Of course,' he replied. 'Which is why we're not only going back to Crete but we're staying in the same resort.'

'Malia?' I spat in outraged disbelief. 'Malia? You're telling me that of all the places in the world you could have chosen you had to choose the one place you know I would least want to go?'

'Hair of the dog,' said Andy firmly. 'Take your poison and turn it into a cure.'

'Andy, mate,' I said as calmly as I could, 'apart from the obvious that I won't go into right now, you know as well as I do that we can't spend a week in Malia. Malia's the unofficial capital of the Club 18–30 world. And in case you haven't noticed, Andy, none of us is between the ages of eighteen and thirty.'

'Exactly,' replied Andy, 'which is why I had to lie about our ages. So if anyone asks if you're thirty, Tom's twenty-nine and I'm twenty-eight next birthday.'

I looked over at Tom to make sure that I wasn't alone in thinking that this was the worst kind of bad news we could be hearing. Rather than being shocked, however, Tom apparently found the whole thing amusing.

'You think this is funny?'

'No,' said Tom chuckling to himself as he looked at Andy. 'I think this is what happens when you let McCormack book a holiday for you.'

'Tom's right,' said Andy calmly. 'This *is* what happens when you let me book a holiday for you. I mix things up. I make things happen. Think about it, Charlie. You had

the best holiday of your entire life in Malia when you were twenty-five. What better way could there be of getting over Sarah than going back there and meeting someone else?'

39

Wish You Were Here

the best holiday of your entire life in Malta when you were
twenty-five. What better way could there be of getting
over Sarah than going back there and meeting someone
else?

## The ice cube game

It all happened two years after Tom, Andy and I graduated
from Sussex University and were living in a shared house
in the Bevandean area of Brighton. At the time Tom was
back at the university doing a post-graduate course, Andy
was on the dole and I had got my first job in the lower
echelons of the council's Economic Development unit.

Up until this point I'd never been on holiday with the
two of them together. In my first year I'd spent a month
Interrailing around Europe with Tom as he wasn't a lying-
on-a-beach-soaking-up-the-sun type; and in my second year
I'd spent a week on Kos with Andy as he wasn't a-museum-
and-monument type. And so, as far as the idea of the three
of us going on holiday together went, it just never seemed
likely to happen.

But one summer evening Andy put forward the suggestion. While I was into the idea straight away I was sure
Tom wouldn't be. But I was wrong.

'Sounds like a great idea,' he said. 'A week in the sun
will give me the chance to catch up with all the engineering
text books I'm supposed to have read by September . . .
and have a few beers too.' With that settled, we came up
with a list of criteria for what we wanted from the holiday.
The list, as far as I can remember, went something like
this:

1) Girls.
2) Places to meet girls.
3) Cheap alcohol.

Andy volunteered to book the holiday because he had the most free time and the following day, over dinner, he pulled out a list of three resorts that he had managed – with the help of the girl he'd chatted up in Thomas Cook – to whittle down from a cast of thousands:

1) Faliraki, Rhodes.
2) San Antonio, Ibiza.
3) Malia, Crete.

Whether it was because of the girl in Thomas Cook or because of his desperate need to go on holiday, Andy knew his stuff. He gave us a detailed presentation of not only the pros and cons of each resort, but each hotel and apartment block, too. Casting aside Ibiza on the grounds that we suspected the type of girls who went there might possibly be a bit too trendy for guys like us, we narrowed our options down to Faliraki and Malia. We debated the issues as best we could. Tom pointed out that the flight and hotel package in Faliraki was a bit cheaper than the one in Malia. Andy countered by making the point that the girls on the Malia page of the holiday brochure seemed marginally more attractive. We put it to a vote and despite Tom's earlier defence of Faliraki decided unanimously that Malia would be our destination.

We were already having the best holiday on record when, after two days, I first noticed Sarah and her friends lying on sun-loungers by the side of the hotel swimming pool.

She was absolutely amazing to look at. Shockingly so. And I was well aware that none of my tried and tested cheesy chat-up lines would have worked on her in a million years. A girl like Sarah required a special kind of approach. A one-off that would get me noticed without making me look like the sort of bloke from whom she'd run a mile. And so began my campaign . . . of smiling. That was it. Nothing else. I smiled when I passed her table as she and her friends had lunch by the pool; I smiled when I passed by her in the hotel's reception; and if we were out for a drink in the evening and our two groups met in the street, I'd smile at her then too.

I always gave her the same kind of smile too. Short, friendly, and not in the least bit suggestive, as though we were work colleagues or vague acquaintances. After the smile, I'd follow up with a quick exchange of eye contact and then look away. Initially she didn't notice me but then gradually her friends picked up on what I was doing so she started to notice too. Soon it got to the stage where if I looked up to smile at her she'd be all ready to smile straight back at me. And that was when I knew I was right where I wanted to be: slap bang in the middle of her consciousness.

Of course being in her consciousness wasn't the ultimate aim of my campaign. What I needed was the opportunity to take things further. And it came in the form of a night out organised by the tour operators billed as: 'The Club Fun Big Night Out' – a gigantic pub crawl involving about forty of us from the hotel.

Halfway through the night, having already consumed more flavoured vodka shots and luminous-coloured jello shots than would normally be advisable on an empty

stomach, we were herded by the tour rep into a bar called Flashdance. Over his loudhailer the rep informed us that once we had downed the bar's free strawberry-flavoured jello shots we would have a couple of rounds of The Ice Cube Game.

The rules were as simple as they were off-putting to the sober. Two teams had to form a line behind each other in a 'boy/girl' fashion. The two people at the front of the line would then be handed a beer glass filled to the brim with ice cubes and instructed to pass as many ice cubes down the line as quickly as possible without using their hands. On realising that this so-called game was just a huge excuse for a free-for-all snogging session a number of the more attractive girl members of the pub crawl bailed out immediately. Sarah was one of them. I was just about to drop out myself as a fearsome-looking Welsh girl sidled up in front of me and grinned suggestively in my direction. In desperation I looked across at Sarah and realised she was already looking at me. She smiled. But this was a different smile to the others we had exchanged. Without saying a word she came and stood at the front of my queue. And without saying a word I squeezed out from behind the Welsh girl and – much to the chagrin of a short guy in glasses – slotted in the queue right behind Sarah.

Once everybody was ready to begin the game the rep handed out the ice-cube-filled glasses, returned to the podium and blew furiously into the whistle around his neck. A commotion broke out. The whole bar was yelling, screaming and cheering. While the guy at the front of the queue next to us was already doing battle with the girl behind him, Sarah had yet to begin. Tipping the glass up to her glossed lips she slowly sucked a solitary ice cube

into her mouth and then turned to face me with a wry grin on her face. I put my lips to hers and closed my eyes as the ice cube slid a cool trail from my mouth to hers. For a moment I wondered whether I had misread the situation but then her tongue darted quickly into my mouth after the ice cube and I knew that I wouldn't be sharing any frozen water with anybody else.

# SUNDAY

## Long-stay car park blues

'Over there by that green Range Rover!' cried Andy.

'Forget the Range Rover,' said Tom. 'Head for that silver people wagon on the other side.'

'Sod it.' I slammed on my brakes. 'I'm just going to dump the car here and hope for the best. Because at this rate we really are going to miss the plane.'

It was now late in the afternoon on what had so far already been an extremely long day. Following Andy's revelation at The George that our holiday destination was to be Malia, he made things worse by badgering me into matching him drink for drink for the rest of the evening. Once we'd left the pub, he dragged me into an off-licence and bought yet more alcohol to finish off back at the flat. Anytime I looked even vaguely as though I was going to stop drinking he'd simply harangue me into having another. And though we did end up having a great time (I hadn't laughed so hard, sung so loudly or sworn quite so vociferously in a long time) I couldn't help but wish that sometimes he would turn his personality down a couple of notches.

At around three in the morning Tom declared that he was going to bed and although I wanted to go too, Andy held me captive for another hour until I could take no more and fell asleep on the carpet next to him. With no one to

47

keep him company Andy allegedly did the only thing he could: he cracked open a few more beers, dug out a bunch of old *Fast Show* videos from a shelf in the hallway and stayed up by himself for another three hours until he finally succumbed to exhaustion.

Thanks to our late night, none of us stirred until well after midday. And when we did wake up, Andy insisted that we stick to our plan, the first part of which was breakfast at Stomboli's, a café in Bevandean that we used to frequent on a regular basis. It was comforting seeing the old place again with its fake wood-panelling wallpaper and cheery wipe-clean gingham table cloths. And even better to see that Georgiou the owner was still in charge. The only problem with our nostalgic late breakfast was that it dragged on far longer than the half an hour we had allotted for it. This wouldn't have been so bad if I'd already packed my suitcase but of course I hadn't. So once we got back to the flat I had no choice but to empty the contents of my wardrobe, chest of drawers and ironing pile into my suitcase and then randomly eject items of clothing until I could actually get the lid shut. Then I had just enough time to race around the flat making sure everything was safe and secure before finally squeezing all our cases into the back of my car and heading to the nearest petrol station. With a full tank of fuel I drove like the proverbial bat out of hell in the direction of the A23, thereby guaranteeing myself a sizeable number of points on my licence, if not a complete driving ban.

'You worry too much,' said Andy as we climbed out of the car and began unloading our luggage on to the tarmac. 'I promise you that speed-camera did not go off.'

'Of course it did,' I replied. 'I saw it flash.'

'You're wrong,' said Andy. 'Tom, tell him he's wrong, will you?'

'You're joking,' said Tom. 'It was a guaranteed licence-loser.'

Still arguing I locked up the car and then we made our way to the shuttle-bus stop. The warmer weather that had opened August had gradually faded away as the month progressed and as I looked up at the sky I could see that the sun was fighting a losing battle with the scattered cloud above. Regardless of the restrained sunshine all three of us donned our sunglasses without comment.

Just as I was beginning to believe that we might actually miss the flight, the shuttle-bus arrived. Even as we climbed on board, lodged our luggage in the space provided and took our seats my heart was racing. The thought of having to stay in England even one more day was bringing me out in cold sweats.

As we finally approached the front of the airport it was clear that pretty much everyone in the world was going on holiday. There were taxi drivers, family members, friends and lovers all parked in the bus's designated dropping-off zone. Right in front of us was a long white stretch limo that just screamed students with too much disposable income. Lo and behold a bunch of glamorous-looking types emerged from inside, spilling out on to the pavement. One of them pulled out a camera while the others congregated in front of the limo to have their photo taken. They all looked fresh-faced and energised, as though they were about to begin a new chapter of their lives. And despite myself I couldn't help but make the connection between them and my twenty-five-year-old self, recalling my own youth and eternal optimism. On the outside we didn't look

all that much different; on the inside we couldn't have been more dissimilar. 'That's what a decade does to you,' I thought as I watched them laughing and joking. 'It changes water into oil.'

## Strays

Standing in the entrance to the departure lounge with Andy and Tom ahead of me and the electronic doors hovering expectantly on either side I became gripped by the conviction that I had forgotten something important. I wracked my brain trying to work out what the missing item might be, but it was difficult to concentrate against the barrage of announcements over the Tannoy – delayed flights, opening check-in desks, heightened security – it was all putting me off. I double-checked my passport and tickets but they were safely tucked away in the back pocket of my jeans and I even opened up my suitcase and checked that I had my 'Death To the Pixies' T-shirt. When I closed the case I recalled what or rather who was missing – Sarah. It had always been Sarah's job to double-check that we had everything that we needed. That was why being here at the airport felt so odd. Without the safety-net of her presence, how could I be sure that I hadn't left anything important behind?

By the time I made my way over to the check-in desk there were only five minutes left until it closed but the queue was still some twenty to thirty people deep. Tom overheard something from the people in front of us about airport staff apologising over the late opening of the check-in desk that afternoon. We could finally relax. We'd been handed a reprieve.

The queue in front of us was made up of every sort of person. Old folk with luggage trolleys packed right up to the rafters; families over three generations who all seemed to be talking at once; well-groomed young couples clearly taking their first joint holidays abroad; preening young men with salon tans and highlighted hair pouting and posing to their hearts' content; scruffy-looking student types flirting with each other in a prelude to holiday foreplay; gangs of girls who looked as though they'd just stepped out of a nightclub; worried parents assisting their over-excited offspring with their luggage for their first holiday alone; rough-looking lads in baseball caps laughing and joking with each other; and then finally there was us: three relatively well-dressed but hardly stunning thirtysomething men suffering from varying degrees of hair loss. I'm sure we stood out a mile in our queue because we looked so incomplete – like stray dogs abandoned by their owners: grown men without their other halves.

Gradually the queue whittled down to us and a bunch of lads in their late teens who had attempted to push in ahead of us only to be set straight by Andy. The woman at the check-in handed the return tickets, boarding cards and passports to Andy, assuming in the way that everybody did that he was our leader.

'I'm going to get a paper,' said Andy. 'Anybody else want anything?'

'I'll come with you,' said Tom. 'I want to see if I can get a guide book to Crete.'

'What for?' asked Andy. 'All we're going to do is eat, drink, and lie on a beach. You don't need a guide book for that, do you?'

'If you think I'm going to spend all week staring at the

sun you've got another think coming, mate,' said Tom flatly. He turned to me and winked. 'You'll come with me on a few trips won't you, mate?'

'I'm easy,' I replied in a bid to keep the peace. 'I'll go anywhere with anyone.'

As Andy and Tom made their way to the newsagent's, I stood and watched a group of people who had obviously just returned from their holidays and had lost their way from the arrivals lounge. Some were wearing their market-stall-purchased straw hats as though they were still basking in the glow of the sun that they had long left behind. They looked relaxed and carefree, in stark contrast to the guys in the reflective yellow tops collecting the abandoned trolleys who looked miserable and hassled. Seeing these fresh-from-holiday people made me smile because what they had – their sunshine state of mind – was exactly what I wanted for myself. Maybe in seven days' time I too wouldn't feel quite so at odds with the world. Maybe I would return to Gatwick wearing clothing inappropriate for the non-existent British summer. Maybe I would come back changed somehow. Different.

In the pub the night before Andy had promised me that this holiday would turn my life around. He promised laughter and new experiences. New stories to tell and new women to tell them to. Though at the time I'd found myself thinking instinctively, 'Andy mate, that's asking a lot of a cheap last-minute package holiday,' but afterwards, as we walked home through the chilled Brighton night air I'd thought to myself, 'Maybe he's got a point after all. Every-body has expectations of holidays. We want them to restore us, entertain us and even find us new loves. So why should this holiday be any different?'

\*

On Andy and Tom's return from the newsagent's we made our way through to passport control, now with only a security check between us and the departure lounge. When Andy stepped through the metal detector he set off the alarm, as did Tom – they had both neglected to empty out money from their pockets – so as I took my turn to walk through the detector I convinced myself that I too would somehow set it off even though my pockets were empty. It was with no small relief that I made it through without a single electronic beep or flash to the other side. I was through. I was safe. There could be no going back without a great deal of difficulty. Now I was standing in the kingdom of discounted perfume and aftershave; of multiple packs of fags and litre bottles of booze. This wasn't England any more. It was a shopper's paradise.

'Does anyone fancy a stroll around the shops?' I asked as Andy located a row of seats in the lounge to use as a base while we waited for our flight number to be called.

'No thanks,' replied Andy. 'I'm going to read my paper.'

I looked over at Tom. 'I'll give it a miss, mate. There are a few things I'm quite keen to check out in my guide book.'

Undeterred by my friends' lack of consumerist urges, I did the rounds of the various high street names inside the departure lounge alone. And although I didn't actually need anything at all I still managed to return from my sojourn with several packs of fruit pastilles, two bottles of mineral water and three books from Waterstone's.

'How long is the flight?' asked Andy looking up from his newspaper as I sat down next to him.

'Four and a half hours,' I replied. 'You're trying to work out if we'll have time to get to our hotel and then go and get slaughtered aren't you?'

'A wise man always knows how much drinking time is available to him.'

'Have you never heard of pacing yourself? I'm still feeling a bit rough from last night.'

'I would've been better off going on holiday with that lot,' chided Andy pointing to a group of girls featuring more peroxide highlights, spandex, gold rings, tattoos and naked flesh than any group of people had any right to. 'Do you think they're planning to go to bed as soon they reach Crete?'

'They're young,' I replied. 'They'll learn.'

'I doubt it,' said Andy. 'They might be young but I guarantee you they won't learn anything at all. Look, at me, I'm thirty-six next birthday and I'm proud to say that I haven't learned a single thing in my entire life.'

**People to say goodbye to**

We'd been discussing the phenomenon of how, when you've been away on holiday, someone famous always dies, when Andy was cut short by the announcement over the Tannoy of the departure gate for the flight to Heraklion. There was an instant flurry of activity in our corner of the departure lounge as people began to troop towards the gate.

'This is it then,' said Tom folding up his newspaper. 'Better give Anne a quick ring.'

'I suppose I'd better try Lisa too,' said Andy, pulling out his phone.

'Okay,' I said standing up. 'I'll see you guys at the gate.'

Tom and Andy both had people to say goodbye to but I had nobody and for a brief moment I felt as if the one thing I wanted most in the world was to have someone who wanted to hear from me. Someone who would miss the fact that I was no longer there. I considered calling Sarah and as I reached the queue for the gate I even pulled out my phone and scrolled through the address book for her number. But then I imagined her answering the call. And I imagined hearing the disappointment in her voice. And I imagined my reaction. And I knew I didn't want that feeling to be the last thing in my head as I got on the plane. So I turned off the phone before I could do any

damage and slipped it into the carrier bag in my hand, next to my books and bottled water.

Even with the phone off, Sarah remained in my thoughts. She was there as we handed in our boarding cards and as we trooped aboard the shuttle-bus. She was there as we crossed the tarmac and climbed the stairs to the plane. She was there as we listened to instructions to turn off all mobile phones and electrical devices. And she was there as the emergency manoeuvres were drilled into us and the nearest emergency exits pointed out. She was even there as we prepared for take-off and taxied along the runway. But as the cabin began to shake and the roar of the jets filled our ears, her presence finally began to fade, so that by the time we had lifted up into the air and broken through the clouds above she was gone altogether.

## Because when you go on holiday stuff like this happens

According to our pilot we would land at Heraklion airport at a quarter past eleven in the evening, local time. The flight had been fairly uneventful. With an initial burst of energy after take-off the three of us became quite talkative, taking great pleasure in unearthing a flurry of embarrassing anecdotes and memories from our student years, but as the journey progressed an oddly uniform lull spread across the plane and, with the exception of the odd screaming child, few passengers did anything other than eat, sleep, read or watch the in-flight entertainment: *Miss Congeniality 2*, an ancient episode of *Only Fools and Horses* and a documentary about clocks. I had entertained myself with the first of my three books: *Touching The Void* by Joe Simpson. A completely absorbing account of two friends who climbed the 21,000 ft Siula Grande Peake in the Andes only to get themselves in trouble on the way down. I'd seen the documentary they had made of the book a few years earlier at the cinema with Sarah. After the film Sarah had said to me that if it had been me and Andy on that mountain, Andy wouldn't have thought twice about cutting the rope and seemingly sending me to my doom. I'd told her she was wrong. Andy would never have cut the rope in a million years. It wasn't his style at all. But as I read

58

the first few chapters of the book it dawned on me that I'd never really considered the situation the other way round. With Andy's life in my hand would I have cut the rope? I couldn't come to any kind of conclusion even after hours of internal debate. In the end I abandoned the book and distracted myself by watching *Miss Congeniality 2* without the aid of headphones.

With the sound of the electronic 'ding' the seat-belt safety sign switched off, plunging the entire plane into a flurry of frenzied activity. Passengers were frantically unbuckling, unloading the overhead storage lockers and squeezing into the aisles in a bid to be the first off the plane.

'What's the big rush?' said Andy a little too loudly. 'It's not like they're going to get to their hotels any quicker. They're still going to have to wait for everyone else.'

'I suppose,' I replied but the truth was, I was as eager to get off the plane as they were; like them I wanted to get my holiday started right away. Now I was on holiday my time was my own. I could go wherever I wanted to go and, more importantly, I could be whoever I wanted to be. I couldn't wait. And as our turn arrived to file into the narrow aisle and head towards the exit, it was all I could do not to run. As the cabin crew said goodbye I was too excited to reply, distracted by the exotic thrill of walking out of the air-conditioned cool of the plane straight into a thick fug of Mediterranean night air. The warmth was real. Almost palpable. Good things were going to happen to me in this country. I could feel it in my blood.

As soon as we passed through passport control Andy, Tom and I turned on our mobile phones and stared at them expectantly. But while Tom and Andy, despite their

lack of messages, took great delight in comparing names and logos of the Greek mobile phone operators they had been assigned, I simply stared at my phone in disbelief. Unbeknownst to me, while we'd been in the air I'd received a text message from Sarah:

**Message Sarah:** Charlie, I need to talk to you about something important. Please ring me when you've got a moment. S x

'What's up mate?' asked Tom, obviously reading the concern on my face.

'Nothing.' I shook my head as if waking from a dream. I quickly switched off. 'I'm fine. Just a missed call.'

Andy walked over to me and ruffled my hair as if I was a five-year-old. 'We're on holiday now, mate. Cheer up. Once we reach baggage claims me and Tom will get the luggage and you can go and get a trolley.'

Though I was already pretty sick of being organised by Andy, I didn't have the energy to protest. There were at least two flights that needed to be unloaded ahead of us and so it took quite a while for our luggage carousel to get started. And when it finally did get going, much to Andy's annoyance a good few of the passengers on our flight managed to get their luggage without a single sighting of our own. I however had my own problems to contend with. Sarah's text had sent my world into a spin. While I was curious about her message I was fearful of it too. I stared at my phone and silently cursed the progress of technology. A decade ago she wouldn't have been able to send me a guided missile via the airwaves. A decade ago I would have been blissfully ignorant of her desire to make contact. But it was now, not then. And despite my best

intentions the message had been received. Loud and clear.

As I reached across with my thumb to switch off my phone I felt a tap on my arm. Standing in front of me was a girl wearing a straw cowboy hat. She had curly black hair, flawless mahogany skin and looked altogether amazing.

'You were on the flight from Gatwick weren't you?' said the girl-in-the-cowboy-hat in a bold south-London accent.

'Yeah,' I replied cautiously as I looked over her shoulder at a gang of girls in their mid-twenties who were trying their best to give the impression that they weren't watching us.

'I thought so,' said the girl-in-the-cowboy-hat. 'Which resort are you staying at?'

'Malia.'

'I knew it!' she exclaimed. 'Me and my friends are too. Have you been before?'

'Once, a while ago. How about yourself?'

'This is the third year in a row for me and the girls,' she replied.

'You must like it.'

'It's great. I guarantee you'll have the best time ever here.'

'That's good to know.'

She paused. 'Do you like clubbing?'

'Yeah,' I replied, mainly because I suspected that at least in her eyes this was the correct answer.

'Where do you go out in London?'

'I don't,' I replied. 'I'm from Brighton.'

'I know Brighton,' she replied. 'I've been clubbing there loads of times. I bet you're a regular at places like Purple Paradise and Computer Love.'

'Yeah, I know those,' I bluffed.

'Excellent,' said the girl-in-the-cowboy-hat. 'I don't suppose you know a bar in Malia called Pandemonium do you? It's on the main strip. You can't miss it. It's the one with the neon rabbit sign.'

'I could probably find it,' I replied.

'Well, I just thought you might like to know me and my friends will be in there around midnight tomorrow night if you want to join us.'

'That sounds great,' I said coolly. 'Midnight, tomorrow, Pandemonium.'

'Right then,' she smiled, 'I'd better go.'

'It was nice to meet you,' I said trying my best to hide my confusion.

'It was nice to meet you too,' she replied. She paused and then added: 'Oh, and bring your mates too. My friend Liz quite likes the one with the shaven head . . .' Tom. '. . . and my friend Luce quite likes the guy in the red top.' Andy. 'So, I might see you tomorrow night then?'

'Yeah,' I replied. 'Tomorrow night it is.'

Watching her walk away I was barely able to breathe as I considered what had just happened. It appeared as if an amazingly attractive young girl had just asked me out. I turned round to search out Andy and Tom to tell them my good news but they were standing right behind me wearing looks of pure bewilderment.

'Who was that?' asked Andy immediately.

'I don't know,' I replied. 'She didn't tell me her name.'

'She was spectacular,' continued Andy. 'What did she want?'

'I think she wanted to ask me out . . .'

'You're joking!'

'No, she invited me to join her and her friends in some bar in Malia around midnight tomorrow.'

'Now that is pretty amazing,' said Tom. He patted me on the back. 'Well done, fella.'

'You see?' said Andy. 'No offence, Charlie mate, but back in Brighton girls who look like that don't normally come up to blokes who look like you and say meet me in a bar around midnight, do they? The only place that things like that happen is right where we are now – on holiday.'

'This is too weird for words,' I said, still somewhat stunned. 'She even said that one of her mates fancied Tom.'

'Brilliant,' laughed Tom. 'It's always nice to know that you can still turn a few heads when you want to.'

'Just wait until they find out you're a married born-again Christian though,' teased Andy. 'So,' he continued, turning to me, 'which one of the girls fancied me?'

I opened my mouth to reply but stopped as I recalled my promise to Lisa. 'Sorry, mate,' I replied, 'she didn't mention anything about you at all.'

'Not a single word?'

'Nothing at all.'

'That's just because they've yet to feel the full force of my personality,' said Andy philosophically. 'You wait until tomorrow night when they finally meet me in the flesh. I guarantee you, my friend, the girls of Malia will be all over me like a rash.'

## Steve-the-barman

With our luggage piled precariously high on a single trolley we made our way through customs and out the other side. It was easy to spot where we had to go next as waiting expectantly underneath an awning set up at the main exit were dozens of brightly jacketed holiday reps, clipboards and pens at the ready. Ours was a diminutive Glaswegian called Debbie who didn't bat an eyelid when we gave her our names and she pointed us in the direction of the coach that would transfer us to the hotel.

'Who'd have thought it would be this easy to shave five or six years off your age?' said Andy once we were out of earshot. 'There'll be no stopping us now.'

It took a good half hour for everyone assigned to our coach to arrive. Once we had our full contingent of passengers, however, our driver seemed determined to make up for lost time at all cost and drove with a recklessness that showed scant regard for his own or anyone else's safety. Despite the threat of impending doom, a combination of the constant growl of the diesel engine, the darkness outside and simple exhaustion sent me to sleep and I only woke up on hearing the driver bark in heavily accented English: 'Apollo Apartments! Quick! Quick!' from the front of the coach.

The three of us hurriedly gathered our things together and

launched ourselves off the coach. Leaving its air-conditioned cool we were once again plunged into the Cretan heat and within seconds were dripping with sweat.

'Home sweet home,' said Tom looking up at the lilac building in front of us; it had two floors and an outdoor terrace café that faced on to the road.

I was just about to ask Tom whether it was obligatory for all hotels to have some sort of reference to Greek mythology in their name when a male voice with a strong Welsh accent came from behind me.

'I see you've brought the weather with you then?'

I turned round to see a short, crumpled-looking middle-aged man with an overly red face. He was wearing a wide-brimmed straw hat tied underneath his chin to keep it in place, a bright pink T-shirt and Union Jack shorts.

'What an idiot,' he said taking into consideration our natural English sense of reserve as we stared at him blankly. 'It's all right, guys, I'm not just some random nutter. I'm Steve the bar man . . . but you lads can just call me Mr Barman if you like.'

Out of politeness we laughed and then watched as he introduced himself to our fellow residents (a group of six lads in their late teens and a couple of girls in their twenties). Along with the other new arrivals we followed Steve-the-Barman into the hotel lobby. Inside there was a small unmanned reception desk and standing next to it a large bright orange board with our tour operator's logo at the top. A cavalcade of leaflets was pinned to it, advertising a host of parties, barbecues and bar crawls. While Steve-the-barman took the group of lads and the two girls to their rooms the three of us remained in the lobby with our luggage momentarily lost in our own thoughts.

'I'm knackered,' said Tom eventually. 'It's two o'clock Monday morning back home. Normally I'd be in bed next to my Anne right now.'

'I'd probably be alone in bed right now,' I replied, 'which bizarrely doesn't seem like such a bad prospect at all.'

Andy sighed. 'What's wrong with you two? You're like a couple of old women. We're on holiday. There's no work tomorrow. If you want to sleep late you can. If you want to get up early and just stare out of the window you can do that too. This is what being on holiday is all about – getting the chance to do what you want when you want.'

'But it's two o'clock in the—' Tom stopped as Steve-the-barman returned.

'Right then, lads,' he said cheerily. 'I'll give you the guided tour shall I?' We all nodded. 'That over there,' he said, pointing to the gigantic wide screen TV which was showing an old Robert Wagner film, 'is fifty inches of top-class satellite televisual entertainment. It's got the lot. All the films. All the music. All the channels . . . all the sport.'

We all looked at the TV. He was right. It was stupidly large. Ridiculously so. It was probably visible from space. But the picture seemed wrong. The colours seemed too bright and the picture had a soft sheen about it that was distracting.

'Which teams do you follow?' asked Steve.

'Arsenal,' said Tom. 'But I don't go to the matches.'

'Man City,' said Andy. 'Although I haven't been to a game in a few years.'

Steve looked at me expectantly. 'No one,' I replied feebly.

'I'm a Spurs man myself,' continued Steve quickly glossing over my lack of footballing allegiances. 'Although they haven't exactly had their best season have they?' He

laughed. 'Anyway, there'll be plenty of European friendlies on during the week so you won't miss any of the action.' He paused and for a moment looked like an overgrown cherub. 'I hope you don't mind me asking, boys, but what made you choose Malia for your holiday?'

Tom pointed to Andy. 'It was his idea.'

'I only ask because . . . well, because we don't tend to get many people your age here.'

'What do you mean?' replied Andy shiftily. 'I'm twenty-eight.'

Steve-the-barman chuckled heartily. 'If you say so, mate.'

'Give it up, Andy,' said Tom. 'He knows we're over thirty because we stick out like a sore thumb – a thumb that's been battered senseless by a sledgehammer. Didn't you notice on the coach on the way over here that there wasn't a single person on it under twenty-five? They might call it an eighteen-thirty holiday but no one goes on these things past the age of twenty-five.'

'It's true,' said Steve-the-barman. 'Compared to ninety-nine per cent of the lads and lasses in Malia you are ancient.'

'Even if we are a bit mature,' replied Andy, 'it makes no odds. Charlie here managed to pull some cracking bird at the airport without even trying.'

'Only because it probably wouldn't have occurred to her that people as old as us would dream of going on to somewhere like Malia,' said Tom.

'Do you remember when we used to go out on the pull when we were at university and we'd see packs of greasy old men eyeing up the girls we were with?' I said to Andy with a sigh. Andy nodded. 'Well, I've got a horrible feeling that we're the greasy old men now.'

'Enough of me yakking on at you, eh?' said Steve-the-

barman uncomfortably. 'I bet you want to get to your rooms and freshen up a bit.'

We all followed him back to the reception, through an open archway and up a flight of stairs. 'Here we go,' he said, unlocking the door to apartment six. 'This way.' We all stepped into what appeared to be the kitchen but then right in front of us was a small table so I concluded that it was a dining room too. Then just behind the table was a large uncomfortable-looking sofa-bed which was clearly for the third person in the party, making it also a bedroom. We exchanged worried glances. The main bedroom was much better. There were two single beds, a wardrobe and a dressing table and very little else but at least it was clean. The only worrying thing was the temperature in the room.

'How do people sleep in this?' I asked Steve-the-barman. 'It's like a furnace in here.'

'They don't,' he replied, 'not unless they pay the extra to have the air-conditioning turned on.'

'We'll pay,' I said, without consulting the others.

'A wise decision,' said Steve-the-barman, giving me a wink, 'I'll get you the key and the remote control for the unit in a minute.'

The rest of the apartment was equally uninspiring. There was a TV but it had only three channels; a very basic tiled bathroom with a shower which Steve warned didn't really give out any hot water until about three in the afternoon; and then finally he slid open the doors to the balcony.

'You've done well here, boys,' he said, 'you've got a sea view. Not that you can see it now of course.'

I looked at the skyline and at the very bottom where the dark blue appeared to meet the black I could just about make out the lights of a passing ship.

'He's right you know,' I replied. 'We have got a sea view.'
I looked down below. 'And a view of the hotel pool too.'

'Well, I'll leave you to it,' said Steve. 'The bar will be
open as late as you like tonight if you want a drink in a
bit.'

He's right and knows it replied, 'we have got a sea view.'
I looked down below. 'and a view of the hotel pool too.'
well, I heard you to it,' said Steve. 'the bar will be
open as late as you like tonight if you want a drink in a
...

## Yassou

We finally made it downstairs to the bar an hour and much arguing later. The problem was that no one wanted the sofa-bed and we couldn't agree a fair way of solving the problem. Tom suggested a rota but Andy hated that idea. I suggested drawing straws, but Tom said that the way his luck was running at the moment he would be bound to draw the short straw. Andy suggested that we arm wrestle for it but as I hadn't been near a gym for years I shot down that idea. In the end Tom announced that he would volunteer to take the sofa-bed if it meant that we could all stop arguing. Andy just laughed and muttered something about Christian charity in action. Relieved that we wouldn't have to sleep in the kitchen, Andy and I promised to compensate Tom by making sure that he didn't have to buy a single round of drinks for the rest of the holiday.

'What are you having?' I asked my friends. The bar was virtually empty apart from a group of lads in one corner and the girls that had arrived on our coach in another. Maybe people were put off drinking there by Steve-the-barman's dress sense, or the Billy Joel greatest hits album that was playing over the sound system.

'I'll have a pint,' said Andy.

'We're in Europe,' I replied. 'It's litres and half litres here.'

Andy sighed and sat on one of the tall stools in front of the bar. 'I'll have a litre, then.'

'Me too,' replied Tom.

'I knew you'd guys would be down,' said Steve cheerfully. 'Oh, and sorry about bringing up the age thing. Just to give you boys a proper welcome – and to show you that the Apollo Bar welcomes anyone no matter how prehistoric – I've got something special for you.'

Intrigued, we watched as Steve walked over to a large chest freezer and pulled out a plastic bottle filled with clear liquid. He carried it back over to the bar and then set three shot glasses up in front of us and began pouring.

'It's Ouzo isn't it?' asked Andy.

'Close,' replied Steve. 'Raki.'

He pushed the glasses over to our side of the bar, poured himself a glass too. 'Yassou,' he said, holding up his glass, and then on his cue we all knocked back our shots.

The small explosion at the back of my throat was instant. And as the flames licked their way down to my lungs, up to my nostrils and tickled the back of my eyeballs, it was all I could do not to cough and splutter like a schoolboy trying his first cigarette.

'You get used to it,' said Steve. 'You sort of have to because they serve it everywhere around here.'

Still chuckling, he began pouring our beers while Tom and Andy asked him questions about the best places to go in Malia.

Feeling removed from the conversation I announced to my friends that I was going for a leak and made my way to the lounge area where I promptly sat down on one of the large sofas near the pay-per-go pool table. The truth was I didn't need the toilet at all; I just needed to be on

my own for a while. As much as I was enjoying being with my friends, the prospect of spending all day every day with them over the coming week was already beginning to overwhelm me. Things had changed a lot since our college days when we'd lived in each other's pockets. I'd got older. More grumpy. Less likely to put up with other people's nonsense. Now I was thirty-five I'd completely lost the tolerance required for living with anyone other than the woman I loved. Unfortunately for me, somewhere during the decade we were together, the woman I loved had somehow lost the tolerance for living with me.

I reached into my pocket, pulled out my phone and re-read Sarah's text message, imprinting every word in my brain. Then, taking a deep breath, I pressed 'delete', and she was gone.

# DAY ONE:
# MONDAY

## Reptilian sensation

I woke up shivering. I peered through the dim bedroom at the flashing light on the front of the air-conditioning unit that indicated that it was on (thanks to Andy) its maximum setting. Grimacing, I looked over at Andy and watched as he snored oblivious of the arctic chill in the air. With a sigh I pulled on my T-shirt from the floor and then looked at my watch. It was just after ten o'clock.

As I slipped out of bed and continued getting dressed, I wondered how long Andy had been asleep. It wouldn't have surprised me if it had only been a couple of hours. As it was, the three of us had remained in the hotel bar talking with Steve-the-barman until nearly four in the morning. Once again Tom had been the first to bed, followed half an hour later by me. But I could tell from the look of determination on Andy's face as he labelled me a lightweight and finished off my beer that he was prepared to see in the daylight, because he had a point to prove: that when it came to excess he was a giant amongst dwarves. It was a message wasted on me: I already knew this and was more than content with my vertically challenged status.

Still, it felt wrong being the first one of us awake – almost unmanly. On the original holiday to Malia there had been an unspoken daily struggle between Andy and me to win

75

the coveted title of Last Man Up. Although I managed to beat him on a number of occasions, and once even clocked up a staggeringly tardy six-thirty in the evening, it was always Andy who was the more consistent winner. I was nothing more than his pace-maker. Now a decade on, here I was awake while Andy and *even* Tom were both still asleep. I felt like a genuine lightweight.

Other than the cold, the main reason I was awake was due in no small part to the vast array of things on my mind. Everything from my encounter with the girl-in-the-cowboy-hat to my alcohol consumption over the past few nights and right through to a genuine sense of excitement at being on holiday had managed to wake me up and get me thinking. But right at the top of the list, straight in at the number-one position, was Sarah and her text message.

What did she want? Should I reply? Did she know that I had gone on holiday? Did she know when I was getting back? Why hadn't she called me directly? And was it bad news? Or was it good news? Did she want me back? Did I want her back? Were things not going well with Oliver? Was it about money? Or bills? Or change of address cards? There were just too many questions and not enough answers. And although I knew all it would take to put my mind at rest would be to pick up the phone and dial her number I was also well aware that all it takes is a slight shift in perspective for the easiest things in the world to become the most difficult.

The one thing I wanted from this first day of my holiday was for it to be untainted by Sarah in any way, shape or form. Today was too special for that. Too hopeful.

Picking up my sunglasses from my bedside table I walked over to the patio doors, held back the curtains, opened

the latch and stepped out on to the balcony. Instantly I was transported from the middle of the harshest winter on record to the kind of record-breaking temperatures that result in people dropping dead from heat exhaustion. The sun seemed a million times brighter and more intense than anything I'd ever experienced. I'm pretty sure it was my imagination but for a few moments I could have sworn that I smelt the hairs on my arms singeing in the sun.

The balcony furniture consisted of two white plastic chairs, a small round table, a clothes airer, and a bucket into which dripped water from a pipe connected to the air-conditioning unit. I sat down on one of the chairs and carefully manoeuvred myself so that I could peer over the edge of the balcony and get a better view of the swimming pool below. Though the pool itself was empty, the loungers around the edge – there must have been at least forty of the things lined up together – were occupied either by a vast array of bikini-clad girls of all shapes and sizes or large beach towels with colourful logos.

Feeling too fragile to cast anything more than a cursory glance across the girls below I adjusted my chair to its lowest reclining position, leaned back, closed my eyes and instead basked in the almost reptilian sensation of my sun-starved body being brought to life. Within minutes the sensation of being baked had shifted from pleasant but tingly, to searing and uncomfortable, as though I might be seconds away from bursting into flame. But I didn't care. This was it. I was warm. I was free. I was on holiday.

## That's just it

I ended up spending the next few hours shifting between a range of activities that included getting a few chapters further into my book, staring aimlessly into the sky, and wondering what I could possibly wear that might make me appear cool for my 'date' with the girl-in-the-cowboy-hat. I would've continued like that for a few hours more, too, if a bleary-eyed Tom, wearing only a T-shirt and boxer shorts, hadn't put his head through the gap in the patio doors and informed me that he was hungry.

'What are we doing for breakfast, mate?' he asked. 'I'm starving.'

'I was waiting for you and Andy,' I replied.

Tom ducked his head back into the room. 'Andy's out like a light,' he said, reappearing. 'I'll die of hunger before he wakes up. What time did he make it to bed? Dawn?'

I shrugged. 'How about we give him another ten minutes and then go out and get something?'

'All right then,' said Tom joining me on the balcony. He sat down gingerly on the hot plastic chair next to me.

'How long have you been up?' he asked shielding his eyes from the sun.

'A few hours,' I replied. 'Couldn't sleep.'

'And you've been sitting out here all this time? It's like being grilled on a barbecue.'

*Wish You Were Here*

'It gets all right, after a while,' I assured him. 'And even if it does burn you, to a sun-hungry Brit like me there's nothing better than being toasted like this.'

Tom laughed and leaned back in his chair. 'So when was the last time you went on holiday?'

'Last August. Sarah and me went to Malta. It was nice. The hotel was fantastic.'

'Isn't Malta meant to be big with the grey brigade?' asked Tom. 'I know my grandparents have been going there every summer for the last ten years. They meet up with a whole bunch of friends that they made out there and spend all their time visiting places they've already been a million times before.'

'It is a bit like that,' I replied. 'When we first booked the holiday, the girl at the travel agent's tried to talk us out of it. She was really polite, but you could see in her eyes she just wanted to say: "Look, you'll hate it. It'll be full of British pensioners sucking humbugs." But it wasn't like that at all. It was really chilled out actually. Sarah and I loved it. We ate great food. Slept late everyday. And in the afternoons we just lay on the beach and read. We didn't go to a single nightclub, get drunk or stay up past midnight once. It was fantastic.'

'Sounds great,' said Tom. 'Before Anne and I had the kids we spent a month touring around Tuscany. The trip was worth it just for the food, let alone the scenery and the weather.'

'We were supposed to go to Tuscany this summer,' I said despondently. 'Some friends of Sarah's parents had a villa out there and they were going to let us have it on the cheap. It would've been great too.' I paused and allowed myself the necessary indulgence of a small sigh. 'I can't

79

tell you how different life is without her, Tom. It's like I've got all this time on my hands and no one to spend it on. When we lived together I always felt like I didn't have enough time to myself. If she ever went away for the weekend to see her parents I'd go mad trying to fit in all the things that I felt I was missing out on. I'd go to the cinema and watch stupid action films; I'd watch *South Park* box sets back to back; I'd eat takeaway food until it was coming out of my ears; I'd listen to music until the early hours. And then an hour before she was due back I'd steam around like a demon and tidy the whole place up. By the time she'd got back to the flat everything would be immaculate.'

'But that's good, surely?' said Tom. 'Now you can do all that stuff all the time.'

'That's just it,' I replied. 'Now I've got all the time in the world I don't want to do any of that stuff any more. Instead I just sit around hoping that Sarah's going to come back through the front door.'

Feeling suddenly self-conscious I opted to change the subject but before I could do so the patio door slid open and Andy appeared in the doorway, scowling at the sun and naked except for his boxer shorts.

'Now that is hot,' he said sliding a hand inside his boxers and scratching. 'How long have you two been up?'

'Half hour,' said Tom.

'A while,' I replied, in a bid to sound cool.

'Let's do breakfast,' said Andy firmly. 'I'm starving.'

'We were waiting on you,' said Tom. 'What time did you get to bed?'

'Half-five . . . maybe six . . . can't remember really.' He paused. 'I'm going to have a shower then.'

'Can't you do that after breakfast?' I asked.

'Nah,' he replied, 'after breakfast we should go straight to the beach.'

'So if you're going to the beach why would you bother having a shower?'

'You're joking aren't you? Now we're on holiday I can't take any chances. I mean, what if we bumped into the girl-in-the-cowboy-hat and her mates? No, from now on I'm on full-time duty, which means dressing to impress twenty-four-seven.'

## I'll have what they're having

There is no greater sartorial challenge for the British male than deciding what clothing is appropriate for a day at the beach. Living in a country where the sun rarely makes an appearance has had the effect of shaking our confidence so much that when it comes to removing layers of clothing in the public arena we have no idea what to do. Show us a hail storm in deepest Aberdeen and we'll be appropriately attired in a matter of minutes. Put us in the sunshine in Crete and we'll be flailing through our suitcases for hours on end. Andy, for instance, interpreted the theme of 'dressing for the beach' as 'dressing for a game of five-a-side in the park' (white Reeboks, dark blue Adidas football shorts and a white England T-shirt). Tom took it to mean 'wear what you might put on if you were about to play a round of golf followed swiftly by some fell walking on the Yorkshire moors' (a pastel blue polo shirt, beige khaki shorts and a pair of chunky 'all-terrain'-style sandals). And I interpreted it as 'dress as if you're a thirty-five-year-old male trying to hang on to the last vestiges of his youth' (a T-shirt with a doctored image of Bruce Lee riding on a skateboard, a pair of cut-off camouflage print shorts, and a pair of knock-off Birkenstock sandals). Looking at the reflection of the three of us and our differing interpretations of the theme, the one thing

I was sure our individual looks didn't say was: 'We are going to the beach.'

Collecting together our essentials for the day (books, magazines, suncream) we made our way downstairs. In the hotel lobby there were a few lads milling about wearing only gold jewellery, shorts and trainers. Judging from the peeling skin on their backs they appeared to be veterans of this summer's assault on Malia rather than new recruits like us. Before we left the hotel I thought it wise to ask the Greek girl on the reception desk for directions to the beach. She just laughed and said: 'Out of the door, take a right, and follow the road to the sea. You can't miss it.'

Stepping outside into the intensity of the sunshine I immediately lowered the sunglasses on my head on to the bridge of my nose and looked around. Last night when we'd arrived I hadn't paid a great deal of attention to our surroundings. In the full glare of daylight I took it all in. The Apollo appeared to be lodged on one of the main roads in the resort as every other frontage was a hotel, car-hire shop or takeaway food emporium. Scattered along the pavements were various groups of young Brits chatting to each other, sipping water or simply posing. Occasionally a delivery truck laden with bottled water or the odd hire car went by but the main source of noise pollution (other than the constant club DJ mix albums being pumped out of speakers located inside every shop) was from the roar of chunky-wheeled quad bikes being driven by lads like the ones at our hotel.

'From scooters to quad bikes,' said Tom as two guys riding pillion passed by flicking the 'v's to their friends. 'Do you remember the scooters we hired last time we were here?'

'I still bear the scars from when I skidded off mine racing you and Charlie,' laughed Tom.

'Maybe we should hire one of these each for a bit of a laugh?' said Andy, enviously eyeing up a quad bike parked up in front of our hotel.

The last thing I wanted to do was let Andy talk me into hiring a quad bike so that we could relive our youth. My days of taking part in pointlessly reckless activities were long behind me. Now I no longer had a live-in girlfriend to look after me should the need arise I needed to be careful.

As we headed along the road towards the beach with the general aim of finding somewhere reasonably nice and cheap to have breakfast we played holiday resort bingo. Clothes shops selling T-shirts bearing comedic gems like 'I'm with stupid'? Tick. 'Authentic' Greek restaurants advertising 'English-style roast dinners with all the trimmings'? Tick. Grocery stores selling copies of the *Sun*, the *Star* and the *Daily Mirror*? Tick. Bars with ridiculously traditional English pub names like 'The Royal Oak?' Tick and bingo! Every cliché, everywhere, and they were all repeated on a constant loop along every single inch of the road. It was like a reproduction Blackpool but with better weather. It was a simulated Skegness without the North Sea. It was Little England in the sunshine.

We ate breakfast at Stars and Bars, an American-themed bar and diner with a British slant. The whole of the outdoor terrace had been empty when we'd sat down but the bar's owners had compensated for this by attempting to import a 'happening' ambience into the bar via three large TV screens positioned above our heads, showing various MTV

channels. Their attempts were hampered by the fact that the sound had been turned down on all three screens.

Half distracted by the soundless MTV screen, we had barely glanced at the menus by the time our waiter arrived to take our order. Andy and I ordered lager (because it was cold and large) and then followed up with the 'Killer' English breakfast (bacon, eggs, sausages, tomatoes, mushrooms, hash browns, toast, tea and jam). Though Andy and I spoke to the waiter in English, for some reason Tom made the whole process more complicated by pulling out his *Rough Guide* book and earnestly murmuring a few sentences in Greek. At first we assumed that Tom's pronunciation was so awful that the waiter had failed to understand a single word he'd said but it turned out that Kevin wasn't Greek at all. He was actually from Bloxwich near Wolverhampton and was spending the summer in Crete helping out in his uncle's bar to earn some money before going to university. It was all Andy and I could do to stop ourselves from spluttering with laughter as Tom sighed and mumbled: 'I'll have what they're having.'

## Susie

Following on from our late breakfast we ventured to a grocery store to buy bottled water and a couple of day-old English tabloid newspapers and continued on our journey towards the beach. At various junctures along the way, one of us would point out a landmark that we recalled from our last visit. Tom indicated Kato's, a small nightclub that Andy had once got thrown out of for falling asleep on the dance floor, which had now changed its name to Eden. Andy pointed out the once open ground where we had played mini-golf every afternoon, now a new block of holiday apartments. And finally I spotted Ming House, the all-you-can-eat Cantonese restaurant that was now Luigi's, a takeaway pizzeria.

'They've even renamed the beach,' said Andy as we finally reached our destination.

I glanced up at the official-looking sign above Andy's head. 'Laguna Beach – this way'. 'What was it called before?' I asked trying to recall its name.

Andy shrugged.

'I think it was just called "the beach",' said Tom. 'That's how sophisticated things were back then.'

Laguna Beach was exactly what I expected of the Malia I had encountered so far. It was less a beach in the traditional sense of the word and more an alfresco nightclub. Two huge speakers were carefully positioned at the top of the

beach to ensure maximum exposure of the kind of club tunes that I spent my whole life trying to avoid.

Resignedly we began making our way across the beach in search of a patch of sand without a sun-lounger parked on it. Ten feet on to the sand, however, we were intercepted by a tall bare-chested bronzed guy wearing black wraparound sunglasses, cut-off shorts and a bum bag.

'Five Euros each,' he said in heavily accented English.

'We've got to pay?' said Tom incredulously.

'For that you get a pass, a sun-bed and umbrella.'

'No thanks, mate,' I replied. The idea of paying to lie on a beach just seemed wrong on all kind of levels.

'Come, come,' he said confidently. 'I will show you someone who will explain.'

I looked at Andy and he shrugged and then Tom looked at me and he shrugged too and because we were English and didn't like to offend people if we could help it, we followed him across the sand to three empty sun-loungers. The man waved across the sand to a pretty blonde in a bikini top and cut-off denim shorts who came running across with all the urgency of a lifeguard in action. When she reached us the bronzed guy gave me a cheeky wink and then disappeared, leaving the girl to introduce herself.

'Hi,' she said. 'I'm Susie.'

'Nice to meet you, Susie,' said Andy shaking her hand. 'Is that a Newcastle accent I detect there?'

Susie nodded. 'I've just graduated so I thought I'd come out here for the summer. I'm here during the day and then in the evening I work at Eden.' She paused and smiled. 'So how long are you guys here for?'

'A week,' said Andy. He winked at Susie. 'But it could be longer if you play your cards right.'

Even I could see that Susie was merely chatting us up in order to soften the blow when she asked us for money for our so-called beach card but Andy was lost in a fantasy world where he imagined that this girl really fancied him. I was reasonably sure that his flirtatious manner was more out of habit than actual intention. But thankfully before he could get round to proving me wrong she got to the point.

For the princely sum of five Euros each we would receive a card that would entitle us to three sun-beds and umbrellas for a week, ten per cent off any meal at Spetzi's Chicken Grill and a free cocktail (choice determined by the barman) at the Cool Breeze beach bar. We all signed up without the slightest hint of struggle. It was pathetic really. The fact that this very attractive girl was even talking to us seemed to render our cognitive faculties redundant.

Susie thanked us for our money, assured us that she would see us later and then shimmied back across the beach to where the tall bronzed Greek guy was standing with some other tall bronzed Greek guys. Suitably emasculated we arranged ourselves on the sun-loungers (left to right: Andy, me, Tom) and took in the view.

There were literally hundred of girls on loungers. Girls of every shape, size, race, colour and, presumably, denomination. Some were tanned to perfection. Others lobster pink. It was as if a women-only container ship had run aground and carefully thrown up its precious cargo on the beach right in front of us.

'You can't even see the sea,' complained Tom as he pulled out his *Rough Guide* book from his rucksack and began reading.

He was right too. You couldn't see the actual sea at all

from where we were because there were too many bodies around us. But there was a sea in front of us – a sea of flesh, long legs, tantalising upper thighs, tattooed backs, toned midriffs, lower buttocks peeking out through g-string bikini bottoms, side breast and (yes) even the occasional full breast with nipple. And though technically it should have been a glorious sight to behold I couldn't help but feel intimidated. It was as if every single one of the young women who surrounded us was fully aware of the power and allure of the feminine form. And uncharacteristically I longed to see these women clothed, if only because it would have provided a moment's respite from the feeling that I was never going to stand a chance with any of them.

The three of us had been keeping ourselves to ourselves, quietly reading on the beach for over an hour when suddenly a group of yobs barely old enough to buy alcohol legally in England began play-fighting in front of us in a bid to impress a group of girls sitting across from us.

'This is like a school field trip from hell,' said Tom slamming down his *Rough Guide*.

'I know what you mean,' I replied peering at them over the top of my sunglasses as one of the yobs dropped his shorts and mooned his friends. 'I keep looking at them and thinking: "Where's your responsible adult? Who's actually in charge of you lot? Surely at some point someone's going to round them all up and take them back to whichever borstal or secure unit they've escaped from."'

'But it's not just these yobs that are winding me up,' replied Tom, warming to his theme, 'have you seen that lot over there?' Tom discreetly gestured to a group of guys, roughly in their twenties, who were all defined upper body

muscles, tattoos and perfect tans. They were flirting with a group of girls who, with their perfect hair, bodies and flawless skin, appeared to be their female counterparts.

'That bloke there has got a washboard stomach,' I said squinting in the group's direction. 'I don't think I've ever seen an actual six-pack that wasn't on the cover of some sort of fitness mag.'

'But do you know what's worse?' added Tom. 'Look around us and what do you notice that makes us the odd ones out here?'

I did as Tom instructed but as far as I could tell there were so many things that made us the odd ones out that it was difficult to choose just one. 'Is it the fact that we're the only blokes on the beach who look like off-duty geography teachers?'

'Nearly,' replied Tom. 'It's actually that we're the only people here wearing T-shirts.'

I looked all around. Tom was right. Most of the girls were in bikinis and every guy was topless. 'Do you think we should de-robe so we blend in a bit?'

'You can if you like,' replied Tom. 'But I'm keeping my T-shirt firmly on. I thought I wasn't in bad shape until I saw this lot. But this bunch of body fascists will probably call the police on us.' Tom paused and adopted a high-pitched Monty Pythonesque voice: 'Hello, is that the police? I'd like to report three lumpy thirty-five-year-old men on the beach lying around making the place look untidy.'

Tom and I laughed and then fell into an uneasy silence.

'But it's easy to look like that when you're twenty-one,' I said after a while. 'You don't have to exercise, you can just eat what you want and burn it all off arsing about all day.' I paused as a different bunch of guys ran past, pursued

by a group of giggling girls. 'Do you know what? I'm half tempted to whip off my top and yell: "Enjoy yourself while you can because this will be you in ten years time!"'

'So why don't you?' asked Andy, his first contribution to conversation.

'It wouldn't make any difference if I did. They're already enjoying themselves as much as they can. Anyway, one way or another they'll learn that the party's got to end sometime.'

Andy had just returned from a trip to the grocery shop near the top of the beach to get various essentials like water, crisps and sandwiches when he paused and said in reverent tones: 'Now *that* is a work of art.'

Tom and I sat up and followed his line of vision as a blonde minus the top half of her bikini strode past our loungers towards the outdoor shower.

'She might be a work of art,' I replied as the girl stood underneath the shower and turned it on, 'but she knows it.'

'Doesn't matter,' said Andy unashamedly standing up to get a better view. 'If I was a girl and I had a body like that I'd spend most of my life walking around completely naked. I mean it – *all the time*. I'd be there prancing around stopping traffic, watching guys crash their cars and blokes on motorcycles smash into lampposts. I'd cause mayhem.' Andy laughed and finally sat down. 'The world is so lucky that I wasn't born a woman.'

As Andy returned to his newspaper and Tom returned to his *Rough Guide*, I settled back in my lounger and momentarily found myself thinking about Sarah. On our last holiday I found myself staring at her while she was

engrossed in some book that she'd bought at the airport. And I remember thinking to myself that she was mine. This beautiful woman lying next to me was mine and nobody else's. And unlike the girls around us playing frisbee in the sea or the girls sunning themselves on the loungers or even the girl my friends and I had just watched take a shower, Sarah didn't know how beautiful she was. I liked to believe she didn't think stuff like that mattered. And in my eyes at least that made her even more beautiful. As that thought began to fade, I deliberately tried to stop thinking about Sarah because I wasn't sure how much I could take. And so I closed my eyes and enjoyed the calming sensation of the heat of the sun on my eyelids. And though my head was still full of thoughts, my heart remained as broken and as empty as ever.

The rest of the day slipped away without a fight. We lay on our loungers, stared at the sea and watched the girls go by. And now that we had experienced our first full day in the sun I felt as if I could relax. I could easily imagine how our daily routine might go and because of that I was sure that for the 'daytime' section of our holiday there wouldn't be too many surprises to encounter ahead. The 'night time' section however would be a completely different beast altogether. And I was well aware that, like Dr Jekyll and Mr Hyde, daytime Andy and night-time Andy were two different creatures altogether.

Leaving the beach towards the close of the afternoon we headed back to the apartment and came up with a plan for the evening: 'free time' until nine o'clock, then a drink in the hotel bar, followed by a meal out at the nearest half-decent restaurant. Then the main event: the bars and

clubs of Malia until the early hours. Tom called his wife and kids and then took himself off for a walk; Andy meanwhile went to bed and promptly fell asleep; and I returned to the balcony to continue with *Touching The Void*. A short while before we were due to leave I came in and had my first (vaguely warm) shower of the day and got ready to go out. By ten minutes past nine all three of us were standing in the kitchen (aka Tom's bedroom) in our best glad rags (me: T-shirt and jeans; Tom: button-down polo shirt and chinos; Andy: T-shirt and cut-off camouflage trousers).

It had felt good having some time to spend getting ready for our big night out. As if the effort I'd put into making myself look half-decent would somehow pay off in admiring glances. Ultimately, however, the focus of my efforts for the evening was the girl-in-the-cowboy-hat. In spite of some initial reservations I was beginning to believe that something might actually happen between us. So much so that I began to imagine her name on what I hoped would be a long list of women whom I'd always refer to as 'The ones that came *after* Sarah'.

## Hiya, boys

It was now just after eleven and Andy, Tom and I were in a taverna near the beach called Taki's Place, having just consumed our first authentic Greek meal of the holiday: chicken souvlaki in pitta bread with chips and tatziki followed by a litre of Carlsberg. As we waited for the bill to arrive we watched as a continuous stream of shirtless revellers screeched by on their quad bikes yelling to each other at the top of their lungs whilst attempting to run over anything that attempted to get in their way. It was like watching a junior facsimile of a hell's angels rally.

Leaving Taki's we began our expedition towards what Steve-the-barman had referred to as 'the main strip' – the dozens of cafés, bars, clubs and takeaway restaurants that made up the heart of Malia nightlife. It was like on the streets around Wembley on Cup Final day: with each step we were joined by legions of merrymakers whose destination was the same as our own. Young guys and young girls, all ready to party like it was a Saturday night back home. We passed smaller bars and restaurants that tried to tantalise us with offers of cheap beer, football matches on TV and pirate films that hadn't even been released at the cinema yet but not a single one could match the allure of our objective. As we reached the crossroads at the heart of the resort we were finally able to see our promised land in all its

neon glory and hear it in all its stereophonic disco splendour.

Crossing the road to the main strip was like journeying across a checkpoint between two different countries: in one there was law and order and in the other anarchy reigned supreme. Even before we'd reached the other side of the road we saw a girl throwing up on the pavement while her friends held her hair out of the way; two paramedics attending to a shirtless guy propped up against the window of a fried chicken takeaway; and a gang of guys with their trousers around their ankles mooning a group of giggling girls.

'I've got a horrible feeling that tonight is going to be pretty grim.' Tom shook his head in despair as we stepped over a patch of sick on the pavement.

'You are so wrong, my church-tastic friend,' countered Andy. 'I've got a feeling tonight is going to be a night to—' he stopped suddenly as an attractive dark-haired girl caught his eye with a killer smile and reeled him in right in front of us.

'Hiya, boys,' she said standing directly in our path. The accent was English and northern. 'I'm Tasha. Where are you guys from?'

'I'm Andy,' said Andy. 'And I'm from Hove.'

'I'm Tom,' said Tom uncomfortably. 'And I'm, er . . . from Coventry.'

'I'm Charlie,' I added nervously, wondering if all this personal information would be used against us. 'And I'm from Brighton.'

'I've been to Hove,' she said ignoring Tom and me and focusing her attention on Andy. 'I've got an auntie down there. I'm from Chorley in Lancashire. Do you know it?'

'Yeah,' replied Andy. 'I've got family there too.'

'That's brilliant.' Without any hesitation she reached out and held his hand. Unable to believe my eyes I looked to Tom to reassure me that this whole exchange was as weird to me as it was to him. He flashed me a puzzled look by way of return that said: 'Surely it can't actually be this easy to go on the pull in Malia?'

'How long are you here for?' asked the girl, still holding Andy's hand.

'A week or so,' said Andy coolly. 'Maybe longer if you're lucky.'

I couldn't believe it. Andy was recycling the lines that he had used on Susie from Newcastle right in front of us.

'So is this your first night out?' asked Tasha.

'We arrived late last night,' said Andy. 'I would've gone out last night but these guys weren't up to it.'

'Well at least you're here now,' said Tasha confidently. 'And as this is your first night out then you lads should kick things off tonight in style . . . at the Eclipse, where we've got a two-drinks-for-the-price-of-one promotion going on all night.' Without pausing for a reaction, Tasha started dragging Andy in the direction of a dark, empty neon-clad cavernous bar. I could see the dilemma writ large on Andy's face. On the one hand he was flirting with one of the most attractive girls we'd seen so far but on the other she was only talking to him in order to drag him and his hard-earned money into an empty bar. Though he was clearly offended that she was so openly exploiting her sexuality (and his own), at the same time it was quite clear that there was part of him that just didn't care.

Andy looked at Tom and me forlornly as though he couldn't bring himself to walk away without our assistance.

'I think we're going to have to give your bar a miss tonight, Tasha,' I said, wrestling Andy's hand away from her. 'We're going to Pandemonium. Maybe another time, eh?'

'He's right,' said Andy in a voice that registered genuine disappointment. 'Maybe another time, eh?'

It was as though Tasha had just flipped a switch. In the blink of an eye she went from sex kitten to ice queen. The flirting stopped. The smile turned to a grimace. And Andy's face free-fell into disappointment. If we hadn't forced him to start walking away I'm sure he would've rushed back to Tasha and begged her forgiveness. In fact, even when we were well out of her reach he couldn't help turning around to watch as Tasha waylaid a group of lads coming the other way using the exact same technique that she had so skilfully employed on him only moments earlier.

The situation was so tantalisingly ripe for Tom and me to use as ammunition against Andy that we didn't have the heart – it would've been too easy. Instead, taking into consideration the fragility of his ego, we made the decision to move briskly on without further comment. This was difficult, because in the space of the next three bars we were stopped by two bikini-top-wearing girls from south London offering us free introductory vodka shots on behalf of Bar Go-Go, virtually manhandled into Galaxy bar by three Scottish girls in pink sparkly hats who offered three drinks for the price of one, and nearly lured into Club $H_2O$ by a gorgeous girl from Birmingham with huge false eyelashes and an offer of a free fruit cocktail.

'It's quite insulting really,' said Tom as we extricated ourselves from the grip of the girl-with-the-false-eyelashes. 'These girls think just because they have great bodies and

are drop-dead gorgeous that they can get us to do anything they like.'

'Well they can,' said Andy. 'The only reason I'm not standing in that first bar drinking the second of my two-for-the-price-of-one beers is because of you guys. Alone, I'd have folded like a pack of—' Andy stopped and pointed across to the other side of the road. We were here. We'd finally reached our destination: Pandemonium. Yet another neon-lit bar that, while not exactly empty, wasn't all that full either. But that didn't matter. What mattered was that I was convinced that it would be here where my luck would finally begin to change. Here I would rid myself of the spectre of my ex-girlfriend. Here I would meet the girl-in-the-cowboy-hat.

'Are you ready, Charlie?' asked Andy.

I looked at my watch. It was five minutes to midnight. 'I'm as ready as I'll ever be,' I replied and then, taking a deep breath, I looked both ways and crossed the road to meet my date with destiny.

## Budweiser, okay?

Even from my short experience of the strip so far I knew that most bars in Malia relied heavily on loud pounding club music to provide ambience. The difference with Pandemonium was that the music was turned up just that little bit louder, as though the extra volume might make it stand out from the crowd. It was only when we reached the bar and were pointed by a barman in the direction of some banquette seating that we discovered that Pandemonium had one further trick up its sleeve: waitresses in bunny-girl outfits.

'Now this is what I call a holiday,' bellowed Andy as a waitress resplendent in pink fluffy ears, hot pants, fishnet stockings and heels passed by our table carrying a tray of tequila shots. 'What do you think to that, church boy?' Tom didn't reply. 'The girls in the bunny outfits,' said Andy this time nudging Tom with his elbow. 'Fit or what?'

'Hmm,' said Tom in a noncommittal fashion. He turned his head slightly and gave the waitress a cursory once-over, shook his head and then looked away as if to ponder some higher vision. It was only when Andy and I followed his line of sight that we realised that the higher vision Tom was pondering was the highlights of the England test match playing on a miniature TV screen above the bar.

'I like sport as much as the next man, but how can you

99

be watching cricket when there are women like this . . .' said Andy indicating yet another waitress slinking by our table, 'less than three feet in front of you?'

'Leaving aside that I'm happily married with two kids,' said Tom, '. . . fact is we're doing really well.'

One of the bunny waitresses approached our table. 'All right, lads?' she asked in a pronounced Liverpool accent as she leaned in towards us in an effort to be heard over the music. 'What can I get you boys tonight?'

'Anything you like, darling,' leered Andy.

'Three beers will do,' I replied quickly, giving her an excuse to ignore Andy.

'Budweiser do you?' she asked smiling in my direction.

'Yeah,' I replied giving her the thumbs-up. 'That'll do nicely.'

She turned and headed in the direction of the bar to deliver her order.

'Why don't girls at home look like that?' wondered Andy as he turned his head to get a better view of the waitress's legs.

'Because all the girls at home who do look like that are here,' I replied. 'I'm guessing they come for a holiday and stay because they can't stand the thought of going back to another grey summer in England.'

'But do you think it's in the rules that you have to be a babe in order to be allowed to stay? Pretty much every girl who has spoken to us since we got here has been amazing.'

'Don't know,' I shrugged, 'but I don't suppose it can hurt can it?'

We both fell silent as we spotted our waitress wending her way through the now-crowded bar with an almost balletic grace.

'There you go, lads.' She set the bottles down on the table along with a bill. Andy snatched it up immediately and then, presumably possessed by the spirit of Hugh Hefner, handed her a large Euro note and told her to keep the change.

'What?' protested Andy once she was out of earshot.

'What do you mean, what?' I replied.

'So I gave that girl a tip, big deal!'

'No, Andy, you gave that girl a gigantic tip because she was wearing a bunny outfit. You've been like a dog on heat since we landed last night.'

Andy rolled his eyes in despair. 'For once in your life, Charlie, why don't you have a go at being a bloke? It's actually quite a bit of fun when you know how.'

'What's that supposed to mean?'

'It means stop being such a self-righteous eunuch and grow a pair, because you're beginning to drag me down,' replied Andy.

'I'm dragging you down?' I repeated. 'I thought this holiday was supposed to be for my benefit?'

'It is,' replied Andy, 'but as the saying goes "You can lead a horse to water . . . "' He paused and looked around the room. 'I'm just saying instead of moaning about being thirsty all the time why don't you get yourself a drink?'

'And *I* will do,' I replied, willing the girl-in-the-cowboy-hat to choose this moment to walk into the bar, 'but don't forget *you've* got a girlfriend.'

Andy nearly choked on his beer. 'Are you bringing Lisa into this?'

I wished I'd kept my mouth shut. I wished Lisa hadn't asked me to keep an eye on Andy. And I sort of wished this night was over because it was already becoming too much of a strain.

'Forget it,' I replied, realising I hadn't got either the energy or the inclination to argue. 'I shouldn't have said that. And I'm absolutely in the wrong.'

'Too right you are.' Andy looked genuinely infuriated. 'I'm here to have a good time so just leave Lisa out of—' Andy stopped as two things happened simultaneously: first, the guy behind the bar turned the music down so low that for a few moments we could actually hear the conversational hubbub in the bar, and second, a huge commotion erupted near the entrance.

'What's going on?' asked Tom as the bar was suddenly deluged by a huge influx of revellers dressed in swimming goggles, snorkels and cheap-looking white T-shirts.

'Finally,' said Andy, rubbing his hands with glee, 'the entertainment.'

'What's he talking about?' asked Tom.

'Check out the T-shirts,' I replied, pointing to a couple of guys standing by the bar.

'The Club Fun Big Night Out,' said Tom reading the slogan. 'You're telling me that after all this time the mother of all bar crawls is still going?'

'Makes you feel sort of proud doesn't it?' said Andy. 'And they say young people have no sense of tradition.'

The Club Fun Big Night Out organisers ended up commandeering the rear half of the bar near where we were sitting. A young guy wearing a blue version of the white T-shirt appeared to be leading the proceedings and after a short while he turned on the microphone. Tapping it several times to make sure it was working he then jumped on to a raised platform to the left of us and bellowed in a broad Yorkshire accent: 'Welcome to the Legendary Club Fun Big Night Out! Are! You! Ready! To paaaaaaaarrrrrrrrtttttttttyyyyyyyy!'

The crowd gave a half-hearted cheer, which wasn't good enough for the holiday rep. He put the microphone back up to his lips: 'That's rubbish!' he chided. 'You need to make more noise. Now on the count of three . . . one . . . two . . . three! Welcome to Club Fun! Are! You! Ready! To paaaaaaaarrrrrrrrrrrttttttttttttyyyyyyyyy!' The crowd cheered back but the rep still wasn't satisfied. 'One more time!' he boomed into the microphone. 'Come on! Give it all you've got. Club Fun Big Night Out! Are! You! Ready! To paaaaaaaarrrrrrrrrrttttttttttttyyyyyyyyy!'

Clearly motivated by the need to have this idiot stop shouting at them, the crowd yelled, screamed and whooped at the top of their voices like game-show contestants.

'That's more like it! Now let's get things started with one of my favourite party games and I'm sure it's one of yours . . . you know what it is . . . the ice-cube game!'

My jaw dropped.

'How brilliant is that?' said Andy, laughing uncontrollably. 'Mate, we should get up and join them for old times' sake.'

'No way,' I replied. 'And neither should—' I stopped as I realised that the back pocket of my jeans was vibrating. I reached for my phone and looked at the screen. It was a phone number I didn't recognise.

'Who is it?' asked Andy.

I shrugged, wondering if Sarah had perhaps bought a new phone. 'It's too loud in here,' I said to Andy, 'I'm going to answer it outside.'

'See you in a bit,' he replied.

Tom was sipping his beer, still engrossed in the cricket and I whispered in his ear: 'Keep on eye on Andy for me and make sure he doesn't get into any trouble, okay?'

'Yeah,' replied Tom, his gaze fixed to the TV screen.

'Will do.' I moved away but then returned: 'Oh . . . and keep an eye out for the girl-in-the-cowboy-hat and her mates.'

'I'll keep an eye out for everybody,' said Tom, wincing as one of the England team was bowled out. 'Go and answer your call, and trust me, everything will be just the same by the time you come back.'

## That's the problem

The strip was now so busy it resembled Trafalgar Square on New Year's Eve. There were gangs of lads singing football chants, groups of girls singing along to Kylie Minogue, young guys in cars blasting out music from their in-car CD players and, watching over the entire proceedings, a small collection of stone-faced police officers. In a bid to get away from the noise I ducked down a side street next to Pandemonium and answered the call.

'Hello?' I began.

'Charlie,' said a female voice. 'It's me, Lisa.'

It took a few moments for her voice to register. 'Lisa?' I replied eventually. 'What's going on? How are you? Is everything all right?'

'I'm fine, honestly,' said Lisa.

'You had me worried there for a second,' I replied, 'I thought something must have happened.'

'I'm sorry.' She sounded genuinely apologetic. 'I knew I shouldn't have called you like this. It was a bad idea. I'll let you get back to doing whatever it was you were doing.'

'No, no, no,' I replied. 'It's fine. I don't mind you calling at all.' I paused. 'I take it this is about Andy?'

'Am I that obvious?'

'Transparent.'

'This is so pathetic.'

105

'No it's not,' I replied. 'You're worried and you're looking for a bit of reassurance. It's better you call me up and find out what's going on than sit at home driving yourself mental.'

'So how has he been?' she asked. 'I hoped he might call me tonight but I've not had so much as a text message to let me know you guys got there okay.'

'Well, let me bring you up to speed,' I replied. 'The flight was all right, the accommodation is okay, the weather is glorious and most of today we spent hanging out on the beach.'

'And that's all?'

'Yeah,' I replied. 'That's—' A group of lads passing by at the end of the street let off an air horn, cutting me off mid-flow.

'So where are you now?' asked Lisa. 'You sound like you're at a football match.'

'I think a football match would be less crowded than this. I'm outside a bar called Pandemonium. When I left to take your call Andy was staring into space and Tom was watching the cricket.'

Lisa laughed. 'So you're telling me I've got nothing to worry about?'

'Yes,' I replied, 'I'm telling you you've got absolutely nothing to worry about.'

'And you'd tell me if there was something to tell, wouldn't you?'

'I promise you, Lisa, other than tales of excessive drinking, I doubt that there will be anything to report back to you. And you don't want to hear about that do you?'

'No,' replied Lisa. Her voice was lighter now and less anxious. 'I'm really sorry, Charlie. You've been a sweetheart. You really have.'

'Look,' I replied, 'it's no problem at all.'

'Thanks, Charlie. I'm going to let you go, but just promise me this one thing, will you? Promise me you won't tell Andy I called.'

'Of course,' I replied.

There was a long silence.

'Okay,' said Lisa finally. Her voice was shaky. She sounded small and lonely. 'Well, have a good night then.'

'We will,' I replied. 'And you can call me as much as you want to. You know that.'

We said our goodbyes and then I ended the call and made my way back to the main street. For a few moments I stood on the pavement, jostled by passersby in both directions, thinking about Lisa. I couldn't get over how much she loved Andy. She loved him so much that she couldn't even bear to think about losing him and despite his many faults her love remained. And I thought to myself that that is what love must be – resilience in the face of opposition; knowing when you should give in and refusing to do so. Andy didn't know what he had in Lisa. He didn't know that she had what it took to make love work. He'd taken her for granted and would always do so because, unlike me, he'd never had a Sarah in his life to show him just how tough life could be.

Still mulling the call over I returned to Pandemonium and worked my way across the crowded bar area to the seats where I'd left my friends. A few feet away from my destination I realised that half of them were missing.

'Where's Andy?'

Tom dragged his eyes from the cricket and looked at me. 'He said something about going to the—' he stopped abruptly and instinctively I followed his line of vision across

Mike Gayle

the room to the other side of the bar. Andy was frantically kissing a tall, dark-haired girl who was wearing a Club Fun Big Night Out T-shirt while holding a glass full of ice cubes.

'This isn't going to be a relaxing holiday at all, is it?' sighed Tom.

'No,' I replied despondently. 'I'm guessing this is going to be as stressful as they come.'

# DAY TWO:
# TUESDAY

# DAY TWO: TUESDAY

## Let's hope it doesn't last long, eh?

Déjà vu. That was the feeling I woke up with on the morning of my second day in Crete – the sense that I had pretty much already seen this day begin before. I looked at my watch. It was just after ten o'clock. I sat up in bed and the sheet covering me slipped off my shoulders exposing my skin to the arctic chill of the room. I glared at the air-conditioning unit gurgling happily on the wall as it continued on its mission to turn the bedroom into a glacial wasteland. Sighing, I pulled up my sheet and relaxed into my pillow, listening to the various sounds coming from outside: music from the bar down below, people laughing and shouting next to the pool, the occasional splash of someone jumping into the water. Everything was just like the day before . . . with one glaring exception: Andy wasn't here. His bed was empty and he was nowhere to be seen – a clear indicator, should I have needed one, that the events of the night before had been no passing nightmare. They were very real indeed.

Last night. What. A. Total. Disaster. Tom and I had watched slack-jawed as Andy had kissed, fondled and generally manhandled the tall girl with the dark hair for a good five minutes before we finally managed to tear our eyes away from the car crash that had occurred right in front of us.

111

I really couldn't believe that he had so unambiguously crossed the line. I knew that Andy liked to flirt with members of the opposite sex like most people liked to breathe, but I'd always assumed that when it came to The Line – between being technically faithful and technically unfaithful – he had enough sense to remain on the side that would bring least trouble. And yet there he'd been standing right in our line of vision, kissing a girl I'd never seen before only moments after I'd assured his teary live-in girlfriend that he would be faithful to her for the entire holiday.

Neither Tom nor I had any idea what we should do. It wasn't as if we could have dragged him forcibly from her clutches – although that was actually the first suggestion I'd come up with. So after taking time out to assess the situation over a stiff drink, we came to the conclusion that the only thing we could do was let him get on with it in the hope that he would come to his senses and return to the fold. After some time it became clear that Andy and the girl weren't going to come up for air any time soon. Just as we'd reassessed the situation and made the decision to issue Andy in his absence with a toothless NATO-style sanction ('If he doesn't stop snogging that girl in, say . . . the next hour or so I think we should register our protest by going back to the hotel') Andy and the girl stopped kissing.

'Finally,' I said, relieved, 'his conscience is kicking in.'

'He hasn't got one,' said Tom. 'I suspect he had it surgically removed years ago to make room for his ego.'

Tom was right. As the girl disappeared in the direction of the ladies' toilet Andy didn't look the slightest bit repentant. In fact he looked incredibly pleased with himself, as though he deserved a round of applause. Returning to

our table, he picked up his beer and downed the remains of his Budweiser in one go.

'Now that hit the spot,' he said, setting down the bottle firmly on the table in front of me.

'Are we supposed to be impressed?'

Andy sighed wearily. 'I knew you'd make a big deal out of this. It's nothing, Charlie, okay? Just a bit of fun. There's no need to be concerned.'

'Come on, mate,' I replied. 'You don't have to do this. You've made your point. She was gorgeous and you're the king of pulling birds. Let's just leave now and call it a night before you get yourself in any more trouble.'

'Leave now?' said Andy. 'You must be joking. There's no way I'm going anywhere tonight without her. Have you seen her, Charlie? She's amazing.'

'You're right. She is amazing. And I can't believe that you're making me remind you but here goes: you've got a girlfriend.'

'Will you try and be a bloke just for one second?' snapped Andy. 'This is the kind of thing I'd expect from church boy Tom, not you. Come on, mate, we're blokes. This is what blokes do. Especially when they're on holiday.'

I looked over to see if Tom had any words of wisdom that might back me up.

'You want me to say something to stop Andy going off with this girl?' said Tom, reading my face. 'Maybe something about his girlfriend, and how he's risking losing her for a meaningless fling?' Tom shook his head. 'No, I'm afraid I won't be doing that.' He gave Andy a wink. 'Do whatever you want, mate. Just leave us out of it, okay?'

For a brief moment I was sure that I saw a faint flicker of doubt spread across Andy's face. And it might have

113

taken hold had that not been the exact moment that Andy's kissing companion chose to stride across the bar and join our table.

'Are these your friends?' asked the girl, slipping her fingers between Andy's.

'Nina, this is Charlie and Tom,' said Andy neutrally. He then gestured to Nina. 'Charlie and Tom, this is Nina.'

Tom didn't take his eyes off the cricket during the whole exchange and as I felt bad on behalf of everyone involved I ended up issuing an overly enthusiastic hello.

'Hi,' I said, shaking her hand. 'It's really good to meet you.'

'It's nice to meet you too,' replied Nina.

Even in an ill-fitting Club Fun T-shirt there was no disguising how attractive Nina was. 'How long are you here for?' I asked.

'A week,' she replied. 'I'm here with my sister and some friends. You guys are only here for a week too aren't you?'

I nodded. 'Having a good time so far?'

'Great. It's just nice to take a break isn't it?'

'Yeah, it is,' I replied. 'Where are you from?'

'London. East Finchley to be exact. Are you from Brighton too?'

I nodded. 'Although I'm originally from Derby.' I paused and asked the six-million-dollar question. 'When do you go back home?'

'Wednesday,' she replied, even though I'd been willing her to go first thing in the morning so at least I could be sure of this nightmare not dragging on too long. 'And I'm back at work on the day after. It'll be murder.'

'Right then,' interrupted Andy, clearly bored with me and my small talk. 'I'll see you guys later.'

'It was nice to meet you,' said Nina, giving Tom and me a little wave which Tom dutifully ignored. 'Maybe I'll see you again.'

'Yeah,' I replied. 'That would be nice.'

Hand in hand Andy and Nina crossed the bar, pausing only to kiss at the exit before disappearing from view. Once they had gone I looked at my watch and realised that, thanks to Andy's antics, I'd been too distracted to realise that yet more bad news had managed to come my way without my even noticing it. The girl-in-the-cowboy-hat was nowhere to be seen. I'd been stood up.

'We can wait a bit longer if you want,' said Tom, reading my mind.

'No.' I finished off my drink in preparation to leave. 'Let's just go before this night gets any worse.'

We were about to move when I looked up to see a young woman approaching our table. She was wearing a tight black sleeveless top, dark blue jeans and heels. Three things immediately struck me: first, there was something oddly familiar about her; second, unlike everyone else in the club she didn't appear to be in her early twenties. Late twenties, yes. Early thirties possibly. Early twenties, definitely not. Third: she was very pretty.

'Excuse me,' she said, 'I know this is going to sound a bit weird but your friend who left a little while ago, is he an all-right-sort of guy?'

'Yeah,' I replied as I exchanged baffled glances with Tom. 'Why do you ask?'

'He's with my sister and, well, she sometimes doesn't have the best judgement in the world, if you know what I mean.'

'Believe me,' said Tom. 'We know what you mean.'

'So?' said the girl looking at Tom. 'Your friend?'

Tom licked his lips as though already relishing the sweet savour of his answer. 'Andy,' he began, 'is an—'

'Okay sort of bloke,' I interrupted.

The girl raised her eyebrows. 'Well, put it this way,' she said, 'is he the "okay sort of bloke" you wouldn't mind being with your sister?'

I had to laugh at the thought of my sister Jeanette (minus her husband and her two kids) together with Andy. 'I think I'd mind pretty much anyone being with my sister,' I replied. 'But yeah, Andy really is an okay sort of bloke.'

'Thanks,' said the girl. 'Well I'd better get off then. It was nice to meet you.'

'Yeah,' I said. 'Nice to meet you too.'

116

## Thanks again for last night

As I lay in bed still shivering from the cold, having just reviewed the previous night's escapades, I found myself thinking about the girl from the club whose sister had gone off with Andy. There had been something about her that had immediately marked her out in my head as different, and it hadn't just been an age thing (although that did help), or that she had been attractive (although that helped, too). What had marked her out from the other girls in the club was that she looked as though she had a story to tell. Things had happened in her life. Things that had left their mark. I couldn't tell what that story might be. Whether it was happy or sad. But what I did know was this: I hoped that somehow I would get to hear it this holiday.

An electronic beep from my mobile signalled the arrival of a text message and broke my chain of thought. My pulse quickened. It had been a while since I'd spent any time contemplating Sarah's 'Call me' text message and I couldn't help but wonder if this were a reminder. I scrabbled around on the floor with my hands and eventually found my phone wedged in the back pocket of my jeans. I looked hopefully at the screen but was disappointed to discover that it was a text message from Lisa:

**Message Lisa:** Charlie, sorry about last night. Do you forgive me? Hope it didn't spoil your evening. Thanks for being such a treasure. Have a great rest of holiday. L x PS. Did you pull?

I sat up in bed and read it several times – just to make sure that I was fully aware of every single guilt-inducing nuance of the message – and then sent a reply in return.

**Message Charlie:** Hi, don't worry about a thing. Night out was pretty poor anyway. Your phone call was highlight. C x

I pressed send and then climbed out of bed and got my things together for a shower. On my return to the bedroom, naked and dripping water over the floor, I noticed that my phone was beeping again to let me know I had another message:

**Message Lisa:** Why pretty poor? L x

Feeling uncomfortable about her question I sat down on my bed and keyed in a response:

**Message Charlie:** Everyone here is decade younger than us. Feel like a mature student at university/school teacher. Delete as inapplicable. C x

I pressed send and then put on a clean pair of shorts and a T-shirt. Grabbing my book and sunglasses I decided to sit on the balcony and read until either Andy came back to the apartment or Tom woke up. As I slid back the patio doors I remembered that I'd left my phone lying on the bedside table and went back to get it. As I

picked it up, it beeped in my hand once again.

**Message Lisa:** Don't you know that older men can be quite a novelty to youngsters?

And again:

**Message Lisa:** Don't put your back out though! L x

I was glad that she seemed to be in such a good mood. And I have to admit I was also glad to be the one helping her not to worry, even though I hadn't exactly kept Andy out of harm's way.

**Message Charlie:** Never mind mocking the afflicted, young lady. Why aren't you busy working for a living instead of hassling me? C x

I pressed send and waited expectantly for a reply. When one didn't come I decided that she had probably had enough and so I picked up *Touching The Void*. I'd scarcely got more than a few pages further into the book when I received another message:

**Message Lisa:** I don't leave for work until 8.30 a.m.! We're two hours behind you lot.

And another:

**Message Lisa:** But I promise am going to stop bothering you now. Okay??? So have a good day and stay out of the midday sun. L xxx

119

And another:

**Message Lisa:** PS What are your plans for this evening?

I had no idea what my plans would be for the evening but I guessed that if Andy were still with Nina then there would be every chance that he would spend the evening with her. And as Nina had friends who (at least in Andy's eyes) would need entertaining, Andy would more than likely try to get Tom and me to come along. As I was in no mood to help Andy out like that, it was therefore looking highly likely that the evening ahead would consist of me and Tom moaning about Andy's behaviour over a quiet pint somewhere.

**Message Charlie:** No plans as yet. Will probably go somewhere quiet that doesn't require the use of ear trumpet to hear conversation as I fear it puts girls off! C x

I didn't even get a chance to pick up my book again as a reply came back in less than a minute.

**Message Lisa:** Have to go to work now. Thanks again for last night. And remember that you WILL meet someone nice soon. L x

For some reason the last line of her text message made me feel incredibly sad. Not for me, but for her. There she was, trying to cheer me up, oblivious of the mess Andy was making of their relationship. I think I ended up rereading it three or four times but just as I was about to put the phone away I received one last message from her:

**Message Lisa:** P.S. Can you remind Andy to reapply his sun cream too. He always forgets. L x

As I reached the end of the message I decided that enough was enough. I went through them all one last time and deleted them, because my overactive imagination had created a horrific scenario consisting of Andy picking up my phone by accident, seeing the messages and jumping to the wrong conclusion. That done, I switched off my phone, put my feet up on the railing in front of me, picked up my book and, for a short while at least, escaped into the pages of the true-life snow-covered-mountain adventure.

121

## My 'cup-of-tea' face

Midday came and went with no sign of Andy. The thought of calling him on his mobile had briefly crossed my mind but I had rejected the idea on the basis that (a) I wasn't his mother and (b) the last thing I needed was him pointing this out to me. By this time Tom was up, showered and dressed but had yet to show any interest in Andy's whereabouts. Instead he lobbied constantly for us to go for breakfast despite the fact that one of our number was missing. By this point it was difficult for me to tell which one of my friends was annoying me the most: Andy, because he was being Andy, or Tom because he was annoyed at Andy for being Andy. I'd always felt that part of Andy's charm was his essential Andyness and to be anything more than moderately exasperated at him for being who he was seemed to be missing the point entirely.

'Come on, Charlie,' said Tom impatiently, 'he's probably still with that girl from last night having breakfast at her hotel while we're sitting here starving. If he really wants to find out where we are all he needs to do is call your mobile.'

'Okay,' I finally relented. 'You're right. Let's go.'

Without further protest I packed a small rucksack with a towel, my book and a bottle of water. Tom and I left the apartment and made our way to the downstairs lobby. We

would have gone straight out but there were at least two dozen people crowded around as though a meeting was about to begin or had just ended. When Tom asked a girl standing near the pool table what was going on, she told him it was a welcome meeting organised by a Club Fun tour rep.

'Look at this,' said Tom, calling me over to take a closer look at a series of forms on the reception desk. 'They're doing day trips and organised events. All you have to do is sign your name and you can pay on the day. Leaving aside the stuff like boat parties, barbecues and bar crawls, some of this stuff looks okay.'

I wasn't convinced. 'Like what?'

'Well for starters there's a trip to Agios Nikolas.'

'Which is?'

'A town I read about in the *Rough Guide*. It's got a lake that locals claim is bottomless.'

Tom looked at me expectantly. I pulled a face that clearly said: 'Not really my cup of tea.'

'Okay, how about this one?' continued Tom, reading off the list. 'A visit to the palace of Knossos.'

'You want to go to a palace?'

'It's more ruins than anything,' explained Tom. 'It was supposed to have been home to the Minotaur.'

'That's the bull-thing isn't it?'

Tom nodded. 'Half-man and half-bull and liked to devour young virgins.'

'That'll be Andy then.'

'So what do you say? Fancy it?'

My 'cup-of-tea' face made an unwelcome return. 'Is there nothing . . . ?' I searched for the right word. 'You know . . . a bit groovier?'

'You want groovy? Okay, tomorrow they're organising a sixteen-kilometre trek through the Samaria Gorge, which is apparently one of the longest gorges in Europe. It'll be great.'

My 'cup-of-tea' face made an immediate reappearance.

'It'll be good exercise,' countered Tom.

'It might be,' I replied. 'But isn't sixteen kilometres quite far? I didn't really pack with hiking in mind.'

'Neither did I,' said Tom. 'I've done hiking in my trainers before now, you'll be fine. It says here that a coach would pick us up outside about eight and we'd be back sometime around five.'

Tom looked at me expectantly but my 'cup-of-tea' face was still firmly fixed in place.

'You don't want to go do you?' asked Tom.

'Not really,' I replied.

There was a long pause.

'Fine,' said Tom eventually, 'I'll go on my own.'

Suddenly I felt bad. Tom didn't ask much from me (in fact a lot less than Andy) and it seemed like a million different types of wrong to turn him down, but the truth was, hiking along a gorge in the heat of the Cretan sun seemed like madness to me.

'Look, I'll come,' I replied, making the decision to try to be a better friend to Tom. 'You can put my name down at the top.'

Tom picked a pen up off the desk and hovered over the form, but then he put it down with a resigned sigh. 'It's nice of you to offer,' he began, 'but to be truthful if you're not into it, it'll just bring me down. I'll be fine. I'll go on my own.'

'Are you sure?'

'Yeah,' he replied. 'I'm sure.'

As Tom scribbled down his name at the top of the list I looked through the lobby towards the pool where a group of girls was screaming and laughing as they took it in turns to be thrown into the pool by a couple of lads. Every last one of them looked as though they would no sooner spend the day walking along a gorge in thirty-six-degree sunshine than they would spend the day reading *War and Peace*.

'What about Andy?'

'What about him?'

'Maybe he'll want to go with you.'

Tom laughed. 'Do you know what, I'll put his name down on the off-chance that between now and then he completely loses his mind.'

## King of the road

Leaving the Apollo, Tom and I made our way along the same route to the same diner that we'd eaten at the previous day, where we were served by the same waiter. We then ordered the same breakfast and beer combo and ended up watching MTV again with the sound off. And at the end of the meal we even left the same amount of money as a tip as we had done the day before. As we stood up to leave, I found myself thinking that we'd been in Malia only one full day and yet we were already in danger of finding ourselves stuck in a rut.

'What are you thinking?' asked Tom as we lingered at the entrance to Stars and Bars, roasting in the afternoon sun. 'Back to the beach?'

'We could do,' I replied, conscious of the fact that we had done just that yesterday. 'What do you reckon?'

'I'm easy either way,' said Tom, 'although if I'm honest I quite fancy doing something a bit different.'

'Different,' I echoed determinedly. 'You're right. We do need to do something different. Any ideas?'

Tom thought for a moment. 'I've got it,' he said eventually, 'let's rent a couple of those quad bike things and visit somewhere else for the day.'

'That, my friend . . .' I began as a gang of youths passed by yelling and shouting to each other, '. . . sounds like a great idea.'

Renting the quad bikes was the best thing we could've done to get us out of our post-Andy funk. Riding along with our throttles wide open and the wind in our faces we were young again and we were free. We cruised along the coastal road out of Malia and headed for Stalis, the next resort along. Every now and again, as we sped along, we would pass girls on lower-powered quad bikes than our own and as we'd overtake them I'd feel, if only for a moment, as though I really was king of the road.

As Tom and I sat down on the beach that we didn't have to pay for and got out our books, it occurred to me that if Malia was a metaphor for youthful excess then Stalis was its older, wiser sibling who had long since given up late nights and all-day drinking for the delights of good food and family life. The contrast couldn't have been greater. Slightly less Anglo-orientated than Malia (on our walk through the town centre we passed a Dutch-owned bar, saw German translations on several menus and passed a couple arguing in French), Stalis itself was populated solely by couples and families. The only people we saw under twenty-five were kids on holiday with their parents or other quad-biking migrants from Malia.

Although neither of us said it aloud, I could see that Tom was thinking the same as me: 'This is where we should've come on holiday.' Not that the attraction of Malia to the eighteen-to-thirty crowd was lost on me but the fact was neither Tom, Andy nor I *was* between the ages of eighteen and thirty any more and as we hadn't been for a long time, there was no point in pretending anything else. Stalis was a resort built for grown-ups. People who had left their twenties well behind and moved

on. But as I sat there on the beach devoid of loudspeakers and club music and surveyed the couples and families that surrounded us, it hit me that I actually didn't belong here either. Tom, with his family, yes. Possibly even Andy with Lisa. But me without Sarah? There was no place in this holiday world for a thirty-five-year-old single man. There was no resort designed for those recently dumped but disinclined to party until dawn. There was no middle ground at all because people like me simply weren't a big enough demographic to cater for. Market forces had dictated that we were invisible – we didn't exist. We weren't young and we weren't settled. And because we weren't at the beginning of our stories or in the happily-ever-after end zone, we'd been simply edited out all-together.

'So what's your take on last night?' I asked Tom in a bid to derail this particularly depressing train of thought.

'I think Andy's an idiot,' replied Tom putting down his book. 'I haven't got much more to add than that.'

'I suppose,' I replied. I thought for a moment. 'How old do you reckon that girl Nina was?'

'Twenty-three or twenty-four,' suggested Tom. 'I can't really tell how old anyone is these days.'

There was a long silence. Taking this to be the end of the conversation Tom returned his attention to the *Rough Guide* but I was far from finished with the topic of Andy and his infidelity.

'Lisa asked me to keep an eye on him you know,' I said looking out to sea. 'When she dropped him off at mine on Saturday night. She said she'd sort of guessed what he wanted to get out of the holiday and asked me to try and stop him. And ironically, the reason I didn't manage to do

what she wanted was because at the crucial moment I was on the phone with her.'

'Lisa called you?'

I nodded. 'She wanted to know how things were going. And what's worse is that I told her everything was going to be okay. She even sent me a couple of text messages this morning too.'

'You didn't tell her anything about last night did you?'

'Of course not but I feel bad about making out like everything's okay when it obviously isn't. I know Andy is my friend but . . .'

'But what?'

'But part of me feels like she deserves to know.'

Tom nodded. 'I know what you mean, but if you want my advice I'd say don't get involved.'

'I know but—'

'She won't thank you, Charlie. And I doubt that Andy would either. Just stay clear. These things usually have a way of coming out without anyone's help.'

'I know you're right,' I replied. 'But it just feels wrong. No one likes being the last one to find out do they? No one ever likes to be the last one in on the joke.'

Tom and I ended up staying in Stalis for the rest of the afternoon. He carried on reading his *Rough Guide* while I dozed in the sun, flicked my way through a day-old copy of the *Daily Mail* and went for a number of contemplative footwear-free walks along the shoreline. At around five o'clock the beach began to empty so we took that as our signal to return to the madness of Malia. As we handed the quad bikes back in at the hire shop I couldn't help but feel slightly disappointed that we hadn't managed to cultivate a single envy-inducing anecdote during the day

that might provoke Andy to jealousy. All we'd done was hire quad bikes, travel the short distance to Stalis and then sit on a beach that had a lower ratio of beautiful girls to middle-aged German men than the one we had left behind. Andy meanwhile had probably spent all morning and all afternoon feasting on a rotating diet of drinking, sex and post-coital napping. Of course he'd be gutted.

## It was just an observation

As I opened the front door to the apartment, I half
expected to see Andy and his new lady friend entangled
in convoluted sexual congress on the kitchen table
because that would've been Andy all over – an exhib-
itionist in need of a shockable audience – but there was
nothing on the kitchen table save a half-empty bottle of
water and two plastic carrier bags from the local mini-
market.

'You'd think he'd call us just to let us know he's not
dead,' I snapped as we walked through the kitchen into
the bedroom.

'Not Andy,' replied Tom, choosing to stretch out on our
absent companion's bed. 'He's far too self-involved to
worry about what we think.'

I sat down on my own bed and looked over at Tom. 'Do
you think we should call him?'

'And let him think we've got nothing better to do than
sit around and wait for him to turn up?' asked Tom. 'You
can do what you like but leave my name off the petition.'

Tom was right. Calling Andy would be a bad move
which would only serve to further inflate his ego. At the
same time, I had to admit that I was beginning to miss
having Andy about. This was the conundrum faced by
everyone who invited Andy into their lives: he was twice

as entertaining as he was annoying but it was impossible to separate one part of the equation from the other.

'Okay,' I replied, 'you're right, I shouldn't phone him. It's a bad idea. But the thing is I feel like I ought to at least try and do something, because I've got this horrible feeling the longer this thing carries on, the worse the consequences are going to be.'

'I'm not so sure myself,' said Tom. 'My guess is Andy will carry on seeing Nina until she goes home and then he'll hang out with us for the rest of the holiday. Come Sunday night he'll fly home and carry on as though nothing happened. And what's more, he'll get away with it. Because Andy always gets away with everything.'

'Maybe you're right,' I sighed. 'I don't even know why I'm that bothered what he gets up to. I mean, why do I care?'

I'd meant the question rhetorically. I didn't really want to know why I cared at all. But then I looked at Tom as I said it and there was something about his face that changed just for an instant, that made me curious.

'What?' I asked.

'Nothing.'

'*What?*'

'Look,' said Tom, 'you didn't mean it as a proper question so it doesn't matter.'

'No,' I replied. 'Come on. Let's hear what you've got to say.'

'Fine. I think you care because you sort of wish it was you that had pulled last night and you're sick and tired of always being envious of Andy.'

'That's rubbish,' I replied. 'I'm not envious of Andy.'

'Fine,' said Tom. 'It was just an observation.'

'But I'm not.'

*Wish You Were Here*

'I said, fine.'

'But you don't believe me.'

'It doesn't matter what I believe, does it? All that matters is what's true.'

'And you think it's true that I'm envious of Andy?'

'Why else would you still be hanging out with him after all these years when most of the time all he does is rub you up the wrong way? He does the things you wish you could do.'

'You've never liked Andy though have you?' I countered. 'It's been the same ever since college.'

Tom shook his head. 'You're wrong actually. It's not him I don't like. He's an idiot and nothing much is ever going to change that.'

'So who is it you don't like then?'

'You . . .' said Tom fixing me with a disappointed stare '. . . when you've been round him too long. That's always been your main problem. You lose sight of who you are too easily and let Andy lead you around like a lost sheep.' He sighed and then climbed off the bed as I looked on speechless. This wasn't like Tom at all. Yes, he was sometimes confrontational with Andy but he'd never been like that with me before.

'What's wrong?' I asked. 'Why are you being like this? This obviously isn't about me or Andy, so what's it about?'

'Nothing,' sighed Tom. 'I was well out of order.' He paused and laughed. 'You'd think someone had died and made me minister of home truths the way I've just carried on. It's not like I couldn't be told a few myself.' He shrugged and looked at me. 'Are we all right?'

'Yeah of course,' I replied. 'But don't you want to talk about whatever it is that's bothering you?'

'No,' said Tom. 'I'm fine. I'm probably just tired or something.'

There was a long silence.

'So what now?' I asked eventually.

'I thought I'd have a shower, call Anne and the kids and then have a sleep,' said Tom. 'Assuming his lordship is otherwise engaged tonight what do you want to do later?'

I shrugged. 'I don't care, really. Just not the strip if we can help it.'

'Well, this might not be your thing,' began Tom. 'But I was reading in the *Rough Guide* this afternoon about a little village not too far away from here called Mohos.' Tom reached down to the floor, pulled the book out of his bag and flicked through it until he got to a page where he had turned down the corner. 'We could get a taxi there, have a bit of a wander round, a drink and something to eat. What do you think?'

'Sounds okay,' I replied. 'Be ready to leave about eight?'

'Sounds good to me,' said Tom. 'So what are you going to do until then?'

I looked around the room for inspiration and spotted some through the patio doors. 'Finish the day the way I started it,' I replied pointing to the balcony, 'making the most of the sun.'

## Look after my man

As Tom began getting ready for his shower I finally got off my bed and plucked *Touching The Void* from my bag. I was getting tired of all the tension between the two friends on their snow-covered precipice. I wanted something a bit lighter . . . a bit less full-on and so I opened my suitcase, pulled out *The Da Vinci Code* (the second of my three holiday reads), went out on to the patio and closed the door behind me.

Sitting down in my favourite patio chair with my feet up against the railing, I began reading the first paragraph of my book. A few sentences in, Tom turned on the shower and so distracted me that I stopped reading. I tried again a few moments later but then a group of girls talking loudly passed by underneath the balcony and I stopped again. When I eventually picked the book up some five minutes later, my heart was no longer in it. I was bored but I didn't want to read. I wanted to be entertained without actually leaving the comfort of my balcony seat. And then the answer came to me. I pulled out my mobile phone from my pocket, typed out a text message and pressed send.

**Message Charlie:** Hi, just thought you'd like to know I'm lying on a beach, drinking fluorescent cocktails served by topless hula ladies. How about you? C x

A minute later I got the following reply:

**Message Lisa:** I'm at work. My back aches, I have a headache and it's raining. Keep holiday chirpiness to yourself! L x

To which I replied:

**Message Charlie:** I'm actually sitting on the balcony of our apartment watching (in strictly non-pervy way) a bunch of nineteen-year-old girls have a water fight. C x

To which she replied:

**Message Lisa:** What have you guys been up to today? Did you remind Andy about the suncream? L x

To which I replied:

**Message Charlie:** Hung out on beach all day. And yes, I did remind Andy about suncream. C x

To which she replied:

**Message Lisa:** What are you up to tonight? L x

To which I replied:

**Message Charlie:** Haven't decided. What about you? C x

To which she replied:

**Message Lisa:** Staying in wishing I was sunning myself in Crete too. L x

To which I replied:

**Message Charlie:** You should guilt-trip Andy into taking you away.
C x

To which she replied:

**Message Lisa:** Can't. He has no conscience. L x

To which I replied:

**Message Charlie:** I'll get him one for Christmas! C xxx

To which she replied:

**Message Lisa:** I'd better go. Have a great rest of holiday. PS.
Look after my man. L x

The time that elapsed between the first text message and
the last was just under an hour and during all that time I
didn't return to *The Da Vinci Code* even once.

137

## It's not *Match of the Day*

The sound of keys rattling in the front door signalled Andy's return to the apartment. I looked across at Tom. Though neither of us spoke, I knew that we both wanted to achieve the same thing: to look as sufficiently uninterested in Andy, Nina (should he have brought her along), and his where-abouts for the last twenty-four hours as was humanly possible. Tom opted to frown at his book as though mulling over a particularly well-structured paragraph, while I chose to un-mute the TV and stare at it, looking vaguely bemused.

'You can call off the search party,' said Andy striding into the bedroom. 'I'm back.'

Tom (who I have to say excelled in his attempts at projecting general uninterest) finished the sentence he was reading before looking up at Andy. I preferred to stare blankly as though I only vaguely recognised him.

'Okay, I get it,' said Andy bullishly, 'you're both wound up at me for being away so long.'

'Yeah, that's it in a nutshell,' replied Tom. 'We've been lost without you.'

Ignoring Tom, Andy deliberately focused his attempts at ingratiation on me. 'Come on, Charlie,' he nearly but not quite pleaded. 'You can understand can't you, mate? I mean you've seen her right? She's amazing.'

Without replying I got up, walked over to the chest of

drawers, put my sunglasses back inside their case and began sorting out my suitcase.

Realising I was ignoring him, Andy sighed in my direction as though he was really disappointed in me. 'How long are you two going to be like this?' he asked.

'Like what?' I replied.

'Like you're my dad,' he said. 'Do you know what? Nina didn't want me to leave her and come here.'

'So why did you?' I asked.

'Because I hadn't seen you guys all day.'

Tom laughed. 'And are we supposed to feel flattered?'

'You're not supposed to feel anything,' replied Andy. 'Look, I—' He stopped suddenly, rolled his eyes in frustration and tried a different approach to the problem. 'Hey, Charlie,' he began. 'Did that girl you were supposed to meet last night ever turn up?' he asked. 'You know, the one in the cowboy hat?'

'No,' I replied.

'Bad luck, mate.'

'It was no big loss.'

'Still, you shouldn't give up yet. How about this? Why don't you come out with me tonight and meet Nina's mates? We're going to Flares. Do you remember it from last time? It's that seventies bar we used to go to sometimes where they played that *Match of the Day* theme tune and then everyone would do that dance – do you remember?'

'It's not *Match of the Day*,' corrected Tom. 'It's *Ski Sunday*.'

'Same difference.'

'No,' replied Tom. 'I think you'll find that one is dedicated to the sport of football and the other skiing.'

I wanted to laugh but I could see that Andy was running

out of patience. 'Come on, guys,' he said adding a hint of joviality to his plea, 'both of you come out tonight. I guarantee you we'll have a laugh. Nina's mates are good fun.'

'What about her sister?' I asked, hoping that Andy wouldn't make a big deal about it. 'Tom and I met her last night after you left Pandemonium: shortish, dark-hair, nice-looking, dry sense of humour. More our sort of age than most girls in Malia.'

'That sounds like Donna all right.' Andy grinned. 'You don't fancy her do you?'

'Of course not,' I lied, making a mental note of her name. 'She just seemed nice, that's all.'

'I haven't had much to do with her,' said Andy. 'But since I'm currently in with her sister I'm sure a word from me could put you in good stead.'

'No thanks,' I replied. 'I'm good.'

'You're nowhere near good,' said Andy, 'Look, mate, unlike some people . . .' he paused and looked pointedly at Tom, '. . . I haven't forgotten what this holiday is all about – it's about you moving on. And the best way of doing that would be for you to come out with me tonight. Forget Sarah. Forget the girl-in-the-cowboy-hat. And forget Nina's sister too. Because I've spent all day telling Nina's mates about how wonderful "my mate, Charlie" is. Mate, I guarantee they're practically gagging for you. I've built you up so much they already think you're the greatest thing since sliced bread. All of which means at least one of them has got to be a dead cert.'

'A "dead cert"?' I repeated disdainfully at the thought of Andy's selling me to Nina's friends as though I was a sack of potatoes past their sell-by date.

'Yeah,' replied Andy stubbornly refusing to pick up on my sarcasm. 'A "dead cert".'

'Well, much as I'd like to be the beneficiary of your charitable efforts to get me sex,' I replied, 'I'm going to have to say no this time.'

'Why?' asked Andy.

'Because Tom and I have already got plans.'

Andy looked confused. 'What plans?'

At this point it would have been perfect if the plans Tom and I had in mind had been the type that involved excessive drinking, lap-dancing clubs and the possibility of rubbing shoulders with a female celebrity or two.

'We're going to a village up in the hills that Tom's *Rough Guide* recommends,' I explained feebly. 'It's got a church . . . and some shops . . . and a taverna. You can come if you want.'

'Let me get this right,' said Andy his eyes straining with incredulity. 'You're turning down a night out with hot girls for a trip to a village with a Christian?'

'Well, if you'd given us a bit more notice . . . like this morning . . . or even this afternoon we might have been able to come,' I replied. 'But the fact is we've made plans, mate. It's just the way it is.'

'Fine,' snapped Andy, 'you stick to your village people plans and I'll stick to mine.'

There was a long uncomfortable silence while we all sort of stared at each other.

'Anyway,' I began softly in a bid to appease Andy. 'I'd be rubbish company for girls tonight anyway. I'd just end up cramping your style.' I paused and, a diversionary tactic I'd cultivated over the many years I'd known Andy, I decided to flatter his ego. 'Nina's a bit spectacular,' I

said raising my eyebrows suggestively. 'Tell us about her.'

'Like what?' said Andy, making a token effort to resist my flattery.

'Like what does she do?'

'She works in TV.'

'Doing what?'

'She's a production secretary.'

'How old is she?'

'Twenty-five.'

'When's her birthday?'

'November the—' Andy stopped suddenly and began laughing. 'All right, Mansell, you've had your fun. Let's move on with the questions.'

'Hang on,' said Tom, 'I've got one I'd like to ask.'

'Go on then,' said Andy.

'I know I said I wasn't going to get involved but I'm curious to find out how long you're going to carry this on?'

Andy turned to face Tom but neither man spoke for several moments.

'I'm not in the mood for this, Tom,' said Andy coolly. 'So for your benefit and the benefit of Charlie I'll say it once: this is just a holiday thing. It's not going to last forever so there's no need to tell anyone anything. I know you two think that you're somehow morally superior to me but this is something I've got to do, okay? And none of it is any of your business—' Andy stopped abruptly and pulled out his mobile from his back pocket. 'It's Lisa,' he said looking at the screen. 'I'll be back in a minute.'

Tom and I exchanged wary glances as Andy left the room to take the call on the balcony.

'I think we're being too hard on him,' I whispered to

Tom as Andy slid back the patio doors. 'After all, none of this is our business.'

'Look,' said Tom, 'if you want to go to the club with Andy then you should go. But whether you come or not my plans for this evening involve going to Mohos.'

'I'm still coming to the village,' I replied. 'Nothing has changed there. All I'm saying is I think this night out Andy has planned is his way of saying sorry for being away all day. I think he really wants us to come out tonight.'

'Maybe he does,' said Tom. 'But do you know what, Charlie? I don't think I could put up with his nonsense tonight even if I wanted to.' Tom smiled mischievously. 'But you should go, mate, if you really want to.'

'What are you smiling about?' I asked.

'You, and your big speech about Andy wanting us to go with him. You just want to see Nina's sister again, don't you?'

'Yeah right,' I replied. 'I only met her for about five seconds.'

'There's no need to be defensive, mate. She seemed really nice. I can see why you'd be into her.'

'And why would that be?'

'She's just your type.'

'And my type would be?'

'Oh come on,' protested Tom. 'You've always had a type. Even back in college. They were always pretty but not too pretty. Usually dark haired. Good dress sense. Look like they might be able to hold their own in a conversation about the meaning of life until the early hours . . . you know the sort of thing.'

'Okay, okay,' I grinned. 'You're right. I have got a type and Nina's sister did pretty much fit the bill. But I'm not

going out with Andy tonight and that's final. Tonight it's just you, me and a village—' I stopped as Andy opened the patio doors and returned to the room, yawning.

'Everything okay with Lisa?' I asked.

'Yeah, fine,' replied Andy. 'She was just ringing for a chat. I kept it short though. Told her we were going out in a minute.'

'So what did you tell her?'

'I said we'd spent the day hanging out by the hotel pool and then—'

'You said what?' I spluttered.

Andy looked confused at my concern. 'I told her we'd spent all afternoon by the hotel pool,' he repeated. 'Which it so happens is actually what me and Nina did when we weren't—'

'But why did you tell her we'd been by the pool?' I asked nervously.

'Why shouldn't I have?' replied Andy. 'It's not like she's going to know any different is—' Andy stopped abruptly and looked at me. 'What aren't you telling me?'

It was a good question. There were a million things that I wasn't telling him. But at this moment everything would be a lot easier if I kept it down to just the things he needed to know.

'Lisa sent me a text message this afternoon.'

Andy looked confused. 'Why's she sending you text messages?'

'It was something to do with Sarah,' I lied. 'But you're sort of missing the point. In my reply to her message I told her that we'd spent the day at the beach.'

'So?'

'Well you've just told her we spent the whole day by the pool.'

'So I mixed up swimming pool and beaches, so what?' said Andy. 'I do that kind of thing all the time. Honestly, Charlie, you nearly gave me a heart attack acting like that.'

'But aren't you even a little bit worried that she knows what's going on?'

'Not at all,' said Andy sighing with relief. 'I guarantee you, my friend, that she does not suspect a thing.'

## Useful phrases

Andy had long since gone back to Nina's when Tom and I finally left the apartment just after nine. As we waited for a taxi by the roadside I noted that as usual the streets of Malia were buzzing with young Brits on their way up to the strip. As they passed by I found myself scanning them in what I considered a detached academic manner, as though I were a TV documentary maker scouting locations for a reality TV series called 'Malia Uncovered'. This pseudo-anthropological stance was, of course, simply a cover for me to stare at attractive girls in short skirts in the hope that one of them might be the girl-in-the-cowboy-hat.

I'd been wondering on and off all day why she hadn't turned up when it had been she who had made the initial contact. My more cynical side presumed that it was all part of some elaborate joke but my more optimistic side was willing her to have been run over. I guessed that the truth would be somewhere in the middle.

A white Mercedes with a taxi sign on the roof came by after a ten-minute wait and we jumped in the rear seats and asked the driver – a grim-faced local in his late fifties – to take us to Mohos. He did a sort of comedy double-take. As he pulled away from the pavement he checked several times that Mohos was definitely our destination and even tried to put us off making the journey. 'No

nightlife in Mohos,' he said brusquely. Once we'd reassured him that we weren't expecting dancing girls and wild parties from a village in the hills he just shrugged and turned on his car radio.

Because there were so many revellers on the streets we had to drive through the strip at a snail's pace on our way to the motorway. I wondered briefly whether the taxi driver had taken this route deliberately as if tempting us to stay where we belonged. If so, the implied message of our detour was: 'This is what you'll be missing out on tonight: tall girls, short girls, fat girls, thin girls, girls with dark hair, girls with light hair, girls with short skirts, girls with long skirts . . . in fact every kind of girl you can think of.' And I'll admit for a moment there I was tempted to yell out, 'Stop the car. You've made your point and it's a good one.' I didn't, of course, even though I was well aware a night out in the hills would inevitably mean one fewer opportunity for me to meet someone. Sighing inwardly, I kept my mouth shut until we'd left the deafening music and neon haze of Malia long behind and replaced it with the comforting xenon glare of motorway streetlights and the gentle purr of Goodyear radial on bone-dry tarmac.

Slowly negotiating a long narrow residential street, the taxi finally emerged into a small village square. Though I tended not to have much of an opinion on matters aesthetic when it came to village squares, even I appreciated that this one was indeed pretty. Everything about it from the trees glinting with decorative fairy lights to the quaint old church was picture postcard perfect. In fact, had the girl-in-the-cowboy-hat and I ever made it to a second date, this would've been the perfect place to take her.

As Tom dug around in his pockets for money to pay our taxi driver, he attempted to engage him in some Greek banter culled from the 'useful phrases' section of his *Rough Guide*. To say that the taxi driver wasn't interested would be something of an understatement. In fact he seemed to be bordering on the outskirts of outrage, as though the very act of Tom attempting to speak Greek was somehow permanently soiling his mother tongue.

Still somewhat stunned by his naked contempt for us, we headed first to a small gift shop across the road from the taverna, because it seemed as though it might have the fewest people in it who hated us. We had become aware that we were the only non-locals in the square and the row of elderly men sitting on a bench outside a butcher's shop blatantly watching our every move as though we were the evening's entertainment did little to make us feel less self-conscious.

The gift shop was filled with standard tourist items: Greek lace, a million different kinds of olive oil, little dolls in 'traditional' Greek clothing, the lot. As we walked around, Tom voiced his concern that the tendrils of commercialism had extended so deeply into the countryside that there was a real danger of losing any sense of authentic Crete. I didn't want to argue with Tom because it was hard enough arguing with Andy all the time, but I was sure that his idea of simple peasant people, living simple peasant lives, untainted by the modern world hadn't existed anywhere other than in the heads of tourists searching out the 'real' Crete for some time.

Still closely observed by the old men on the bench we left the shop and headed over to the church. There appeared to be some sort of service going on so we didn't

go in, but as we turned to leave an old lady standing in the vestibule at the back spotted us and nudged her friends: as one they all turned and stared at us for an uncomfortably long time.

Bemused by the interest we seemed to be creating we finally made our way to the taverna and sat down at one of the many outdoor tables. Much to our great relief, within seconds of sitting down a friendly middle-aged man came over and took our order. Still keen to try out his phrase-book Greek, Tom relayed our choices from the menu as best he could. And although he struggled greatly with a whole gamut of unfamiliar words and phrases, our waiter seemed to be genuinely pleased that Tom was making the effort.

The food and drinks arrived quickly and were a definite improvement on anything we had eaten so far. There were spinach and feta pies, meatballs, stuffed vine leaves and a few dishes that we couldn't match to the menu but tasted great anyway. Just as we ordered a second round of beers to wash down the remains of the meal, a couple of guys carrying acoustic guitars emerged from inside the taverna and began playing a batch of songs that some of the locals spread across the other tables seemed to know well. Within a few moments virtually all the customers were clapping and singing in unison.

'Charlie?' whispered Tom in my ear as we finally overcame our natural reserve and joined in with the clapping to a particularly upbeat song. 'If I tell you something, I need you to promise that you won't make a big deal out of it, okay?'

'Of course,' I replied, still clapping. 'It'll be a small deal all the way. What's on your mind?'

Tom stopped clapping and I did likewise. 'You know earlier today you asked me if I was okay?' I nodded. 'Well the truth is I'm not.'

'What do you mean?' I replied.

'I mean I've had something on my mind for a while that I haven't told a single soul about and it's sort of driving me mad.'

'What is it?' I asked.

'It's like this,' he began. 'The day we fly back home I've got to make a phone call.'

'What kind of phone call?'

'It's nothing really it's just . . .' his voice faltered. '. . . It's just I'm supposed to call my doctors' surgery to get some test results.'

'Test results?' I said a little too quickly. 'For what?'

'I really don't know how to say it,' said Tom fixing his eyes on the guitar players in front of us. 'I really don't. I haven't even dared to say the word aloud even when I'm on my own.'

'This is me you're talking to,' I replied. 'You know you can tell me anything.'

'Cancer,' said Tom quietly as the song came to a close. 'I've got to phone my doctor to see if I've got cancer.'

# DAY THREE:
# WEDNESDAY

## She is a holiday

Through the dimness of the darkened bedroom I could just about make out the shape of a figure at the bathroom door. I squinted at my watch. It was just after seven in the morning. The good news from my perspective was that for once during this holiday I wasn't the first person awake. The bad news was that had I not been woken up, I'm sure I would have slept on for hours. Realising that I was unlikely to get back to sleep any time soon I climbed out of bed and, without saying a word, slipped on my shorts, opened my suitcase and pulled out my 'Death To The Pixies' T-shirt.

'Morning, mate,' said Andy, emerging from the bathroom wearing shorts and a T-shirt. His hair was wet and he was frantically rubbing it dry with a towel.

'You woke me up,' I replied cheerlessly.

Andy fixed me with a hard stare. 'I've just had a shower. Since when was that a crime?'

'Since you started stealing my towel to do it,' I said snatching the damp towel from Andy's hands. 'What are you doing up so early anyway? I didn't expect to see you until tonight. That's how it goes doesn't it? Every twenty-four hours you check in with us just to make sure we're still alive.'

'I'm back because Nina and I agreed that we're both

153

knackered,' said Andy, side-stepping my early morning fractiousness. 'And my plan – if it's actually any of your business – was to have a shower and then sleep until late in the afternoon but if you want me to go back to Nina's I can do that just as easily.'

'Well if you really want to go,' I replied. 'Be my guest.'

There was a long silence. Andy stared at me as though trying to work something out. All of a sudden his face suggested he'd found the answer and he whispered knowingly, 'I get it.' He looked pointedly over at the kitchen door. 'This isn't about me at all is it? It's about you having to spend all this quality time with Hans Christian Andersen, visiting villages, hiking up hills and talking about Jesus.' He paused and laughed. 'This is great. You're finally as sick of it as—'

'Just leave it, Andy,' I threatened cautiously. 'Today is most certainly not the day for you to be saying all this.'

'Really? And why would that be? Tom's never been my biggest fan and I'm certainly not his so what's the point in pretending anything else? If you ask me he's a—'

'Look,' I interrupted, 'I've asked you once and now I mean it, drop it.' I stepped towards Andy and pushed him in the chest as if to punctuate the point.

'Tell me you didn't just do that,' said Andy as his face flushed with anger.

'I did it,' I replied, even though I could feel that the situation was beginning to get out of control, 'and do you know what? I'll do it again if you carry on talking about Tom like that.'

'Is that right?' said Andy squaring right up to me as though he might actually throw a punch in my direction.

'Yeah,' I replied firmly, 'that's right.'

I'd never stood up to Andy like this before. I don't suppose I'd ever needed to. And I could see in his eyes that even though he was used to getting his own way, he actually wanted to back down as much as I did. Unfortunately I wasn't sure Andy actually knew how to back down so the only way it was going to happen was if I did it first.

'Look,' I began. 'I shouldn't have pushed you like that, Okay? I'm just a little weirded out that's all.'

'Weirded out by what?'

'By Tom,' I replied. 'Last night he told me that he thinks he might have cancer.'

Andy's face fell in shock. The tension between us immediately evaporated. The confrontation was finally over.

'Cancer?' said Andy barely able to get the words out. 'How can Tom have cancer?'

Walking over to the patio doors I opened them up and gestured for Andy to follow me on to the balcony. There I sucked in a deep breath of air and held it in my lungs and looked around me. It was odd being outdoors this early in the day. The morning air seemed fresher. The sun, though bright, had yet to reach its usual intensity. All the loungers beside the pool were empty. Everything familiar seemed as though it had been turned on its head.

'Listen,' I began, as I closed the patio doors behind Andy, 'I'm not sure that I'm supposed to tell you about what Tom said. He didn't say one way or the other. I suppose given how you've been on at him all holiday he didn't think the occasion for a heart-to-heart would come up somehow.'

'I know, I know,' said Andy shamefacedly, 'I have been a bit of an arsehole. But that's not the point is it? The point is how can Tom have cancer? He looks fine to me.'

Andy sat down on one of the plastic chairs while I took the other and I told him the whole story, the same way Tom had told me.

One morning about a month earlier Tom had been to the toilet before breakfast and noticed afterwards that the water in the bowl had a slightly pinkish tinge to it. He ignored it for a few days, hoping it would sort itself out, but it didn't; it got worse and gradually became pinker by the day until one day he saw spirals of red. He made an appointment to see his doctor that same morning, without telling his wife and she immediately referred him to a specialist at his local hospital. The doctor checked him over and informed him that they'd have to run a whole batch of tests to rule out the worst-case scenario – cancer of the bladder.

'So they don't know for sure what he's got?' asked Andy.

'No,' I replied. 'But I don't know whether you know this, but cancer of the bladder is what Tom's dad died of . . . and he was only fifty-two.'

Neither of us spoke for a few moments.

'When do his results come back?'

'The morning we land back at Gatwick.'

Andy thought for a moment. 'That's why he agreed to come on the holiday with us, isn't it?'

I nodded. 'He told me he thought he'd be better off being distracted by the two of us than moping around at home waiting for the results.'

Andy stood up and went back inside the bedroom, reappearing with his cigarettes and a lighter. He lit a cigarette and handed it to me, then lit one for himself. As the balcony briefly filled with a pale blue haze of smoke we sat looking out at the misty horizon in front of us.

'My nan died of cancer,' said Andy quietly. 'It was in her liver. Saddest fucking day of my life.'

'You lived with her, didn't you?'

'From about seven, when my dad left and my mum lost the plot, to when I left to go to college. Honestly, Charlie, my whole life she was such a strong woman – a real tower of strength – nothing ever fazed her. Not raising my brother and me. Not working two jobs. Not my granddad dying. She took everything in her stride. She used to bang on about God all the time and about how he would look after her because he always had done in the past. But he didn't. As she gradually got sicker she was like a different person. She wasn't my gran any more. She was a frail old lady. I'd never thought of my nan like that – as being an old lady. But the first time I saw her in hospital after her first round of treatment that's what she was.

'She'd always been this woman who wasn't scared of anything or anyone. I remember this one time her house got burgled – they nicked a video recorder and some cash that had been sitting on the fireplace – and she had a pretty good idea which one of the kids in our close had done it, because my nan had lived there all her life and knew everyone's business. She must have been pushing seventy at the time but that didn't stop her from walking round to this kid's house and banging on his front door until his parents opened up. Right there on the door step she threatened to batter the mum, the dad *and* the kid black and blue unless the video and the money were returned to her by the end of the day, along with a bit extra to cover the cost of a pane of glass that had been smashed. And do you know what? She got it too. That was my nan, a force of nature.' Andy paused to flick the long

stem of ash from his cigarette and then took a long drag. 'But you wouldn't have recognised her in hospital. You really wouldn't. And every time she had a treatment she looked worse not better. And then one day a few months in, I'd been to visit her and it just dawned on me that despite all the talk she was never actually going to get better. And after that I never went back. My brother did. He was with her at the very end. But me?' Andy shook his head. 'I just couldn't stand to watch her go like that.'

I didn't know what to say. I'd known bits about Andy's background. The stuff about being raised by his gran (although he'd never mentioned anything at all about his parents before) and just how much his gran had meant to him, although that was mainly through the way he reacted after her death. It knocked him sideways. It really did. He stopped eating. He drank to excess. And was so obnoxious to pretty much everyone in his life that along with losing his job, he lost nearly every friend that he had made in the last decade with the exception of me and Lisa. It was nearly a year before he was able to get himself together, and only because Lisa threatened to leave him. And while it had long since occurred to me that there had to be a reason why Andy was so anti-religion, and anti-Tom especially, now that I knew, or at least could guess his reasoning, I couldn't say that I felt any wiser. He had his reasons and I'm sure they felt justified to him but that didn't make him right.

'Do you think he'll be all right?' said Andy, stubbing out his cigarette on the balcony railing.

'Yeah, of course,' I replied. 'He'll be fine.'

'How old are his kids again?'

'I think one's four and the other is three.'

'And he still believes in God?' said Andy shaking his head in disgust. His response was posed as a question but also as a statement of fact. But whatever it was I chose not to respond.

'You think I'm being an idiot cheating on Lisa, don't you?' he asked.

I left a gap of a few moments before replying in the hope of convincing Andy that I was wavering between two options. 'Yeah,' I replied eventually. 'I think you are.'

'You think she deserves better.'

'I think if you don't want to be with her, fine, end the relationship and move on. But if you have any respect for her at all then you'll stop this thing with Nina now.'

'Or . . . ?'

I looked at him, puzzled.

'You make it sound like you're going to do something about it if I don't,' he said.

'What could I possibly do?' I replied. 'It's not like I'm in any position to force anyone to do anything.'

'Lisa is what I want,' said Andy calmly. 'And I know that we'll have kids and all the rest of it.'

'But?'

Andy smiled ruefully. 'There's always a but isn't there? And for me it's the routine. I can't stand it. Mondays: work and the gym. Tuesdays: work and then TV in the evenings. Wednesdays: work and one of her mates will come over for dinner. Thursdays: work and she goes out with her mates and I'll go for a drink with you. Fridays: work and then a takeaway in front of the TV; Saturdays: gym, shopping, and if we can be bothered we might go out in the evening; Sundays . . . who knows what happens to Sundays? Every day just melts away into nothingness because before

159

you know what's happened it's Monday again and you're right back where you started. Who wouldn't want a holiday after that?'

'Is that what Nina is? A holiday?'

'It's as good a word as any,' replied Andy. 'She is a holiday . . . from real life . . . from routine and yeah, even from Lisa. Everybody needs a holiday, mate. Even you.' He paused, picked up his cigarettes and stood up. 'I'll see you, later, maybe?'

'Are you going to bed?'

'No,' he sighed. 'I'm going back to Nina's.'

# I ♥ Malaysia

It was ten o'clock and I was back on the balcony, lying in the sun, with my nose stuck between the pages of the *The Da Vinci Code*. Tom had long since set out on his trip to the Samaria Gorge leaving me alone for the day.

Things had been awkward between the two of us to say the least. I didn't know how to behave around someone who'd just told me they might have cancer. I was so confused by the situation that I ended up alternating between being overly concerned about his well-being and acting like his personal court jester in order to lift his spirits. By the time he left the apartment (having turned down a constant barrage of offers from me to come to keep him company) he must have been over the moon to see the back of me.

With a full day alone ahead of me and no one to distract me from indulging in thoughts of Sarah, I knew that it would only be a matter of time before she took up her usual residency in my thoughts. So, resting my book on the table at my side, I decided that if thinking about Sarah was inevitable then the best thing I could do would be to get it out of the way. Without any further ado I settled back in my chair and commenced thinking.

I never told this to anyone but on the day Sarah left me I actually went out to book a holiday. It had been a day

full of arguing and shouting and crying (on both our parts) and then she had delivered the final blow with the words: 'I don't think I love you any more.' I knew straight away she wasn't bluffing. It was just like when I was a kid and I'd been up to no good, deliberately doing something that I knew would get me in trouble. My dad would catch me in the act and he'd say something like, 'Right, that's it,' and from the tone of his voice I'd know straight away that this wasn't an empty threat. Within seconds I'd feel the effect of my dad's open palm connecting with the bare flesh of my upper legs long before I'd hear the sonic boom of the slap. And that's exactly what it was like hearing Sarah tell me she no longer loved me. It was a blow to the heart followed by a sonic boom. A slap so hard that I thought it would never stop stinging. My head was reeling, my heart was racing and my life was lying shattered in tiny shards at my feet.

As Sarah slammed the door at her exit I remember feeling strangely calm. People who have nearly died on operating tables in hospitals sometimes say, as they're lying there with doctors and nurses screaming all around them trying to bring them back to life, that they can feel themselves leaving their bodies and floating up above the scene of what they think are their last moments. Well that was me. I was floating out of my own body watching myself slumped lifeless on a chair at the dining-room table only there was no one trying to bring me back to life. There was just me, an empty flat, and too many memories. And in that state I heard myself saying the words, 'You've got to do something,' over and over again and I couldn't work out whether I meant I'd got to do something to get Sarah back or that I should just stop sitting there and take some

action. And while I sat there trying to work out exactly what I meant, out of the corner of my eye I spotted a holiday brochure in a magazine rack by the TV. It was called something like *Luxury Holidays Plus*, and was filled with expensive five-star breaks to places like Barbados, the Seychelles and the Maldives – holidays that we could never have considered under normal circumstances. That was when I realised that Sarah hadn't picked up the brochure with the two of us in mind at all. Within seconds of this bombshell dropping, I'd put on my shoes, grabbed my coat and was heading into town.

The travel agent's I went to were called Holidays Now. Above the door to the shop was a sign that said: 'The home of holidays', and stuck to the windows with Blu-Tack were dozens of marker-pen-inscribed cards featuring late-booking offers. My eyes lit up as I reviewed the offers in the window: fourteen nights in Costa Rica, ten nights in Ibiza, seven nights in Gran Canaria, a fortnight in Portugal and eight days in Malta but there was a problem with every single one of them. All the discount prices were offered on the basis of two people sharing. And yet here I was, just one person, looking for a way to escape.

The moment I entered the travel agent's I felt as if all eyes were on me. It was as if I'd tripped some sort of infrared alarm. The three of the female sales agents had looked up and flashed me their whitest, toothiest, shiniest smiles. For a few moments I genuinely felt loved, and then I realised that they were not so much smiling as responding to some sort of Pavlovian trigger they had been taught on one of those long-distant training schemes at the beginning of their careers. They reminded me of the androids in *Blade Runner*. Human, but not quite human enough.

A deftly manicured finger pointed me in the direction of their waiting area – a space in the centre of the store somewhat bizarrely made up to look like a beach-style café bar. There were three aluminium café-style tables with chairs and sunshades and in the middle of them was a pile of sand, a bucket and spade, a beach towel and a Jackie Collins novel.

Unsure whether this was an art installation or a genuine waiting area, I looked enquiringly back at the saleswoman and she gave me a hearty smile and a wink. Taking a deep breath I crossed the floor and sat down at one of the tables, feeling peculiarly self-conscious. Here I was, a now single, thirty-five-year-old man, sitting alone at a fake outdoor café, next to a fake beach, in a travel agency in the middle of a busy Brighton shopping centre on a wet July afternoon.

As I poured myself a cup of water from a dispenser I tried to work out which one of the sales girls would serve me first. My guess was the one nearest the entrance, as there was something ridiculously efficient about her manner that told me she was probably the store's top sales person. But as I looked around the room I noticed that the assistant sitting at the desk at the rear of the shop was actually quite pretty. She had dark brown hair, caramel-coloured skin and a killer smile. Even in her work uniform of purple polyester skirt and red checked blouse she looked amazing.

The pretty sales assistant must have sensed she was being watched because for no reason at all she looked up and caught my eye. Our eyes met for a few moments and then instinctively I looked away, which only served to make me look guilty. To balance things out I looked at her again but then incorporated this look into a whole batch of long

stares around the room to make me look less suspect. I stared at the large banner above her head, featuring soft focus families walking across an idyllic palm-tree-strewn beach; I stared at three men in the queue at the Bureau de Change (one of whom was carrying a large carrier bag emblazoned with the slogan: I ♥ Malaysia); and I stared at the Jackie Collins novel in the display.

Having sufficiently distanced myself from any deviant-seeming behaviour, I hedged a glance back at the pretty saleswoman. She was still deep in conversation with a young couple she was serving and didn't look in my direction once in the three seconds I spent imagining what it might be like to kiss her. And so with the heat off I took a long sip of my water and studied the rows of brochures on the rack behind me. Just as I was about to pluck out one about skiing holidays (even though I didn't ski and hated the idea of skiing) I stopped. A young couple, laden with fashionable shopping bags and dressed as if they were going out on a Saturday night, sat down at the table next to mine. Our eyes met, and I was temporarily frozen in embarrassment until a female voice entered my consciousness.

'Hello there.'

The pretty sales assistant was talking to me. She was barely into her twenties and was even prettier up close.

'I'm Denise,' she said cheerfully. 'How can I help you today?'

There was a long pause as the cogs in my brain began to rotate, reminding me of several key factors I'd neglected to consider that would considerably hinder any attempt to book a holiday: first, it was three weeks until pay day, second, I hadn't checked with work when I could get the time off, and third, I didn't want to go on holiday alone.

I smiled. 'I'm afraid I've wasted your time. I've just realised that I'm in completely the wrong place to book a holiday.'

Then I stood up and left.

## Camera phone

Around midday I came to the conclusion that if I was going to enjoy this holiday at all then I was going to have to stop thinking about Sarah. I briefly contemplated going down to the beach with *The Da Vinci Code* but I was getting tired of reading about religious conspiracies and wanted to do something that required physical exertion of some description. Looking around the room for inspiration, I spotted Tom's beloved *Rough Guide* that he'd inadvertently left on the table on the balcony and began flicking through it. There was a whole host of 'must see' cultural suggestions from museums and ruins right through to hills and famous birthplaces. Though Tom had circled a number of his favourites in blue Biro, most held no interest for me whatsoever.

The only place I was even vaguely interested in visiting was Heraklion, the capital of the island. And that was because I thought it might have proper shops and things to buy that weren't just the usual old tourist tat. In essence what I wanted from Heraklion was a small glimpse of England – a homogenised city centre that despite its architecture, culture and customs would have the same chain stores, brands and regular 'old tat' shops of any high street back home. Why? Because what I wanted more than anything was a little retail therapy. And with several hundred pounds' worth of holiday Euros doing very little other than

securing me access to alcohol, ice cream and local cuisine, I was now desperate to exercise my real buying power.

I took a taxi into Heraklion and my hunch that it might be a modern city, with modern shopping facilities, paid off. It was just as I had hoped. The downside was that once I was there, I couldn't actually find a single thing I wanted to buy. I visited electrical shops and computer shops, clothes shops and book shops, and I visited a bunch of One-Euro shops and a market and left all of them without buying a single thing.

Coming to the conclusion that my excursion had been a mistake, I made my way down a back street in a bid to find the taxi rank where I had been dropped off. After a quarter of any hour, it became clear to me that I was well and truly lost. Nothing in my surroundings seemed even vaguely familiar and with the midday sun beating down on my head I was beginning to feel quite disorientated. In a last-ditch attempt to find out where I was, I took a left down a narrow passageway that opened up into a large civic square dominated by a grand-looking cathedral.

As I edged my way further into the square, the cathedral's bells chimed twice as if beckoning me towards it. Reasoning that I had nothing better to do I made my way across the shady square and up the steep steps to the entrance to the church.

In contrast to the intense warmth and brightness of the day outside, the inside of the cathedral was dimly lit and cool and seemed like the perfect sanctuary. Sitting down on an old wooden bench at the back of the church I looked around me. The cathedral was just as I expected. It had grand painted ceilings, colourful stained-glass windows, ageing frescoes and hundreds of ornate woodcarvings.

Closing my eyes, I took a deep breath and as the peace and quiet of the building began to filter into my head I wondered whether I might ever find myself approaching a religious conversion similar to Tom's. Though it was probably my imagination, for a few brief moments I began to feel as if the weight of my worries was being lifted off my shoulders. Just as I was beginning to explore this new sensation an electronic-sounding camera click broke my reverie. I opened my eyes to see a middle-aged woman armed with a camera phone frantically taking pictures of everything around her as if she was shooting a front cover for *What Cathedral Weekly*.

Even though I was pretty sure I didn't believe in God, on Tom's behalf and behalf of people like him, I was grabbed by the impulse to smash this woman's phone into a million pieces. Fortunately for me, a priest approached her and after a brief exchange she left the building. I felt as though I could finally relax and for a short while that's just what I did. I stared at the characters depicted in the frescoes, I watched a stream of people lighting candles for their loved ones and I thought long and hard about Tom and his situation. And although I felt none the wiser by the time I came to leave, I did at least feel in some small way more at peace with the world. And while I wasn't sure whether it was the right thing to do or not, I lit a candle for Tom.

As I turned round to leave, I noticed a young dark-haired woman standing by the bench in front of me. And recognised her immediately.

'You're Andy's friend aren't you?' said the woman. 'Charlie, isn't it?'

'Yeah,' I replied shaking her hand. 'And you're Nina's sister Donna.'

## Why would anyone want to kill a pixie?

'Are you Catholic?' asked Donna.

'No,' I replied. 'I was just . . . it's a long story.' I paused and looked at her. 'You're not Catholic are you?'

Donna shrugged. 'I think the rules say you're one for life even if, like me, you haven't stepped foot in a church since you were a teenager.' She paused. 'I don't even know what made me decide to come in. It's one of those things you do when you're in a foreign country, isn't it? I'd never think for a minute to look around my local church just because I was passing by.' She smiled awkwardly. 'Are you here alone?'

'Yeah,' I replied. 'My mate Tom has gone hiking and I'm guessing Andy's with your sister. You're not here with them are you?

'Those two?' laughed Donna. 'I doubt they're even up yet. No, I came in on my own. We fly home tomorrow so I thought I'd buy a few presents and see something other than the beach. How about you? What brings you to Heraklion?'

'Same as you really,' I replied. 'Malia can feel a bit small after a while.'

'You're not wrong there.'

'Where are you off to next?' I asked.

'I don't know. How about you?'

'I've got nothing planned as such. In fact I was thinking about heading back.' I paused. 'Look, I don't suppose you fancy getting a coffee or something do you? I haven't eaten yet and could do with grabbing a quick something.'

'That would be great,' said Donna. 'On my way here I saw a café across the square that looked quite nice. It's in the shade, too, which is a blessing in this heat.'

With Donna leading the way, we made our way outside.

'You forget how bright it can get,' she said slipping on a pair of black Jackie O-style sunglasses. They suited her perfectly. With the blue-striped T-shirt and grey skirt she was wearing, she looked like a glamorous sixties film star.

'They suit you,' I said to Donna as I put on my own sunglasses.

'Thanks,' she replied. 'I bought them on holiday last year. They're my favourite thing I own. I love them.' She peered at me closely so that all I could see was my own reflection in her sunglasses. 'Yours suit you too. You look like you ought to be in a band.'

We walked a few steps in silence and then Donna spoke. 'So do you live in Hove like your friend Andy?'

'Brighton, actually,' I joked. 'How about you?'

'North London,' she replied. 'Archway to be exact.'

'I know Archway,' I replied. 'I used to have a mate who lived there for a while. His place was just on the edge of a really rough council estate.'

'Henmarsh?'

'Yeah,' I replied. 'I think so.'

Donna laughed. 'That's where I live.'

'That's so typical of me,' I said, wincing. 'It's a wonder I haven't started randomly insulting members of your family.'

'It's fine,' replied Donna. 'It *is* a bit of a rough estate. But Sadie and I won't be there forever.'

'Sadie?' I asked.

'My daughter.'

As we reached the tables outside the café, some kids behind us rode their bikes towards a large congregation of pigeons, sending them flying into the air. Donna ducked in towards me and instinctively I put my arm around her to protect her.

'Sorry about that,' said Donna as she realised that she was clinging on to my T-shirt. 'I hate pigeons. Can't stand them. My worst nightmare is one of the vile things getting their feet caught in my hair.'

'I don't mind them really,' I replied, 'although I admit I get a bit freaked out when I see the ones with missing limbs hopping about. Does that make me evil?'

'No,' smiled Donna. 'At least not in my eyes.'

We sat down and I plucked a plastic menu, sandwiched between a container of sugar packets and a paper-napkin dispenser, and handed it to Donna.

'Are you just snacking or having a proper meal?' she asked.

'It's too hot to eat a proper meal,' I replied. 'I just want something to fill the gap.'

'I'm going to have the waffles and ice cream then,' said Donna handing me the menu. 'They sound really nice.'

I scanned the menu. 'I'll have that too. And I think I'll have a Coke to wash it down.'

'Good idea,' said Donna, taking off her sunglasses and resting them on the edge of the table. 'Full fat or diet?'

'Full fat,' I replied. 'You?'

Donna smiled. 'Full fat all the way.'

A waitress appeared almost as soon as I returned the menu to its resting place and took our order. As soon as she left Donna turned to me and pointed at my T-shirt. 'So you like the Pixies then? I saw them once at the Brixton Academy when I was eighteen.'

'Were they good?'

'They were brilliant. Have you seen them?'

'I saw them back in Brighton when I was at college. They were okay but I wouldn't call myself a massive fan. I liked the T-shirt more than anything. It just seems like such a mad thing to proclaim don't you think? "Death to the Pixies". Why would anyone want to kill a pixie?'

'Maybe it's like my thing with pigeons,' smiled Donna. 'Maybe somewhere in the world there's a woman wearing big sunglasses who has an acute fear of getting pixies stuck in her hair.'

There was a brief lull in the conversation as we watched the kids on bikes continuing to harass the pigeons who had regrouped to peck the ground around the cathedral steps.

'What do you do for a living?' I eventually asked.

'I'm a paediatric nurse at Whittington hospital,' said Donna. 'I've been there nearly ten years now and I still love it. I just wish it paid more, that's all, so I could move out of Henmarsh. How about you?'

'Try not to yawn, but I set up schemes to help businesses and housing trusts start up in run-down areas around Brighton and Hove. It's an all-right job as they go and the people I work with are good to be around so I don't worry about it too much.'

The waitress returned with our drinks and set them down in front of us. I hadn't realised just how thirsty I was and

had to stop myself gulping down the entire glass straight away. Donna meanwhile sipped her Coke through a straw in a slow considered manner as though she were savouring every drop.

'Can I ask you a question?' said Donna setting aside her drink.

'Depends what it is.'

'It's about your friend Andy,' she began. 'He's got a girl-friend hasn't he?'

I studied her face, trying to work out if she knew this for a fact or was trying to trick me into confirming her suspicions but then I realised that I didn't actually care one way or the other.

'Yeah,' I nodded, 'he has.'

'I thought so.'

'Does your sister know?'

'Any time I ask her about it she gets cagey – which is a sure sign of guilt in my family. She keeps telling me it's just a holiday thing. As if that makes it all right.' She frowned and bit her lip. 'It doesn't does it?'

'It's hard to say.' I shrugged. 'There's that phrase Americans always say when they go to Las Vegas in a big group isn't there? Something like, "What happens in Las Vegas stays in Las Vegas". Malia's a bit like that for us Brits. It's a place where people go a little bit mental just because they can. I think it must be something that's hardwired into the human brain – the need to escape the normal rules sometimes.'

'So is it a case of what happens in Malia, stays in Malia with you and your friends?' asked Donna. 'Or will you be telling Andy's partner what he's been up to?'

I thought for a moment. 'It'll be staying in Malia,' I replied.

Donna nodded. 'And I'm guessing the trade-off is that he won't be telling your partner what you've been up to either?'

'There's no partner for him to tell.'

The information registered on her face. A raise of the eyebrows, some curiosity in the eyes, a small movement in the lips and then . . . gone.

'You don't look single,' said Donna matter of factly.

I had to laugh. 'So what do I look like?'

'You look like the partners of my friends back home – well turned out and looked after.'

I sighed heavily. 'Well, it's not been that long since that was actually the case.'

Donna winced. 'Looks like it's my turn to put my foot in my mouth. I'm really sorry. I went a bit far there didn't I?'

'No, it's fine,' I replied. 'It's not like it happened yesterday.'

'So is that what this holiday is about?'

'Is it that obvious?'

Donna smiled. 'Come on, three guys in their mid-thirties in a place like Malia? What could be at all obvious about that?'

'Well, for starters I can assure you that it wasn't my plan.'

'Let me guess,' said Donna. 'It was Andy's.'

'When he gets an idea in his head it's difficult to say—' I stopped mid-sentence as the waitress returned with our waffles and ice cream and by the time she had left it no longer seemed like a sentence worth finishing.

With the conversational flow between us interrupted we both retreated to our separate corners and tucked into our

waffles in a polite silence. I wanted to carry on talking to her. I didn't want this to end. I decided that the best thing I could do was jump in with both feet.

'Okay,' I said, after Donna forked the first mouthful of her dessert into her mouth. 'You know about how I ended up here but you've still to explain about *you*. After all you're . . . what . . . ?' The face. The hair. The clothes. I had her pegged somewhere roughly in her early thirties but decided to err on the side of caution. '. . . late twenties?'

Donna grinned. 'Early thirties – as if you couldn't tell.'

'Early thirties?' I laughed. 'Then you belong in Malia about as much as I do. Shouldn't you be out renting villas in Tuscany or going on diving holidays in the Maldives or at the very least living it up in Ibiza?'

'I would've loved to have done any of those things you mentioned this summer, but beggars can't be choosers. Nina and I are half-sisters and even though there's nine years between us we're really close. Anyway, about a month ago she told me she was planning to come here with her friends and wanted me to come along. With work and Sadie I don't get to see her as often as I'd like so I thought why not?'

'So who's looking after your daughter now?'

'Her dad. He's a teacher. We're not together any more.' She paused and then added: 'These things happen, don't they?'

'Yeah,' I replied. 'I suppose they do.'

We both picked up our spoons and returned to our waffles and ice cream.

'So how old's Sadie?' I asked after a while as Donna pushed her empty plate to one side.

'She was six in April.' Donna reached into her bag, pulled out her purse and took out a passport-sized photo of her

daughter. She too had dark hair, big brown eyes and a huge smile.

'She looks just like you,' I said staring at the photo.

'A lot of people say that,' replied Donna. 'But I don't see it myself. Have you got any kids yourself?'

Her question took me by surprise. Then I realised that at my age it was a valid question, given that most of my contemporaries were now fathers or at the very least thinking about becoming fathers.

'No,' I replied.

'Were they ever on the list?'

'I think so,' I replied. 'Once upon a time they were, anyway.'

Donna and I talked in general about the holiday and a bit more about our lives back home but then our waitress returned to clear our table and I could feel that our time together was over. We split the bill and then, tucking the money we owed underneath the sugar dispenser, stood up and made ready to leave.

'Thanks for that,' said Donna quietly. 'That was a really nice way to spend an afternoon.'

'It was, wasn't it?' I replied. 'Maybe I'll see you around later in Malia? Andy was saying that you were all going out tonight as it's your last night.'

'Nina did mention something like that. You and your other friend should definitely come along if you're free.'

'Cool,' I replied. 'Well, I'll see you later then, hopefully.'

Donna waved goodbye and as she crossed the square back to the city, the cathedral bells began to chime, sending the pigeons that had been resting in the bell tower soaring one last time into the sky.

## Happy face

It was just after six-thirty when Tom returned to the apartment. He came out on the balcony where I'd been sitting and I offered him one of the two remaining cans of Heineken I'd brought out with me. Though worn out from his day walking he looked happy, almost carefree and we exchanged highlights of our day apart with none of the awkwardness of earlier. He was back to being Tom and I was back to being me. And everything between us was just fine.

'So is it too crass to ask the big question?' asked Tom.

'Which big question would that be?'

'The one about you and Donna,' he said, smirking. 'Do you think anything will happen tonight?'

'I've no idea,' I replied. 'It's not like I got any sort of positive vibes from her . . . not unless you count agreeing to eat Belgian waffles with me.'

Tom shrugged. 'Well I wouldn't discount it altogether. Back when I was single I knew plenty of girls that wouldn't even talk to me, let alone eat waffles in the same vicinity.'

'You see,' I sighed, 'this is the bit I always found difficult, back in my single days: the "how to tell if they're interested part".'

'What does the evidence say?' asked Tom.

*Wish You Were Here*

'Well, other than the waffles she did say that I should come out with her sister and her friends tonight.'

'That's all the evidence you need right there,' said Tom.

'Do you think so? She told me to bring you along too.'

'Even better,' said Tom. 'That's a clear case of using me as a smokescreen to hide her true motive.' He paused. 'So what's Andy got organised for tonight anyway?'

'Nothing too excessive . . . you know . . . a few beers and a bit of a laugh. Tell me you're coming.'

'I can't,' said Tom, wincing. 'This walk really took it out of me. I was at the front of the entire walking party there and back. Tonight all I want to do is have a shower, phone Anne and the kids, and then sleep. Just give Andy a ring and tell him you're definitely coming tonight. If he gets a little too Andy even for you then at least you'll have Donna to chat to.'

'I think I'll do it,' I said reaching for my phone. I dialled Andy's number and he answered after three rings. 'It's me. I'm just calling to see what you're doing tonight. Tom's knackered from his hiking thing so he's going to—'

'Brilliant!' yelled Andy down the line. His voice became muffled but I could still just about hear him informing Nina that 'my mate Charlie is coming out tonight'.

'We're starting off at Club Tropicana,' said Andy coming back on the line. 'It's an eighties-themed bar and restaurant on the main strip, just past Pandemonium. We'll be there around nine-thirtyish. How does that sound?'

'Cool,' I replied. 'Nine-thirtyish. Club Tropicana.'

'That's the one.' He added cheerfully, 'Charlie?'

'Yeah?'

'Make sure you bring your happy face with you, okay, mate?'

179

'Happy face?'

'You know . . . give misery the night off for a change. It's the girls' last night in Malia. They want it to be a good one and I just want to make sure that everything is in position.'

'In position for what?'

'For you to have the best night of your entire life.'

## What plan B?

As I sauntered into Club Tropicana at close to twenty to ten I was quite sure that it wasn't going to be the best night of my life. For a start, my clothes didn't feel right. I'd wanted to wear the same clothes I'd worn on our night out at Pandemonium (a tried and tested ensemble that was virtually my going-out-on-the-town uniform back in Brighton) but after all that time in the bar the shirt stank of cigarette smoke. My back-up ensemble, a pair of beige trousers and a white patterned shirt, had never been matched together before and though technically they should have had no trouble getting on together, for some reason the whole thing didn't quite work. Secondly, on my way to the strip that night I'd been waylaid by two Geordie girls who looked about seventeen. The first girl cheered me up immensely with the greeting: 'You're gorgeous, you are,' but then a second girl leered drunkenly into my face and tittered: 'Stay off the Bacardi Breezers, Tina, he's at least forty.' Thirdly, though not completely up to speed on the rules and regulations for having the best night of your life I was pretty confident that it wouldn't be sound-tracked by a Jive Bunny mega mix.

I found Andy and Nina sitting at a table on the club's outdoor terrace surrounded by Nina's friends, but there was no sign of Donna.

'Charlie!' said Andy, greeting me like I was his long-lost brother. 'How are you, mate? Come and sit down and meet the girls.'

One by one I was introduced to Nina's friends: Stacey, Melissa, Hattie and Beth. They all seemed nice enough and several of them were actually incredibly attractive but none of them sparked off anything in me the way Donna had that first night in Pandemonium – none of them looked as though they had stories to tell.

'I thought there were six of you?' I asked as I settled down in a chair between Andy and Melissa. 'Who's missing?'

'That'll be my sister Donna,' said Nina. 'She wanted to have some time by herself so we said we'd meet her around midnight in Bar Go-Go.'

'Couldn't you have told her we were going somewhere else?' said Andy.

'Why would you do that?' I asked.

'Andy thinks Donna doesn't like him,' said Nina. 'But he's wrong.'

'How can I be wrong since I was there when she took me aside yesterday and said to my face: "I don't like you."'

'It's not that she doesn't like you,' said Nina breezily. 'She's just looking out for her kid sister that's all. Trying to make sure that I'm not being corrupted by an older man.'

Andy stood up and began taking orders for the next round of drinks. But because I was determined to make a good impression I told him that I would get the next round in. We then proceeded to bicker in a pantomime fashion before agreeing to a compromise: I would pay while Andy would come to the bar with me and give me a hand getting the drinks back to the table. It was a perfect

rendition of our 'how-to-look-good-in-front-of-the-opposite-sex' routine lifted straight from our college days and could only have been improved if Donna had been there to witness it.

'So what do you think of the girls then?' said Andy as we made our way to the bar.

'They seem nice enough.'

'Well, my friend, you're in for some luck tonight,' said Andy. 'With them going home tomorrow there's a bit more of a party atmosphere in the air than usual. And if you want my advice I think Hattie – the tall girl in the black dress – is your best bet. She hasn't pulled all holiday so might be up for some last-minute action. If Hattie's not your thing, try Stacey – blond hair, red top, white skirt. Nina says Stacey's pulled a different bloke every night so if you don't mind being number seven you could be well in there. I think you might be out of luck with Melissa – dark hair, black top, white skirt – because she's got a boyfriend back home but I reckon if you turn on that old Mansell charm to its maximum setting she might be persuaded to forget about him. Finally there's Beth – red hair, blue dress – she's actually single but to be truthful, mate, she is so out of your league it hurts. I only say this because she's pretty much out of my league too. I suppose if you're feeling ambitious she might be worth a go but I reckon you'd be wasting time that could be better spent charming Hattie out of her knickers.'

'What are you talking about?' I asked, even though I knew *exactly* what he was talking about.

'You came out tonight to pull didn't you?' said Andy.

'No,' I replied, reasoning that there was no point in weakening my argument with the truth, 'I came out tonight

because I spent today, the third day of a holiday we're supposedly on for my benefit, on my own while Tom went hiking and you hung out with Nina.'

'Well, I'm here now aren't I?' said Andy. 'And the girls are here too. All you've got to do is give it a bit of the old chat and you'll be away.'

'Fine,' I said glancing over to our table in the hope that Donna might have arrived. 'I'll get the drinks and you—' I stopped as I felt my mobile phone vibrate in my back pocket. I pulled it out and looked at the screen.

'It's Lisa,' I said locking eyes with Andy guiltily.

'Why is she calling you again?' he asked staring at the screen on my phone.

'How am I supposed to know?' I replied. 'Do you want me to answer it or let it go to voicemail?'

'Answer it,' said Andy quickly. 'Speak to her. Find out what she wants.'

'Look,' I replied as the phone continued to ring. 'I've been thinking about this and I'm really not comfortable at getting into the middle of all the stuff with you and Lisa.'

'I know, I know,' he said urgently. 'Look, I've got a Plan B sorted that will solve everything, okay? Just answer the call and it'll be the last thing you have to do with her I promise you.'

'What do you mean you've got a "Plan B?"'

Andy winked at me. 'I'd tell you but I think I'd prefer to see the look on your face when I pull off my masterstroke. Now just answer the phone and talk to her for as long as you need to, okay?'

'Fine,' I replied. 'But you'll have to get the drinks in.'

## It's not Malia

'Lisa,' I said breezily into the phone as I watched the hordes of late-night revellers milling in the street outside Club Tropicana. 'How are you?'

'Where are you?' she asked quickly. 'It sounds noisy.'

'Outside a bar,' I replied. 'It's quite crowded around here so—'

'Is Andy with you?' she interrupted.

'He's at the bar getting the drinks in.' I paused. 'Look, Lisa, what's with all the questions? Are you okay? Is something wrong?'

'I'm really sorry, Charlie.'

'Sorry about what?'

'I've got it into my head that you're hiding something from me. You're not are you?'

'What makes you think that anything is wrong?' I asked, side-stepping the issue.

'Nothing really. It was just a small thing that you said earlier that didn't quite add up. You remember the text message you sent me? You said you and Tom and Andy spent the day on the beach, didn't you?'

'Yeah, I did.'

'Well, are you sure about that?'

'Of course I am.' Then I paused and, employing my best acting skills, corrected myself. 'Well . . . actually . . . come

185

to think of it . . . we actually spent most of the day by the pool because we were too wrecked to go anywhere else, but then we did make it to the beach a bit later in the afternoon once our strength was up. But you know how it gets when you're on holiday, everything sort of merges into one doesn't it?'

'You're right.' The acute relief in Lisa's voice was clearly audible. I felt like the lowest of the low. 'You're absolutely right.' She paused. 'I really am so sorry, Charlie. I should let you go. I feel like I'm single-handedly ruining your holiday.'

'You don't have to go,' I said quickly. Her guilt was making my own spiral out of control. 'It's not like I'm missing out on much. I think they're playing Tears For Fears at the moment.'

'Okay,' laughed Lisa. 'Leaving aside Tears For Fears for the moment . . . how has your day been?'

'How has my day been? All right . . . I suppose. Nothing special. It started pretty crappily but then—'

'Why did it start crappily? Andy's not being a real pain is he?'

'No,' I replied. 'It's not Andy . . . it's just that . . . well last night I heard some bad news and it was pretty much the first thing on my mind when I woke up this morning—'

'It was Sarah wasn't it?' said Lisa with genuine pity in her voice. 'She's finally told you.'

'Told me what?'

There was a long pause. I could feel Lisa panicking at the other end of the line.

'It's . . . it's nothing . . .' she stammered. 'I thought that . . . look, it doesn't matter.'

'What do you know about Sarah that you're not telling me?' I demanded. 'She sent me a text message on Sunday but I didn't reply. You know what she wants to talk to me about, don't you?'

'Please, Charlie, don't make me say any more,' pleaded Lisa. 'I'm begging you. I've said too much as it is. It's the sort of news that you need to hear straight from Sarah not me. Call her and I'm sure she'll tell you everything.'

'Just tell me, Lisa,' I snapped. 'Whatever it is I'm not going to blame you, okay? This is Sarah's fault. Not yours. So tell me what she wants and we can move on.'

'I can't,' she said.

'Just tell me.'

'I can't,' she repeated.

'Look, I'm not going to hang up until you do.'

'She's pregnant,' she said finally. 'Sarah's pregnant.'

There was a long silence.

'I'm so sorry, Charlie.'

Silence.

'Charlie, you have to forgive me. You should never have heard this from me.'

Silence.

'I'm sorry.'

'I know you are,' I said softly and then without saying goodbye I switched off the phone.

187

"What do you know about Sarah that you're not telling me?" I demanded. "She sent me a text message on Sunday but I didn't reply. You know what she wants to talk to me about, don't you?"

"Please, Charlie, don't make me say any more," pleaded Lisa. "I'm begging you. I've said too much as it is. It's the sort of news that you need to hear straight from Sarah not me. Call her and I'm sure she'll tell you everything."

"Just tell me, Lisa," I snapped. "Whatever it is I'm not going to blame you, okay? This is Sarah's fault, not yours. So tell me what she wants and we can move on."

"I can't," she said.

"Just tell me."

"I can't," she repeated.

"Look, I'm not going to hang up until you do."

"She's pregnant," she said finally. "Sarah's pregnant."

There was a long silence.

"I'm so-sorry, Charlie."

Silence.

"Charlie, you have to forgive me. You should never have heard this from me."

Silence.

"I'm sorry."

"I know you are," I said softly and then without saying goodbye I switched off the phone.

# DAY FOUR: THURSDAY

DAY FOUR:
THURSDAY

## Voicemail

It was just after midnight. I was sitting on my own in a booth overlooking the strip in the McDonalds at the cross-roads. In front of me were a cold cup of coffee (mine) and the remains of a Big Mac Meal (someone else's).

I pulled my phone out of my back pocket and switched it on. Within seconds it beeped frantically to let me know that I had several voicemail messages. I dialled the mailbox and listened to the messages:

**Message one:** 'Charlie, this is Lisa. Where are you? I'm so sorry for what happened. Please call back and let me know you're okay.'

**Message two:** 'Charlie, it's Andy here. It's nearly half ten. Where are you, mate? I know I said talk to Lisa as long as you want but this is ridiculous. Come back quick. Nina's mate Hattie is definitely interested in you.'

**Message three:** 'Charlie, Andy here again. It's half eleven. You've chickened out on me and gone back to the apartment haven't you? Is it because of Hattie? Well you've missed out there. She's pulled some Scottish guy with an armful of tattoos. Just come back okay? The night's still young and even Beth – the one I said you didn't stand a chance with – is looking a bit desperate. We're off to Bar Go-Go in a bit so look sharpish.'

191

**Message four:** 'Charlie, whatever time you get this message please call me to let me know you're all right. I've tried calling Andy to find out where you are but his phone is switched off. I'm starting to get worried that something bad has happened. Please call.'

I put my phone down on the table and took a moment to look through the window in front of me. A large gang of lads in Newcastle United shirts were passing by the restaurant singing at the top of their voices. Sighing heavily, I picked up my phone again and typed out a text message for Lisa:

**Message Charlie:** 'Hi, don't worry. I'm fine.'

As I switched off my phone and looked out of the window again a huge tidal wave of emotion crashed over me, threatening to engulf me completely. My heart began racing and I felt as though every last one of my internal organs was being slowly crushed inside.

The intensity of my reaction took me by surprise. I couldn't work out what it meant or why it was happening. Even after Sarah first left me I'd been more angry than upset. I'd been more interested in exacting revenge than in responding in any kind of emotional way to her actions. I almost took comfort from the fact that she simply didn't push the button. Yes, she had the power to make me depressed but *she* wasn't the trigger that opened up the flood gates. And for that small mercy, at the time at least, I was grateful because it made me feel as if I was super-human. She had gone and wrecked my life in the process and yet I didn't feel a thing. I was bulletproof. I was invincible. I was Superman. But as I wiped the tears from my eyes in

the crowded restaurant I realised that even Superman had his Kryptonite, and thanks to Lisa I'd now discovered mine.

I dumped my cold coffee in the bin by the exit and strode into the street outside with such purpose that I almost bumped into someone coming the other way.

It was only when I looked to apologise that I realised that the person standing in front of me was Donna. She was dressed in a white top and skirt with matching sandals. Her hair was tied back in a pony tail.

'Charlie,' she said surprised. 'Aren't you going the wrong way for Bar Go-Go or have I missed something?'

'I'm not going,' I replied.

'Are you all right?' asked Donna as though she had a sixth sense for troubled minds. 'Has something happened?'

'I'm just not in the right mood to be here tonight.'

'You're not the only one,' said Donna. 'I'm missing Sadie like crazy and on top of that I'm really getting sick of this place.' Donna paused and looked at me again as if trying to see inside my head. 'I was only going to show my face at Bar Go-Go so that Nina wouldn't keep on about me being miserable,' she began. 'Why don't you come too? We wouldn't have to stay long and if you came I'd at least have someone nice to talk to.'

'Thanks,' I sighed. 'But—'

'Are you sure?'

'Yeah, I'm sure.'

Donna nodded carefully. If she was offended by my sullen mood she did a good job of hiding it. 'Okay, well I think I'll still pop in anyhow.' This was it. This was goodbye. 'Well, it was nice to meet you anyway.'

'Yeah,' I replied, willing myself to say something that would make her stay. 'It was nice to meet you too. Hope

193

everything goes well for you and Sadie back in north London.'

'Look after yourself, Charlie.' She reached up and kissed me on the cheek. 'And make sure you have a great life.' With that she turned and walked away in the direction of Bar Go-Go and for a few moments I stood rooted to the spot, unsure of what I should do next. That was the moment I realised that I couldn't let her walk away without at the very least explaining my behaviour. I ran after her, calling out her name until she stopped and turned around.

'Listen, Donna,' I said unable to take my eyes off her. 'I'm sorry for what just happened. I know it's no excuse but the thing is I've just had a bit of bad news that's sort of turned my whole world upside down.'

'Was it about your ex?'

'Is it that obvious?'

Donna smiled and shook her head. 'Do you want to talk about it?'

'I don't know,' I replied. 'Do you want to listen?'

'How about we take it in turns to do both?' said Donna smiling.

'Now that,' I began as she took my hand in her own, 'sounds like a good idea.'

## Heads or tails?

At Donna's suggestion, we made our way back up to the strip in the direction of all the main bars and clubs, but as we passed the Camelot club we turned right up a street with a slight incline that I'd failed to notice on my previous visits. The early part of the street consisted mainly of fast-food outlets and amusement arcades but those died out the further we walked along and were gradually replaced by small grocery shops and bakeries. Near the end of the street, opposite a taxi rank, was a small bar called Mythos. As we walked in it was obvious that Mythos didn't cater for the tourist crowd: the décor was that of a traditional taverna, the music on in the background was Greek and with the exception of a couple of middle-aged locals the entire bar was empty.

Donna and I sat down at a table near the door and when a waiter came over to us we ordered two beers which he brought to us straight away.

'So how did you find this place?' I asked.

'On my travels,' replied Donna. 'One afternoon when the girls were all down at the beach I took myself off for a walk. I spotted the bakery next door first and bought a few pastries and then saw this place. It just seemed really nice and quiet so whenever I could get away during the day for a little while I'd nip up here and have a drink and write a postcard to Sadie.'

'You wrote more than one?'

'Two a day for every day that we've been here,' she laughed. 'I told you I was missing her.'

There was a long silence.

'Heads or tails?' said Donna after a few moments.

'What do you mean?'

Donna laughed. 'I thought it might make it easier to work out which one of us would be talking first.'

'Heads you go first,' I replied.

'Okay,' said Donna handing me a one-Euro coin. 'But you'll have to be the one to flip it because I'm rubbish at that kind of thing.'

I flipped the coin and caught it moments later in mid-air, wrapping my fingers around it tightly. Donna and I stared expectantly at my clenched fist. I opened my hand and Donna laughed, clearly delighted with the result.

'Over to you then.'

'Fine,' I replied, 'but I'll keep the coin.'

With that I took a long sip of my beer and told Donna everything about my break-up with Sarah, beginning with the day she left and finishing with Lisa's phone call less than a couple of hours ago.

'No wonder you looked so shell-shocked when I bumped into you,' said Donna. 'I'm surprised you're still standing at all after what you've been through.'

'Maybe,' I replied. 'I think the real killer is that I didn't even see it coming.'

'There's no reason you should have done, Charlie. I think it's just one of those things. The important thing is what you do next.'

'There is no next,' I replied. 'That's it. It's all over.'

'But what about the baby?'

'It's not mine. It's his. Oliver's.' I caught Donna's eye and could see that she was curious how I could be so sure. 'We hadn't touched each other in months,' I explained. 'I assumed it was just a phase, but we never seemed to come out the other side.'

## A million years

'For a long time after Sadie's dad left I thought about taking an overdose,' said Donna.

'You're joking?'

Donna shook her head. 'I wish I was.'

'But you didn't do anything did you?'

She shook her head, scanning my face for a reaction. 'I think it was just me not thinking straight, that's all. My GP had prescribed me antidepressants and I wasn't coping very well.' She paused and looked at me. 'You don't think I'm weird do you?'

'No, of course not.'

'I don't think I was serious about it,' she continued. 'I know I'd never willingly leave Sadie in a million years. But there were times after he'd gone when I didn't know how I'd make it through the next minute, let alone the next day. I missed Ed so much I didn't know how to cope. In the end my mum and dad had to come and stay with me to help out with Sadie. Ed walked out because he said he couldn't cope with being tied down. He said that I wanted more from him than he had to give and that he needed his own space.' She paused and laughed. 'He said a lot of things actually. But none of them ever made sense.' She took a sip of her lager. 'It's been two years since it happened and I get on with him now for Sadie's sake

rather than my own. If I didn't think that she would hold it against me, I'd never have anything to do with him again. He's okay now that he's managed to get over his mini-life crisis, find himself a new girlfriend, and finally get his head around the idea of being a parent. But I just can't find it in my heart to forgive him for what he did. He broke my heart, Charlie. Smashed it in two and I never thought that I'd recover.'

## My way of coping

'What's the single thing you miss most about Sarah?' asked Donna.

'Just one thing? Her not being around,' I answered. 'Until she left I don't think I was ever quite aware just how much space she filled in my life.'

Donna nodded. 'No one ever tells you what a lonely place the world can be when you go from being two to one, do they? I think the only reason I managed to cope with the situation was because I had Sadie to look after.'

'I suppose Andy and Tom are my way of coping,' I said, avoiding Donna's gaze. 'It's not so much that they've said or done anything special since I split up with Sarah – I didn't even tell Tom that Sarah had gone until he arrived at my flat the day before we flew here.'

'So what is it they give you?' asked Donna. 'How did they help you to cope when Sarah left?'

I paused and thought for a moment. 'They gave me somewhere to belong,' I replied eventually. 'And I think that's pretty much all I needed.'

## The middle of it

'Where do you think you'll be this time next year?' asked Donna.

'What kind of a question is that?'

'The kind of question I ask all the time,' smiled Donna. 'I think about the future all the time. Probably even more than the present. I never used to be like this. I think it must be something to do with having a kid because you always have to plan ahead – meal times, clothes to wear, everything. Now I love thinking about the future because it's a place where, until you arrive there, anything can happen.'

'I used to think about the future quite a bit when I was at college,' I replied. 'But you do when you're that sort of age don't you? You constantly feel like your whole life is ahead of you.'

'And now?'

'Now I'm in the middle of it. This, right now, this is life and most of the time I've got enough problems dealing with the now to think about anything else.' I paused and laughed. 'I sound like the king of doom.'

'That's because you're too bogged down in the daily struggle.'

'Okay,' I replied. 'So with all your thinking about the future, where do you think you'll be this time next year?'

*Mike Gayle*

'Somewhere out of London,' said Donna. 'I don't know where exactly. Maybe somewhere in the country, or near the sea. A few years ago my parents moved to Aberdovey in Wales. Where they live is only five minutes from the sea and it is absolutely amazing there. Sadie and I try to see them at least every other month and any time we go it's just like being on holiday. That's where I'd like to be if we could afford it.'

'And what about next year's holiday?' I asked mischievously. 'Any chance of you coming back here with Sadie?'

'You may laugh but she'd love it here,' said Donna. 'She'd be telling all of her friends how sophisticated she is.'

'So where then?'

'Do you know what? I haven't actually thought that much ahead. But if you pushed me for an answer I think I'd be happy going on holiday anywhere. Anywhere at all.'

## Let's go

'It's late,' said Donna, looking at her watch. 'Let's go but not home.'

'Another bar?'

Donna shook her head. 'I'm done with bars.'

'How about the beach?'

Donna's face lit up immediately. 'Definitely. I think it's the one thing I'll miss about this place when I've gone.' She stood up, finished off the remains of her drink and then took me by the hand.

'Let's go.'

# The two of us

It was just after two in the morning as Donna and I headed along the crowded strip in the direction of the beach while everyone else was heading in the opposite direction. It felt good swimming against the tide like this. As if it was the two of us against the world. Every step we took towards our destination seemed to bond us closer together just as every step the crowd took seemed to push them further away.

'Do these guys really think girls who look like that actually fancy them?' asked Donna as we watched with some amusement as a girl in a tight white vest and red sparkly hotpants waylaid a group of lads who looked as if they had only just this second turned eighteen.

'They're not completely stupid,' I explained. 'They're just willing participants in the fantasy.'

'You sound like you're talking from experience.'

'Lurking inside most men is a spotty prepubescent teenager who thinks he'll never get a girlfriend.'

'Even you?'

'Especially me.'

A gang of girls carrying glow-in-the-dark batons passed by, closely followed by a similar-sized gang of lads chanting (rather than singing) 'Happy Birthday'.

'So was that ever you?' I asked as one of the girls carrying

the glow-in-the-dark batons suddenly turned around and lifted up her skirt to flash the boys behind her.

'I wouldn't like to say.'

'So you've been on holidays like this before?'

'Full-on, all-girls-on-the-razz type resort holidays?'

I nodded.

'A few,' replied Donna coyly. 'The last one was about seven years ago. Some girls from nursing college and I went to Fuerteventura. We partied so much we inevitably all came back suffering with the symptoms of Fuerteventura 'flu: extreme exhaustion brought on by burning the candle at both ends for fourteen nights on the trot. It took me a good six months before I felt anything near back to normal and a year before I could look a Mai-Tai in the eye without feeling like I was going to throw up. My friends all went back the following year. I would've gone with them too but by then I'd got together with Ed, and the two of us went to Sardinia instead.'

'Was that a good holiday?'

Donna shrugged. 'It was okay, I suppose. We were young and in love and this was the first time that either of us had ever been away on a couple's holiday. When my friends came back from Fuerteventura and I heard about everything they'd got up to I remember feeling for a while like I'd missed out on something special. But when they all went back the year after I didn't have any regrets at all. It was definitely a case of been there, done that.'

'I met Sarah ten years ago here in Malia on an all-boys holiday with Andy and Tom,' I confessed.

'A holiday romance? I'd never have guessed that in a million years. I suppose because I've never done the holiday-romance thing myself.'

I was surprised. 'Not even when you went to Fuerteventura?'

'Not even when I went to Newquay with my parents when I was fifteen,' she replied. 'I don't know . . . I think I always thought they were a bit of a waste of time. My friends all had them and they never worked out. They'd fall massively in lust with some guy and a few weeks later when they were back at home and he hadn't phoned or called they'd be heartbroken.' Donna paused and smiled. 'Still, it worked for you. You must have been one of the good ones that kept the dream alive.'

Donna paused as we returned to the crossroads near McDonalds. There were quite a few cars on the road and no sign of a break in the traffic. As we waited, Donna squeezed my hand and smiled. A closeness was growing between us. And it didn't seem forced or even flirtatious. It seemed natural. As if the only logical place in the world for her hand to be was in my own.

## Typical Libran

As we passed by a late-night grocery shop a few hundred yards from the top of the beach Donna suggested that we stop and get a bottle of wine. Without waiting to hear my reaction she led me into the brightly lit store where a middle-aged woman with a sad face sat at the till, staring into space.

I followed Donna to the wine section where she asked my opinion about what kind of wine to get.

'Let's go for a mid-priced red and a cheap one for afters,' I suggested reaching for a merlot and a cheaper bottle of Rioja. I offered both bottles up for her approval.

'They'll do fine,' said Donna. 'I hate choosing which wine. If you'd left it up to me we would've been here for ages and then I would've spent all night thinking that you secretly hated my choices.'

'Ah,' I joked, 'so instead I'm the one who's got to spend all night worrying?'

'No,' said Donna squeezing my hand. 'Right now, my friend, I don't think you could do a single thing wrong if you tried.'

Along with the wine we bought some chocolate and Pringles in case we became hungry and then left the grocery store with the bottles clanging together in a blue plastic carrier bag. Within minutes we had left the road behind and were on the path down to the beach.

It was odd being at the beach so late at night. The moon was quite bright and in its light I could see the shadowy outlines of the sun-loungers and umbrellas packed away behind a fenced-off area. The rest of the beach was completely empty.

'Do you think I should call Nina and tell her where I am?' asked Donna.

'Definitely.'

Donna took off her sandals and walked barefoot across the sand until she was out of earshot but just about visible.

I don't know why but I suddenly felt like talking to someone too. I pulled out my phone and dialled Andy's number.

'Charlie?' he said, answering the phone after six or seven rings. 'What happened to you? One minute you've gone outside to talk to Lisa and the next you've vanished into thin air.'

'It's a long story,' I replied.

'To do with Lisa?'

'No, to do with Sarah.'

'Oh, right,' said Andy solemnly. 'Bad news?'

'You could say that.'

There was a long pause.

'So where are you now?'

'I'm with Donna down at the beach.'

'Donna who?'

'Nina's sister, Donna.'

Andy burst out laughing. 'You're a sly one. How did that happen?'

'I bumped into her. We got talking.' I paused basking in the glow of being momentarily enigmatic. 'That's pretty much it.'

'Never mind all that,' said Andy. 'Have you and her—?'

'No.'

'But you are going to—?'

'No.'

'What do you mean no? This is it, Charlie. This is your moment. Don't screw it up by being Mr Nice Guy okay?'

I sighed. Andy was draining my batteries down to nothing. 'Look,' I replied, 'I only called to say sorry for running out on you like that.' I looked across the sand in Donna's direction and she waved at me. 'I'll see you later, okay?'

'Yeah,' replied Andy chuckling. 'I will see you later. And you'd better be prepared to tell me everything.'

I pressed the end call button and slipped my phone into the back of my jeans just as Donna beckoned me towards her.

'I think I've just completely freaked my sister out,' said Donna gaily, as she grasped my hand. 'She can't believe that I've gone off with you like this. It's so funny. Normally I'm the one trying to stop her doing crazy stuff.'

'I was on the phone to Andy and I think I freaked him out too. Which is probably a good thing.'

'Well I've got some good news for you,' said Donna. 'You'll be pleased to know that my sister's friend Beth apparently fancies you something rotten.'

'I'll make a note of that for later,' I said laughing.

Hand in hand we walked across the beach until we were about twenty yards from the edge of the sea.

'How about here?' suggested Donna. 'We'll be able to see the water but won't be under threat from getting soaked by the waves.'

We sat down cross-legged on the sand and I proceeded to open the more expensive bottle of wine by pushing the

cork back into the bottle using the keys to the apartment.

'I think you should try it first,' I said, handing her the bottle. 'You can let me know if it's to your liking.'

Donna took a long swig and swallowed. 'It tastes fine to me; see what you think.' She handed the bottle back and I put it to my lips.

'Tastes pretty good to me too,' I replied.

For a few moments we sat lulled into a hypnotic silence by the waves breaking on the shore. I would have been content to stay like that much longer but Donna must have felt self-conscious because for no reason at all she asked me when my birthday was.

'Pardon?'

'Your birthday,' repeated Donna. 'When is it?'

'You're not going to ask me my star sign are you?' I asked warily.

'That's such a sexist thing to say. Not all women are obsessed with astrology. I'm just curious that's all.'

'Okay,' I replied. 'It's the first of June.'

'I knew it. A Gemini. That explains everything.' She paused and then admitted, 'I don't know anything about astrology. I only know you're a Gemini because an old boyfriend of mine used to be into it. He was forever trying to explain away my actions as being down to my star sign. In fact it got to the stage where I promised myself that if he ever said the phrase "Typical Libran", to my face again I was going to dump him. A minute after I made the decision he said it and I told him it was over that very second.'

'That's a bit harsh, isn't it?' I said leaning in closer to her face so that my lips were only inches away from her own.

'I don't think so at all.' She was smiling.

## Waves

I don't know how long we kissed. A minute. Maybe two.
In my head it seemed all too short although I suspect for
Donna it was just long enough for the conscious side of
her brain to gain control of the subconscious side.

'Is something wrong?' I asked as she pulled away.

Donna shook her head and leaned against my shoulder.
'There's nothing wrong. It's just me.' She reached across
and held my hand, carefully interlacing our fingers. 'Do
you mind if we just sit like this for a while and talk?'

'No,' I replied. 'That's fine.' And so pulling closer together,
we sat in silence, watching the waves crash in front of us,
wrapped in our own thoughts in our own worlds.

# Foot prints

'What time is it?' asked Donna sleepily.

'Just after six,' I said reluctantly removing my gaze from the hazy rising morning sun to my watch. 'How rock and roll are we staying up all night?'

'Not very.' Donna stretched her arms above her head and yawned. 'Right now I think I could easily sleep the whole day away.' She looked at me and smiled. 'Are you hungry?'

'Starving.'

'Shall we go and find somewhere to eat?'

'I know just the place,' I replied. 'You'll love it.'

We stood up, stretched our limbs, brushed the sand off our clothes and made our way hand in hand across the beach.

'Look,' said Donna. 'Are those our foot prints from last night?'

'Yeah,' I replied.

'It seems like such a long time ago since we made these,' said Donna. 'It's almost as if they were made by two different people.'

'But they weren't two different people,' I replied. I pointed to the ground. 'Look, there's your foot print and there's mine. Side by side going in the same direction.'

212

'And now we're going back,' sighed Donna. 'It almost makes me wish we could turn around and just keep going forwards until we fall off the edge.'

## Like infinity

The road near the beach was the quietest I'd ever seen it. No Brits, no club music and no quad bikes. The only signs of life were from delivery trucks dropping off supplies and tired-looking shop keepers opening up their stores. Stars and Bars, however, was a different story. Clusters of shattered-looking clubbers were scattered around the various tables as if it had somehow become the final port of call for Malia's more hardcore hedonists before they finally said goodbye to the night before.

Donna and I managed to find a table at the rear of the bar and ordered two of the 'Killer' English breakfasts along with two beers. Falling into an easy silence we were content to eavesdrop on the gang of student-looking types in front of us retelling the story of their night with all its attendant highs and lows. For the first time during the holiday I realised that I was no longer looking on with envy at their lives. I no longer wanted to be them at all. Finally I was happy being me.

'Why can't real life be like this all the time?' I asked as our waiter arrived at our table with our breakfasts.

'Do you really want a life where you're always out eating breakfast at six in the morning?' asked Donna laughing.

'No,' I replied, 'I mean why can't holidays last for ever?'

'Because then they'd stop being holidays and would start

being real life,' replied Donna. 'Holidays are holidays because they're a break from the norm.'

'When I was a kid I used to wonder if people who lived in Spain went on holiday,' I said squeezing a dollop of tomato ketchup on to my plate. 'If people like my next-door neighbours went on holiday to Majorca, then what did people who lived in Majorca do when it came to holiday time?'

'What answer did you come up with?'

'None,' I replied. 'I probably got distracted and accepted that it was just one of those weird conundrums that you're faced with in life – like infinity, or when time began. I must have come to the conclusion that it's probably easier to not think about things like that at all.'

'The head-in-the-sand philosophy?'

'Yeah,' I replied. 'But don't knock it if you haven't tried it.'

## So what now?

'I can barely keep my eyes open,' said Donna as the waiter came to take our empty plates away.

'We should probably think about going.' I looked up at our waiter and asked for the bill. A few moments later, he placed it in the middle of the table but before I could reach for it Donna snatched it up and passed it back to him along with a handful of notes.

'You didn't have to do that,' I said as we stood up.

'But I wanted to,' replied Donna.

'Okay, but next time breakfast is on me.'

It was just a throwaway comment. A joke and nothing more. But I could see from the look of worry that flashed across Donna's face that it carried more weight than I'd intended. How would there ever be a next time when Donna was leaving Malia for good?

'So what now?' We were standing outside the bar basking in the gentle warmth of the early-morning sun.

'This is really difficult for me, Charlie.' Donna took my hand.

'I know.' I changed the subject. 'What time do you leave?'

'I think the coach to the airport is supposed to arrive about nine. I'm going to get some sleep but why don't you come to my hotel about six and at least then we can maybe get something to eat.'

'I'll see you at six then.' Donna stepped towards me and I automatically put my arms around her and we kissed. It was different from our earlier kiss, though. More awkward and self-conscious.

'I'll see you later,' she said waving goodbye.

'Yeah,' I replied. 'I'll see you later.'

## Tell uncle Andy everything

'Go on, Tom. Poke him awake.'

'You poke him awake.'

'But you're closer.'

'And you're obviously more interested than I am.'

'I'm not that interested.'

'So wait until he wakes up then.'

'You're joking. He's been asleep ages as it is. I can't be hanging around here all day. I've got stuff to do.'

'Well, if you want him awake, by all means be my guest.'

'Okay, I'll do it myself but I think it's worth pointing out that there's no need for you to be such a—'

Andy stopped mid-sentence as I blinked open my eyes to see his unshaven face leering inches away from my own.

'Ah, so it lives,' he said smirking at me. 'Nice to see you're awake finally.'

'How could I not be with you two yelling over me like that?' I sat up and yawned. 'What time is it?'

'Ten past three.'

I immediately leapt out of bed and began throwing on clothes.

'What's the big rush?' asked Andy.

'I only meant to sleep a couple of hours,' I said as I struggled to pull on my shorts. 'I'm supposed to be meeting

218

up with Donna again at six and I've got a few things I need to sort out before that.'

'What kind of things?'

I shrugged. 'It doesn't matter what. Just stuff.'

Andy rolled his eyes in despair. 'This is so typical of you when it comes to girls. You were just the same at college: always pointlessly secretive about everything.'

'Look,' I said, grabbing a clean T-shirt from my suitcase, 'I'm not being secretive about anything. In fact I'm actually sort of keen to tell you both what happened last night because I could do with some advice.'

'At last.' Andy rubbed his hands together with mock glee. 'Tell your uncle Andy everything.'

Leaving out the contents of Lisa's call, I told Andy and Tom everything that had happened from the moment I'd met up with Donna right through to our breakfast at Stars and Bars.

'So that's it?' Andy looked at me with an odd mixture of amusement and disbelief. 'All you did was talk?'

'With the exception of the odd kiss, yes.'

'Well there's your problem right there.'

'I knew you wouldn't get it.'

'What's to get?' replied Andy. 'She's obviously not interested.'

'That's rubbish,' said Tom. 'She sounds to me like she is interested but just wants to take things slowly that's all.'

'So slowly that she's not even mentioned seeing him again?' said Andy shaking his head. 'No, mate, you're being blown out, but if you want my advice you're best off out of it anyway. With the kid and her ex and all the rest of the stuff she sounds like she's too high maintenance for you.'

'You couldn't be more wrong,' I replied.

'So if she's that great why didn't you bring the subject up yourself?'

I shrugged. 'Because the timing's so off. We missed the boat on being a "holiday thing" that turns into something more . . . and we're too early for anything else. The choice is either say nothing and risk losing her or say something and risk coming across like some kind of stalker.'

'She's just a girl,' said Andy. 'There'll be others.'

'You just don't get it do you?' I replied.

'Look,' said Andy, 'I'm only telling you this for your own good. You should've stayed with me last night and worked your magic with Hattie like I said. She was so desperate by the end of the night that she ended up pulling some kid in a Newcastle United top. That could've been you there with her. Instead, you were off having moonlit chats on the beach with some girl who may or may not be interested in you. You're thirty-five, Charlie, not fifteen. You should've grown out of this teen-angst melodrama years ago.' He tutted and then, more to himself than to me, added, 'And you wonder why Sarah left you.'

If I'd wanted to hear a pin drop on our tile flooring now would've been the time to do it. Though Tom looked shocked, I could tell Andy was the more horrified. In the past I had allowed him a certain amount of leeway with regard to the offensive and childish stuff he said to my face simply because we were friends, but this time he knew he had overstepped the mark.

'Look, mate—'

'Just go,' I said. 'Go before I say something we'll both regret.'

I could see him weighing up the situation. On the one

hand he didn't want to lose face in front of Tom, but on the other he knew that he had gone too far.

'I'll talk to you when you've calmed down a bit, yeah?' He picked up his rucksack from the floor, slung it over his shoulder and left the apartment.

'Tell me again why you're friends with him?' said Tom as Andy slammed the front door.

'Do you know what? You should give him a break sometimes. The reason Andy's an arsehole to the people who love him is the same reason we're all arseholes to people who love us . . . because it's only the ones who stick around when we haven't given them a reason to that are worth keeping.'

Tom grinned. 'So how are you today, you useless bag of crap?'

'Me? You fat tosser. I'm fine.' I paused and looked at Tom. I wanted to ask him about the cancer thing without actually talking about the cancer thing.

'Are you sure you're really okay?' I asked.

'I wouldn't say I'm great,' shrugged Tom, 'but I'm not down either. I'm sorting of hanging on in there with grim determination.' He flashed me the same look of examination that I'd given him. 'And how about you?'

'About the same.'

'Made a decision?'

I shook my head. 'And if that's not bad enough she's off in six hours.'

'So what are you going to do? Play it by ear?'

'No,' I replied. 'Right now I'm going to try to see if I can buy myself some more time.'

## I'll be fine by myself

The look of surprise on Donna's face when she spotted me pulling up in front of her hotel in a white Fiat Punto, spot on six o'clock, said it all.

'What's this?' she asked, peering over her Jackie O sunglasses as I wound down the window.

'It's a car,' I replied, 'new invention, great for getting from "a" to "b" with.'

'Okay,' said Donna, laughing. 'What I meant to say is . . . why are you driving it?'

'Tom hired it yesterday and put me down as a named driver,' I lied. 'I thought as you're leaving in a few hours it was pointless to let some surly coach driver have the pleasure of your company when I could have it all to myself.'

The disappointment in Donna's face couldn't have been more apparent. 'I don't know what to say,' she said.

'All I'm offering you is a lift to the airport,' I replied.

She didn't look convinced. 'I'm not sure,' she said, as though the mere thought of getting in a car with me was causing her much unneeded stress. 'I'll have to talk it over with my sister, okay?'

'Fine,' I replied tersely, 'you talk to your sister and I'll wait here.'

As Donna walked back across the road to her hotel I

wished that I hadn't bothered hiring the car. Despite my efforts to downplay my big romantic gesture, Donna had spotted the significance of it straight away and run a mile in the opposite direction. Rather than sweeping her off her feet, all I'd succeeded in doing was confirming her worst fears – that perhaps I wanted more than she was willing to give. I couldn't help but think that perhaps Andy had been right. Maybe I was acting like a lovesick teenager. Maybe I had blown my feelings completely out of proportion. Maybe I should've stayed with him last night and tried to pull one of Nina's friends after all.

I looked across the road. Donna was coming out of the main entrance, but much to my disappointment she didn't look any happier than when she'd disappeared inside five minutes earlier.

'So are you coming or not?' I asked brusquely.

Donna gave me a reluctant nod. 'But we can't be late for the check-in, Charlie . . . I really mean it.'

'Fine,' I replied, 'you tell me what time you want to be there and I'll get you there.'

'Ten at the latest.'

'Then ten it is.'

'I'd better go and get my luggage then.'

'I'll give you a hand.'

'There's no need,' said Donna coolly. 'I'll be fine by myself.'

## It's all in the past

'Are you going to tell me what's wrong?' I asked as we finally pulled up on an open piece of rough land near the harbour walls in Heraklion. 'You've barely said anything the whole journey.'

Donna had seemed wrapped up in her own thoughts and as I hadn't wanted to give her any more of an excuse never to see me again, much of our hour-long journey had been spent in silence. Occasionally she'd make a polite comment or two but then as soon as we'd batted the topic around for a while she would immediately fall back into silence. Even when we reached the outskirts of Heraklion and the roar of jet engines became so frequent that barely a minute passed by without hearing one screeching overhead she said little. Instead she stared out of the car window while the roar of every engine made me increasingly aware of just how little time I had left with Donna.

'I know I've been quiet,' said Donna. 'I'm sorry.'

'Is it me?' I asked dreading the answer. 'Have I done something wrong?'

'No.' She touched my hand. 'It's all me. I've got a lot of things on my mind.'

'Can we talk about it?'

Donna shook her head. 'I think it's probably too late for

224

that, but it's no excuse for me being such a misery though. I feel I'm spoiling everything.' She ran her hands over her face as though trying to wake herself up from a dream. 'Thanks for doing this, Charlie,' she said, turning towards me. 'I know it's only been a short time but you really have made this holiday special.'

We climbed out of the car, bought a parking ticket and made our way towards the restaurant I'd discovered in Tom's *Rough Guide*. Donna seemed brighter. She was more talkative, and making jokes and seemed much more like the person I'd got to know the night before.

The restaurant was right next to the harbour wall. There were scores of tables set up underneath a canopy and we were shown to one that the waiter assured us had the best view of the harbour. Instead of sitting opposite each other we sat side by side so that we could watch the same sun set that we had seen rise.

We left the restaurant after an hour, having shared every-thing from home-made tatziki to fried Mako shark and made our way back to the car hand in hand. The silence had a different quality now. Less gloomy and more hopeful – as if we'd stopped speaking because there were too many things to say rather than too few.

'Last night and this afternoon have been really special,' Donna said, as we reached the car. 'I don't know the last time I spent this much time in someone else's company . . . not since . . . well you know. Anyway, I just want to say thanks.' She reached up towards me, wrapped her arms around my neck and then placed her lips on top of my own. We kissed the sort of long slow kiss that had the ability to transport me right back to the night before.

'I think it might be time to go,' said Donna, once the kiss had ended.

'Yeah, you're probably right.'

## I've forgotten my sunglasses

Our time was over. The day had come to an end. And Donna was heading home. But the big question, in my mind at least, was had I succeeded in making Donna want to commit to seeing me again? As we pulled into the car park at Heraklion airport and I looked across at her I couldn't help but feel like the answer to the question was a resounding yes. Surely, I told myself, she had to be feeling what I was feeling?

Still, as we climbed out of the car into the still-baking heat and unloaded Donna's luggage on to the tarmac, I made up my mind that if all really was fair in love and war, then now would be the right time to pitch one last all-out assault. Timing, I reasoned, was everything and fortunately for me I had been dealt the perfect hand: a 'departure gate goodbye'. I prepared the speech in my head: stuff about her being 'special', our need to 'overcome obstacles' and 'how we could make it work if we really wanted to'. It was all made for this moment. Victory was assured.

'I've forgotten my sunglasses,' said Donna, when we were only a few metres away from the entrance to the departure lounge. 'I must have left them in the car.'

'Carry on and check in,' I replied, 'I'll go back and get them.'

'I couldn't ask you to do that,' said Donna. 'You've done enough already. I'll go myself.'

'No problem,' I replied, handing her the keys to the car. 'I'll just wait here for you.'

Sitting on the kerb outside the entrance to the airport with her suitcase and bags by my side, I watched her until she disappeared behind a row of cars. She was gone longer than I expected but soon returned wearing her beloved Jackie O sunglasses.

As we entered the airport we went in search of Nina and her friends amongst the hundreds of British holidaymakers who were heading back home. Each one of them, standing in line at the various check-in desks, was dressed as though they thought that the warm weather of Crete would stay with them forever. My mind flicked back to the tanned and T-shirted hordes I'd seen arriving at Gatwick in the rain – people stuck so solidly in their holiday state of mind that they had forgotten that any climate existed other than the one they had left behind.

'Won't you be a bit cold when you reach England?' I asked, as we studied the departure board to find her check-in desk.

'I put a warmish jumper in Nina's bag before I left,' said Donna who herself was wearing a long skirt, a sleeveless top and flip-flops. 'She'll have it with her now.'

'Right now I wish I was wearing a jacket so I could do the gentlemanly thing and give it to you.'

Donna opened her mouth to reply when a voice yelled her name from across the hall. We both turned round to see Nina waving at us frantically from the front of the furthest check-in desk from where we were standing. Dragging her suitcase behind her Donna rushed over to join them. Nina and her friends all huddled around her immediately, while some threw a bemused glance in my direction.

Once the girls were all checked in they collected themselves together at the side of the queue while Donna made her way back to me.

'Everything okay?' I asked.

'Yeah, fine,' said Donna. 'Nina and the girls are going to meet me on the other side of passport control in a minute or two but I'm just going to the loo first.'

There was something about her face when she spoke to me that didn't seem right. I let it go, reasoning that perhaps this was a good sign: that she was finding it as difficult to leave me as I was finding it to accept that she was going. At this rate, I told myself, our departure gate good-bye could be nothing short of a resounding success.

After about five minutes or so with no sign of Donna's return I became uneasy, so I headed towards the ladies' toilets in search of her. When she failed to emerge after a further five minutes I began to be convinced that something was wrong. Aware that I was once again possibly going too far I approached a couple of English girls on a flight bound for Manchester and asked if they could check the toilets for any sign of Donna. When they emerged a minute later without her, a real panic set in and I searched the whole of the airport frantically, even briefly considering contacting the airport's security. In the end I decided that the best thing to do would be to return to the spot where we had parted and wait. And there I remained for over an hour before I finally accepted that she had gone.

With Donna still occupying my every thought, I made my way back to my hire car. As I opened the car door a folded sheet of paper on the driver's seat fluttered down into the footwell. I reached down and opened it up:

*I know you'll think this was the coward's way out and you're probably right. And I know you probably hate me right now. But the truth is I just can't think of any other way of saying goodbye that won't make things more complicated than they are (and believe me they are complicated enough already). I'm sorry for everything, Charlie. I really am.*

*Donna xxx*

With my heart still racing, I started up the car and wound down the window. A warm gust of night air caused Donna's letter to flutter on the dashboard. I read it one last time, as though saying a final goodbye to both her and the notion that there was any fairness in the world. Nice guys did finish last. Sarah had taught me that and now Donna had rammed the point home.

I told myself that I was tired of being a doormat to the world at large. From now on I was going to switch off my brain and act on instinct. I wasn't going to agonise over every decision or wallow in the past. In short I was going to take a leaf out of Andy's book and start putting myself first.

And so as I tore up Donna's letter into a fistful of confetti, dropped the pieces out of the window and watched them flutter to the ground, there was no doubt in my mind that it was the right thing to do.

# DAY FIVE:
# FRIDAY

DAY FIVE:
FRIDAY

## Why break the habit of the holiday?

I cracked open my eyes. The bedroom was still shrouded in darkness although chinks of light coming through the curtains indicated that morning had broken. I sat up in bed and two things happened: first, the covers slipped down my body resulting in legions of tiny goosebumps springing to life as my skin came in contact with the arctic air. Secondly I was temporarily overwhelmed by a sudden feeling of biliousness that had me racing to the bathroom. I wasn't sick but I wished I had been because then at least the nausea currently gripping me might have gone away. Instead it stayed with me, clinging tightly to the pit of my stomach with a fist of iron.

As I left the bathroom I looked over at Andy's bed. Although it was empty it had clearly been slept in. I carefully opened the kitchen door. Tom's bed was empty too. I opened the fridge, pulled out a bottle of water and attempted to rehydrate myself. It was just after midday.

I threw on some clean clothes and then looked around the room for inspiration as to what to do next. I spotted *The Da Vinci Code* on my bedside table and decided to read for a while. Picking up the book along with my sunglasses I drew back the curtains over the patio doors to reveal Tom lounging in one of the white plastic chairs with his feet up on the balcony. In one hand was his

beloved *Rough Guide* and in the other a cigarette. What was strange about this scene was that Tom didn't smoke and never had done.

'All right?' I said as I opened the patio doors and stepped out into the midday sun. I stared pointedly at Tom's cigarette. 'Anything you'd like to tell me?'

'I'm experimenting.' He paused and inhaled heavily, then slowly expelled the smoke from between his lips. 'I found them on the table,' he said, holding up a pack of Andy's Benson and Hedges. 'I was sitting here looking at them and I thought to myself: if I have actually got cancer then at least the cells that are screwing me up will be too busy attacking my bladder to worry about my lungs.'

'And what if it's something else?' I asked.

'Well, if it is and I've gone through all this for nothing,' Tom plucked the cigarette from his lips, 'then I think the very least I deserve is a cigarette.'

I sat down next to Tom, slipped on my sunglasses and squinted at the sky. 'So – fledgling cigarette habits notwithstanding – how are you this bright and sunny afternoon?'

'I feel like crap,' said Tom. 'Which is I'm guessing how you must feel too.'

'I feel like I'm dead from the neck downwards,' I groaned. 'Any chance you could take me through the details of last night because some of them are more than a bit foggy?'

'I think it started when you came back to the apartment after your evening with Donna and didn't speak for ages,' began Tom. 'I asked you what was wrong and you said that you didn't want to talk about it. So then I suggested that we go for a drink because I was sick of thinking about this cancer thing and you said, "Good idea let's do it." Nine bars,

roughly six hours and many, many, many drinks later we crashed out here.'

'Was Andy with us? I don't seem to remember much about him last night at all.'

'Bizarrely, he chose to stay in,' said Tom. 'Something about wanting to catch up on his sleep.'

'So where is he now?'

Tom shrugged and lit another one of Andy's cigarettes. 'When I was in bed this morning I heard the door open. I assumed it was Andy either coming in or going out but I don't know any more than that.' Tom stubbed out his cigarette. 'That's me done with smoking for now,' he said cheerfully. 'Maybe I'll see what other vices I can succumb to before the holiday's out.' He stood up and picked up his book. 'Hungry?'

'Starving.'

'Stars and Bars?'

'Of course,' I replied. 'Why break the habit of the holiday?'

# The substance of things hoped for

'So,' said Tom, as the waiter brought our 'killer' breakfast and lager combo, 'I think we've now skirted round enough diverse topics for me to ask the billion dollar question.'

'Me and Donna?' I replied. 'It was a disaster. A near-perfect disaster.'

'You told her how you felt and she turned you down?'

'Worse than that,' I replied. 'Much worse. I hired a car, took her out for dinner and then to the airport, only to have her do a runner when my back was turned.'

'You're kidding me,' said Tom looking gratifyingly outraged.

'I wish I was,' I replied. 'Now come on, what she did was a bit harsh wasn't it? Women always talk about how men hate confrontation and will do anything to avoid it . . . but if what Donna did wasn't avoiding confrontation I don't know what is.'

'Obviously I'm not taking her side or anything,' said Tom cautiously, 'but I can't imagine that she did it for a laugh. It must have been hard for her. It's not like it's that long since her kid's dad left her is it? Maybe she's a bit gun shy.'

'Gun shy?' I replied. 'I'll tell you who should be gun shy – me. I found out the night before last that Sarah's pregnant.'

Tom was stunned. 'I don't know what to say.'

'There's nothing *to* say,' I replied, 'other than that I know

for a fact that it's not mine.' Suddenly I didn't feel quite so hungry any more and so I pushed my breakfast plate away to one side. 'I really loved her you know.'

'I know you did,' replied Tom quietly.

'So how could she do this to me after being together so long? A whole decade, Tom. Surely that has to count for something?'

Tom looked on blankly.

'Right now,' I continued, 'I feel like the only thing that has any real substance is the moment you're in right now. That's what Andy thinks, doesn't he? He lives in the moment and that's all he believes in.'

'And look where that's got him,' said Tom. 'He's no happier because of it. He just spends his life chasing something that he's never going to get. I know it's difficult for you right now but you can't always think the worst will happen. Sometimes you've got to have a bit of faith that everything will work out in the end.'

'Faith?'

'The substance of things hoped for.'

'How can I have faith when everyone always lets me down?' I replied. 'How can I have faith in anyone when I haven't got any in myself?'

'Maybe believing in yourself is the best place to start,' said Tom.

'Maybe,' I replied, glancing over at my plate in the hope that my appetite might return sometime soon. 'Then again, maybe not.' My appetite was nowhere to be seen, so instead I took a long sip of my lager and changed the topic of conversation. 'What do you think Andy's up to then?' I asked. 'I've got a bad feeling that he's up to something.'

'Maybe he went out last night after all and hooked up

with some new girl,' suggested Tom. 'You never really know with Andy do you?' Tom paused and looked at me. 'Anyway, why all the curiosity about Andy?'

'I don't know,' I shrugged, 'I guess I'm tired of being annoyed at him.'

Tom smiled. 'Do you remember that time the two of you fell out after you had a go at him for bouncing a cheque on you for his share of the rent for the third time in a row? He didn't talk to you for days.'

'How could I forget it? I was the one out of pocket and yet he was the one who went around slamming doors like it had just gone out of fashion.' I contemplated my drink absent-mindedly. 'You don't really think Andy's with another girl do you?'

'Like I said, with Andy anything's possible, isn't it?'

'Don't ask me why but I kind of get the feeling that he's not going to do it again. I mean, why would he? This thing with him and Nina was about proving to himself that he'd still got it. There wouldn't be anything to be gained by doing it again.'

'I'd agree with you,' replied Tom, 'if Andy was a subscriber to regular logic. But he isn't, is he? He just makes this stuff up as he goes along. Who knows how his mind works? Maybe he wants to get caught out? Maybe he thinks it'll be easier if Lisa dumps him than the other way round. All I know is that there's always been something in Andy that just seems . . . I don't know . . . unhappy. You must have noticed it too.'

'It'd be hard to miss,' I replied.

'Do you think he'll ever get over whatever it is he's got to get over?'

'I hope so for his sake,' I replied. 'I really do.'

Tom finished his breakfast and I ordered another beer. Leaving Stars and Bars just after one-thirty, we headed back to the Apollo stopping off at a mini-market to stock up on bottled water, beer and assorted crisps and confectionery. As we reached the lobby we noticed that there were about half a dozen guys scattered around the sofas by the pool table watching the highlights of a football match on the widescreen TV and we joined them for five minutes or so and bonded briefly over a discussion of England's performance in a friendly match earlier in the week. Eventually we left our new friends to their football highlights and made our way up the stairs to our apartment where we were surprised to discover that the door was open – either our room was being cleaned or Andy was back. My gut instinct told me to go with the Andy option.

I still hadn't quite managed to work out how I was going to behave with Andy following our argument the day before. Part of me wanted to continue being annoyed at him because he deserved it, but the rest of me knew that maintaining any kind of frostiness would end up being too much like hard work in the face of his constant effervescence. In the end I decided that I would go with the first emotion that sprang to mind.

Tom and I unloaded our bags on to the kitchen table and then made our way through to the bedroom. When I saw Andy, the first emotion that registered on my internal radar was complete and utter shock and surprise. My mind shot back to Tom's comment that 'with Andy anything's possible' and I suddenly realised just how was right he was, because standing next to Andy in a vest, a denim skirt and flip-flops – looking for all the world as though she was on her way out to the beach for the day – was Lisa.

## Could you just rub some on my back, babe?

Andy couldn't have looked more pleased with himself if he'd won the national lottery. 'All right, boys?' he announced cheerfully as we looked on slack-jawed. 'Don't just stand there staring like a pair of idiots. What sort of welcome is that to give a lady?'

'Oh, Andy,' said Lisa, as the penny dropped. 'How could you not tell them I was coming?'

'What fun would there be in that?'

'But you promised me you'd clear it with them first. No wonder they're looking at me like I'm some kind of freak. I'm really sorry about this, guys. I'd understand completely if you wanted me to stay somewhere else.'

'We're absolutely fine with you staying here,' I said finally getting my mouth into gear. 'It's just that . . . well . . . we're a bit surprised to see you that's all. Don't take this the wrong way but . . . what *are* you doing here?'

'Yesterday morning Andy called me up out of the blue and told me he was missing me so much that he'd bought me a cheap flight to Crete over the internet,' explained Lisa, still glowering at Andy. 'One call into work faking food poisoning and an early morning trip into Gatwick and here I am.'

I had to give Andy the credit that was due him. Inviting Lisa over to Crete was a masterstroke of strategic thinking

on his part. The perfect win/win scenario. He'd had his fun during the first part of the week and now at a stroke he'd allayed her fears and banked himself a tonne of perfect-boyfriend points in the bargain. It was genius really. Utter genius. And I probably would've given him a standing ovation had his actions not made me feel like the lowest of the low. How did he think he could pull off such barefaced deceit without being crippled by guilt? He obviously didn't know the meaning of the word. But I did, and thanks to him I felt forced to take on the burden of his guilt for cheating on her as well as my own for hiding the fact from her.

'It doesn't matter how you got here,' I said, squeezing Lisa in my arms. 'It's great anyway.'

'That's really nice of you,' said Lisa. 'Even if you don't actually mean it. I know this was meant to be a bit of a boys' holiday and now here I am messing things up. I promise you I'll do my best not to cramp your style.'

'Look, Lisa,' said Tom grinning, as he too greeted her with a hug, 'we've been about as rock and roll as a bunch of old age pensioners. Your presence can only improve matters, believe me.'

'Right then,' said Andy as if he hadn't got a care in the world. 'Who's coming down the beach?'

'That sounds great.' Tom exchanged glances with me warily. 'I could do with a day in the sun.'

'Me too,' I replied acknowledging Tom's look. 'It'll give me a chance to catch up with my reading.'

As we made our way down to the beach there was a certain amount of tension between us. Lisa was obviously conscious of having gate-crashed our holiday. Tom seemed on edge because despite not wanting to get involved he

had now been covertly sucked into keeping Andy's secret from Lisa. And I was anxious because not only had it been me who had promised to keep Andy on the straight and narrow and failed to do so, but in addition I had my own private source of tension with Lisa due to our last conversation on the phone. The only one of us who seemed to be anywhere near relaxed was Andy.

Because of all this apprehension, we all made an effort to talk as a group rather than splitting off into our natural pairings. But the route to the beach was so busy that it was impossible to walk along four abreast. At one point near Stars and Bars, the pavement got so crowded that Tom and Andy broke off and I found myself walking a few paces alone next to Lisa. As I didn't want to talk to her about my mission with Andy, or indeed about Sarah's pregnancy, as she opened her mouth to speak I started fake frantic coughing while carefully speeding up my pace to join the others. When it happened again a few yards later, I was forced to pretend that I had a stone in my sandal. And a few yards after that my solution was to get in first with conversational topics that couldn't be construed as personal. And while these were possibly the least subtle methods I could have chosen to keep Lisa at arm's length – bar my obtaining a loudhailer and yelling the words 'Don't come any further!' – they did at least do the job.

As usual the beach was heavily congested with young sun-worshippers. But whereas before the three of us had felt like intruders into a world of youth and beauty, with Lisa in our midst I felt as though we now had as much right to be there as anyone else. Although at thirty-one Lisa was probably one of the oldest – if not the oldest – women on the beach, she easily looked five years younger

and had the body to prove it. So suddenly we were no longer just a bunch of sad thirtysomething blokes spending the whole day with their noses pressed up against the sweet-shop window, instead we were three thirtysomething blokes who had a three-in-one chance of being mistaken for Lisa's boyfriend. I couldn't have asked for more. And as the three of us trooped across the sand towards the sun-loungers, I could see gangs of younger guys straining to get a better look at Lisa's magnificent figure. It really was all I could do not to turn round to them with their sinewy bodies, their perfect tans and stupidly youthful hair-cuts and kick sand in their faces.

Gathering together four spare sun-loungers, we set up camp for the afternoon. Andy lay down on his lounger first and then Lisa lay down next to him. At this point Tom looked at Lisa and then at me as if to say, 'You know her better than me,' and so I stepped forward to take the lounger next to her and Tom tucked himself on at the end.

'This is fantastic,' said Lisa, as she undressed down to her bikini. 'I wish Andy had invited me to come earlier.'

'I know what you mean,' I replied eyeing my best friend's girlfriend's perfect bikini-clad figure from behind the privacy of my sunglasses and then immediately wishing I hadn't. I closed my eyes and tried to delete the image from my retinas.

'Charlie's only saying that because you're here now,' said Andy mischievously. 'Secretly he's really enjoyed being one of the lads this week. Isn't that right, Tom?'

'Hmm,' said Tom who was already engaged as usual with his *Rough Guide*. 'Definitely, mate.'

'Has he managed to pull any "birds" while you've been here?' asked Lisa pouring a small amount of sun lotion into the palm of her hands.

'Was that your attempt at being one of the boys?' laughed Andy.

'Don't you call girls "birds" any more?' asked Lisa as she began to rub the lotion into her arms. 'I know it's a long time ago but I quite liked being a "bird" when I was young free and single.'

'You're still a "bird" to me,' said Andy. 'Isn't that right, Charlie? Lisa's still got "bird" status, hasn't she?'

'Yeah, of course,' I said wincing as I covertly watched Lisa rubbing suntan lotion into her thighs. 'She's a "bird", all the way.'

'Thanks, guys,' said Lisa. 'That's just what I needed to hear.' She turned to Andy and handed him the suntan lotion. 'Could you just rub some on my back, babe?'

'No problem,' replied Andy as Lisa lay down on her front and deftly untied her bikini top to reveal the full allure of her naked back.

'So, Charlie,' said Lisa as Andy straddled her back and began to massage the lotion into her shoulder blades. 'What's the talent been like?'

'What are you asking him for?'

'Because he's the only one of you that's legally licensed to check out the women here,' grinned Lisa. 'Come on, Charlie, remember I'm "one of the boys", now. You can tell me anything.'

'It's been . . . all right,' I replied.

'The man's on fire, actually,' interrupted Andy who was now massaging the middle of Lisa's back. 'He managed to pull at the airport before we'd even collected our bags.'

'He's exaggerating,' I replied. 'All that happened was that a girl came up to me while we were waiting for our bags . . . she said she wanted to meet up in some bar. It must

have been a practical joke or something because she didn't turn up . . . it's all a bit embarrassing, really.'

'Rubbish,' said Andy. 'She definitely fancied him. She had a look in her eyes like she really wanted a morsel of Mansell. I think something must have happened to stop her coming that night.'

'Was she nice?' asked Lisa.

'Gorgeous,' said Andy, working the sun lotion into Lisa's lower back. 'Like a young Naomi Campbell.'

'Wow,' said Lisa. 'A babe like that could be just the thing you need, Charlie. Maybe we'll bump into her tonight. Talking of which, what exactly have we got planned for tonight?'

I shrugged and passed the question over to Tom in a bid to distract myself from Lisa's glistening back.

'What do you reckon, Tom?'

'My vote is somewhere quiet,' he replied. 'I don't mind having a big night out tomorrow but after last night I could do with taking it easy.'

'This is what I've been up against all holiday,' said Andy climbing off Lisa's back. 'Some people wouldn't know a good time if it bit them on the backside.'

'Actually I think Tom's right,' said Lisa struggling to retie her bikini top. 'Maybe we should save ourselves for the last night and have a big blow-out then? Tonight we could go out for a nice meal and then maybe have a bit of a drink and a chat on the balcony when we get back. It's nice out there.'

'Sounds okay to me,' said Tom.

'I suppose that's all right,' added Andy, 'as long as we're definitely going out tomorrow.'

Lisa turned and looked at me expectantly. 'What do you think, Charlie?'

'Sounds like a great idea,' I replied even though I was already beginning to get the feeling that this quiet night out might turn out to be more eventful than we'd bargained for – Lisa was an unknown quantity in what was already a pretty volatile mix. 'Count me in for sure.'

## Mine has a little extra kick!

It was now just after ten in the evening and we were all sitting at a table on the vine-covered terrace of Taverna Stefanos. The taverna was tucked away in the older part of Malia, far enough from the hectic pace of the main strip to imagine that we might be somewhere rural. Much of the tension from earlier in the day now seemed to have evaporated. Tom was talking to Andy. Andy was talking to me. And I was even talking to Lisa. Everybody seemed to be getting on and the meal, the wine and the entertainment (halfway through our second course a couple of bouzouki players dressed in traditional Greek costumes emerged from the rear of the restaurant) seemed to bind us all closer.

'Now that was a fantastic meal,' said Tom to Georgiou, the owner, as he brought our bill. 'We'd be back in a shot if tomorrow wasn't our last night.'

'Well if you were to bring this lovely lady back with you tomorrow night,' grinned Georgiou, 'you might get yourself a free bottle of wine.' He paused and gave Lisa a cheeky wink. 'What do you say?

'It's tempting,' said Lisa, allowing Georgiou, who had complimented her on both her beauty and her dress sense at regular points throughout the meal, to steal a kiss on the cheek. 'We'll have to see.'

I couldn't blame Georgiou – a middle-aged father of three – for trying it on with Lisa as she was absolutely stunning in her black backless dress. Sitting with the three of us at the table she was the perfect definition of a rose amongst thorns.

'I feel I have died and gone to heaven,' said Georgiou swooning theatrically from Lisa's kiss. 'To which one of you lucky men does this stunning lady belong?'

'This is my boyfriend,' said Lisa, pointing to Andy. 'And these two handsome gents are just friends.'

'Well, my friend,' said Georgiou in a mock whisper as he leaned in towards a clearly embarrassed Andy, 'I hope you know that you are a very lucky man.'

We piled up a small mountain of Euros in the middle of the table to cover the bill and as Georgiou was about to sweep the cash away, Andy asked if there were any chance that we could buy a bottle of raki from him to take away. Georgiou immediately called for one of his waitresses to get a bottle.

'I make it myself,' said Georgiou as she returned with a plastic litre bottle of the clear liquid. 'I make the best raki on the island.' He thumped the table dramatically. 'Mine has a little extra kick!'

'That's good to hear,' said Andy. 'A little extra kick is just what we all need.'

We thanked Georgiou for the meal and then slowly made our way out of the taverna to the quiet street outside.

'What have you bought that rot-gut for?' asked Tom as we made our way through the winding back streets. 'We've still got some beer back at the apartment.'

'I'm not touching a drop of that stuff,' I said, adding my weight to Tom's objections. 'That stuff is lethal.'

'Will you two stop acting like old ladies?' said Andy. 'This stuff is brilliant.'

'What is it?' asked Lisa taking the bottle from Andy's hands to examine it closely.

'Have you ever had ouzo?' asked Tom.

'Not since I was seventeen and my parents went away for the weekend,' replied Lisa. 'A couple of friends came over to keep me company and things got a bit out of hand. We ended up dumping a whole bottle of ouzo that my parents had brought back from a holiday in Athens into the remains of a two-litre bottle of Coke and split it four ways.' Lisa shook her head in shame. 'Before long some boys got invited round, my friend Katie ended up getting a huge love bite from a boy called Kevin and we all ended up in my parents' bathroom taking it in turns to be sick.'

'Well,' said Tom laughing, 'it's just like that . . . only stronger.'

Lisa looked at Andy. 'Do we really have to do this?'

'Of course we do,' he replied. 'It's a rite of passage. You know as well as I do that every holiday needs a good hangover story.'

'Like you haven't got enough already,' sighed Lisa. 'Fine. Count me in. Only because I don't want you moaning that I spoilt things by not getting into the mood. But when you wake up in the morning with a screaming headache don't come running to me.' Shaking her head in disapproval, Lisa joined Tom who was walking slightly ahead of the group. She looped her arm through his and started asking him lots of questions about his kids, which forced Andy and me into walking together. Neither of us spoke for quite a long time but as we paused waiting to cross a road Andy eventually broke the silence.

'Listen, mate,' he began, 'I'm sorry about yesterday. What I said was absolutely out of order.'

'It's okay,' I replied. 'It's no big deal.'

'So we're all right, then?'

'Yeah . . . we're all right.'

There was another silence.

'So, did you always know you were going to bring Lisa out here?'

'Yeah,' replied Andy. 'Pretty much so.'

'So this holiday was never about me?'

'Of course it was about you. But it was about me too.'

'And you don't feel guilty?'

'About Lisa?'

'Of course about Lisa.'

Andy shrugged. 'I don't think about it.'

'I guess that's the big difference between you and me.'

Andy checked that Lisa and Tom were out of earshot.

'Nina called me today,' he began quietly. 'Said she wants to carry on seeing me when I get home.'

'You've said no though, haven't you?'

Andy shook his head. 'It's difficult.'

'What's difficult?'

'I think I might want to see her again.'

'What about all that stuff you said to me yesterday?'

'I think that was more for my benefit than yours.'

There was another long silence.

'Being with Nina . . . it makes me feel like I'm alive again.'

'So what about Lisa?'

'I need her too,' said Andy. 'Like I said, it's difficult.'

'Look,' I said pointing to Lisa and Tom up ahead. 'Just look. That beautiful woman there is your girlfriend. And

more than that she loves you. Why would you want to risk losing all that?'

'I wouldn't be risking anything,' said Andy evenly. 'She'd never find out. All Nina's suggesting is that we meet up once in while.'

'You'll get caught.'

Andy shook his head. 'No we won't,' he said confidently. 'I've thought it through.'

'People who cheat always get caught,' I replied. 'It's a fundamental law of the universe. You take one risk, and then you take another and another until you've convinced yourself that you're invincible. Then one day you'll take a risk too far . . . or you'll get careless . . . or you'll end up hating Lisa so much for not catching you out that you won't care if she finds out . . . but whichever way it happens, the truth will come out because it always does. Just like it did with me and Sarah.'

Andy stopped and looked at me. 'I thought you said you only found out when Sarah left you.'

'That wasn't true,' I replied. 'I lied to you because I didn't want to look stupid. But the truth was I knew Sarah was cheating on me long before she left.'

'How?'

'I went through her things one morning after she left for work. I went through everything – her bags, clothes, underwear, diary – even her computer. I was trying to find evidence that might explain why she had changed so much in the past few months. I felt terrible. I really did. It felt like a real intrusion. Until I found something. It was a letter from him folded inside an empty compact in her make-up bag. It had all the stuff you'd expect. And it was quite obviously not the first letter of its type either. So I had to

ask myself what was so special about this one? I read it and reread it a million times and I couldn't work out why she'd kept it when she'd obviously disposed of the earlier ones. And then it hit me . . . she'd kept it because the thought of destroying the letter upset her more than the idea that I might find it. That's when I knew that it wouldn't be long until she left me.'

'So, why didn't you say something?' said Andy. 'You shouldn't have let her walk all over you like that.'

I could've predicted Andy's reaction down to the letter. He didn't understand because he couldn't understand. And he couldn't understand because he'd never been in love.

'I didn't say anything because I knew that would mean she would leave me sooner rather than later. So I put all of her stuff back exactly where I'd found it and carried on as if nothing had happened. A month later she left me anyway. And do you know what? I don't regret not confronting her about it for a second because the thing you won't understand – I don't think you *can* understand – is this: when you love someone and you find yourself living on borrowed time, you're just too grateful for every last moment you get to worry about anything else.'

## Good friends

When we finally reached the apartment, the first thing Andy did was raid the kitchen cupboard in search of receptacles for the raki. Failing to find any shot glasses he chose to improvise and brought four white 'I ♥ Crete' mugs out to the balcony. Carefully pouring a double shot's worth of raki into each mug, Andy distributed them out amongst us and then on his cue we raised our mugs in the air and simultaneously knocked back our shots in one. Our reactions were instant: Andy's eyes began to water, Lisa and I coughed so violently I thought we might choke and Tom gritted his teeth like a tough TV detective and immediately poured himself another glass.

That first drink marked something of a watershed for the four of us. It was as if we had unanimously decided to give our minds a night off from our various individual troubles and just have fun. And with each shot of raki we consumed, having fun seemed to become a lot easier. Encouraged by Lisa, Andy, Tom and I wheeled out all our old favourite stories from the past. Everything from how we'd met during our first week at college, through our post-college years right up to and including the 'edited' highlights of our first night out in Malia only a few days earlier. Anyone watching this scene would have immediately assumed we were not just friends, but good friends. People who cared about each other. People who loved each other.

## The night is still young

It was just before midnight and we'd been drinking, smoking and talking for well over an hour. Andy was sitting on one of the patio chairs with Lisa lodged on his lap, Tom was sitting on the other chair with his bare feet propped on Lisa's lap, and I was sitting cross-legged on the table looking round at my friends and grinning like an idiot. This was one of those moments that I wished would last for ever. It was the kind of moment that makes a holiday feel like a holiday.

'Never let it be said that I won't admit when I'm wrong,' I said drunkenly to Andy. 'You were absolutely right about the raki, mate. This stuff is spot on.'

'You're telling me,' said Andy. 'For the past half an hour I've been shocked by just how entertaining Tom can be when he's drunk too much.'

Tom raised his mug. 'And with every double shot of raki, Andy, you somehow become a lot less obnoxious.' Tom then walked over to me and gave me a drunken squeeze. 'I'm off to bed,' he announced. And after proceeding to embrace both Lisa and Andy, he slid back the patio doors and disappeared inside.

'And then there were three,' said Andy sharing out the last of the raki.

'How can we have drunk a whole bottle already?' said

Lisa staring disappointedly into the bottom of her mug.

'Maybe it's a sign that we should call it a night,' I said conscious of the fact that this was the second night in a row that I had drunk too much. 'Maybe we should quit while we're ahead.'

'There'll be no talk of quitting,' said Andy. 'The night is still young. Don't worry, for the greater good I'll nip out and get some raki and fags, too, as we seem to be running low on B&H. I won't be long . . . half an hour.'

'No, mate, don't,' I pleaded as I realised that with more raki in the apartment there would be little chance of any of us getting to bed before dawn.

'Too late,' said Andy, standing up, 'I'll be back before you know it.'

Through my raki-addled brain I did a quick calculation: one Tom (already in bed) minus Andy (to get raki and fags) plus me and Lisa would equal an opportunity for an uncomfortable conversation (or two). I did not want this to happen, especially as the alcohol had already done a pretty good job of loosening my tongue. 'I'll come with you,' I said, struggling to my feet. 'Keep you company.'

'Charlie Mansell!' screamed Lisa in mock outrage. 'Anyone would think you're scared to be left alone with me.'

'I'm not scared of anything,' I lied. 'I just fancied a walk that's all. You could come with us if you want.'

'No way,' exclaimed Lisa. 'It's hard enough walking in my heels when I'm sober, let alone in this state. Nope, I'm staying here and you're staying too.'

'You stay,' said Andy. 'I'll be back in a bit.' He patted his pockets as if looking for something. 'Have you seen my keys?'

Lisa shook her head. 'You must have had them earlier because you let us all in.'

'They must be around somewhere, but I can't be bothered to look for them right now. I'll just call you on my mobile when I'm back and you can let me in, okay?' He leaned across to Lisa and kissed her on the lips. 'Oh, and make sure he doesn't sneak off to bed, okay?'

Lisa nodded. 'I'll try my best.'

'Right then,' said Andy sliding back the patio door. 'You two try to be good and I'll be back ASAP.'

## Show me how it's done

'Tell me something I don't know.' Lisa turned to me with a grin as I sat down in the chair next to her.

'I don't understand what you mean,' I replied. 'Tell you something I don't know about what?'

'About you,' she replied, 'tell me something I don't know about you.'

I was confused. 'But why do you want me to do that?'

'Because if you don't then we're both going to have to sit here and endure the mother of all awkward silences. Come on, Charlie, you've been trying to avoid me since I arrived.'

'What are you talking about? I've done no such thing.'

'So that wasn't you practically clutching on to Andy's leg, yelling, "Don't leave me alone with this woman?" I know why you haven't wanted to be around me. The last time we spoke was horrible. I feel terrible about it, I really do. And I know what you guys are like . . . you all hate talking about awkward stuff. You'd sooner chop off your head than talk about how you're feeling. But one way or another, Charlie, we're going to have to talk about these things because I need to . . . if only to apologise for my part in them. So for now I thought I'd warm you up – so to speak – with a much lighter conversation.'

'One where I tell you something about myself that you don't know?'

'Anything at all,' said Lisa. 'The first thing that pops into your head.'

'I'm terrible at these sorts of things,' I explained. 'Nothing's "popping" into my head at all. I'm a complete blank.'

'That's the second rubbish bloke thing you've said in as many minutes,' said Lisa. 'I thought you were better than that.'

'If it's so easy then,' I replied, 'why don't you show me how it's done?'

Lisa laughed. 'You've got me there. There are millions of things you don't know about me: how can I choose just one without you reading too much into it?'

'My point entirely.'

Lisa took a sip of raki. 'Okay, here's one. When I was twelve my parents bought me a Girl's World for my birthday – do you know what that is?'

'My best mate's sister had one,' I replied. 'They look a bit like the head of a shop-window dummy and you're supposed to use them to practise hair and make-up skills.'

'That's the one,' said Lisa. 'So at least you know what one is . . . because my revelation is a bit tragic really . . . I now confess right in front of you that I used to practise French kissing on mine.'

'But it hasn't even got a tongue.'

'I know, I know, I know,' said Lisa momentarily burying her face in my shoulder in shame.

'And did all that practice turn you into an amazing kisser?'

Lisa laughed cheekily. 'I've had no complaints if that's what you mean.'

'Right,' I said knocking back the last of my raki. 'So I

need a revelation that's as good as snogging a plastic replica head . . . ?'

Lisa nodded.

'Haven't got one I'm afraid.'

'Nothing?'

'Nope, nothing. You've won revelation of the day, hands down with your Girl's World story. But you can consider me warmed up if you like.'

There was a long silence.

'I just really want you to know how sorry I am about what happened,' said Lisa quietly. 'I can't tell you how much I wish I'd kept my stupid mouth shut. You should never have had to hear news like that the way you heard it. I could barely sleep that night for thinking about you and what I'd done. I was really worried about you.'

'There was no need,' I replied. 'I was fine.'

'And now?'

'I'm still fine. In fact it was probably the best thing that could've happened because it forced me to do the one thing I hadn't managed to do: move on.'

Lisa reached across and touched my hand. 'Are you saying you were still in love with Sarah?'

'I don't know what I'm saying,' I replied, aware of the warmth of her touch. 'When you've been with someone for as long as I was with Sarah it becomes quite difficult to tell when love stops being love and starts being habit. Either way, it doesn't really matter now does it? She's definitely moved on. And so have I.'

'I can't tell you how shocked I was when she told me,' said Lisa, still touching my hand. 'She and Oliver had only been together five minutes.' She paused and added: 'I'm not sure I should tell you this, but at one point she actually

asked me if she was doing the right thing having this baby.'

'And what did you say?'

'What could I say?' replied Lisa. 'I told her she had to do whatever she thought was right.'

Momentarily lost for a response, I chose to stare into the bottom of my empty mug in the vain hope that it might have replenished itself. The only thing I found lurking at the bottom of the mug was a change of subject.

'It must be weird for you,' I said looking out towards the sea. 'Yesterday you were in Brighton in the cold – today you're in Crete in the sun.'

'It's been great to get away,' said Lisa. 'I'm loving every second of it. I know I seem to be doing a lot of apologising but I really am sorry if I've spoilt your holiday. It's not enough that I've been calling you and sending you text messages about Andy, now I'm here in person spoiling things up close.'

'You're not spoiling anything. In fact it's been nice having you around today.'

Lisa squeezed my hand. 'That's really sweet of you.'

'Well, it's true.' I was silently willing Lisa not to release my hand. 'How are things with you and Andy now you're here?'

'Okay, I suppose,' replied Lisa. 'It's funny, but my first reaction when he told me he'd bought me a ticket to come over was that he was trying to make up for something. Isn't that a horrible way to think?'

We both stopped talking for a moment, content to look out towards the sea where a far-off ship was passing by. Meanwhile underneath us we could hear a group of girls – all clicking heels and laughter – passing by the pool.

'So, what about this girl that you met at the airport?'

asked Lisa with a mischievous tone in her voice. 'The girl-with-the-cowboy-hat? Andy said she was a bit of a babe.'

'She was, and right now she's probably getting chatted up by some tall, dark, handsome twenty-year-old bricklayer with abs of steel.'

'I think you're doing her a massive injustice,' said Lisa. 'Girls don't always go for the physical . . . not that there's anything wrong with you like that, but you know what I mean.'

'Come on, Lisa, which would you rather have – me or the bricklayer?'

Lisa grinned. 'Abs of steel you say?'

'Yeah.'

'Personality?'

'Of a house brick.'

'But he's got abs of steel?'

'Steel covered in burnished bronze.'

'And then there's you?' said Lisa pulling a face.

'Less abs of steel and more abs of custard.'

'But a great personality.'

'I can definitely tell a joke or two if that's what you mean. Two fish walk into a bar—'

'That wasn't a question,' replied Lisa, cutting me off with a grin. 'It was a statement. And on top of that you can talk on the phone without resorting to a series of grunts, you're a good listener, especially when the person at the other end of the phone is in tears . . . and to cap it all you're nigh on perfect at making insecure girlfriends feel that bit less insecure when their useless boyfriends decide to go on an all-boys' holiday. You won't know this but I've always said to Andy that you really would make some girl the perfect boyfriend.'

'I doubt that strongly.'

'Because of Sarah?'

'No,' I replied, 'because . . . oh . . . it doesn't matter.'

'Is this to do with this other girl you met out here? Donna?'

'And they say that women are the worst gossips! What did he say exactly?'

'Well, this is all through an Andy filter so I'll take some, if not all, of it with a huge pinch of salt, but he said that you had some sort of an intense twenty-four-hour thing with her where nothing actually happened.'

'That's pretty much it.'

'I bet it wasn't.'

'She was still getting over her ex.'

'A pretty big obstacle, I'll grant you but not an impossible one.'

'She told me that holiday romances never work out . . . maybe she was right. After all, technically speaking that's what Sarah and I were.'

'Maybe they do work out and maybe they don't,' replied Lisa, 'but they can be a lot of fun while they last.'

As Lisa's words echoed around my head I realised that there was a certain inevitability about what was about to happen. It was as though everything in the past week had been conspiring to bring about this moment. Everything from our embrace in my kitchen, to the easy intimacy of our text messages, to the news about Sarah's pregnancy had had the effect of bringing us closer together. But it had been Andy himself who had ultimately united us through his friendship and through his lies.

I touched Lisa's face with both hands and she didn't shy away. For a moment I wavered, telling myself that what I

was about to do was wrong. But before I could retreat I recalled Andy's response when I told him not to contact Nina: 'I wouldn't be risking anything,' he'd said. At the time he had seemed so sure of the odds and so confident of the outcome that I wanted to know what it would be like to take the risk. Just as Andy had done. Just as Sarah had too. And that was the moment that thought turned into action.

was about to do was wrong, but before I could retract I reassured Andy's response when I told him not to contact Sinead, I wouldn't be telling anything," he'd said. "At the time he had seemed so sure of the odds and so confident of the outcome that I wanted to know what it would be like to take the risk, first as Andy had done, just as Sarah had too. And that was the moment that thought turned into action."

# DAY SIX:
# SATURDAY

## BBC Breakfast News

Most mornings when I wake up, the first thing that hits me is a strong sense of déjà vu, which is only natural, I suppose, because most mornings are exactly the same. Radio clock alarm goes off, I get out of bed and have a shower. Dripping water over the bathroom floor I shave badly in front of a steamed-up mirror and then return to the bedroom where I finally get dry and pull on some underwear. Clad only in boxer shorts I take out the ironing board and proceed to iron one of the five white work shirts I've washed over the weekend. I slip on the shirt, still warm from being pressed, quickly followed by my grey work suit, before heading to the kitchen where I pour myself a bowl of cereal (usually cornflakes but occasionally muesli – I got a taste for it after Sarah moved out). I eat the cereal in front of *BBC Breakfast News* then return to the kitchen, slip two slices of bread into the toaster and take out the margarine from the fridge in anticipation of my toast's arrival. Lurking in the living room, I continue watching TV until I hear the toast pop up, then head back to the kitchen, slap the margarine on the toast and return to the TV. Approximately sixteen bites later breakfast is over and so I put on my shoes, grab my coat and I'm out the door. Sometimes I think I hate this routine. It makes me feel that I'm boring. So occasionally I'll vary it (iron my shirt

the night before or buy a different cereal or watch GMTV) and I'll feel great. Vibrant even. But no matter what happens, the very next day I'll be back to my normal routine with no deviations or variations. It's almost as if the day before had never happened. And that's exactly how I felt when I woke up following my raki-fuelled late night.

Staring at the darkened ceiling I strained my ears listening to noises coming from outside: water splashing in the hotel pool, laughter from fellow holidaymakers and the electronic warning beep of reversing delivery trucks. Lying there with all these familiar noises swirling round the room I thought to myself, 'This is just an ordinary day. A day like yesterday and the day before that,' and for a few seconds I felt a real sense of relief. That nagging feeling of discomfort was wrong. The sick feeling in the pit of my stomach was mistaken. I even smiled at the air-conditioning unit when I realised that once again it had been left on its maximum setting all night.

And because nothing was wrong and everything was okay I reasoned that today was going to be a day just like any other on the holiday so far. We'd get up. We'd have breakfast. We'd go to the beach. In the evening we'd go out, drink too much and go to bed in the early hours. Everything was predictable. Everything was safe.

Just as I finally allowed myself the luxury of relaxing, something – possibly my burgeoning sense of guilt – made me turn my head in the direction of Andy's bed where he and Lisa lay fast asleep and that was the moment that I knew for sure that this wasn't going to be a day like any other. This was the day after the night before. And I'd never seen this script before in my life.

Unwilling (or unable) to start thinking too deeply yet, I climbed out of bed and quietly got dressed in my usual holiday attire of shorts and T-shirt. Grabbing my sunglasses and the keys for the hire car, I made my way from the bedroom into the kitchen. Tom stirred briefly on the sofa-bed but soon fell back asleep, so opening the front door as quietly as I could I stepped into the bright morning light and made my way downstairs.

The big question on my mind was where to go. The beach seemed like the most obvious place. It became less appealing, however, once I imagined it filled with its usual clientele flirting with each other against a backdrop of loud club music. Of course, now I had transport I could go anywhere I pleased. And so without thinking about my eventual destination, I made my way to the car, started it up and pulled into a break in the traffic in the direction of the Malia crossroad.

With only a handful of road signs for guidance, I knew I had to make a decision. Amongst the signs for nearby villages and the motorway, there was one with the symbol for a tourist attraction next to it that said 'The Palace of Malia: 3km'. I had no idea what The Palace of Malia might be given that I was having a hard time imagining that Malia, even in ancient times, had been anything other than the alfresco night club that it is today. Whatever it was, I reasoned that it was as good a destination as anywhere else and so followed the road signs in that direction.

It took no time at all to get there. As I climbed out of the car the first thing I noticed was the intensity of the sun. Despite it being relatively early, the temperature was already

so hot that the car park tarmac had begun to melt and felt sticky underfoot.

I locked the car and made my way along a path to the entrance where a sign said: 'Welcome to the Palace of Malia – a Minoan treasure.' Looking over the fence I could make out various huge lumps of sandstone. Next to the sign was an elderly woman wearing a straw hat who was sitting in a chair reading a book. I asked how much it was to come in and she said something in Greek and pointed towards a doorway a few yards away.

Inside the room along with some literature about the Palace, there was a small ticket booth. As no one was there, I pressed a buzzer mounted on the top of the counter. A small woman with a cheery smile arrived almost immediately and sold me a ticket, which I then handed to the woman in the chair outside. As I gave her my ticket, she muttered something in Greek and then pointed me in the direction of a building behind her.

The building was part of a permanent exhibition that told the story of the palace's excavation. Large black and white photos from the 1900s were mounted on the wall, and reading from the panels underneath them I learned that the first palace of Malia had been built by the Minoans in 1900 BC only to be destroyed some two hundred years later. It was later rebuilt and destroyed again and then in 1450 BC they rebuilt one last time.

This final version must have been the most impressive, because when I followed the exhibition trail through an archway into an interconnected room, I found a scale model of the palace on a table, under a large glass case. It looked like those models of planned shopping centres and housing developments that I used to see at work before everything

became computer generated. I stood for quite a long time, imagining miniature Minoans going about their daily lives. It was sad thinking that all the people who had lived in the palace were no longer alive. And it was a stern reminder of how much things can change in a relatively short space of time.

More knowledgeable about the Minoans than when I'd entered the exhibition, I made my way to the exit, stepped outside and began to pour with sweat. In the short time that I'd been out of the sun the outside temperature had sky-rocketed to unbearable proportions. With the realisation that I might die of dehydration, I wiped the sheen of sweat from my forehead and began looking around the ruins of the palace in earnest. I looked around the remains of court-yards and cellars. I ventured around workshops and dwelling rooms. And somewhere around the court of the tower I decided that it might be time to take a look at the ruination of my own life.

Coming to a huge lump of sandstone that was probably of great archaeological significance, I took the opportunity to take the weight off my feet and sat down. As the sun beat down on my scalp, I took a deep breath and, with much relief, finally let the guilt bottled up inside me run its course.

## Here's to hot summer nights

The kiss on the balcony. That was where it had begun. But it had ended somewhere entirely different. Though we had stopped speaking by this point, there had been no doubt in my mind about how far we intended to go. Guilt didn't even get a look in as we negotiated the short distance from the balcony to my bed and I knew that unless Andy returned any time soon, nothing short of a miracle would stop my betrayal.

Everything that happened once we reached our destination was lost in the blur of sensory overload. (Although later that night as Lisa and Andy slept peacefully in their bed next to my own, I could recall perfectly the sense of urgency that had gripped me at that moment; the actions it inspired however had faded too swiftly to make a lasting impression. It was a moment within a moment. It was everything and then it was nothing.)

Afterwards, as we disentangled our bodies and readjusted our clothing, I found myself waiting expectantly for the arrival of some sort of sense of regret. After all I had just slept with my best friend's girlfriend. But there was nothing. And the longer I thought about it the more I began to wonder whether this was down to the simple fact that I wasn't sorry. Whatever the reason, the deed was done. Events had been set in motion. And no matter what we

did to cover up our actions, something fundamental had changed about the world we both inhabited and could never be changed back, no matter how much we adjusted the sheets of my bed, straightened our clothes and wiped away smeared make-up.

The tension was unbearable. Every knock, creak, scrape or groan of the infrastructure of the apartment building set my heart racing even once we were ready for Andy's return. And as the minutes passed, and the distance between our shared moment and our current state of readiness grew, we became more tense rather than less. I was almost more desperate for him to return and sense that something had gone on than I was to wait for his arrival and escape the consequences of my actions. What I didn't want – what I couldn't stand – was the waiting. It was the not knowing if my betrayal would be exposed that was the real torture.

When Andy finally called to let us know he was back I was convinced that if his senses hadn't been dulled by the raki then he would have guessed straight away that something was wrong. Through my now sober eyes it was as though everything that had been witness to my actions and Lisa's was emitting a steady fog of guilt that only the sober could see. The whole apartment seemed eerily sinister, like the scene of a murder long after the body had been removed.

'Victorious,' said Andy, holding up not one but two bottles of raki. 'Sorry I took so long, kids. On the way back from the mini-market I bumped into Steve-the-barman downstairs and we got talking and so I bought him a beer.' Andy set down the bottles, arranged our mugs in a huddle, poured out a double shot into each one and handed them out. 'Here's to hot summer nights,' he said raising his mug in the air. 'May there be many more of them.'

The three of us stayed out on the balcony for another hour or so, during which time I amazed myself by remaining calm in such a chaotic situation. I made jokes at Andy's expense, I chatted with Lisa about the everyday stuff of life and I breathed calmly at every opportunity. In short I acted as though nothing had happened. But as the night progressed I realised that my ability to fool Andy had less to do with innate acting skills than my fear of being discovered. I just couldn't let that happen. I had betrayed my best friend in the cruellest way possible. So if it meant I had to crack jokes, if it meant I had to make small talk with Lisa, if it meant that I had to callously act as though I hadn't just committed the crime of the century, then that was exactly what I would do.

For the most part, however, as we whiled our way through to the early hours, my mind was focused on two questions: why had Lisa done what she had done? And more importantly, where would we go from here?

## Not a single thing

No one batted an eyelid on my return to the apartment following my sojourn to The Palace of Malia. Tom and Lisa were out on the balcony, while Andy was in the bathroom taking a shower. They all assumed I'd gone down to the beach for a morning constitutional and as it seemed as good an excuse as any I didn't correct them.

Fear of being discovered aside, my biggest worry about the day ahead was centred on how Lisa might act around me in the cold harsh light of day. In my more egotistical moments I'd been imagining that she might be in need of some form of reassurance that last night had meant as much to me as it had done to her. I imagined a whole day of longing looks and secret smiles. Perhaps even a few unexplained tears and temper tantrums. Lisa, however, was as far from giving the game away as possible. From the moment of my return all she did was laugh, joke and be her usual effervescent self. And that was even when Andy wasn't there. As we made our way down to Stars and Bars, Andy told an anecdote about an anti-student loans demonstration we'd gone on in a bid to chat up a couple of girls we both fancied; I tried desperately to catch Lisa's eye as if to say, 'Last night was real wasn't it?' but when I did, though she held my gaze unflinchingly, there wasn't even the faintest flicker of guilt or recognition. It was as

though she had wiped the memory from her mind. And without her corroboration to back up my version of events it began to feel as if last night hadn't happened at all.

'That was excellent,' said Andy lighting up a post-breakfast cigarette following our usual Stars and Bars breakfast. 'I'd suggest that we get the waiter to give our compliments to the chef but I'm guessing he'd think we were being clever.' He yawned and stretched his arms in the air. 'So what are we going to do tonight, boys and girls? It's our last night of freedom. After tonight there's just a plane ride between us and another twelve months of day-to-day grind.'

'Very poetic,' teased Lisa. 'Is that what life is like with me?'

'Of course not,' grinned Andy. 'It's much worse.'

'Well . . . though I'll hate myself for saying it, given last night's excesses,' began Tom, 'I think we sort of owe it to ourselves to head out in Malia tonight.'

'Did Tom just suggest that we have a bit of fun?' asked Andy doing a comedy double take. 'I tell you what, Charlie, he's more fun than you these days.' He paused and took a drag on his cigarette. 'So Malia it is then,' he continued. 'There are still loads of bars that we haven't been in that look like a right laugh . . . in fact there's a club I read about that's throwing a "foam party" tonight.' Andy looked at us all expectantly but we all looked equally nonplussed. He reached into the back pocket of his shorts and pulled out a page torn from a magazine. It was an advert for the Camelot Club featuring a series of photos of young (mainly female) clubbers waist deep in white foam as if an industrial washing machine had exploded only moments before the pictures had been taken.

'Now that,' said Andy waving the advert, 'is a foam party. Tell me that doesn't look like fun.'

'When you say "fun",' said Lisa drily, 'I take it you mean, "Largely populated by twenty-one-year-old girls in bikini tops and cut-off denim shorts?"'

'Not at all, but if there are girls like that around, then that can't exactly be a bad thing for our friend here.' Andy gave my shoulders a squeeze – his physical shorthand for sincerity. 'Come on, babe,' he continued, 'have a heart will you? Let's not forget that Charlie here – the only single person amongst us – has yet to get any action this holiday. We have to go to this party . . . for his sake.'

'Thanks and all that,' I said to Andy in a more determined voice than usual, 'but it really doesn't sound like my thing. Let's just go out, have a few beers and a laugh, okay?'

'You say that now,' replied Andy, 'but when the foam's flying—'

'I'm not interested, honestly.'

'You will be. Trust me.'

'Trust *me*,' I replied as my exasperation edged its way into my voice, 'I won't.'

'Come on, Andy,' intervened Lisa on my behalf. 'If Charlie said he's not interested then you shouldn't force him.'

Andy rubbed the top of my head patronisingly. 'See this guy here? This is my mate Charlie Mansell and there's not a single thing in this world that I wouldn't do for him. Not a single thing. So that's why we're going to the Camelot Club tonight. And that's why we'll have a good time. And that's why I'll make sure that whatever happens he won't leave that party alone.'

Until You Were Here

'Now that,' said Andy waving his shovel, 'is where part v,'
'Tell me that doesn't look like fun.'
'When you say "fun",' said Lisa drily, 'I take it you mean
largely untroubled by throbbing overhérfa clitsx di bikini
tops and suncof denim shorts?'
'Not at all, but if there are girls anywhere and there
that can t exactly been had tying for our little Here-Andy
Give my shoulders a squeeze - hey, typical shorthand for

## To talk

It was mid-to-late-afternoon, the sun was marginally less
intense than it had been all day (which meant that you
could still probably just about fry an egg on the sand)
and the four of us were lying on our sun-loungers. Lisa
had yet to drop a single hint about the events of the
previous night, despite my giving her various opportunities to do so. After leaving Stars and Bars I'd deliberately
lingered behind Tom and Andy so that Lisa and I could
walk down to the beach together without arousing any
suspicion. But before she had noticed me she had play-
fully called out to Tom and asked for a piggyback as far
as the mini-market. At the mini-market I announced that
I was going to buy a couple of bottles of water and might
need a hand. Although Lisa could've easily volunteered,
Tom was forced to come to my aid because Andy had
simply ignored my request and Lisa took the opportunity
to reapply some suncream on her shoulders. Once we
were settled on the loungers, I'd asked if anyone was
interested in going for a walk – knowing full well that
Tom was too engrossed in his *Rough Guide* and Andy
too lazy to stand up – but again she declined preferring
to have Andy undo the strings to her bikini, douse her
back in suncream and vigorously massage it into her
skin. By the time I returned from my walk Lisa was dozing

278

in the sun with one hand resting gently on Andy's arm and the two of them looked like the perfect picture of togetherness.

'Do you know what?' said Tom resting his *Rough Guide* on his chest. 'It's just occurred to me that none of us have actually been in the sea all holiday.'

'What's the point?' said Andy. 'All that happens is you go in, you get wet, you come out, sand sticks to you and then you have to have a shower – sounds like a proper pain in the arse if you ask me.'

'I'd love to go in,' said Lisa, 'but my suncream isn't waterproof and I'd have to reapply the lot.'

'What about you, Charlie?' asked Tom. 'Fancy a swim?'

'Nah,' I replied eyeing Lisa from behind my sunglasses. 'I've always felt there's something undignified about men walking round topless. It's the snob in me.'

Andy sat up, yawned loudly and stretched. 'I'm going to get some more water. Anyone else want anything?' Lisa asked for an ice cream while Tom requested a can of Coke. I declined. All I really wanted was an acknowledgement from Lisa that what had happened last night wasn't a figment of my imagination, so that I could stop feeling as if I was losing the plot.

'Do you need someone to give you a hand?' Tom said. 'I could do with a walk.'

'Actually I've got it sorted,' said Andy quickly. He turned and looked at me and even though he was wearing his sunglasses I could tell that something was going on. 'Charlie will give me a hand, won't you, mate?'

My heart froze mid-beat. 'Yeah, of course.'

'Oh, I see,' joked Lisa. 'You want to have a quiet word with Charlie, is that it?'

'Course not,' said Andy coolly. 'Feel free to come if you want.'

Lisa looked over at me and I saw a flash of anxiety in her blue-green eyes. 'No thanks,' she replied. 'You two go and do your boy thing.'

We trudged barefoot across the hot sand until we were out of earshot.

'So what's going on?' I asked.

'Nothing really,' said Andy, looking over his shoulder at Lisa and Tom. 'I just couldn't think of any other way of getting you on your own.'

'On my own for what?'

'To talk.'

'About what?'

'Nina.'

'So what have you decided? Are you going to carry on seeing her or call it quits?'

'Well, that's sort of what I wanted to talk about.'

Without waiting for my response Andy walked out of the entrance to the beach, crossed the road and sat down on the wall outside the mini-market. There were a couple of girls chatting to each other just to the left of him. Neither of them noticed me as I sat down only a few feet away from them. I was invisible.

'I know I don't act like it,' began Andy, 'but the truth is Lisa really does mean the world to me. You won't understand but this holiday and the things I've done . . . they aren't anything to do with her at all. It's all been about me.' Andy paused and stared at me as if trying to judge whether I was buying into his argument. What he saw I don't know, but when I looked into his sunglasses in a

return bid to see his soul, all I could see was my own reflection.

'Well if all that's true,' I replied, 'why are we talking now?'

'Because somehow things have got messed up,' said Andy. 'Last night I came up with the excuse of getting those extra bottles of raki so that I could call Nina and tell her that I wouldn't be seeing her again. But as soon as I told her she started telling me how good we were together and how we ought to at least give things a try. And even though I kept telling her "no", at the back of my mind I knew that I wanted to say "yes".'

'So you're going to carry on seeing Nina behind Lisa's back?'

'No,' replied Andy. 'I've decided that when we get back from holiday I'm going to leave her.'

281

**It is what it is**

Andy waited for my reaction.

'So what do you think?' he asked eventually. 'Am I losing it? Am I doing the wrong thing? Tell me what I should do?'

I wanted to tell him to leave her. I wanted to tell him that he didn't deserve her. I even wanted to tell him about what had happened last night. But I didn't say anything. Instead I remembered that despite everything Andy was still one of my closest friends in the world and deserved the best advice I could give irrespective of its consequences to me.

'If you leave her it will be a mistake,' I said firmly.

'Maybe, but right now I feel it's the only thing I can do.'

'You're not thinking straight. You can't be. You're talking about leaving someone you've been with for nearly seven years for a girl you've known only a few days. Does that sound like the action of someone who is thinking straight?'

'It is what it is,' said Andy.

'What does that mean?' I replied. 'It doesn't mean anything. It's one of those meaningless phrases people say when they can't justify whatever ridiculous act of self destruction they're about to do next.'

There was a long silence and the two girls sitting next to Andy stood up and walked away. I couldn't think of what else to say. I couldn't think of how I wanted things to turn out. It was all a mess.

'I thought you of all people would understand,' said Andy, looking down at the pavement.

'What's that supposed to mean?' I replied.

'Nina told me about you and Donna. Nina said that reading between the lines Donna seemed to think that you might have fallen in love with her.'

I tried to hold back all of the feelings brought to the surface just by hearing Donna's name. 'Recently dumped guy falls in love with girl on holiday,' I replied sarcastically. 'Has all the hallmarks of a relationship that – even if she hadn't dumped me at the airport – would've lasted . . . what? Five . . . maybe . . . six seconds after we'd got back home and she'd realised that I'm not the bloke she thought I was, just a dull bloke with a dull job . . . and a dull flat . . . still licking his wounds following a savaging by his ex-girlfriend.' I paused and looked at Andy. 'So what was your point?'

'My point was . . .' his voice trailed off. 'Look you know what I'm like. I'm hardly perfect boyfriend material, am I? Lisa deserves someone better than me.'

'And Nina doesn't?'

'It'll be different.'

'How?' I replied. 'What makes you so sure you won't do the same with her too?'

'Because that's the whole point of starting again,' said Andy, 'to give yourself a clean slate in the hope that maybe this time around you'll get it right.'

I could see from his face that his mind was made up, so we made our way into the mini-market in silence, bought all the things we were after and then left the shop. On our way back to the beach neither of us mentioned Nina or Lisa again. Instead we talked about recent films we had

*Mike Gayle*

seen, TV we had watched and famous women we found
attractive. And that small host of conversations managed
to occupy the void between us right up until we got back
to the beach. I retreated to my corner and Andy retreated
to his and even though neither of us spoke again we both
knew that the conversation was far from over.

284

## . . . and that was all it took

Lisa was holding Andy's arm aloft so that she could look at his watch. 'Time to go, boys,' she said disappointedly.

'What time is it?' asked Tom.

'Just coming up to five.'

'So that's the end of beach life for us for a while,' said Andy. 'I was actually kind of getting into it.'

'We could still come down tomorrow,' said Lisa. 'What time are we supposed to be out of our rooms?'

'Eleven,' said Andy.

'Midday,' I corrected.

Andy shrugged. 'Either way we'll have nowhere to wash once we've been kicked out so I doubt if I'll be bothering with the beach tomorrow.'

'That's a shame,' said Lisa. 'So what time's the actual flight home?'

'Eleven o'clock at night,' said Andy.

'Actually it's just after midnight,' I corrected again. 'And the coach picking us up for the airport is coming some time around nine.'

As Andy and Lisa began collecting their things together, it became clear that the tension between me and Andy hadn't gone unnoticed because Tom lifted up his sunglasses and raised his eyebrows in querying fashion. Andy and Lisa were still too close for comfort for me to

respond so as they began making their way towards the top of the beach I lingered by the loungers with Tom.

'So what's happened now? You've barely said a civil word to each other since your trip to the shops.'

'I don't even know where to begin,' I replied. 'It's all wrapped up so tightly together it's almost impossible to unravel. I'm not even sure where the beginning of the story is . . . but I'm pretty certain what the end will be if Andy finds out.'

'This doesn't sound good at all. What has he done now?'

'It's actually all my fault this time,' I replied. 'I slept with Lisa.'

'You *what*?'

'I know,' I replied. 'I shouldn't have done it but I did.'

'When did this happen?'

'Last night, after you went to bed. Andy went out to get some more raki and I don't know . . . we started talking and it all snowballed from there.' Tom couldn't have looked more disappointed in me if he'd tried. 'I promise you, if I'd thought for a second that Andy even remotely cared for her I would never have let it happen.'

'That's easy to say,' said Tom. He looked up ahead to where Andy and Lisa stood waiting at the top of the beach. 'I take it he doesn't know?'

'No,' I replied.

'So why all the tension this afternoon?'

'Well that sort of brings me to the twist in the story . . .'

'Nothing you say could surprise me now.'

'Not even if I told you that not only is Andy going to carry on seeing Nina when we get back home, but he's decided that he's going to leave Lisa?'

'This whole holiday is a mess from beginning to end.

We would've all been better off staying at home.' Tom bent down and picked up his bag. 'So where does all this leave you and Lisa?'

'I don't know,' I replied. 'We haven't had a chance to talk yet.'

'And if you had, what would you say?'

'I don't know,' I replied. 'I really don't know.'

## It's not going to blow over

It was evening now and the four of us were making ready to leave The Bengal Castle (one of the few Indian restaurants in Malia and yet another one of Tom's discoveries). Our next stop was the strip, where we planned to visit a few bars before heading off to Andy's beloved foam party at the Camelot Club.

So far the evening had been uneventful. Andy and I had barely spoken to each other until we all sat down to dinner, when we both mellowed significantly for the sake of the evening that lay ahead of us. As for Lisa, I was still none the wiser about her feelings about last night. She hadn't said a single thing to me and there hadn't been the opportunity for me to say a single thing to her. Instead, while the others hung around the bedroom watching TV, I sat on the balcony alone under the guise of reading *The Da Vinci Code* when in reality all I was doing was staring out to sea and thinking about Lisa.

'So come on then, Charlie,' said Tom as he pushed his chair underneath the table and leaned on the backrest, 'what do you think will be the first thing you'll do once you get home?'

'I don't know.' I hadn't been particularly talkative all evening. I glanced at Lisa. 'Maybe you should ask someone else.'

Tom turned to Lisa and smiled. 'You'll give me an answer won't you, mate?'

'Okay,' replied Lisa. 'The first thing I'll do is open the post. I love it when you go away and there's a ton of stuff waiting for you. It's almost like it's your birthday . . . only there aren't any cards . . . only junk mail and utility bills and letters from your auntie telling you how well all your cousins are doing.' Lisa batted the question back to Tom. 'What about you? What will be the first thing you do when you get home?'

'It's a bit boring,' replied Tom. 'I'll kiss Anne and the kids. That's the first thing I always do when I walk through the door.'

'That's not boring,' said Lisa. 'It's sweet. I'd love to come home to a family like that one day.'

'Ask him what the second thing is,' said Andy. 'I bet it won't be quite so cuddly.'

'He's right,' laughed Tom. 'The second thing will be to check all my work e-mails in case there's anything important in there. Last time Anne and I went away I came back to an in-box groaning under the cyber-weight of two hundred-and-sixty-seven unopened e-mails and attachments. Ninety per cent of them were the usual: "It's Brian's leaving do on Friday – please make the effort to come along."'

'That sounds like my place too,' replied Lisa.

'What about you, Andy?' asked Tom. 'What will be your first move when you get home?'

'I can answer that one for you,' said Lisa. 'It's easy. The first thing Andy always does is go around the house checking every single room to see if anything's changed. It's a weird sort of superstition he's had going for as long as we've been living together.'

'She's making this up,' said Andy, clearly embarrassed, 'I don't do that at all.'

'He does,' teased Lisa. 'He even does it in the same order every time. It's living room, kitchen, front bedroom, back bedroom and then bathroom. It's like he's checking for burglars or something.'

'Look,' interrupted Andy, 'can we stop talking about going home and start having some fun here? Tonight's our last night together. And I'm pretty sure that none of us is ever going to come back here again. So let's just enjoy ourselves okay?' He patted me on the back. 'And that means you too, mate. Tonight is going to be a night you're never going to forget.'

Things were busy now. The pavements were packed with so many young Brits that it was hard to imagine there could be anyone between the ages of eighteen and thirty left at home. They were all here, fuelled with booze and ready to party.

The bar girls of the strip were in force. It was easy to pick them out amongst the streets crowded with holidaymakers because they stood out a mile: long legs, incredible bodies, cheeky personalities, provocative dress sense. It was all there and it was all working for them. We watched in admiration as a stunning girl in a pink top, short skirt and cowboy boots managed to single-handedly herd about ten guys into Bar Logica in a matter of seconds. Meanwhile across the way three girls wearing tight jeans and matching polka-dot bikini tops were picking off groups of guys at random and leading them into Hotshot's cocktail lounge at such a rate that there was a huge backlog of blokes crowded in the bar like sheep waiting to be shorn. But despite the strong bar-girl presence, unlike on our previous visits, not a single one of them even

looked in our direction. The message was clear. Even though there were three of us – and only one of Lisa – in their eyes at least, we all belonged to her. We were no longer strays as I'd imagined at the airport. We had an owner. A leader. Someone in charge. And the girls in their short skirts and tight tops knew and respected that. And although I didn't miss the attention – my mind was too focused elsewhere – I did resent the assumption that Lisa owned all three of us, even if in truth they were actually only one third out.

Lisa's presence affected my perception of the strip too. Bathing in the neon glow of the bars and the clubs we found ourselves jostling with rowdy gangs of youths shouting and swearing at the top of their voices; we were breathing in the hot fat smells of a thousand and one takeaway meals, and we were forced to endure the constant thump of countless anonymous club tracks. Thanks to Lisa, I suddenly saw Malia with new eyes and felt embarrassed that we had brought her here at all. Everything around us was evidence of both my and Andy's lack of maturity – the exact opposite of the dictionary definition of 'sophistication'. We were Beavis and Butthead at thirty-five. Grown men in schoolboy trousers. Overgrown teenagers trying desperately to hang on to the last vestiges of our youth. And I realised (albeit too late) that some activities in life, like holidaying in Malia, skateboarding or drinking until you throw up over your shoes, are too youthful for a man this deep into his thirties to participate in without looking like a fool.

'Let's try this place.' Lisa came to a halt as if she had overheard my thoughts and was now desperate to compound my shame. 'It looks like fun.'

'Are you sure?' replied Andy, staring at Pandemonium's

eye-catching neon sign. 'I mean, it looks a bit tacky, don't you think?'

'Cheesy, yes,' corrected Lisa. 'Tacky? No. What does everyone else think?'

'I don't mind,' said Tom.

Lisa looked at me expectantly, but I had long since given up trying to hide how I was feeling.

'Right then,' said Lisa, 'Pandemonium it is then.'

Pandemonium hadn't changed since we were last there. The music was still loud, the bar was still packed and the waitresses still wearing very little. We set up camp in the same seats that we had occupied on our first night, Tom and I facing the bar and Andy and Lisa sitting opposite. A bunny-girl waitress came and took our drinks orders and once they arrived we tried several times to start a group conversation but soon tired of yelling over the music. Out of necessity, then, Lisa and Andy fell into their own private conversation while Tom and I fell into our own.

'It's like history repeating itself,' said Tom as he looked up at the TV screen above his head showing highlights of the day's test match. 'At least tonight should be less eventful than last time.'

'Maybe,' I replied.

'What do you mean, "maybe"?' asked Tom looking at me suspiciously. 'You're not going to start something tonight are you?'

I took a sip of my beer. 'I really like her, Tom. I really like her.'

'Lisa?'

I nodded.

'Do you mean you like her in the same way you "really liked" Donna?' said Tom, playing devil's advocate.

'That's hardly fair is it?' I responded. 'I *did* like Donna
. . . but she didn't want me. What should I be doing
instead? Sitting around crying into my beer?'

'No,' replied, Tom, 'but I just don't think Lisa's the
answer. Think about it, Charlie, you haven't even spoken
to her about last night yet and you're already thinking
about rocking the boat with her and Andy.'

I glanced across the table. It seemed too bizarre for
words that I could be discussing my feelings for her so
openly with her sitting less than three feet away and yet
so oblivious.

'You're absolutely right.'

'Absolutely right about what?' asked Tom.

I didn't reply. Instead I stood up, walked around to Andy
and Lisa's side of the table and tapped them both on the
shoulder.

'All right, mate?' said Andy. 'What's up?'

'You're right about me putting some effort into having
a laugh tonight. In fact I'm so in the right frame of mind
that I actually fancy a dance . . . which is why I was just
wondering if I could borrow your girlfriend for a bit.'

Andy laughed. 'How much have you had to drink? I've
never seen you on the dance floor unless you're practically
slaughtered.'

'I know,' I replied. 'But there's a first time for everything.'

'In that case you have my full blessing, mate.'

Lisa looked on helplessly as I took her by the hand and
led her in the direction of the Pandemonium's packed
dance floor. At the last minute, however, I changed direction and instead guided her through some large glass doors
to the bar's outdoor patio area where dozens of couples
sat at tables talking by candlelight.

'I'm sorry for dragging you away like that,' I said as we came to a halt next to a row of potted olive trees. 'I didn't know what else to do.'

'This is insane, Charlie,' protested Lisa. 'What if Andy came out here right now?'

'I know, I know,' I replied, fighting hard the urge to kiss her. 'But what could I do? I've got to know what last night was about.'

'It was a mistake,' she said quietly.

'A mistake?'

Lisa nodded. 'I wish with my whole heart that it had never happened.'

I walked over to an empty table, sat down and closed my eyes in a bid to block out what was happening. As I squeezed my eyes shut a million and one emotions washed over me.

'It can't have been a mistake,' I said desperately. 'I felt something for you last night and I know you did too. I can't have got it that wrong, surely? It wasn't just all in my head.'

'You're right,' she replied. 'I think when Andy told me he was flying me over here I was more excited about seeing you than I was him. You were there for me when I needed you. I wanted to be there for you, too. But I took things too far. You're Andy's best friend. I should never have put you in that position.'

'But you did,' I replied. 'And even though I'm Andy's friend I don't regret anything about last night.'

'You and Andy have been friends too long for me to believe you mean that.'

'You don't need to tell me what's at stake,' I replied. 'I already know. And maybe Andy will never get over it or

maybe he will. But all I know is that it's worth the risk. Last night wasn't just about sex. It was about something more than that. It must have been.'

'I don't know what to say.'

'Say you'll leave him.'

I could see from Lisa's face that she hadn't seen that coming. 'You don't know what you're saying, Charlie.'

'Maybe not,' I replied. 'But I know you don't love him.'

There was a long silence.

'You're right,' she said eventually, 'I don't, at least not like most people would mean it. We're probably more like a car crash. We're too mangled together to tear apart without doing ourselves some permanent damage.' Lisa paused as a group of girls carrying luminous cocktails came out through the glass doors and filled the patio with cackling laughter.

'We'd better go back inside, Charlie,' said Lisa, standing up. 'Andy could start looking for us any second. Are you coming?'

'You carry on,' I replied. 'I'll see you in a minute.'

Lisa headed back inside the bar while I looked up into the night sky and contemplated what had just happened. She was right, of course. What had happened was just a messy situation in which some degree of misery was inevitable for everyone involved. But what she didn't know was that she was living on borrowed time, just like I had been with Sarah. Andy was going to leave her and yet she had chosen him over me. This didn't seem right or fair. Once again he was going to walk away with everything he wanted while everyone else cleared up the chaos behind him.

I crossed the patio towards the door back into the bar but stopped when I saw Tom coming the other way.

'Are you all right?' he asked. 'When Lisa came back to the table alone I thought something might be up.'

'She's not going to leave him,' I said succinctly.

Tom sighed. 'I know it must be tough for you but it's probably for the best.'

'How can that be true when he's going to leave her anyway?'

'You don't know that for sure, do you? Andy says a lot of things he doesn't mean. And even if he does, there's no need for you to get involved is there? If he does leave her then maybe there'll be a chance you and Lisa can get together when all this has blown over.'

'It's not going to blow over,' I replied. 'Can't you see that? This whole thing is a mess. I didn't mean for it to happen but I don't regret it because it wasn't me who cheated on Lisa in the first place. And it's not me who's planning to leave her when we get back home. And while this might not be the best way for me and Lisa to get together, now it's happened there's no going back. The only thing I regret is all the lies. It's time for me to be honest, Tom. It's time that someone told Andy the truth.'

'You're not thinking straight,' said Tom grabbing my arm. 'This is going to cause nothing but trouble. What about Lisa?' Tom increased his grip. 'You haven't even talked it through with her.'

'I know all I need to know,' I replied.

When I look back at that moment when I broke free of Tom, stepped back inside the bar and began making my way over to Andy and Lisa, the two things I remember most clearly are the sound of blood rushing to my head and the feeling of urgency fuelling my actions. This was something I needed to do, regardless of the consequences.

'All right, mate?' Andy grinned as I reached our table. 'So how was the dance floor?'

'I wasn't on the dance floor,' I replied much to Andy's confusion. 'We need to talk.'

'No, he doesn't,' said Tom, catching up with me. 'Just ignore him, Andy.' He grabbed me by the arm again and tried to pull me away but I was too determined to carry out my mission to budge an inch.

Lisa flashed Tom a look of concern. 'Is he all right?' she asked, as though I was unable to speak for myself.

'*I'm fine,*' I replied. 'I just need to talk to Andy alone, that's all.'

'This isn't the time or the place, mate,' said Tom. 'Why don't you leave it until later?'

'Leave what for later?' said Andy standing up. 'I feel like I'm missing out on something. What's this all about?'

'It's about you,' I said calmly.

Andy's eyes flitted from me to Tom and back again as he tried to weigh up whether this was to do with him and Nina, or something else altogether.

'Let's take this outside, mate,' said Andy, hedging his bets.

'You'd like that, wouldn't you?' I replied. 'Is it because you don't want Lisa to hear what I've got to say?'

'You'd better watch yourself, Charlie,' warned Andy. 'You're going too far.'

'You're wrong,' I replied. 'I've already gone further than I thought I ever would and now I'm here I'm not going to back down. I've always backed down with you, haven't I? I used to back down with Sarah too. I feel like I've spent my whole life backing down from everything and everyone. But not this time. This time I'm going to stand my ground.'

'Look, mate,' intervened Tom. 'I'm begging you, please don't do it. You'll regret it. You know you will. Just leave it and walk away.'

'I can't, Tom,' I replied. 'I have to do this.'

'You have to do what?' said Andy defiantly.

'Tell you that last night I slept with Lisa,' I replied, facing Andy head on.

Andy didn't say anything for a few moments. He didn't need to as it was all written across his face: the relief of realising that this had nothing to do with Nina, followed quickly by the hurt of a double betrayal, and then finally the anger and indignation of being wronged.

Before he could ask Lisa the question on his lips, she grabbed her bag, and brushed past me and ran towards the entrance to the bar. Pausing only to throw me a look of pure distilled hatred Andy followed after her, while Tom and I stood by in silence.

# DAY SEVEN: SUNDAY/MONDAY

## It's good for the soul

It was early morning and I'd been sitting on a towel in the middle of an empty Laguna beach watching the tide come in for well over an hour. Sensing that I was no longer alone, I turned to see an elderly Greek guy standing less than five feet away from me. He was wearing a white sun-hat, sunglasses and pale blue swimming trunks and was carrying a towel and a bundle of clothes underneath his arm.

'You like early swim too?' he asked in heavily accented English.

'Yeah,' I replied, even though I was startled at the sight of a genuine old person. I didn't know that Malia had any genuine old people and this guy with his leathery sun-beaten skin and silvery body hair looked to be at least in his seventies. 'I do like swimming early in the morning,' I continued, 'it's good for the soul.'

'I swim every morning,' said the old man, carefully laying out his towel on the sand by his feet and placing his clothes on top of it. 'It makes me feel good about the day ahead.' He took off his hat and sunglasses and laid them on his towel. 'Enjoy the water when you get there,' he said, giving me a gentle wave of his hand, 'the Mediterranean is the best sea in the world.' With a sudden burst of energy – particularly for a man verging on his

301

seventies – he gently jogged towards the sea. Within a few moments he was chest deep in the blue-green waves and soon all I could make out was the shape of his head bobbing in the water.

Seeing the old guy enjoying the water like that was like a challenge to me. If he could get into the water then so could I. As I'd arrived at the beach already wearing my trunks, all I needed to do was kick off my sandals and slip my T-shirt over my head. Feeling the warmth of the early morning sun against my skin made my whole body feel alive again and now I was back from the dead I was more than ready to begin my journey to the water. Walking across the warm sand I came to a halt once the sea was lapping at my feet and watched, momentarily hypnotised by the rise and fall of the water. A few yards in front of me a large wave crashed on the shore sending a huge surge of water over my ankles. As the sand underneath my feet began to give way, and I felt myself sinking, without further encouragement I took my first steps into the water.

The sea felt cool but not cold and with the sun overhead getting warmer with each passing minute, the water gradually became more inviting. The deeper into the water I walked the more quickly I became acclimatised to its temperature and within moments I too was nothing but a head bobbing above the water. So there I was, treading water, facing out towards the open sea, while being gently buffeted from side to side by the swirling currents around me, grateful for the opportunity, if only for a few moments, to feel weightless.

It had been a long night. Tom and I had waited at Pandemonium in the hope that Andy and Lisa might come back. We must have made a ridiculous sight for the bar's usual

'up for it' clientele: two miserable-looking guys in their mid-thirties not talking or drinking while everyone else in the bar partied at their very hardest.

When it became clear after an hour and a half that Andy and Lisa weren't going to return Tom and I headed back to the apartment, hoping to find them there. They weren't of course. The empty apartment was shrouded in darkness. Tom suggested that we go out and look for them, in case anything had happened. In retrospect I can see that this idea was more about making me feel like I was actually doing something than it was about finding our friends. Malia was a big resort and Andy and Lisa could have been anywhere in it. A search party of two stood no chance at all. In the end we both agreed that the best thing we could do would be to get some sleep but once Tom had retired to his sofa-bed I dropped all pretence of getting ready for bed and instead opened up the doors to the balcony, positioned myself in front of the horizon and tried my best to work out how once again I had managed to get things so completely and utterly and spectacularly wrong.

By organising the holiday, Andy had given me the one thing I needed most in my life: hope. His holiday plans had set me in a completely new context, one where I could forget about the past and could allow myself to be more optimistic about the future. Because of this newfound positivity, I'd seen opportunity at every turn and regardless of the consequences had pursued it to the end. The girl-in-the-cowboy-hat had got things going but it had been Lisa's phone calls and text messages where I'd really begun to hit my stride towards lunacy. So by the time Donna had arrived in my life I'd been so ready for action that not even the setback of Sarah's pregnancy could stop me from

my mission. But when all my efforts with Donna came to a halt, all I did was refocus on Lisa. That's the only way I could find to explain what had happened. Sleeping with friends' girlfriends wasn't the kind of thing I did normally. It wasn't me at all. I had succumbed to the ever-present holiday temptation to take leave of my senses.

I sat out on the balcony for most of the night and as each hour passed without heralding Lisa and Andy's return I felt increasingly worse about my role in the night's events until somewhere around seven in the morning I could take no more. From my vantage point on the balcony, I looked around for something to do and found a huge blue-green expanse of inspiration right in front of me. 'That's it,' I thought, as the sun continued its rise over the horizon, 'for the first time this holiday I'm going to go in the water.'

In total I spent just under an hour in the sea – far longer than I'd expected – but every time I contemplated leaving the comforting buoyancy of my surroundings I kept imagining how every step towards the shore would bring me closer to the burden of carrying my own weight. When I eventually came out of the water I felt ungainly. Beached almost. And it took a few moments to get used to the sensation of supporting my own weight on dry land. Returning to my towel and clothes I found myself wondering about whichever one of my evolutionary ancestors it had been who had first come up with the idea of leaving the safety of the ocean. I was convinced that if I had been in their shoes (or flippers) at the time, as soon as I'd experienced the unbearable strain of life on land I would've turned my salamander-like tail right around and headed straight back into the ocean.

The beach was already beginning to fill up. The guys who ran the sun-lounger business were setting out their wares and a few early-bird sunbathers had already laid claim to the best spots on the beach. Not wanting to get changed in front of even the smallest audience I used my beach towel to soak up as much of the water as possible, pulled on my T-shirt, shoved my feet back in my sandals and left.

There were few people on the streets although Stars and Bars, as usual, was home to a number of young clubbers determined to deliver a two-finger salute to the supposedly moribund concept of sleep. A few of them waved at me as I passed by and I waved back, even though it may have been a joke at my expense. It was a good sign, however. I was feeling positive again. The night before had repre-sented rock bottom but now I was definitely on my way up.

## This is between me and Charlie

I was beginning to flag by the time I reached the front door to the apartment. As I put my key in the lock I was yawning and barely able to keep my eyes open, so as I opened the door and slipped past Tom on his sofa-bed my intention was to throw myself into my bed even though I was in desperate need of a shower. Once in the bedroom I realised that I wasn't going to be getting any sleep any time soon. Standing in front of me, packing their suitcases, were Andy and Lisa.

'You're back,' I said inanely.

'Not for long,' replied Andy. 'We'll be out of your way in a bit.'

'Look, Andy,' I began, 'I just want you to know that I'm completely aware how much I've messed up. What I did was . . . well . . . it was unforgivable. I've let you down in the worst possible way. And I completely understand if you want nothing more to do with me. I just want you to know that it was nothing to do with Lisa. It was all me. I'm the one to blame.'

Andy stopped packing. 'Have you finished?'

'Yeah,' I replied. 'That's all I wanted to say.'

'Good,' said Andy, 'I can carry on with my packing.'

'Look,' I said. 'Can't we at least go somewhere else and talk this through?'

'I'm not interested in hearing anything you've got to say,' said Andy. 'So I suggest that you leave me alone before I show you just how unimpressed with you I really am.'

'Please, Charlie,' said Lisa stepping in between us. 'Just do what he says.'

'Come on, Andy,' I pleaded, 'this is me and you we're talking about here. Surely there has to be a way that we can work this all out?'

'Are you joking? Tell me, Charlie, how do you think we're going to work this all out? You slept with my girlfriend. How are we going to resolve something like that?' He then struggled past Lisa and pushed me in the chest with such force that I staggered backwards into the side of his bed.

'Calm down, Andy,' I yelled, struggling to my feet.

'I'll calm down when you answer the question,' said Andy through gritted teeth.

Tom entered the room. 'What's going on?' he shouted as Andy made another lunge for me and connected with my chest, sending me flying on to the bed again.

'Just stay out of it, Tom,' spat Andy as he drew back a fist ready to thump anyone who got in his way.

'If you think I'm going to let the two of you batter each other senseless, you've got another think coming,' barked Tom.

'Stop it all of you!' yelled Lisa grabbing on to Andy. 'Just stop it.'

Lisa's intervention seemed to have the effect of bringing us to our senses.

'I understand that you're angry, Andy,' began Tom in his role as peacemaker, 'and from where I'm standing you have every right to be. What Charlie did was . . . well, you

know what it was. But fighting each other won't change a single thing, you know that.'

'So why don't you help us out here?' suggested Andy. 'Come on, Tom, you're the Christian. Tell me what would you do if you were standing in my shoes? What would you do if our friend here had slept with your wife? Would you turn the other cheek? That's what you're supposed to do isn't it? Come on. I really want to know the answer. Would you forgive him?'

'No,' replied Tom, his eyes filling with disappointment. 'I don't think I could forgive him—'

'See that, Charlie?' replied Andy. 'Even Tom thinks you're scum.'

'That's not true,' said Tom. 'You didn't let me finish. What I wanted to say was that if I was in your shoes I didn't think I could forgive Charlie . . . *on my own.* But that doesn't mean that it's impossible. It just means that I'd need help to do it. We all need help sometimes – even you.'

No one spoke for a while. We all stood staring at each other, wondering how this was going to end.

'You're probably right when you say there's no way back from this.' I finally found my voice. 'I should know that better than most. When I found out Sarah was cheating on me, it really did feel like my life was over and to have done the same to you was the lowest thing I could've done to anyone. So you don't need to tell me how hard it is to forgive, because I already know. But do you know what though? That doesn't mean I can't ask.'

'You can ask all you want but the answer will always be no,' said Andy.

'Will it?' Lisa turned to Andy. 'Is that really the way it

is? You know it's not that straightforward, Andy. We're all as bad as each other. And to make out Charlie is somehow worse than anyone else makes me think that you didn't mean a single thing we talked about last night. They weren't just words, were they?'

There was a long silence.

'No,' said Andy eventually, as he avoided Lisa's gaze. 'Of course they weren't.'

Lisa reached out and held his hand. 'Well then, if you really did mean it when you told me you wanted for us to start over, if you meant it when you said that you wanted to give us another go, then for our sake I think that you have to find some way to forgive Charlie, because otherwise you'll always be holding on to the past.

'I know you, Andy. You won't be able to move on if you don't deal with this now. You'll just end up hating Charlie, and hating me and hating yourself at the same time and I don't want that for you or me.' Lisa paused and looked from Andy to me and back again and then, leaving Andy's side, she walked over to Tom. 'It's up to you,' she said. 'If you want us to work this will be the only way it will happen.'

## Not the way we were

The balcony was a tip. Our solitary week of occupation had taken its toll. There were beach towels draped over the chairs, ashtray overflowing with cigarette butts, abandoned crisp packets and beer bottles littering various surfaces and right in the centre of the table, gently warming in the mid-morning sun, lay the dregs of Andy's second bottle of raki from two nights earlier.

'Looks like someone had a bit of a party out here,' said Andy moving a towel from one of the chairs and hanging it over the railings.

'A party?' I replied. 'More like a wake.'

We sat down and slipped on our sunglasses but neither of us spoke. It had been my idea to come out here while Tom and Lisa went for a walk. I felt I'd done some of my best thinking during this holiday while looking out across our perfect sea view and hoped that the power of the balcony would assist Andy and me in the seemingly impossible task ahead.

Lowering my sunglasses on to the bridge of my nose I stared down at the swimming pool. A new batch of twenty-something girls had taken up residency on the prime spot of sun-loungers opposite our balcony and were gently grilling themselves in the sun.

'New Arrivals,' I said, in a bid to start us talking.

310

'Looks that way,' replied Andy. He reached into his pocket, pulled out a pack of cigarettes and offered me one which I declined.

'Given up?'

'Never really started.' I paused and then added, 'It was just a holiday thing more than anything.'

There was a long silence as we both realised that once again one of us was using the holiday to excuse some form of anti-social behaviour. We both knew it was ridiculous. The holiday wasn't to blame for anything. We were.

Looking out to sea, Andy lit his cigarette, took a long, deep drag and held his breath before sending a swirl of smoke into the morning sky.

'Let's get this straight,' said Andy lowering his cigarette. 'I'm out here because of Lisa not you.'

'I know.'

'If it was up to me I'd never say a word to you again.'

He meant it too. He meant every word.

'So what do you want to do?' I asked. 'Sit here until Lisa comes back and then make out like we've sorted things out?'

'Have you got a better plan?'

'No.'

'Well then that's what we'll do.'

There was a long silence. We both looked down at the pool as a couple of guys who could have been Andy and me in our younger days simultaneously dive-bombed into the water, making such a huge splash that all the girls lounging at the side of the pool looked at them.

'So where do we go from here?' I asked as, mission accomplished, the two young lads swam across to the steps

on the other side, exiting the pool to the cheers of their friends.

'I don't know,' said Andy. 'I think the best we can do is try making it up as we go along. But one thing I know is we will never be friends again. It just won't happen.'

## Still hungry

Content to be amused by the antics of the young guys showing off below, Andy and I sat quietly on the balcony for some time. Eventually we both stood up and made our way back indoors; Andy continued packing while I finally had a shower. By roughly midday the four of us were all standing in the bedroom with suitcases packed ready to leave the apartment.

Although we had only been living in our apartment for just over a week, somehow during those seven days it had managed to transform itself into a home. As we checked all the rooms one last time in case we had forgotten anything, I knew that I would soon end up feeling nostalgic about the lukewarm/cold shower and the uncomfortable single bed, the overzealous air-conditioning unit and the TV with its three crappy stations. But the one thing I would miss most of all was the balcony – the few square metres of private outdoor space that had provided the backdrop for so much of the holiday. Grabbing my camera, I slid back the patio doors and stepped out on the balcony. Breathing in the outside air I tried to capture the view in my head: the perfect blue of the sky meeting the perfect blue-green of the sea and illuminating it all the perfect summer sun. I took the picture in my mind's eye. Then I took the picture with my camera and although I was sure that there would

be a discrepancy between the two, I was content to make do until the day when I could see it once again with my own eyes.

The photo taken, I returned to the others, who had been silently observing my eccentric behaviour from the kitchen doorway. No one made any comment and we made our way outside where Tom handed me the keys, allowing me the honour of locking the door one last time.

Downstairs there were already quite a few people waiting by the reception desk to check out. I recognised some of the people in the queue ahead of us: the young lads and the two girls who had arrived at the Apollo at the same time as us as well as a group of student-looking types who'd been lingering by the pool most days. Eventually the queue whittled down and we handed in our keys, settled our quite extensive bar tab, paid the extra we owed for the use of the air-conditioning unit and put our luggage in the hotel's storage room.

'So what are we going to do for the rest of the day?' asked Tom as we all gravitated towards the steps at the front of the Apollo. 'I could murder some breakfast.'

'Me too.' I tried to read Andy's face but he wasn't giving anything away, nor was Lisa. 'What do you guys reckon?'

'Actually,' said Andy coolly, 'Lisa and I have got a few things to do. How about we meet you guys back here later this afternoon, around three? The coach to the airport isn't coming until about nine so we'll still have time to do some stuff later.'

'Okay,' I replied. 'We'll see you in a few hours then.'

Andy and Lisa turned left out of the hotel and headed in the direction of the strip.

'What do you think that was all about?' asked Tom.

'I don't know,' I replied. 'Maybe they just need some more time on their own to sort stuff out.'

'So what are we going to do until three?'

I looked at Tom and smiled. 'Still hungry?'

'Ravenous.'

'How does a "Killer" English breakfast followed by a litre of lager chaser sound?'

'Perfect. Stars and Bars?'

'Of course.' We descended the steps to the street. 'And after that . . . well who knows? We're still on holiday so we might as well make the most of it.'

## A great plan

At three-thirty in the afternoon, Tom and I were sitting in the hotel lounge drinking beer and watching the sports channel on the big screen TV. Since our final breakfast at Stars and Bars all we had done was wander around Malia hunting for souvenirs that might be appropriate for Tom's kids. It was a harder task than we'd assumed as most shops seemed to specialise in little more than glow-in-the-dark-condoms, T-shirts with slogans even students would be embarrassed to wear and statuettes of Priapus, the ridiculously over-endowed Greek god and symbol of fertility. In the end we managed to find a One-Euro shop and bought two packs of felt-tip pens and two T-shirts emblazoned with a map of Crete.

'Do you want another beer?' said Tom looking at his watch. 'Or should we hang on until they arrive?'

'We might as well have another,' I replied. 'Who knows how long they'll—' I stopped mid-sentence as I spotted Andy and Lisa entering the lobby.

'I'm really sorry, guys,' said Lisa. 'We sort of lost track of time.'

'No worries.' I could tell straight away that there was some-thing different about Andy even without him speaking. His black mood from this morning seemed to have completely disappeared. He almost looked as though he was happy. As though he had made some sort of life-changing decision.

'What have you guys been up to?' asked Tom.

'It's a long story,' said Andy, 'which we'll explain later.' He paused and looked at me. 'Look, Charlie, I think we should both put everything that's happened in the past now. Agreed?' He held out his hand for me to shake.

'Agreed,' I replied shaking his hand even though I knew this charade was for Lisa's sake, not mine.

'And the same goes for you, Tom,' continued Andy, offering his hand to Tom. 'I know I've been a bit of an arsehole in the past and I'm sorry.'

Tom looked at me perplexed. 'Yeah, okay,' said Tom shaking Andy's hand warily. 'Who are you again?'

'He's still the Andy we know and love,' said Lisa rolling her eyes, 'believe me.'

'And now that you've finished dissecting my personality,' said Andy, 'do any of you mind if we actually get on with the rest of the day?'

'What have you got in mind?' asked Tom cautiously.

'Nothing that you need worry about,' replied Andy. 'It's just that Lisa has come up with a great way to kill the afternoon: we all choose one thing we really want to do and then we do it.'

'Sounds like a great idea,' said Tom. 'Where's the catch?'

'There is no catch,' replied Andy. 'And just to show that there isn't, I think you should go first.'

'You mean I get to choose somewhere to go and we'll all go without any arguments or moaning?'

Andy nodded. 'Anywhere at all.'

Tom thought for a moment. 'Well, there is somewhere I actually do want to go but I guarantee you'll hate it.'

'We'll enjoy it, okay, Tom?' grinned Andy. 'But whatever it is just spit it out because time's running out.'

'Okay,' said Tom, 'I want to go and see a tree.'

'A tree?' said Andy, incredulously.

'Yeah, a tree,' replied Tom. 'It's two thousand years old. Apparently its circumference is so wide that it would take sixteen adults linking hands to span it. I'd really like to see it. Charlie's still got his hire car until tonight. And it shouldn't take longer than a hour to get there.'

'Well, if Tom wants to see a two-thousand-year-old tree,' said Andy, shaking his head in mock despair, 'let's take him to see a two-thousand-year-old tree.'

318

## It's not an olive tree

It took just under an hour for us to reach the village of Krassi. We pulled up in a dusty car park on the outskirts that was all but empty apart from us and one other car.

'Are you sure you've got the right place?' asked Andy leaning out of the rear passenger window. 'Or could it be that there's not exactly a huge demand amongst tourists to see some knackered old olive tree?'

'It's not an olive tree,' said Tom.

'So what kind of tree is it?'

'How am I supposed to know?'

'It could be an arse tree for all I care,' replied Andy. 'How interesting can any kind of tree be?'

'Give it a rest, Andy,' said Lisa calmly. 'Think about it, how often do you get to see something that's as old as this tree's supposed to be and still be alive?'

'Nice try,' said Andy. 'But I guarantee you that this tree is just going to be a tree, no matter how old it is.'

We climbed out of the car into the searing sun and began making our way up the steep hill to the village. On the way up we were all on constant tree alert but other than the occasional gnarled-looking oak we didn't see anything at all that fitted our expectations. As we reached the top of the hill with no sign of it, however, we began to wonder if we had somehow missed it.

'Do you think it was the pine tree by that house on the hill?' asked Tom. 'That was pretty tall, after all?'

'It can't have been,' I replied. 'Surely a two-thousand-year-old tree is going to be more substantial than that?'

'Well, how about that chestnut tree by that gate?' suggested Tom.

'That can't have been it either,' said Andy. 'Two of us linking arms could've spanned that easily.'

'I give up then,' said Tom. 'I have no idea where this thing is.'

'Maybe we should ask someone,' suggested Lisa.

Andy, Tom and I looked at her blankly. It was clear that none of us wanted to do anything as potentially embarrassing as asking people for directions to a two-thousand-year-old tree.

'Okay,' said Lisa pointing across the road at a shady terrace the size of a small football pitch. It was surrounded by a line of trees (none of which looked to be over thirty years old let alone two thousand) and had tables and chairs set out as if it were some sort of outdoor café. 'Why don't we go over there, get a drink and cool down a bit and work out what to do next?'

Following Lisa's lead we all crossed the road and made our way to a table at the edge of the terrace. A waitress came over to us and handed out menus and we were in the process of deciding what to order when Andy froze and pointed across the way. And there it was, right in front of us: a two-thousand-year-old tree looking exactly like you'd expect a two-thousand-year-old tree to look – tall, stately, ancient and wise.

'If you'd told me this morning that I'd be impressed by

a tree I'd have called you a nutter,' said Andy quietly. 'But I have to admit, Tom, you were right, mate, because that . . . really is one amazing fucking tree.'

## The small thumb

'So come on then,' said Andy on our return to the hire car. 'It's your choice next, Charlie, what's it going to be?'

'How come it's me next?'

'Well, we could do mine if you like,' conceded Andy. 'But I think it'd be more fitting if we did it last.'

'It isn't dangerous is it?' asked Tom.

'I wouldn't say it was dangerous,' said Andy, revelling in the mystery. 'At least not if it's done properly. But there'll be no backing out of it okay? I've seen your tree, we'll do Charlie's thing next and finish up with mine.' Andy turned to me. 'So come on then, hurry up.'

'What I really want to do,' I said having now rejected over a dozen different ideas in my head, 'is sit on a beach where there aren't massive speakers blasting out music, people trying to flog you loyalty cards to use sun-loungers, hot girls in bikinis or cool boys with six-packs. That's what I want. Just us and a beach and as much peace and quiet as we can manage.'

Unsurprisingly the criteria for my beach excursion proved difficult to fulfil given that all the decent beaches were next to densely populated resorts and therefore packed with people. Any stretch of water that had sand next to it seemed to be either too grim for words (broken bottles in the sand, plastic bottles washing up on the surf, chockful of sinister-

322

looking seaweed) or right next to some smoke-belching industrial plant. Just as we were about to give up and return to Malia, Tom spotted a sign for a stretch of beach that wasn't visible from the road and suggested that we give it a try.

In front of us was a small lagoon that was empty apart from a mum and dad watching their young son skimming stones across the surface of the still water. There was no sand, only large, perfectly smooth pebbles.

'Is this good enough for you, Charlie?' asked Lisa as she slipped off her sandals.

'I think this is what I've been looking for all holiday,' I replied. 'A bit of peace and quiet and a nice view.'

Andy laughed. 'Are you sure you're actually a bloke, Charlie? Because you do a brilliant impression of a girl sometimes.'

'Don't listen to him,' said Lisa, 'this place is fantastic.'

I turned to Tom. 'What do you think, mate?'

'I think we need to get our shoes off and get in that water,' said Tom.

Barefooted, all four of us walked down to the water's edge and then in unison waded into the cool shallows right up to our knees.

'You don't get pebbles like these on Brighton beach,' said Lisa dipping her hand into the water and picking up a large smooth grey stone with a long white swirl in it. 'This one looks like a bar of soap,' she said, offering to me. As I took it, my fingers grazed her warm skin, sending a shiver down my spine. 'You keep it,' said Lisa. 'It'll be something to remember the holiday by.'

'Have you got your camera on you?' called Andy as he skimmed a handful of stones across the water. 'We should take a picture.'

I pulled out the camera from my bag and handed it to Andy who walked over to the small boy and asked him to take a picture of us all.

Knee deep in the water we lined up in a row with our arms around each other – Tom, me, Lisa, Andy – and then in his best English the boy yelled: 'Cheese' and took the picture. He handed the camera back to Andy before running off to rejoin his parents and we all grouped around to get a better look at the camera's display. Though it might not have been the most brilliantly composed picture of all time – a small thumb was clearly visible in the corner of the picture – it still managed to capture the essence of what we were about: four people who were connected with one another more closely than any of us might like to admit.

## Dragons aren't really me

It was just after six o'clock by the time we made our way back to Malia. And even as we parked the car a few doors down from Stars and Bars, Andy still wasn't giving much away about our final task.

'So where is it we're going next?' asked Lisa, yawning.

'I'm afraid there's no "we" in this next bit,' replied Andy. 'This one's strictly for the boys.'

'It's not a strip club is it?' asked Tom.

'Of course it isn't,' said Andy rolling his eyes. 'It's better than that.'

'So what then?'

'It's over there,' said Andy, pointing to the Angel tattoo parlour across the road. 'And it's the perfect way to commemorate this holiday.'

I'd never given much thought to the idea of paying to have my skin permanently scarred in order to make some sort of indelible fashion statement, but if I had I would've definitely have been one of those people who rejected it on the grounds that: 'It might look great now but what about when you're eighty-five, and about to take residency in a nursing home?'

This was the argument that I attempted to present to Andy and Tom as we crossed the road to check out various pictures of the proprietor's (a Mr Rodney Cross, originally

325

from Dulwich, East London) handiwork. There were full colour 6"x4" pictures of arms, legs, calves, backs, faces and full bodies covered with everything from animals and Celtic symbols right through to sportswear logos and film stars.

'Look, Charlie,' said Andy, 'if you do end up in a nursing home with a tattoo on your arm it'll be a fantastic reminder as you freefall into dementia that once upon a time you actually had a life worth living.'

Tom laughed. 'I'm with Andy on this one. If you make it to eighty-five and all you've got to worry about is a tattoo you had done over fifty years ago then as far as I'm concerned, you're doing pretty well.'

'So that's two against one,' said Andy. 'Are you in or out?'

'I'm in,' I replied. 'One hundred per cent.'

'For the record,' said Lisa, 'can I just say that I think this is one of the stupidest overly bloke ideas the three of you have ever had?'

'Your objection is duly noted, babe,' replied Andy. 'But what you don't understand is that sometimes a man's gotta do what a man's gotta do. And right now what these men have to do is choose a cool tattoo design.'

Agreeing that Mr Cross's work was of a sufficiently high standard to let him loose on our skin, we made our way into the shop and told the woman standing by the till our requirements: three reasonably straightforward tattoos, no colour, done as soon as possible. In return she took our money, booked our time slots and handed us several large portfolios of designs to look at.

'I've found my design,' said Andy after five minutes of flicking backwards and forwards.

'Me too,' said Tom.

They both looked at me.

326

'I haven't seen anything so far that says, "Please be on my skin forever," I replied. 'I could be here a while.'

'Not that I'm endorsing what you're all doing in any way at all,' said Lisa, taking the portfolio in Andy's hand away from him and flicking back a couple of pages, 'but I have to admit I quite liked that one.' She pointed to a design in black ink of a Celtic-looking sun. 'It's quite subtle and wouldn't look too hideous.'

I wasn't convinced.

'How about this one then?' said Andy turning the page to a small circular Chinese-looking design of a dragon chasing its own tail. 'I was seriously considering having it for myself before I found the one I really wanted.'

'Cheers,' I replied, 'but I don't think dragons are really me either.'

I looked at Tom. 'Come on, mate, you must have some sort of suggestion too?'

Tom shook his head. 'I think you already know what you want but you're just too scared about making the decision.'

I couldn't help but laugh. Tom was spot on. 'Okay, you're right,' I replied. 'I was just playing for time but my mind's made up now. So let's go and get ourselves a tattoo.'

When I emerged from the back of the tattoo parlour three quarters of an hour after Andy and Tom had had theirs done, all Andy would say was that his tattoo was in the middle of his shoulder blades while Tom told me that his was on his right shoulder. Given that we were all being so secretive, I suggested that we have a grand unveiling in a few weeks' time as a sort of post-holiday reunion. Tom thought that was a great idea but Andy just laughed and said that he would have to see.

327

## As good a place as any

'What time is it?' asked Andy as we emerged from the tattoo parlour. The early evening sun had long since disappeared and we were now standing right in the middle of the constant bustle of night-time Malia.

'Dinner time,' said Tom looking at his watch. 'I'm starving and we've only got half an hour before the coach arrives to pick us up.'

'What kind of food do you want?' asked Andy.

'The fastest food possible.'

As we headed back to the Apollo feasting on takeaway McDonalds we were laughing and joking so much that the events of the morning seemed as though they had happened a million years ago, to someone else entirely. Were Andy and I back to being friends? It was hard to tell. The damage we'd inflicted on each other was hardly going to heal overnight. The important thing to me, though, wasn't that we were back to normal. Rather that it seemed that we were both willing to make the effort to fake our friendship until such counterfeit feelings were no longer necessary.

Liberating our suitcases from the Apollo's secure room we sat on the steps outside to wait for the coach. Within five minutes the Club Fun tour coach finally reared into view and it pulled up directly in front of us.

'We should have said goodbye to Steve-the-barman,' I said as the coach driver opened up the vehicle's storage bay and began loading up a small mountain of luggage.

'No worries,' replied Andy, 'I'll do it for you later.'

'How are you going to do that? You'll be—' I stopped and looked at Andy's face and suddenly realised what he meant. 'You're not coming back home are you?'

'No,' said Andy, 'we're not.'

Lisa's face confirmed that Andy wasn't joking. Andy reached across and gently traced a small line along Lisa's right hand. It was a small gesture. A gesture of love, I suppose. But even though I tried to fight it the gesture broke my heart.

'What are you saying?' asked Tom. 'That you're extending your holiday?'

'We're thinking something more permanent,' said Andy.

I don't know why I was surprised. If I'd learned anything from this holiday it was this: given the right degree of provocation, anyone could lose the plot. All it took was a partner leaving, a doctor diagnosing cancer, or the betrayal of a close friend and it appeared the rule book for normal behaviour could be abandoned completely.

'I know it's a lot to take in,' began Lisa. 'We can hardly believe it ourselves but we've talked about nothing else and it's what we want.'

'To stay here?' I asked.

'It's as good a place as any,' replied Andy.

There was a long silence. I could feel the time slipping away.

'I know it's none of my business but are you really sure?'

'There are just too many distractions at home,' explained

Lisa. 'Too many ways to get lost. That's what went wrong with me and Andy: we both ended up being too focused on things that didn't matter. We need to take this time out together if we're ever going to make things work between us again.'

'We're thinking a year to begin with,' added Andy. 'And if we're still happy . . . maybe we'll even make it permanent.'

'What about your jobs?' I asked.

'We'll sort something out,' said Lisa.

'And your house?'

'We were sort of hoping you'd keep an eye on it for us,' said Lisa. 'We've rented somewhere here for a few months – that's what we were up to this afternoon – it's not much but I can't see us needing to do much in there apart from sleep. And as for work . . . look where we are . . . there must be hundreds of bars and restaurant jobs going. And if there aren't, well, we'll just have to sort something else out.'

The more I tried to reason the whole situation out in my head, the more I came to realise that every hole I tried to find in their plan seemed to point out my own inadequacies rather than theirs. The truth was I was jealous of their spontaneity. I was envious of the fact that they had succeeded where I'd failed. For both Andy and Lisa, whether they stayed together forever or split up after a week, this would always be the holiday that changed their lives. The Andy standing in front of me right now was different from the one who had left England over a week ago. And that's what bothered me. He had changed and I was still the same. I'd be going back to the same flat, job and life that I had left behind seven days ago.

'Are these going to the airport?' asked the coach driver pointing to our luggage.

'Yeah,' I replied. 'Just these two please.'

'Are you sure?' he asked eyeing Andy and Lisa's luggage. I looked at Andy and then Lisa waiting for their confirmation.

'Yeah,' replied Lisa. 'We're sure.'

The driver shrugged, loaded up the last remaining suitcases on to the coach and closed the hatch. There was no going back now.

'So this is it,' said Andy thoughtfully.

'I'll say my goodbyes first,' said Lisa. She put her arms around Tom and squeezed him tightly, burying her face into his chest. 'I hope everything goes well tomorrow. I'll be thinking of you.'

Initially confused, Tom looked at me and the guilt must have been written on my face. 'I told Andy earlier in the week,' I apologised.

'That's okay,' said Tom. 'I'm glad in a way. It'll be nice knowing I've got friends rooting for me.'

'Well, count me among them,' said Andy shaking Tom's hand firmly.

'Look after yourself, Charlie,' said Lisa embracing me.

'You too,' I replied. 'I really do hope everything goes well for you guys.'

'It will,' she replied. 'I'm sure of it.'

'Look after yourself, mate,' said Andy stepping towards me.

'I will do,' I replied. 'And if you need anything at all while you're out here, just let me know and I'll sort it out for you.'

'Cheers.' Andy paused as if he wanted to say something

else but then at the last minute his face changed and he shook my hand. 'Don't go thinking things will change,' he said. 'Because they won't. From now on you're dead to me. Absolutely dead!'

332

## I'm sure you really are a nice guy

At the sound of the electronic ding the seat-belt light over my head switched off, thereby setting off a commotion of seat-belt unclicking. Even though it had been half an hour since the plane had taken off, my mind was still very much on the ground, wondering from minute to minute what Andy and Lisa were up to and when might be the next time I would see them. Releasing my seat-belt I stretched my arms in the air, yawned and turned behind to see if I could see what Tom was up to. Due to a computer error, we'd been allocated seats in different parts of the plane and Tom was now sandwiched between a dour-looking youth wearing multiple gold chains and a smiling middle-aged woman with painted-on eyebrows and a deep orange tan. Looking at Tom's companions, I realised I'd fared much better: a pretty but hassled-looking mother, with a sleeping baby on her lap and a napping toddler on the seat next to her.

As people began passing by on the way to the toilet I reached under the seat in front of me and pulled out *The Da Vinci Code*. With all that had been happening over the past few days I'd somehow managed to neglect the book so much that I suspected I'd have little chance of getting back into it. So I pulled out the third and final choice for my holiday reading: *White Teeth* by Zadie Smith – a book

I'd selected less because I was desperate to read 'an epic comic tale telling the story of immigrants in England' and more because the bespectacled authoress on the cover looked quite foxy. I only managed to get as far as the end of the first paragraph before I had to stop as I'd become aware that somebody was lurking by my side. I looked up to see a man roughly my own age, with a few days' worth of stubble and a slightly drawn complexion, staring down at me.

'Sorry to trouble you,' he began, 'but I was wondering if you wouldn't mind swapping seats with me? It's just that my wife and kids are here.' We both looked across at his wife and she gave me the same wearily apologetic smile that her husband had just given me. I smiled back, somewhat surprised to find myself feeling envious of the guy who had just spoken. He was where I was supposed to be at thirty-five. But where was my hassled wife? Where were my sleepy children? Where was my family holiday? 'We were all supposed to be sitting together, you see,' the husband continued, 'but they made a cock-up at the check-in desk and said that we should wait until take-off to see about swapping seats.'

Envious or not, I wished them happiness. 'Of course you can have my seat,' I replied as I bundled my things together. 'Just show me where you were sitting.'

Cringing from the huge amount of appreciation that the couple lavished on me, I followed the husband back to his original seat – a middle seat – some five rows in front of my own. As we approached, an austere-looking woman, who had obviously spent too much time in the Cretan sun, stood up making little effort to hide her annoyance at being disturbed for a second time. Apologising

again the man quickly grabbed his things, thanked me and made his exit, leaving me to squeeze into my middle seat and re-organise my things.

'Sorry about this,' I apologised as I knocked the girl in the window seat next to me several times with my elbow. 'They don't actually give you very much room to do anything in these seats beyond breathing.'

'That's a good thing you've done,' said the girl. 'He'd been fretting about moving seats ever since—' She stopped abruptly and a horrified look spread across her face. And though it took a few seconds, I suddenly realised the reason.

'You're not wearing your cowboy hat,' I said, unable to believe my luck. It was the girl-with-the-cowboy-hat or rather the girl-formerly-known-as-the-girl-with-the-cowboy-hat.

'Oh, it's you,' she began. 'I really am sorry for what happened.'

'There's no need to apologise,' I replied. 'It's fine.'

'It wasn't really me,' she continued. 'You see I was being egged on by my friends.'

'Honestly,' I replied. 'It's all fine.'

'Look, I'm really sorry if I embarrassed you.'

'I wasn't embarrassed,' I replied grinning. 'I was flattered.'

'But you didn't turn up at the bar, did you?' I shrugged and she buried her face in her hands. 'Oh, you did, didn't you? You must think I'm a terrible person. I'm so sorry. I did sort of think about going but I lost my nerve. I feel awful now.'

'And so you should. I waited all night for you to turn up.'

'You didn't, did you?'

'No,' I replied. 'As it happens that whole night went a bit weird so I probably wouldn't have been much fun anyway . . . *even if you had turned up.*'

There was a long silence. Fully aware that in terms of conversation etiquette a choice was being presented to us – to continue chatting or not – the girl-with-the-cowboy-hat chose to stare pointedly out of the window into the darkness. Accepting that our conversation was now officially over, I pulled out my book again and began reading. She did the same with her book. Just as it seemed that we would both spend the entire flight not talking I became convinced that I was looking a proverbial gift horse in the mouth. Here I was, sitting next to an attractive girl who had selected me to ask out on a date following a dare. Conversational openers didn't really get much better than that.

'Just in case you've forgotten,' I said, closing my book, 'I'm Charlie.'

She turned and looked at me, embarrassed. 'Look, Charlie,' she began hesitantly, 'I don't want this to come out the wrong way . . . and I'm sure you really are a nice guy but I think I ought to tell you I met someone . . . in Malia . . . and we're sort of together.'

'Oh,' I replied. 'Well, that's good to hear.'

There was another long silence. The girl-in-the-cowboy-hat smiled at me uncomfortably. It was difficult to know which of us was more desperate to get away from the other.

'I'll be getting back to my book then,' I said, after a few moments.

The girl-in-the-cowboy-hat half nodded, dug into her bag and plugged a set of headphones into her ears.

I folded back the cover of my book and read page one all over again.

We landed at Gatwick ten minutes early because of something to do with wind speeds and early time slots. As we taxied along the runway, I tucked my book into my bag. I would never finish *White Teeth*. Not because it was a bad book, but rather because judging from the little I'd read I'd come to realise that, along with being quite foxy, the author was also incredibly talented and most definitely out of my league. This news depressed me: once again, by virtue of just being me, I was ruling out yet another one of the several billion women alive on planet Earth.

As the cabin crew switched off the seat-belt sign there was once again a frenzy of activity among the passengers. The austere-looking woman next to me was out of her seat and rummaging in the overhead locker in an instant but the girl-in-the-cowboy-hat, I suspect keen to give me a head start off the plane, remained in her seat looking out of the window.

Along with everyone else, I shuffled into the narrow central aisle of the plane towards the exit. Welcome home. There was a chill in the air and floodlights were glistening in a dozen puddles dotted across the wet tarmac.

Waiting for me at the bottom of the steps was a tired and drawn-looking Tom. I looked at my watch. 2.38 a.m. There was now roughly six hours until he would be making the call that could change his life forever.

'How was it for you?' I asked as we boarded the bus that would take us to arrivals.

'I slept for most of it. How about you?'

'It was . . . interesting.' My eyes flitted across the tarmac

337

to the girl-in-the-cowboy-hat who was waiting for her friends.

'Is that who I think it is?' asked Tom.

'Yeah,' I replied. 'But don't get your hopes up.'

'Why not?'

'Because I did and I ended up severely disappointed.'

Tom laughed. 'If it wasn't to be then she probably wasn't right for you.'

'Maybe not,' I replied, 'but if she isn't, who is?'

I could tell from the look on his face that Tom wasn't interested in discussing his feelings about making the call. So instead we walked in easy silence until we were through passport control and out the other side.

We both turned on our mobile phones. 'Any messages?'

'Looks like it,' replied Tom as he dialled his voicemail. Positioning himself out of the way of fellow passengers, Tom's face lit up as he listened to voicemail messages that were obviously from his family.

Tom grinned. 'One from Anne, two from the kids . . . and one from Andy.'

'What did he say?'

'Even though he doesn't believe in God, on the off-chance there is one, he said he'll say a little prayer on my behalf.'

'That doesn't sound like him.'

'No,' replied Tom. 'That doesn't sound like Andy at all.'

We made our way through to the luggage carousels and waited patiently for our bags to arrive. Once again I spotted the girl-in-the-cowboy-hat pushing a trolley with her equally attractive friends but on seeing me she steered them to the opposite end of the carousel.

It took over half an hour for our luggage finally to emerge, by which time most of the passengers (including the girl-in-the-cowboy-hat) had claimed their bags and disappeared through customs. I could feel all the good work that my seven days of relaxation had achieved slowly beginning to unravel. And as we finally pushed our luggage through the brightly lit 'Nothing to Declare' channel at customs, I was gloomily convinced that by the time we reached the long-stay car park, I would be back to my usual hassled and severely stressed state of mind.

Stepping through the large doors from customs into the arrivals lounge, Tom and I were forced to walk the gauntlet of waiting husbands, wives, boyfriends, girlfriends, parents and minicab drivers all scanning constantly for a glimpse of the people who mattered to them most. We had no one waiting for us. Or so I thought. But right at the end of the crowd queuing behind the security barrier was Donna.

It was odd seeing her in the flesh, here. As I walked towards her, I was forced to readjust the picture of her in my head that had grown somewhat blurred these past few days. She was prettier than I remembered, and her hair was different. And while I was still wearing shorts and a T-shirt appropriate to summer in Crete she was wearing jeans and a coat more appropriate to autumn in England. The oddest thing of all was that she was wearing glasses.

'You hate them, don't you?' said Donna, as I came to a halt in front of her.

'What?' I replied.

'My glasses,' said Donna. 'All day I've been agonising over whether to wear them or my contacts. Nina said contacts because she's pretty vain, so that immediately made me want to go for my glasses.'

I didn't know how to respond to her glasses, the knowledge that she had been preparing all day to meet me from the plane or the fact that she was here at all.

'What are you're doing here?' I said, eventually.

Donna opened her mouth to reply but paused and looked expectantly over my shoulder where a clearly embarrassed Tom was lingering with our luggage trolley.

'I just wanted to say that I'm going to get a coffee,' said Tom.

'Cheers, mate,' I replied. 'I'll see you in a bit.'

As Tom headed off in search of a café, Donna and I stood watching the people around us: an elderly man pushing a trolley piled high with suitcases; a young couple kissing next to a newsagent's; and a group of young lads taking photos of each other with their mobile phones.

'I'm sorry about leaving like that,' said Donna quietly. 'There was no excuse for it. I should have been more honest with you.'

'So why did you do it?'

'Do you want the truth? Because you seemed more sure of me than I was.'

'So it was my fault?'

Donna shook her head. 'I got scared, Charlie. Really scared. I was beginning to feel things for you that I haven't felt for anyone in a long while. I just wasn't sure that I was ready for anything this big this soon. Sadie's dad and I were together a long time. And we had a child together. And even though everyone thinks I should be moving on and looking for something new I couldn't do it. I felt like I was stuck in the past and I just couldn't find a way of moving forward.'

'So what changed your mind?'

'You did,' said Donna, looking into my eyes. 'You changed my mind. I don't know how you did it but you did. You've been in my head every second since I left you. I've replayed the time we spent together a million times and that's when I realised that the feelings I have for you weren't going to go away just because you weren't there. So last night I called my sister to get Andy's number and called him to find out what time you guys were landing at Gatwick. And now here I am. That is, if I'm not too late?'

It was a good question. Was she too late? Did what had happened between Lisa and me make a difference? Had my feelings for Donna just been a holiday thing? All I had was questions and not enough answers that I could be sure of.

'You met someone else, didn't you?' whispered Donna, observing my indecision.

'It's complicated,' I replied. 'But yes, I was with someone else after you left. It was a real mess and it's over now.'

'So why do I feel like there's something you're not saying?'

'Because there is . . . being here with you . . . having you here right now . . . hearing you say these things. It's like having my dreams come true in an instant. But the thing is, Donna, we're not on holiday any more. We're back in reality. And when I left seven days ago the one thing I wanted most of all was to come back different . . . to come back changed. And I've done it. I'm not the person who went on holiday any more.'

'I don't understand,' said Donna. 'So what's the problem?'

'The problem's this.' I let go of her hands and pulled

341

off the top I was wearing. I rolled up the right sleeve of my T-shirt to reveal the cottonwool dressing fixed over my tattoo. I pulled it away gently and showed Donna what was underneath.

'It's a question mark,' said Donna. 'I still don't understand.'

'I'm not sure I do either.' I shrugged. 'I've never tried to reduce myself down to a symbol before . . .' I paused and peered down at the black ink of my bold 18pt Helvetica question mark '. . . and looking at this I don't think I'll ever do it again.' I taped the dressing back in place, rolled down the sleeve of my T-shirt, then looked at Donna. 'The thing I need you to understand is that once upon a time I used to think I was an okay boyfriend . . . but then Sarah left and I realised I was wrong about that. I used to think I was a pretty good friend, too, but things have happened this holiday that have made me rethink that too. The truth is: I actually have no idea who I really am any more. Not in a real sense. I can't guarantee that the guy you met on holiday really is me and not just some faker. I can't guarantee that you won't wake up one day and hate my guts. And what hurts most is that I can't even guarantee that I won't do something that might hurt you one day. I can't offer you any guarantee of any kind at all, Donna. So why would you want to get involved with someone like that?'

'Because I don't need your guarantees,' she replied. 'I've got my own.' She paused. 'I know I don't know you that well. And maybe you're right about what you're saying. But what I do know is this: you're the first person I've met in a long time who has made me feel like wanting to trust again.'

There was a long silence.

'So where does this leave us?' I asked.

'It's up to you,' she said.

So there it was, right in front of me. A big decision that, as Donna had pointed out, was indeed 'up to me'. And I wanted to do the right thing . . . whatever that might be.

'This is all wrong,' said Donna, interpreting my reticence as the awkward silence before the delivery of bad news. 'I feel like I'm crowding you into making a decision, which isn't what I want to do at all.' She sighed. 'I should go.'

'Maybe you should,' I replied with a smile.

Donna looked confused.

'You drive, don't you?' I asked.

She nodded.

'And you know Brighton pretty well too?'

She nodded again.

'Good.' I rummaged in my pockets and pulled out the keys to my car and my flat. 'Well, I don't know what your plans are for tonight but I'd really like it if you'd take my car back to Brighton and stay at mine.'

'While you do what exactly?'

'I've got something I need to sort out. I'll tell you everything when I get back in the morning. But for now you'll just have to trust me.'

Donna smiled softly and looked at the keys in her hand. 'Just like you're trusting me?'

'Exactly,' I replied. 'Sometimes you've just got to have a little bit of faith.'

I gave Donna the details of where the car was parked and how to get to my flat and told her to ring me if she needed anything at all. With that done we made our way outside and joined the queue for the shuttle-bus to the car park.

Mike Gayle

It was raining and cold and I realised why Donna was dressed so warmly. Though it was technically August, the weather was more late September. I began to shiver as the cold quickly made its way through my thin summer clothing. Donna put her arms around me. As she pressed her body against mine she looked up and we kissed. While part of me was sure this was a bad idea, given we still had so much to sort out, most of me was simply happy to be caught up in the moment.

As we parted from the kiss Donna bit her lip guiltily and without saying another word, jumped on to the shuttle-bus. As she settled into a seat at the rear of the bus, I was conscious of being scrutinised by her fellow passengers as though I was part of some new form of reality television. I didn't care though. Standing my ground, I shivered patiently until the bus finally pulled away and then, taking in a long, deep breath of cool night air, I made my way back inside the terminal to find Tom.

344

## Five hours and forty minutes and counting

'How did that go?' asked Tom when I found him sitting at an empty table in the only café still open.

'Okay, I think. I hope you don't mind, but I've sent her off to mine in the car. I thought we could wait here to make the call if that's okay?'

'Here's as good a place as any.'

'We could always get a hotel or something,' I added. 'There must be loads around here.'

'Here's fine,' said Tom. 'I doubt I'll sleep much anyhow.'

'So we'll just sit here until morning?'

'Probably not here, exactly,' replied Tom. 'The guy at the counter said he's shutting up shop pretty soon.' I looked at my watch. It was twenty minutes past three. 'Five hours, forty minutes and counting,' said Tom meeting my gaze. 'Doesn't seem all that long since I woke up this morning,' he paused and laughed. 'I guess time really does fly fast when you're having fun.'

I told Tom everything that had happened with Donna. When the café finally shut we ended up moving from the arrivals concourse to departures and eventually set up camp on a bench overlooking rows of closed check-in desks. Other than the occasional cleaner pushing large industrial floor sweepers back and forth no one took much notice of us

and so we were free to sit and talk uninterrupted for the rest of the night. We talked about our university days, reminding each other of several embarrassing occasions best forgotten, we talked about what we both wanted from life and how we might get it, and then finally as night turned into early morning, we talked about Tom's beliefs and my own. It was an interesting and at times heated discussion and Tom made a number of points to which I genuinely could find no retort. I can't say that he changed the way I thought about religion, because he didn't; what he did was change the way I thought about him. Regardless of my opinions, Tom's faith worked for him in a way that I truly envied. And that's not to say that he didn't seem scared about how the call to the doctor's might go, it was more that I could see in his eyes that – even if the news was bad – the things he believed in would somehow give him comfort.

The café reopened at 6.00 a.m. and we were its first customers of the day. But as the hours passed things gradually became busier until sometime around 8.00 a.m. the café reached critical mass – every table occupied, huge queues at the tills, and the café staff beginning to look hassled.

With only twenty minutes left before Tom made his call, he decided to phone Anne and the kids.

I wondered whether I too should use this opportunity to make a call. The events of the early hours seemed so far away that I almost feared they were an elaborate dream. Though I was happy imagining Donna asleep in my bed, part of me (possibly all of me) wanted to call her and wake her up just to say good morning. Now that a new day had

begun I wanted to make a new form of connection with her. But even though I took out my phone several times I just couldn't bring myself to make the call, for fear that things wouldn't be the way I hoped.

When Tom returned to our table he looked even more tired and drawn, as if he had suddenly driven headlong into a brick wall of mental exhaustion.

'Everything okay?'

Tom shook his head and for the first time I thought he was going to break down. 'I just can't believe that any of this is really happening,' he said. 'I feel fine. I feel healthy. Surely if I had something bad I'd feel sick, wouldn't I? I keep telling myself to expect the worst because at least then I'll be prepared for it. But I can't do it. The worst is just too terrifying to think about.'

We sat and stared at our collection of empty coffee cups.

'How are the kids?' I asked, eventually.

'They're fine,' replied Tom. 'They've been playing their gran up big time this morning, which can only be a good thing. Anne and her mum took them to a butterfly farm yesterday. Apparently Katie now wants to be a butterfly farmer when she grows up and Callum wants to be a cater-pillar . . . because they get to spend all day eating.'

'Does he like his food, then, Callum?'

'He can eat for England.'

'I'd love to see them again. I bet they've grown loads since I last saw them.'

'They'd love to see you, too. They're really curious about you. When I told them I was going to Crete with my friend Charlie you took on this strange mystique in their heads. Now they think you live in Crete and for some reason

they've got hold of the idea you're very tall.' Tom stopped abruptly. 'Will you do something for me?'

'Yeah, of course,' I replied. 'Whatever you want.'

'If this does turn out to be bad news, will you promise me you'll always keep in touch with my kids?'

'Of course.'

'It's just that they're young. They'll forget.'

'Of course they won't. You're their dad. And anyway Anne will remind them about you all the time.'

'I know. And she will do a great job. But I want them to know *all* about me. I want them to know what their dad was really like. I want them to know that I struggled with life just like they'll have to. I don't want them to grow up thinking I was perfect.' Tom looked at his watch again. 'It's time,' he said quietly.

'Where do you want to do this?'

'Here's fine.'

'Are you sure?'

He nodded, almost glaring at his phone in anger. I found myself holding my breath as he began dialling his doctor's number. Even though the air was ringing with the constant chatter of dozens of different conversations, I could still make out the high-pitched tones of each number pressed on his keypad. I couldn't begin to imagine what he might be going through. At least not on any meaningful level. How would I know how it might feel to have everything that I loved balancing precariously on a knife-edge? I didn't have a wife. I didn't have kids. There was only me.

Entering the final digit into his phone Tom breathed deeply and put the phone up to his ear. His face contorted in rage and he threw the phone down on the floor. 'They're fucking engaged,' he said kicking the empty chair

next to him with such force that it toppled over. Everyone in the café turned and stared at him.

'It's all right, mate,' I said grabbing him by the arm in a bid to calm him down. 'Look, I'll make the call and as soon as someone answers, I'll pass them over to you when they answer.'

Tom nodded and calmed down. 'Thanks,' he replied as he rescued his phone from the floor. 'I'm sorry about that.'

'Don't worry about it,' I replied. 'You wait here and I'll keep trying until I get through.'

Making my way out of the café, I headed in the direction of the nearest newsagent's in search of a morning news-paper as a distraction. On the way I tried the number twice and each time got the engaged tone. In a bid to try to calm myself down, I told myself that I wouldn't try again until I'd read the headlines on every single newspaper in the shop. And that's just what I did. It was the usual mix of politics and celebrity scandal, although one newspaper headline was dedicated to the poor weather the nation had been suffering in recent days. Even after seven days away, none of it was a surprise. Just more of the same.

I pulled out the phone again and pressed redial. And my heart began to race when, instead of the engaged tone, I finally got a connection. As I ran back to Tom at full pelt a voice at the other end of the line answered my call.

'Brookdene Road Surgery,' said a female voice brightly.

'Hi,' I replied, as I finally reached the café. 'Could you just hang on a second?'

I barely dared to breathe as Tom took the phone from my hand and told the woman his name, the reason for his call and his date of birth. And I continued to hold my breath as Tom closed his eyes as he waited for the news.

In a split second everything changed. He'd been given the test results. And the news was good. To this day I've never seen an expression more life affirming than the one on Tom's face. What the customers in the café must have thought as I threw my arms around Tom I don't know. And I don't care either. All that mattered was that he was okay.

## A brand new start

I felt exhilarated as Tom and I grabbed our suitcases and made our way towards the train station. I was so euphoric that I wanted to stop complete strangers and tell them his good news.

At the station I bought a single ticket back to Brighton, while Tom bought a ticket into London so that he could get his train back to Coventry.

'Thanks for everything, Charlie,' said Tom, as we arrived at his platform just as the service into central London came to a halt and the doors opened. 'I wouldn't have been able to get through any of this without you.'

'You did it all yourself, Tom,' I replied. 'I didn't do a single thing. I'm just glad you're okay.'

'You'll come up and see us though won't you?' He picked up his bags. 'Anne was saying this morning that she would love to see you again.'

'I'll definitely come up. And you should bring them all down to Brighton one weekend too. Brighton beach might not be quite up to the standard of the ones in Crete but it'll do for a half-term break.'

We shook hands and Tom looked at me thoughtfully. 'I hope everything goes well with Donna,' he said. 'You deserve to be happy.'

As Tom boarded the train I remained on the platform,

lost in my own thoughts, long after it had departed. I was thinking about the holiday again, and about Donna, Lisa and Sarah too but most of all I was thinking about Andy. I still couldn't believe what I'd done to him. I still couldn't believe that I'd betrayed him like that. And even though I knew it was likely that I would never see him again I couldn't stand the thought that I'd let him down so badly. As I made my way out of the station to get a taxi I pulled out my phone. *'It'll be mid-morning now in Crete,'* I thought as I looked at my watch and I couldn't help but raise a small smile as I wondered whether Andy would be up yet. I dialled his number and determined to find out. The phone seem to ring forever but eventually someone answered.

'Hello?' said a groggy female voice.

'Lisa, it's me, Charlie.'

'Oh, Charlie . . . I'm sorry, I was fast asleep. Are you back home? How's Tom? Has he had his results yet? Is he okay?'

'He's fine. The results were negative.'

'That's fantastic!' There was a long pause while I heard her relay the news to Andy. I found myself smiling as I heard Andy let out a huge roar as though he'd just scored a goal in a world cup final. 'I'm so pleased, Charlie. I really am. If you speak to Tom tell him we'll ring him soon.'

'I will do.'

There was a short pause.

'I wasn't just calling about Tom's news,' I continued. 'I was sort of hoping to speak to Andy too if that's okay.'

'Of course,' said Lisa. 'I'll put him on.'

As I listened to the static at the other end of the line I began to wonder if this call really would give me the

absolution that I felt I so desperately needed. The facts of the matter at hand hadn't changed now that I was back home; the feelings they had generated, though less intense on my side, were bound to be still boiling over inside Andy. And though my self loathing was riding at an all-time high, I still wasn't at all sure I had what it would take to face yet another rejection of my efforts to make things right. *Maybe I'm just making things worse*, I thought. *Maybe we'd all be better off if we just let this go*. I was about to put the phone down when Andy finally came on the line.

'Charlie,' he said evenly. 'It's good to hear the news about Tom.'

'Yeah it is,' I replied.

There was a long pause.

'Is Lisa still there?' I continued.

'No, she's gone for a shower. Why?'

'Because I want . . . I need to talk to you.'

'I know,' said Andy. 'I do too. I was going to call you later in the week. This feels wrong doesn't it? I want to hate you and I feel like I've got good reason to but I just can't quite do it . . . and last night I think I worked out why. The fact is after everything that happened I could've lost Lisa . . . someone who has been with me through all the bad times in my life . . . and if I had I couldn't have blamed anyone but myself. Not you. Me. No one but me. I've treated her badly so many times and always left you to clear up the mess so it's hardly surprising that she turned to you in the end.'

'But it was my choice wasn't it? I didn't have to do anything, did I? I could've stayed away from her.'

'I think you saw how I was treating Lisa and convinced yourself you'd be the one to step in and fix things. She

told me everything you said to her. How you wanted her to leave me and be with you.'

'She wouldn't though. She chose you.'

'You could've made your job a lot easier if you'd told her about Nina. But you didn't. So why didn't you?'

'I'd been lying to her about what you were up to. What else could I do?'

'Nice try,' said Andy. 'But I don't believe you for a second. You could've easily talked your way out of looking guilty. You were only covering for me because you had no choice. You didn't tell her about Nina because you hoped I'd come to my senses. She would have understood that because seeing other people's point of view is what Lisa does best. And you're not stupid, Charlie. You knew that.'

'I don't understand. What are you trying to say?'

'I'm trying to say what I know to be true: that even after everything that happened you still couldn't bring yourself to betray me. That night in the bar you didn't tell Lisa what I'd done. You told *me* what *you'd* done. Even though you could have betrayed me you didn't, you betrayed yourself. And that's why I can't hate you, Charlie. I know better than most about letting people down.'

'I know what you're saying,' I replied. 'You're saying I let you down.'

'No,' replied Andy. 'You've got it all wrong. You've always had standards and yet you let yourself get dragged down to mine. That's my problem here. It's not me you've let down, it's yourself. And I know in my heart that it's a lesson learned. You'll never do it again because now you know how it feels. So don't beat yourself up about it. What's done is done. Pick yourself up and do like me: make a brand new start and promise yourself that you'll never go back there again.'

## Just us

As the taxi I'd caught from the station pulled up outside my flat and I saw Donna standing on the doorstep, all the doubts that had pushed their way to the front of my mind melted away. As I struggled to pull my suitcase out of the cab, she descended the steps from my door down to the street so quickly that by the time I was free of the taxi her arms were around my neck and we kissed.

'I thought you were never going to come,' she murmured.

'And I thought there was a chance that you might not be here,' I replied.

'I'll always be here if you want me to be,' smiled Donna.

'Well in that case,' I replied, taking her hand, 'I think you should know that the way I'm feeling right now I will always want you to be here.'

'I don't need any guarantees from you, Charlie,' said Donna scrutinising my face.

'Then what do you need?' I asked.

'For us to be able to start again. You and me, right here, right now. No baggage. No worries. Just us.'

I thought about Andy. He was right. New beginnings. A brand new start. And now here was mine.

'Hi, I'm Charlie Mansell,' I said holding out my hand for Donna to shake. 'Pleased to meet you.'

'Hi, Charlie Mansell,' replied Donna shaking my hand,

'I'm Donna Finch and I'm pleased to meet you too.'

'How was that for a new start?' I asked.

'Good,' replied Donna.

'Really?' I replied. 'I think there's room for improvement.' Grinning I leaned across and kissed her firmly on the lips. 'And how was that?' I whispered as our lips parted.

'Better,' replied Donna. 'Much better.'

# EPILOGUE

## As long as we're together

So that's it really. The story of how, a year ago, a cheap package holiday changed my life. Changed it for the better. And it is better. By a long way. Donna and Sadie (a great kid, by the way, whom I couldn't love any more if she were my own) ended up moving from East London to Brighton after we'd been together six months. I offered to move to London, but Donna reminded me that Sadie had always fancied living by the sea and after a lifetime of land-locked living was ready to try something different. We talked briefly about moving in together, but with Sadie and Donna's ex to consider, we decided that it was a bit too early for all that and she ended up renting a flat three doors down from me. She got a new job too, working in a bookshop in the centre of Brighton because she wanted a break from nursing. She took a cut in pay and has to work every other Saturday but she enjoys it much more than her old job and the people that she works with are fun to be around.

As for me, I carried on working at the council, even though after the holiday I daydreamed about packing the whole thing up and moving permanently to a country where at the very least you were guaranteed decent weather in August. Helped by Donna, I ended up doing quite a bit of work to the flat: all the things I'd been meaning to do but

had never got round to. So now every single room has been painted from top to bottom; I've had new kitchen and bathroom suites installed and finally got round to replacing the furniture that Sarah took with her when she moved out. Guests no longer have to sit on dining chairs or the carpet when they come round. I have a proper sofa, and a dining table and loads of other stuff that civilised people have in their homes.

Donna and I bought the sofa one Saturday morning in the early part of the new year. Sadie was spending the weekend with her dad and Donna had come down to Brighton for the weekend. Feeling good that we had finally managed to tick 'Buy Charlie a sofa' off the long list of things 'To Do' we'd decided to go for lunch at a really nice café in the Lanes. Just as we were about to go in, the door opened and a couple pushing one of those trendy prams that looks like a lunar landing vehicle emerged. It was only when Donna and I stepped aside and the couple pushing the pram looked up to thank us for doing so, that I realised that the woman was Sarah.

Though I'd been expecting to have an inevitable 'ex-encounter', as time passed and she faded from memory, I assumed (or should that be hoped?) that Sarah had left Brighton altogether. So when I saw her that day I have to admit it took me by surprise. Donna said that I acquitted myself pretty well but I'm not so sure. Surely the sharp pang of pain I felt must have shown on my face? I don't know what caused it. Whether it was the shock of seeing Sarah, or Oliver, or even their baby, a little girl they'd called Daisy, I don't know. But I know it did hurt. Probably more than it should have done.

Sarah and I talked for a while and did all the introductions

required. She appeared happy and healthy and I have to say that they seemed more suited as a couple than we'd ever been. After five minutes or so of polite catch-up chit-chat we parted company. But it was very much a case of, 'Good to see you, have a nice life.'

Donna and I carried on into the café and I was grateful that she didn't make a big thing about it, even though she would have had every right to. In fact, Donna didn't mention it at all until I brought it up one evening about a month later. We were standing in my kitchen talking about nothing in particular when I came out with it. I told her I was sorry for the way I'd reacted and how seeing Sarah had taken me by surprise. Donna seemed to understand what I was trying to say and it sparked a discussion that went on until the early hours. Things from our pasts that we'd never spoken about before emerged and although at times it was upsetting, the end result of this tidal wave of confession was a declaration from Donna that she loved me and one in return from me that my feelings were the same.

As winter turned to spring and even Brighton got a bit warmer, we talked about going on holiday together – the three of us – Donna, Sadie and me. Initial thoughts ranged from a week at a posh hotel in St Lucia right through to a fortnight camping in south Wales. We just couldn't make up our minds. Then, around Easter, Tom and his wife and kids came to stay for a few days and they made us an offer neither Donna nor I could refuse.

'How about we all go on holiday together?' suggested Tom, as we all sat eating chips on the beach overlooking the old Brighton pier. 'Andy and I have been e-mailing each other about it for a while and he says there's a villa in Stalis owned by a friend of his. He thinks he might be able

to get it for us all for a week on the cheap. It's got four bedrooms, a swimming pool and is only five minutes from the beach. What do you reckon?'

Things had remained pretty awkward between Andy and me. We hadn't spoken much at all. Neither of us was particularly suited to long telephone calls and I had more to say to him than I could ever limit to an e-mail. And although I'd seen them both at Christmas when they had returned to the UK to see their families and tie up a few loose ends to do with putting their house on the market, the time had flown by so quickly that I felt I'd barely seen them at all.

'You want to go, don't you?' asked Donna.

'Yes, of course,' I replied. 'But I'd understand if you didn't. After all, it's our first holiday together.'

'You're mad,' said Donna smiling. 'Of course I want to go. It doesn't matter where we go as long as we're together.'

So that was that. The plans were made for us all to stay at Andy's friend's villa in August. The night before the flight, Tom and his family stayed at mine and the next day we drove together to Gatwick and boarded a midday flight to Crete. From the moment I spotted Andy and Lisa waiting for us at arrivals it was clear that their new life in Crete agreed with them. With their matching deep bronze tans, and their T-shirts advertising 'Andy's Bar – the number one night-spot in Stalis', they looked every inch the perfect couple.

The whole week was faultless from start to finish. The weather was great every single day; the villa really *was* only five minutes from the beach and we all got on together better than we'd ever done. Andy was no longer quite as

cocksure as he used to be; in fact for the whole of the holiday he was almost (but not quite) consistently likeable. Of course we had the odd bit of conflict (Tom and Andy argued over the best way to barbecue fish and Andy and I argued over who would win the premiership next season) but other than that things were fine. The three of us even managed a quick trip to Malia one evening for old times' sake, but we didn't even get out of the car. Instead we sat with the windows wound down, content to watch the teeming hordes of young Brits having the time of their lives.

Building sandcastles on the beach with the kids on the morning of the final day of the holiday, we were all shocked when Andy suddenly shouted out: 'What about the tattoos?'

Since we'd had them done, none of us had remembered to look at each other's tattoos. Eager to get the ball rolling, Andy promptly took off his T-shirt to reveal a Chinese symbol between his shoulder blades. 'It's the Chinese symbol for love,' said Andy. 'But my Chinese is terrible so it could say pretty much anything.'

Tom then rolled up the sleeve of his T-shirt to reveal three names on his bicep, one under the other: Anne. Callum. Katie. Anne laughed. 'You couldn't have just had an anchor or a dragon, like everyone else in the world, could you?'

'Don't you like it?' asked Andy. 'I think it looks great.'

'It's not that,' replied Anne, blushing. 'It's just that in seven months' time he's going to have to add another name to his list.'

'That's great news,' I said, patting Tom on the shoulder as everyone else joined in with the congratulations. When the commotion died down Tom demanded that I reveal my tattoo.

'I'm going to have a bit of a problem with that,' I replied, as I rolled up the sleeve of my T-shirt.

'Where is it?'

'I had it removed.'

'How come?' asked Andy. 'It had better be for a good reason.'

'It was actually,' I replied, looking over at Donna and Sadie and smiling. 'It was for the best reason possible: I just didn't need it any more.'

At this Tom laughed and Andy rolled his eyes in despair and as I walked over to Donna and kissed her on the lips I made a mental note to book us all on another holiday as soon as this one was over.

## Acknowledgements

A round of applause to the following: Sue, Phil P, Swati and all at Hodder for their hard work on the book; Simon and all at PFD for making stuff happen; The Fitz for being such a great travelling companion; Euan, Jane, Jackie, Danny, Cath, Chris, Nadine, Vic, Elt, Ruth, Richard, Andy, Phil, Shelia, Alexa, Rod, John and Charlotte (for general mate/advice/family stuff); Arthur, Steve, Kaytee, Gary, Marcus, Ian D, Ian H, Jo, Amanda for being the Sunday Night Pub people; everyone at the Board for being there 24/7; and finally, for actions above and beyond the call of duty: Team Gayle.

# The Life and Soul
# Of the Party

**MIKE GAYLE**

If you have enjoyed WISH YOU WERE HERE,
here is a taster of Mike Gayle's next novel,
THE LIFE AND SOUL OF THE PARTY,
available in trade paperback in August 2008
from Hodder & Stoughton.

arrival of yet another twelve months heralding the arrival of yet more debt, more university assignments and a greater sense of being left behind by my peers, the only thing I hate more than New Year's Eve itself is the thought of spending it alone.

my mind up about the various potential outfits I had laid out there for the party. There was a black boob tube and trousers, a green dress I'd bought last summer in

# Ed and Sharon's New Year's Eve Party December 2005

**Melissa:**

It was just after six on New Year's Eve and I was in my bedroom in the flat that I shared with 'creepy' Susie, my flatmate/landlady. I call Susie 'creepy' not out of any particular malice towards her but because that's exactly what she is. Despite being ten years my senior, Susie has a creepily large collection of teddy bears and a creepy boyfriend called Steve, who somehow always manages to be lingering outside the bathroom whenever I emerge from the shower. On top of all that I'm convinced she snoops around my room when I'm out which I'm pretty sure is the definition of creepy.

The only reason I put up with Susie's creepiness is because, as a thirty-four-year-old mature student with no boyfriend and money, I've no choice in the matter whatsoever. And anyway, having lived in enough nightmare houseshares in the fifteen years I've been in Manchester I know that as bad as Susie is, there are a lot of people out there who could be a good deal creepier.

My plan for the night ahead was simple: along with my friends Vicky, Chris, Cooper and Laura, I was heading to Ed and Sharon's house for their annual New Year's Eve party. And even though as a rule I hate New Year's Eve and can't think of many things I'd rather do less than celebrate the

arrival of yet another twelve months heralding the arrival of yet more debt, more university assignments and a greater sense of being left behind by my peers, the only thing I hate more than New Year's Eve itself is the thought of spending it alone.

Looking down at the bed in front of me I tried to make my mind up about the various potential outfits I had laid out there for the party. There was a black floaty top and trousers; a green dress I'd bought last summer in the sales teamed with opaque black tights and boots; and a dark blue dress that I was 99 per cent sure I could no longer fit into and green shoes with a bit of a heel. Unable to decide, I tried to imagine myself in the clothes without having to go through the ordeal of actually putting them on. The longer I pored over them, however, the more I realised that actually nothing I had chosen was quite right. All the clothes seemed just a little bit too showy for a house party . . . which might have been okay for Vicky and Laura – who could pull off 'showy' – but would make me seem for all the world as though I was trying too hard.

Returning the rejected clothes to the wardrobe, I spotted a black long-sleeved top that had fallen off its hanger and was lying crumpled across a pair of black pumps that I hadn't worn in years. I was slipped off my dressing gown and tried it on. It just felt right, so I searched around some more and found a green knitted cardigan from Oxfam I'd bought a couple of months earlier; it went perfectly with the top, and, inspired, I made a final trip to the wardrobe and rejected all manner of trousers and skirts and even trouser/skirt combos, before closing the door in defeat. That was when I spotted the jeans that I'd been wearing all day. They were lying on the floor by the door. I straightened them

out, slipped them on and checked myself in the mirror. I couldn't believe it. They looked great. The whole outfit was coming together very nicely indeed. Now all I needed was the right footwear. After some moments of deep deliberation I opted for my Converse baseball boots, which I eventually found by the radiator underneath the window swamped by a large mountain of ironing.

My baseball boots were almost as frayed and worn-out looking as my jeans. They were a faded brick red colour and so heavily scuffed and battered that I couldn't wear them in the rain because the seam on the right one had a tear in it. Still, grateful that it wasn't actually raining I slipped them on, tied the laces and surveyed my new outift in the mirror one last time. I looked like a student—which wasn't exactly the look I was going for—but I took some solace in the fact that at least I didn't look like I was trying too hard.

I tied my hair back in a ponytail and then began searching for my make-up bag which I eventually found underneath a stack of magazines by the side of my bed. Rooting around for an eyeliner that hadn't spoiled I finally tipped the whole lot out on to the bed in frustration, just as my mobile phone rang.

'Hey babe, it's me.'

It was Vicky.

'Hey you,' I replied. 'How are things?'

Vicky sighed. 'I've just put William to bed and told him mum's babysitting tonight and he went off on one as though I was leaving him in the care of the big bad wolf. I wouldn't mind but his Gran will spoil him to death like she always does.'

Of all my friends here in Manchester, I'd known Vicky

the longest. We met during the first year that I'd spent studying Business and Economics at UMIST before I was kicked off my course for being completely and utterly hopeless. Vicky and I had both lived in the same halls of residence and I'd been drawn to her because, unlike most of the other eighteen year olds I met during freshers' week, Vicky didn't act like she was trying to cram several years' worth of repressed teenage rebellion into seven days of debauchery. In fact she didn't act like she was eighteen at all. She seemed older and wiser somehow and even though she'd only been in the city for the same amount of time as me, she seemed to know the clubs and bars around Manchester like the back of her hand. So, rather than following the student hordes to grotty pubs and clubs playing the same music you heard everywhere, thanks to Vicky we ended up in clubs in the depths of rough housing estates, warehouse parties in the middle of industrial estates and the kinds of bars you had no chance of finding without being in the know. In short, back then, she had been an education in how to be cool. Fifteen years on, she was a wife, mother to William, my four-year-old godson, and hadn't set foot in a nightclub since the late nineties, but to me, she would always be the girl who knew everything.

'Anyway,' continued Vicky. 'I'm just calling about the plans for tonight. Chris talked it over with Cooper earlier and they've decided we're all meeting at eight in the Old Oak.'

'I thought eight was when the party started?'

'It is, but you know what the boys are like. Apparently it's far too emasculating to arrive at a party at the time actually written on the invitation.'

'That's fine by me.' I paused to consider what tone of

voice to use in order to ask the question on my lips. I decided to go with casual indifference. 'And what about Paul and Hannah? Are they coming?'

'I don't know. Chris left a message on Paul's mobile but he hasn't got back to him yet. I'm sure he'll turn up though. I don't think there's ever been a New Year's Eve that we haven't all spent together. And somehow I can't imagine Hannah is going to change all that.' Vicky paused. 'You are okay about him coming aren't you?'

'Of course I am,' I replied. 'I'll see you later, then, yeah?'

'Yeah, see you later.'

**Vicky:**

After I put the phone down I couldn't get the picture of Melissa out of my head. She'd be sitting alone in her tiny bedroom, thinking about Paul and Hannah, worrying about where her life was going and why he was now so happy and not her. And much as I loved Paul as a friend, I couldn't help feeling angry with him on Melissa's behalf. It was awful the way things had ended between them. Absolutely awful. And even though five years had passed since they split up, for all the moving forward Melissa had done it might as well have been yesterday.

I was with Melissa when she and Paul first met. We were both twenty-three, living in that post-student nether world where you're no longer in full-time education but you don't exactly feel like a fully paid-up member of the workforce either. Mel and I were living in a houseshare in Longsight and spent most of our time buying clothes and records and above all chasing boys. One night a bunch of us met up for a drink in the Horse and Jockey in Chorlton with the plan of moving on to a club night

in Hulme afterwards. However, just after last orders, we heard about a party going on round the corner from the pub and we decided we'd give it a try; if it was any good we'd at least save ourselves money on the cab fare getting over to Hulme.

I'd never seen so many people crammed into such a small space. It was only a two-bedroom terrace, but it felt as though the entire population of the pub had transferred to the party too. I wanted to leave straight away and probably would have done had I not managed to lose Melissa within moments of arriving. I eventually found her half an hour later out in the garden, even though it was freezing cold. She was talking to a couple of guys I'd never seen before and called me over.

'Vicks, this is Paul and Chris,' she said with a grin. 'They lured me out here with the promise of a hidden stash of booze.'

'She's lying,' protested Paul. 'It was her banging on about "hidden booze" that lured us out here!'

Paul and Chris seemed cool and funny without being pompous and annoying and they were good-looking enough to make me want to join in with the conversation. I could tell straight away that Melissa was doing her best to try and impress Paul which was fine by me; Chris—tall and handsome, thoughtful without being morose—was more my type anyway.

Later, around three in the morning, with the party showing no signs of flagging, the four of us decided to leave and headed towards Chorlton Park for a change of scenery. We climbed over the gate and sat on the kids' swings, knocking back lukewarm Red Stripe that we'd liberated from a sink full of melted ice in the kitchen at

the party, and for the next hour or so we put the world
to rights with the kind of heated political debates that
you can only have when you're drunk and in your early
twenties. Eventually we calmed down and started talking
about the future.

'So, where do you see yourself in ten years' time?' asked
Paul, directing his question at Melissa.

Melissa shrugged. 'Why do you ask?'

'Curiosity.'

Melissa thought the question over. 'Ten years from now
I'll be . . .' she paused '. . . what? Thirty-three? That sounds
like a lifetime away.'

'So what will you be doing "a lifetime" from now?'
prompted Paul.

Melissa took a swig from the can in her hand. 'Okay,
okay. Ten years from now I'd like to be . . . right here.'

'What, in Chorlton Park?'

'No, in Chorlton. By then I'll have gone back to university
and finished a degree in something more interesting than
Business and Economics like—I don't know—Art History.
I always loved the academic part of my Art 'A' level more
than the sitting around drawing stuff bits. I like knowing
the stories behind paintings, the reasons why artists create
the things they do.'

'So what would you be doing for a job?'

'I don't know. Something worthwhile I hope. Maybe something for a charity. And I'd be living in one of those sweet
little terraces on Beech Road.'

'On your own?'

Melissa laughed. 'No, with my bloke.'

'And what's he like, this bloke?'

'He's nice and caring and funny. Likes animals and is

good to his mother.' She paused, then added: 'And he never ever, ever forgets my birthday.'

'Sounds like a made-up bloke to me,' said Paul, grinning at Chris.

'Nope,' replied Melissa. 'He's out there somewhere. And do you know what? One day I'll find him.'

The interesting thing was that although two relationships started at that party, they both went in completely different directions. Chris and I were rock solid from day one, moving in together after nine months and then getting married a few years later, but Melissa and Paul's relationship was always volatile. In the early days it seemed like every other week they would have one kind of argument or another, only to make up by the end of the night. Thankfully, after a year or two they appeared to calm down and for a long while things were good between them. I remember them laughing. I remember them being happy. I can even remember thinking to myself when they moved in together (partly out of love but mostly out of convenience) that this was it. They would settle down into the kind of comfortable groove that Chris and I were already in. Finally there would be no more fights, no more arguments, and no more conflict. I even thought that one day the two of them might actually get married and have kids. And like I said, for a long while it really did look as though things were working out for them.

Quite when they began to fall apart I was never really sure, but Melissa always claimed that it was somewhere around the time that Paul turned thirty. It started with small rows about nothing, which eventually progressed into bigger rows about everything. Paul would get annoyed at Melissa and then Melissa would get annoyed right back, thereby

guaranteeing that every petty quibble ended in full-scale war. As bad as it was though I never guessed that Paul would want to get out of the relationship: by this time—to me at least—they came as a pair. You never got one without the other. And I found that comforting because that was exactly how things would always be with Chris and me.

I assumed the arguments were just a 'phase' or a 'bad patch' or 'one of those things' that all couples go through, only to come out of the other side stronger. I'd lost count of the times when friends of ours would appear to be on the verge of splitting up, only to announce a few weeks later that they were getting married or having kids or leaving their jobs to go travelling for a year. I didn't realise that Paul was so genuinely unhappy with the way things were between him and Melissa. And certainly not that he was capable of speeding up the demise of their relationship with a catalyst so lazily constructed that to this day I still find it hard to forgive him.

Out one night with Chris and Chris's brother Cooper and some other mates, Paul got talking to a girl in a club and went home with her. He didn't know that one of the girl's housemates, Sara, was a friend of our friend Laura, and although Paul hadn't recognised her when he'd chatted to her next morning as she left to go to work, she had recognised him and told Laura everything. Laura then checked the story with Cooper (who lied) forcing her to ask me to check the story with Chris (who told a different lie) which in turn validated the story enough for Laura and me to present our evidence directly to Melissa.

Melissa was devastated; it really cut her to the bone. She challenged Paul the moment he got in from work and

the second he confirmed it, she packed her bags and came to stay with me and Chris.

For most people that would have been the end of the story, but not Melissa. Because she was still in love with Paul, she just couldn't seem to let go. Paul must have felt the same, because about six weeks after the split Melissa told me that she had had a long talk with Paul and, despite all that had happened, they were going to try to be friends. I assumed that this was just her way of saying that they would carry on sleeping together but it wasn't that at all. She really did want them to be friends and nothing more. And even though in the months that were to follow she stayed over at his house on numerous occasions, sometimes even sharing the same bed, nothing ever happened between them. According to Melissa all they ever did was talk with an honesty and openness that they had never been able to achieve when they had been together. With the single-mindedness of a scientist on the verge of making a medical breakthrough, Melissa made it her mission to discover why things hadn't worked between them. Taking Paul's confessions and half-mumbled revelations, she did her best to make sense of them all and then, not far off the first anniversary of when things had fallen apart, she made a pronouncement that seemed to take even her by surprise. She said to Paul: 'You think you don't want what other people want. You think that all you want is to be alone. But it's not true. The day will come when you'll be so sick of being alone that you won't know what to do. And when that happens, come and find me and we'll pick up right where we left off.'

When Melissa told me what she had said, I got so angry that I lost it completely and told her to her face how

pathetic she was being letting Paul walk all over her. The last thing she should do was promise to hang around waiting for him to get his act together. I told her straight. Paul didn't deserve her. He wasn't going to miraculously turn into some kind of Prince Charming overnight. And if she was under the misguided notion that she was the woman who was going to fix whatever was broken inside Paul and make him want to settle down, then she was wrong. The best thing she could do was move on to someone else as soon as possible. Melissa got up, walked out and didn't speak to me for the best part of a month.

**Billy:**
It was just after seven, I was on the phone and my New Year's Eve was not off to a good start.

'So what are you up to tonight?'

'Gina and Danni have got me tickets for some club in town,' said Freya. 'Apparently it's going to be really good.'

'What sort of thing?'

'Don't know.'

'Dancey or indie?'

'Indie.'

'Which club?'

'I don't know.'

There was a long pause.

'What about you then?' she asked. 'Are you hitting the town with the gruesome twosome?'

She meant my housemates Seb and Brian.

'Yeah,' I lied.

'Anywhere good?'

'Some club in town.'

'Indie or dancey?'

'Dancey, I think.'

There was another long pause.

'Well, have a good New Year, yeah?' she said. 'I'll be thinking of you come midnight.'

This was far from true. Freya would not be thinking about me at all. She would be thinking about whichever tight-trouser wearing, big-haired, 'Look at me I'm in a band' loser she'd have selected as her next victim. 'And I'll be thinking of you too,' I replied, realising just how much I didn't want this call to end. 'Are you going to make any resolutions?'

'No,' said Freya firmly. 'I'm not into all that. You?'

'I'm making a few.'

'Like what?'

'You know, the usual.'

Freya briefly considering digging a little deeper before she finally said: 'Well good luck with all that then. And we'll catch up soon yeah? Go for a drink or something, yeah?'

'Definitely. Let's catch up soon.'

I put my phone down on the empty computer printer box that doubled as my bedside table, picked up the remote for my CD player, and pressed play. As 'A River Ain't Too Much To Love' filled my ears, I lay down on my bed, closed my eyes and wondered whether Bill Calhoun had ever had problems with 'the ladies' when he was twenty-four.

I'd never been entirely convinced that what I'd felt for Freya had been love (after all, how could it be real love if she didn't love me back?) but what I felt now was torture.

I first got to know her when she took a job at the Duke and Drake in Chorlton. At that time Brian, Seb and I virtually lived there, and we'd got to know most of the staff, so

when I turned up one Saturday night and saw Freya standing behind the bar it sort of took me by surprise. She was absolutely amazing. She had shoulder-length black hair that, along with the way she dressed, made her look as if she had just stepped out of a time machine from 1963. She had that whole Bridget Bardot, sexy indie-chick thing going on and the most beautiful face I had ever seen.

I guessed that she was into music so over the course of a couple of conversations as I got my round in, I'd drop in the names of a few bands that I thought she might like and when those worked I dropped in a few more and then a few more. One night, after about a month of name-dropping bands like crazy, she mentioned that a band we'd both been raving about recently were playing at Night and Day and asked me if I fancied coming along. I couldn't believe it. A date. With Freya. This kind of luck was absolutely unheard of. I was completely over the moon.

Though we'd arranged to meet at Dry on Oldham Street at eight, Freya didn't turn up until minutes to nine.

'I'm really sorry I'm so late.'

'It's fine,' I replied.

'No, it's not, you see the thing is . . .' she started to get a bit tearful, '. . . I've just had a massive row with Justin.'

'Who's Justin?'

'My boyfriend.'

The news that she wasn't single knocked me sideways, even though it made perfect sense that a girl like Freya would have guys throwing themselves at her left, right, and centre.

On the way to Night and Day, Freya gave me a potted history of her and her boyfriend, right up to and including the fight that they had just had. I listened attentively and

gave her advice, even though this guy sounded a lot like some of the idiots who had been on my course at university—all rock star poses and daft haircuts without a shred of personality between them.

At about ten o'clock, when the headline band came on stage, Freya suggested that we move towards the front, grabbed me by the hand and led me right to the front of the stage. And from the band's opening song to their closing encore she didn't let go of my hand once.

At the end of the night we filed out of the venue and headed to a fast-food place for curry and chips, which we ate sitting on a bench next to the bus stop before getting the 192 back to Withington. As we got out to go our separate ways, she told me she'd had a great time and that she would call me in the morning. The call never came.

The next time I saw her was about a week after the gig, when I turned up at the Drake with Seb and Brian to see her behind the bar.

'I'm sorry,' she said. 'I didn't call you did I? It's just that ... well ... Justin and I sort of got back together.'

'Great,' I replied, with as much enthusiasm as I could muster. 'I'm really, really pleased for you.'

'Well, good because it was all down to you.'

'To me?'

'I followed your advice to the letter and before I knew it we were having this massive heart-to-heart and we realised that we were both really wary of getting hurt, that's all. Ever since that night things have been just perfect.'

It didn't last. Like most devastatingly pretty girls, Freya had spectacularly bad taste in men and soon Justin was superceded by a whole litany of posers who could smell

her lack of self-esteem and father-issues from a mile away. And although the names changed (Oscar, Tom, Jamie and Lucien) the pattern always remained the same. They'd fancy her, she'd fancy them; they'd get off together at some crappy indie club in town, then a few weeks later she'd find them snogging some other girl; or she'd find out they already had a girlfriend; or they would simply stop calling. Upset and distraught, she would turn to me for comfort and support. And while I'd be hugging her and telling her how it'd all be all right in the end, she'd be telling me how special I was and how different I was from the other guys. And all the time I'd be thinking 'If I can just hang on a little longer, maybe she'll finally see just how mad about her I really am.'

So anyway, to cut a long story short, a few nights before Christmas Eve, following the demise of yet another short-lived hook-up with a skinny, scruffy, waste of skin and bone called Luke, Freya dropped round at mine to claim both consolation and a free bottle of wine. We joked about how love was a game for losers and made plans for a perfect New Year's Eve.

'How about I come to yours?' she said. 'We can order a takeaway.'

'And drink as much as our livers can take!' I added.

'And then when we're well and truly wrecked,' said Freya really getting into the rhythm of things, 'we can watch *Eternal Sunshine of the Spotless Mind* for the millionth time.'

At that particular moment we were the closest we had been, so I decided that six months of unrequited love was more than enough for anyone and attempted to convert a good-night embrace into something more. Honestly, I couldn't have misjudged the situation worse if I'd tried. The

second my lips touched hers, Freya pulled away and was all 'I'm really flattered Billy, but I don't really see you like that', and I couldn't say a thing in reply because I was too busy willing the earth to open up and swallow me whole.

With five hours to go before midnight, I still had no idea what I was going to do with my New Year's Eve. I called Seb and Brian to see if there were any tickets left for the club night they were going to but apparently the whole thing had sold out months ago and tickets were now changing hands for ten times their face value. I didn't really fancy the idea of bankrupting myself just so that I didn't have to see the New Year in watching *Jools Holland* so I told them to have a good time and decided to put on more suitably melancholy music, turn off the lights, climb back into bed and allow myself the minor indulgence of feeling totally and utterly depressed. After a few minutes realising that I wasn't exactly being a man about all this, I got out of bed and called my older sister Nadine to find out what she was up to.

I chatted about life in general for a bit, to give her the illusion that I wasn't after anything (covering topics as diverse as our parents, the love life of my middle sister Amy, and Nadine's own impending thirty-fifth birthday) before jumping in with both feet and asking her the big question.

'So, sis, what are you up to tonight?'

'I'm off to a party.'

'You're nearly thirty-five!' I exclaimed. 'Do people your age still have parties?'

Nadine laughed. 'You're such a cheeky little sod sometimes.'

'But you love me for it don't you? So this party,' I continued. 'Is it local?'

'It's in Chorlton—my friends Ed and Sharon. Why do you ask?'

'It's just that . . . well . . . I'm sort of at a loose end and I was wondering if I could come with you.'

'You'll hate it,' said Nadine.

'I won't.'

'You will. I'm not saying it'll be a bunch of people standing around talking house prices and swapping notes from the Habitat catalogue but it's not far off, Billy. There won't be any drugs, raids by the police or young girls throwing up in the bathroom.'

Looking around my sad bedroom, my eyes came to rest on the portable TV sitting on top of the chest of drawers in the corner. *Jools Holland* could wait. A boring party full of boring people my sister's age it might be, but at least it was somewhere to go.

'It sounds perfect,' I replied. 'Give me ten minutes to sort myself out and I'll be ready.'

**Melissa:**
I arrived at the Old Grey just after eight. The pub—a favourite with the older crowd in Chorlton—was packed out like it would be just before last orders on a Saturday night. Vicky and Laura were sitting at a table near the jukebox, hemmed in on all sides by large groups of what Helena liked to call 'People like us' but which could have more accurately been labelled 'Slightly worn at the edges, *Big Issue*-buying, left-leaning, thirtysomething graduates who still feel like they're still students even if they aren't.' I eventually managed to find an empty stool, and made my way over to join Vicky and Laura.

'So where are the boys?' I asked.

'At the bar,' replied Laura. 'Although they seem to be taking forever about it.'

'And still no word of Paul and Hannah?'

Vicky shook her head. 'Not yet but I'm sure he'll be here sometime soon.'

It must have been obvious that I couldn't work out whether I was relieved or not, because Laura reached across the table and touched my hand. 'What do you want to drink, babe?'

'I'm fine for the minute,' I replied. 'Maybe I'll get one a bit later.'

'Don't be silly. Getting drinks is what boys do best.' She pulled out her mobile and dialled. 'Coop it's me. Melissa's here now, can you get her a drink?'

Cooper and Chris, patiently waiting to be served, smiled and waved at us.

'What are you drinking?'

'I'll have a Becks, if that's all right?'

Laura rolled her eyes as though my politeness was trying her patience. 'Melissa wants a bottle of Becks and a packet of prawn cocktail crisps and be quick about it!'

I poked Laura in the elbow. 'You tell him right now that I don't want any crisps, least of all prawn cocktail.'

'You might not, but I certainly do. I'm starving.'

Vicky looked perplexed. 'I thought you were on that Courtney Cox diet? Are prawn cocktail crisps part of the bargain?'

'Tomorrow,' grinned Laura. 'The diet starts tomorrow.'

Laura and I had been friends for as long as she had been going out with Cooper, which was roughly six years. Cooper had met her when he first moved to Manchester after

splitting up with his girlfriend. I hadn't been too sure about Laura at first, she seemed much more of a 'boy's girl' than a 'girl's girl,' thriving on any male attention that was available. And although she'd probably be the first to admit that this was true, she was also a lot of other things besides and over time these made me warm to her. For starters she could be really funny, which I considered to be a good sign as beautiful people like Laura rarely bother cultivating a sense of humour. She was also burdened with more than her fair share of insecurities (she hated her nose, was a borderline bulimic through her teenage years and constantly put herself down for not being smart enough). Once I discovered what I considered to be her human side, I found it much easier to like her and with the minimum of adjustment, space was made in the tight bond that existed between Vicky and me to include Laura in our gang.

While we waited for our drinks we began exchanging stories about our various days.

'Well the highlight of my day,' Vicky began, 'was watching Chris trying to teach William how to fly the kite we got for him for Christmas. It would've been hilarious if it hadn't been so cold. Chris was running around the park like a demon trying to get the thing in the air and William kept asking if it was time to go home because he was freezing to death.'

'Well, given the fact that I only got out of bed about four hours ago,' began Laura, 'I'm guessing this is probably the highlight of my day.'

Vicky was incredulous. 'You only got out of bed four hours ago?'

Laura nodded sheepishly. 'I went out with a few of my old work friends from the teaching staff at Albright High

last night and it turned into a bit of a late one and I didn't get in until three.'

'How about you, Mel?' asked Vicky. 'What have you been up to today?'

'Nothing much,' I sighed. 'I read about ten pages of that Monica Ali book that you lent me, watched a double episode of *Deal or No Deal* and finished off the entire top layer of the selection of chocolate biscuits that my evil stick-thin sister gave me for Christmas. Not exactly the most fruitful of days but I'm not complaining.'

Vicky grinned. 'I'd kill to spend the afternoon watching Noel Edmonds and eating biscuits.'

'You're welcome to my life anytime you want it,' I replied. 'Really, just say the word and it's yours. You have my life and I'll move into yours and raise William as my own.'

'If you're going to be me then you do realise you'll have to sleep with Chris?'

I pulled a face. 'Ours would be a chaste marriage.'

'So anyway,' said Laura, 'moving on from that distasteful picture, how are we all feeling in general about the year ahead? Optimistic?'

'As you know,' I began, 'I hate New Year's Eve and thinking about the future so it would be fair to say that I'm pretty pessimistic.'

Vicky smiled. 'I love the idea of being handed a clean slate every year and setting myself a whole new set of goals.'

'There speaks Wonder Woman. So what's your goal for this New Year then, Vick? Something involving those cook-books of yours? Maybe it's time you finally applied to *Ready Steady Cook*. You'd be ace on that.'

'Cheeky cow! No *Ready Steady Cook* for me.'

'Well then you should have another baby,' suggested Laura. 'You and Chris make great babies. It's a proven fact. William is quite possibly my favourite human being on the entire planet.'

'Well I'm afraid you're not his.' Vicky gave me a wink. 'Before we came out tonight it was Auntie Mel this and Auntie Mel that. I think he's got a massive crush on you, Mel.'

'Fine by me,' I replied. 'What is he, four? I'm more than willing to hang on another twenty-six years for the right one.'

'That is so wrong on about a million different levels,' protested Vicky.

'So, are you going to have another baby then?' Laura probed.

Vicky shook her head. 'I've only ever wanted one.'

I looked at Laura. 'Looks like you and Cooper will have to take up the slack, then.'

'Cooper would have kids at the drop of a hat,' said Laura despairingly. 'Your William's so much like a walking advert for procreation that I've lost count of the times Coop's dropped subtle-as-a-brick-hints like, "How great would it be to have one of those around the house?" and I'm like, "Are you insane? I can barely look after myself let alone another human being."'

'So you don't want kids then?' asked Vicky.

'There's too much I haven't done for me to even think about any of that. In fact if there's one thing I want to do this year it's go travelling. I want to see a bit more of the world, spend a bit of time in a place where it isn't always raining, live a little. Do you know what I mean?'

I nodded. 'You and Cooper should definitely do it.

389

Grown-up gap years are all the rage for the discerning thirty-something.'

'Tell that to my boyfriend. If it wasn't for the fact that he's making us save up a stupid deposit for a stupid house I'd do it in a heartbeat.'

Vicky sighed. 'You know you really shouldn't give him such a hard time. Cooper's just doing what Cooper does. He wants the best for you both.'

Laura shrugged and fingered the label of the beer bottle in front of her. 'I don't know, maybe he does. But why does he have to be so boring about it?'

'Look,' Vicky tried to lift the mood around the table, 'let's not get all depressed. It's New Year's Eve and we're all together so let's just enjoy ourselves.'

**Chris:**
It was just after nine by the time we left the Old Grey and made our way to Sharon and Ed's. On the way I tried Paul's mobile a couple of times but kept getting his voicemail. This was 100 per cent typical of Paul. He never returned people's calls if he could help it and when he turned up and you had a go at him, he'd just look at you like you were acting like some kind of girl making a big deal out of nothing and say: 'I'd let you know if I wasn't coming wouldn't I?'

Whilst hitting redial I thought about how long I had known Paul. We first met through mates of mates one summer night outside the Black Horse in the days before they knocked down Shambles Square and moved it over the road. I was in my second year of my law degree and I'd just finished my exams, so a whole bunch of us had been drinking on the benches outside the pub since late after-

noon. Heading up to the bar to get a round in I'd ended up standing next to Paul. We had both drunk quite a bit by this point in the evening and out of nowhere Paul turned around and told me a joke about a nun and a polar bear that was so ridiculously puerile that even thinking about it now can put a smile on my face.

We got talking and he told me a bit about himself. He was in the second year of a Social Studies degree at MMU and though he was born in Telford he had moved around the country quite a bit with his parents before ending up back where he started at around the age of fifteen. That was pretty much it for biography, because after that all we talked about was football and motor-racing before the conversation as a whole disintegrated into the usual mix of music and films, clothes and trainers, in fact all the stuff employed by certain types of men to separate the wheat from the so-called chaff.

Despite us both proving our credentials to each other with talk of obscure Italian horror films, the back catalogue of the Stones and several shared sitcom favourites, we didn't have a great deal to do with each other after that night out, apart from the odd nod of the head or short conversation whenever we bumped into each other (usually either coming in or out of Piccadilly Records). It wasn't anything personal. I doubt either of us had given it any consideration, but I'm guessing if we had it would have been along the lines of if we were meant to be friends then it would happen whether or not we did anything about it.

A few months later, on an unseasonably mild afternoon at the beginning of our final term, we once again found ourselves sitting outside the Black Horse. But this time we somehow ended up making plans to go for a drink, and

go and see bands and we somehow both followed through with these haphazard arrangements and gradually became mates.

I tried his number one last time. Sure enough it switched to his voicemail. Ending the call without leaving a message I returned my phone to my pocket and caught up with the others.

**Melissa:**

There were already quite a few people lingering outside Ed and Sharon's tiny two-bedroom terrace by the time we arrived. Some were congregating by the door saying hello to each other, while others were enjoying the first of many 'last' cigarettes before they resolved, once again, to give up forever at midnight. I recognised two of the smokers as Fraser and Helen, who I'd shared a house with in our early twenties. The boys claimed it was too cold to stand outside talking so they headed straight inside, taking Vicky and Laura with them. As I hadn't seen Fraser and Helen since they'd gone travelling over a year and half ago, I stood chatting for a while. It was good to see them and I was dying to hear their travelling stories; although they were a bit self-conscious at first, wary of coming across like the kinds of people who constantly evangelise about the wonders of travelling, they seemed so much happier with their lives in general and with each other specifically that it made me sort of hopeful about my own future too.

I left Fraser and Helen finishing their cigarettes outside and entered the house. The hallway was crammed wall to wall with party-goers. Even though I didn't know most of them, they all appeared to be the same vintage as me, which was comforting. At least if I got drunk and ended

up dancing I would feel my peers' sympathy rather than their embarrassment.

In my search for Vicky and the others, I ended up bumping into an inordinate number of people I hadn't seen in ages. I once read a newspaper survey that each person in the UK knows at least 120 people. I remember thinking at the time that that seemed like a lot but standing here at this party maybe it wasn't such an outrageous figure after all.

I eventually found Vicky and Laura talking to Sharon and a group of her friends I'd never met before. They all seemed nice enough and encouraged me to join in the conversation, but conscious of the fact that I hadn't got a drink in my hands and that my plan for the evening was to drink myself stupid, I made an excuse and made my way to the kitchen.

Ed and Sharon's kitchen was, like the rest of the house, packed with people but eventually I spotted all the booze lined up on the kitchen counter next to the sink. I'd asked Vicky to give Sharon and Ed my contribution to the party— a bottle of Sancerre that had cost me nearly a tenner— when we first arrived and I was dying to try it. Scanning the various bottles and cans, I eventually found it, empty and minus its cork, poking out of a green recycling box on the floor at my feet. Resigning myself to the situation I selected a sophisticated looking oak-aged Chardonnay with a posh label as compensation, even though there was an open bottle of Sainsbury's own label right in front of me.

Just as I was cringing at how much I was letting myself down by three-quarter filling a plastic pint glass (I couldn't find any others) with wine that I had no proper claim on,

a male voice said: 'All right, fella, what are you looking so guilty about?'

I spun around, almost spilling the wine all over me, only to find Chris and Cooper grinning like idiots. 'Okay, okay,' I replied. 'You caught me in the act. Someone drank the whole of that bottle of wine I brought with me. It wasn't like I was going to keep it to myself but I didn't even get a sip.'

'So now you're wreaking your revenge by searching out the most expensive bottle you can find?' 'What are you? Some kind of student waster?'

'You're such a git to me sometimes.'

Chris put his arm around me. 'You know I only do it because I love you.'

Chris and Cooper were more like older brothers than friends. The pair of them often teased me mercilessly (their jokes focusing mainly on the notion that I was a bit flaky, lack ambition and hopeless with men), but the flipside of this abuse is that as their honorary little sister it is their duty to protect me. I'd lost count of the times that one or other of them had walked me home in the rain, picked me up from the airport, put up shelves in my bedroom, even sorted out dodgy guys giving me hassle.

Obviously I'd known Chris longer than Cooper. In fact it was hard to remember there was ever a time that Chris was apart from the unit I'd come to know and love as 'Chris and Vicky.' He was the complete opposite of Paul. Whereas life with Paul was like being on a rollercoaster with highs that thrilled every nerve ending in your body and lows that took you to the very depth of despair, Chris was a lot more even and steady. You always knew exactly where you stood with him and how he would react in any

given situation. He seemed to give off this aura of authority—so much so that whenever any of us had a real world problem, like when I was being hassled by a debt collection agency over an unpaid mobile phone bill, I didn't take my problem to Paul, or Cooper, I took it straight to Chris, and he sorted the whole thing out in a few phone calls.

Chris picked up a bottle of champagne from behind my back and held it aloft. 'Still,' he said, giving me a wink, 'if you're going to do this revenge thing at all, at least do it properly.'

'You can't do that!' Chris pulled off the foil and began removing the twisty metal surrounding from the cork. 'What if Ed and Sharon are saving it for midnight?'

'It's okay, Mel,' Cooper chipped in. 'No need to get your knickers all bunched up, mate. Laura and I brought it with us. We've had it sitting in our fridge since last summer, but you can consider it your belated Christmas present if you like.'

Before I could protest Chris popped the cork. Everyone in the kitchen looked at us with disdain, as though we were acting like a bunch of yobs, which I suppose in a way we were.

Chris took a swig then handed the bottle to me. 'Happy new year, Mel.'

'I really shouldn't be doing this, you two are always leading me into bad ways.'

Chris laughed. 'Us? Never.'

I took another swig. 'So, are either of you going to make any New Year's resolutions?'

Chris shook his head. 'Don't believe in them. I mean, what's the point?'

'They're only supposed to be a bit of fun.'

*Mike Gayle*

Chris didn't look convinced. 'Okay, so what's yours?'

'I've got a list as long as my arm: I'm taking up jogging, I'm going to start cycling into uni, I'm going to cut down on takeaways and read more books, watch less TV and . . . do you want me to carry on?'

Chris did a mock cringe. 'Please don't.'

I turned to Cooper. 'What about you? Unlike your useless brother here I know you must have a few.'

'No resolutions as such, just some plans.'

'Like what?'

'To buy a house. I'm sick of renting. It's money down the drain. Laura and I should have enough saved by the middle of the year for a deposit as long as house prices don't carry on going through the roof.'

I thought about Laura's comments back at the Old Oak. Knowing both of them as well as I did, I sensed trouble on the horizon but said nothing.

'Still,' I replied, 'getting a house of your own isn't the be all and end all, is it?'

'I think you're making Mel feel bad about the fact that she's wasting valuable time playing at being a student again rather than getting on the property ladder,' Chris teased.

I punched him on the shoulder as hard as I could. 'It's unbelievable how much of a tosser you can be sometimes.'

'Just ignore him, he's not worth the effort.' Cooper looked at me sheepishly. 'I suppose you're right: getting a house isn't the be all and end all but it's a step forward isn't it? And that's all I want really, a couple of steps forward.'

There was something about the look on his face, like a child desperately trying to hide a secret, that made me curious.

'What other "steps forward" are you thinking about?'

Cooper smiled enigmatically.

'You're not . . .?'

'What?'

'Going to ask Laura to marry you, are you?'

'Yeah, right. Do I look like a mug?'

'What do you mean? You and Laura make a brilliant couple. Plus, it's been ages since I've been to a good wedding where I actually cared about the couple getting hitched. You should do it.'

Cooper rolled his eyes. 'Well, much as I'd like to help you out by throwing a good party, Mel, I'm afraid that won't be happening any time soon. But I'll be sure to let you know if I do change my mind, okay?'

I looked at Chris in the hope that he might back me up but he just shrugged and offered me the champagne bottle again. I took a swig then set it down on the counter, glancing up at the clock on the wall. It was twenty minutes past eleven and there was still no sign of Paul and Hannah.

'So where's his Lordship then?' I asked, directing the question at both Chris and Cooper.

'Haven't heard from him.'

'But he is still coming isn't he?'

Chris shrugged. 'That's what he told me but you know what he's like, your guess is as good as mine.'

'Maybe Hannah didn't fancy the idea of spending the biggest night of the year with a bunch of her boyfriend's friends who don't really like her,' suggested Cooper. 'I don't think I'd be here if I was her. After all, she's not you, is she?'

'Cheers for the solidarity Coop, but she's Paul's girlfriend so we should be nice to her. He's always been nice to the guys I've seen in the past.'

'Maybe to your face,' said Chris solemnly.

'What do you mean?'

Chris shook his head. 'Look, I'm saying nothing. But take it from me he's never been anywhere near as happy as he makes out when you're seeing someone.'

This didn't exactly make me feel any better.

'Doesn't matter anyway,' I replied. 'The truth is I like her, and I can definitely see what Paul sees in her.'

'Well that's hardly rocket science, she's very easy on the eye.'

'I mean above all that superficial stuff,' I replied. 'I was talking to her round at Chris and Vicky's and she was telling me about some of the stuff she's doing on her MA and I didn't have a clue what she was talking about. It was like she was speaking a different language. She's so clever it's frightening.'

Chris put an arm around my shoulder as though he was drawing me close to impart an important piece of wisdom. (One of the downsides of being Chris and Cooper's little sister was that every once in a while I had to endure their unsolicited advice.)

'Considering what a Hannah-fan you are,' observed Chris, 'I bet you'd have a face on you that could turn milk if she walked in with Paul right now.'

I pretended to look for the champagne but could feel myself starting to flush.

'Listen, Mel,' he continued. 'I know this might sound a bit harsh and for the life of me I don't mean it that way but seeing as we're about to begin a new year, why don't you do yourself a massive favour and just move on? Hanging on to Paul is doing you no good at all.'

I could feel tears pricking at the back of my eyes before Chris had even finished.

'If it was that easy, don't you think that I'd have done it by now?'

'Of course it is,' replied Chris oblivious of the look of disbelief on Cooper's face. 'You just have to want it badly enough, that's all. All I'm saying is that you and Paul are mates, and that's great, but I think that now he's finally moved on, maybe you should too.'

**Chris:**

I have no idea who had died and made me Minister of Home Truths, but whoever it was I really wished they hadn't bothered. Melissa looked absolutely crushed when I finished delivering my big piece of advice and all I could think was, why didn't I just keep my big mouth shut?

'Maybe you're right, maybe I am wasting my time here with Paul. Maybe I should just go home right now.'

I could tell that Melissa was absolutely serious about leaving and could already picture the scene Vicky would make when she found out it was my fault that her best friend was spending New Year's Eve on her own.

'You can't go, Mel. First off it's just wrong, second, you shouldn't listen to anything I've got to say because what do I know? And finally, if you go home early and Vicky finds out that it's because of me she will go insane.'

'She would, wouldn't she?' said Melissa, with the beginnings of a smile on her face. 'She'd make your life a misery for days.'

'Days? Try weeks.'

'Look, Chris, I know you mean well and that you're probably right about me and Paul, it's just . . . well, you know . . . some things are easier said than done. You can't really think I want to be like this. You can't think even for

a minute that I enjoy waking up on my own only to end the day in bed alone, too. You have no idea how lucky you are having Vicky and William. No idea at all.'

'Look,' I replied. 'I really am sorry, mate. You just do what you've got to do and from now on I'll keep my mouth shut.'

'Okay, you're forgiven, but if you start with any of that "Melissa's a flaky Southern layabout stuff" again I will grass you up in a second.' She picked up her plastic cup of wine. 'Right boys, I'm off to find some proper people to talk to, okay?'

'No hard feelings, mate?'

'Of course not. We're fine. I'll see you later?'

'Yeah. Later.'

I watched Melissa leave the kitchen then turned to Cooper and sighed: 'It's not like it takes a genius to work out that Melissa doesn't want to hear the truth about her and Paul.'

'Certainly not tonight, of all nights,' replied Cooper. 'New Year's Eve always puts people in a weird frame of mind.'

I raised an eyebrow, relieved at the opportunity to talk about something else. 'Like you? What was all that stuff going on with your face when Mel was talking about you and Laura getting hitched? For a second I thought that you might be—'

'I am,' he replied.

'You are what?'

'Going to ask her. Not tonight. But this year, definitely.'

'You're joking?'

'No, I'm absolutely serious. I was thinking of asking her on her birthday in April. That way it'll give me enough time to save up for the ring without raiding our savings.'

'You do know you can't just get any old rubbish and

hope that she'll be so flattered that she won't notice it's gold-plated?'

Cooper grinned. 'That's why I'm planning to give it to her over a candlelit dinner.'

I picked up Melissa's bottle of champagne and took a swig. 'Well best of luck to you, bruv. I hope it all goes well when you do the deed.'

'Cheers,' replied Cooper taking the bottle from me. He took a swig and winced. 'Nope,' he said resignedly, 'still can't stand this stuff.'

**Melissa:**

Determined to think about something other than Paul, I ended up circulating the party on my own for about an hour, dipping in and out of conversations here and there. Most of the people I spoke to were friends I only met up with at the occasional party or summer barbecue. Most of them were settled now, coupled up with kids or tethered down by massive mortgages but there was a small yet resilient battalion who were still fighting the good fight like the last ten years hadn't happened. It was these in particular that I was always pleased to see. It was great to hear that Cathy and Brendan were still in bands, that Dean and Lewis were still actively pursuing their dream of becoming full-time artists and even that Alistair and Baxter were still running the same city centre indie club nights that they had been involved with when I'd first got to know them as a nineteen-year-old student. It felt good knowing that they were all getting on with their lives. It made me feel like I was part of something larger than myself.

In the middle of a conversation with Carl and Louisa, whose big news was that Louisa was pregnant, I realised

that I needed another drink to keep me going. I made my excuses and tried to make my way out of the room but every few steps someone emerged from the wings with an air kiss and a desperate need to catch up. Manjeet and Aaron were moving down to London, Joel and Rowena had just bought a house over in Withington and Tina (formerly of Tina and Alan and currently of Tina and Susan) had left teaching and was now trying to write a novel. Beginning to feel like I was suffering from information overload, I managed to reach the door to the hallway but before I could complete my exit there was a tap on my shoulder. Standing in front of me was a tall young-looking guy wearing a pinstriped jacket with a green T-shirt with yellow writing on it. I didn't recognise him, but the way he was looking at me, convinced me that I must have met him before at some long forgotten party. I was about to kiss him on the cheek and ask him how he was doing before politely making my excuses when he did something really odd. Raising his foot in the air so that I could see that he was wearing brick red baseball boots just like my own, he said: 'Snap.'

**Billy:**
It had taken me over two hours, three cans of Carlsberg, and all the courage I possessed in order to approach the girl in the red Converse.

I'd spotted her the moment she entered the living room sometime after nine. I'd been bored out of my mind making small talk with my sister's mates when boom, there she was. I thought she was amazing pretty much straight away, different from the other women at the party. Prettier. More thoughtful. Older than me but without making me feel like

it would require a huge leap of the imagination to picture us together. That, along with the style of her hair, the cardigan, her frayed jeans and the fact that she seemed the total opposite of Freya, made me think that if I was going to pull at this party then this girl would be it.

Normally I would never have dreamed of trying to chat up a girl like that in a million years, especially with a line that boiled down to "Wow, look at us, we're wearing the same footwear." And what made it worse of course was the fact that it was so obviously just a cheesy chat-up line. I might have been better off just saying: "Do you think that at some point this evening you might be drunk enough to consider getting off with me, a complete stranger?" At least then I might have gained a few points for sheer brazenness.

Still, since the girl in the Converse was unknown to my sister and her friends (I'd already checked out that avenue) I knew that if I was ever going to have a hope of talking to her I had no choice but to try something on my own. So looking over at the three remaining cans of Carlsberg I'd brought with me and placed on the mantel, I decided that if Dutch courage was what I needed to make this work then Dutch courage it would be. I pulled one can out of its plastic carrier, opened it and gave myself the deadline of eleven o'clock to make my move.

**Melissa:**
You can imagine how weird this was. There I was, trying to escape the room, when this guy just appears from nowhere, taps me on the shoulder and says: 'Snap.'

I was confused to say the least.

I decided to humour him. 'Great minds, eh?'

403

'I was thinking the same thing,' he replied.

I played for time and gestured to his chest with my empty plastic cup. 'What does your T-shirt say?'

He pulled his jacket open so I could read the words of his t-shirt—a cryptic fake film review that said: 'An athlete, a criminal, a brain, a princess and a basketcase bond in detention at a Chicago High School (1985).'

'*The Breakfast Club*,' I said, grinning. 'I love that film.'

'Me too,' he replied. 'What's your favourite bit?'

'I haven't seen it in ages. How about you?'

'The bit when they're all dancing—and pretty much any scene with Ally Sheedy in it.'

'So you're a Sheedy man?'

'All the way.'

I remembered how at school you could always divide boys into the ones who considered themselves to be tortured poets (and therefore fancied Ally Sheedy) and the boys who were just boys (and therefore fancied Molly Ringwald). I had to smile at the thought that this guy in front of me fancied himself as a tortured poet.

'This is really awful of me,' I said after a few moments, 'but I seem to have completely forgotten your name.'

'That's because we've never met before,' he said looking slightly uncomfortable. 'Can I be straight with you? I only came over because ... well ... you seem nice and it's New Year's Eve ... and we'll all be singing 'Auld Lang Syne' in a bit ... so I just thought I'd come over and say hello.' He offered me his hand and was about to tell me his name when he stopped and looked over my shoulder. Instinctively I turned around too and there, standing right behind me, was Paul. And Hannah was nowhere to be seen.

**Billy:**

Even without knowing anything about either of them I could tell straight away that these two had history. The second Melissa saw Paul she lit up like a switch had been flipped. Freya was the only person who could make me feel the way this girl was feeling.

'We all thought you weren't coming,' said Melissa.

'I'm just a bit late, that's all,' he replied.

Melissa bit her lip. 'No Hannah?'

'No, she ... er ... she couldn't make it.'

Melissa looked concerned. 'Nothing wrong is there?'

'No, nothing's wrong,' replied Paul. 'She's fine.' He paused. 'So what have I missed?'

'Nothing much really, Helena wants to go travelling and Cooper wants to save up for a deposit for a house and it's all going to end in disasters; and Chris and Vicky are well, you know ... *Chris and Vicky* and I ... I ...'

I could tell that Melissa had just recalled the fact that prior to Paul's arrival she had actually been in the middle of a conversation with me and now I was just dangling, like some kind of spare part, wishing one of them would put me out of my misery.

Melissa looked at me apologetically.

'Paul this is ...'

'Billy,' I replied. 'My name's Billy.'

'That's it, Billy,' said Melissa. 'This is Billy. And Billy, this is Paul. He and I are old friends.'

'Very old friends,' added Paul. 'How long has it been? Ten or eleven years?'

'Twelve,' replied Melissa. 'Twelve long years.'

**Melissa:**

Half past midnight. Thirty minutes into a brand new year. And Paul and I—having shouted, cheered and done the 'Auld Lang Syne' thing with everyone else at midnight— were in Ed and Sharon's back garden sitting on their damp patio furniture with a freshly purloined bottle of wine, watching a series of fireworks explode in the night sky. I could feel the damp of the table soaking right through my jeans to my underwear but I didn't care. There was something different about Paul tonight. I could sense it.

'Genius idea of yours,' I said, as yet another firework popped and sparkled in the sky. 'Leave the comfort of a nice warm house and sit outside in the rain.'

Paul shrugged. 'You could've said no.'

'And miss out on all this? Never.'

Paul took a sip of wine and handed the bottle to me. I put it to my lips, took a long, deep swig and swallowed. It felt good to drink wine like this. An instant reminder of the days when finer graces genuinely didn't matter.

'I haven't drunk straight from the bottle since the year we all went to Glastonbury. And for some reason I've done it twice tonight.'

'I remember that year at Glastonbury,' he said raising a small nostalgic smile. 'That was the year we bought those bottles of home-made wine from that hippie guy near the main stage and Cooper refused to drink it in case it was laced with weed killer. Do you remember? Like a hippie hasn't got better things to do than poison a bunch of middle-class layabouts.'

'I remember the hippie ... and I sort of remember handing him the cash but other than pushing the cork into the bottle with my keys, I don't remember much about

that night at all.' I paused. 'Still, somehow I just get a sense that it might well have been one of the best nights of my life.'

'Easily up there in the top ten.'

I took another swig and glanced at Paul. He looked thoughtful and pensive.

'So, are you going to tell me what's going on?'

'What do you want to know?'

'Well, where's Hannah for starters?'

'I'm guessing she's at home. I don't know for sure. We split up just before Christmas.'

There it was. Paul and Hannah had split up. It didn't seem to make any sense, given how happy they had been last time I had seen them together—all loved up and fawning over each other.

'How did she take it?' I asked carefully.

'How do you know it was me?'

'Come on, Paul,' 'this is me you're talking to.'

'She'll be fine,' he said obliquely. 'It wasn't like I was the love of her life.'

'And you'd know that how?'

'You think I was?'

I shook my head. 'I doubt you'll ever be the love of anyone's life. It would be tantamount to making a public admission that you didn't really have much of a life to begin with. I have to admit I'm surprised though. I would've put money on you and Hannah going the distance.'

'Even though she was so young?'

'She was twenty-three. That's not so young.'

'Do you think?'

I sighed. 'It looks like it was more your problem than hers.'

Paul pulled at the label on the wine, eventually tearing off a small strip. 'I wasn't right for her. And I think she knew it.'

'Ah, so it was Hannah's fault you split up?' I replied. 'You were actually doing her dirty work for her? Come on, surely not even you believe that?'

Paul didn't reply and I didn't say anything to ease the tension.

Paul proceeded to tap his left foot in time to some imaginary soundtrack in his head, which made me want to sit as still as I could just to be awkward. It was only when Ed and Sharon's back door opened, spilling light and music into the garden, that we both jolted back to life and only relaxed when we saw that it was Vicky.

'Everything okay?' she called out.

'Yeah we're all good,' replied Paul.

'I'm just letting you know that Chris and I will probably be getting off in a minute.'

'We'll be in soon,' I replied. 'Don't go without saying goodbye, okay?'

Neither of us spoke as Vicky closed the door, plunging us both back into the darkness and silence. Paul coughed nervously. 'Do you know Chris and Vicky will have been married ten years this coming year? A kid. A proper home. A proper life. All in ten years.'

'Does that make you feel a bit weird?'

'Not really. I suppose it's just got me thinking—you know—about wasted time.'

I put on a rubbish American accent in the hope of lightening the mood and said: 'You're preaching to the choir.'

Paul smiled and I went to take another swig of the wine but misjudged the manoeuvre, missed my mouth altogether

and spilled some down my chin. I wiped my face with the sleeve of my cardigan and looked over at Paul to see if he'd seen. He was watching me with an odd look in his eyes.

'Have I still got wine on my face?' I asked, wiping around my mouth.

Paul shook his head.

'Then what?'

'You wouldn't believe me if I told you.'

'Try me.'

He stood up, turned to face me and held my hands. 'You think you don't want what other people want,' he began. 'You think that all you want is to be alone. But it's not true. The day will come when you'll be so sick of being alone that you won't know what to do. And when it happens, come and find me and we'll pick up right where we left off.'

'Do you think that's funny?' Pulled my hands away from him. 'Is that what you think? That I'm some kind of pathetic joke?'

'Of course not Mel,' he said urgently. 'If you would just listen to me for a second I'm trying to tell you that you were right.' He grabbed hold of my hands again. 'You asked me earlier why I'd split up with Hannah and here's your answer: I split up with Hannah because of you. I did feel for Hannah, it's true. I liked her a lot. But the thing I couldn't escape was that she wasn't you.'

'I don't understand,' I replied. 'I don't understand what you're saying.'

'Well understand this,' he said kissing me as a firework roared up into the sky and exploded, filling the air with a rainbow of tiny stars. 'Understand that right here and now I'm asking you to pick up right where we left off.'

## FREE!

### 4 Books
#### and a surprise gift!

We would like to take this opportunity to thank you for reading this Mills & Boon® book by offering you the chance to take FOUR more specially selected titles from the Medical™ series absolutely FREE! We're also making this offer to introduce you to the benefits of the Mills & Boon® Reader Service™—

- ★ FREE home delivery
- ★ FREE gifts and competitions
- ★ FREE monthly Newsletter
- ★ Exclusive Reader Service offers
- ★ Books available before they're in the shops

Accepting these FREE books and gift places you under no obligation to buy, you may cancel at any time, even after receiving your free shipment. Simply complete your details below and return the entire page to the address below. You don't even need a stamp!

**YES!** Please send me 4 free Medical books and a surprise gift. I understand that unless you hear from me, I will receive 6 superb new titles every month for just £2.89 each, postage and packing free. I am under no obligation to purchase any books and may cancel my subscription at any time. The free books and gift will be mine to keep in any case.

M7ZEF

Ms/Mrs/Miss/Mr ........................................Initials ...............................
**BLOCK CAPITALS PLEASE**

Surname ........................................................................................

Address ........................................................................................

........................................................................................

.....................................................Postcode ...............................

### Send this whole page to:
### UK: FREEPOST CN81, Croydon, CR9 3WZ

## 1. Belgian Shoes

Angus Lordie, portrait painter, citizen of Edinburgh, husband of Domenica Macdonald and owner (custodian, perhaps, according to modern sensibilities) of Cyril, the only dog in Scotland to have a gold tooth; *that* Angus Lordie stood in a room of his flat at 44 Scotland Street, wondering what to wear.

All the clothing he possessed was either hanging from a number of wooden hangers or was neatly folded and stacked away in a series of drawers within a large wardrobe, called, in the second-hand trade, *brown furniture*. Nobody, apparently, wanted brown furniture any longer, as it was considered too cumbersome, not to say too dull, for contemporary tastes. If the Scottish diet had become Mediterranean, then Scottish furniture had become Scandinavian – light and minimalist, consigned to its owners in flat boxes and requiring to be assembled before use – and then reassembled, once the instruction booklet had been read. This was the very opposite of Angus Lordie's wardrobe, as gloriously over-engineered, in its way, as the Forth Railway Bridge, and of similar vintage.

This wardrobe consisted of a series of drawers in which Angus kept what he called his *accoutrements*: his shirts and socks, handkerchiefs, ties, vests and so on, while jackets and trousers were hung from a railing on the opposite side. His kilt, along with his sporran, hose, kilt pin and *sgian-dubh*, were also in one of the drawers, protected, ineffectively, by moth-repelling balls of cedar.

He had two suits – a dark one that had been made for him twenty-two years ago and that was described by Domenica as his *kirk suit*, and a three-piece, tweedy outfit that Domenica had disparagingly labelled his *bookie's suit*. Neither of these descriptions was entirely helpful: the kirk suit was well-made and discreet, rather than Calvinist; the bookie's suit was not in the least bit flashy, being made of Harris tweed and designed to withstand Hebridean weather – the horizontal rain and Atlantic gusts that beset the West of Scotland, and the North, South, and East for that matter. There was nothing wrong with these suits, although Angus seldom wore them. Suits, he thought, might be going the way of men's hats and ties – both of which were now seen only infrequently on any man under forty. This was a matter of regret, Angus felt, even if he himself was doing nothing to stem that particular tide of fashion.

Alongside the suits were hung four jackets, all of them in frequent use. Two of these were linen, and formed the core of his summer garb, while the others were of an unidentified fabric that Angus referred to as one hundred per cent unnatural. They were comfortable enough, though, and went with virtually anything, but particularly with the crushed strawberry corduroy trousers by which Angus signalled his status as a resident of the Georgian New Town, as a member of the Scottish Arts Club, and as a man of artistic bent. If these trousers raised eyebrows amongst the ranks of the staid, then Angus did not care in the slightest. There was no fixed ordinance stipulating that men should wear sober trousers: fund managers, lawyers and accountants could dress in grey and black if they wished – he, as an artist, preferred something livelier.

On the floor of the wardrobe was the shoe rack on which Angus kept shoes other than those in regular use. His regular shoes – described by Domenica as his *daily boots* – were a pair of brown brogues made by the Northampton shoemaker, Joseph Cheaney. English shoes, Angus maintained, were second to none. They may not be as elegant as Italian footwear, but Italian shoes would never stand the rigours of Scottish conditions. English shoes were made to last; they were modest, often understated, and they were, above all else, *honest* shoes. That quality of honesty was difficult to define – in shoes at least – but one knew it when one encountered it. That was why English shoes were still sought after when everything else, as far as Angus could see, was being made in distant, unspecified workshops. *Designed in X and made in Y* ... Angus had never fallen for that particular attempt to sugar the pill of local deindustrialisation and the deskilling that went with it.

The English shoes of which he was proudest were a pair of black brogues, made of soft and supple leather, and bought by his father from the London firm of John Lobb. Lobb made shoes to measure, and while Angus could not afford the expense of bespoke shoes – the price tag ran effortlessly into thousands – his father, a Perthshire sheep farmer, had been able to do so after a particularly good season at the Lanark stock sales. His prize Scottish Blackface tup, Walter of Glenartney, renowned for his noble bearing, his fine Roman nose, and his contempt for lesser sheep, had broken all sales records and had provided him with the funds to order a pair of Lobb shoes.

By great good fortune, Angus and his father had near-identical feet, and when Angus left school, his father passed his shoes on to him. Angus accepted the gift with a degree of concealed embarrassment: at the age of eighteen, when one is busy shaking off parental influence, who wants a pair of bespoke Lobb shoes? At the Edinburgh College of Art at the time, shoes were being worn, of course, but these shoes were *concepts* or *statements*, rather than shoes *simpliciter*. So Angus relegated the Lobb brogues to a cupboard and wore, instead, a pair of Hush Puppies of tobacco-coloured suede, threaded with red laces – a touch that met with the wholehearted approval of his fellow students. 'Radical,' they said – high praise in those innocent days.

At a crucial stage in life – somewhere in one's mid-thirties – the merits of well-made shoes dawn on one, and that was what happened to Angus. He wore the shoes to his father's funeral, and as he and farming neighbours carried him to his final rest, a tear fell from Angus's eye onto the cap of one of the shoes. Not every man, he thought, will live to see such a thing: his tears falling onto a shoe into which he had, both metaphorically and otherwise, stepped.

Alongside the Lobb shoes, in as complete a contrast as could be imagined, was a pair of Belgian shoes, those light-weight, indoor shoes that are made only in Belgium and are completely unsuitable for active use. Angus had been given these by Domenica, whose eye had been caught by them on a trip to London.

'You can't wear them out of doors,' she said, as she presented him with them. 'The Belgians, it would seem, don't get out much.'

Angus smiled. 'How *drôle*,' he said.

Domenica accepted the compliment with an inclination of her head. 'Belgium is a bit of a mystery to me,' she said. 'I don't feel I've ever really *grasped* it, if you see what I mean.'*

## 2. Galileo, Orthodoxy, Dinner

Angus was choosing his clothes for a specific purpose – he and Domenica had been invited by Matthew and Elspeth to have dinner at Nine Mile Burn. Matthew had stressed that it would be a casual evening – 'kitchen supper', as he put it – but

---

* Angus Lordie, it may be remembered, was the author of the hymn *God Looks Down on Belgium*, the first verse of which is: *God's never heard of Belgium/ But loves it just the same;/For God is kind and doesn't mind/ He's not impressed by fame.*

even so, Angus wanted to make an effort in order to show that he appreciated the invitation.

'People like you to dress up a bit,' he said. 'It shows that you regard them as worth the trouble.'

Domenica was in complete agreement. As an anthropologist, she understood the significance of uniform, and of the way in which clothing sent signals. 'When I go to my dentist,' she had once remarked to Angus, 'I expect to find him in one of those natty blue jackets with buttons down the side. Such outfits reassure those facing the drill.'

Angus nodded. 'And pilots should wear blue uniforms with a bit of gold braid. That, too, is reassuring. I would not feel confident if I boarded a plane to find the pilot wearing jeans with rips in the knees.'

Domenica rolled her eyes. 'Rips in the knees! Have you ever worked out what's going on there, Angus?'

He shook his head. 'It's very fashionable. You buy them with the rips ready-made. It's most peculiar.'

'Perhaps it signals indifference to formality,' suggested Domenica. 'Rips proclaim that you don't care about being smart.'

'And that you're not ashamed of your knees,' added Angus. 'Rips say: I don't mind if you see my knees.'

Domenica looked thoughtful. 'Are the knees an erogenous zone?'

Angus was not sure. 'I've never been attracted to knees myself,' he said. 'But there may be some who are.' He was not sure whether gallantry required him to say something here about the attractiveness of Domenica's knees, but he decided to say nothing. Anybody could tell the difference between sincerity and insincerity when it came to comments about their knees.

Domenica did not seem interested in pursuing the subject of knees, as she now asked, 'What about trousers that hang down low, and display the wearer's underpants? I saw a young man at Waverley Station once who was wearing trousers with the crotch roughly level with his knees. He was finding it very difficult to walk. He did a sort of penguin waddle.'

'Another statement,' said Angus. 'But I'm with the prudes on that one, I'm afraid: underpants are definitely private. Exhibitionists may not agree, of course.'

Now, as Angus reflected on what he was to wear to Matthew and Elspeth's dinner party, Domenica had already changed into her favourite trouser-suit that she found fitted the bill for just about every occasion except those specifying evening dress. And she had few such invitations, she thought, with a momentary regret. Her full-length dress, with its optional tartan sash, lay folded away, and she had no idea when it would next be needed.

While Angus chose between his two linen jackets, she stood before the window from which, by craning one's neck, one might look up towards Drummond Place Garden, which was touched at that moment – it was six o'clock – by summer evening light. She was not looking in that direction, though, but was gazing, rather, at a patch of empty blue sky. She was contemplating something that she had put off thinking about until that very moment – a request to write a letter that she did not want to write.

Domenica still considered herself to be a practising anthro-pologist. She held no institutional position – and had not done so for some years – being one of those rare *private scholars* who pursue their subject without the comfortable safety-net of an academic salary. It was not easy being a private scholar: for one thing, you had to overcome a certain scepticism rooted in people's assumption that if you were any good you would have a university post. Why, after all, do research for nothing when there were institutions that would pay you to do the exact same work, give you grants to attend conferences in exotic places, and, if you stayed the course, dignify you with a professorial title?

The private scholar also had to put up with the condescension of those holding academic positions. When applying for research grants from public bodies, he or she had to write *none* in that part of the form that demanded disclosure of institutional affiliation. It was a statement of independence, but one that had long borne considerable risks. And yet the private scholar was now being recognised as being of increasing importance, for all this marginality. In an age of intellectual conformity, the private scholar could ask questions that probed received ideas. That was what Galileo had done, and yet there was no room for contemporary Galileos, it seemed. If those who called the tune, which now meant those who could shout loudest, said that the sun revolved around the earth, then the sun really *did* behave in that way, and it was no use echoing Galileo's *eppur si muove – and yet it moves.*

She sighed. It was precisely because she was a private scholar that they had written to her and asked for a letter. She would have to respond, although not just yet. She would do that tomorrow, for now they were about to go out to dinner and there were other things to think about.

And one of these was what Bertie was up to, because there was the small boy from the flat below, leaving the front door of No. 44, accompanied by his grandmother, Nicola, and that spindly-legged little friend of his, Ranald Braveheart Macpherson. They paused briefly, as Nicola bent down to say something to the two boys, and then continued their way up the sharply sloping street.

Angus came into the room and stood behind her.

'I've decided not to wear a tie,' he said. 'Matthew won't be wearing one – not in his kitchen. But I'm going to wear this jacket, I think.'

She did not look round. She knew his clothes off by heart. One day she would replace them, lock, stock, and barrel. She would buy him an entirely new wardrobe and throw out those two dreadful suits and those threadbare jackets. Wives had to do that sort of thing from time to time, as that was the only way husbands could be kept looking vaguely presentable.

Then Angus said, 'I'm going to take Cyril for a quick walk around the garden. Then I think we should think of setting off for Nine Mile Burn.'

Domenica nodded, without turning round. 'I see that Nicola has had the same idea with the boys,' she said. 'Boys are just like dogs, don't you think, Angus? They need to be exercised.'

Angus laughed. 'Possibly,' he said.

## 3. The Terraces of Purgatory

With Cyril straining at the leash, Angus made his way up Scotland Street towards Drummond Place.

'You don't have to be quite so impatient,' Angus said to Cyril. '*Festina lente*, remember ...'

Cyril looked up briefly, but then leaned forward with renewed enthusiasm. He was aware that Angus had addressed him, but there were none of the words that he recognised, his vocabulary being a poor bag of words such as *wall* and *biscuits* and *sit*; and, of course, he had no Latin to speak of. The limited range of canine understanding, though, does not stop people from talking at considerable length to their dogs – a fact which had always amused Angus, even if he himself did exactly that with Cyril. The day before he had overheard a woman in the garden berating her West Highland terrier at length for his over-exuberant behaviour.

'You really need to bark less, Douglas,' she admonished. 'There's no point in barking at chimeras, is there? Don't you understand that?'

Angus, who was walking past her at the time, almost stopped to answer that question for her. 'He doesn't, I'm afraid,' he might have said. 'Or perhaps try him in Gaelic.'

And yet dog owners persisted in these long one-sided conversations as if the dog really did grasp what they were saying, some even enunciating their words particularly carefully in order to give the animal every chance to get what was being said.

But here he was doing it himself, as he unselfconsciously remarked to Cyril, 'It's a very nice evening, don't you think, Cyril?'

Cyril looked up at him again, and then continued to pull on his leash. His world was one of smells, delectable and tantalising, rather than sounds, and he was picking up intriguing hints of what lay ahead. There was something dead somewhere – a rat probably – and a discarded, half-eaten ham sandwich further up wind. And seagulls – an acrid, annoying scent he did not like at all. And car fumes. And squirrels somewhere or other – an infuriating scent because they always got away. And what was that? Cat? That was an outrage, pure and simple, a challenge that could not be ignored. He would get that cat one day. He would teach it to be superior. He would teach it about arrogance. There was no place for cats in the new Scotland, thought Cyril ...

They reached the gate to the garden and here Angus extracted the key from his pocket. A key to Drummond Place Garden was highly sought-after in the area, as the garden was private, and access to it was a constantly contested matter. Those with a Drummond Place address had a clear right to a key, as long as they paid their share of the upkeep charge, but the occupants of flats just a few doors away, in Dundonald Street or Scotland Street, were ineligible. That had been long settled, after lengthy internecine struggles, but what about those who lived in one of the surrounding streets, but who had a window overlooking Drummond Place?

Dante, contemplating the terraces of Purgatory, might have addressed just such a question of boundaries, but even he – or Solomon, perhaps – might not have reached a decision that was acceptable to all, and there were many who were disappointed at not being able to avail themselves of the garden.

Angus had a key by the application of the overlooking window rule, and the same applied to Bertie's parents. So Angus and Cyril frequently came across Bertie in the garden, just as he met other local residents, such as the Italian socialite nun, Sister Maria-Fiore dei Fiori di Montagna, and her friend and flatmate, Antonia Collie. The two women had garden access on the strength of their occupation of a flat on the north side of Drummond Place, and in fine weather they were often to be seen sharing a picnic served from a large wicker hamper and laughing at some *recherché* witticism from Antonia or aphorism from Sister Maria-Fiore dei Fiori di Montagna's seemingly limitless store of such observations.

Once inside the gate, with Cyril's extending leash played out to its maximum length, allowing him to investigate the undergrowth, Angus made his way slowly round the perimeter pathway. He soon met Nicola, who was standing underneath a tree, gazing up at a couple of wood pigeons that had alighted on a branch above her.

'Such lovely birds,' she remarked. 'Altogether more engaging than those troublesome feral pigeons.'

Angus nodded. 'I see that you have young Bertie's friend with you.'

Nicola smiled. 'Ranald Braveheart Macpherson? Yes, he is a funny wee boy, isn't he? He and Bertie are the greatest of friends. Do you remember how important those childhood friendships were? They meant the world, didn't they?'

Angus did remember. 'And we never find them again, do we?'

Nicola thought about that. Angus was probably right; we never recovered the things of childhood – we were never readmitted to that lost Eden.

From behind some bushes came the sound of children's voices raised in what sounded like a dispute.

'That's Olive,' said Nicola. 'Olive and Pansy. Bertie doesn't quite see eye to eye with those two.'

'Olive and Pansy?'

'Olive is Pansy's great friend,' said Nicola. 'Pansy's family has just moved into Drummond Place. Olive lives on the south side but comes over to see Pansy. Bertie was dismayed when he realised they had descended on his turf, so to speak.'

Angus felt sorry for Bertie. He had had his mother to contend with, and now this. He looked at Nicola, trying to gauge whether he could speak directly about Irene. She was Nicola's daughter-in-law, of course, and he would have to be careful, but he had heard that there was no love lost between the two of them.

'How is Irene?' he asked. 'Any news from Aberdeen?'

'She's busy with her PhD,' Nicola said. 'And long may that continue. A PhD should not be rushed – particularly that one.'

Angus smiled. 'Scotland Street isn't the same without her,' he said.

'It's vastly improved,' Nicola muttered, and then, looking contrite, added, 'Not that we should be uncharitable.'

'Of course not,' said Angus.

'She's impossible,' said Nicola.

Angus said nothing.

'Although I'm sure she has her good points,' Nicola added.

'Of course.' Angus was relieved at this sign of charity. Irene was difficult, but, like the rest of us, she was probably just doing her best.

But then she said, 'Not that I ever noticed them.'

Angus looked at Nicola. There was something worrying her, and he wanted to ask her what it was. But how to put it? 'Are you troubled?' Could one say that to somebody one did not know very well – in Drummond Place Garden, out of the blue?

## 4. Debtors and Creditors

In another part of Drummond Place Garden, separated from Nicola and Angus by a yew hedge and a cluster of rhododendrons, Olive and Pansy presided over a game they were trying to inveigle Bertie and Ranald Braveheart Macpherson into playing. They were unwilling victims: the two boys had been dismayed to discover Olive and Pansy in the garden, and would have scurried off had they not been spotted by Olive and prevented from escaping.

'We can see you, Bertie Pollock,' Olive shouted when she

first spotted them. 'Stay where you are – it's no good trying to run away.'

'You're surrounded,' cried Pansy. 'And don't pretend you can't see us, because you can, and we know you can, don't we Olive?'

'Yes, we do,' Olive confirmed. 'You must come over here and play with us. We need two more people for our game, don't we, Pansy?'

'Yes,' said Pansy. 'And if you don't do as we say I'll report you to the Gardens Committee.' She paused, and then uttered a final shot, 'You're history, Bertie.'

Ranald looked at Bertie, who lowered his eyes. 'We'll have to do as they say, Bertie,' he said, adding, 'I hope Olive gets struck by lightning.'

Unfortunately, Olive heard this, and uttered a cry of outrage. 'I heard that, Ranald Braveheart Macpherson! You're in trouble now!'

'Big time,' said Pansy.

Ranald looked flustered.

'You mustn't pick on Ranald,' said Bertie. 'He didn't mean it.'

'It sounded like he meant it,' countered Olive. 'But I'll let him off this time, Bertie, as long as you both come and join in our game.'

Bertie walked slowly over towards the bench on which Olive and Pansy were sitting. Ranald Braveheart Macpherson followed him reluctantly.

'What is this game?' asked Bertie.

'Debtors and Creditors,' Olive replied. 'This bench is the Abbey at Holyrood, and where you're standing now is the Cowgate.'

Bertie waited for further explanation. 'And so?' he said.

'You must be patient,' said Olive. 'I was about to tell you, Bertie, before you interrupted me.'

'I didn't interrupt you, Olive,' protested Bertie.

'Don't argue with her,' snapped Pansy. 'You think that just because you're boys, you can argue with people who know better than you do.'

Olive gave him a scornful look. 'I'll tell you the rules,' she said. 'And you should listen to them carefully, because I won't repeat them.' She paused. 'Are you listening, Bertie?'

Bertie nodded.

'Right,' Olive continued. 'Did you know that in the old days – that's over twenty years ago – the Abbey of Holyrood was a place where you could go and be safe if you owed people money? They couldn't get you there, Bertie, and send you to debtors' prison. They called it a sanctuary.'

'That's right,' said Pansy. 'A debtors' sanctuary. For people like you.'

'But you had to stay there all week,' Olive went on. 'The only day you were allowed to go out was on a Sunday. Your creditors weren't allowed to get you on a Sunday.'

'So you could go swimming if you liked,' interjected Pansy. 'Tell him about how one of the debtors went swimming, Olive.'

'He went swimming on a Sunday,' said Olive. 'He went down to Cramond. But his creditor came and took his clothes while he was in the water.'

Bertie was intrigued. 'So what happened, Olive?'

'The poor debtor had to stay in the water until people took pity on him and gave him some clothes to get back to Holyrood.'

Bertie and Ranald looked at one another.

'You're going to be the debtors,' said Olive. 'Pansy and I are going to be the creditors. You have to stay on the bench and then try to get out. If we catch you, you're in trouble.'

'Why can't we be the creditors?' asked Bertie. 'Why do we have to be the debtors?'

'Because you have to,' said Pansy. 'So just shut up and play.'

'I'm not going to play,' said Ranald. 'I don't see why we should always be the debtors.'

'I don't care,' Olive retorted. She had lost interest in the game and wanted to talk about something else.

'You know that you're going to have to marry me, Bertie Pollock,' she said. 'You promised. I've got it in writing. You're going to have to marry me when we're twenty.'

'That's right,' said Pansy. 'And I'm going to be a brides-maid. It's the bridesmaid's job to make sure that the groom doesn't run away. You know that, Bertie?'

Olive wagged a finger at Bertie. 'I've been looking at venues for the reception, Bertie. I've been considering Dundas Castle. That's just outside town, and it has a marquee for dancing. I've been looking at that. And then there's the Signet Library. Do you know the Signet Library, Bertie?'

Bertie was silent.

'The Signet Library is a very good place for weddings,' said Olive. 'You can dance afterwards, once they clear the tables away. I've been looking at bands, Bertie.'

'And at wedding cakes,' Pansy chipped in.

'Pansy's aunt knows somebody who makes those cakes,' Olive said. 'If we put in our order soon, we'll get a discount.'

Now Pansy changed the subject. 'I see your granny over

there, Bertie,' she said. 'What a pity. I feel really sorry for her.' She paused. 'My mummy knows her. She feels sorry for her too. And your granny told my mummy something that you're not going to like one little bit, Bertie. Do you want to know what it is?'

This was the signal for Olive to intervene. 'He may not be ready for it yet, Pansy. Not yet.'

## 5. Being Aeneas

At the wheel of their custard-coloured car, Domenica drove herself and Angus through the West End of Edinburgh, through bustling Tollcross, and on towards the polite braes of Morningside. Angus had a driving licence, but he did not particularly like driving and was pleased that Domenica should actually relish it – even to the point of her donning completely unnecessary driving gloves. He had held his licence since the age of nineteen, and it was valid, he assumed, in spite of a misprint. He was described as *Aeneas Lordie* instead of Angus Lordie, and although he had intended to correct this bureaucratic mistake, he had given up after a single unsuccessful attempt.

Angus had written to the driving licence authorities, pointing out that he was Angus rather than Aeneas, and asking for a new licence to be issued under the correct name.

He had received a reply two weeks later, which began, 'Dear Aeneas Lordie, I have received your recent letter, which is receiving attention. We shall contact you when the matter to which you refer has been resolved.' And with that the official had signed off. At the top of the letter, printed in large type above the address, was the mission statement of the government department in question: *Working for You and for the Community.*

No further letter was received, and Angus had decided to leave the matter at that. He knew that in Scotland you could call yourself whatever you liked, provided you did not do so in an attempt to commit fraud. There were no necessary formalities – and all you had to do was to start using your new name. A lawyer friend had confirmed this when Angus had asked him, but had pointed out that you could make a formal declaration, authenticated by a notary, in which you asserted the new name. In Angus's case, though, he had never been Aeneas, and so it seemed that no declaration should be necessary. The lawyer considered this, and suggested a declaration with the simple wording: *I, Angus Lordie, do hereby state and affirm that I am Angus Lordie.*

'That should do the trick,' he said.

Angus had smiled. '*I, Franz Kafka, do hereby state and affirm that I am Franz Kafka.*'

The lawyer looked at him blankly. 'I don't see what Franz Kafka has to do with this,' he said.

Angus had not pursued the matter. He rather liked this alter ego, this shadowy Aeneas Lordie, who led a parallel life in a government computer somewhere. He liked the classical associations of the name, and imagined the complications that

Odysseus may have faced in his own documentation when required to linger on Calypso's island for years because his boating licence described him as Aeneas, instead of Odysseus.

Now, sitting in the front passenger seat of the car, he crested the brow of Church Hill and descended into Morningside. He liked Morningside, which was not only a geographical area but a state of being, a state of looking at the world. That could happen to neighbourhoods – their name could become associated with a particular set of attitudes and might stand thereafter for a world view rather than a bounded collection of streets.

'Morningside,' he remarked to Domenica.

She smiled. 'We should not mock, Angus. It's unseemly for us to come over from the New Town and condescend to Morningside.'

'I was not mocking,' said Angus. 'I was simply muttering the word … as one might say *om*, for example, in incantation. *Om* induces a state of peaceful acceptance.'

'*Om*,' intoned Domenica, as she drew up at the lights at the Morningside Clock, and then, in much the same register, '*Morningside*.'

Angus looked out of the window. Not far from where they were was the street on which Ramsey Dunbarton had lived. He had been a partner in a firm of lawyers, a man of a certain dryness, with an interest in amateur dramatics and singing, whose great moment of glory had come when he played the part of the Duke of Plaza-Toro in the never-to-be-forgotten Church Hill Theatre production of *The Gondoliers*. Poor Ramsey, thought Angus, as they waited for the lights to change; poor Ramsey …

Domenica distracted him. 'Are they having anybody else tonight?' she asked.

Angus shook his head. 'Not as far as I know. Matthew said that they like having just one couple. I think it will be just us.'

Domenica was pleased with that. 'We'll have the chance to catch up. I haven't seen Elspeth for ages. Of course, the triplets must take up most of her time.'

'It can't be easy,' said Angus. 'Sometimes Matthew looks exhausted when he comes into Big Lou's for morning coffee. He said to me the other day he'd been up since four in the morning, coping with the boys. By the time he got into work he was already finished.'

'They have an au pair, don't they?'

'Yes, so I believe. A young man – James. They share him with Big Lou. He works half the day in the coffee bar and the rest of the time he's the au pair out at Nine Mile Burn.'

'It's rather exciting – going out to a dinner party,' said Domenica. 'Remember how we used to go out to dinner parties almost every weekend? Remember?'

Angus did remember. 'And then suddenly people stopped having them.'

'Or stopped inviting us.'

That was an unsettling possibility. 'Do you really think . . . ?' he began.

'No, I don't,' said Domenica. 'I suspect that the formal dinner party just became too much for most people.'

'People became too busy?'

'Yes,' said Domenica. 'Everybody is busier than they were, say, ten years ago. Our lives have expanded to embrace the increased possibilities of our times. There is more information, to start with. We simply get more messages – all the time. We have more to think about. And we can move about more easily too. Places are cheaper and more accessible.'

Angus thought this was probably true. Of course, he went nowhere, but he imagined he could go to all sorts of places if he chose to do so. He could go to Iceland, for instance, which he had never visited, but which he would like to see. There was a line of poetry about Iceland that stuck in his mind ... *where the ports have names for the sea*. It was a haunting line – a typographical mistake that had been left as it was. The poet – W. H. Auden – had written *where the poets have names for the sea*, but had liked the typographical error, which gave the line greater poetic impact, and had kept it. It was rather like being called Aeneas by the driving licence authorities and keeping the mistake for its poetic possibilities. It was the same thing, really, Angus decided.

## 6. *Blue Remembered Hills*

They parked beside the house. As Angus got out of the car, the sun had just dipped below the top of East Cairn Hill, casting a lengthening shadow over Carlops and the winding road to Biggar. In the distance, across a landscape of wheat and barley, of secret lochs and hidden glens, the Lammermuir Hills were still bathed in evening gold.

Angus turned to Domenica. 'This view always makes me feel sad. I don't know why, but it does.' He drew in his breath, savouring the freshness of the air. Freshly mown grass was upon it, and the smell of lavender, too, from Elspeth's kitchen garden. 'Well, perhaps not sad – more wistful, perhaps, which is one notch below actual sadness.'

She followed his gaze over to the hills. 'What's the expression? Blue remembered hills? Where does that come from?'

'It's Housman,' said Angus. 'I happen to know that because I used it as the title of a painting I did once – a long time ago. I painted those very hills we're looking at, as a matter of fact.' He had been an admirer of William Gillies, who had visited those hills in watercolour time and time again, in all their seasons and moods.

Domenica gazed at the hills. They were blue, just as watercolour hills should be.

'*What are those blue remembered hills?*' Angus recited. '*That is the land of lost content,/ I see it shining plain.*'

She looked at him; the moment of shared feeling had arisen unexpectedly, as such moments sometimes did. It was the beauty of the country before them that had done it. Scotland was a place of attenuated light, of fragility, of a beauty that broke the heart, as MacDiarmid had said it would, with its little white rose, sharp and sweet. And sometimes she felt this Scotland slipping away, which was why Angus should feel sad, she thought, and why she should feel that too.

She reached out and touched his forearm, gently, without words, to show that she understood what he felt. Then she said, 'We should go in.'

And as she said that, the front door opened and Elspeth

came out to greet them. 'Perfect timing,' she said. 'Matthew has left drinks on the terrace.' She made a show of looking relieved. 'James is cooking. I'm off-duty.'

Domenica smiled. 'I'm sure you deserve it.'

Elspeth said, 'Sometimes the boys can be a bit ... demanding. Triplets tend to go through the same stages together, and all the challenges are multiplied by three. They're currently going through the biting stage – so Tobermory bit Rognvald, who bit Fergus, who in turn bit Tobermory. They all ended up screaming.'

Domenica's eyes widened. 'Red in tooth and claw ...'

'Yes,' said Elspeth. 'That's exactly what little boys are. It's the way their brains are wired. They are impulsive, violent, endlessly energetic, and prone to bite. That's just the way they are.'

'And yet ...' said Angus. 'When you see them, butter wouldn't melt in their mouths. I could use them as models for *putti*, if I were ever to paint something like that. Will we see them this evening?'

Elspeth glanced at her watch. It was eight o'clock. 'They'll be dropping off to sleep. Next time, perhaps. Matthew has been upstairs reading to them. He'll be down soon.'

She led them into the house and then out through French doors onto the terrace. Four chairs ringed a table on which a tray with glasses had been placed. There was a sparkling wine for Angus and Elspeth, and a soft drink for Domenica. As driver, Domenica was to restrict herself to bitter lemon, which she enjoyed anyway; in general, she was not one for alcohol.

Elspeth raised her glass to her guests.

'*Slàinte mhath*,' said Angus.

Domenica touched her glass against Elspeth's. '*God blesim yu*,' she said, adding, 'That's *cheers* in Melanesian pidgin. In Chinese pidgin, it's *chin chin*, which is what you might have said in Shanghai in 1925.'

Elspeth smiled. 'Lovely! *God blesim yu*, too. I suppose you used that on your fieldwork.'

Domenica nodded. 'All anthropologists went to Papua New Guinea in those days – if they could. It was the real thing – the copper-bottomed experience of fieldwork that enabled you to outstare anybody at an anthropological conference. If you were really lucky, you were able to study a cargo cult. Less fortunate people ended up dealing with initiation ceremonies or rain-making rites. Have you read *The Innocent Anthropologist*, by any chance?'

Elspeth shook her head.

'It's by an anthropologist who went as a young man to spend some time with a remote people in Cameroon. It caused a bit of a stir.'

'Oh? And why was that?'

'He was too frank. Anthropologists take themselves immensely seriously. He didn't.'

Elspeth laughed. 'Isn't that a fault of many academics? Don't they think that everybody is hanging on their every word?'

Domenica looked thoughtful. 'Some of them are like that, I suppose. And I suppose they never realise that people may actually not pay much attention to what they say and just get on with their business. I think I understood that. I was never under any illusions that my conclusions on the societies I studied were of much interest to anybody – other than fellow anthropologists.'

Elspeth looked at her. 'But you completed your fieldwork *rite de passage*?'

'Yes. Papua New Guinea – I wrote a book about it – eventually. Nobody read it, as far as I know. At least, I never met anybody who had done so. Except my cousin in Melrose. She read it, I believe.'

'And you learned pidgin for that?' asked Elspeth.

'Yes. I haven't used it for rather a long time, of course, but it comes back. Languages don't disappear altogether; once you know them, they tend to become embedded in the mind, like fossils in rock.'

Matthew arrived from upstairs. The boys had gone to sleep, he said, and he had called in on the kitchen on his way out to the terrace. 'James is rustling up something pretty tempting,' he said. 'He loves his garlic. Smell it?'

Domenica sniffed at the air. 'Delicious,' she said.

'It has to be handled carefully,' said Matthew. 'But you won't be disappointed. He is very creative in the kitchen.'

'Will he eat with us?'

Elspeth shook her head, rather firmly, thought Domenica. 'He wants to go into town after he's served us,' she said. 'He's up to something. I have no idea what it is, but he's planning something. That boy has a secret – I'm sure of it.'

Angus was curious. 'Have you asked him?'

Matthew shook his head. 'It's not our place.'

'Yes, it is,' Elspeth contradicted him.

Matthew sighed. 'The point about secrets is that people don't talk about them.'

'We could try,' said Elspeth.

'What possible secret could a nineteen-year-old have?' asked Angus.

'You'd be surprised,' said Elspeth. But she did not answer his question.

## 7. *The Holy Family Boxing Club*

James had prepared the menu carefully. He enjoyed cooking, and found that Elspeth needed little persuading to allow him to cook dinner at least three times a week, on top of the cooking that he did for the boys. They, of course, liked nursery food, and James was only too happy to rustle up macaroni cheese with tomato sauce, fish fingers, or pizza, followed by semolina pudding into which he dribbled quantities of strawberry jam. Matthew had never lost his taste for the dishes of his childhood, and often succumbed to that temptation familiar to all parents of raiding the children's plates for the odd morsel. Elspeth disapproved: she fought a battle for healthy food rather than this carbohydrate-rich fare, and served the boys grated carrot, kale purée, and vitamin D-enriched, low-GI oatmeal sausages. All of these were toyed with, and often left uneaten, rather than consumed with any degree of enthusiasm. Between these extremes, though, the boys had a balanced diet, in the sense that they received roughly equal quantities of healthy and unhealthy food, and appeared to be doing well on it.

It was on occasions like this, though, that James's prowess in the kitchen came to the fore. Elspeth had given him free rein on the choice of courses for their dinner party, although she had reminded him that Angus was keen on seafood and Domenica was known to have a soft spot for garlic. James had chosen scallops for their first course, followed by a saddle of lamb into which he had inserted liberal quantities of sliced garlic and sprigs of rosemary. A selection of cheeses from Valvona & Crolla would follow, each one vouched for by Mary Contini, who could give a full provenance for the cows, the milk, and the manufacture.

As he stirred the scallops, James reflected on the day's events. He had been busy, as he had spent the morning working in Big Lou's coffee bar before assuming responsibility for the boys for several hours after lunch. Fortunately, the weather had been good enough to allow most of the afternoon to be spent out of doors, and the boys had passed their time making a fort underneath the rhododendron bushes, destroying it, and then moving on to an energetic hour of hide-and-seek. That had not been without its incidents, including an alarming ten minutes or so when Rognvald had hidden himself away so successfully that he could not be found at all. Eventually he was located in a dustbin, and was given a strong warning by James on the dangers of such hiding places.

James was happy, and was conscious of his happiness. He had the impression that many of those with whom he had been at school, at James Gillespie's, were discontented for one reason or another. They were anxious about the future or felt that their present was not quite what they would like it to be. Some of them believed that others were having far more fun than they were; some thought that nobody would ever love them; others railed at the world for being unjust or indifferent to the suffering that they could see so clearly all around them. These were all normal feelings for nineteen-year-olds – even if James himself experienced none of these reservations about the world. It never occurred to him that he would be judged unworthy of anything, including the devotion of a suitable girl, or even, *seriatim*, of more than one suitable girl. Nor did he ever doubt that he would be able to pursue whatever career he decided upon, and that doors would open to him when he wanted them to.

This self-confidence could easily have been the result of a sense of entitlement, but in his case it was not. James felt as he did about the world because the world felt as it did about him. The world liked James because of his youth, and the optimism that went with it. That was how the world responded – there was no justice in that, no question of desert: that was just the way things were.

Now everybody was at the kitchen table, James came over, bearing a large tray. He served the first course with a flourish.

'Hand-dived,' he said. 'All the way from Mull.'

Angus sniffed appreciatively at his plate. 'Wonderful,' he said. 'The fact that they're hand-dived is so important, isn't it, James?'

James nodded. 'And they've been nowhere near any fresh water.'

'Very wise,' said Angus.

'If you wash a scallop, it absorbs water like blotting paper,' James explained. 'A quarter of the weight of the scallops you buy at the fishmonger's or in the supermarket is just water. Never wash scallops.'

'And the sauce?' asked Domenica.

'Cream and brandy,' James replied. 'With a bit of basil.'

'Oh my!' exclaimed Domenica.

'I heard about them from somebody at the boxing gym.'

Angus raised an eyebrow. 'You box?'

'James belongs to a boxing club,' Matthew explained.

'Michty!' said Angus.

'I'm not sure how I feel about boxing,' said Domenica.

Elspeth nodded. 'I know what you mean,' she said. 'It's definitely a contact sport . . .'

'And yet,' said Angus, 'boxing clubs can be a force for good. I happened to read about a book on the sociology of boxing. I came across it by chance and found it fascinating.'

'Why?' asked Matthew.

'It provides a way out of hopelessness for some young men,' said Angus. 'It channels their energy. It provides structure.'

Elspeth looked doubtful.

'No, I'm serious,' Angus continued. 'One of the chapters in that book was about a boxing club in West Belfast. It was called The Holy Family Boxing Club.'

Domenica laughed. 'Surely not?'

'No, that was its name,' Angus said. 'And during the Troubles in Northern Ireland, it was one of the few places where young Catholics and Protestants could meet.'

'And punch one another,' said Matthew.

30

Elspeth turned to Matthew. 'Don't be so cynical,' she said. 'It might have done a lot for reconciliation.'

Matthew shrugged. He sliced into a scallop and put it into his mouth.

'Divine,' he said.

'The Holy Family Boxing Club,' muttered Elspeth. 'How very strange.'

'And yet, in the event, how ecumenical,' said Domenica. 'And what did the rest of us do to make that situation better?'

## 8. Students Eat Anything

The scallops did not last long.

'I loved that sauce,' said Angus. 'Delicious.'

Elspeth pointed towards the kitchen. 'I told you: James is a superb cook. He can do anything, that boy. He could probably get a job at Prestonfield or Gleneagles. Anywhere, really.'

'I went to Prestonfield a few months ago,' said Matthew. 'A client took me for lunch. He wanted to talk about buying a Peploe that had come up at auction. We had a wonderful lunch. There were peacocks strutting around on the lawns, people getting married in the marquee. We didn't finish lunch until four o'clock. We'd paid no attention to the time.'

'Sometimes time does that, doesn't it?' said Elspeth. 'It forgets to whisper in your ear.'

Angus looked down at his plate. 'That sauce – it was superb. It makes me want to lick the plate. Just to get the last drop of it.'

'Please do,' said Elspeth. 'We're not formal here.'

Angus smiled. 'I sometimes do that at home. In fact, I often do.'

Domenica gave a look of mock disapproval. 'He does, believe it or not. Most people stop doing that when they're about ten.' She paused. 'I've always assumed that he picked it up from his dog, Cyril.'

Angus defended himself. 'I don't see what's wrong with it.' He gave Domenica a reproachful look. 'We all have little things we do when nobody else is looking – harmless little habits that we wouldn't want anybody else to see.'

There was a sudden silence at the table, as they each contemplated the truth of what had been said. Matthew blushed. Angus noticed, and wondered what it was that Matthew did, the mere thought of which caused embarrassment. Did he lick the plate too, or was it something worse – not that there was anything *wrong* in licking the plate. It was mere social custom that dictated that you should not do it. But waste not, want not: why not enjoy every last morsel rather than put the scraps in the food-waste bin?

It was as if Elspeth had read Angus's thoughts. 'I caught Matthew going through the food-waste bin the other day,' she said. 'He takes out scraps and eats them. I caught him.'

All eyes turned to Matthew, who blushed again. So that was it, thought Angus. It was nothing to be ashamed of – nothing involving something that could not be talked about at the dinner table. Mind you, he thought, was

32

there *anything* that could not be talked about at the dinner table today?

Domenica laughed, perhaps slightly nervously. 'I can understand that,' she said. 'We throw away far too much.'

'But it's not the purpose of the food-waste bin,' said Elspeth. 'The council collects scraps for a purpose.'

'I've often wondered what they do with the scraps,' said Angus. 'You can't feed swill to pigs these days, can you? They don't want the wrong things getting into the animal food chain.' He paused. 'Somebody said that they took it off somewhere and reprocessed it as food for students.'

'I doubt it,' said Elspeth. 'If you can't feed it to pigs, then should you be able to feed it to students?'

'Students eat anything,' said Domenica. 'And drink anything as well. They are utterly undiscriminating.'

James reappeared with the next course – the rolled saddle of lamb. Matthew wanted to carve it at the table, which he now did, observing as he did so the perfection of the meat.

'This comes from just up the road,' he said. 'From Baddinsgill. Local produce.'

James served the vegetables.

'Will you cook for us forever?' asked Domenica.

James smiled. But Domenica thought: I really would like things to be forever. I would like to be able to sit at this table once a week, perhaps, with these friends. I would like to talk about the things we talk about, the small things, whatever happened in the world. I would like to wake up in the morning and not think that things were getting worse. I would like not to have to listen to the exchange of insults between politicians. I would like to hear of people co-operating with

33

one another and helping others and bringing succour and comfort to the needy and ... and I would like to think that we were not still in the seventeenth century here in Scotland, as divided amongst ourselves as they were at that time, pitted against each other, with one vision of the good battling another, and people despising others for their opinions. If only we could put that behind us and ...'

She sighed.

'You sighed,' said Elspeth.

'Yes, you did,' said Angus, his mouth half-full. 'Or were you just breathing?'

'I was thinking of the seventeenth century,' said Domenica. 'I was thinking of what it was like to live in Scotland in those days.'

'Unpleasant,' said Matthew. 'No antibiotics. No anaesthetics. Unremitting toil. Religious extremism. No midge repellent, if you lived in the Highlands.'

'It was the religious extremism that was worst,' Angus suggested. 'And the plotting of the various factions. Those ghastly nobles.'

'Have we changed all that much?' asked Domenica. 'I mean, obviously things are better in some respects. People have rights; they have freedoms. We don't have public executions. We aren't forced to profess a particular religion.'

'Oh, that's all infinitely better,' Elspeth said. 'But I wonder whether there isn't the same tendency to bicker, and whether the moral energy that gave us the religious extremism isn't still there, just the same, but showing itself differently. There are still plenty of people who are keen to tell other people what to do.'

Angus agreed. 'There certainly are. We may not be lectured from the pulpit any longer, but we're certainly lectured. And we might be every bit as intolerant of dissent as we were back in those days.'

The silence that had attended the earlier recollection of social solecism now returned, but only for a few moments. Then Matthew said, 'Our history is so violent.'

'Isn't everybody's?' asked Domenica. 'We're a violent species.'

Elspeth looked pained. 'There must have been some peaceful societies. Domenica, you're an anthropologist – you must know of some society where …' She shrugged. 'Where people share and co-operate and look after one another.' Sometimes, she thought, such *desiderata* seemed so unlikely as to be impossible.

'Eden?' suggested Angus.

'The Peaceable Kingdom theme,' mused Matthew. 'Do you know those pictures? There's that famous one in the Phillips Collection in Washington. I've actually seen it. All the animals are together – the lion and the lamb, and so on. All are at peace with one another.'

'That's wishful thinking,' said Domenica. 'Not painted from life.'

'Perhaps,' said Matthew. 'But then don't we have to have some idea like that – somewhere in the back of our minds? An idea of civilisation? An idea of what things might be?'

'Nobody uses the word *civilisation* these days,' said Domenica.*

Matthew reached for his glass of wine. 'That's the

---

* Not entirely true: see, for example, *In Search of Civilization* by the Scottish philosopher John Armstrong, a profound defence of the tarnished concept.

problem,' he said. 'We don't believe in anything ... except *things* – the material.'

Angus looked at him. He was right. We had forgotten about the spiritual; we had forgotten about the idea of civilisation; we had forgotten about how important it was to be courteous to one another and to love your neighbour. And nobody talked about these things except in a tone of embarrassment or apology, but at least they could do so here, in this kitchen, in the warm embrace of friendship, under the gaze of these gentle hills, this lovely country, this blessed place.

## 9. *An Orcadian Spell*

Discreetly, like a barely visible waiter, James cleared away the plates before returning with a large platter of cheese. Placing the platter in the centre of the table, he recited the names of the cheeses. Angus tried to follow, and to remember which was which, but found himself remembering only a rare Orcadian cheese and a Mull cheddar. One might forget so many exotic cheeses, he thought, but the memory of cheddar always remained.

'Should one be embarrassed by choosing cheddar every time?' he asked.

Matthew laughed. 'There's no need to apologise for simple things.'

'But is cheddar simple?' Domenica enquired. 'Just because there's a lot of it, does that make it simple?'

Elspeth thought it did not. She, like Angus, preferred cheddar to the other cheeses. She did not like runny cheeses, nor those that smelled too strongly; she did not like cheese that had blue veins running through it. She wondered what exactly was in those blue veins. Bacteria? Of course, there was nothing wrong with bacteria – we were full of bacteria, ourselves – populated by millions, no by billions, of tiny organisms, leading remote, bacterial lives inside us and covering our skin.

She gave an involuntary shudder, and changed the subject. 'This Orkney cheese,' she said. 'Is it nicer than the Mull cheddar?'

'I love Orcadian cheeses,' said Angus, realising, as he spoke, that he could name none. But he could broaden his declaration of love. 'In fact, I love everything to do with Orkney. The Italian Chapel. Scapa Flow. George Mackay Brown. Peter Maxwell Davies ... *An Orkney Wedding, with Sunrise* ...'

Matthew nodded. 'I heard that at the Festival last year,' he said. 'The Scottish National Orchestra played it. That beautiful, swelling music, rising to a climax, and then the piper comes in. It takes the breath away.'

'The pipes always do that,' agreed Elspeth. 'I don't mean just do that to the piper – it's the same thing with the listener. There's nothing more stirring.' She paused. '*Mist Covered Mountains* does it for me. There's an extraordinary ...' She struggled for the right word.

'Gravity,' suggested Matthew. 'I know what you mean.

There's a grave beauty to that tune. All the sorrow of Scotland is somehow distilled in that music.'

Angus nodded. There was a deep well of sorrow in Scotland ... or was it wistfulness? Perhaps wistful longing was what Matthew was talking about: longing for something that had been there in the past, but was no longer.

But Domenica now said: 'This Orcadian cheese – why was it so rare?'

Elspeth smiled. 'Because the woman who made it had only one cow.'

Angus laughed. 'A good enough reason.'

'I love the idea of that,' said Matthew. 'Can't you see it? An idyllic scene. A croft house surrounded by green fields. And a woman going out to milk her only cow.'

'And not far away,' Elspeth said, 'cliffs at the end of her field, with the sea moving below, and the sun on the sea, and Norway only a few hundred miles away.' She paused. 'And the woman with her single cow and her little shed in which she makes the cheese – tiny blocks of it – that are sent off to Edinburgh, where people can eat it and think about Orkney and how beautiful it is and how ...'

They were silent. Then Matthew pointed at another cheese and said, 'That one's a goat's milk cheese.'

The Orcadian spell was broken, and as Angus cut off a slice of Mull cheddar, reassuringly yellow, he said, 'I'm reading a book about friendship.'

Matthew looked at him enquiringly. 'About a particular friendship?'

'No. Friendship in general. It's by a Professor Dunbar. He invented something called the Dunbar Number.'

They waited.

'It's one hundred and fifty, apparently,' Angus said.

Elspeth looked puzzled. 'One hundred and fifty?'

Angus explained. 'That's the number of people with whom one can maintain stable social relationships. You can have about one hundred and fifty people in your life. After that, it becomes impossible to relate to them properly.'

'You mean close friends?' asked Elspeth.

Angus shook his head. 'No. These are just people with whom you can sit down and have a chat. These are the people on your Christmas-card list.'

'And how many closer friends can you have?' asked Elspeth.

'I forget exactly what he says,' Angus replied. 'But I think it's not much more than ten. We just can't cope with more than that.'

For a moment, nobody said anything, as each of them discreetly measured themselves again this standard. Angus thought: does Cyril count as one of my ten? A dog could be a very close friend, but maybe that was a separate category. Perhaps Professor Dunbar had a figure for the number of dogs one could have in one's life. Ten would be a bit much. Even two dogs could be emotionally demanding, he thought. And then he started to compile his list: Matthew would be on it, of course, and Elspeth too ... unless a married couple counted for one in this context. He would count them as one, he decided. And then there was Domenica. Did one's spouse count? That could be tricky. If you didn't count your spouse or partner, then that implied a lack of friendliness in the relationship. No, a spouse definitely counted.

Elspeth was thinking: Domenica and Angus were friends, but would they be part of her allowance of ten? Did she know them all that well? Probably not. There was Molly, of course, with whom she had been at school, where they had been not only friends but best friends. Good old Molly, with those awful shoes of hers and that irritating way of saying, *You know what I mean?* They had drifted apart, particularly after Molly had married Steve, who made model aeroplanes and talked about Hearts football club all the time – but *all* the time, or at least when he was not talking about model aeroplanes. Poor Molly. She was embarrassed by Steve, Elspeth thought, because her voice always dropped when she mentioned his name. That was a sign; that was definitely a sign.

Then she thought: Big Lou. Elspeth liked Big Lou, but she very rarely saw her. She would like her to be among her ten, but she was not sure whether, realistically, she was. Perhaps one would be allowed two lists: a list of those with whom one was currently a good friend, and then a list of those whom one would like to have as a close friend. There might even be a waiting list, like the waiting list for membership of Glyndebourne or for membership of Muirfield Golf Club, both requiring a wait of some years. Elspeth would have loved to be a member of Glyndebourne, but was indifferent to Muirfield Golf Club.*

But *chacun à son goût*, she thought – in this, as in all matters.

---

* Aka The Honourable Company of Edinburgh Golfers, located just outside Gullane (pronounced Gillin).

## 10. Scotsmen Can Skip

At the very time at which Elspeth was thinking of Big Lou, Big Lou herself was thinking of Elspeth – an example of the synchronicity that Jung believed meant something, but which may occur simply because there is a limited number of people to think about and things to do, and some of these thoughts and things are destined to occur at the same time. Big Lou, who had been endowed through her upbringing on Snell Mains with a healthy capacity for scepticism, would have agreed with that.

That evening, Big Lou was sitting in her second-floor flat in Canonmills, which had a distant view of the river, the Water of Leith, on its winding progress through the city towards its appointment with the Firth of Forth and eventually the sea. At her feet, on the floor of her living room, her adopted son, Finlay, was struggling to complete a large jigsaw puzzle. The theme was the Massacre of Glencoe, an unfortunate incident in Scottish history, portrayed here in a nineteenth-century painting entitled *How Not to Behave Towards Your Guests*. Finlay was now attempting, without much success, to find a place for a piece that looked as if it came from a Campbell kilt. It was a 500-piece puzzle, and Big Lou had already had to speak to him on the need for patience in tackling jigsaw puzzles.

'It's not simple, Finlay,' she said. 'And it's no good trying to force a piece to fit. That never works.'

As she said this, she reflected on the fact that this was advice that held for most things, not least for our personal lives. Forcing yourself to be something you were not was never entirely satisfactory, and was likely to lead to at least some degree of unhappiness. Very rarely, people got away with it – they acted a part, and then, at length, discovered that the created persona had put down deep enough roots to become the authentic person. But for the most part, the result was more likely to be inauthenticity or bad faith. Big Lou had read Sartre, whose works were amongst the collection of books she had inherited when she bought the bookshop that became her café. She knew about existentialism, but was not convinced by the arguments around authenticity. These left so many questions unanswered, and in particular she wondered what existentialists had to say about those who felt authentic only when being cruel or exploitative. In other words, what was the essential merit in authenticity, if the self to which one was being honest was flawed in some way? Would it not be better overall to pursue an aspirational, pro-social ideal, even if that was something that you felt was not authentic to you? Was there a moral distinction between the authentically bad, on the one hand, and those on the other hand who were authentically bad but behaved in an inauthentically good way?

She thought of this as she gazed down at the spread-out puzzle. Finlay had finished a corner in which a sheepdog belonging to the unfortunate MacDonalds was cowering in a

42

corner watching its owner being put to the sword. The artist had been particularly skilful in revealing the dog's expression, which was one of abject terror.

'Poor dog,' she muttered.

Finlay looked up. 'I wonder if the Campbells killed the MacDonald dogs too. Do you think they did, Lou?'

Finlay had called Lou by her first name from the beginning, when she had first fostered him. Now and then he had called her Mum, and her heart had leapt with delight when he did so, but he had always corrected himself, and she thought it best not to ask him to address her thus. If, in due course, he chose to make that change, she would quietly accept it, and rejoice in the bond that it created, but until then she would not raise the subject.

She addressed his question. 'I doubt it, Finlay. The Campbells were certainly a ruthless bunch, but I don't think they would have slaughtered the MacDonald dogs. Stolen them, perhaps, but not massacred.'

'There's a boy at school who's called Campbell,' said Finlay. 'He says it's not true. He says that the Massacre of Glencoe never happened. He said that the MacDonalds had stolen the Campbells' cattle and they were just trying to get them back.'

Big Lou shook her head. 'I'm afraid it did happen,' she said. 'But I don't think we should make too much of it, you know. A lot happened in history.'

She looked at her watch. It was time for Finlay to have his bath and then be tucked up in bed. He would have a story, of course – she was currently reading him *The Wind in the Willows*, and they were at a crucial moment for Toad. Justice was about to be done, with reckless driving getting its comeuppance, and Big Lou found herself looking forward to each night's chapter every bit as much as Finlay was.

'Ten minutes more with the jigsaw,' said Big Lou, 'and then it'll be time for your bath.'

But Finlay had had enough. 'I'll never finish this,' he said, tossing the problematic piece down on the ground. Then, getting to his feet, he suddenly leapt into the air, brought his toes together, separated them in a scissor movement of the legs, and landed back on his feet. Finlay studied ballet.

'Very neat,' said Big Lou, with a smile.

'And then there's this,' said Finlay, quickly managing a further *échappé* and *cabriole*.

Big Lou smiled. 'You're making such good progress,' she said.

Finlay inclined his head in acceptance of the compliment. She watched him, and thought about how difficult it would have been for a boy like him in the time of her own childhood. She could not imagine any of the boys with whom she had been at school in Arbroath all those years ago being able to do what Finlay was doing and profess an interest in ballet. That would have been greeted by cries of derision, by ruthless teasing from the other boys, and by smirking looks of disapproval from the girls. Insults would have been hurled, each with a barb and a not-so-subtle innuendo, and the boy would have gone home each day with those hurtful words ringing in his ears.

How things had changed. Scotland was now simply a kinder place. And that was true of just about everywhere, except for those few countries, redoubts of old-fashioned machismo and reaction, where men strutted, where cruelty still reigned. And that kindness – how had it been brought into existence? The answer, Big Lou thought, was easily discerned: feminisation. Scotsmen, previously encouraged to be strong and silent, afraid to cry, afraid to be seen to be weak, afraid to *feel* ... Now released from the tyranny of their gender straitjacket, men had been allowed to be something different. *Scotsmen can skip*, Big Lou had read on a poster somewhere. Absurd, embarrassing; but it was true. They could.

She stopped herself. Men had become liberated by a side-wind to the liberation of women. Or *some* men had been transformed: she was not sure just how far this applied to her new boyfriend, Fat Bob. If there were indeed new Scotsmen, then Fat Bob was definitely not one.

## 11. Fat Bob

Big Lou had met Fat Bob outside her café one morning. She had arrived at seven-thirty, as she usually did, in order to be open by eight, and had found him standing at the railings, peering down the stone steps that led to the café entrance, slightly below street level. At first, she wondered whether he was up to no good – there had been an attempt to force the door a few weeks ago, and Big Lou had arranged for the installation of a more secure lock. But that sort of thing, she imagined, would hardly happen in broad daylight, when there was a regular stream of people walking up Dundas Street on their way to work.

He turned to her, as if surprised that anybody should come to open up the café.

'This your place?' He spoke in an accent that was familiar to her – Dundee perhaps.

She nodded. 'Aye, it's my place.'

'You Big Lou then?'

Again, she nodded. 'That's what they call me.'

He looked at her and smiled. She saw that he had a tooth missing to one side, in the upper row. The effect was not unpleasant – giving him a slightly raffish, almost piratical look. But just as she noticed this, her gaze fell to the broad shoulders and the powerful, stocky build. This was a man who would be more at home on a building site, or the docks, rather than a New Town coffee bar. He was the size – and shape – of a large industrial fridge, and she found herself thinking that one could probably attach fridge magnets to him.

'They call me Fat Bob.'

Big Lou raised an eyebrow. Her inspection had continued, and had picked up the tattoo on his right forearm, just below his rolled-up sleeve. It was a large thistle, under the legend, SCOTLAND FOREVER. 'Your friends?' she said. 'That's what your friends call you?'

Fat Bob shrugged. 'Everybody. I don't mind.' He grinned. 'And it's muscle, not fat.'

'Well,' said Big Lou, extracting her keys from the bag she was carrying. 'Folk often get it wrong, don't they?' She paused. 'We're not open yet, you'll have seen. Eight o'clock.'

Fat Bob looked at his watch. Big Lou noticed that it was a large, round watch of the sort that sportsmen – or the slightly showy sort of sportsmen – liked to wear. She had heard Matthew describe such watches as Dubai Airport watches, and she had been struck by the description. Yet there was something unusual about this watch: it was a Mickey Mouse watch, with Mickey's rotating arms being the hands.

Fat Bob intercepted her glance. 'Aye, Mickey Mouse,' he said, a note of apology in his voice. 'But I've always liked him.'

'Nothing wrong with Mickey Mouse,' said Lou. She hesitated for a moment. Then she said, 'You can come in, if you like. I'll get the coffee going – if that's what you want.'

'I've heard about your bacon rolls,' said Fat Bob. 'I'd like one of those. But no hurry, of course.'

Big Lou was pleased by the mention of her bacon rolls. Since James had come to work for her, their food menu had improved greatly, but the most popular item continued to be their bacon rolls. These were carbohydrate-rich rolls that made no concession to whole-grains, in which two rashers of bacon were inserted, curling crisply at the edge, untrimmed of surplus fat, dripping in grease. When they were cooked, the smell permeated the coffee bar, pushing that of freshly ground coffee into the background. And like the distant sound of the sirens on Scylla, this olfactory lure enticed people off the street and into the café. Some of this passing trade felt guilty, and would explain, as they placed their orders, that it was years since they had treated themselves to a bacon roll; that they otherwise had a perfectly healthy diet, consuming a lot of roughage and *plenty* of Omega-3 oil; and anyway, wasn't there research somewhere that showed that one bacon roll a week was positively beneficial, in the same way as two glasses of red wine *per diem* (and, of course, *per os*) were – or was it that the two glasses of red wine would cancel the cholesterol-raising effect of the occasional bacon roll – something like that? And anyway, could I have my bacon quite crisp, if you don't mind, and is that tomato sauce I see: I haven't had that for years – for years! – or not since I was at school and we used to cover our chips with it – you should have seen us. We had such an unhealthy diet in those days, with all those E numbers that went into everything. Mind you, nobody had allergies in those days, did they? It's only now that people are developing all sorts of allergies because their food is so pure and their immune system is not getting the challenge it needs to build up a memory.

Big Lou unlocked the door and pushed it open. It occurred to her that it was perhaps slightly unwise to be letting this stranger into the coffee bar when there was nobody else around. What if he suddenly pushed past her, slammed the door behind them, and demanded money from the till? That sort of thing happened, she knew, because she had read about it recently in the *Sunday Post*, the newspaper on which she had been brought up, and still read each weekend, cover to cover, along with *Scotland on Sunday* and the *Sunday Herald*. A shopkeeper in Oban, of all places, had let a customer into his shop before normal opening hours and had been rewarded for his consideration with the theft of the entire contents of his safe.

She looked over her shoulder. Fat Bob was immediately behind her, but there was nothing in his demeanour that suggested malicious intention, and she relaxed. There was something about him that Big Lou liked. She did not like thin men – at least she did not like thin men in *that* way. Nor did she like men who took too much trouble with their grooming: men simply did not do that in Angus, where she had been brought up. There had been a man in the coffee bar recently who quite clearly plucked his eyebrows, and Big Lou had been unable to keep her eyes off them. What sort of man plucked his eyebrows? She was not sure how to answer her own question, but she was certain that Fat Bob would not do something like that: some men might be in touch with their eyebrows, she thought, but not him.

Fat Bob was looking around the coffee bar appreciatively. 'Braw,' he said.

Big Lou smiled. Yes, it was braw. Of course, it was braw, and the fact that he used the Scots word to describe what he saw further endeared him to her.

'I'll heat up a bacon roll for you,' she said, as she went behind the counter, adding, 'Two maybe.'

He thanked her. 'You're a great lass, Big Lou,' he said.

'Thank you, Bob . . . er, Fat Bob.'

The compliment was completely sincere. Fat Bob himself was completely sincere. He was authentic – in a way that only those who have never heard of Jean-Paul Sartre can be. Here was no hesitant aesthete; here was a man who could manage two bacon rolls, and who had SCOTLAND FOREVER, not SCOTLAND PRO TEM, tattooed on his forearm.

## 12. The Story of Mags

Fat Bob, having eaten his bacon rolls, paid the six-pound bill entirely with fifty-pence coins. These were extracted from a wallet that he produced from his back pocket. The wallet was tartan, and had been engraved with *Bob*, and, beneath that, with a lover's heart symbol, complete with Cupid's arrow. Big Lou's eye was caught by this, and Fat Bob noticed.

'Nae doot about who that wallet belongs to,' he said, winking at Lou. 'That's my tartan, you see. Macgregor, of course.'

Big Lou nodded. She pretended to busy herself with wiping the coffee bar counter. 'It's bonny.' And then she added, rather absently, 'Macgregor. Of course. Macgregor.'

She had been dismayed to see the heart. That suggested that somebody had given the wallet to Bob – somebody who loved him sufficiently to have his name engraved, along with a heart. That meant a girlfriend or wife, and Big Lou suddenly felt that she did not want this man to have a wife or girlfriend. She did not stop to ask herself why; she just did not want him to have somebody else.

'And the ... the heart?' she stumbled on the word. All the men I meet are *taken*, she thought. There are no men left. None.

Bob laughed. 'Oh that. That was a long time ago.' He paused. 'It doesn't mean anything.'

She saw a faint glimmer of hope. 'You were married?'

Bob shook his head. 'Never quite married. Almost.'

'Engaged?'

This brought a similar shaking of the head. 'Never quite.'

She looked away. She did not want Bob to see that this disclosure had pleased her.

'She was a great girl,' he said, in a voice tinged with regret. 'Mags, she was called. We had something going – we really did. And then . . .' He shrugged. Now he was wistful. 'Her career got in the way.'

Big Lou sighed. 'A familiar story.' She wondered what Mags had done.

'She was doing so well,' Bob continued. 'She had to make a choice, I suppose. And I can't blame her, to be honest. If I had been in her position, I would probably have done the same.' He fixed Big Lou with an intense look. 'You never know what you're going to do until the chips are down. Then . . .' He shrugged. 'Who knows how they'll react?'

Big Lou made an understanding noise. Then she said, 'Of course, it depends on what the career is, doesn't it? Some things you can shelve for a few years and then take them up again – others you can't. What do they say: there's a tide in the affairs of men?'

'Aye,' said Fat Bob. 'You can say that again. You have to make a choice or you may lose a once-in-a-lifetime opportunity. That's what happened to Mags.'

Big Lou waited, but it seemed that further information was not going to be vouchsafed.

'What was it?' she asked.

Bob's tone was matter-of-fact; it was as if Mags had pursued the most mundane of occupations. 'Weight-lifter,' he said.

Big Lou's eyes widened. 'Weightlifter?'

'Aye. She was the Scottish champion – female, of course. And she would have been European champion if it weren't for the fact that one of the Russians cheated. She was entered as a woman, but she was really a man – people heard her being called Ivan. That's a man's name in Russia, you know. A dead giveaway. In fact, Mags inadvertently came across her in the showers at one competition, and she saw that he was definitely a man. She said you don't get things like that wrong – usually.'

'Did she complain?'

Fat Bob nodded. 'She went to the organisers of the competition and told them what she had seen. They made enquiries but were met with a blank denial. They said it was bad sportsmanship on Mags' part. So nothing was done.'

'That must have been hard for Mags.'

Fat Bob agreed. 'She was pretty cut up. But then she got this offer, you see, and she accepted. It was a weightlifting scholarship to a university somewhere near Boston. That's in America. You heard of the place?'

Big Lou nodded.

'It has a great reputation, they say. And they offered Mags full tuition fees and living expenses. How could she say no?'

'I don't think she could,' said Big Lou. She wondered what Mags had studied. 'And her degree?'

'Oh, that's nae bother with these scholarships. You register for whatever you like – either that, or they allocate you to some programme where they don't have enough students. That's not the important part.'

'So what was it?'

'Philosophy,' said Fat Bob. 'Mags liked it. She had always been an ideas sort of person, and philosophy was just right for her.'

'Very fortunate.'

'Yes, and Mags found that they didn't mind too much if she didn't go to any lectures – they said they would tell her what they were about later on. What they really wanted her to do was to lift weights and, in particular, to win against a place called Yale. Have you heard of that place?'

'Aye,' said Big Lou. 'Yale.'

'She spent a lot of time practising. She went to some classes, she said, but she used to sit at the back and lift those small portable weights while the professor was talking. Nobody minded, she said, because they all knew that she was their big hope to beat Yale, and they were in on it – the professors, the works.'

Big Lou said nothing. She had a deep respect for education, and she would have leapt at the opportunity to go to university, although she would much prefer Aberdeen to this Boston place. Had she been in Mags' position, she would have made use of the academic opportunity and immersed herself in her studies. But nobody would ever offer her a scholarship to anywhere, and so all that was hypothetical.

'What happened to her?' she asked. 'Did she come back to Scotland?'

Fat Bob shook his head. 'No,' he said. 'She stayed in the US.

She took a job teaching at Princeton. She runs a course called *Intellectual Heavy Lifting*. It's very popular, I'm told. There's always a waiting list.'

'Will she ever come back to Scotland?' asked Big Lou.

Fat Bob looked doubtful, perhaps rather regretful. But then he brightened. 'I don't think so. But she was a great woman,' he said. 'One of the very best – and I miss her an awful lot. Right here.' He placed a hand across his chest. 'A man needs a woman, you know, Big Lou. He needs somebody to go through life with – know what I mean? Just to share things with. Have a laugh with – that sort of thing.'

*Me*, thought Big Lou. *Me*.

## 13. *Great Lass, Big Quads*

'But what about you, Bob?' asked Big Lou.

He seemed taken aback by the question – as if he were surprised that anybody should take any interest in him.

'Me?'

Big Lou smiled encouragingly. 'Yes, Bob. You've told me about Mags, but what about you?'

He still seemed surprised. 'You want to know about me, Lou?'

She was taken by his modesty. 'Unless you're in a hurry to get away.' She glanced at her watch. There were still fifteen minutes before her normal opening time.

'There's not much to tell,' he said. 'I'm not one of those people who've done very much. Not really.'

Lou pointed to his empty plate. 'Could you manage another bacon roll? On the house?'

Bob grinned. 'Now I know why they're legendary,' he said.

Big Lou took a container of bacon out of the fridge and put two generous rashers into the grill. From the high stool on which he had seated himself, Fat Bob watched Big Lou at work.

'I tell myself that eating bacon rolls is part of my job,' he said. 'That makes me feel a bit better. Somebody said I could claim them against tax.'

Big Lou smiled. 'I doubt that, Bob. The tax people don't like you claiming things that you need anyway, if you see what I mean. You need food whatever you do. They don't treat food as a business expense.'

Bob frowned. 'But I was told that I could claim *extra* food. There's the stuff I need to keep alive – that's not an expense as far as the tax people are concerned. All right. But the food that you need to build up strength for the job, so to speak – that's different.'

Big Lou waited for an explanation.

'You see,' continued Fat Bob, 'I need to have extra energy for my job. I'm a professional strongman.'

Big Lou could not conceal her astonishment. 'Professional ...' She did not complete the sentence. She had not anticipated the effect that his announcement had on her. Had Fat Bob said that he was a builder, or a driving instructor, or a pastry chef – or anything of that sort – she would have not thought much about it. But a professional strongman was quite different, and considerably more interesting than any of those other, unexceptional occupations.

'You mean you . . . you tear up telephone directories? That sort of thing?'

Fat Bob laughed. 'Oh, Jeez, Lou – there's more to it than that. I go to Highland Games.' He reeled off a list of Highland events. 'Strathmore. Deeside. The Braemar Gathering. Inverary. Mull. The whole circuit.'

Big Lou put a hand to her forehead in a gesture of realisation. 'Of course,' she said. 'Of course. I should have guessed. You're one of those fellows who goes around winning prizes for tossing the caber and so on.'

'Hoping to win prizes,' Fat Bob corrected her. 'But that's not guaranteed. There are quite a few of us who are professional. I don't always win. Sometimes it's Wee Eric or Billy Mactaggart – people like that. Then there's a young guy from Lochearnhead who's doing rather well these days. He works for the South of Scotland Electricity Board. That's how he discovered his talent.'

Big Lou did not see the connection.

'Electricity poles,' explained Bob. 'He was working with those big poles they use for electricity wires. You know the sort? Telephone poles, they used to call them.'

Big Lou nodded. 'And he . . . ?'

'Yes. They found that he was good at moving these things. If they wanted a pole moved from one place to the other, this guy just picked it up and threw it. Amazing. He's called Jimmy Wilson. Not a particularly large fellow, and still in his early twenties. But pure muscle. Built like a tractor.'

'And the hammer?' asked Big Lou. 'You throw that too?'

'Yes,' said Bob. 'I do caber and hammer. I actually prefer the caber, but I won several big hammer events last year.' He paused. 'You don't think I'm boasting, Lou? You did ask me.'

She reassured him. 'Of course not. I'm interested – that's all. How much does that hammer weigh, by the way?'

'Twenty-two pounds,' said Bob. 'These things are all strictly controlled. It's sixteen pounds for the women's events. There's Lilly Mackay at the moment – she's from Inverness. Great lass. Big quads. She's the one to watch when it comes to the hammer. I wouldn't get on the wrong side of her.'

The bacon roll was ready, and Lou passed it over to Fat Bob. He leaned over the plate and sniffed. 'This is the first thing you get when you get to heaven,' he said. 'A bacon roll.'

Lou laughed. She had been right, she thought. Fat Bob was fun.

'Yes,' said Bob, as he took his first bite out of the roll. 'It's a very well-regulated sport. And there's no cheating. Most sports these days are full of cheats – aren't they? And people who are too competitive. Look at Formula One racing. Look at it, Lou. They do their team-mates down all the time. Cut corners. All that stuff. It's not a sport for gentlemen.'

Lou noted his use of the word *gentlemen*. It was an unfashionable word, and only used apologetically, in most cases. But she knew what he meant, and she was pleased that he was not embarrassed to use a word that was widely sneered at. Big Lou believed that it was still a good thing to be a gentleman, which involved treating other people with courtesy and consideration. That was all that it entailed.

She looked at Fat Bob. He was a gentleman. That was perfectly apparent.

'The caber weighs even more,' Fat Bob was saying. 'It's between one hundred and one hundred and eighty pounds. And there are regulations about its length.'

'How long is it?' she asked.

'Between sixteen and twenty-two feet,' said Bob, as he swallowed the last of the bacon roll. 'That was terrific, Lou. And are you sure I can't pay?'

Big Lou politely refused his offer.

'In that case,' said Fat Bob, 'would you let me buy you dinner? This evening? No notice, of course, but . . .'

Big Lou hesitated. 'I have a wee boy,' she said. 'I can't.'

Fat Bob stared at her directly. 'Have you got a man, Lou? I'm sorry if . . .'

'No,' she said quickly. 'I'm single. But there's Finlay, you see.'

'Bring him along,' said Fat Bob. 'We can eat early. Six o'clock. Seven. There's an Indian restaurant down in Leith that I like. Does he like Indian food?'

'He loves it,' said Big Lou.

She turned round, so that he should not see the emotions within her. That she had been sent a man like this, and that he should be prepared to include Finlay in their date, was more than she could ever have dared hope for. Big Lou had been unlucky in matters of the heart, but runs of bad luck came to an end – statistically, that was more likely than not – and now, perhaps, her own turn for happiness had at last arrived.

## 14. The Wolf Man Again

After their brief sojourn in Drummond Place Garden, Bertie
and his friend, Ranald Braveheart Macpherson, were taken
back to the flat in Scotland Street by Bertie's grandmother,
Nicola Tavares de Lumiares, formerly, and once again,
Nicola Pollock. She had reverted to her earlier married name
after her second husband, a Portuguese wine producer, had
gone off with his housekeeper. Most men who go off with
somebody else will have some justification: *my wife doesn't
understand me* is said to be the typical excuse, although, in
fact, few men actually say that. Men are now far more subtle,
and will use explanations, such as *we drifted apart*, that provide
a good smokescreen for the avoidance of blame. Very rarely
does a man give the real explanation for his conduct, which
might be something like *I wanted somebody younger.*

In the case of Nicola's husband, his excuse was disarming
in its effrontery. He had, he said, been instructed by the
Virgin Mary, no less, to go off with his young housekeeper.
It is difficult to argue with such an explanation, other than
to suggest, perhaps rather lamely, that the Virgin Mary
can hardly be expected to get everything right, and that
her advice should not always be followed to the letter, well-
intentioned though it undoubtedly might be.

Nicola returned to Scotland from Portugal. She was pleased

to be back, although during her marriage she had immersed herself in Portuguese culture, spoke the language fluently, and had even begun writing a critical biography of Fernando Pessoa. She was financially secure from two sources: the generous settlement that the Virgin Mary instructed her former husband to make, and from an inheritance that Nicola had received in Scotland. This included ownership of a Glasgow pie factory, formerly known as Pies for Protestants, but now called, more appropriately, Inclusive Pies. Nicola did not have the time to adopt a hands-on approach to the pie factory, and had proposed a scheme in which the firm's management and employees were given a major stake in the enterprise. It was just the right solution: the staff in Glasgow now shared in the profits and participated in management decisions. From Nicola's point of view, she was happy to involve herself in certain aspects of the company's affairs while leaving the day-to-day running of the business to those who knew about Scotch pies and the people who ate them.

The life she had planned for herself in Edinburgh was to have been one in which she enjoyed the cultural offerings of the city while re-establishing contact with old friends with whom she had lost touch on leaving for Portugal. It was to have been an unhurried existence: morning coffee with friends, followed by a visit to a gallery. Then lunch with further friends and, after that, something she had become accustomed to in Portugal – a siesta. In the evening, there might be a visit to the Lyceum Theatre, or a concert, perhaps even a dinner party with entertaining guests. It would have been a comfortable, fulfilling existence – not particularly strenuous, but also not markedly sybaritic. It would have been what is sometimes called *me time* – the time so appreciated by those whose lot it has been to look after others – by exhausted mothers, in particular, who have had to juggle child-care with work and the running of a household. Such persons richly deserve *me time* but often do not have the chance to claim it because those they are looking after are enjoying *me time* themselves.

That had been the plan, but then everything changed when Bertie's mother decided that the time had come for her to move to Aberdeen to begin a PhD with Dr Hugo Fairbairn, recently appointed to a chair at the university there. Dr Fairbairn had been Bertie's psychotherapist, and Irene had discovered they both shared an interest in the work of Melanie Klein. This gave an added point to the weekly visits they made to Dr Fairbairn's Queen Street consulting rooms. While Bertie sat in the waiting room, paging through the old copies of *Scottish Field* provided for patients to peruse while awaiting their appointment, Irene would sequester herself with Dr Fairbairn and discuss matters of interest. This suited Bertie, who did not enjoy his sessions with Dr Fairbairn, whom he thought to be certifiably insane. Bertie had read about the State Hospital at Carstairs, and thought it only a matter of time before attendants in white coats arrived to take Dr Fairbairn away for much-needed attention. That this never happened was put down by Bertie to inadequate resources.

And now, of course, Dr Fairbairn was safely in Aberdeen, where Bertie had read hypothermia was a real issue. Cold shock therapy might help him, he imagined, but in the mean-time he was pleased to be spared those weekly sessions in which Dr Fairbairn invited him to tell him about his dreams, and Bertie, obliging as ever, made up enough dreams to keep Dr Fairbairn scribbling away in his notebook. Bertie had discovered a book about Freud's cases on his mother's bookshelf, and had read with great interest about the famous Wolf Man, who had described a dream in which he had been observed by wolves *sitting in the trees*. This had intrigued Bertie, who thought that the Wolf Man was probably just fibbing: wolves did not sit in trees – everybody knew that, even Larch, a boy in his class at school who was famous for knowing nothing at all about anything, but who, on request, could burp the melody of *La Marseillaise*, perfectly in tune and with surprising attention to the dynamics of the music.

Bertie had told Dr Fairbairn about a dream he had had in which wolves had stolen his underpants and had hung them in a tree. The narration of this dream had been received with rapt attention by Dr Fairbairn, who twice broke the lead in his propelling pencil in his eagerness to write down the details. He was pleased that he had been able to satisfy Dr Fairbairn so easily – he did not bear the psychotherapist any ill-will; Bertie bore ill-will towards nobody – but if a few tall stories needed to be invented in order to keep Dr Fairbairn from becoming too unstable, then he saw no particular harm in that. Everyone made things up, Bertie had concluded – especially adults – and a few helpful stories of this sort would do no harm, particularly since they appeared to give such inexplicable pleasure to Dr Fairbairn. Adults, Bertie thought, are often desperate for something to do, and psychotherapists, it seemed, were no exception.

## 15. Dear Little Argonaut

Nicola might have been expected to feel disappointed when she heard of Irene's departure for Aberdeen. She might have been expected to regret the dashing of her plans for a relaxed, even if slightly self-indulgent, existence in Edinburgh, but, as it happened, she felt quite buoyed by the news, and lost no time in volunteering to fill the child-care gap that Irene had so selfishly created.

Stuart was reluctant to take advantage of his mother. 'I could always employ somebody,' he said. 'I gather that there are plenty of qualified people searching for jobs looking after children. I heard of somebody who received thirty-two applications for a job they advertised. Thirty-two!'

'It doesn't exactly surprise me,' said Nicola. 'People like working with children.'

'But thirty-two, Mother!' exclaimed Stuart. 'Thirty-two – and apparently they were all pretty impressive. One had a master's degree in early education.'

Nicola made a dismissive gesture. 'Everybody has a master's these days.'

'Another was a qualified music teacher,' Stuart continued.

This did not impress Nicola. 'Frankly, I don't think you need any formal qualifications to look after children. You don't need them to be a parent – and I don't see why you should need them to be *in loco parentis*.' She paused. 'No, Stuart, you don't need to get anybody in. I shall be only too happy to do my grandparental duty. I shall make myself available and, with any luck, we can start undoing the damage that . . .'

She stopped herself, but Stuart had heard. 'Go on, Mother,' he muttered, tight-lipped. 'Say it.'

'Well, I thought that perhaps a small corrective might help to deal with the influence of the last little while . . .'

Stuart interrupted her. 'Irene's influence?'

Nicola lowered her eyes. 'One might say that.'

Stuart bit his lip. He knew what his mother felt about Irene, and it made him feel uncomfortable, even if he also knew that her animosity had every justification. Irene was intolerable – at least from most people's perspective, and it was only loyalty, and a certain embarrassment, that prevented him from acknowledging that fact.

He fixed his gaze on his mother. 'You never liked her – right from the start, you never liked her, did you?'

Nicola hesitated. Then she said, 'No, I didn't. I couldn't stand her. But I did try, you know. I made an effort.'

He granted her that. 'Yes,' he said. 'I noticed. I don't think anybody would fault you on that. You did your best.'

She looked relieved. 'I'm glad that you saw that,' she said. 'It's an odd thing – having to like somebody as a matter of duty. We all know that we have a duty to the people we have to live with, but sometimes . . . Well, sometimes, it's an awful effort.'

Stuart thought about this. 'Like, or tolerate? I'm not sure that anybody says to us that we have to *like* others. They do say, though, that we have to tolerate them.'

'I think that Christianity has something to say about that,' said Nicola. 'Love your neighbour as yourself. Isn't that the second great commandment?'

Stuart said, 'If you're talking about religion, yes. But not otherwise. Not in ordinary morality. That's less ...'

'Less strenuous?'

'Yes, that's what I meant. We're not meant to be unpleasant to others, but we're not told to *like* them.' Stuart paused. 'Well, you did your best. You tried – I know you tried.'

'And so did you,' said Nicola. 'You worked at your marriage.'

Stuart was silent.

'I saw how you bit your tongue,' Nicola continued. 'I saw how you struggled when she was going on and on about Melanie Klein and Bertie's psychotherapy. And his yoga and his saxophone lessons, and his Italian. All of that. You bit your tongue when another might have exploded and said that enough was enough and all that Bertie needed was to be left alone and allowed to be a little boy. To have a Swiss Army penknife and join the Wolf Cubs or whatever they call them these days. To do all of the things that little boys like to do and that people like Irene try to stop them doing.'

Nicola stopped. She understood that there were limits to what she could say about Irene because everything that she said – the entire catalogue of Irene's failings – could be taken as an indictment of Stuart's bad judgement in choosing to marry her, and, after that event, of his weakness in not standing up to her barrage of criticism. Bullies got away with what they got away with because people allowed them to do their work of bullying without standing up to them. Stuart should have put his foot down a long time ago. He should have told Irene that she could not expect him to share all of her attitudes, and that a civilised marriage involves acceptance by each party of the fact that two people might have different views of certain subjects. Jack Sprat could eat no fat, and his wife could eat no lean. They got on all right in spite of these different tastes. People could do that – at least they could in the past. It was different now, of course, and today the Sprats might well be expected to be searching for more personal space.

Nicola moved into 44 Scotland Street, taking over a room that Irene had previously used as a study. Her days became busy, as Ulysses was getting bigger and was requiring more attention. That kept her busy all morning until it was time to set off to collect Bertie from the Steiner School. She did that by bus, taking Ulysses with her. As often as not, Ulysses would be dressed in a neat sailor suit, on the sleeves of which Nicola had embroidered the name *Argo*.

'Dear little Argonaut,' she muttered, kissing him on the top of his head, as the bus wended its way up the Mound.

Ulysses beamed. He had been in a much better frame of mind since Irene had gone off to Aberdeen, and was sick far less often. Prior to Irene's departure, he had manifested the trying habit of being sick whenever Irene picked him up or addressed him directly. That behaviour seemed to have been completely corrected, and now nobody could remember when Ulysses had last brought anything up. That was not to say that he was completely without vices. He still made somewhat embarrassing bodily noises whenever a friendly adult face beamed at him, and it was generally impossible to take

66

him into any form of human society, owing to the somewhat overpowering smell that tended to emanate from him. Apart from that, though, he was an ideal baby and a little brother of whom Bertie was quite proud.

It had not always been thus. Until recently, Bertie had been rather too ready to speculate in public about what might happen if Ulysses were to be left somewhere – inadvertently – and never recovered. Could they sell his toys, he asked, and if he did the selling, could he get commission on his brother's estate?

'I'm not saying that I want Ulysses to go away, Daddy,' he told his father. 'I'm not saying that we should get rid of him. All I'm saying is that I don't really see the point of him. I've tried, but I just can't.'

Bertie looked miserable. He was a kind boy. So he concluded, 'I'll carry on trying, though. I promise. Scout's honour.'

He was not a scout. Irene had always forbidden it. But a moral profession is often aspirational, and all the more forceful for that.

## 16. *Aberdeen Beckons (or Threatens)*

Now, while Bertie and Ranald Braveheart Macpherson started a game of *Jacobites and Hanoverians* in Bertie's room – a popular game among Edinburgh children, and almost as frequently played as *Accountants and Clients* – Nicola prepared a cup of tea for Stuart.

'I'm ready for that,' said Stuart, glancing at his watch. It was not quite yet a respectable time to pour a gin and tonic, but tea would always do. He had been looking after Ulysses and had eventually managed to settle him for a much-needed nap.

'Dear little Ulysses,' said Nicola. 'He can be a touch exhausting.' And then added, quickly, 'Not that I mind in the slightest. He is, after all, my grandson.'

'I wish we still had old-fashioned gripe-water,' mused Stuart. 'Did you give it to me when I was a baby?'

Nicola smiled. 'It was a great tragedy when they changed the formula. You can still get it, but it's a pale imitation of the original thing.'

'Everybody says it settled babies miraculously,' said Stuart.

'Yes, it did. It worked a treat.'

'What was the magic ingredient?'

'Gin,' said Nicola. 'Babies love gin. It stops them girning.'

Stuart laughed. 'I can see why they stopped it.'

'Perhaps,' said Nicola. 'There used to be all sorts of questionable things in popular products. Coca-Cola used to contain cocaine, I'm told – right up to the nineteen-twenties. And then there was a wonderful mixture that my mother swore by for upset stomachs, until it disappeared from the pharmacies. It was invented by one Dr John Collis Browne, and he called it Dr J. Collis Browne's Chlorodyne. It was a horrible brown liquid and you put a few drops in water and drank it. It worked because it contained chloroform and opiates into the bargain. It put your stomach to sleep, so to speak.'

Stuart thought that a rather good idea. 'What was that stuff in *Brave New World*? Soma, wasn't it?'

'It's a long time since I read that,' said Nicola. 'But I think you're right. The whole population was dosed with soma to keep them happy.'

'Huxley may have been more prescient than we thought,' said Stuart. He paused and looked morosely into his teacup before continuing. 'We need to talk, Mother.'

Nicola knew what was coming. She had been dreading this conversation, which she and Stuart had been having on and off for more than a week, but which had yet to be concluded. Now she took a sip of tea and put down her cup with a clatter.

'You're right, Stuart. We need to talk. I've been dreading it, but we can't pretend that Irene does not exist. She may be up in Aberdeen, but it's as if she's in the room with us here. Pachydermatically, so to speak.'

Stuart nodded glumly. 'Denial never works,' he said.

Nicola was not sure about that. 'Oh, I don't know. I think denial has its place. There's no point in fretting unnecessarily. People who deny things often strike me as being quite cheerful.'

'But there's a difference between denial and that sort of attitude. You might accept that something exists but don't worry too much about it. I'm not sure if that's denial. You might call it optimism, or putting on a brave face, or whatever.'

Nicola sighed. 'Possibly. But here we go again. We're talking about something else when we know that we should be talking about ...'

'About Irene's plan.'

Stuart nodded again. He looked up at the ceiling, but then realised that looking up at the ceiling was a form of denial. He looked down at the floor, and thought the same. He closed his eyes. That was pure denial. 'All right,' he said. 'She phoned me this morning.'

'And?'

'She hasn't changed her mind.'

For a few moments, neither spoke. Then Nicola said, 'So she's insisting that Bertie go to Aberdeen?'

'Yes. For three months.'

Nicola pursed her lips.

'I told her that we all thought it was a ridiculous idea,' Stuart continued. 'I told her that Bertie's teacher said that it would set him back if he had to go to a new school up there and then, just when he would be settling in, to bring him back to Edinburgh.'

'Of course it would,' Nicola exploded. 'Anybody can see that. Children need routine. They need security. They don't need to be carted off to Aberdeen for three months.'

Stuart said that he had argued along those lines when Irene first raised the issue, but had got nowhere. 'The thing about Irene,' he said, 'is that she thinks she is always right. Most of us experience the occasional moment of self-doubt, but I'm afraid she doesn't.'

'No,' agreed Nicola. 'It must be marvellous to have such complete confidence in oneself.'

Stuart continued with further details of the morning's conversation. Irene had hinted that if Stuart were to contest her decision to have Bertie with her in Aberdeen for three months, she would review their entire agreement as to custody. 'It might be simpler for me to come back to Edinburgh,' she said. 'There's a strong case, I think, for my returning to Scotland Street full-time.'

Stuart had been aghast. 'But your PhD? What about your PhD and Dr Fairbairn ... ?'

'*Professor* Fairbairn,' Irene corrected.

'Yes. What about Professor Fairbairn?'

She did not reply immediately. Then she said, 'I'm not proposing to return. All that I'm asking is for Bertie to come and live with me for three months in Aberdeen and do a term at a school up here. It's all arranged. It'll broaden his horizons.'

*And end his world*, thought Stuart.

Stuart had noticed that nothing had been said about Ulysses. 'But what about Ulysses?' he said. 'What about your baby?'

Irene snapped back, '*Your* baby too, may I remind you. It takes two people to produce a baby, Stuart, as I have pointed out to you before on numerous occasions. It's only because of the patriarchy that people refer to *mother and child* and so on.'

Stuart gritted his teeth. 'I think that perhaps you should take both of them for three months. Poor little Ulysses will wonder where his brother has gone. Wouldn't it be better for him to be up there with you?'

'Certainly not,' replied Irene. 'I have my PhD. I'm extremely busy. You have your mother living with you. I'm sure she's looking after Ulysses in a very satisfactory way, thank you.'

After that, there was little to be said, and now Stuart explained to Nicola that the rest of the conversation had been about details, rather than the principle that Bertie should go. Irene would come to collect him, she said, the following week. Could Stuart please pack a suitcase of Bertie's clothes?

71

'Do I have to tell him now?' Stuart had asked.

'Of course,' said Irene. 'He has to be involved in this decision. He has to take his share of the ownership of it.'

'You won't be here to see his tears when I tell him,' Stuart muttered.

'Did you say something?' asked Irene.

Stuart put down the telephone. Now, remembering that conversation, he stared at Nicola. She was resourceful. She was constant. She was what a real mother should be – everything that Irene was not. But in this particular matter, she was powerless.

## 17. The Coolest Boy by Far

Amongst those who particularly enjoyed Big Lou's bacon rolls was Bruce Anderson, an alumnus of Morrison's Academy in Crieff – where he was voted, amongst other things, *Coolest Boy by Far* by the girls in the two top forms of the school; a qualified surveyor with a particular eye for undervalued property; a one-time wine dealer (not very successful); a member of the Merchants Golf Club, with a handicap of twelve; a devotee of a particular brand of clove-scented hair gel, not used by many (in fact, by virtually none); and now contemplating a new business venture, the details of which would shortly be revealed.

Bruce had gone into Big Lou's coffee bar shortly after Fat

Bob had left but before Matthew was due to arrive for the cup of coffee that started his working day at the gallery.

'The usual, Lou,' Bruce said, tossing his newspaper down on the table he habitually occupied.

Normally Lou said, 'Right you are, Bruce,' and started to prepare the double-strength cappuccino that she knew Bruce enjoyed before preparing the roll that served as his breakfast. On this particular morning, Bruce noticed that she merely nodded.

'You all right, Lou?' Bruce asked.

Big Lou looked up. 'Aye, I'm just fine. And yourself?'

'It's just that . . . well, you seem a bit preoccupied.'

Big Lou shrugged. 'Thinking,' she said.

Bruce grinned. 'A dangerous thing to do, you know.'

'You should try it sometime,' said Big Lou.

'Hah!' Bruce paused. 'Who was that guy I saw coming out just before I arrived?'

Big Lou busied herself with the coffee machine. 'Guy? What guy?'

'That big chap.'

Lou pressed the button that produced the steamed milk. 'A customer.'

'I've not seen him before,' said Bruce. 'And he's not a type you'd miss.'

Big Lou remained silent. Bruce glanced at her. 'Just asking, Lou.'

He took the cup of coffee she slid across the counter and returned to his table. He glanced at his watch. Ed had said nine-fifteen, and it was now five past. He would have time to flick through the paper before then, and at least make a start on the easy Sudoku. Bruce had only recently started doing Sudokus after reading an article in a magazine that suggested that the brain started its decline at about eighteen years of age and it was downhill all the way from there. Bruce was, in his view, exactly the right age – not yet having experienced any of the significant birthdays about which people became nervous or concerned, although his last birthday, he reflected, was one that some people regarded as significant. But whatever view one took of that, the fact remained that if your brain cells were dying off at a rate of thousands every day – and some people could really ill afford to lose that number – then at least you should do what you could to make sure that those that remained were capable of firing correctly. It was all a question of neural networks, the article explained, and these could be kept in good order by doing things like crosswords and Sudokus.

Simple, thought Bruce, and had turned to the crossword on page two of his newspaper. He had never done crosswords before, but he imagined that the clues would be simple enough if you had his intelligence. He had achieved an A grade in every one of his Higher subjects at school – every single one! And then he had waltzed through his university examinations doing virtually no work because . . . and here Bruce felt that he simply had to recognise reality without any false modesty – *simply because I am exceptionally bright*, he thought. That was all there was to it. Some people were dim, and others were so-so, not exactly *dim*, in so many words, but what Bruce liked to call 2.5 amp types. Like that fellow Steve, who was married to Molly What's-Her-Face, who was friendly with Elspeth because they had been at school together. Like him. Poor

Steve. That stupid Hearts supporter. Molly was all right, if you liked that sort of girl, Bruce thought. She had been interested in him at one point, he remembered, but then most girls were. They couldn't help themselves. Poor Molly. It would have been so easy to throw her a crumb of attention – perhaps to have asked her out when they were both nineteen, something like that – but one had one's *standards*, and there was never enough time to spend with every single girl who showed an interest. Well, Bruce knew what they wanted, these poor girls. That was not their fault – of course it wasn't. You can't help biology, thought Bruce, and thought: *I am biology*.

Yes, *I am biology*. And then he looked at the crossword, at 1 across, which would probably be the best place to start, he decided, before he progressed to 2 down, and so on. He might time himself. Fifteen minutes? He was already doing the Level One Sudoku in eighteen minutes, and a crossword would not be much more difficult than that. It would probably be easier, in fact. So, here goes, he said to himself. And then, as an afterthought, *I am biology*. Yes, he liked that. *L'état, c'est moi*. Who had said that? President de Gaulle? That tall chap with the large conk? That was good as well, but *I am biology* had a certain ring to it.

1 across: *Did a former girlfriend sit for an artist to bring things to light?*

Bruce reached for the pen he carried in an inside pocket. What? Old flame? Bring things to light? *Lighten?* No, this was meant to be six letters. *Lighten* was seven.

He looked at 2 down. *Was the first clever girl in the form.* Five letters.

What? This was stupid.

75

Bruce looked up and saw that Big Lou was looking at him.

'Having difficulty with your Sudoku, Bruce?'

There was something in her tone that irked him. Big Lou had left school with no Highers, he said to himself. Zilch. None. She made great bacon rolls, but that was about it.

'The crossword, actually, Lou.'

Big Lou smiled. 'What's the problem?'

'You won't get it, Lou. It's the cryptic one.'

'Probably not. But what's the clue?'

'Did a former girlfriend sit for an artist to bring things to light?' Then he added. 'See?'

Lou began to butter the bacon roll she was preparing for Bruce. '*Expose*,' she said.

## 18. An Incident in Crieff

'Bruce Anderson, no less!'

Bruce looked up. He had become absorbed in the crossword, and the ten minutes had passed without being noticed. He had not solved any of the clues, which irritated him, particularly since Big Lou had so effortlessly come up with the answer to 1 across. *Expose*. What a stupid clue, thought Bruce. Perhaps that was the problem – the clues were just too basic, and that if he were to tackle one of those more complex crosswords – like the ones in the heavier Sunday papers, composed by people with impressive, classical *noms de plume* – then the solutions would come to him.

Bruce had not seen Ed Macdonald for almost a year, and he noticed that he had grown a small moustache. It did not suit him, thought Bruce, but then nothing suited Ed. He looked as dim without a moustache as with one. And he always wore those excessively heavy brogues in that strange-coloured leather. Ed called it *light tan*, but it was really pale yellow; and those socks with pictures of dogs on them. A serious lack of taste, thought Bruce. Poor Ed, but perhaps what you should expect from ... where did Ed come from originally? Somewhere near Falkirk. He claimed to be from Crieff, but he wasn't really. It was somewhere nobody had ever heard of. Poor Ed.

Bruce and Ed had been at school together at Morrison's Academy, where Ed, Bruce recalled, had come last in just about everything. Not that anybody believed in ranking any more, but if they did, Ed would certainly be at the bottom. What had they voted him – those girls, Priscilla and her friends? *Worst-dressed Boy*, wasn't it? Or was it *Creepiest Guy*? Or did that go to Ed's friend Vince Treadmill? What happened to Vince, Bruce wondered. Poor Vince. Poor Ed. How tragic. Both of them. Tragic.

Ed sat down. 'Doing the crossword, I see,' he said. And then, sniffing at the air, 'This place stinks of bacon.'

Bruce looked anxiously in Big Lou's direction, but decided she had not heard.

'Keep your voice down, Ed,' he said. 'It's because of the bacon rolls. You should try them.'

'I'm a vegetarian,' said Ed. 'I don't eat dead animals.'

77

Bruce was surprised. 'You used to eat hamburgers. I remember it. The grease used to run down your chin and cover your pimples. I have a very clear memory of it.'

Ed smiled. 'Used to, Bruce. Used to. You used to ... No, I won't say it. Not here.'

Bruce blushed.

Ed glanced again at the crossword. 'You don't seem to have made much progress.'

Bruce waved a careless hand. 'I've been doing it mentally. I haven't written anything in.'

Ed reached for the paper and looked at the crossword. 'What's this?' he said. '*Interdict girl, lacking small number, fruity!*'

He looked at Bruce. 'Did you get that one?'

Bruce shrugged. 'Not yet.'

'Banana,' said Ed.

Bruce looked at him. 'Banana?'

'Yes,' said Ed, tossing the paper aside. 'Interdict Anna? Ban her. Take one *n* out of Anna, and you're left with *banana*.'

Bruce pursed his lips. 'Yes, I see. I would probably have reached the same conclusion. No, I definitely would have.' He paused. 'You said you were going to bring somebody.'

Ed nodded. 'Gregor? Yes, he said he's going to be a bit late. He'll be here in ten, fifteen minutes. Don't worry. You read his email I sent on to you? The one with the details of that house in the Grange?'

'We call them *particulars*,' said Bruce. 'In the business, details are called particulars.'

Ed shrugged. 'Same difference. You read it anyway?'

Bruce said that he had. 'It's interesting. Just off Dick Place. Near the cricket ground.'

'That's the place,' said Ed.

'I played cricket there a few times,' Bruce remembered. 'Scored sixty-two runs once. Then I was bowled by that guy MacQueen. I wasn't ready, but the umpire was looking the wrong way.'

'They often do,' said Ed.

'I could have made a century. I was in with Rob Houlihan. Remember him?'

'The guy with one leg?'

'No, Rob had two.'

Ed nodded vaguely. 'Maybe. I get them mixed up. There was Rob Robson. You'll remember him. He stayed in Crieff. He was run over last year, you know. Outside Valentine's. Remember the outfitters – T. Palmer Valentine?'

Bruce looked down at Ed's shoes. 'You got those shoes there?'

Ed nodded. 'They always stock them. Anyway, Rob – Rob Robson, that is – was there with his new wife. I don't know her name – Gemma, or something like that – but she worked at the Hydro, I think. She was quite a stunner – how Rob got her is anybody's guess. He's a real minger. Anyway, he was there walking along the street, and this guy in an Alfa Romeo came round the corner and ran Rob over. Broad daylight. Bang. *Buonanotte, Roberto.*'

Bruce winced. 'Poor Rob. What with his dandruff and now ... now being run over.'

'But don't worry,' Ed said quickly. 'You know what? Rob picked himself up from under the car. Just like that. Picked himself up. He was unharmed – completely unharmed. Can you believe it?'

'Rugby,' mused Bruce. 'He was in the scrum, remember? Those guys can take anything.'

'Yes, well, you know what Rob did next? This Alfa Romeo chap had got out of the car and was rabbiting on about how the sun had been in his eyes or whatever, and Rob just socked him in the jaw. Right there and then. Knocked him down.'

Bruce laughed. 'Rob never hung around.'

'No. Not this time either. He had a lot of anger in him, I think. Years of it. All pent up. Maybe because of having his head crushed in the scrum. You know how it affects them. So this anger all came out and this guy hits the deck. Knocked out.'

'No!'

'Yes. And somebody had called an ambulance for Rob, but when it arrived Rob didn't need it, so it just picked up the Alfa Romeo chap and took him off to Perth Royal Infirmary. He was okay, but the Alfa Romeo got a parking ticket.'

Bruce sipped the last of his coffee. 'I'm still hungry. What about you, Ed? Carrot roll?'

Ed smiled. 'Very funny, Bruce.'

Bruce became serious. 'This place in the Grange – you want to buy it?'

'No,' said Ed. 'We're going to sell it. It belongs to Gregor, you see.'

'The Gregor who's coming here?'

'Yes. He's an interior decorator. Paint, wallpaper, presentation. All that. He can transform anything. Saughton Prison? No problem. That old gasworks down near Trinity? Bijou flats. No question. Flair, you see. You need flair, and Gregor has serious flair.' He paused. 'He comes from Glasgow.'

Bruce looked thoughtful. 'And this place in the Grange – you say that it could be converted into flats?'

Ed nodded. 'It could be. But not by us.'

Bruce waited for an explanation.

'No, we'll be working on another place down the road. This one is different. We're the sellers. Or Gregor is, but we're involved. He acquired it six months ago.'

Bruce asked why, if it had only recently been acquired, it should now be sold.

Ed touched the side of his nose. 'Wait until Gregor comes. Then I'll tell you.'

He looked at Bruce. 'I hope you're discreet.'

'Of course I am.'

Ed hesitated. 'Because what I have in mind is ... how shall we put it? Creative. Have you got the guts for that? If not, end of story.'

Bruce stared at Ed. He would not let Ed Macdonald, of all people, think he was scared of a challenge.

'Who do you think I am?' he answered scornfully.

'Good,' said Ed.

## 19. The Money Rolls In

Gregor arrived ten minutes later.

'That's him,' said Ed, half-turning in his chair. 'See what

I mean? A bit of style. You can't *create* that, Bruce – you've either got it or you haven't. You and I can simply look on.'

Bruce bristled with resentment. What was Ed thinking of – lumping him in with himself? He began to say something, but Gregor had spotted them and was making his way towards their table.

Gregor looked at his watch. 'I'm sorry to be late,' he said. 'My car wouldn't start.' He sighed. 'For the *nth* time. It's got a new starter motor, but no luck.'

Ed reassured him that he understood, and then explained to Bruce, 'Gregor has a Morgan – an old one.'

'1953,' said Gregor, smiling at Bruce. 'A very good year for Bordeaux, but not necessarily for Morgans. Or not for *all* Morgans.'

'That was the year they introduced the new Plus 4 with the Triumph TR2 engine,' said Ed. 'You probably didn't know that, Bruce.'

'Yes,' said Gregor. 'They already had the one with the 2088cc Standard Vanguard, of course.'

Ed nodded. 'Sure. You heard of Vanguard, Bruce?'

Bruce smarted. 'Of course.'

Gregor sat down and looked in Big Lou's direction. 'Does the girl come over? Or do I go to the counter?'

Bruce caught his breath. 'Girl? That's Big Lou,' he whispered.

Gregor smiled. Bruce noticed his perfect teeth, white against the tanned complexion. He noticed the green eyes, the confidence.

Ed offered to order coffee, and when he got up, Gregor looked at Bruce and smiled again. 'I like your hair,' he said.

Bruce looked down at the floor, and blushed. You did not say that sort of thing. You did not.

'What do you put on it?' asked Gregor.

Bruce cleared his throat. He felt strangely embarrassed. 'Gel,' he said. 'Same as everybody. A lot of people use gel these days.'

Gregor was still staring at him. 'Oh, I know that. I use a lot of products myself. But yours has an odd smell. Is it cloves?'

Bruce drew a deep breath. He was used to being in command of social situations, but now he felt at a distinct disadvantage.

'Might be,' he said.

'I think it is,' said Gregor. 'I rather like cloves. I've never encountered them in hair gel, though.' He paused. 'Ed said you're a surveyor.'

'I am. And you?'

Gregor adjusted the cuff of his shirt. Linen, thought Bruce: green linen. 'I do interior work,' said Gregor. 'Hotels, offices, private houses. I source things.'

'Interior decoration?' asked Bruce.

'It's a bit more than that,' said Gregor. 'I source furniture. Say you have an office suite and you need twenty desks. You come to me. I get you what you need. Or flooring. You're renting an office that needs new flooring. You phone me. You get a floor.'

'I see.'

'Or you have a house, right? You think: I could do with some new stuff, e.g. a couple of sofas. Where do you go? You come to me, and I get you sofas that aren't going to *argue* with one another. Most furniture, Bruce, is argumentative. Give it a chance, and it'll argue with what's around it.'

Bruce smiled. He thought the remark a bit arch, but it was funny.

'So,' continued Gregor, 'I facilitate. You could call me a facilitator.'

'Or an interior decorator,' said Bruce.

Gregor's manner changed. There was a coldness in the green eyes. 'Let's get one thing clear, Bruce. I don't need any of that, see. E.g. implications, right?'

'I wasn't . . .' Bruce stuttered.

'You were, actually,' said Gregor. 'I'm not naïve.' His eyes narrowed. 'There are some people who are anxious about where they stand, e.g. in relation to sexuality. They make remarks that tell you more about them than the person they're making remarks about. See? Freud, e.g., opened our eyes to that one, I can tell you.'

'I didn't . . .' Bruce began.

Gregor cut him off. 'I'm not saying you did. I'm just saying: don't.'

Any further developments in this conversation were stopped by the return of Ed, carrying Gregor's cup of coffee. 'All right,' he said as he sat down. 'I'm going to explain to Bruce.' He glanced at Gregor, who nodded.

'Bruce can keep his mouth shut,' Ed went on.

Gregor glanced at Bruce. The hostility that had crept into his manner seemed not to have dissipated. He smiled. 'Good.'

'So this is the story,' Ed began. 'Let's say you're selling a property in Scotland. The standard method is to put it on the market and ask for offers. Right?'

'I know all that,' said Bruce. 'Remember I worked for a property company.'

84

'All right. But there's nothing wrong with a bit of background. So the house or whatever goes on the market and the lawyer gets the offers – all sealed. Then they look at them after the closing date and see who's put in the largest. That person gets the place – subject to whatever conditions they may have put in.'

'It works,' said Bruce. 'The system works.'

'Yes, I know,' said Ed. 'But what if you have somebody working in the solicitor's office who sees the offers and tells a potential bidder what the highest one so far is? What then? I'll tell you. That person then knows that he only has to offer one hundred pounds more – or even one pound – and he gets it.'

Bruce was silent.

Ed lowered his voice. 'So the idea is this. Gregor has this place in the Grange. He bought it six months ago. Now the market has moved – upwards. If he sold it now he would make ...'

'Sixty thousand quid,' said Gregor. 'I.e. sixty thousand above what I paid. Sixty grand profit.'

'But,' Ed said, now descending to a whisper. 'If we have somebody ...'

'E.g. you,' said Gregor.

'Yes, somebody e.g. you who puts in a really high offer. But then we have someone who works in the lawyer's office – big friend of Gregor here – who goes to the person putting in the next-highest offer and says the highest offer so far is ...'

'What you ... i.e. you, Bruce, have put in,' supplied Gregor.

'Then the under-bidder puts in a slightly higher offer than the figure he's been told, and *bingo!* Gregor makes one hundred thousand rather than sixty thousand. Maybe more.'

Bruce thought about this. 'That depends on the under-bidder doing what you expect him to do.'

'Under-bidders always will,' said Gregor. 'In today's market they are often desperate to be the one who makes the best offer. Some of these people have lost three, four, maybe more auctions. They are at the end of their tether.'

Ed sat back. 'We pull it off in this one,' he said. 'Then we do it again. Discreetly. Carefully. And the money rolls in.'

'You in, Bruce?' asked Gregor. 'Some of it will roll in your direction. Percentage to be agreed.'

## 20. Torquil at the Door

Domenica Macdonald was seated at her desk when the door-bell rang. She was struggling with the composition of a letter that she did not wish to write, because she knew the power of words – even just one or two – to end a world. She had always been in awe of the ability of a document – perhaps no more than a few lines of print on paper – to bring down a whole edifice of human arrangements, even to turn upside down the lives of millions. The protocol to the Molotov–Ribbentrop Pact had been such a document – a few lines on a piece of paper, once revealed, many decades later, precipitated Estonia's departure from the Soviet Union and the events that eventually brought down the entire empire. And, in a more domestic setting, the uttering of a few words could do the same – could change the whole landscape of a life. *I love another*, for instance: three words that could bring an ocean of tears in their wake. Or a monosyllabic *no* might do the same thing: the sound of *no* was tiny, but its echoes could be huge.

Domenica sighed. Did she have an alternative but to do what was asked of her? She thought not. If she failed to respond to the request for an opinion, she herself could be accused of indifference to presuppositions and values that lay at the heart of anthropology. It would be easier to decline the request that had been made of her – there were numerous excuses to which she could resort: being overcommitted, being out of touch, being on holiday or sabbatical. Eyebrows might be raised, but eyebrows held no terrors for her. Yet she could not do that; she could not dissemble or lie outright. Not to do something was impossible – she would have to act.

She sighed again, and reached for her pen. And at that moment, as if scripted by a dramatist careless of implausibility, the doorbell rang. Domenica's next sigh was one of relief. Angus was out, and she would have to answer the door. The letter could be put off in good conscience.

She opened the door and saw before her on the landing her neighbour, Torquil. Torquil was one of a group of students who had moved into the ground-floor flat a few months earlier. There were five of them: three young men – Torquil, Dave and Alistair; and two young women, Phoebe and Rose – all of an age, all barely twenty, Domenica thought. Domenica had met Torquil on several occasions before this – he seemed to be the spokesman and was the only one who bothered to sweep their shared stair according to the rota agreed by all the flats. He was a student of classics, he had told her, while Alistair was a mathematician. Or was it Dave who was studying mathematics? No, Dave had been described by Torquil as being 'too thick to study anything but environmental science' – an extraordinary assessment. Domenica did not think that environmental science was an easy or intellectually unchallenging option. Surely that was media studies – or so people said, perhaps unfairly. And if Dave was at university in Edinburgh, then he would have had to have satisfied high entry standards, otherwise he would have gone elsewhere – and enrolled in a course on media studies.

Dave had come to the party that she and Angus had thrown, and although on that occasion she had not had the chance to speak to him at length, their conversation had been enjoyable. She had found him good company, in fact, with a wry sense of humour of the sort she appreciated. Torquil had mentioned that one of the young women, Rose, had been keen on Dave and that they had been, as he put it, an *item*. It was not an expression she liked, as it had her think of shopping trolleys, and she imagined Dave sitting in a shopping trolley being pushed by a triumphant Rose. Alongside him would be other household necessities obtained from the supermarket: washing-up liquid, kitchen towel, detergent, and so on, all gathered from shelves so labelled, until one came across the shelf that said *Men*, with some, perhaps, being advertised as *On Offer*.

She could understand what Rose saw in him. Like Torquil, Dave was good-looking in a way favoured by the compilers of men's clothing catalogues or advertisements for expensive watches. No thin or ungainly men are ever featured in such publicity – only those with decisive jaws, who gaze, into the middle- or far-distance, from the teak deck of a yacht or from the driver's seat of a desirable sports car. Such men not only have impeccable taste in clothing, which they wear with insouciant elegance, but they also display a penchant for Swiss watches that tell the time only incidentally to the information they provide on such matters as barometric pressure and its concomitant, height above sea-level. Domenica had never needed to know her altitude, and although she had once toyed with the idea of buying Angus a watch with elaborate functions, she had decided not to, as Angus, too, was indifferent to altitude, and indeed to the hour. As far as she could make out, he relied on the sun to tell him what time it was, and seemed unconcerned by the margin of error that such a method of time-keeping involved.

'As long as I know what day it is,' he once said, 'and as long as I know roughly what the month is, then do I really need to burden myself with more information?'

Now, as she stood in her doorway, she saw that Torquil was holding a parcel – what Angus called a *Maria parcel* ('brown paper packages tied up with string').

'They left this with us yesterday,' he said. 'You were out and it didn't fit through your letter box.'

'Very little fits through there,' said Domenica. 'I think people used to get very thin letters in Georgian times.'

'And no junk mail,' said Torquil, grinning.

'Junk mail is a recent curse,' said Domenica, reaching out for the parcel he was offering her.

'It feels like books,' said Torquil, and then immediately

89

qualified what he had just said. 'Not that I actually felt it – not deliberately, if you see what I mean.'

Domenica laughed. 'I don't mind. I think one is entitled to feel a neighbour's parcels if they are left with one. That is entirely understandable human curiosity.'

'But you're not entitled to hold their envelopes up to the light?' asked Torquil, in a tone of mock disappointment.

'Only *in extremis*,' answered Domenica. 'For a *very* good reason, that is.'

She smiled at Torquil. She liked this young man – so much so that she would offer him coffee. There were people to whom one offered coffee, and people to whom one did not offer coffee. She felt in the mood for conversation. So she said, 'Can I tempt you with a cup of coffee?'

And he replied, 'Yes, you can tempt me.' Adding, 'With coffee.'

They were getting on extremely well. And why not? she asked herself. Many twenty-year-olds were rather dull company because they knew so little about anything. Torquil, she decided, was different.

## 21. Aunts and Spies

Torquil said to Domenica, 'Arabica?'

Domenica shrugged. 'Possibly. I must confess, I never look

at the provenance. Life is complicated enough without having to find out what sort of coffee one's drinking.'

Torquil sniffed at the cup of freshly percolated coffee that Domenica had passed him. 'I'd say so,' he said. 'There's a hint of caramel there.'

Domenica shrugged again. 'Coffee is coffee, as far as I'm concerned. As long as it isn't instant coffee, which isn't really coffee at all. I don't think I would be able to tell the difference between the various types.'

Torquil took a sip, as a wine connoisseur might interrogate a Médoc. 'You probably think it a bit showy of me,' he said. 'But I'm interested in the various types of coffee and what they taste like. It's not coffee snobbery.'

'Of course not,' said Domenica. 'People should not have to apologise for knowing a lot about something.' She paused. 'And yet there is a certain anti-intellectualism in some quarters that makes fun of expert knowledge – that regards it as pretentious.'

'I wasn't accusing you of that,' Torquil reassured her. He took another sip of his coffee before continuing, 'I love this stuff, but it makes me feel so guilty.'

Domenica looked at him. 'Because you feel you should be doing something else – rather than sitting around drinking coffee?'

'Maybe,' said Torquil.

'Or guilt over the origins of what you have?'

She waited.

'Each cup of coffee,' Torquil said, 'takes a hundred and forty litres of water to make. That's a hundred and forty litres of the world's finite supplies of fresh water.'

Domenica looked up at the ceiling. 'A water-print?' she said. 'Is that what we should call it?'

'I like that. A water-print. A liquid footprint. Everything will have one. We get through a lot of water.'

'Don't we just?' agreed Domenica. 'So, should I cancel the coffee?'

'*Da mihi castitatem et continentiam, sed noli modo*,' said Torquil, smiling. 'Oh Lord make me chaste, but not just yet, as St Augustine said.'

Domenica remembered that Torquil was a student of classics. She topped up his cup. 'In that case, here you are.' She racked her brains. She wanted to keep up with this clever young man. '*Carpe calicem* ... if that's correct.'

Torquil laughed. 'Seize the chalice? Why not?'

'I'm not sure if my blue Spode should be described as a chalice,' said Domenica. 'But *faute de mieux*.'

'Precisely,' said Torquil, and smiled, revealing the dimples she had observed when first she met him. Their placing was perfect, she thought.

Torquil was looking at her too. 'You remind me of somebody,' he said.

Domenica looked away. She had not intended to flirt nor to provoke flirtation on his part: her interest in this young man was not of that nature. And she was too well aware of the absurd to engage in such a fantasy, even if she had been inclined to do so. She had Angus, and was content with him, and he, she believed, with her. There was no call for any dalliance outside that – no call at all. And she was *not*, to the slightest extent – even in thought – a ... what did they call such women? A *cougar*. She was not that. And yet, subject to all those qualifications, it was flattering to be *noticed* by a young man, and she felt, slightly, and, she hoped, imperceptibly, a blush on her cheeks.

'Yes,' said Torquil, taking a further sip of his coffee, and looking at her again, as if trying to dredge an answer from memory. 'You remind me of . . .' And then it came to him. 'Of my aunt,' he concluded.

Domenica came down to earth – so quickly that she felt the bump might even have been detectable through the floorboards.

'Oh,' she said, adding, lamely, 'I see. Your aunt. How . . .' How what? She decided: 'How evocative.'

There was no sign that Torquil had noticed her dismay. 'She has the same high cheekbones,' he said. 'And the same lines around the side of her mouth.' He indicated on the side of his own mouth where the aunt's – and Domenica's – lines were. 'Here. There's one in particular that goes up at an angle of about seventy degrees, like this.'

'Erosion happens,' said Domenica reflectively. And thought: except to the young. For them, the ravages that afflict the skin are theoretical – things that happen to other people – like death itself. Of course, when it came to any discussion of the ageing of the skin it was best to be disarming in one's frankness – to own, in a courageous way, the ravines and gullies to which the flesh was heir. How was W. H. Auden's famously cracked face described? As looking like a wedding cake left out in the rain. And of course Auden himself had referred to his face as having experienced a geological catastrophe. That was the way to refer to oneself. *I am falling to bits.* If you said that before anybody else said it, then the process of disintegration was far less painful.

Torquil frowned. 'I hope I'm not being tactless,' he said. 'You don't mind, do you?'

'Mind?' exclaimed Domenica. She waved an insouciant hand. 'Why on earth should I mind? This aunt of yours ... tell me about her. No, let me guess. Where does she live? Helensburgh? That's a very suitable place for an aunt to live. Helensburgh and Rhu are stuffed full of aunts. I know somebody who has *three* aunts in Rhu. Can you believe that? Or North Berwick? Once again, aunts haunt North Berwick, I'm led to believe.'

'She lived in Broughty Ferry,' Torquil began. '*Lived*. I'm afraid she's no longer with us. She's dead.'

'Oh, I'm sorry.' So, she had invoked memories not only of an aunt, but an aunt who had expired. Oh well ...

Torquil was philosophical. 'Old age. She was pretty ancient, and nobody was all that surprised when she died.'

Domenica sighed. 'It doesn't do to surprise people. If one is going to die, then ideally one should try to give some indication in advance – like a character in an opera who sings *I am dying* for a number of bars before expiring. Poor Mimi in *La Bohème* is a case in point.'

'I was very fond of her,' Torquil reminisced. 'She worked for British intelligence. She knew Anthony Blunt. You know about him?'

'Of course I do. The art historian spy. The authority on Poussin. The Soviet agent who was a cousin of the Queen Mother.'

'She told me a lot about him,' said Torquil. 'They got on

94

rather well, although she knew him well after he had retired from espionage. He was at the Courtauld Institute then. She understood why he did what he did, she said, even if it was the wrong thing to do. At the time, he believed that that was what was morally required of him. He later regretted it bitterly.'

'I can see that,' said Domenica. 'I don't think that he saw Stalin for what he was. Quite a few people made that mistake.'

'She told me that Blunt went to the cinema after he had been outed as a spy,' Torquil went on. 'It was in Notting Hill. People recognised him and slow-clapped him out of the auditorium.'

Domenica winced. People loved to shame and humiliate others. It was universal. *The fact that you are so bad makes me feel a whole lot better about myself . . .*

## 22. Oedipus, the Minotaur, Guilt

'We were talking about guilt,' said Torquil.

'Yes,' said Domenica. '*Inter alia*. We also touched on aunts and Soviet agents.'

Torquil smiled. 'But you're the one who brought up guilt.'

'I think you did. Or did I? Anyway, the topic did come up. I think it was in the context of drinking coffee and how getting coffee beans to market used so much precious water. That sort of guilt.'

'That's right. I find that interesting.'

Domenica agreed that it was. 'Guilt is definitely one of the great subjects. It's pervasive, ubiquitous, and profoundly unsettling.'

'I'm doing a course in classical mythology as part of my degree,' said Torquil. 'Guilt figures prominently.'

'I'm sure it does,' said Domenica. 'Oedipus springs to mind. He certainly felt guilty once he discovered that Jocasta was his mother. It made him put his eyes out in expiation.'

'I felt sorry for him, but then, who wouldn't? I also felt sorry for the Minotaur. Did you? The pain of being a genetic freak.'

'I haven't given much thought to the Minotaur,' said Domenica. 'I suppose I never really related to him. But I definitely felt sorry for Oedipus.' She paused. 'I can think of very few societies where incest fails to give rise to a particular horror. Did you know that in Scots law, until not all that long ago, the offence of incest was simply defined by reference to Leviticus, chapter 18?'

Torquil raised an eyebrow. He was not sure about Leviticus.

'Yes,' said Domenica. 'It was convenient, I suppose, and it expressed a repugnance that would have been widely shared.'

Torquil thought of something. 'Could you base an entire system of criminal law on the Ten Commandments?'

'No,' said Domenica. 'Coveting one's neighbour's ox is hardly criminal. Nor are most forms of lying. Nor adultery, come to think of it.' She paused. 'Criminal law requires clear definition – the lines we're not meant to cross should never be vague ones. Mind you, we have some pretty odd corners in Scots criminal law. There's an offence known as *lewd and libidinous conduct*. A vivid description.'

'How do you know all this?' asked Torquil.

'I'm an anthropologist,' Domenica replied. *'Homo sum, humani nihil a me alienum puto*, as you – or Terence – might say.'

'Ah, Terence,' mused Torquil. 'You know he was a slave? He was freed and went on to write six comedies.'

'His sense of humour obviously survived.'

Torquil returned to guilt. 'We go in a lot for guilt, don't we? I mean, by comparison.'

'By comparison with whom?'

Torquil looked out of the window. 'Oh, just about anybody, I think. Mediterranean cultures don't seem to me to be very concerned with it. The Italians rarely mention Mussolini. It's almost bad form to do so, I believe.'

Domenica agreed. 'It's not exactly a guilt-ridden culture,' she said. 'You have to go further north for that. It's to do with the Protestant conscience, of course.' She paused. 'Look at Germany. Look at how they have been burdened with guilt for what happened. By and large, they then faced up to it. They berated themselves. Others perhaps less so ... The Poles have suffered so much, and there are those who might consider apologising to them. Not that I'm thinking of anybody in particular.'

'Whereas we ...'

'We don't have a conspicuous record of apology. We haven't been keen to see ourselves as wrongdoers,' said Domenica. 'We've brushed a lot under the carpet, even if we have occasionally felt the odd twinge of guilt. Not enough, some people say.'

'Didn't Tony Blair apologise to Ireland – for failing to help during the famine?'

Domenica smiled. 'I remember him with a certain nostalgia – along with all the others. Yes, he apologised, as did Mr Clinton – for various wrongs previous American governments had committed. All governments, it seems, have acted shabbily on occasions. As have we all.'

Torquil looked momentarily uncomfortable, and Domenica wondered what this young man could have done. But he was not about to confess, moving instead to a general observation on apology. 'Of course, there's a lot for which nobody has apologised, isn't there?' he said. 'Child labour? Land grabs? Opium wars? Slavery? Highland Clearances? It's a long list, once one starts it.'

'We've begun to be more aware of just how awful all that was,' said Domenica. 'We preferred to put it out of our mind in the past, but now ... Well, we're looking in the mirror a bit more.'

'And?'

'Everything we have is tarnished,' Domenica continued. 'Once you start to follow the money, so to speak, that becomes clearer and clearer. And yet ...'

'And yet what? Are you saying we should forget about it?'

Domenica shook her head. 'No, I wouldn't say that. All that I'd say, I suppose, is that there must be a limit to the extent to which one shoulders a burden of guilt. You can make out a cogent case for saying that any financial advantage a society like ours enjoys is ill-gotten and that if we were being morally scrupulous, we would rid ourselves of all our assets – absolutely everything. But what would that do? It would lead to immense suffering – in the here and now, amongst ordinary people who may not share the sense of guilt of those with a more developed historical awareness.'

'So you're saying that excessive guilt is impractical?'

'Yes, I suppose it is, because you don't really help anybody living today – any actual people – if you destroy yourself through guilt. That's pathological guilt – it would be crippling – and crippling oneself hardly makes sense if you want to change the way the world is.'

She watched his expression as she spoke. Sometimes it was hard to argue with somebody of his age. Everything was so clear-cut to the student mind; the truth was passionately proclaimed, rather than half-believed in, which was how more experienced people thought of things. The more experienced had generally discovered that there were no longer any privileged, exclusive truths – there were just the various shades of possibility.

But Torquil appeared to understand. 'Do you know Luc Ferry's book, *The Wisdom of the Myths*?' he asked.

Domenica did not.

'He deals with the world-view of Greek mythology,' Torquil said. 'And the whole point about their myths was that they set out to illustrate how humans fitted into a world that was governed by elemental forces – certain givens that just *were*.'

'I see.' He understands, thought Domenica: this young man *understands*.

Torquil continued with his observation. 'The Greeks wanted to show how a balanced, good life could be led by somebody who accepted his limitations and the arbitrary nature of the world in which he lived. That was at the heart of the good life – acceptance. They thought that you shouldn't go around feeling miserable because of what had already happened, about what happened in the past.'

*He's very good-looking*, thought Domenica, even when talking about ancient Greek cosmology. But then she remembered that she reminded him of his late aunt, and within herself she sighed – a sigh that was like the movement of the most imperceptible of breezes on a still day, when the air lay heavy over Scotland and nothing moved.

## 23. *Torquil and Domenica Converse*

Like all good conversations, that between Domenica and her student neighbour, Torquil, moved easily, as if borne on a slow-flowing river – a broad waterway that knows where it is going, is confident that it will get there, and is in no particular hurry to reach its destination. They sat and talked in Domenica's kitchen, watching a shaft of light inch gradually across the floorboards, past the place where Angus had once stood on a tube of paint, spreading a Rorschach blot of vermilion across the wood, inadequately lifted by paint stripper; past signs of ancient woodworm; past the tip of the nail hammered in squint over a hundred years ago by the hand of a disgruntled apprentice.

Torquil shared Domenica's interest in the neighbours – unusual for one still at an age when solipsism is standard. 'I've met a lot of them,' he said, 'including people round the corner in Drummond Place. There's a nun ...'

Domenica smiled as she interrupted him. 'Sister Maria-Fiore dei Fiori di Montagna?' she said. 'A slight figure with a rather sharp nose?'

She realised, of course, that the description was otiose: there were fewer and fewer nuns about, and none, she thought, in the immediate vicinity.

Torquil nodded. 'That must be her. And that's a name-and-a-half. She didn't introduce herself when we met. She just said she was Antonia's friend. That's all.'

'Antonia Collie,' said Domenica. 'My former neighbour through the wall. We go back some time.'

Torquil picked up a note of reservation in Domenica's voice. 'You're close to her?' he asked.

Domenica took a sip of her coffee. 'I must be charitable,' she said. 'What are we without charity?'

Torquil laughed. 'Charity should not prevent one from saying what one thinks.'

Domenica thought about this. It was quite wrong: that was exactly what charity should do. She said, 'Do you really think so? I'm afraid I must disagree. It's charity, surely, that stops us giving voice to our thoughts. If I took exception to your appearance for some reason, I should not tell you what I was thinking. If you did something really badly, charity might prevent me saying anything about your lack of skill. *Und so weiter*, Torquil.'

'What?'

'And so on. It's German. One might say *et cetera et cetera.*'

'Or *And so on and so forth*?'

'Yes. It just sounds a little less ... how shall I put it? Dismissive?'

'Tell me about Antonia,' asked Torquil. 'I think she must be the woman I saw walking down Great King Street with Sister Maria-Fiore dei ...'

'... *Fiori d'et cetera et cetera*,' supplied Domenica. '*Schwester und so weiter*, indeed.'

'Yes, her. I saw the two of them walking along Great King Street, deep in conversation.'

'Plotting,' said Domenica. 'Those two do plot a great deal.'

'About?'

'I have no hard evidence,' said Domenica. 'But I think a lot of it is about strategy for Sister Maria-Fiore dei Fiori di Montagna's social advancement. She's a ruthless social climber, positively Alpine in her ambitions. In fact ...' Domenica paused to grin, 'In fact, I said to Angus the other day that we might expect her at any moment to appear in the street hooked up to oxygen cylinders – you know, of the sort that climbers use when they get above a certain altitude on Everest. She'd need those for her high-altitude social climbing.'

Torquil burst out laughing. 'It would be a dead giveaway for the really serious social climber, wouldn't it?'

Domenica nodded. They were having such fun. 'She's scaled unimaginable heights since she arrived. Remember that she came from conditions of great obscurity – she was an unpromoted nun from the Little Sisters of the

Bourgeoisie, or whatever her order was called. They kept a house outside Florence where they looked after people who had been afflicted with Stendhal syndrome while visiting the Uffizi. Poor Antonia was one of those.'

'That's where you're overcome by great art?' asked Torquil.

'The very condition. Shortness of breath caused by looking at *Primavera*. Raised temperature caused by exposure to Ghirlandaio and Raphael. That sort of thing. It's a very refined syndrome. Antonia got it and was looked after in Florence before they sent her out into the country to this place run by these rural nuns. They kept bees and had a lettuce farm, I believe, but I gather their life was not quite the simple affair that we expect nuns to be content with. No, they looked after themselves quite well, I gather. Not only did they make gin, which they had the bad taste to call *Communion Gin*, but they also made tonic water. And grew lemons. That gives the overall picture, I think.'

'Well, why not?' said Torquil. 'People talk about a broad church.'

'Indeed, they do. And the Catholic Church has always been quite happy to allow sybarites to flourish. Cardinals traditionally kept a good table. And they had a place for all sorts of intellect – from simple brothers whose job it was to pick carrots and scrub floors to calculating Jesuits who could twist on the head of a pin. It has always been broad.'

'I'm Episcopalian myself,' said Torquil. 'In a sort of way. I like a high service. Music by Byrd. Incense and so on.'

'Nothing wrong with incense,' said Domenica. 'I love the sight of wafting smoke. It reminds us that not everything is linear and purposeful. It drifts. Suffuses. I most definitely do not approve of the habit of spraying incense from aerosol cans.'

'No! Nobody does that, surely?'

Domenica smiled. 'It's conceivable. A convinced modernist might.'

Torquil brought the conversation back to reality. 'So Antonia met her there? In the convent?'

'It was more of a villa than a convent,' said Domenica. 'But yes, that's where they met. And she brought her over to Scotland out of gratitude for what they had done for her. She actually joined them in some capacity or other – a lay sister or a member of the supporters' club, or whatever they call it.'

'Did she take on a name?' asked Torquil. 'Something like Sister Maria-Fiore's?'

Domenica thought for a moment. They were not only having fun – they were having *great* fun.

'Sister Antonia of the Blue Spode,' she suggested.

Torquil's eyes shone. Blue Spode? Life in Edinburgh was so intriguing – who would have thought? But Domenica, by contrast, now reproached herself. She had overstepped the mark: it was only too easy to make fun of somebody like Antonia. She should not.

'Antonia has many good points,' she said. 'And I wouldn't want to be dismissive of her. We all have our faults – some, of course, having rather more than others.' That qualification was somewhat self-defeating: charity, she reminded herself, *charity*, and was ashamed.

## 24. Agrippina and Nero

'But then,' said Torquil, 'what about downstairs? Stuart, is it? And his two boys? And his mother, who seems to have moved in permanently? Somebody said that Stuart's wife has gone off to Aberdeen with a lover. Is that true?'

Domenica poured both of them a fresh cup of coffee. She was enjoying this conversation with her neighbour, even if it was ... well, if one were to be honest with oneself, it was gossip. But then what was wrong with that? A life devoid of at least the occasional gossip would surely be a bit bland – like an endless stock-market report, or some such recitation of simple fact, or a meal without salt, pepper, or any other seasoning. Gossip allowed one to be amused by the human comedy, involved irony and other shadings of the palette, and was permissible, surely, as long as it refrained from cruelty. Gossip cemented our links with one another, reminded us of community. In the foibles of others, after all, we saw ourselves – or should do.

'Yes,' said Domenica. 'Irene – Stuart's wife, and mother of Bertie and Ulysses – is now doing a PhD in Aberdeen. She comes down here from time to time – I saw her a few weeks ago, briefly – but it's Nicola – Stuart's mother – who is looking after the boys. Stuart himself, of course, is a conscientious, hands-on father, but he struggles a bit.' She paused. 'In fact, he has struggled for years, that man. Irene was a touch on the dominant side. In fact, she was completely appalling. A termagant. The day she left was liberation day as far as Stuart was concerned. And the boys. And the rest of us too. There was dancing in the street. Fireworks.' She looked at Torquil, who was listening wide-eyed. 'I exaggerate a touch. But we were certainly pleased.'

'I see,' said Torquil.

'I suppose she meant well,' said Domenica, slightly reluctantly. 'But she was devoid of tolerance of other people's views. She hectored. And that poor little boy, poor wee Bertie. How he suffered! He's composed of pure goodness, and he never complained about that mother of his – he bore it all with fortitude. Italian lessons from the age of four – yes, four! He's seven now, and, if anything, the pressure is worse – or at least it was until Aberdeen beckoned Irene. Psychotherapy every week – every week! Yoga sessions down at Stockbridge. It was relentless. And all the time he just wanted to be an ordinary little boy, doing the things that ordinary little boys do.'

Torquil shook his head. 'It's rather hard to be a boy these days, I think.'

'Virtually impossible,' Domenica agreed. 'There may be a place where boys roam free – but it's not here.'

Torquil looked thoughtful. 'She sounds a bit like Agrippina.'

Domenica tried to remember who Agrippina was. A Roman clearly, but beyond that . . .

'She was Nero's mother,' Torquil explained. 'I've been writing an essay on Nero in my ancient history course. You have to do ancient history if you do classics – you can't do just the languages and literature, you have to do the Caesars and the corn supply and the decline of the Republic and all that. Nero's rather interesting. He's being rehabilitated at the moment, believe it or not. There's been a big exhibition in London of Nero-related material, and the line is: Nero wasn't as bad as he's been portrayed.'

'Revisionism,' said Domenica. 'People can't resist the temptation to change the way we see figures of the past. They've been doing that with the Vikings. There are quite a few historians now who argue that the Vikings meant well.'

'That they weren't just about burning and pillaging?'

'Exactly. Apparently, that was not the whole point of Viking raids. The real point was to spread Scandinavian culture. The Vikings were very keen on art and music, according to this view.'

Torquil shook his head. 'I doubt it.'

'So do I.'

'Nero, of course, was interested in the arts.'

'All I remember learning of him at school,' Domenica said, 'was that he played the fiddle . . .'

'While Rome burned. Yes, that was his metaphor, so to speak. But he was actually rather interesting.'

'And Agrippina was his mother?'

'She was married to Claudius. You may have read . . .'

'Robert Graves? Yes, I did.' It was a long time ago, though, and she remembered nothing about the book except its title, and the fact that Claudius stammered.

'She was a great poisoner. They murdered Claudius by

feeding him a poisoned mushroom. Of course, he had a food-taster, who sampled the mushrooms and pronounced them fine, but they slipped in a large, choice one that he knew Claudius would go for. And he did. And that was the end of him.

'She was ruthlessly ambitious,' Torquil continued. 'She loved power, and her sole objective in life was to acquire more of it for herself and her son, Nero. That was the agenda. So, once Claudius was out of the way, Nero took over with Agrippina standing behind him, so to speak. He was just a teenage boy when he found himself ruler of a vast empire. He was a bit wild. I read that he used to disguise himself in ordinary clothes and go out at night with the boys, and get into all sorts of fights.'

'Others have gone out in disguise,' Domenica mused. 'The Gudeman of Ballengeich? James V? He used to dress in humble clothes and go out among the people.'

'Of course. And the Duke of Edinburgh used to drive himself round London in a taxi cab.'

'Agrippina?' Domenica reminded him.

'She tried to control Nero. She was the ultimate interfering mother. Unfortunately, Nero murdered her. He had a special boat built that was designed to break in two and tip her into the sea. He saw her off on this after inviting her for dinner at his seaside villa. Halfway across the Bay of Naples, the boat performed as intended. Agrippina found herself in the water, but managed to get herself picked up by some obliging fishermen. Nero sent men round to her house to finish her off. It was very unpleasant. One should not treat one's mother like that.'

'Definitely not,' said Domenica. 'One should appreciate one's mother. One should not tip her into the sea.'

'And ye cannae shove your granny aff a bus,' added Torquil.

Domenica laughed. 'That goes without saying,' she said.

## 25. Bertie's Fate

As the conversation between Domenica and Torquil was taking place, downstairs in the Pollock flat Stuart and Nicola were breaking to Bertie the news of his forthcoming exile to Aberdeen. Both adults were putting on a brave face and trying to present the uncomfortable news in as positive a manner as possible.

'Just think,' Stuart gushed. 'Aberdeen! You're a very fortunate boy, Bertie. There are lots of boys who would give anything to go to Aberdeen for three months.'

'Yes,' said Nicola. 'Lots.'

Bertie had his eyes fixed firmly on the floor. 'Name one,' he said.

Nicola glanced at Stuart. 'Well, we weren't thinking of anybody in particular. But that doesn't mean that there aren't lots of boys who would give their eye teeth to have the chance to spend three whole months at a different school.'

'Yes,' enthused Stuart. 'Three months at another school will mean a whole lot of new friends. Just think of that.'

'I don't want new friends, Daddy,' Bertie pleaded. 'I've got Ranald Braveheart Macpherson. He's my friend. He's the best friend anybody could ever have.'

Stuart assured Bertie that he was second to none in his admiration for Ranald. 'But it's always good to have a bit of a change, you know, Bertie. Meeting new people broadens the horizons. New people are exciting. You'll have a lot of fun with your new friends in Aberdeen.'

'I have a lot of fun with Ranald,' said Bertie.

'Of course you do,' said Nicola. 'But Daddy has a point, you know, Bertie. New friends are always interesting.' She paused. 'Aberdeen is a very friendly place, you know. It's a bit like Glasgow. I know how much you admire Glasgow, Bertie – well, Aberdeen is very similar to Glasgow, I think.'

Bertie looked at his grandmother. Did she really believe that? Did she really think that Glasgow and Aberdeen were in the slightest bit similar? Was there something wrong with his grandmother? Was this the cognitive decline he had read about in one of Irene's psychology books?

'I don't think they are, Granny,' Bertie said politely. 'You don't find people like Mr O'Connor in Aberdeen, I think.'

Stuart forced himself to laugh. 'Oh, Mr O'Connor – my goodness me – I'd forgotten all about him.' Bertie had met the late Lard O'Connor (RIP) in Glasgow when Stuart had mislaid their car there, and the meeting had made a deep impression on him.

Nicola took over. 'Places have different merits, Bertie,' she said. 'You wouldn't want everywhere to be the same, would you?'

Bertie considered this. 'But you're the one who said

Glasgow and Aberdeen were the same,' he pointed out. 'You said that, Granny.'

Nicola sighed. 'I was just trying to reassure you, Bertie. And what I said is a bit true, even if not completely true. Glasgow and Aberdeen have some things in common – and other things that are a bit different. What I'm saying is that you will find the equivalent in Aberdeen of things you might expect to find in Glasgow.'

Bertie looked unconvinced. 'Are there polar bears in Aberdeen?' he asked.

Stuart laughed. 'Good heavens, Bertie. Where on earth did you get that idea? No, there are no polar bears in Aberdeen. It's in the north, but not that far north.'

Something else was bothering Bertie. 'Will I get enough to eat?' he asked.

Stuart and Nicola exchanged glances. Poor little boy – how prey were children to the most extraordinary insecurities.

'Of course you will,' said Stuart. 'Mummy will be looking after you. You know what a good cook she is.'

This was quite untrue, and all of them knew it, including Bertie; Irene was completely incompetent in the kitchen. But it was not his mother's lack of cooking prowess that was worrying him – it was the general question of what would be available.

'Ranald said that everybody thinks they're mean,' Bertie explained. 'Ranald said that people in Aberdeen can survive for a whole month on three plates of porridge. He said that there has been research on this. He said that it's because they don't like spending money. They save on food.'

'That's absolute nonsense, Bertie,' exclaimed Stuart.

'People in Aberdeen are *not* mean, Bertie. They are the most generous, warm-hearted, joyful people you could possibly hope to meet.'

Nicola gave Stuart a sideways look.

'And Ranald says it's very cold,' Bertie continued. 'He said that they won't spend money on heating their houses.'

'Nonsense,' said Stuart.

'Ranald says that people in Aberdeen don't need to buy fridges,' Bertie continued. 'He said that food keeps for ages in Aberdeen.'

'Pure nonsense,' said Stuart. 'Ranald clearly doesn't know what he's talking about.'

Bertie became silent. Then he said, 'I don't want to go, Daddy. I don't want to upset Mummy, but I think it's best if I didn't go. I'm very happy here with you and Granny, and even with Ulysses. I don't see why I have to go to Aberdeen.'

Stuart tried to explain. 'Mummy loves having you with her, Bertie,' he said. 'She's keen that you go and spend some time with her. She thinks you'll love Aberdeen and you'll have great fun together.'

Bertie shook his head. 'I won't, Daddy. I really won't. I like being here with you – and with Granny. I like going to Valvona & Crolla. I like having my own room and all the things in it. I'm really very happy, Daddy.'

'I'm sure you are, Bertie,' said Stuart. 'And let me tell you this: if it were up to me, you'd stay. But it isn't entirely up to me, Bertie. Mummy is allowed to have her turn. That's only fair, isn't it?'

'Couldn't she take Ulysses instead? Wouldn't she be happy with that, Daddy?' It was, Bertie knew, a vain hope. Ulysses, with his regurgitation and his smells, was not everybody's cup of tea, and certainly not his mother's.

'But . . .' Bertie stopped. It was hard for him to go on. He knew that there was nothing that he could do to stop his being sent to Aberdeen. He had never – not once in his life – been able to stop the things that happened to him. They simply happened, as if ordained by some cosmic force, some destiny, that was beyond him to influence. In that respect, he felt as any small child feels. He knew he would not like Aberdeen, even if it was only for three months, and three months, people said, could go quite quickly.

He was content in Edinburgh. He was happy at school, in spite of the terrible people in his class – Olive and Pansy, whose delight, it seemed, was to taunt him at all points; Tofu, whose criminality in all matters lay just below the surface, and who put pressure on Bertie to bring sausages to school so that he might purloin them; Larch, who was generally unpredictable; Luigi, who had recently joined the school from a Montessori School in Palermo, who had set up a small protection racket in the playground, and who spoke, darkly, of his cousins upon whom he could call if thwarted. There were others, of course, of whom the adult world, in its innocence, was quite unaware. In spite of all that, Bertie was happy, and he saw no reason why his life should be turned upside down simply so that his mother could show him off to her new friends. He was not a Pinocchio, an animated toy on strings. He was a boy, and he wanted to stay with his dad, of whom he was so proud.

He looked at his father, willing him to declare that there was a change of plan and Bertie could stay where he was, in Scotland Street. But Stuart came up with no such statement.

## 26. Stuart Goes Out

Stuart felt exhausted. The attempt that he and Nicola had made to persuade Bertie that three months in Aberdeen was something to which he should look forward had failed, as he feared it would. At length, after they had said all they possibly could about the attractions of life in the northern city, resorting even to reference to the delights of Aberdonian bread rolls – *butteries* – silence descended, capped with Nicola's comment, 'Well, Bertie, you're old enough to know that there are some things that we just have to do. We may not like them, but we have to do them.' That remark, true enough in its way, had nonetheless undone the entire official line presented to that point that Aberdeen, like Glasgow, was a shining city on a hill, and that Bertie should look forward to three months there in the company of his mother.

Nicola was in charge of bedtime that day. Ulysses was already asleep, snoring loudly in the way in which, atypically for a young child, he had always done. Medical advice had been sought, and his nose had been closely examined by a paediatric ear, nose and throat specialist at the Sick Kids. It had been pronounced to have slightly unusual properties but nonetheless to be within the range of normality and would not require any medical attention.

'It's very large,' Bertie had observed. 'That's why he

snores, I think. Could they not cut a bit off at the hospital? Just a bit?'

Stuart had smiled, but his smile had faded with Bertie's next comment, innocently made, but nonetheless not the sort of remark that Stuart wished to hear.

'It's funny, isn't it, Daddy,' Bertie had continued, 'that Ulysses' nose is so like Dr Fairbairn's. It's the same shape, I think, particularly if you look at it from the side.' He paused. 'I wonder if Dr Fairbairn snores. Mummy probably knows that. I could ask her, I suppose.'

This had been said in the hearing of Nicola, who was setting up the bread-maker at the time, and who, distracted by what had been said, spilled a large quantity of flour on the floor. She did not know Dr Fairbairn well, but had met him on a couple of occasions and knew that what Bertie said about the similarity was quite true. She also suspected that any resemblance between Ulysses and the psychotherapist was not merely coincidence, although she had not voiced her doubts in this respect to Stuart. But now that was exactly what Bertie was doing, and Nicola waited anxiously to see how Stuart might respond.

Stuart had looked up at the ceiling. He had always done that, Nicola reminded herself. Even when he had been a small boy and had been found to have committed some minor transgression, he had looked up at the ceiling while being reprimanded. And Nicola remembered how at his wedding, when vows were exchanged, she had glanced at her son from her position in the front pew of the church and had seen that he was looking up at the ceiling. That had struck her as a bad sign, and for a moment she had reflected that perhaps her instinct to wear black to that particular wedding had been a sound one. But one did not wear black to a wedding, however strong the temptation.

Stuart had stared at the ceiling and had then said to Bertie, 'I don't think we should talk about other people's noses, Bertie – I really don't.'

That was typical of Stuart, thought Nicola. Much as she loved her son, she was not blind to his faults, and one of them was an unwillingness to address painful issues. It was that failing that had led, she thought, to his putting up with Irene and her ways as long as he had. If he had only had the courage to stand up to her at an early stage – their honeymoon would have been a good time to start – then he might not have been relegated to the subsidiary role that had then been his lot for the remainder of the marriage. And even now, when the two of them were leading separate lives, it seemed to be Irene who was calling all the shots.

Of course, it was difficult to see what he could possibly do about this tricky issue of paternity. Even if it were the case that Ulysses *was* Dr Fairbairn's son, as she suspected was the case, it was not at all clear how the admission of that fact would change anything. Parentage could never be a child's fault: none of us, after all, chose the bed in which we were born, and nor did that have any bearing on the immediate needs of a child. It was unthinkable that she or Stuart could ever claim that Ulysses was nothing to do with them: he was their son and grandchild whatever his provenance, and it would be quite wrong to open that issue.

Now, with Ulysses' snores reverberating from his small bedroom at the back of the flat, Bertie had been tucked up in his own bed and left to read for half an hour or so before lights out. When Stuart next checked up on him, he found Bertie was fast asleep, having dropped the book that now lay on the rug beside his bed. Stuart picked it up, glancing at the title. Bertie was a prodigious reader, picking up anything he came across, and devouring books well beyond anything one would normally expect a seven-year-old to read. That evening it was Eric Linklater's *The Prince in the Heather*, a book that Bertie had discovered in the help-yourself library box at the end of Scotland Street and in which he had quickly immersed himself, giving regular précised accounts of the contents to Ranald Braveheart Macpherson, who had yet to learn how to read.

Stuart looked down at Bertie's tousled hair upon the pillow. He looked at the space-rocket motif of the pillowcase: little astronauts in bubble-helmets, floating in space alongside their space dogs, similarly clad in shiny inflated space-dog suits. He looked at the lobe of his son's right ear, with its tiny indentation, a genetic peculiarity of the Pollock family, passed down from generation to generation like a family badge, from the earliest ancestor they had identified, a Covenanting minister from the south-west of Scotland. The minister had been captured in a pencil sketch by his wife, who had drawn his ear with its characteristic mark. In these little ways, we were bound up in the notion of family and continuity, of identity – the things which we held so tenuously against all the confusion of this world. We had to believe in something, thought Stuart; we had to think that something was important, that something counted, because otherwise what were our lives but tiny events of no significance at all?

He reached down and switched off Bertie's light before returning to the kitchen.

'I'm going out,' he said to Nicola.

She looked at him. She did not ask him why, or where, but he told her nonetheless.

'I'm going to walk round Drummond Place Garden. I need some air.'

She sighed. She knew what was going to happen. He was going to get in touch with Irene and go back on everything that had so far been agreed. Irene would resume the running of their lives from Aberdeen, returning to Edinburgh from time to time to exert her control. He would never leave that woman – never. She sighed again. Even an anticyclone of sighs would not be sufficient to express the regret engendered by this situation; Irene was permanent; Irene was immutable; Irene was omnipotent.

## 27. Sister Maria-Fiore dei Fiori's Secret

Stuart was pleased to find that he was alone in Drummond Place Garden, where the late evening light, slanting in from the west, was still touching the highest branches of the sycamores. The sky above the city was empty of clouds and marked only by the high vapour-trail of a passenger jet bound for America. The jet itself could just be made out, a tiny arrow of steel slicing through the attenuated blue, and Stuart thought of what it would be like to be unencumbered in this life, to be free, to be able to step aboard a plane like that and leave everything behind you. The manacles we forge for ourselves might be comfortable ones, may not chafe too much, and yet they are manacles nonetheless – bonds of family, of profession, of debt, of personal obligation. Or they may be woven of the simple and only too familiar lassitude that prevents us from doing anything to disturb the established patterns of our life.

He began his walk round the perimeter of the garden, following the path widdershins, as he usually did, enjoying the crunch of gravel underfoot. Somewhere off to his left, a bird called out a greeting – or was it a challenge? It was as difficult, he thought, for us to interpret what birds were saying as it was for them to make sense of our human babble. He hoped it was a thrush, because he loved thrushes and believed that a pair of these birds had taken up residence somewhere nearby, possibly in the garden itself.

Irene was in his mind, her disapproving gaze fixed resolutely upon him, even here, in the solitude of the garden. He now suspected that the three months that Bertie was to spend in Aberdeen would be the beginning of a longer sojourn there – one that would soon become, if he were insufficiently vigilant, six months, and then a year, and ultimately an indeterminate time. He feared that he might lose Bertie altogether; Irene had never been one to share, in spite of her communitarian rhetoric, and she would not hesitate to unpick their carefully negotiated custody agreement. And the mere thought of losing Bertie was too awful to contemplate, because Bertie, he realised, was his world. Yes, he had his career as a statistician; yes, he had a few friends whom he saw from time to time; yes, he had the constant and unstinting support of his mother, Nicola; yes, he had interests that diverted and sustained him, but none of these things was as central to him, as important, as his son. Without Bertie, he would be bereft, at a complete loss, devoid of any real reason to continue with life.

His eyes fixed on the ground beneath his feet, Stuart only saw Sister Maria-Fiore dei Fiori di Montagna when he was more or less upon her. She had been walking deasil, in the opposite direction to him, and he almost bumped into her as he turned a corner in the path.

The nun smiled. 'I had thought myself alone,' she said. 'And now, here you are.'

Stuart felt a slight irritation at her presence. The garden, although privately owned, was open to anybody who was fortunate enough to possess a key, as both he and Sister Maria-Fiore did. And yet there were times at which the presence of others seemed like an intrusion, and that was how he now felt.

'Yes,' he said. 'Here I am.'

Sister Maria-Fiore dei Fiori di Montagna clasped her hands together, as if about to pray. But it was not into words of prayer that she now launched, but rather an aphorism. 'Those we find before us are often those who we have been seeking,' she said, adding, 'even if we did not know that we were seeking them.'

Stuart stared at her. 'Possibly,' he said. 'Although you and I disprove the proposition, I would have thought: neither of us has been seeking the other.'

This might have deflated the nun, but it did not. '*A contrario*,' she said, unclasping her hands to make the point. 'We may have been seeking one another because we know – even if we do not know – that the other is the one we need to find.' She paused, and then, in a lower, more matter-of-fact register, continued, 'You look upset, Stuart. Is there something wrong?'

Stuart was about to say that nothing was wrong, but found that he lacked the energy to dissemble. 'I feel awful,' he said, and then, without waiting for further encouragement, told her about Irene's demand that Bertie go to her in Aberdeen for three months. Sister Maria-Fiore listened sympathetically, and then said, 'She's punishing you, of course.'

Stuart's eyes narrowed. What did this nun know of the history of their troubled marriage?

'I don't know . . .'

'No, she is,' insisted Sister Maria-Fiore. 'She is making you and Bertie suffer because she is unhappy – and you do not share her unhappiness. You never will – nor will Bertie. And so she is determined to make you unhappy in the way in which she herself is unhappy. It's fairly basic psychology. I've seen it time and time again.'

For a while Stuart was silent. Then he said, 'What should I do?'

'Do not fight her,' said Sister Maria-Fiore. 'When we fight others, we are simply fighting ourselves.'

'I see.'

'Allow her to make her point. Do not harbour resentment in your heart. Allow healing to take place.'

Stuart looked doubtful.

'That is the only way,' said Sister Maria-Fiore.

She looked at her watch. 'The sun's over the chapel tower,' she said.

Stuart looked confused. 'The chapel tower . . .'

'Do you not say *the sun's over the yardarm* when it's time to have a drink?'

Stuart laughed. 'Oh, that. Yes, some do. It's a naval expression, I believe. Rather old-fashioned.'

'I wonder whether you would care to come and have a gin and tonic with me,' said Sister Maria-Fiore. 'Antonia is in Broughty Ferry, visiting her aunt – such a needful lady, bless her – and so it's just me, I'm afraid.'

Stuart hesitated. He felt at ease coping with most social situations, but this one was rather unexpected. To be invited to have a gin and tonic with an Italian nun à deux was a new experience, and he was not quite sure how to respond.

'Please say you will,' implored Sister Maria-Fiore dei Fiori di Montagna.

There was something in her voice that made Stuart hesitate even more, but it seemed that time for hesitation was over, as the nun now seized his elbow in a surprisingly firm grip and began to guide him back down the path towards the gate.

'I have a little secret to impart,' said Sister Maria-Fiore dei Fiori di Montagna.

Stuart said nothing.

'Antonia and I are thinking of moving,' she continued. 'We've found a delightful double-upper flat in the Grange. It's just come on the market. I can't wait to tell you about it.'

Stuart smiled. He was relieved that Sister Mari-Fiore's agenda was so innocent. A move to the Grange? What could be less controversial, less unsettling than that?

## 28. *Bruce Prepares*

Mr Murthwaite, who had once almost played rugby for Scotland, and would have done so had a slight knee injury not interfered with his summer training, had been Bruce Anderson's physical education teacher at Morrison's Academy. He liked Bruce, although he occasionally berated him for failing to maximise his potential. 'You could perform far better, Anderson,' he said, 'if you spent less time preening yourself in front of the mirror and more time in the gym.' This reproach, publicly delivered, caused giggles amongst those girls present and smirks of *Schadenfreude* amongst the boys. It was entirely deserved criticism, though, and Bruce took it in the spirit in which it was offered. But it nonetheless failed to spur him to the efforts that might have led to greater sporting distinction, even if he still maintained not only his membership of a gym but also, as a non-playing winger, of a small and not very successful rugby club, the North Edinburgh Stalwarts.

On that Monday morning, Bruce set his Apple Watch to wake him an hour earlier than normal, as he wanted to fit in a visit to the gym before his planned on-site meeting with his new business partners, Ed Macdonald and his friend, Gregor. The Apple Watch, obedient to its electronic vows, awoke him at exactly the right time, invoking, via a Bluetooth link, an mp3 file of the Red Army Choir singing the Russian folk song, 'Kalinka'. This had been recorded on that remarkable occasion when the famous military singers had met, and sung with, the Mormon Tabernacle Choir at a choir festival in Seville. The resultant musical energy was significant, and the volume and enthusiasm of 'Kalinka' was such that it would have been impossible for even the drowsiest sleeper to remain in bed once the choir reached the first full-blooded chorus.

Little more than an hour later, Bruce returned to his flat in Abercromby Place, having successfully completed the four demanding circuits that his personal trainer had prescribed for him. Now he was ready for his shower, which usually took at least fifteen minutes, and which involved the application of a special garlic-and-rosemary pre-shower toner, followed by shower treatment, shower gel, and an olive-oil based post-shower skin conditioner. Drying with a high-GSM ring-spun cotton defoliant bath towel was next and then a careful self-examination before the full-length mirror Bruce had installed in what he called the post-shower room, a large, walk-in cupboard directly off the bathroom.

Bruce liked what he saw. A combination of diet and exercise meant that he carried not an ounce of spare flesh, unlike so many of his fellow members of the rugby club who had allowed muscle once exercised in the scrum to turn to flab. These were people, Bruce thought, who had no inner Mr Murthwaite to reproach them over their various shortcomings – their failure to walk to work rather than take a bus, their refusal to eschew fattening carbohydrates, their disinclination to use the stairs at the office rather than the lift. These people ended up with the bodies they deserved, Bruce told himself, with some satisfaction. I, by contrast, end up like this ... And here he tensed his muscles, delighting in the rippling effect that he had come to realise so entranced women. Women, he said to himself, simply couldn't *ripple* in the way in which men could – if they looked after themselves.

The toilette performed at Versailles in its heyday was but as nothing compared to that witnessed each morning in Abercromby Place. The last stage of this elaborate process was the application of hair gel (clove-scented, by tradition), the smoothing down of the hair (it always sprang up, *en brosse*, whatever Bruce did), and then, with the regret that must be felt whenever any masterpiece is concealed from public view, the selection of clothes and the act of dressing.

That morning, Bruce wore a pair of charcoal chinos, red-striped bamboo socks, polo-brown calf-suede Crockett & Jones loafers, a sky-blue shirt from a Jermyn Street mail-order catalogue, and a mustard-coloured casual linen jacket that he had first seen in the window display of Stewart Christie in Queen Street and that he had known, with utter certainty and at first sighting, was destined to be his.

Fully dressed, he took a final appreciative glance at himself in the mirror, while his coffee percolator gurgled promisingly in the kitchen. He found it hard to imagine any way in which the image that he presented to the world might be improved upon. Nothing was overstated, and yet everything spoke of his assuredness, of his confidence that he might be regarded from whatever angle and the admiration would always be the same.

Breakfast was a brief affair – a boiled egg, a small portion of smoked Argyll salmon, and a large cup of black coffee. Then Bruce set off for the Grange, where, at the address given him in Ed's earlier email, he joined Ed Macdonald and Gregor in front of a large South Edinburgh villa. The house, set back from the road, was partly concealed from view by a yew hedge and two well-established copper beech trees.

Ed, who was busy with his mobile phone, greeted Bruce perfunctorily; Gregor was more attentive. 'Like your chinos,' he said.

Bruce acknowledged the compliment with a smile.

'And your jacket,' Gregor added. 'Mustard suits you.'

Bruce inclined his head. He was not quite sure what to make of Gregor. 'Some people can't wear it,' he said, and glanced briefly at Ed.

Gregor grinned. 'Ed can't wear anything,' he said. 'Poor guy. He looks sad in everything. Even beige.' He laughed. 'Those shoes? Is that the colour they call snuff? Or is it tobacco?'

'Polo-brown,' Bruce said.

Gregor gave a sigh that might have been envy or simple admiration. 'Cool,' he said.

Ed finished his telephone call. He turned to Bruce. 'Like what you see?'

Bruce gazed at the house. 'Private,' he said.

Ed looked pleased. 'Privacy easily adds an extra hundred grand to the price – sometimes more.'

'A rare commodity these days,' said Gregor.

Gesturing for the other two to follow him, Ed led them up the paved path to the front door. 'Greg divided it,' he explained to Bruce.

'Yup,' said Gregor. 'Me.'

'There's a double-upper and a ground-floor flat,' Ed continued. 'We're going to hold on to the ground-floor flat until the market moves up a bit. Aren't we, Greg?'

'Yup,' said Gregor. 'A rising market. Helped on its way a bit. Cool.'

'Oldies love ground-floor flats,' Ed went on. 'No stairs, you see. Oldies hate stairs. But the double-upper will go in a week – and at a pretty hefty price.' He winked at Bruce. 'All the ducks, so to speak, are lined up.'

Bruce was gazing up at the front of the house. His surveyor's eye caught a small section where the mortar had flaked out of the join between blocks of stone.

'Pointing needed,' he said. 'There. Over there, too. And there.'

Ed followed his gaze. 'Yes. We have that on our list for this week. There's still a bit to do here and there, cosmetic stuff, that's all. But let's not waste time. Let's go in and take a look round.'

## 29. The Merits of the Double-Upper

Ed explained that with the conversion of the house into two separate flats, the entrance to the top flat – the double-upper, as such flats are called in Edinburgh – was round the side of the house.

'Gregor has done it fantastically well,' he said to Bruce. 'Sometimes it can be hard to convert these places and you end up with an outside staircase climbing up the side of the house.'

'Not at all attractive,' said Gregor. 'Ugly, even. To be avoided, if poss.'

'And it was poss here,' Ed continued. 'Gregor got the builder to knock a hole in a side wall and make a new entrance hall on the ground floor, just to the side of the main staircase. Then he separated the staircase from the ground-floor flat by building an internal wall, and there you have it – two flats. Brilliant.'

'Not rocket science,' said Gregor, modestly.

'Still, pretty smart work,' Ed insisted. 'Give credit where credit is due. You've got a great eye, Greg, for this sort of stuff.'

Gregor smiled. 'That's what I do. I love doing this stuff. It floats my boat.'

Bruce glanced at him. People had said that he had a good eye too, but he did not think he should mention it. Clearly

Gregor thought that his eye was better. 'Are you an architect, Gregor?' he asked.

He asked this question while Ed was fumbling with the front-door key. Gregor turned round and fixed Bruce with a glassy stare.

'What do you mean?'

'I was just wondering whether you were an architect. That's all.'

Gregor gave a toss of the head. 'Architects!' he said. His tone was dismissive.

Ed managed to get the key into the door. 'Architects aren't always what they crack themselves up to be. They get things wrong.'

Gregor addressed Bruce. 'I told you: I do interior decoration.'

Bruce laughed uneasily. 'I wasn't accusing you of architecture.'

Gregor stared at him. 'What's that meant to mean? Have you got a problem with interior decoration, Bruce?'

Bruce shrugged. 'No. Of course not. It's just that architects know about load-bearing walls and things like that. You have to be a bit careful if you start knocking holes.' He paused. 'Just saying.'

Ed raised a hand. 'Gregor knows what he's doing, don't you, Gregor?' And then he answered his own question. 'He does, you see. And he has this builder out at Penicuik who knows about that stuff, doesn't he, Gregor? Bill knows all about load-bearing walls.' And then he added, 'He's an Orangeman.'

Gregor was reassuring. 'Of course he does. He deals with load-bearing walls every day. That's what he does.'

'And he would have got the building warrant,' said Bruce. 'He'd know about that, of course.'

Gregor said nothing.

'This is the hall,' Ed announced. 'You see, Bruce? The hall. Look what Gregor's done to the floor. See it? You like it?'

Bruce looked down at the floor. 'Encaustic tiles.'

'Yes,' said Gregor. 'I designed the pattern myself. You get these designs in a lot of houses on this side of town. The Victorians loved these floors. They thought of them as mosaics – which in a sense they are.'

'Seriously brilliant,' said Ed. 'Now let me show you the staircase.'

They climbed the stairs, which had already been carpeted. Gregor pointed out the brass stair rods. 'Those are not repro. Those are the real thing – Victorian stair rods.'

'Dead gen,' said Ed. 'We had them in our house in Crieff. They'd been there since the house was built. Way back. 1875.'

'I remember your place,' said Bruce. 'I remember going there after school every Friday. Remember? You had those tartan carpets. All the way through the house.'

Gregor made a face.

'You've got unresolved issues with tartan carpets, Gregor?' Ed challenged.

Gregor shook his head. 'If that's what you like, they're fine. *Chacun à son goût.*'

'But you personally?' Ed pressed. 'You think that people who have tartan carpets . . .'

Gregor looked away. 'I wasn't saying anything about the sort of people who have tartan carpets. You're too sensitive,

Eddie. Not that people who have tartan carpets are known for their sensitivity . . .'

Ed spun round. 'What exactly are you saying?'

Gregor sighed. 'It's nothing personal. It's just that I don't do tartan carpets. Some people do. I don't. I don't do flying ducks on the wall or . . .'

Suddenly Ed reached out and grabbed the lapels of Gregor's jacket. Bruce, who was in the way of this attack, pushed the two of them apart. 'No need to fight, boys,' he said. 'We've got a house to look at.'

'I'm sorry,' said Gregor. 'I didn't mean to offend you, Ed.'

Ed glowered briefly, and then assumed a business-like manner. 'We should go upstairs,' he said, and began to lead the way up the broad, now-enclosed staircase with its Victorian stair rods and its mahogany balustrade. At the top of the staircase was a spacious hall giving access to the rooms on that level – a drawing room, a dining room, a kitchen, a bathroom, and two rooms of unspecified usage.

'You could live perfectly comfortably on this floor alone,' said Ed. 'But there are three further bedrooms up that small stair over there. Three, Bruce. And another bathroom. If you have kids, you could put them there and close the door. Or guests, if you like. There's serious room in this flat.'

Gregor took them into the drawing room. 'The *pièce de résistance*,' he said. 'Typical Victorian high ceilings. Lots of room to breathe. And the light. That's what I like about a double-upper – you get this gorgeous light. Really gorgeous.' He paused. 'This is south-facing, of course. So you get the southern light. It's great if you're facing north and you're an artist. Different light. Slightly blue, like a nineteenth-century Danish painting. This light makes me think of . . . of Tuscany. The warm south. Sun-tanned bodies completely at ease with themselves. Vine leaves rattling like dice. Warm evenings.'

Bruce looked about him. He noted the elaborate cornice, undisturbed by any nineteen-sixties or seventies experience. 'Nice,' he said.

'More than nice,' said Gregor. 'That's the original marble – at least the mantelpiece is. The hearth has a Thomas Bogie metal surround. All intact.'

He pointed to a small brass fixture beside the fireplace. 'See that?' he said. 'That's a speaking tube. It connected to the kitchen down below – just like the system you found on ships. They spoke into a tube that ended up in the engine room.'

Bruce smiled. He crossed the floor to pick up the small mouthpiece. 'Hello,' he said. 'Bridge here. Anybody down below?'

From somewhere in the depths of the house, faint from distance, came the reply. 'It's me.'

Bruce turned and stared speechlessly at Ed and Gregor.

## 30. What Tam Didn't Do

On that very first evening with Fat Bob, Big Lou felt that she had done the right thing in accepting his invitation to join him for dinner at an Indian restaurant in Leith. He had invited Finlay as well, and she had been touched by that. There were few men, she thought, whose face might not fall, even slightly, on finding out that the person whom they were inviting out was encumbered by a young child; Fat Bob's insistence that Finlay should join them on this outing had been as sincere as it was spontaneous. 'Of course he must come,' he said. 'Especially as he likes Indian food – poppadoms and so on. He can have as many of those as he likes.'

Big Lou had smiled. 'He loves poppadoms. Of course, he goes for the milder curries – most youngsters do. But Indian restaurants understand that. They usually have a children's curry somewhere on the menu – one of those dishes with plenty of yoghurt.'

Fat Bob agreed. 'A strong curry is an acquired taste, isn't it? You have to get used to it. I go for the milder curries myself, although my friend Tam can't get enough of those really hot ones ...'

'Vindaloos?'

'Yes, that's the stuff. The ones with the government health warnings. He loves those. You see the smoke coming out of his mouth.'

The meal had been a success. Fat Bob had been kind to Finlay, and the young boy had responded accordingly. Children, Big Lou knew, had an innate ability to understand when an adult was condescending to them and when they were addressing them as equals. Finlay had told Bob about his ballet lessons, and Bob had revealed that he had gone to see Scottish Ballet perform *Swan Lake* in Glasgow and had enjoyed every moment of it. 'Those people can dance,' he had said with admiration. 'Boy, can they dance!'

Finlay had asked about his career in the Highland Games, and he had told him about his first big win – a fifty-pound prize purse in the Mull Highland Games, when he had first competed against the same Tam Macgregor who so enjoyed strong curries.

'I won the caber event,' Fat Bob said. 'Tam was expected to win, as he had won at Mull the previous year, but do you know something? When I threw my winning throw, he came up to me and shook my hand. Straight away. Straight away he came up to me, and he said, "Fat Bob, that was a great toss. I'll no be able to match that, and that's the truth."'

'A true sportsman,' Big Lou observed. 'Do you hear that, Finlay? That's how a gentleman behaves when he loses. He congratulates the winner – and he means it.'

'True,' said Fat Bob. 'That's the way to do it. Tam's a good man. One of the best.'

There was something in the way he said this that gave Big Lou the impression that he was harbouring a reservation. And that was revealed on their second date – this time without Finlay, for whom Big Lou had been able to arrange a babysitter. On this occasion, they went to a bar at the west end of Princes Street before going to another Indian restaurant near Haymarket Station.

'Your friend, Tam Macgregor,' Big Lou began. 'When you were telling Finlay about him the other day ...'

'Aye?'

'I wondered if ...'

He interrupted her. 'You picked it up. Yes, there's something.'

She waited. It seemed to her that he was uncertain as to whether to reveal whatever it was. But he did.

'Tam was up in Perth Sheriff Court. Three years ago.'

Big Lou frowned. She was not sure what to say.

'He was charged with an offence he didn't commit,' said Fat Bob. 'He was innocent.'

Big Lou said nothing. Fat Bob was obviously being loyal to his friend.

'I'm not just being loyal,' he said.

She felt that he had read her thoughts. 'I wasn't going to say anything,' she said quickly.

'His brother did it,' explained Fat Bob. 'His brother, Stuart, pinched a police motorbike. It was a stupid thing to do, as the police don't like it if you pinch their motorbikes.'

'I can imagine that,' said Big Lou.

Fat Bob nodded. 'They found the motorbike at their mother's house. It was hidden in the shed, under some sacking. It was Tam, though, who confessed. He was fined three hundred pounds and given one of these payback orders. He had to wash police cars for six months.'

'But why did he confess – if his brother did it?'

'Because of their mother,' Fat Bob said. 'She has Parkinson's and relies on the brother, you see. He's the carer. If anything happened to him it would be really hard for the mother. Tam said they couldn't risk the brother being sent to prison. The police were really cheesed off, you'll understand, about their motorbike, and they may have pressed to make an example of him. Tam took the blame. Now he has the criminal record. But he's really a good man – an honest, good man.'

Big Lou thought about this. He should not have confessed to something he did not do – that was called perverting the course of justice, she thought – but she could understand why he did it.

'Did their mother know about this?'

Fat Bob shook his head. 'They managed to keep it from her. She's never found out.'

'And the brother?'

'Stuart said he felt really bad about it. He didn't want Tam to do it, but by then it was too late. Tam had made a statement to the police, and if he withdrew it, then they would be even crosser with the brother.'

Big Lou saw that. She remained puzzled, though, as to why the brother should have done something so ill-advised as to steal a police motorbike. Was it not clearly marked?

'Yes, it was,' answered Fat Bob. 'But it was in Gaelic. You know how all police vehicles now have *police* written in Gaelic on them? They had done that with this motorbike, but had run out of space, and so they just had *police* in Gaelic on it – there wasn't the space for the English translation. The brother said he didn't know what it meant.'

Big Lou raised an eyebrow. 'I find that hard to believe,' she said.

Fat Bob agreed. 'So do I. I think the brother's lying.'

'Could be,' said Big Lou. She gave the matter further thought. 'It's an odd way to make a statement,' she said. 'Bringing motorbikes into cultural politics. A bit odd, don't you think?'

'It's making up for the wrongs of the past,' said Fat Bob. 'It's all to do with what happened after the Forty-five. The attempt to obliterate Gaelic culture. Remember?'

'Yes,' said Big Lou. 'I suppose points have to be made.'

They looked at one another, each aware, at that particular moment, that they were at an historical crossroads, when the past came back and met the present. Such a realisation can come to any of us, at any time, and in any place – including in an Indian restaurant when we are looking at the menu and trying to decide which of the curries are unpalatably hot and which are not.

## 31. Garlic Naan

Over a kadai paneer with a side-dish of onion bhajis, Big Lou tactfully set out to discover more about Fat Bob. She realised that she knew virtually nothing about him – other than that he liked Indian food, that he came from a small town in Perthshire, and that during the summer he did the circuit of Highland Games, tossing the caber and throwing the hammer throughout Scotland. Was that enough to know about somebody before you allowed yourself to fall in love with him? Lou was not sure.

'Do you have brothers or sisters, Bob?' she asked as the waiter produced a bowl of Indian breads.

Bob nodded. 'Four sisters,' he said. 'Amelia, Annie, Maddy, and Ginger. All of them, apart from Ginger, are younger than I am. Ginger is two years older. Maddy is the baby of the family.'

'Where does Ginger get her name?' asked Big Lou. 'Is she a redhead?'

'Very slightly,' said Bob. 'Just a touch. Her hair's lovely – a bit like a fox's coat, you know – that sort of red.' His voice was filled with pride. *This is a man talking about his sister*, thought Big Lou.

'Pretty.'

Bob offered the bread basket to Lou before helping himself to a piece of garlic naan. 'Yes,' he said. 'Just like you.'

Big Lou caught her breath. Had he said that Ginger was pretty – just like her? Had he really said that?

She blushed in her embarrassment.

Bob reached out to put his hand upon hers. His touch only lasted for a moment, and was gentle. *The strongest of men are the gentlest of men*, she thought.

'I mean it,' he said. 'You're a very beautiful woman, Lou.'

Big Lou knew neither what to say nor where to look. She was unused to compliments, and indeed could not recall when last she had received one. She was accustomed, of course, to hearing her bacon rolls commended – and her cups of coffee, too, on the milky surface of which she often traced a trademark thistle – but a personal remark of this sort was quite different. She was not one for flattery, and would never have sought plaudits of any sort, least of all ones pertaining to her appearance. And yet to hear Bob say this was intensely pleasing, and she felt a sudden welling of affection for this well-set man with his fresh, open face and his rather old-fashioned manner; with his gentleness and his regard for his sister. She could certainly fall in love with this man, she decided – and indeed perhaps she already had.

'You're very kind,' she said. 'But you don't have to say things like that to me.'

She realised immediately that this sounded ridiculous. Of course, he did not have to say things like that – and to draw attention to the fact made her sound ungracious.

Bob was undeterred. 'I know I don't. But I want to. I want you to know what I think.'

She seized the opportunity to show her appreciation. 'It was really kind. And thank you.' Then she added, 'You're not so bad yourself.'

He smiled. 'Och, away with you. Not me. I'm …' He hesitated. Then he went on, 'I'm nothing. Not me. I'm just nothing.'

Big Lou was adamant. 'You're not nothing, Bob. You're strong.'

Once again, it was not what she intended to say. Of course he was strong. He was, after all, a professional strongman – or semi-professional – and that was what such people were: they were strong.

'I do my best,' said Bob, taking a bite of garlic naan. 'But there are guys who are stronger than I am, you know. There's this fellow in Glasgow who can pull a train. I never thought I'd see it, but I did. It was for charity – for the lifeboats, I think. He pulled a railway carriage along the length of a platform at Queen Street Station. It was in all the papers.'

Big Lou shook her head in wonderment. 'You'd think that would be impossible.'

'You would,' agreed Bob. 'But he did it. And then there's Neil Ainslie. You heard of him, Lou?'

She shook her head. 'I don't know much about these things.'

'Well, Neil could tear a telephone directory in two. I saw him do it many times. He ripped them up.'

Big Lou took a sip from the glass of mango juice the waiter had brought her. 'Amazing,' she said.

She wanted to move the conversation on, and so she asked him about Aberfeldy. Had they lived in the village itself? He explained that they had lived just outside town, on a large farm, where his father was the stockman. 'My dad never had his own farm,' he said. 'He would have loved that. Nothing big – just enough to keep some cattle and maybe grow a bit of hay, some neeps, maybe; that sort of thing. But he never had the money. Nor the land. So he worked as a stockman on this farm owned by a woman who had inherited it from her father. She was a good farmer, and she treated the people who worked for her very well. But she died. It was a tractor accident.'

Big Lou winced. 'Poor woman.'

'Yes,' said Bob. 'It was bad luck. She left the farm to her nephew in Glasgow. He drank, and he owed a lot of money. So he sold it to a man who wanted to do the whole thing himself. He gave my father his notice, and, well, he became ill. My mother said it had nothing to do with losing his job, but it was a bit of a coincidence, if you ask me. There are people who can die of disappointment, Lou. I'm sure of it.'

Big Lou agreed. 'They used to call that dying of a broken heart. It's the same thing, don't you think?'

'Yes. And it was what did it for my father, I think. I was sixteen at the time, and it was really difficult for my mother. We lived in a tied cottage on the farm. And so we had to move out. That was hard, and we ended up living in a tiny, damp flat in Perth. My mother had to scrape about to get enough money just for food, let alone anything else, so I left school and got a job so that I could contribute something to the household. We were really poor. We had nothing, you know.'

Big Lou waited for Bob to continue. 'I'm sorry,' she said. It was difficult to think of anything else one might say.

'There was no work where we were,' said Bob. 'I tried to get an apprenticeship in a panel-beating workshop, but the owner took on his nephew instead of me. I tried to get a plumbing apprenticeship. Nothing doing. So I went off to Glasgow. I was sixteen and still wet behind the ears. I had one suitcase and fourteen pounds that I had saved up. That was all. Fourteen pounds, Lou.'

'What happened, Bob?' She experienced an uncomfortable sense of foreboding. Cities beckoned to the children of farmers. They always had. The promises they made were rarely kept. But Bob smiled.

'Don't worry, Lou. Sometimes the world surprises us, don't you think? Not all outcomes are bleak; not everybody is ready to take advantage of the weak; there are good people about, Lou – there really are.'

'Yes,' said Big Lou. Bob was right; but why, she wondered, was it even necessary to say what he had said? How had cynicism, suspicion, and distrust assumed such a role in our lives? What had happened, she wondered, to trust, goodness, and courtesy?

## 32. Harry and Josephine

'I arrived at Queen Street Station in Glasgow,' said Fat Bob, 'thinking that everything would be just fine.'

Big Lou smiled. She remembered what it was like to be sixteen. You were still immortal then – just; your future was something that you would shape, and its possibilities stretched out before you.

'My mother had written to a cousin of hers,' Bob continued. 'She lived not far from the river, and my mother had asked her if I could stay with her for a few weeks while I found a job and some lodgings. She was called Cousin Josephine, I was told, and she was married to a man called Harry. Harry had a good job with a furniture company on Byers Road. They were good people, my mother said, and Harry might help me to find work. She was unwilling to ask him directly, but she was sure that he would do his best. He had been in the Navy, she said, and he was still in contact with a lot of his naval friends. He had influence.

'Their flat was above a laundrette. It was a nice enough place, I suppose. Some of those Glasgow tenements have ornamental tiles on their stair, and this was one of those. You know the sort, Lou? Those tiles with whirly designs?'

'*Art Nouveau*,' said Big Lou.

'If you say so,' said Bob, and grinned. 'Anyway, I turned

up there with my suitcase and my fourteen pounds and rang their bell. I had been excited and, as I said, quite confident when I arrived at the station, but now that was fading a bit. Now I was faced with explaining myself to people I had never met and on whom my future seemed to depend. Josephine was a relative, and might be expected to behave like one, but what about Harry? Why should Harry welcome a complete stranger into his house and be expected to help him to get a job? What could I do? I had no trade, no skills, and no real idea of what I wanted to do.

'Josephine answered the door. I'll always remember her expression when she saw me. You know how people say, *They looked at me as if I was something the cat brought in?* Do you know that expression, Lou?'

Lou nodded. 'Aye, Bob. I know that one.'

'Well, that's how she looked at me. I started to introduce myself, and she said, "I ken exactly who you are. You're Betty's boy and your name's Bob. I ken all that. And you're to stay with us for a day or two, so you'd best come in."'

'A day or two!' exclaimed Big Lou. 'Oh, Bob, what an awful start.'

'Yes, it was. I didn't say anything. I didn't correct her and say that my mother had told me that it would be a few weeks – I did not feel that I could say anything, really; I felt that anxious. But anyway, she took me to a room at the back of the flat and showed me my bed and the cupboard where I could store my clothes. Then she said that she and Harry would be having their tea in ten minutes and that I should come into the kitchen when I had unpacked my things and washed my hands.

'Harry was sitting at the kitchen table when I went in. He

was reading the paper, and when I came in, he looked up and nodded. Then he went back to his paper. Josephine pointed to a chair opposite Harry's. "We don't speak at meals," she said. "Some folk do, as you may know, but not in this house, you'll understand."

'Harry looked at me sternly, as if to underline the warning. I said the first thing that came into my mind, which was, "My ma says hello."

'Harry turned to his wife. "So his ma says hello," he said to Josephine. Then he addressed me. "You tell her hello when you see her next, will you? You tell her that Harry and Josephine say hello."

'I said that I would. I felt miserable. I had not asked to come to these people. This had all been arranged by my mother and had nothing to do with me. It would have been far better, I thought, if they had told my mother that it was inconvenient for me to come to stay with them. I could have found somewhere myself. I could have gone and asked somebody if they knew of a room to rent. That was the way that most people did things, I thought. Of course, I knew nothing of how things worked, but I thought I did. We all think that when we're sixteen, don't we?'

Big Lou frowned. 'They were very unkind. Imagine treating a wee boy like that. Just imagine it. Shame on him, Bob – shame on him.'

'Thank you, Lou. Anyway, there I was, and somehow I got through the meal without crying. Boys are told that they're not meant to cry. They still said that in those days, Lou. I think these days boys are allowed to cry, but it was different then. So I didn't cry, and I put up with it.'

'Did Harry do anything for you?' asked Big Lou. 'Did he find you a job?'

Bob laughed. 'The subject came up the following day. He asked me what I wanted to do, and I said that I would do anything. This seemed to amuse him. He said that if you wanted to get anywhere in this life you had to know what you wanted to do. He said that if you didn't know what you wanted to do, then that meant that you would never be good at anything.

'I asked him whether I might get a job in the furniture trade. He was very discouraging. He said that you needed skills to get into the furniture trade. He said that it took years to make a good French polisher or upholsterer. He said that he didn't think that I would find anything there. Then he said, "Have you thought of joining the Navy?" He said that he knew a chief petty officer who had something to do with recruiting and that he would have a word with him. I told him that I was not sure about the Navy, but he brushed my doubts aside. He said that a lot of people who signed up were unsure about it, but they quickly got used to naval life. It was a good career, he said, and they would teach you a trade if you were lucky. He said that he would speak to his friend and he was sure something could be fixed up. There would be a medical, of course, but he thought I looked strong and fit enough and that they would almost certainly take me. I should get a haircut before the interview, he said, and that he could take me to the barber the next day because he knew somebody who would cut hair half-price if you went before ten in the morning.'

Big Lou was appalled. She did not like the sound of Harry. 'Uncle Ebenezer,' she muttered.

Bob looked puzzled.

'It's a familiar story,' Big Lou explained. 'Young man has introduction to a relative. The relative tries to get him to fall down the stairs. Stevenson's *Kidnapped*.'

'Nobody tried to make me fall down the stairs,' said Bob.

'Aye, but some stairs are metaphorical,' said Big Lou. She dwelt on the word *metaphorical*, allowing its syllables room to breathe. Words need air.

Bob looked at her with growing fondness. He loved big words almost as much as he loved big women.

## 33. Sleeping Rough

Big Lou's coffee bar had been a second-hand bookstore before she bought it, and with the purchase she acquired the complete remaining stock of books. She had disposed of some of these, bestowing on charity shops multiple copies of Edward Heath's book on sailing, Delia Smith cooking tomes, stained by countless splashes and splodges, and any number of out-of-date guidebooks. Books of a more challenging nature were transferred to her flat in Canonmills, where she methodically made her way through piles of titles on philosophy, history, and theology, while making occasional sallies into nineteenth-century poetry, biography, and popular psychology. Her formal education had been limited, but now she made up for that with her voracious reading and her openness to new ideas. The autodidact always fears that the knowledge that he or she has taken such pains to acquire may prove to be pointless; Big Lou had no such concerns. She thought that the more you knew, the better, even if your mind came to be filled with irrelevant detail. Big Lou had no desire to impress anybody with the breadth of her learning: scholarship, of whatever nature, was a good in itself, she thought.

She had recently read rather a lot about life in the Royal Navy, having reached that region of her bookshelves where books on naval history were to be found. She had already read three of Patrick O'Brian's Jack Aubrey novels, and was saving up the remaining seventeen for a later date. These books were full of naval detail, and she soon learned the difference between *aloft* and *aloof* and between *astern* and *athwart*. She learned about what went on in the gunroom and the captain's cabin, about beating to quarters and bagpiping the mizzen, and about how press-gangs captured men of marine experience as well as those who had no desire to gain marine experience. She had assumed that sailors now were all volunteers, and was alarmed to hear that Bob might have been cajoled into a life at sea.

Bob sensed her concern. 'Don't worry,' he reassured her. 'I wasn't going to let myself be forced into anything. I removed myself that night.'

Big Lou was relieved. 'You ran away?'

'Yes. I went along with Harry's suggestion, trying to appear enthusiastic in case he should lock me in until such time as he could get me to the recruiting office. I waited until they had both gone to bed before I repacked my suitcase and slipped out of the flat. I tripped in the corridor, dropping my suitcase with a loud thud, and I froze where I was, in the darkness, my heart beating wildly in my chest. I thought my heartbeat alone would be enough to wake them up, but no sound came from their room, and I was able to make my escape.'

'Did you head for home?'

Bob said that he felt he could not do that. 'It would have been a real humiliation to go straight home. Remember that I had gone off because I wanted to relieve my mother of a mouth to feed – if I returned, I would have achieved nothing, and we would have been back where we started. No boy setting off on his life's journey wants to come right back with his tail between his legs.'

Big Lou said that she could understand that. But where did he go? He was alone in Glasgow, and he was only sixteen. Did he mean to sleep rough?

'That's exactly what I had in mind,' said Bob. 'I thought I might find a corner that might give me shelter somewhere. In a park, perhaps, or under a bridge. I thought that a big city like Glasgow was bound to have nooks and crannies where you could tuck yourself in. I knew that people lived on the streets – I had read about it in the papers – and I thought that I'd probably find a place to sleep if I poked about enough.

'I actually found somewhere quite quickly. I'd only been walking for half an hour or so –with no real idea of where I was going – when I found a yard behind a pub. It was the place where they stored the empty beer kegs and various other bits and pieces, but it had a small shed in a corner, and this was unlocked. It was dark, and it had a musty smell to it, but it was dry. Better than that, there were several old hessian sacks piled up in a corner, and that made a comfortable bed for me. I moved in there and then.

'When I woke up the next morning, I heard voices coming from the back of the pub. A man brought out a dustbin and a sack of rubbish. He stood in the middle of the yard and looked up at the sky, as if he was doing yoga. I held my breath. I thought that if he came into the shed I would simply push past him and run. It was not as if I was a thief, or anything like that – I was simply somebody who wanted to take advantage of an empty shed. I was not harming anybody.

'But there's the thing, Lou. A lot of the things that people want to do can't possibly cause any harm to other people, but they are still not allowed. Don't you think that's unfair? Don't you think we should let people do the things they want to do as long as they don't cause harm to any other folk? I believe that, Lou – I really do.'

Big Lou thought for a moment. 'John Stuart Mill,' she said.

Bob looked at her. He was waiting for an explanation.

'Yes. What you said is exactly what a philosopher called John Stuart Mill said. I read a book on the subject.'

'Oh yes? So, he agrees with me?'

'You could say that. It might be better, though, to say that you agree with him. He said it first, you see. And he says that the only justification for exercising power over another – in a civilised community – is to prevent harm to others.'

'He's dead right, Lou. This John Stuart ... What's the boy's name? He was dead right, I think.'

Big Lou smiled. 'John Stuart Mill. Well, there you are, Bob. Sometimes we do philosophy without knowing it, if you see what I mean.'

Bob held up his hands. 'I'm no philosopher, Lou. I'm an ordinary working man.'

'Anybody can be a philosopher, Bob. You, me . . . anybody.'

He made a self-deprecating gesture. 'Not me, Lou. I haven't had the education.'

She wanted to say to him: never, ever sell yourself short. You can think just as clearly as any of them. And what is philosophy but common sense? Hadn't there been a Scottish school of common-sense philosophy? Surely that would embrace people just like Bob? But there was so much we *could* tell people that we can't tell them. That is what she thought.

'What happened next?'

'I'll tell you, Lou,' he said. 'I'll tell you.'

## 34. Bertie's Outing

Nicola was determined that Bertie's last day in Edinburgh before his three months in Aberdeen would be as enjoyable and memorable as she could make it. She had arranged for Ulysses to spend the day at a high-security nursery so that she could devote her full attention to Bertie, and to this end she had booked him into the Stockbridge Advanced Infancy Experience (High Security), a child-care centre for challenging under-threes. Two programmes were available – Normal Advanced and Gifted Advanced, with all but one or two of the children being booked into the latter. Nicola had no time for parental pushiness and had arranged for Ulysses to spend the day in the Normal Advanced programme. She had read the centre's syllabus with some amusement. 'Our aim,' it had stated, 'is to provide a stimulating and supportive environment for your child. We are acutely aware that your future doctor or lawyer will need every encouragement to meet the exacting intellectual standards of their professional futures. Those futures start now.'

Bertie had chosen a visit to Valvona & Crolla's delicatessen and restaurant. After that, he said, they might go on to the National Museum on Chambers Street.

'Two very good choices, Bertie,' said Nicola.

'And I'd like Ranald Braveheart Macpherson to come with us,' added Bertie. 'He's my friend, you see.'

Nicola smiled. 'I know that, Bertie. I know that Ranald is very important to you.' She paused. 'And I imagine you'll miss him badly.'

Bertie lowered his eyes, making Nicola immediately regret what she had said.

'Of course, three months will be over in a flash,' she gushed. 'And before you know it, you'll be back in Edinburgh. You and Ranald will be reunited again, and you'll have so much to tell him about all your adventures in Aberdeen.'

Bertie was unconvinced. 'Ranald may have another friend when I come back,' he said. 'He's bound to forget me.'

'Oh, I don't think so,' said Nicola breezily. She wanted to sound as cheerful as possible, although she knew that what he said might prove to be true. Children were notoriously fickle in their friendships; we all remembered the pain we experienced when the friends of childhood found others to divert them. For many of us, it was our first experience of disloyalty, and, like all first experiences, not easily forgotten.

Bertie did not share Nicola's optimism. In Olive's crowing, he had already had some warning of the shoals that lay ahead.

'When you go away to Aberdeen, Bertie,' she had intoned, 'you're going to lose all your friends. That's one-hundred-per-cent definite. You know that, don't you?'

Pansy had agreed. 'Olive's right, Bertie. People who go to Aberdeen never hear from their friends again. That's a well-known fact. I read about it on Wikipedia.'

Bertie doubted that. 'But you can't read yet, Pansy,' he pointed out mildly.

Olive papered over this crack in her lieutenant's credibility. 'Mind you,' she continued. 'You don't have all that many friends anyway, do you Bertie? Perhaps you won't notice it so much.'

Pansy nodded. 'That's true,' she said. 'There's always Ranald, though.'

'Hah!' exclaimed Olive. 'Ranald Braveheart Macpherson. Him indeed. I can tell you that Ranald is already advertising online for new friends. I imagine he's probably already deleted you from his list of contacts. In fact, I'm sure he has.'

'I feel sorry for you, Bertie,' said Pansy. 'It's no fun being deleted.'

But now, doubts as to Ranald's loyalty put to one side, Bertie was on his way with his grandmother and his friend to Valvona & Crolla's delicatessen at the head of Leith Walk. As they made their way, Nicola tried to ensure that the conversation was as cheerful as possible, avoiding all reference to

Aberdeen, journeys, cold, or the North Sea, gamely making upbeat comments about how time flew and how easy it was to communicate with friends in the electronic age.

'People used to use pigeons,' she said, 'to send messages to one another. Can you believe that, boys? Pigeons with messages tied around their legs.'

Ranald and Bertie remained silent.

'Pigeons have an inbuilt sense of direction,' Nicola continued. 'They can always find their way home. It's quite miraculous.'

'Not really,' said Bertie, glumly.

'But it is, Bertie!' Nicola persisted. 'You or I would never be able to find our way home if . . .' She stopped herself. This was not the direction in which she wanted the conversation to go.

'They use the stars,' said Bertie flatly. 'They may also use energy fields that we can't see, Granny.'

Nicola raised an eyebrow. She was constantly finding herself astonished at the things that Bertie seemed to have picked up. He at least was well-informed; Ranald Braveheart Macpherson, by contrast, seemed to know rather less.

'Well, fancy that,' she said.

'Birds know more than we think they do,' Bertie went on. 'They may have very small heads, but their brains are quite clever.'

Ranald Braveheart Macpherson seemed surprised. 'Do birds have brains?' he asked. 'Just like us?'

'Yes,' said Bertie. 'Everything has a brain, Ranald.'

'Even a worm?'

Bertie nodded. 'They have tiny brains that have three hundred and two cells. We have billions.'

Ranald whistled. 'Even Larch?'

Larch was a boy at school not noted for his intellectual sophistication.

'Even Larch,' said Bertie.

'And Olive?' Ranald asked, a certain yearning in his voice. He very much hoped that Olive and Pansy might be revealed to have fewer brain cells, but Bertie had to tell him that even the two girls, long their heartless persecutors, had the same number of brain cells as they did.

'That's a pity,' said Ranald.

Nicola smiled indulgently. 'There's no difference between boys and girls,' she said.

Bertie looked at her. This was further evidence, he thought, of his grandmother's cognitive decline: everyone, possibly even Ulysses, knew that there was an important difference between boys and girls; one could hardly miss it, not that one should stare. How could anybody be unaware of that? He looked away. It was sad, really, that by the time he returned from Aberdeen it might be too late. She might have only a few weeks left, if she was saying things like that. That was another reason for him not to go – so that he might spend more time with his grandmother in her declining months.

His thoughts were interrupted by their arrival at Valvona & Crolla. The sight of the gastronomic mecca, home of all things warm, Italian, and tasty, helped him momentarily to forget Aberdeen and the three months of exile that lay ahead, a cloud no bigger than a man's hand, but imminent now, and almost upon him.

## 35. Bertie's Farewell to Ranald

Ranald Braveheart Macpherson had never stepped inside Valvona & Crolla before and was wide-eyed with wonder as they crossed the threshold of the famous Edinburgh delicatessen.

'Can you eat all of these things?' Ranald asked, his gaze moving from the shelves stacked with pastas, via the stacked wedges and circles of cheese and the bowls of bright peppers, to the hams and salamis hanging up behind the counter.

Bertie, who had regularly accompanied his mother on forays to the shop, was on familiar ground. 'You can eat all of these things, Ranald. And they're very tasty – I can tell you.'

Nicola pointed to the boxes of Panforte di Siena on a low shelf behind them. 'That's Bertie's absolute favourite over there,' she said. 'Panforte di Siena. It's a sort of flat cake.'

'Full of fruit, Ranald,' said Bertie. 'Orange peel and raisins and things like that. You'd like it, I think.'

Ranald Braveheart Macpherson had started to salivate. A small trail of saliva ran down from his lower lip, dribbled over his chin, and fell in a tiny drop on the front of his shirt. Noticing this, Nicola extracted a handkerchief from her pocket and dabbed at Ranald's chin.

Bertie looked at his friend with sympathy. 'I know how

you feel, Ranald. I know that you don't get much nice food at home.'

'Bertie!' exclaimed Nicola reproachfully. 'I'm sure that's not true.'

'But it is, Mrs Pollock,' said Ranald. 'My mother's not a very good cook. She drinks, you see. She drinks wine when she's meant to be cooking, and she gets the ingredients wrong. She doesn't mean to, but she does.'

'That's rotten luck, Ranald,' said Bertie. 'Having a drunkard for a mother.'

'I know,' said Ranald. 'We're both jolly unlucky, aren't we? My mummy's a drunkard, and yours is a well-known hate figure. We've both had bad luck, I think.'

Nicola glanced around them. 'Now, boys, you mustn't talk like that. Ranald, I'm sure that your mother only has the occasional glass of wine. There's nothing wrong with that.'

'Oh, no,' said Ranald. 'She drinks far more than that, Mrs Pollock.'

'And Ranald's father was had up in court,' said Bertie. 'Tell my granny about that, Ranald.'

Before Nicola could stop him, Ranald started to explain about his father's prosecution, for a technical company law offence, and the resultant community payback order that had been imposed on him at Edinburgh Sheriff Court. 'He has to do over one hundred hours of Scottish country dancing,' Ranald said. 'He hates it.'

'He shouldn't have been a crook then, Ranald,' said Bertie, helpfully.

'No,' said Ranald. 'You're right, Bertie.'

Bertie remembered something else. 'And now he's planning to overthrow the British Government, isn't he, Ranald?'

Ranald Braveheart Macpherson nodded. 'My daddy wants Scotland to rise up,' he explained to Nicola. 'He thinks the rising might start in Morningside and then spread to Fairmilehead. He says there are lots of people in the area who are ready to rise up.'

'Goodness me,' said Nicola.

'He and some friends tried to raise a standard in Morningside Road,' Ranald continued. 'But the traffic wardens came and moved them on.'

Nicola suppressed a smile. 'I see,' she said.

'He says the French will come to Scotland's aid,' Ranald continued. 'He says that they will definitely send ships.'

'That's interesting,' said Nicola. 'I'm not sure if Scotland can count on the French. That was one of the problems that Bonnie Prince Charlie had, I think.'

Ranald remained confident. 'The English will run away when the French come,' he said. 'My dad says he has heard this from the man who cuts his hair. He knows all these things. I've heard him – he cuts my hair too. He's one of the people who will rise up, my dad says.'

'Very interesting,' said Nicola. 'We shall have to watch this space, as they say. In the meantime, I think we should buy some olive oil and some Panforte di Siena. Then we can go through to the restaurant, and you boys can have some special Italian ice cream, and I shall have a cup of coffee.'

Their purchases made, they made their way into the restaurant at the back of the delicatessen and sat down at one of the tables. A waitress appeared and took their order for ice cream (three flavours) and a *latte* for Nicola. Bertie placed the order in perfect Italian, much to the delight of the waitress, who pinched his cheek, kissed him on the top of his head, and patted his wrist in admiration. Then she kissed him again on the forehead, ruffled his hair, and exclaimed, *Accidenti, è carinissimo!*

Bertie blushed red with embarrassment as the waitress left him to make her way back to the kitchen.

'The Italians are a very demonstrative people,' said Nicola. 'They're tactile, Bertie – which means they like to touch things. The important thing is that they mean well.'

After their visit to Valvona & Crolla, Nicola took them, as promised, to the Chambers Street museum, where they spent an hour or so in the machinery department, marvelling at the vehicles and the antiquated rockets. They saw an instrument for the administration of chloroform and a Van de Graaff generator. They saw a model of the workings of a coal mine, with a tiny cage in which men, minute painted dolls, their faces darkened with coal dust, were poised to descend into the depths. Nicola gazed at this, while the boys moved on to another exhibit. She thought, *There were so many stunted lives.* She saw a picture of a Highland blackhouse, a windowless but and ben, outside which the members of a family were standing, and she thought of the Clearances and all the sorrow of life in Scotland. And then she thought: perhaps that is what one should think in a museum, and one should not be surprised to feel that way.

Then they caught a bus that took them to Morningside, where Ranald Braveheart Macpherson lived. On the doorstep of Ranald's house, Bertie said goodbye to his friend. Nicola, sensing the importance of the moment, stepped to the side, pretending to admire a fuchsia in the Macpherson garden, while Bertie spoke to Ranald.

'I hope that you come back, Bertie,' said Ranald, grasping Bertie's hand in a handshake.

'I'm sure I shall, Ranald,' said Bertie, not with any real conviction.

There was a silence. Then Bertie turned and began to walk down the path. He stopped. He looked back at Ranald Braveheart Macpherson, standing there on his doorstep with his spindly legs.

Bertie looked up at the sky. It was blue and empty. He raised a hand to wave, and Ranald Braveheart Macpherson, his friend, his only true friend, did the same. Nicola watched. She struggled with the tears that were just below the surface; a struggle that most of us have, when one comes to think of it, most of the time.

## 36. Retro's In

When Bruce heard the unexpected voice at the other end of the speaking tube, he gazed in astonishment at Ed and Gregor, who seemed to share his surprise. For a moment, Bruce entertained the possibility, absurd thought though it was, that he had fallen into a time warp. Time warps were a regular hazard in television dramas, and Bruce, being a follower of at least one of these, was able to believe in the possibility of slipping back a few years, or centuries – at least for an hour or so. He had read, too, of physicists who suggested that such ideas were not entirely fanciful. According to them, our present world could well exist just a hair's breadth away from a completely different dimension from which we were separated by wormholes and a few unintelligible mathematical equations. Such theories were taken seriously, Bruce believed, along with other ideas about space and time that most of us found impossible even to envisage, let alone to understand.

Had he somehow slipped into that other dimension a century or so ago, when in this very house a kitchen maid on duty in the nether regions of the building might pick up the speaking tube and reply to a request for a tray of tea for the drawing room? Of course not, he thought, as he stared at the tube in his hand and wondered whether he should say something more – just in case he had imagined the whole thing. But he could not have imagined it, he decided, because Ed and Gregor had obviously heard it too, and the whole point about auditory hallucinations was that you heard them when nobody else did.

Then Ed laughed. 'Give me the tube,' he said.

Bruce handed him the instrument warily. 'There's somebody there,' he said. 'I heard ...'

'Of course there's somebody there,' said Ed, giving him a condescending look. 'You don't get voices coming out of nowhere.'

And then, raising his voice, Ed bellowed down the tube, 'Is that you, Katie?'

A compressed voice came back up the tube. 'No need to shout, Ed. I can hear you perfectly well. Who was that?'

Ed was enjoying Bruce's surprise. 'That was Bruce,' he replied. 'He's my surveyor friend. Remember?'

'Oh yes,' came the reply.

'What are you doing in the kitchen?' asked Ed.

'Checking on something. I've just arrived.'

'See you up here, then,' said Ed, putting the speaking tube back in its place. Then, turning to Bruce, he said, 'That's going to be a feature in the sale, you know. How often do you see that in a set of sale particulars? "Speaking tube in good condition." That's the business. People like things like that. Original features, see? Lots of places have had them ripped out.'

Greg now expressed a view. 'Retro,' he said. 'That's what people are yearning for. They want retro. E.g. speaking tubes.' He paused. 'Retro is now, Bruce. Right now.'

'Greg's right,' said Ed. 'This city is full of retro people. It's a real magnet for them. Take the New Town, for instance. There are people down there – people like you, Bruce, no offence – who lead an entirely retro life. They live in Georgian flats. Their furniture is in period, or as close as they can get to period. They'd drive around in carriages if they had somewhere to keep the horses.'

Greg liked that. 'Yes. Spot on, Ed. And they pay for retro style. They don't want modern.'

'Who wants modern?' asked Ed.

Bruce thought of his shower, with its power features. He thought of his Italian coffee machine – gleamingly modern. He thought of the robot vacuum cleaner he had recently bought and of how it sensed where the chair legs were and successfully worked its way around such obstacles. He felt slightly embarrassed by his taste for these modern conveniences. Had he missed the zeitgeist so completely?

But there were more pressing questions. 'So, who's this Katie?' he asked.

'She's the person who works for the lawyers,' said Ed. 'She's the one who'll be showing people round this place. She has keys.'

Greg took up the explanation. 'They're the selling agents. They're acting for me as owner and developer. She's in their conveyancing department. She's my friend.' He paused. 'She's in on our ... our plan.'

'Greg was at school with her,' Ed remarked. 'Like I was at school with you, Bruce. Big pals.'

Greg looked out of the window. 'She used to be engaged to a guy called Laurence. It's over now. He was bad news. He was a lawyer. He used to criticise her all the time.'

Ed confirmed this. 'Yes, I heard him. He kept telling her that she was wearing the wrong things. He even laughed at the way she pronounced certain words. She came from somewhere in Fife, didn't she, Greg?'

'Yes. Kirkcaldy, I think. He came from Barnton. He had airs. He thought himself superior. I couldn't stand him. I wanted to punch him. You know the feeling, Bruce? There are some people you just want to punch in the gob.'

Bruce nodded. 'Like that guy at Morrison's. Remember him, Ed? The one who clyped on Danny Fairgrieve when he put purple dye in the swimming pool?'

'Yes,' said Ed. 'Him. He shouldn't have clyped. They almost suspended Danny. It was that close.'

'The dye did nobody any harm,' said Bruce.

'It made that girl purple, though,' Ed admitted.

'She deserved it. Catriona Hodge. You know she married a guy who owned a garage in Perth? He had had really bad skin, and you could still tell, you see. I think she felt sorry for him.'

'You forget about teenage skin issues,' Greg mused. 'I never suffered from them. I was lucky. But there was this boy in my class who had those issues, and he was so embarrassed, poor guy. He avoided eye contact for years. Then you know what? He got some pills that fixed his skin, and he went on to do engineering in Glasgow.'

'What sort of engineering?' asked Ed.

'Mechanical. He was a serious petrol-head, and he ended up getting the job he always wanted. He's a design engineer for one of those Formula One teams down near Oxford. No, seriously, that's what he does. They're always fiddling with those cars. They have whole teams of engineers. It's big money.'

'It's a stupid pastime,' said Ed. 'Those cars go round at two hundred miles an hour. You can't see who's where. Then it's all over.'

'And not one of those drivers,' said Greg, 'is in touch with his feminine side.'

Bruce looked at him, but Greg just laughed. 'You don't want to take yourself too seriously, Bruce,' he said, and added, 'Ever heard of irony?'

## 37. Bruce Snubbed

Bruce turned round to see Katie coming into the room. He saw a young woman in her mid-twenties, perhaps, with auburn hair swept back under an Alice band. She was tall – slightly taller than Ed, although Bruce still had a few inches on her. She was wearing a white linen blouse and black jeans. Her appearance and bearing suggested calm and confidence.

Bruce fingered the cuffs of his jacket. It was a mannerism that affected him when he felt anxious. Why should he feel that way now? He was not sure. This young woman was attractive enough, but he was often surrounded by attractive young women – that was his regular lot. *I can't help all that,* he sometimes said to himself; *bees go to pollen, don't they? Some things just are.* So, why do I feel ill at ease meeting this Katie?

Ed introduced Bruce. 'You two have spoken on the tube,' he said, and laughed.

Katie glanced at Bruce, and then quickly transferred her gaze to Gregor.

*Excuse me*, thought Bruce. *No point barking up the wrong tree.*

'Hi, Greg,' she said.

'Hi, sweetie,' replied Greg.

*Hi, sweetie!* thought Bruce. How *cheesy!*

'How's things?' Katie continued, still addressing Gregor.

'*Comme ci, comme ça,*' Gregor replied. 'Actually, not too bad – all things considered. I went to the dentist yesterday.'

'Oh, poor you,' said Katie. 'I hope it wasn't sore.'

*Oh really!* thought Bruce.

'I'm a bit of a wimp. I go for the injection the moment I sit down in the dentist's chair.'

'I don't mind a bit of pain,' interjected Bruce. 'It doesn't last long.'

Katie threw him a quick, dismissive glance and then turned back to Gregor. 'There's no shame in asking for a local anaesthetic,' she said. 'And besides, injections are like quiche, you know.'

Bruce smarted. He had detected a note of contempt in her voice, and he was not at all sure what she meant in comparing injections to quiche. What a ridiculous thing to say. Was she trying to be clever? Who did she think she was? She was *nobody*. He had never seen her in any of the places in town that counted. Never.

Ed moved about impatiently. 'We need to get down to business,' he said. 'What's the situation, Katie?'

Katie had been carrying a small attaché case. Now she opened this and extracted a piece of paper. 'I've done twelve viewings over the last two days,' she said. 'There's really strong interest in this flat.'

'Good,' said Ed. 'That's exactly what we expected – and wanted.'

'You only need one offer,' Bruce pointed out. 'When I was in practice, that's what I said to sellers: "You only need one offer." Land that offer and the place is sold.'

Katie looked at him almost pityingly. 'I don't agree,' she

said. 'In fact, I can't think of anybody who would agree with that these days. You need competition to get the price up.'

Bruce seethed. He did not like being corrected by this rather superior young woman – he was a surveyor, after all, and she was ... what was she? A paralegal at best.

'Excuse me,' he said. 'I've bought and sold rather a lot of properties in the past. And I can tell you: you only need one good offer.'

'One *good* offer,' said Katie. 'But what if it's not that good? Oh yes, you only need one buyer if you are to get rid of a property, but it may not be the result you want. Sellers want a good price – and a single offer doesn't always have the right sum attached.' She looked at him in a challenging way. 'See? That's how it works.'

Bruce struggled to control himself. 'I know all that,' he said, from between pursed lips. 'I wasn't born yesterday.' What was wrong with this woman? Why had she taken against him in this way? It was probably resentment, he decided: people resented what they did not have. She wanted him to notice her, and evidently he had not done so markedly enough. Her behaviour, then, was a cry for attention – that was it. It was as simple as that. Well, that was easily enough remedied.

He smiled at her. 'You know a lot,' he said. 'And those jeans ...' He rolled his eyes.

She stared at him briefly, and then looked pointedly away, addressing Ed now. 'We've had seven notes of interest, Ed. Seven is pretty good, bearing in mind it's only been on the market for three days.'

This information pleased Gregor. 'Supply and demand,' he said. 'There aren't enough double-uppers available. And some of them are going on the private market. They're not even advertised.'

'You're quite right,' said Katie, glancing at Bruce as she spoke, as if to suggest that at least somebody knew what he was talking about.

Bruce seethed – again.

Ed did not appear to notice the undercurrents. 'So,' he said briskly, 'seven notes of interest. Good. Who are they?'

Katie passed Ed a piece of paper. 'Here we are,' she said. 'I've shown all of these people around. One of them came to see it twice.'

'Keen,' said Ed.

'It was two people together, actually. Two women.'

Ed waited. 'Buying together?'

'I think so,' Katie said. 'They were going on about what they'd do to the place. There was a lot of discussion.' She paused. 'Those people will be serious bidders. You can always tell.'

'Good,' said Ed. 'So, this is what we'll do. Let's set a closing date for offers. Next Friday at twelve. Agreed?'

Gregor nodded. 'It's the usual time.'

'The offers will come in to your firm,' Ed continued. 'By email, right? PDFs?'

Katie nodded. 'I get them. I usually pass them on to my boss. He always has lunch on a Friday at Mortonhall Golf Club. He doesn't get back until three. That's when he looks at them.'

'That gives us three hours,' said Ed. 'Just before twelve you identify the highest bid. You pass on the info to Bruce here, who puts in a bid that's twenty grand higher. Then you go back to the original highest offer and tell them they're going to have to up things or they'll be the under-bidder.'

'We can probably drive the thing up by fifty grand,' said Gregor.

Ed agreed. 'At least.' He turned to Bruce. 'Katie's boss has no reason to suspect anything. He comes back from lunch and sees an increased offer from one of the bidders, but won't know that it's come in after twelve or that it's higher because they heard what you had offered. So, if anybody suspects anything, it all looks dead gen. And nobody can pin anything on Katie.'

'Nor on you and Gregor?' said Bruce.

'Exactly. The trail stops dead and nobody would be able to prove anything.'

'Convenient,' said Bruce, adding, 'For you.'

'Well, yes,' said Ed. 'But you get a cut, Bruce. We all benefit.' He paused. 'It's good to co-operate, remember. It's called enlightened self-interest.'

Gregor smiled. 'We are *very* enlightened,' he said archly, winking at Katie, who responded with a coquettish giggle, cutting Bruce dead where he stood in his tracks.

## 38. In the Elephant House

Bruce was not in a good mood as he made his way back to his flat on foot. He drew a couple of admiring glances while crossing the Meadows, one from an earnest-looking young woman on a bicycle, who swerved, but made a quick recovery, and another, more wistful perhaps, from a matron walking a rheumatic schnauzer. Bruce ignored these shy tributes – there was nothing unusual in them, but he was not in the mood to enjoy the attention. On George IV Bridge, as he walked past the Elephant House, the café where he occasionally met a friend who lived nearby, he noticed his reflection in the window and stopped, through ancient habit, for a brief moment of self-admiration. What he saw reassured him and put Katie's rebuff in its proper place: the problem was hers, not his. Her antipathy, he decided, spoke not to any defect on his part, but to ... well, it could only have been frustration on hers.

Poor girl: she was to be understood and forgiven rather than disliked, and that was what he would do. He would forgive her, which made him the moral victor in that brief and rather distasteful encounter – and the psychological victor, too: Bruce had always found that forgiving somebody who slighted him resulted in the most delicious feeling of superiority. Poor girl, he thought; how sad.

On impulse, he decided to go into the café for a cup of coffee and a piece of cake. His light breakfast, of a boiled egg and smoked salmon, had left him hungry, and although it was too early for lunch, Bruce felt that a mid-morning snack was justified. He rather liked the Elephant House, which was a bustling place popular with students and literary tourists. Occasionally there would be queues, but he saw that there was none now, and within a few minutes, with a steaming cup of coffee in one hand and a plate in the other, he made his way to a table near one of the large rear windows.

There was a newspaper on a nearby table, and Bruce paged through this while he waited for his coffee to cool. He began to read a report on a potential volcanic eruption in Iceland, and was barely halfway through this when he became aware that somebody was approaching his table.

'So this is another of your haunts,' said a familiar voice.

He looked up. It was Sister Maria-Fiore dei Fiori di Montagna, whom Bruce knew from an occasional meeting in Big Lou's coffee bar or in the natural food store in Broughton Street. He had seen the nun shopping for lentils and dried beans there on more than one occasion, and they had exchanged snippets of conversation.

Bruce set aside the newspaper. 'Sometimes,' he said. 'I haven't been here for ages, though.'

'The places we go to infrequently are more frequently in our minds than those to which we go more regularly,' said Sister Maria-Fiore. 'The tracks of the heart are not always well-trodden.'

The nun sat down. Bruce felt a momentary irritation that she did not ask his permission: one did not sit down at another's table in a café without at least some enquiry as to whether one's presence might be welcomed. He almost said, *Please sit down*, in a pointed tone, but stopped himself. It was ill-mannered to be rude to nuns.

'I have been in the library,' said Sister Maria-Fiore dei Fiori di Montagna. 'I needed to do some reading for a trustees' meeting tomorrow at the National Gallery.'

In the course of her meteoric rise in the higher reaches of

Edinburgh society, the nun had been appointed to the Board of Trustees of the National Gallery, where she had quickly made her mark as a conscientious board member, always ready to deliver an aphorism that might clarify the debate. She also had proved to be a useful mediator, somehow managing to bridge the gap between differing opinions in such a way that neither side felt either humiliated or triumphant. 'A decision that we both think is our own idea is always best,' she observed. 'Two snails do not argue about whose shell is the more attractive.' The relevance of this latter observation may not be immediately apparent, but it brought nods of agreement from all sides of what had been, until then, a divided table.

Recently there had been intense discussion by the board of a plan to lower the paintings on the gallery's walls in order to make them more readily accessible to people from cities where the average height was on the low side. Sister Maria-Fiore dei Fiori di Montagna found the discussion fascinating. Rarely had she witnessed, outside Italy, a discussion as heated as the one that followed a committee recommendation that the paintings be lowered by four inches. Not only had a raw nerve been touched by this proposal – an entire nervous system had gone into spasm.

The plan had been condemned as tactless at best, and outrageous at worst. 'You know who will think it's aimed at them?' said one opponent. 'They'll think this a typical bit of Edinburgh arrogance. This is the most offensive plan anyone could imagine.'

That view met with some support, but a few voices were raised against it. 'Nobody said anything about the Weeg …

I mean, the Glaswegians,' said one member. 'This is emphatically not aimed at them.'

This brought silence, followed by a few embarrassed groans. 'You can't say that sort of thing,' said a voice from the end of the table.

'Even if it's true?' asked the maker of the original comment.

'But it isn't true.'

'Why can't one take account of the evidence of one's own eyes? Why is that unacceptable?'

There was sigh. 'Because it doesn't help to draw attention to stature issues. It shows a lack of respect. And anyway, where's the hard evidence?'

'There's plenty of evidence. Urban Scotland has big problems. Life expectancy figures tell the story. Poor diet, smoking, damp housing, chronic unemployment, drug abuse: these are all pieces of the whole tragic picture.'

'And whose fault is all that? Who deindustrialised Glasgow, may I ask? Answer me that.'

And so the debate continued until Sister Maria-Fiore dei Fiori di Montagna caught the chairman's eye. 'May I suggest a compromise?' she said. 'If there are indeed dear brothers and sisters who might find themselves craning their necks to see the paintings, then why don't we have a supply of elevator shoes at the entrance that people can put on for the purpose of their visit? The shoes can then be returned at the end of the visit.'

There was complete silence in the room. Sister Maria-Fiore smiled benignly as she looked around the table at her fellow trustees. Then she said, 'The idea occurred to me when I thought of Poussin's painting of blind Orion searching for the rising sun with Cedalion, the servant, perched on his shoulders, showing him the way.'

There was a further silence.

'Dear Poussin,' she mused.

## 39. The Omnipresence of Hierarchy

Now, sharing a table with Bruce in the Elephant House, with the light falling in shafts, butter-yellow and thick, through the windows, Sister Maria-Fiore dei Fiori di Montagna took a sip of her coffee and exhaled with pleasure.

'When I drink a good cup of coffee,' she said, 'I am always reminded of dear Sister Angela of Charity. She was one of the cooking nuns in our order back home in Tuscany. We used to call her Sister Angela of the Medium Roast, because that was the sort of coffee she preferred to make. She made such a delicious *latte*. I can still both smell and taste it when I close my eyes.'

In spite of himself, Bruce was being drawn into Sister Maria-Fiore's conversation. 'Cooking nuns? Is that all they did?'

'And other domestic chores,' said Sister Maria-Fiore. 'The order was a bit old-fashioned, you might say. We had the nuns whose main job it was to deal with our dear, deluded patients – the ones who had been affected by Stendhal syndrome. And then we had the nuns who did the cooking. They were mostly – indeed entirely, as I recollect – women from very ordinary backgrounds: the daughters of small farmers, for example – what we call the *contadini* – or from working-class parts of Milan and Turin: the daughters of men who laboured in factories of one sort or another. All postulants were divided into two groups on their third day with the order. All were invited to have lunch with the Mother Superior, who set them a simple test by laying each place at the table with five or six knives and forks and then asking what it was about Dante that most appealed to them. Those who failed the test – who had no idea how to deal with the cutlery, or who were not too sure who Dante was – would be allocated to the cooking stream, as we called it. Dear limited ones – even if they managed that first hurdle, there would be other tests down the line that could separate the wheat from the chaff, so to speak. And by and large, the system worked. People found their niche.'

Bruce raised an eyebrow. 'Rather hierarchical, surely?'

Sister Maria-Fiore dei Fiori di Montagna replied calmly. 'Hierarchies are everywhere, Bruce. They are to be found in the natural world as much as the human world. Be under no illusion about that.'

'But still, I would have thought . . .'

She cut him short. 'Even amongst angels there are hierarchies – very complicated ones, too. There is no Presbyterianism in the ranks of angels, I can assure you!'

'Well, I imagine . . .'

He did not finish.

'We are so fortunate to have had Pseudo-Dionysius,' said

Sister Maria-Fiore dei Fiori di Montagna. 'I can't imagine where we would have been without him.'

'No,' said Bruce.

'It's a great pity that his *De Coelesti Hierarchia* is not more readily available,' she went on. 'It really is most helpful when it comes to sorting out the exact order of precedence. I have a little *aide-memoire*, of course, which sets out the various angelic ranks, but there are plenty of people who don't have that.'

Bruce decided to let this all flow over him. Every conversation that he had had in the past with this extraordinary woman had been largely one-sided – it was too late to change that now. 'You're most fortunate,' he said.

'Yes. There are Seraphim, Cherubim and Thrones at the apex. Seraphim, you may recall, have six wings. That's how I remember them.'

'Rather like those more expensive drones?' Bruce ventured.

Sister Maria-Fiore nodded. 'You could say that, yes. Cherubim, by contrast, have two sets of wings. Not two wings – that's a common mistake – two *sets* of wings.'

Bruce nodded.

'And the Thrones. They represent humility and submission, while Dominions, another order of angels, have a sort of administrative role. At least, that's the way I look at it. They are the civil servants, so to speak. Just like people who work for the Scottish Government down at Victoria Quay, although the Scottish Government doesn't use quite the same terminology, I believe.'

'I believe not,' said Bruce, patiently.

'Indeed. Sometimes, I expect it overlaps. So Principalities, for instance, who are lower down in the pecking order perform, I suspect, some of the tasks that Dominions undertake. They are more accessible to us, though – they understand our language, so to speak.' She paused. 'And then we have the ordinary angels – the foot soldiers of the heavenly choirs. These are the ones who watch over the likes of you and me, Bruce – who offer their assistance in difficult times.'

She took another sip of coffee. 'Enough of angels, Bruce. I must let you into a little secret.'

Bruce was encouraging. 'I can't resist a secret, Sister Maria-Fiore.'

'I'm sure you can't. Who can? Our secrets are the truths we dare not reveal; and the secrets we dare not reveal are the truth.'

Bruce was still thinking about this when Sister Maria-Fiore dei Fiori di Montagna leaned forward and whispered, 'Antonia and I have found a delightful flat in the Grange. We have decided to buy it.'

Bruce caught his breath.

'And we have so many plans for it,' the nun continued. 'I've already ordered some curtain material and shall make the curtains myself. I learned stitching from Sister Perdita. We used to call her Sister Perdita of the Threads – such a suitable name, that she loved, actually. We never chose a hurtful name for any of the sisters, you know – we always spoke with charity.'

Bruce was silent. It was a terrible, unanticipated coincidence. He hardly dared ask her where the flat was, as he dreaded the answer she would give him, but he steeled himself and asked the question. He was proved right.

*I am about to defraud a nun*, he said to himself.

'I don't know whether you have experienced this yourself,' Sister Maria-Fiore continued, 'but there is a particular sense of contentment in finding just the right place for oneself. It's a sort of homecoming, I think. You have been on a long journey, and then you find yourself in the place that you know is just right for you. You have come home. You know it. You feel that there simply cannot be another place for you – that this is it.'

He heard, with a sinking heart, how this double-upper flat in the Grange was, for Sister Maria-Fiore, that place – that haven in an unsettled and sometimes trying world.

'Are you certain?' was all that he could think of saying.

And she replied. 'I am completely certain, Bruce.'

He hesitated, but then said, 'Of course, you realise in our system that you might not get the property. There may be others who will put in higher bids.'

'Impossible,' said Sister Maria-Fiore. 'We have funds at our disposal. There are my modest assets and Antonia's slightly larger resources. We are in a very good position to buy this house which, *Deo volente*, we are assured of getting.'

She added, 'If you want a house, Bruce, then you can be sure that the house wants you.'

And with that she finished her coffee, wiped her lips, and smiled a smile of serene confidence.

## 40. Poppadoms and Theology

As the onion bhajis were consumed and the pile of poppadoms steadily lowered, Fat Bob continued the story of his arrival in Glasgow. He had been a youth of sixteen, he told Big Lou, with no more than a few pounds in his pocket and an introduction to an unhelpful cousin, and now he found himself sleeping rough in the courtyard of Wee Jimmy's pub. He was already homesick and fearful of discovery, but felt unable to return to the home he had only so recently left.

'Oh, Bob,' said Big Lou. 'I can just imagine how you felt. When I went up to Aberdeen as a young lass at least I had somewhere to go to. You had nowhere. And you had nothing – or next to nothing.'

'That's right, Lou. But when you're that age, you don't necessarily realise how little you have. It doesn't seem to matter so much.'

Big Lou said that she thought that by and large that was true. 'And yet, where was your next meal coming from?'

'I wasn't so much worried about that,' said Bob. 'What I wanted was a job. I thought that if I got work, everything else would sort itself out. So I decided that I would simply go down the street and knock on every likely-looking door. I thought that sooner or later I would find somebody who could do with some help.'

'And did you have any luck?'

Bob laughed. 'A lot. The first door I knocked on was a builder's merchant's. He was a big fellow, and he looked at me and laughed. 'Does your mammy know you're oot?' he said. He was very pleased with himself for that remark. But then he said that, as it happened, he needed somebody to shift piles of timber. He would pay me in cash, he promised, at the end of each day for the first week, and that if I worked hard, he would take me on properly.

'Then he asked me where I lived. I said that I had been staying with a cousin, which was true, I suppose, but that I was hoping to find somewhere else. He looked at me as if he didn't quite believe me, and then asked me whether the police were looking for me. I think that my indignant reaction to that convinced him that I wasn't on the run, and so he didn't wait for me to deny it. He explained that he had to be careful. A few months previously he had taken on a boy who had stabbed somebody and the police had given him a lot of trouble over that. Glasgow had gang issues at the time – it still does – and people were jumpy.'

Big Lou saw Bob look longingly at the last of the poppadoms. 'You have it,' she said. 'I've had enough.'

He reached for the poppadom and broke it in two. 'Let's share,' he said.

Big Lou was pleased: sharing the last poppadom was a good sign. She had known plenty of men who would have eaten it all themselves.

'It was hard work,' Bob went on. 'I was given thick work gloves – I can still smell them – and shown the timber that had to be moved. Then I was left to get on with it, which

I did. At twelve o'clock I was told I could take an hour off if I wanted to go and buy myself something to eat. The boss gave me money for this and to buy a pie for himself. He said that I would have to pay for my own lunch the following day, but by then I would have my first day's wage in my pocket.

'He was as good as his word about paying me. I got the cash in my hand and was told that he was pleased with the work I had done. He said that the following day he would fix me up with a set of overalls as he didn't think my clothes were quite suitable for the job I was doing.

'I went out into the street. I had no idea of where I was going to find a bed for the night, so returned to the shed I had left that morning. It had started to rain, and I was getting wet. At least that would give me a roof – of sorts – over my head.

'There was nobody around in the yard. I slipped in and let myself into the shed and lay down on the sacking. The work had tired me, and although I felt hungry, I decided to rest before I went out in search of fish and chips for my supper. Oddly enough, I felt quite happy. I had done a day's work; I had money in my pocket; and I had somewhere to go that night. Obviously, I would have to find somewhere better to stay, but for the time being, I thought the shed would do fine.

'I slept rather longer than I had planned. When I woke up, it was almost ten o'clock, and I thought that I would have to rush if I were to find a chippie open. I need not have worried – there were plenty of places still serving, and enough people coming out of pubs to keep them open for a good while yet. I ordered fish and chips and a pie for good measure.

I stood outside and ate the meal, watching what was going on about me. Somewhere down at the end of the street there was a brawl – an angry shout and the sound of glass being smashed. Then the police arrived, the blue light of their car illuminating figures in the road. A woman was shouting at the police. It had never occurred to me that you might shout at the police; that never happened where I had been brought up. But this was Glasgow, with rules of its own, and I thought that I would have to learn a whole new way of behaving if I was to fit in here.

'I went back to the yard behind the pub. Nobody was about, and I was able to slip back into my shed. I took off my boots and prepared for bed. In those days, Lou, I said my prayers every night – my mother had always insisted on that. She was a Catholic and said that if you died in the night, the state of your soul might depend on having said your prayers before you went to sleep. I don't believe any of that now, Lou, but I did then.'

'You were sixteen,' said Big Lou.

'Yes. And I believed what they told us about Hell. It was a place of eternal torment, they said, and any of us could end up there if we weren't careful.'

Big Lou sighed. 'The Devil's just a tattie-bogle. And there's no such place as Hell, Bob.'

Bob hesitated. 'No, I don't think there is. But why did they tell us all that?'

'It was a useful threat, Bob. Fear works. It secured compliance.'

'What a wicked thing to do,' said Fat Bob.

'Aye,' said Big Lou. 'But the Catholic Church has

changed, Bob. It's not the same. It's now more about love and charity, which is what it should have been all along.' She paused. 'You can't condemn the present for the wrongs of the past.'

Fat Bob listened. He wanted more love and charity in this world. He wanted that.

'Mind you, it's high time they allowed women priests,' said Big Lou.

'You're right there, Lou,' agreed Fat Bob, adding, 'Shall we order more poppadoms?'

She looked at him fondly: here was a new man who was nonetheless strong, and who liked poppadoms. It had been a long search.

## 41. Given Lodging

Big Lou would have been happy to discuss theology at greater length with Fat Bob had it not been for her eagerness to find out what happened next. This was *Oliver Twist*, she thought – the universal story of the young man cast adrift in the city. Predators circled, ready to dazzle and then devour the innocent in all their guilelessness. Being press-ganged into the Navy might not be as unattractive a fate as it seemed, when conscription into a street gang was a possible alternative.

'Tell me one thing, Bob,' she said. 'Does this have a happy ending?'

Bob looked puzzled. 'My story? A happy ending? I'm not quite there yet, Lou, not quite at the end . . .'

She smiled. 'Oh, I know you're not, Bob. But this particular chapter of your life – this bit in Glasgow: does it end well? You see, I can't bear an unhappy story. I just can't.'

Bob reassured her. 'There's no unhappy ending, Lou, so you can stop worrying. You see, I don't like unhappy endings either.'

'People tell me it's burying your head in the sand,' Big Lou continued. 'They say that life is hard – cruel even. They say that the only story worth telling is one of how things go wrong.'

Fat Bob snorted. 'That's just not true, Lou.'

'Of course it isn't. There are plenty of good stories. There are plenty of people who go through life without . . . well, without anger. Who are kind to other folk. Who don't rant and rage.'

Fat Bob nodded his vigorous agreement. 'You're right. Because if there weren't, then would any of us carry on? I don't think so, Lou. There'd be no point.'

He spoke with such feeling that Big Lou felt there was nothing she could add. And she knew then, as if she had not known before, that this was the man whom she had always hoped would exist. The others – the Elvis impersonator, who had shown his true colours at that desperate Elvis convention at the Crieff Hydro, the slightly seedy chef, the Jacobite plasterer – were all a distraction. This man was the person for whom she had been destined all along. She had read somewhere that all of us, no matter what our personal predilections might be – and creative Eros bestowed so many options – all of us cherished the hope that there would be one whom we could love with all our heart because he or she was just *right*; that we knew what we were looking for, even if we sometimes seemed to pursue the very opposite, and consequently, and with utter predictability, were unhappy, unbelieving of the optimistic lies we told ourselves.

As she looked at Fat Bob, thinking just this, he looked at her and thought much the same thing. He closed his eyes. She was real, because she was still there when he opened them; she, who could have been sent by some divine agency charged with the consolation of those from whom the world, thus far, had withheld much consolation.

'I'll tell you what happened, Lou,' Bob continued. 'I got back to my shed and lay there in the dark, wondering what I would do the following day about some clean clothes. I could get away with what I was wearing for one more day, perhaps, but I had left the rest of my things in the house I had run away from, and I was not going to go back there.

'We take a lot for granted, don't we – those of us who have somewhere to live; who have a washing machine to launder some clothes; and somewhere to wash ourselves and clean our teeth? If you live on the street, you don't have any of that, and you have to work out every day how you're going to do any of those very ordinary things.'

Big Lou nodded. 'I can imagine it, Bob.'

'I got to sleep eventually and slept through until I heard a delivery lorry grinding its gears in the road outside. I opened the door of my shed and looked out – and saw a girl staring at me. She was about my age, and she was standing there, holding a lead with a small black dog at the end of it. I did not know what to do. I wondered whether I should run away – it would have been easy enough to push past her and disappear down the road, but something stopped me from doing that. I think it was the fact that she was looking at me with concern.

'The first thing she did was to ask me my name. I told her, and then she said, "Why are you in my Uncle Jimmy's shed?" I said that it was because I had nowhere else to sleep. She took a moment or two to take this in, and then she asked where I had come from. I answered that question, telling her that I had come to Glasgow to find a job and to send money back to my mother and family. Then she said, "You can't live in a shed, you know. You can come back and stay at our place. It's just round the corner."

'I said, "But what will your parents say? They won't want me."

'She did not seem to be worried about that. "They won't know," she said. "You can have my big brother's room. They never go in there. It's full of his stuff – you can hardly get in."'

Big Lou's mouth was wide open with astonishment. 'You went?' she asked.

'Yes, and I moved in. She meant it. She let me in at nights and brought me food. She brought me some clothes from a charity shop.'

'And they never found you?'

'Not for a whole week,' said Bob. 'Then her mother came in and found me asleep on her big brother's bed. I woke up to find her father standing over me. He was called Jock.'

'And then?'

'He listened to my story and then went off to discuss the situation with his wife. Then he came back and said that it was an awful pity that people like me had to sleep rough and that there should be a law against it. He said I could stay.'

'And did you?'

Fat Bob nodded. 'For four years,' he said. 'They were so kind to me. They treated me as a member of the family. They also gave me a job in their bakery. And that was where I discovered my strength. They had large sacks of flour, you see, and these needed to be shifted from time to time. Usually, it took four people to do this – one at each corner of the sack – but I could do it by myself. Jock said that he had never seen anything like it, and it was his idea that I should compete in the Largs Highland Games. They took me down there in the bakery van, and I won all the events I entered. That was the beginning.'

He had been talking for some time. Now he stopped.

'You were so lucky to have found those people,' she said. 'It could have worked out very differently. For so many young people, it probably does.'

'There are plenty of folk like that in the world,' said Bob. 'We don't hear enough about them because we're so busy looking at all the wretched things that happen.'

'Yes,' said Big Lou. 'The good things that happen – the acts of kindness, the concern for others . . .'

'Are forgotten about,' said Bob. 'I wish it were otherwise.'

'So do I,' said Big Lou. 'But it isn't, is it?'

## 42. Bruce Reflects, and Conducts

For Bruce it was an entirely unfamiliar feeling: shame. As he made his way out of the Elephant House on George IV Bridge, past a group of giggling Japanese teenagers, leaving Sister Maria-Fiore dei Fiori di Montagna at the table that they had, until a few moments ago, shared – the table at which she had revealed to him her dreams of a double-upper flat in the Grange – Bruce barely had time to glance appreciatively at his profile in the reflective front window of the café. Had he allowed himself to dwell on that image, he might have experienced that shock that greets us all when we engage fully and frankly with our face in the mirror, and are confronted, if we are prepared to open our eyes, by our faults laid bare for all to see.

But he did not, such was his eagerness to get away from this place, the site of his perfidy. *I sat there*, he thought, *and listened to the voice of my intended victim.* And then he added to this dire soliloquy, *And I said nothing.*

He walked on. It was early afternoon, and the Old Town was bathed in the charitable light of summer. Obscure corners, moody when in mist, sinister in night-time darkness, were now friendly under the warm benison of the sun. If there were secrets and sorrows in these winding streets, these sharp descents and mysterious closes, then these seemed a long way off. Bright flags fluttered briskly; from a side street somewhere drifted the accusing notes of a pipe tune – Edinburgh *en fête*, welcoming the world's visitors, inviting them to the party.

Bruce was in no mood for any of that. As he walked down the Mound, a Glasgow-bound train, emerging from its tunnel, gave a blast of its two-tone whistle, a familiar enough sound in the Princes Street Gardens, but to Bruce, in his mood of regret and self-recrimination, a note of sharp reproach, like the trumpet that summons the guilty to judgement. He thought now of how easy it had been to fall in with Ed's plan. How quickly had he agreed to be part of it, without any weighing of pros and cons. Why had he done it? Was it because he was concerned that Ed would think him too cowardly to join in? Was it because he always wanted to be one of the boys, whatever the boys were getting up to? When was he happiest? The question came to him out of the blue, and he answered it without hesitation. Bruce liked the fellow feeling of the rugby team. And more than that, he was happiest when in the communal bath at the rugby club, after a game, in the warm soapy water with the rest of the team. The thought almost stopped him in his tracks. It could not be true; it simply could not be true. And yet he had thought it.

He put it out of his mind. He had to. There were times when one thought the opposite of what one really felt. That was very common, and this was an example of exactly that. It was true that he had acted impetuously by agreeing to Ed's plan, but there was no point in engaging in self-analysis to work out why he had done that. And it was not too late to pull out. He would phone Ed and tell him that he wanted no further part of the scheme. He would be careful not to be too judgemental – he would not criticise Ed for what he was planning to do – he would simply stand back from it himself. But then he would have to decide what to do about Sister Maria-Fiore dei Fiori di Montagna and Antonia Collie. Should he warn them? If he did, he might end up exposing Ed and Gregor, who might then be prosecuted for fraud. He would have to give evidence and denounce them in court. Did he really want that? *Anderson the clype*: the playground insult, no more than a threat at this stage, made him shiver.

He crossed Princes Street and began to walk up Hanover Street. His mobile phone rang, and he took it out of his pocket to glance at the caller's number. He recognised it as Ed's, and for a few moments he hesitated. It would have been easy enough to answer and to inform Ed of his decision. 'I'm out,' was all he would need to say. And then Ed would … Well, he was unsure what Ed would do, but there were not many options open to him. This was not like leaving the Freemasons. No callers would drop in to remind one of solemn oaths. All he had to do was to say to Ed that he was no longer involved.

For a moment he allowed himself to fantasise. Ed might say that he knew too much. That's what criminals said when members of their gangs threatened to leave. And if they even thought that, then they might – even if reluctantly – order that he be … what was the term they used? That he be *terminated*? That was ridiculous. This was not a gangster operation; this was a perfectly ordinary middle-class fiddle – an attempt to drive up the price of a house. There were probably plenty of countries in the world where that sort of thing was perfectly permissible. It was just bad luck that Scotland was so holier-than-thou, thought Bruce.

The thought cheered him, and with his improving mood, he began to abandon the resolve to withdraw from the scheme. He should get a grip of himself, he decided. He should stop these unhelpful, self-recriminatory thoughts; he should stop being such a *wimp*. It was bad luck that Sister Maria-Fiore was involved, but it was probably mostly Antonia Collie's money, and that woman was clearly more than comfortably-off. She could easily afford an extra fifty thousand or so for the privilege of securing that double-upper in the Grange. In a year or two it would be worth what she paid, anyway, if house prices continued to climb as they were currently doing.

He reached the top of Dundas Street. Now the Queen Street Gardens were on either side of him as he made his way down the hill. He looked up at the sky, which had suddenly become dark and threatening. A great cloud had moved in briskly from the south-west and was towering above, an ominous anvil of cumulonimbus. Bruce gazed up at the swirling cloud mass, and was marvelling at its size when the bolt of lightning descended with a gigantic crack. It struck him with a crash, flash, and shower of sparks, making of him a brief and glorious firework. Then it flung him into the air, twenty feet or more above the pavement and the road, giving him a last vision of grey sky and trees and, tilting wildly, the distant shores of Fife.

## 43. Against All Medical Odds

Annette McFarlane was a nurse. She was twenty-seven and had recently become engaged to Rab Cameron, a civil engineer from Falkirk. Annette was from Oban, where she had been a keen member of a kayak club. She had met Rab at a kayak rally on Skye, and they were engaged within three months. Annette's mother ran a small garden centre, and got on particularly well with Rab's mother, whose hobby happened to be the cultivation of roses. Annette had studied nursing at Queen Margaret University, Edinburgh and had been given her first job at the Royal Infirmary. That had been in the Accident and Emergency Department, to which she had returned after a brief spell in Paediatrics, which she left after being bitten by several of her young patients.

'I like the drama of A&E,' she remarked to Rab. 'You get all of life there, you know. And then some.'

Rab was not sure whether he wanted to see all of life. 'But you must see some pretty horrible things,' he said. 'People with knives sticking out of their backs and so on.'

Annette laughed. 'That's actually quite rare. You do see knife wounds from time to time, but it's usually people cutting themselves with the bread knife, or something like that. Those very expensive German bread knives – you know, the ones that actually cut the bread – they're the worst. We had a guy in the other night who was making himself some toast and he took the bread knife and . . .'

Rab stopped her. He was squeamish. 'Okay, I get the drift.'

'I was just going to tell you about his thumb,' Annette continued. 'You see the knife went . . .'

'I don't want to hear about it,' said Rab. But he added, 'He was all right, was he?'

'Yes,' said Annette. 'Although there was a bit of a panic when we weren't sure where we'd put the thumb. They wanted to sew it back on, you see, and this nurse I was working with – she's called Julie – she had it. I swear I gave it to her, but she said I didn't. She should have owned up – she really should. Anyway, we found it on the floor and I gave it a bit of a wash. Have you ever washed somebody else's thumb under the tap? It's really odd, you know . . .'

'All right,' said Rab. 'He was fixed up. Good.'

'And there was this boy who swallowed a light bulb,' Annette continued. 'No, I'm serious. He swallowed a light bulb. One of those screw-in ones. He was about sixteen, which is a bit late to be swallowing things. Over at the Sick Kids Casualty they get small kids who have swallowed all sorts of things – but he was brought in to us. He had an X-ray, and there it was – an actual light bulb.'

'What did they do?'

'I don't know,' said Annette. 'I went off duty shortly afterwards.'

But now Annette was on duty and was standing outside one of the examination rooms when Bruce was wheeled in on a trolley by the paramedics who had retrieved him from Dundas Street.

'He's had a shock,' one said.

'A big shock, I think,' said the other.

Annette looked at Bruce, who was staring back at her, his eyes wide and unfocused. She noticed his hair, which was standing straight up, bristling like the coat of a cat that has had a bad fright. She smelled something unusual – was it cloves?

She reached out to take his pulse. 'Hello,' she said. 'What's happened to you?'

Bruce struggled to say something.

'I think his tongue's swollen,' said one of the paramedics. And then he addressed Bruce. 'Don't bother to speak, Jim. You can tell us later.'

He drew Annette aside. 'Lightning,' he said. 'This chap's been struck by lightning. Down in Dundas Street. He was in the middle of the street – in the middle – and there was a muckle great burnt patch about five or six metres away. That's where he was standing when the lightning hit him. There were two witnesses.'

'They swore it was lightning,' whispered his colleague. 'They said there was a great bang and sparks – the lot. This poor guy was thrown up in the air like a doll.'

Annette looked down at Bruce. 'Where does it hurt?' she asked. It was not perhaps the most intelligent thing to say to somebody who has been struck by lightning, but she found that it was usually a good way of getting a history.

Now Bruce managed to speak. 'My ribs,' he said. 'I landed on my front. I've hurt my ribs.'

A junior doctor arrived. 'What have we here?' she asked.

'A lightning strike,' said Annette.

The doctor looked at her. 'You serious?'

The paramedics repeated their report. The doctor listened, frowned, and then began an examination of Bruce.

'You're very lucky,' she said. 'You appear to be largely unscathed. I think you may have broken some ribs, but not much else.'

Bruce groaned. 'It's sore when I breathe.'

'That's cracked ribs for you,' said the doctor.

A consultant was called. Lightning strikes were unusual, and word quickly got round the hospital. Notes were taken, and a medical photographer was summoned. Bruce attempted to tidy his hair before the photographer got to work, in spite of being assured that it did not matter. What interested the consultant, and in due course the photographer, were the thin lines, like exposed veins, that ran down Bruce's side. That, the consultant said, was where the current had passed down into the ground. They were surface burns, but so slight as to be inconsequential. 'Lightning is a very peculiar thing,' said the consultant. 'I attended a case in India where a mother who was holding her baby was struck. She was badly burned, but the baby was completely unharmed.'

Bruce listened to this. This was no accident, in his view. It was a judgement – a punishment. These people would not understand that, but he did.

Once the consultant and the photographer had left, Bruce said to Annette, 'I'm really sorry.'

She looked at him. 'You've been no trouble. And it wasn't your fault.'

'No, I'm sorry about what I did. I'm sorry about what I did to make this happen.'

She looked bemused. 'Lightning is . . . just lightning. It's nothing to do with what you did.'

But then she thought: *I wonder what he did.* So she said, 'I'm sure it wasn't all that bad.' And added, after a brief pause, 'What was it, anyway?'

## 44. *'You are troubled in your soul'*

Bruce was kept in overnight in the Royal Infirmary. An X-ray had confirmed the diagnosis of cracked ribs, and an ECG had established normal heart function, apart from a slight and, as it happened, temporary irregularity. This was what justified his remaining in hospital, even for a brief period. Further observation, though, revealed nothing untoward, and by ten o'clock the following morning Bruce was informed that he could return home, but was to take things easy for the next few days. 'And avoid lightning,' added the doctor, somewhat unnecessarily.

The incident had been picked up by the press. *The Scotsman* had reported it under the headline *Man Struck in Capital Strike*, while *The Sun* wrote 'Bolt Batters Bruce'. Always interested in near-escapes of any sort, there were several journalists and photographers waiting to greet Bruce on his return to his flat in Abercromby Place. He replied courte-ously to their questions, and posed without demur for the photographs in which he was pictured looking up at the sky, as if awaiting further intervention from that quarter. His hair still seemed to be holding an electrical charge and was sticking up from his scalp in an irrepressible fashion, and this was of some interest to the photographers, who took close-up pictures of the phenomenon.

One of those to read the news reports of Bruce's misfortune was Sister Maria-Fiore dei Fiori di Montagna. She saw the item in Antonia Collie's copy of *The Scotsman* and immediately drew her friend's attention to it.

'Toni, there's the most remarkable thing here,' she said. 'You know that young man who lives in Abercromby Place – the one with the hair ...'

'And the curious hair gel? Brian, or Bruce or ...'

'Bruce Anderson. Yes.'

Antonia nodded. 'I call him Apollo.'

Sister Maria-Fiore said that she thought this very appropriate. Then she continued, 'He was struck by lightning yesterday. In Dundas Street, of all places.'

'Oh, my goodness,' said Antonia. 'One doesn't expect people one actually knows to be struck by lightning.'

'No, one does not. Fortunately, to no ill effect, according to the paper.'

'He must have been well grounded,' remarked Antonia, and then added, 'Not that I mean to make light of it. I would wish lightning on nobody.'

'Wish lightning on another,' said Sister Maria-Fiore, 'and you wish it upon yourself.'

As Antonia thought about this, Sister Maria-Fiore continued, 'I must have been speaking to him no more than a few minutes before it happened. For in the midst of life, we are in death; of whom may we speak for succour?'

'Indeed,' said Antonia.

Sister Maria-Fiore put down the newspaper. 'I shall go and see him,' she said. 'I shall take him some honey, I think. It has curative properties for those who are in a state of shock. We always gave it to our Stendhal syndrome people when they came to recover with us.'

'I'm sure he would appreciate it,' said Antonia.

It was not only honey that Sister Maria-Fiore took to Bruce's flat, but also a salami, a bunch of grapes, and a copy of a small booklet entitled *The Pensées of Sister Alphonsine of Tours*. Bruce welcomed her warmly and was clearly touched by the gifts.

'I love honey,' he said. 'I always have. And salami too. You're very kind, Sister Maria-Fiore dei Fiori di . . .' His voice trailed off.

'Dei Fiori di Montagna,' Sister Maria-Fiore prompted. 'But I have always been content to be simply Sister Maria-Fiore. A name is only as good as the heart of the one who bears it.'

'Of course,' said Bruce. He gestured towards Sister Alphonsine's book. 'There will be many fine thoughts in this book, I imagine.'

'That is indeed true,' said Sister Maria-Fiore. 'Dear Sister Alphonsine spent years in Indochina. She was much loved there and makes frequent reference in the book to her many friends in that part of the world. She died in Algeria about ten years ago. She wrote a book called *My Dear Pieds-Noirs*, which did not meet with the success it deserved. But you will find a great deal of value in these *Pensées*.'

Bruce invited Sister Maria-Fiore to sit down on the sofa next to him. 'I have had a terrible experience,' he said. 'It happened a few minutes after you and I had our conversation in the Elephant House.'

'I know,' said Sister Maria-Fiore. 'I read about it in the papers. What a ghastly accident.'

Bruce hesitated. 'Except, it was not an accident.'

'But it was lightning, wasn't it?'

Bruce stared out of the window, seemingly deep in thought. 'Not all accidents are accidents,' he said. 'Some are sent. They are sent because of something that we have done.'

'Surely not,' protested Sister Maria-Fiore. 'God does not intervene so directly in our affairs. He sets the stage. He gives us our freedom, and then it is up to us.'

Bruce shook his head. 'I used to think like that,' he said. 'I used to reject anything that seemed vaguely superstitious. Not now.' He looked at Sister Maria-Fiore, who knew immediately that he was troubled.

'That lightning strike was a judgement,' said Bruce. 'I was part of a plan to drive up the price of that double-upper you and Antonia are interested in. I feel so ashamed, but I was part of that.'

'*Were* interested in,' Sister Maria-Fiore corrected, in a matter-of-fact way. 'Now no longer.'

Bruce frowned. 'You've decided against it?'

'It decided against us,' said Sister Maria-Fiore. 'The building was declared unsafe yesterday. We heard from the solicitors.'

Bruce wanted to say something, but found that he could not speak.

'Yes,' continued Sister Maria-Fiore. 'It's an awful shame, but apparently a load-bearing wall collapsed. Nobody was hurt, but there was substantial damage.'

'Oh heavens,' whispered Bruce, struggling to take this in.

'Yes. But we must remember this: God destroys a building here, and builds another there. In this way the equilibrium of the world is maintained.'

Bruce rose to his feet. 'A great burden of guilt has been lifted from my shoulders,' he said.

'Then give thanks for that,' said Sister Maria-Fiore.

'May I ask you one thing?' said Bruce. 'Will you forgive me if I confess that I lied to you? Not a direct lie – more a withholding of the truth.'

'Of course I shall,' said Sister Maria-Fiore. 'Forgiveness is the greatest of the virtues – greater even than love. Forgiveness enables us to get on with the future unembittered.'

There was more. 'If something is true,' the nun continued, 'then it does not matter how you express it – its truth will shine out, even in the darkest of darkness.'

'You put it so well,' said Bruce. He paused. It was not easy for him to utter the words he was about to say. 'I feel so ashamed of myself.'

She looked at him. 'You are troubled in your soul, Bruce. I can tell, you know.' She looked at him with compassion. 'And those who are most troubled in their soul are often those who deny they have a soul. Did you know that, Bruce?'

He lowered his gaze. She was right. He had been so proud; he had never spoken like this to another. He felt himself beginning to cry. Him! Bruce Anderson! Crying! Was that the effect of lightning? Was that what it did?

She reached out to embrace him. Her arms were so thin, as are the arms of pity, wherever, whenever.

## 45. The Road to Aberdeen

The day after Bertie's visit to Valvona & Crolla with Ranald Braveheart Macpherson, Nicola drove him up to Aberdeen. She had not been looking forward to the trip. Not only would she be saying goodbye to her grandson for a full three months, but she would have to hand Bertie over to Irene, and maintain a cheerful disposition during what was bound to be a trying meeting with her ex-daughter-in-law. Nicola was prepared to be tactful – for Bertie's sake – but she had always found that more than fifteen minutes in Irene's company strained comity to near breaking point. Irene would lecture her or condescend to her, or, more likely, do both. For her part, Nicola would bite her tongue, purse her lips, and resort to whatever other muscular and facial contortions might help her get through the encounter, and then, in the car journey home, would think about what she should have said to the various comments that would be bound to come her way. That was always the case, she thought: the perfect riposte, the *mot juste*, inevitably occurred well after the event, and one could not really write to somebody and tell them what you would have said had you thought about it in time.

As they drove across the bridge spanning the Firth of Forth, Bertie gazed out of the car window at the water far below, a rippling field of greyish-blue. Two working boats, a tug and a pilot vessel, ploughed the surface of the sea, a white line of wake behind them; a little further out, attached to an oil terminal, a long tanker poked out into the water-way. In the distance, pale shadows against the sky, were the islands of the Forth, half-veiled in a mist rising from the sea. The ragged coast of Scotland stretched out to the north, an indistinct, disappearing line that would eventually become Aberdeenshire. Bertie shivered.

'How long before we're there?' he asked.

'About three hours,' said Nicola.

Bertie considered this. 'Could you not drive a little slower?' His tone was pleading.

Nicola glanced at the speedometer. She was travelling at forty miles an hour – slowly, by most standards – but would speed up to sixty once she was off the bridge.

'I don't think I'm going too fast, Bertie. Are you feeling nervous?'

'Couldn't we break the journey somewhere?' Bertie continued. 'We could spend the night in Montrose or some-where, and then go on tomorrow – or the day after that.'

Nicola made light of this. 'But we don't need to break such a short drive, Bertie. We don't need to do that.'

'I'm sure Mummy wouldn't mind if we didn't arrive for a few days. That would give her more time to get things ready.'

Nicola tried to change the subject. 'Oh, look, Bertie. Look down there. That's Rosyth, if I'm not mistaken. That's where the Royal Navy fixes ships.'

The distraction succeeded. 'There's a boy at school called Robbie. His dad is a sailor, and he works there,' said Bertie. 'Or he thinks his dad works there.'

Nicola frowned. 'How can he not be sure? Hasn't he asked him?'

'Oh, he knows that he goes there to work. It's just that he's not sure that it's his dad.'

Nicola waited, but Bertie offered no further explanation. 'Has this person – the man who works in the dockyard – said that he might not be his dad?' she asked.

'No,' said Bertie. 'It's just that Robbie says that when the man who says he's his dad goes off to sea, a friend of his mummy comes to stay. Robbie says that he thinks this friend might be his dad.'

The car swerved, but Nicola quickly regained control. She tried not to smile. What Bertie said was perfectly feasible, as she had heard that there was a lot of swapping of partners and spouses in Rosyth. One sailor might move out, but another was always available to move in.

'Does Robbie like this ... this other dad?' she asked.

'Yes,' said Bertie. 'He has red hair – just like Robbie.'

'And the other dad?'

'He has black hair, Robbie says.'

'I see.' And then, 'And do you get on well with Robbie?'

Bertie thought about this. 'Mostly,' he said. 'He has a tattoo.'

Again the car swerved.

'Are you sure about that, Bertie? It's against the law to give children a tattoo, you know.'

'His mum's friend gave it to him,' said Bertie. 'He did it himself with a pin. It's a small anchor.'

'Not a good idea,' said Nicola.

'Robbie likes it.'

'Be that as it may,' Nicola insisted. 'That's not the point.'

She decided to change the subject again. 'We shall be going fairly close to Falkland Palace, Bertie,' she said. 'We can't stop this time, but maybe someday I'll take you there. After you come back to Edinburgh.'

Bertie was silent. He would not be back for three whole months – an eternity at his age.

'Falkland Palace,' Nicola continued, 'was where James V heard of the birth of Mary, Queen of Scots. He was on his deathbed, and they brought him news of Mary's birth. He was hoping for a son, but he got Mary instead, and the whole unhappy story began.'

Bertie looked thoughtful. 'Why are so many stories unhappy, Granny?' he asked.

'There's no simple answer to that, Bertie,' Nicola replied. 'Perhaps it's because of all the things that are wrong with us. Not you and me, of course, but people in general – what we call humanity.' She paused. 'People are unkind to one another. They are thoughtless in their dealings with others. They want what other people have, and they try to take it from them.'

'Ranald Braveheart Macpherson says that the English have always tried to take Scotland from us,' said Bertie.

Nicola thought about this. 'There's some truth in that,' she said. 'The English have many virtues, Bertie, but they may be said to have shown a slight tendency to take things from other people.'

'Like the Benin bronzes?' said Bertie.

Nicola was unprepared for this. And yet it was typical of Bertie – his eclectic reading meant that he picked up all sorts of snippets of information. 'Yes, Bertie, you could say that.'

'I think you should give back the things you've stolen,' said Bertie. 'It's only fair.'

Yes, thought Nicola: it was only fair. And yet when you had stolen so much ...

She decided on another change of subject, and the conversation moved on to all the news that Bertie would have to give his mother once he was safely settled in Aberdeen. 'There's so much for you to tell her,' said Nicola. 'What Ulysses has been getting up to, for instance.'

Bertie agreed. 'She'll be pleased to hear that he's so much better now that she's gone,' he said. 'He's not sick as often. And he doesn't scrunch up his face so much and yell.'

'Possibly,' said Nicola.

'And I could tell him about some of Daddy's new friends. That nice lady who wrote poetry. I could tell Mummy about her.'

'Best not to burden her with too much news,' Nicola counselled.

'I could tell her about how you threw away most of her things,' Bertie went on.

'I did not throw them away,' Nicola pointed out sharply. 'I rearranged them. That's all.'

'I saw some of the things you rearranged in an Oxfam shop in Stockbridge,' Bertie said.

'Let's listen to Radio Scotland,' said Nicola, leaning forward to switch on the car radio. And then, 'Oh listen, Bertie. Jimmy Shand and his Band! *The Braes o' Auchtermuchty!* How about that, Bertie?'

### 46. My Ordeal, by Bertie

Irene had initially lived in a flat when she arrived in Aberdeen but had since moved to a small terraced house in Granite Drive, Ferryhill. The house itself was solidly built – of granite – and so constructed as to withstand the gales and storm-force winds that regularly assailed it from the North Sea. Irene had converted one of the house's two bedrooms into a study, where she was writing her thesis on Melanie Klein, and so Bertie was to be accommodated in the scullery, in which she had installed a folding bed and a small chest for his clothes.

'This,' she said to Nicola, 'is where Bertie will be staying.' And to Bertie, she said, 'Your new bedroom, Bertie. Isn't it snug?'

Nicola's eyes narrowed – involuntarily. She struggled to control herself. It was so important, she felt, that Bertie be spared overt arguments within the family.

'How very sweet,' she said. She lingered on the word sweet, knowing that Irene would pick up her disapproval.

'Isn't it just?' said Irene. 'Such a change from Scotland Street.'

Nicola was not sure what this implied. She pursed her lips. 'It's a pity the window is so small,' she said quietly.

Irene turned round. 'I don't think one wants large windows in a bedroom,' she snapped. 'Such windows leak heat, Nicola – as I'm sure you know. The emphasis now is on insulation.'

'Of course,' said Nicola. 'Mind you, I don't see an obvious heat source here. No radiator – as far as I can make out. Therefore no heat to leak, surely?'

The gauntlet had been thrown, and Irene was not slow to pick it up. 'It's bad for children to be in overheated rooms,' she said. 'They are far healthier in a more invigorating environment. There's no substitute for fresh air, Nicola – as I'm sure you know.'

Nicola addressed Bertie. 'Remember to wear a vest,' she said. 'At all times.'

Irene glowered at her. 'You'll be wanting to get back down the road to Edinburgh,' she said. 'I won't delay you by offering you tea ... or anything.'

Nicola drew in her breath. 'I assumed that,' she said icily. 'I took the precaution of packing some sandwiches. And I have a flask of tea. I can stop on the way back.' She paused. 'But do tell me, Irene, how is your PhD going?'

'Extremely well,' said Irene. 'But let me not detain you.'

'Oh, don't worry about that. I'm so glad that you're happy here in Aberdeen. No need to rush back to Edinburgh.'

Irene looked down at the floor. 'I really must get on,' she said. 'And Bertie needs to settle in.'

Bertie had remained silent throughout this encounter. Now he heaved his small suitcase onto the bed and opened it.

'My goodness,' said Irene. 'All those woollens, Bertie! You should have let your grandmother pack for you.'

'I did indeed pack,' said Nicola. 'Bertie was concerned about being cold. I sought to reassure him.'

Irene bit her lip. 'Quite unnecessary,' she muttered. 'However, let's not waste time on these small things. Bertie, shall we see your grandmother to her car? She'll want to get home before it gets dark. A dark road is not easy if you have ageing eyesight.'

Nicola froze. This was too much. But then she looked down and saw Bertie, standing in dejection, and thought: it's hard enough for him as it is; a showdown would simply make it worse. So she limited herself to saying, 'Your mother is so considerate, Bertie – always to be thinking of others. I wish I could be as selfless as she is. Very few are, I fear.'

Irene threw her a suspicious look, but said nothing, and the three of them made their way out to Nicola's car.

'Goodbye, darling Bertie,' said Nicola, bending down to embrace her grandson. And whispering to him she said, 'I know you'll be strong. Just remember that three months is not very long and we'll be waiting for you in Edinburgh. Tell yourself that every morning when you get up, and it'll help you through the day.'

'What's that?' asked Irene, struggling to hear what was being said.

'Nothing,' said Nicola, and Bertie, taking his cue from his grandmother, his co-conspirator, also said, 'Nothing.'

That night, after he had been put to bed, Bertie switched his bedside light back on and opened a small notebook he had hidden in his suitcase. On the cover of this notebook he had written, in large letters, my ordeal by bertie pollock. This was to be his diary, his secret record of his durance in Aberdeen. If he had to be here, then he might as well use his time to keep a record of his experiences. He had read somewhere that there was a large market for what were called *misery memoirs* and he thought, therefore, that there might be many potential readers of an intimate diary kept over three months. He would hide the notebook under his mattress, as people did when they wrote their diaries in prisoner-of-war camps. He might even begin to dig an escape tunnel, as some of those brave men did in those days.

He opened the notebook and began to write on the first page. 'Chapter One,' he wrote. 'I was transported from Edinburgh by road ...' He liked the sound of that. Being *transported* seemed just right for a story of this sort. 'My driver took me over the new bridge over the Forth and then headed straight for Aberdeen, where my Mummy was awaiting me.' He liked the sound of all that. He did not mention that his driver was his grandmother, as that rather spoiled the tone, and although readers would want a certain amount of detail, they did not need to know everything.

He wrote a few more sentences. There was a description of his room, which he said was cold and dark. 'I know that my Mummy wants me to be happy. I think she likes me. She also likes Dr Fairbairn, who phoned her today while I was eating my dinner. I knew it was him because he has a way of clearing his throat while he is speaking (Ulysses does the same thing – it's very strange). Dr Fairbairn is mad, although he tries to hide it. One of these days they will get him and take him off to Carstairs, but in the meantime he is living up in Aberdeen quite openly.

'My Mummy says that Dr Fairbairn is keen to see me to discuss some more of my dreams. I do not want to see him, but I know that I shall have to. I shall make up some dreams for him so that he is kept busy writing them down in his notebook. If he is kept busy like that, he is less dangerous.

'I have to go to school tomorrow. I am not looking forward to that. There is a school called Robert Gordon's, and I am going to be going there for three whole months. I will put a chalk mark on my wall for each day, and I shall strike out each group of five, which will be a full school week. But now I shall stop writing this because it is time to go to bed and my fingers are already so cold that I can't hold the pencil properly. And this is summer here. End of Chapter One: (signed) Bertie Pollock (7).'

## 47. Edinburgh Past; Glasgow Future

While Bertie was committing to paper in Aberdeen the first pages of *My Ordeal*, in Edinburgh Angus Lordie was making his way up Dundas Street in the direction of the National Gallery of Scotland. Angus was that evening due to attend a lecture there entitled *New Directions in Scottish Conceptual Art: Glasgow Leads the Way*. The lecturer was unknown to Angus, but had been described in the advance publicity for the event as 'one of the most exciting artists to come out of Scotland in recent years' and 'hotly tipped for a future Turner Prize'. Both of these recommendations had sounded warning signals to Angus, as had the title of the lecture itself. To describe somebody as an artist who had 'come out of Scotland' was, he felt, vaguely ridiculous. How did one come out of Scotland? The expression seemed to conjure up a picture of a large map of Scotland with a hidden trapdoor through which, Houdini-like, an artist emerged. And if one came out of Scotland, where would one be going? As for being a front-runner for the Turner Prize – that was even more damning, in Angus's view. He was convinced that it was impossible for anybody with any interest in painting in any form, or any feeling for the role of art as an expression of the beautiful, to get any-where near the Turner Prize – even onto its longlist. Those were his views. He knew that not everyone shared them, and that there were others who thought the opposite, but he told himself that there always would be people who were utterly wrong – whatever one was talking about.

By the time he reached Hanover Street and was begin-ning the descent to Princes Street and the Mound, Angus had worked himself up into a mood of despair. How could it be that the artistic establishment – or a substantial part of it – should be so incapable of seeing pretentious posturing for what it was? How could it enthuse so over people whose sole talent seemed to lie in the arranging of found objects, the switching on and off of lights, or the making of unintel-ligible, self-obsessed videos of themselves or their domestic surroundings? He had recently seen one such video – highly praised by the critics – which was entitled *My Chair*, and which consisted of a twenty-minute film of a kitchen chair, shot from different angles. In the final scene the chair disappears and the room in which it stood is solemnly filmed for a further five minutes, during which the artist performs a small dance. 'Utterly memorable,' said one of the newspapers. 'Immensely promising,' said another.

The audience was composed of familiar gallery supporters and a small cohort of intense and slightly disapproving-looking people occupying the front seats. These Angus immediately identified as the lecturer's friends: they had that special conceptual-art look about them – a look he had long since learned to spot at any formal artistic function. It was born, he suspected, of discomfort at being in the presence of others who might not understand – or, at least, understand in the way in which they understood. As such, it was not a sentiment that was out of place at any occasion where a mystery of any nature was being celebrated. These people, Angus thought, are convinced of their vision, but know that they are vulnerable in the way in which the Emperor with No Clothes knew he was vulnerable: at any point a small boy, with the innocence of youth, might point out that the emperor was naked. Huddled together in the front rows, they cast occasional glances towards the audience filing in behind them. Seeing nobody of any consequence, they turned to talk to one another in hushed, expectant tones.

The lecture began. 'I am not a painter,' said the lecturer. 'Nor would I wish to describe myself as an artist. I am one who has a practice, and that practice is art. Why is it art? To quote a well-known practitioner, it is art because I say it is art. Art is not something that needs the endorsement of an establishment, of an academy. An academy is nothing but a self-appointed bureaucracy that purports to endorse one particular view of the world and in doing so to delegitimise the work of those who do not meet with its approval. That may have worked in the past, but no longer. Now we are free of the constraints of the officialdom that stifled and distorted the creative impulses of people in the past. Now we are free to be ourselves – to look at the world through eyes that are beholden to nobody, through eyes that can truly see. And to show you – the public – what we see, we do not need to put paint on a canvas. That has been done, and done again. There are no new landscapes to depict; there are no new jugs and flowers to portray. All these things have been done. They are stale. They are the fixations of the stale mind located in a stale world-view. We no longer need paintings. We need experiences. We need ideas that spring not from the material, but from the inner experiential universe. That is why the focus of Scottish art is now firmly on Glasgow. Glasgow is alive. Edinburgh is dead.'

Angus looked about him. The front rows were nodding; behind them, though, there were several stony faces. A well-dressed woman turned to her neighbour and whispered something; the neighbour smiled. Angus stared at the lecturer, who had appeared in his short sleeves, with no jacket. There were damp patches under his arms. He was sweating. He was free, of course, but he was still sweating, Angus noted.

Then Angus saw that Sister Maria-Fiore dei Fiori di Montagna was there, seated towards the back, and next to her was Antonia Collie, looking a bit bored. He realised that

he should not have been surprised to see Sister Maria-Fiore –
the nun was everywhere, and of course she was now on the
gallery's board of trustees. He made no attempt to catch her
eye, but she spotted him shortly after he had noticed her, and
she waved in a friendly way. That was not something that happened all that often at an Edinburgh lecture: people did not
wave to one another. Perhaps that happened in Glasgow, of
course: he might ask the lecturer at the reception afterwards.
Or he could present it to him as confirmation of the point
he had made about the vitality of intellectual and artistic life
in Glasgow.

Angus waved back. He was fed up with accusations that
Edinburgh was stuffy. It may have been a bit like that in the
past, but things were different now. Edinburgh had taken off
its metaphorical tie, and what the lecturer had said was just
an old canard. It was he who was stale. He was stale through
and through – with a stale practice. 'You have a stale practice,
you know,' Angus might say to him.

Why were these people so dismissive of painting? Angus
asked himself that question as the lecture drew to its conclusion. Was it because they could not paint? Was that the real
reason underneath the pretentious banality of conceptual
art? Everyone, Angus thought, who cannot do something,
experiences at least some resentment of those who can do it.
Human nature.

Angus felt that he needed a drink. There was a reception,
although he realised that the word *reception* was a bit old-
fashioned. It suggested ownership of the space and the event
to be held in that space. *Gathering* was perhaps more acceptable. Or what about *rammy*?

## 48. Sister Maria-Fiore Confides

Clutching a glass of National Gallery of Scotland white wine, Angus surveyed the crowd gathered outside the lecture theatre. The lecturer was surrounded by acolytes congratulating him on the content of his talk. He accepted their plaudits with a grave nod of the head, shaking hands with one or two, blowing a kiss to more favoured others. Angus turned away. Perhaps he's right, he thought. Perhaps I am exactly what he was talking about – I'm a *stale man*. My time has passed. Nobody wants to hear from me because I paint the sort of things that have been done to death. I am a portrait painter, and who is going to get excited about anything a portrait painter does – particularly a portrait painter who happens to be a *man*? Ramsay and Raeburn were all very well in their time, but now people want a whole new approach, and that approach does not include portraits, particularly portraits of other *men*.

He was thinking these somewhat destabilising thoughts when he became aware that Sister Maria-Fiore dei Fiori di Montagna was at his side, accompanied by Antonia Collie. Angus greeted them warmly. He did not want to talk to anybody new, he had decided, and the familiar presence of these two was just what he needed. Both had glasses of wine considerably larger than his – reserved for trustees and their guests, Angus decided.

'You've heard about our friend, Bruce?' asked Sister Maria-Fiore.

'Struck by lightning,' said Antonia. 'In our very midst. In his prime, so to speak.'

Angus said that he had read about the incident. 'A narrow escape,' he said.

'Of course, in one sense he's fortunate,' observed Antonia. 'They say, do they not, that lightning never strikes twice in the same place. That means that statistically Bruce can discount any possibility that he will ever again be struck. It's rather like having measles – you are unlikely to get it again.'

'But the chance of being struck by lightning is infinitesimally small,' said Angus. 'About the same as you or I being the victims of a shark attack.'

Sister Maria-Fiore thought about this. 'Of course that depends on where you live,' she said. 'If you live in a land-locked country – let's say Switzerland – then surely the chances of being attacked by a shark are non-existent. Whereas you or I, being residents of an island, at least face some such odds, small though they may be.'

Antonia took a sip of her wine. 'I think this is Italian,' she said. 'Goodness knows where from.' She paused. 'Perhaps you might be able to identify it, Floral One.'

It was the first time Angus had heard Sister Maria-Fiore addressed by this soubriquet. It was, he thought, rather touching.

Sister Maria-Fiore sniffed at her wine before tasting it. 'Veneto,' she said, after a moment or two of thought. 'I have an uncle who produces wine exactly like this. Not on a big scale, of course – no more than four hundred bottles a year.

But his wine is much appreciated. We bought some for the convent a few years ago. The sisters enjoyed it greatly. It was a change from the red wine that we produce ourselves.'

Angus looked at her with fascination. She really was a most *refreshing* nun. And her social ambitions, although plain for all to see, were harmless enough. Sometimes those with social aspirations simply wanted to be loved – that was all there was to it.

Angus sought their views on the lecture.

Antonia shrugged. 'I was thinking of other things,' she said. 'There's a limit to what one can take in.'

Sister Maria-Fiore smiled. 'Dear Antonia has so much on her mind,' she said. 'What with her book on the lives of the Scottish saints and one thing and another. As you know, Angus, we were thinking of moving over to the Grange, but that will no longer happen.'

'The house fell down,' said Antonia, in a melancholy tone.

'Not altogether,' Sister Maria-Fiore corrected her. 'It was declared structurally unsound after somebody interfered with a supporting wall. One should never do that. Supporting walls are called supporting because of the support they give. And without support, they are unsupported.'

'No,' said Antonia. 'That is not quite correct, dear Floral One. Supporting walls are not themselves supported – they *give* support. It is the overall structure that is not supported.'

'You are quite right, Toni,' said Sister Maria-Fiore. 'I sometimes speak in general terms and lose sight of the particular.'

Angus now asked Sister Maria-Fiore what she thought of the lecture.

'He has a point,' said the nun. 'Art can become stale.

We all know that. When I contemplate the endless Holy Families painted by Neapolitan Baroque artists, for instance, I am overwhelmed with a sense of déjà vu.' She paused. 'St Joseph usually looks so uninspiring in those paintings. He looks rather like the chairman of a branch of Rotary International.'

Angus was inclined to agree. There could be a sameness to certain stock images. But then so many of our cultural images were afflicted by that sameness: there was a limit to the human imagination, after all, and we revisited and revisited certain popular themes. What was the current word for those? Tropes? Memes?

Sister Maria-Fiore had more to say. 'But at the end of the lecture, I found myself thinking: who is the stale one here? And do you know what? The answer that came to me was: *they are*. Yes, the conceptual artists who are so busy attacking conventional painters for being stale have themselves become stale. They are the ones who are saying the same thing over and over again. Whereas anybody now who paints in a conventional style is the radical, the outsider.'

Antonia was nodding her agreement. 'Maria-Fiore is absolutely right, you know,' she said.

Angus smiled. 'Am I then in the avant-garde?'

'Of course you are,' said Sister Maria-Fiore. 'Anybody who has painterly skills is the progressive now, ploughing a lonely furrow. You are definitely in that category, Angus.'

He was pleased. It was rather like being rehabilitated after a long exile.

Sister Maria-Fiore looked about her. She had the look of a conspirator, and now she leaned forward and whispered to Angus. 'Antonia knows about this, so she can hear. But I wouldn't want some of those people to hear just yet.' She glanced over at the lecturer and his knot of supporters. 'I learned only a few days ago that I have been chosen to be on a rather significant committee.'

Angus waited. It seemed to him that there was barely a committee left in Scotland on which Sister Maria-Fiore had not been invited to serve. 'Tell me all about it,' he pressed. 'I'm the soul of discretion.'

'I have been appointed to the panel of judges of the Turner Prize,' said Sister Maria-Fiore. 'The board of the National Gallery of Scotland was invited to nominate a member, and I proposed myself. It was at the end of a trustees' meeting, and people were keen to get away. Nobody objected, and I was on.'

Angus struggled to regain his composure. 'You?' he stuttered. 'A Turner Prize judge?'

'Yes,' said Sister Maria-Fiore. 'And I can tell you this, Angus, the prize will not be going to people like tonight's lecturer who belittle the tastes of ordinary people. These people are incorrigible elitists. They are the epitome of intellectual arrogance. No, I'm going to do everything within my power to make sure it can go to somebody who can actually paint. Perhaps even to a landscape artist. Who knows?' She paused. 'And I shall use such skills as I have to ensure that I am elected to chair the panel.'

Angus clapped his hands together, forgetting he was holding a glass of wine. The wine went everywhere, but it was worth it.

'This is very welcome news,' he enthused. 'And I suspect you might just be able to pull it off.'

Antonia Collie beamed. 'Of course she will. She's a Daniella come to judgement.'

Sister Maria-Fiore dei Fiori di Montagna lowered her head demurely. 'I merely do my duty – to art and to beauty,' she said. 'That's all.'

## 49. A Martini Is Planned

While Angus was receiving the extraordinary news of the appointment of Sister Maria-Fiore dei Fiori di Montagna to the Turner Prize panel of judges, Domenica Macdonald was back at their flat in Scotland Street mixing a martini for her student neighbour, Torquil. They had met on the stair earlier that day, and she had invited him to come in for a drink that evening. He had readily accepted.

'I wouldn't want to distract you from your studies,' she said. 'But I thought that ...'

He cut her short. 'I never do any work after six,' he said. 'And neither do any of my flatmates. In fact, some of them never do any work *before* six either.'

'I'm sure you exaggerate,' said Domenica, smiling.

'Of course I do,' replied Torquil. 'But some of them are ... well, I think they don't over-exert themselves. Take Rose, for instance. She gets up really late, you know, even when she has a lecture at ten. She says, "I can learn the stuff out of a book. I don't need to be told." And so she doesn't go into the university until well after eleven. She's writing a novel by the way – or claims to be doing that. She's fairly secretive about it, but if you press her, she'll tell you a bit about it. It's science fiction, I suppose – about a woman who finds that her new car has a time-travel feature. She thinks it's the air-conditioning switch, but it isn't. It's a time-travel device that will take you back to minutes before some important histor-ical event is about to occur. She gets transported back – in the car – to Dallas on a November day in 1963. That was the date that President Kennedy was assassinated. This woman finds herself parked outside the Texas Book Depository, and she sees a man going inside carrying an object that looks as if it might be a rifle.'

Domenica smiled indulgently. 'How far has she got?'

'Page three,' Torquil replied, and laughed. 'Anyway, what time shall I come up?'

'Six-thirty,' said Domenica. 'Angus will be at a gallery lecture and usually doesn't come back from those until eight, or so. He and I shall be having a late dinner, which means there's plenty of time for a cocktail. Do you like a martini?'

Torquil nodded. 'Do I like a martini? I certainly do. I had a mystical experience once after drinking a martini. I've never forgotten it.'

'You can tell me about it later. Gin or vodka?'

'Oh, gin,' said Torquil.

'I have a bottle of McQueen Gin,' said Domenica. 'They make it up near Callander. I don't suppose you remember *Dr Finlay's Casebook*. That was set in Callander. With Janet and the miserable Dr Snoddie, and Dr Cameron being every bit what a country doctor is supposed to be. It was an old Scotland that, well, seems to be slipping away.'

Torquil was listening. He said, 'I think I know what you mean.'

She looked at him. 'Do you?'

'Yes.'

She returned to the subject of martinis. 'With an olive perhaps?'

'Good idea.'

The plan was laid, and at various points in the day Domenica thought with pleasurable anticipation of what lay ahead. Every so often, she reflected, one met somebody to whom one felt one had just so much to say. It was a curious phenomenon, and occurred quite unexpectedly. People talked about being on the same wavelength, and perhaps that was all it was – being attuned to the interests and concerns of another. She and Angus talked, of course, but much of their conversation was what she would describe as comfortable, covering well-worn tracks, involving references that both understood perfectly, involving no surprises. They were fortunate in that: some couples, she knew, lapsed after a time into near-silence, as if they had said to one another anything they possibly could say. When all the words were used up in a marriage, what was left?

Domenica remembered a previous discovery of a conversational soulmate. It had occurred before her first marriage, when she had been involved in a research project with a young anthropologist from Cambridge, a man a year or two older than she was, but seemingly so much more worldly and sophisticated. He had been a junior fellow of one of the colleges and had a set of rooms overlooking a quad. He had the ease and self-confidence of the expensively educated and the privileged, but none of the negative qualities that sometimes went with that background. He was modest and unassuming, and it was only by accident that she discovered that his family lived in an Elizabethan manor with a dovecot and tennis court. He referred to the tennis court as a *lawn tennis* court because he played real tennis, a different game altogether with its strange score calls and its half-roofed court. She remembered now how she had looked forward to the time they spent together and the ease with which their conversation ranged over every conceivable subject.

That was different, of course. She had been single then, and she could afford to immerse herself in the company of a brilliant and entertaining young man. They were near coevals; she and Torquil were not, and this friendship, if that is what it was, had predetermined boundaries. It would be unwise to become too close to this young man because ... She asked herself why, and she came up with the answer immediately. It was because they inhabited different worlds, and she understood that; he might not. She had to remember the inescapable realities of age: he was twenty – she was not.

And there was scope for misunderstandings. How would she feel if Angus started meeting a much younger woman for coffee, or – and here she brought herself up sharply – martinis? Platonic friendships existed between men and women, but even the most trusting of spouses or partners might feel a twinge of jealousy in such circumstances.

She thought about cancelling the invitation. She could find some credible excuse that would not involve any embarrassment for her nor offence to Torquil. She could truthfully claim a deadline or, less honestly, a forgotten prior engagement. And then she would simply not reissue the invitation and could avoid any situation in which a substitute invitation might be expected or extended. But although she considered these possibilities, she did nothing to bring them about, with the result that when six-thirty arrived she found herself looking anxiously at her watch, her breathing shallow, an odd feeling in the pit of her stomach, like somersaulting butterflies – if such a thing does not strain to breaking point the tendons of analogy.

## 50. *Post Martinis Omnia Animalia . . .*

'You said that you once had a mystical experience after drinking a martini. You did say that, didn't you?'

Domenica was addressing Torquil as she handed him the martini she had just mixed for him. He took it, smiled appreciatively, and replied, 'Yes, I did.' And then, after a moment's hesitation, he continued, 'I'm not sure if I should tell you, though. We don't like to hear about the dreams of others, do we? Perhaps the same goes for mystical experiences.'

Domenica disagreed. 'No, mystical experiences are different. We're not interested in others' dreams because we know that dreams are unreal. That's why we forget them so quickly. Have you noticed that?'

He had. 'It's odd, isn't it? You wake up remembering a dream and then, in two seconds flat, it's gone.'

'That,' said Domenica, 'is because the brain knows that it can't clutter itself up with useless phantasmagoria.'

Torquil, taking a sip of his martini, looked at her over the rim of his glass. 'What a great word.'

'Phantasmagoria? Yes, it is, isn't it? It was invented by a French playwright to describe magic lantern shows of disturbing images – ghosts and what we would call bogles. People liked to frighten themselves with them.'

Torquil rolled his tongue around the word. 'Phantasmagoria . . .'

'Whereas,' Domenica went on, 'a mystical experience is something that really happens, even if it is elusive. So we're interested in that. And most of us have had one, even if we wouldn't necessarily describe it as such.' She paused. 'All of which means you can speak about it, you know. My eyes won't glaze over.'

Torquil took another sip of his martini. 'All right. It was in New York.'

'Ah. Place is important for such things. It's easier to imagine having such an experience in exotic locations. Trebizond. Dar es Salaam. Does New York belong in such company?'

Torquil thought it did. 'I know that if you live in New York – work there – then it's probably just the place you live or work. But if you don't, then it hits you when you first see it. You can't be indifferent to it. There it is. Those buildings. The scale of it. The feel. The sounds. The sirens. The yellow cabs. The steam coming out of the subway vents. The smell of hot dogs on street corners.'

Domenica dipped the tip of her tongue into her martini. The alcohol was sharp. A madeleine cake dipped in tea. A bar in London. A man in a fur-lined coat, his hair still wet from the rain outside. A red London bus going past the window. She shook her head. 'You were in New York. Go on.'

'It was at the end of my first year at university,' Torquil said. 'Two years ago. As a birthday present my parents offered me an air ticket to New York. They said they would pay for my cousin Chris to come too, although we would have to live in a cheap backpackers' hostel – not that anywhere in New York is cheap.

'I accepted the offer like a shot, and Chris and I went off for two weeks. My parents had friends there, and they were in touch to ask us to drinks at their apartment on the Upper East Side. We went to the address expecting to find just a . . . well, an ordinary apartment. It wasn't. It was massive; on the very top of a building, and with a garden terrace of its own. They had invited other people too – members of their crowd – and these people were milling around making us look seriously shabby, as you can imagine.

'They had a piano on the terrace, played by a small man in a double-breasted blazer and a bow tie. He had an oddly shaped head – rather like a bullet – and a pair of tiny round glasses. He was playing show tunes, singing some of the lines in a thin, reedy voice that sounded as if it was coming out of an ancient radio. Chris said, "That guy is the real McCoy, you know." I agreed. He was. I think he may have overheard us because he turned and said to us in his thin, rather whiny Midwest voice, "Thank you, boys. Take care now." Then he carried on playing.

'Chris went off to talk to a girl in a green dress. I walked over to the parapet around the terrace. It was topped by an ornate bronze rail, with Art Deco features – the style you see on the Chrysler Building. I looked over the edge, down twenty-six storeys to the street below, which was Madison Avenue. It was early evening, about seven o'clock, and the slanting sun was on the tops of the skyscrapers, making them warm and gold. The sky was empty, and I remember thinking it was so pale a blue as to be almost white.

'I turned round. I had just finished the martini I had been given when I arrived. I saw that Chris was on his second, but one was more than enough for me, as it had been generous. I looked at the people there, at these New Yorkers, and I suddenly felt a rush of affection for them. It was very strange – a feeling of love, in the *agape* sense – a feeling of being *with them* in a curious way. It was a feeling of tenderness; I suppose you might call it that.

'And everything, it seemed to me, was just right. The people, the terrace garden, cars crawling along the road down below, New York in all its extravagant, unapologetic glory, was all *just right* – benevolent and well-meaning and utterly human – not the indifferent, money-making machine it is sometimes portrayed as being, but a place of human tenderness. These were kind, generous people who had just given me, a perfect stranger, a life-changing martini; and now the pianist had started to play 'As Time Goes By' from *Casablanca*, and was singing the words, almost under his breath, as if unconcerned whether any of the guests might hear him. *A kiss is just a kiss*, he sang; *the fundamental things apply* . . .

'He looked up. Chris had come back to join me. "The

fundamental things apply. Remember that, boys," the pianist said, from the corner of his mouth.'

Torquil stopped. He put down his glass and rose to his feet. Then he took Domenica's hand in his. She caught her breath. Then she said, 'Perhaps not.' And he looked away. He seemed neither hurt nor surprised.

They started to discuss something quite different – an essay that Torquil was writing on how cruelty is portrayed in the final scenes of Homer's *Odyssey*.

'Odysseus was very unforgiving,' said Torquil. 'I ended up not liking him at all.'

'Neither did I,' said Domenica. 'A very unsympathetic type.'

At seven-thirty he left. Angus came back half an hour later.

'I had Torquil up for a few minutes,' said Domenica. 'We chatted for a short while.' Then she added: 'We held hands. Very, very briefly. It was his doing, not mine.'

Angus seemed uninterested. 'You'll never guess what I heard from Sister Maria-Fiore dei Fiori di Montagna,' he said.

## 51. Room Issues

Torquil went downstairs. He had declined a second martini, not because the atmosphere had soured after his ill-advised taking of Domenica's hand – it had not – but because he found that the boundary between the feeling of exhilaration

227

following the consumption of one martini and the collapse into maudlin incoherence following two was a fine one, and easily crossed unawares. Domenica had similarly shown restraint, and they had ended up having a cup of tea before Torquil looked at his watch and remembered that Rose and Dave had agreed to make dinner for the entire flat that night. They would be expecting him to be there.

'He's back,' Dave called out from the kitchen when he heard the door open and close. 'Torquil has returned from his intimate little tête-à-tête with his friend upstairs. Let's hear all about it, Torquil, you dark horse, you.'

Rose appeared from her bedroom – the one she shared with Alistair. 'What do you two talk about?' she asked. 'Or do you just, you know, commune with one another?'

Torquil ignored the taunt. 'We talk about all sorts of things. She's an anthropologist, you know. She's worked in some amazing places. Papua New Guinea. The Malacca Straits.'

'And you know all about that sort of stuff?' asked Rose.

'No. But we talked about other things.'

Rose took Torquil aside. 'Torquil, can we talk?' she said, her voice lowered.

Torquil nodded. 'Of course.'

'In there.' She nodded in the direction of the room she had just left. Torquil followed her back into the room, closing the door behind him. Rose gestured for him to sit down.

'I don't want to talk about this in front of the others,' she said. 'But I feel I can talk freely to you.'

'Of course you can.'

'And you can talk freely to me,' Rose continued. 'You know that, don't you?'

He nodded. 'We always have. You remember when we discussed your relationship with your sister. And I told you about how I felt when Sally chucked me. That wasn't my fault, you'll remember.'

Rose frowned. 'You have to move on, Torquil. You can't live in the past. Sally is history as far as you're concerned. And Phoebe said that your star signs were completely incompatible.'

'That's nonsense,' he snapped back. 'You don't believe any of that rubbish, do you? She picks up all those ideas from Findhorn. You know how weird they are up there. The problem with Sally was that she was looking for somebody exactly like her father. I worked that out eventually. She wanted somebody who was just like him. I wasn't.'

Rose looked doubtful. 'I'm not so sure of that.'

'Well, I am. I met her father. I think that he liked me. He said he did. He said to me, "I quite like you." Those were his exact words.'

'You have to forget Sally. You have to move on.'

'I have moved on,' protested Torquil. 'I used to be ... be *there*.' He pointed to one side of the room. 'Now I'm here. I've moved on.'

'Then stop talking about her.'

'I wasn't. You brought her up.'

Rose sighed. 'This is not about Sally. It's not about you. It's about me and Alistair. Or mostly about Alistair.'

Torquil waited.

'I don't dislike Alistair,' Rose began. 'I wouldn't want you to think that.'

'I never thought you did.'

'It's just that I don't see why I have to share a room with him.'

He gave her a reproachful stare. 'You chose to share with him.'

'I know I did. But that was at the beginning – when we first moved in. Remember? And it was you, I think, who said that we weren't going to allocate rooms on a gendered basis.'

'I did. Yes, that was me. But it was also you. You were in favour of it, remember. You and Phoebe both said that was fine by you.'

'I know. But that was because we were so keen to show that we had risen above all that stuff – all that single-sex nonsense.'

'Well? Nobody said they were unhappy with it, did they?'

Rose laughed. 'You're talking about the boys. Of course they're not going to object. Ask a guy if he wants to share with a female, and he'll say "Sure". Ask a girl the same thing, and you won't get the same answer.'

'But you both said you wanted to,' Torquil pointed out.

'That's because we didn't want to appear uncool,' she said. 'Then we discovered it wasn't such a good idea.'

Torquil hesitated before saying, 'Is Alistair making things difficult for you?'

She shook her head. 'No, he's not like that.'

'Then?'

'I think he's thinking things,' said Rose.

'What things?'

'Things. I'm not sure exactly what – but you can tell he's thinking. He looks at me sometimes, and I realise that he's ... he's thinking.'

Torquil resisted the temptation to laugh. 'Do you think he fancies you?'

Rose shook her head. 'No. Well, maybe. Who knows?'

'So what do you want me to do?' asked Torquil.

'Why don't you let Alistair share with you? You're both guys, and your room is bigger than the other two bedrooms put together.'

'And you?' asked Torquil. 'Who will you share with? With Phoebe?'

Rose shook her head. 'No, with Dave. Phoebe can have a room to herself. She's too weird to share with anybody really.'

'Let me get this straight,' said Torquil. 'Alistair moves in with me. You move in with Dave. Phoebe has a room to herself. Is that what you want?'

'More or less. In fact, yes, that's what I want.'

'But I don't want to share with Alistair. Why can't he share with Dave and you and Phoebe share? Two guys sharing and two girls sharing. What's wrong with that?'

Rose gave Torquil a sullen look. 'Why can't I share with Dave?'

Torquil thought for a few moments. Then he said, 'You fancy Dave, don't you?'

Rose looked away. 'Maybe. In the past. Not now.'

'You've moved on?'

'Yes.'

'And do you think he wants to share with you? Have you spoken to him about it?'

'Not in so many words. I thought if you said that you were doing a reorganisation, he'd accept it.'

Torquil asked what Rose thought Phoebe would want – if she were to be asked.

'You don't ask Phoebe for an opinion,' came the reply. 'She can't handle these things.'

'And Dave? Did you ask Dave what he wanted?'

Rose shrugged. 'Dave doesn't mind either way.'

'Do you think Alistair's into guys?'

'Maybe.'

'Maybe he'd like to share with Dave. Have you thought of that?'

Rose's tone was dismissive. 'I don't do hypotheticals,' she said.

'Why don't you share with me?' asked Torquil, adding, 'Hypothetically.'

'Because you aren't Dave,' Rose replied. 'Sorry, Torquil. No offence, but you just aren't.'

## 52. Elspeth Reflects

Elspeth had enjoyed having Angus and Domenica to dinner. She liked both of them, but in particular she found Domenica's company stimulating. At the same time, she found the evening of friendly conversation curiously unsettling. As she and Matthew said goodbye to their guests, waving them down the drive towards the narrow passage through the encroaching rhododendrons, she felt a nudge of regret. Only twelve miles or so separated them from Scotland Street, Drummond Place and the world in which Angus and Domenica lived, but it seemed to Elspeth to be rather more than that. Angus and Domenica led an urban existence – one in which the facilities of Edinburgh were there at hand, only a short walk away. They could go out of the front door of 44 Scotland Street and expect to meet, within a block or two, people with whom they could pass the time of day. They could drop into Big Lou's coffee bar whenever they wanted, and the odds were there would be somebody whom they knew. Or if there wasn't, there would be Big Lou herself, whose reassuring presence, it seemed to Elspeth, was so much a part of Edinburgh life – like the One o'Clock Gun or the Floral Clock. Big Lou always had time to chat, even as she made her bacon rolls and coffee, and of course Matthew was now part-owner of her business, which meant they could, if they wished, go round to the other side of the counter and lend a hand.

It seemed to Elspeth that Domenica had a far more interesting life than she did. She knew that this was not a line of thought one should pursue: all of us know of others whose lives seem more colourful, more fulfilling than our own. Other people, it often seems, have more friends than we do. Other people have more going on in their lives; have more interesting things happen to them; have more disposable income, more attractive clothes, fewer problems with their weight, their cholesterol levels, or their hair. Other people, Elspeth thought, don't have triplets, or live in a place where for large parts of the day there is simply nobody around with whom to have a chat. If she felt lonely, as she often did with

Matthew off at work in the gallery, then to whom could she talk? James, the au pair, might be around, but his working time was now shared between them and Big Lou's coffee bar, and anyway James was young and there was a limit to the company he could provide. He was planning something, Elspeth felt, but she had no idea what it was.

'Are you happy with these arrangements?' she had asked him.

'What arrangements?'

'The deal we agreed. You work here so many days a week and then so many at Big Lou's.'

He assured her he was. 'This suits me fine. It really does. I love helping out in the coffee bar – I really do. You meet all sorts of people. And I like Big Lou. She makes me laugh. We have a great time.'

She was pleased with that, because they liked having him about the place. He was by far the most successful au pair they had had: he was good with the boys, who adored him; he was a talented cook; he was good with his hands, and had recently fixed not only a washing machine but also a leaking water tank, a malfunctioning computer, a fence, and a window that had been broken by a ball kicked by one of the boys. James was in every respect perfect, and if Elspeth was discontented with her lot, it had nothing to do with him. She had heard stories from other young mothers of nightmare au pairs, including one who had been dealing in stolen goods from the house, another who drank, and a third who spent several hours a day, every day, washing her hair. Elspeth knew that she was lucky to have James, but what she needed were friends, and that, it seemed, was more difficult, living in the country.

There was the Duke of Johannesburg, of course, who was James's uncle, and who lived just a few miles away. He was always happy for her to call in for a cup of tea, and he sometimes called in to see her on his way back from West Linton, where he played bridge two afternoons a week. Recently, though, he had had trouble with transport, and these calls had become less frequent. His Gaelic-speaking driver had gone back to Stornoway and had taken the Duke's old Land Rover with him, promising to return it, but failing to do so. That left the Duke only with the car that he had bought from a man at Haymarket Station, and that had proved to be temperamental. It was a strange-looking car: it was difficult to tell at first glance which was the front and which was the back, and it was only when one opened the door and saw the position of the steering wheel that one could work out which way it was meant to go. A further problem was the fact that nobody had as yet identified what make it was. The garage man to whom the Duke went, a mechanic whom he had used for years, had expressed the view that it was Belgian, but he was not certain about that. When spare parts had been needed, they had found that Alfa Romeo parts appeared to fit, but then so did some made by Ford. This had left the *garagiste* scratching his head.

'The important thing is that the car goes,' he said. 'That's the bottom line, Duke – believe me. If your car goes, you're happy. If it doesn't, you're unhappy.'

'True,' said the Duke.

That afternoon, on the day after the dinner with Angus and Domenica, Elspeth was thinking about her situation when she heard the crunch of tyres on gravel and looked out to see the Duke of Johannesburg's unusual car drawing up outside. It was exactly what she wanted. She felt in the mood for a chat. James had taken the boys to play in the woods, and she had been sitting there, looking at the hills. The arrival of the Duke was very well timed.

She went outside to greet him.

'Car's playing up again,' he said. 'I had to drive half the way from Carlops in reverse. Then it got unstuck and went forward again.'

Elspeth expressed sympathy. But then she said, 'There comes a time when you have to get rid of a car.' She paused. 'Have you thought of going electric?'

'It would be an awful bother changing the batteries,' he said.

Elspeth smiled. 'Let's have tea on the terrace. Have you been playing bridge?'

'Dreadful hands,' said the Duke. 'I had the wrong cards. But you have to make do with the cards you get.'

Yes, thought Elspeth. You do.

## 53. We're All of Us Lost

'It's an odd thing, corrosion,' remarked the Duke. 'I'm fairly convinced that the problem with my car is that some of the leads have corroded.'

Elspeth poured his coffee as they sat out on the terrace, taking advantage of the warm mid-afternoon sun. An area of high pressure had settled over Scotland, and the sky was devoid of cloud. Elspeth had put on a battered sun hat, and the Duke had taken an ancient Tam o' Shanter out of his pocket, brushed it down, and then planted it firmly on his head.

'This tam belonged to my father,' he said. 'He was with Fitzroy Maclean in the desert during the war. And in the Balkans.'

The Duke looked at Elspeth. 'Do you know who Fitzroy Maclean was?'

Elspeth looked embarrassed. 'It sounds as if I should.'

The Duke shook his head. 'No, I wouldn't say that. I wouldn't expect your generation to know about him. He was one of our finest men, though. He had an adventurous life – the sort of life nobody leads today. He sat through Stalin's show trials; he fought in the Western Desert and with Tito in Yugoslavia; he was in Parliament for a long time. He wrote travel books and spoke numerous languages and ran a hotel in the Highlands ... My father knew him well. I went to his funeral. It was the last funeral Scotland will ever have for a hero, a clan funeral that everybody attended, with a piper playing a lament, and crofters and fishermen rubbing shoulders with smart Edinburgh people, and everybody aware that the country had lost a great man ...'

He stopped. 'I shouldn't be talking about the past. It's only too easy, but I don't want to wallow in nostalgia.'

'You started off talking about corrosion,' said Elspeth.

The Duke took a sip of his coffee. 'Yes, corrosion. Living here, a few miles from the sea,' he continued, 'we don't see as much corrosion as they do down on the coast. I have a friend over on Mull who is right on the shore. He gets wind coming in from the Atlantic, and it's laden with salt. You don't see it, of course, but the salt is there. And do you know what? He went to open his front door one day, and the door fell off. Right off. It landed on the ground with a great bang. The hinges had corroded.'

'No!'

'They were meant to be brass. He always went for brass, because it's not meant to react to salt. It's the same with stainless steel. But the problem is that they sell stuff that claims to be stainless, but isn't.'

The Duke took another sip of his coffee. 'Talking of doors, do you know I'm having some alterations done to the house? I've been putting it off for some time, but I've decided to bite the bullet. You may recall that when you and Matthew came to dinner at my place, we ate in a rather poky little dining room at the back of the house. Remember?'

'I rather liked it.'

'Oh, it's all right. It's just that I find it a bit small. If you have more than four people for dinner, as I sometimes do, it gets a bit crowded. So I decided to incorporate a large pantry with the dining room. Together the two will make a good-sized room.'

'That seems reasonable enough. Who's your architect?'

'Actually, I'm not employing an architect. No need to, in my view. If you get a builder who knows what's what, then they can do the drawings in-house. A competent draughts-man can do much of what an architect does.'

'Perhaps that's what *we* need. Matthew has been talking

about building a conservatory. On that side of the house, over there. It's south-facing.'

'And has lovely views too,' said the Duke. 'The Lammermuir Hills.'

'I can imagine sitting out there a lot,' said Elspeth. 'We have this terrace, of course, but it can get a bit chilly – even in summer – if there's much wind about. Anything from the north or north-east can be a bit chilly.' She paused. 'Have you got a good builder, Duke?'

'The best. He lives in Penicuik. People speak highly of him around here. An Orangeman, I believe. He's had a look at the house, and it was he, in fact, who suggested that we simply remove the wall between the existing dining room and the pantry. He says we don't need planning permission. I assume he's right. Anyway, he says he can do it as early as next week. He said the messy bit will last only two days – then it can all be finished off pretty quickly. I must say . . .'

The Duke suddenly stopped talking. He looked at Elspeth quizzically, as if unsure about something. 'Elspeth,' he said, 'may I ask you a very personal question?'

She nodded. 'I don't mind.'

'Are you unhappy?'

She had not expected this, and for a few moments she was unsure what to say. Then she answered, 'For the most part, no. But sometimes . . .'

'It's just that you seem unhappy to me. I'm not sure why I think that – perhaps it's something in your eyes. The eyes give us away, you know.'

She looked away, unsettled.

'I don't mean to embarrass you,' said the Duke. Then, 'Is it your marriage?'

She shook her head. 'No, it's not Matthew. He's a good husband to me. And I love him dearly.'

'Good, so it's being out here, with the boys. Trapped? Am I right?'

She sighed. 'Perhaps.'

'And not having any sense of purpose? Or is that putting it too strongly?'

'Maybe. I mean, no, you're not putting it too strongly.'

The Duke sat back in his chair and looked up at the sky. 'We're all of us pretty lost, I think. We have no purpose to our lives because we don't believe in anything. And because we don't believe in anything, there are no challenges for us. It's all flat and featureless. Empty.'

'Isn't that a bit extreme? Some people still have a cause.'

'Yes, they do. And in Scotland, what is that cause for many of our compatriots? A new Scottish state – because the existing state is not one that some people find easy to believe in any longer. We want to have a sense of something we can create ourselves. A chimera, perhaps, but *our* chimera. We want to have a mission in our lives, and the national cause provides one. I can see that.'

'And where do you stand?' asked Elspeth.

The Duke hesitated. 'I can see both sides, quite frankly. And surely one shouldn't deny that there are always two sides to such issues.' He paused again, before adding, enigmatically, 'Head or heart?'

Elspeth waited. And then the Duke continued, 'There are patriots on both sides, we might remind ourselves. Perfectly reasonable people have quite differing ideas of the good. And remember that people may take up a position enthusiastically because it is something that they are invited to believe in. And when you haven't believed in anything for some time, that's an attractive invitation. Therein lies the appeal of identity politics throughout the world.'

'Heal Scotland, and I heal myself?'

The Duke turned to look at Elspeth again. 'These are big questions, and the real issue is what can be done to make *you* feel better?'

'Talking to you seems to help,' said Elspeth. She barely thought about the words before she uttered them, but, once she had spoken, she immediately realised that what she said was true.

## 54. At Doddie's Hoose

It was on the third day of his sojourn in Aberdeen that Bertie reached the view that his only hope was to escape – by whatever means possible – and make his way back to Edinburgh. He had by then started at his new school, Robert Gordon's, where he had been handed over to a small group of boys in the class who had been instructed by the teacher to ensure that 'this poor boy from Edinburgh' be made welcome. 'So you're the new loon,' the leader of these boys, Doddie, had said. 'Is it yersel', then?' Bertie had been uncertain how to respond to what was clearly intended to be a friendly greeting, but had replied, 'Aye, it's mysel'.' This appeared to satisfy Doddie, who looked him over while muttering, 'So, a new loon ...' Bertie had not known what this meant. Loon? What was a loon? Was it an insult, or was it something else – perhaps even a compliment? But if it was a compliment, why was he described as *peer*? Bertie's grasp of Scots was sufficient for him to know that *peer* meant *poor*, but if it was Scots that these boys were speaking, it was certainly a very strange version.

His subsequent conversation with his new friends was equally unenlightening.

'Fit are ye cried?' asked Doddie at this first encounter.

Bertie stared at the other boy. 'I'm not crying,' he said.

Doddie frowned. 'Naebody said you're greeting. Fit are ye cried?'

'He's cried Bertie,' said Jake.

'Aye,' agreed Jeems. 'Bertie Pollock. He's cried Bertie Pollock.'

'Aye, ye're nae far wrang there,' joined in Andra. 'Bertie Pollock fae Edinburgh.'

Doddie now had a further question, 'Fa div ye bide?' he asked politely.

Bertie looked up at the sky. He had no idea what Doddie meant and hoped that inspiration might come from above. But it did not. All he saw was a cold, empty sky. And he wondered, for a moment, how far they were from the North Pole. Fifty miles, perhaps.

Getting no response to his question, Doddie went on to say, 'Foo ye deeing?'

Bertie smiled. In desperation he said, 'Aye.' This appeared to satisfy Doddie, who himself then said, 'Aye' – a sentiment echoed by Jake, Jeems and Andra, each of whom in turn said, 'Aye.'

Having broken the ice in this way, the four Aberdonian boys then told Bertie a bit about themselves. Doddie explained that he lived at Mannofield, but that he spent every weekend at his grandfather's farm near Cults. Or that was what Bertie thought he said, although he was by no means sure. Jake came from Milltimber and had two brothers, he said, Hamish and Willie. Jeems told Bertie that he was not sure where he came from – or again that is what Bertie thought he said. 'He kens fine,' said Doddie. 'Aa folk ken where they bide.'

This exchange was followed by a suggestion – from Doddie – that they play *steelers*. Not having any steelers himself, Bertie was given a couple of round metal marbles by each of the boys on the understanding that he could pay them back once he had won a few more himself. The game was ready to start, but before that happened, Doddie solemnly pronounced a formula that was taken up by the others, as a Greek chorus might pronounce on a character's fate:

> *Eetle, ottle, black bottle,*
> *Eetle, ottle oot;*
> *Tak a roosty roosty nail*
> *And pit it straight oot,*
> *Shining on the mantelpiece*
> *Like a silver threepenny piece,*
> *Eetle, ottle, black bottle,*
> *Eetle, ottle oot!*

In the silence that followed, Bertie asked what this meant.

Doddie shrugged. 'That means you start, Bertie, and I dinnae ken fit it means. We've aye done it.'

Back in the classroom, it was time for instruction in Charles Murray's *The Whistle*. The class appeared to know several verses of this poem, and recited it with vigour while Bertie, embarrassed at not knowing what was going on, made an attempt to mouth the words. He felt ashamed. He felt isolated and ignorant. And the following day, when Doddie kindly invited him to come home to tea at his house – the invitation having been approved by Irene, who had engaged in conversation with Doddie's mother at the school gate – Bertie's sense of alienation simply grew.

Doddie was welcoming, and showed Bertie his collection of birds' feathers, his electric train set, and the rugby ball signed by Stuart Hogg and Gregor Townsend that his father had bought at a charity auction. Then he escorted Bertie into the garden, where Bertie helped him take the tea bags off the line.

'Why do you hang tea bags on the washing line?' Bertie asked, as they released the small shrivelled squares from their pegs before putting them into a jar.

Doddie seemed surprised by the question. Was this not something that everyone did? Perhaps Edinburgh, he reflected, was different. 'To dry them,' he replied.

He was now speaking English to Bertie, and there was no difficulty in their understanding one another.

Bertie was puzzled. 'But you've already used them,' he pointed out. 'Why dry them out?'

'To use them again, of course,' said Doddie. 'You dry them,

see, and then you can use them again. We use our tea bags three times. Jeems says that at his house they get six cups of tea out of each bag. That's a lot, I think.'

Bertie had heard that there was a certain degree of parsimony in Aberdeen, but he had not expected this. Nor had he expected what happened next, which was for Doddie to show him how to repair a hot-water bottle after it perished.

'You can fix them with a bicycle puncture repair kit,' Doddie explained. 'We keep our hot water bottles for thirty years, you know. This one here, Bertie, belonged to my grandfather. My dad still wears his slippers. Patched up a bit, of course, but still all right.'

Tea consisted of a bowl of oatmeal porridge and half a rowie, a buttery roll on which a very small amount of jam had been spread.

'My granny makes that jam,' Doddie explained. 'She collects the berries from the hedges. The only thing she has to pay for is the sugar.'

Bertie was collected by Irene at six o'clock.

'You'll have had your tea?' Irene asked.

Bertie nodded.

Irene drove them home. 'I'm so pleased you're enjoying yourself here, Bertissimo,' she said.

Bertie said nothing. Before he had left Doddie's house he had had an urgent conversation with his new friend. Doddie, it transpired, knew how to use his father's solar-powered computer and had agreed to Bertie's request that he send an email to Ranald Braveheart Macpherson, who not only knew the combination number for his father's safe, but knew, too, all his computer passwords. Ranald's reading was not all that good, but he could get that girl next door to read it to him. And Ranald had, of course, told Bertie that if he needed help, he was only to send a message. With this in mind, Bertie had written out a message for Doddie to send.

'Please help me, Ranald,' it read. 'Please help me to get home. Very unhappy here. Your friend, Bertie.'

## 55. *Ranald Leaves a Note*

When Ranald Braveheart Macpherson received Bertie's email, as dictated to Doddie and as read out to him by his neighbour and amanuensis, Shirley, he lost no time in packing his school satchel with a change of clothing, a compass, and a water bottle. Then, making sure that his parents were fully engrossed in their favourite soap opera, he crept into his father's study and began expertly to twirl the dial of the safe's combination lock. With a satisfactory series of clicks, the mechanism slipped into place and the door of the safe swung open. Inside, Ranald saw the neatly stacked piles of euros that he knew his father kept for some unexplained eventuality, along with several expensive-looking men's watches, and a pouch of Krugerrands. Behind the euros were smaller piles of five- and ten-pound Bank of Scotland notes, and it was to these that Ranald now helped himself, tucking them into the zip-up compartment of his satchel. Then he went out briefly – to speak to the girl next door – before returning to his own house for final preparations.

Being as quiet as he could, Ranald let himself out of the door, and darted down the garden path. Within a few minutes he boarded a bus that would take him down to Princes Street and to Waverley Station. Once there, he used some of the purloined Bank of Scotland notes to purchase a one-way ticket to Aberdeen.

'How old are you, son?' asked the official in the ticket booth.

Ranald hesitated. 'Eighteen,' he said, eventually, making his voice as deep as he could.

The official burst out laughing. 'Do you want to pay an adult fare?' he asked. 'Is that what you want, son?'

Flustered, Ranald shook his head, and was given a half-fare ticket.

'You're not running away, by any chance?' asked the official. 'And what's your name, by the way?'

Ranald cleared his throat. 'Ranald Braveheart Macpherson,' he replied. 'And I'm going to Aberdeen on a humanitarian mission.'

The official laughed again. 'Oh, goodness! Humanitarian. That's a big word, Ranald Braveheart Macpherson! I must remember that.'

Ranald made his way to the platform from which the Aberdeen train was scheduled to leave. Once on the train, he made himself as unobtrusive as possible, sheltering behind a newspaper left in the carriage by a previous traveller. Ranald could not yet read, and was concerned that he might have the newspaper upside down, but a glance at a photograph on the front page reassured him. It was the First Minister, and she was opening something, or closing it – Ranald could not be quite sure. As the journey began, he gazed out of the window, thinking of what he would do when he arrived in Aberdeen. He had an address for Bertie, and he had a street map of the city that showed quite clearly where Irene's house was. He would go there, he thought, and help Bertie to escape through a window. Then they would return to the railway station and start the journey back to Edinburgh. With any luck they would have a head start on any pursuers – especially Bertie's mother, for whom Ranald had a healthy respect. He would not like to be caught by Mrs Pollock, Ranald thought, because he had heard it said that mad people sometimes had the strength of ten ordinary people, and there was very little doubt in Ranald's mind that Bertie's mother, even if not entirely mad, was at least half-mad, and was therefore very probably as strong as five normal women.

Ranald had given some thought to what his parents might think and do when they realised he was not there. He was a conscientious boy, and had asked Shirley, the girl who lived next door and who was famous for her neat handwriting, to pen a note for him. This note, written in what Shirley described as 'my exemplary joined-up writing' had cost thirty pence. 'And no credit terms are available, Ranald Braveheart Macpherson!' Shirley warned. Ranald had given her one of the five-pound notes from his father's safe and told her that she could keep the change.

Shirley had outdone herself. 'To whom it may concern,' the note began. 'This is to inform you that Ranald Braveheart Macpherson has been called away. He will be back tomorrow. During the period of his absence, he will not have access to

email or to a telephone, but will attend to your issue immediately on his return to Edinburgh.'

'What do you think of that?' Shirley asked proudly.

'It's very good, Shirley,' Ranald said. But then he asked,
'Are you sure it says what you say it says?'

Shirley looked at him disdainfully. 'Of course it does,' she
snapped. 'Why would I tell fibs in one of my notes? I've got
more sense than that, Ranald Braveheart Macpherson. I want
to get customers coming back. If you fib, then they don't.' She
paused, and finished, 'Your call is important to me.'

Ranald had left the note on the dining-room table where
it would be sure to be seen by his parents. He did not want
them to worry, and he thought that they would probably be
reassured by the tone of the message. This was not a simple
*back soon* note – this looked, and sounded, official.

Slowly the train wound its way through Fife. Kirkcaldy
came and went, and then there was the Tay Railway Bridge,
curving across the river, with Dundee nestling on the other
side. Then the towns of the east coast, with their hinterland
rolling out behind them; farms and villages amongst which
lives were led according to nature's designs: spring, and plant-
ing, summer and growth, the harvest of autumn.

Ranald felt increasingly anxious. What if he could not
find Bertie? What if he arrived too late and Bertie's mother
had sent him off to boarding school, or apprenticed him to
a cruel ship's captain and he was, even now, being forced
to climb the rigging on some Jamaica-bound ship? Ranald
had been read a story very much like that not all that long
ago, and he could just imagine poor Bertie in the position
of the boy in that tale. Bertie's mother was a desperate

character – everybody knew that – and she was quite capable of packing him off to sea.

Ranald shivered. He was beginning to feel homesick. Scotland was much bigger than he had imagined it to be. And what was that smell? Fish. They were approaching Aberdeen now, and it occurred to Ranald that Bertie might even have been put to work on a fishing boat. That was very tough work – and dangerous too. And you came home and you smelled of fish for days, Ranald had heard. It wouldn't matter to him, of course, because Bertie was his friend, and if your friend smells of fish you should try not to let it affect your friendship. Everybody, thought Ranald Braveheart Macpherson, knows that.

## 56. *Thank You for Having Me*

Bertie heard the pebble hit his window. He looked up sharply. A second pebble clattered against the glass, and he caught his breath. His heart raced as he approached the window and stared out into the darkness.

An urgent voice came from below. 'Bertie!'

He peered into the darkness. 'Ranald? Is that you?'

Now Bertie saw his friend's face emerging from the shadows. He should never have doubted that Ranald would come. Of course he would come. Ranald had never let him down, even in small things, and now, in this, his moment of greatest need, he was here. Bertie opened his window and reached down to help Ranald clamber up to the sill. Then with a wriggle and a twist, Ranald was in the room, dusting himself off, beaming with pleasure at his achievement.

Bertie stuttered his thanks. His heart was almost too full for him to say very much, but he left Ranald in no doubt as to the intensity of his relief.

'We can go back tomorrow morning,' Ranald said. 'I've got money for our tickets, and I've also got a compass and a torch.'

'You think of everything, Ranald,' said Bertie appreciatively.

Ranald accepted the compliment with a nod of his head. 'We can set off tomorrow,' he said. 'It's easier to travel by daylight.'

Bertie agreed. He remembered what he had read in *Scouting for Boys*, a clandestine copy of which he had secreted under his bed in Edinburgh. Baden-Powell had said something about how easy it was to get lost during the night, especially when there was no moon or the moon was obscured by clouds. He knew what he was talking about, thought Bertie, as he must have been lost many times in Matabeleland. And Matabeleland and Aberdeenshire were probably more similar than many people realised.

'You're right,' said Ranald. 'You could end up going in the completely wrong direction if you can't see where you're going.'

'You can sleep at the other end of my bed,' Bertie said. 'There's plenty of room.' He paused. His mother usually came in to say goodnight, and Ranald would have to hide until that visit was over. He could go under the bed, Bertie decided. Then, when Irene had switched off the light, he could be made more comfortable.

As it happened, Ranald had just enough time to hide under the bed before Irene appeared and told Bertie it was time to turn off his light. The following day was a Saturday, and although there would be no school, Irene said that she was planning an hour of Italian *conversazione* after breakfast, and Bertie would need to be alert for that. 'We have so much to catch up on, Bertie, *troppo*, in fact.' Afterwards, she announced, they would go out to have morning coffee with Dr Fairbairn.

'You remember Dr Fairbairn, don't you, Bertie? You loved going to talk to him in his consulting rooms.'

Bertie remained tight-lipped. Not wanting to prolong his mother's presence in the room, he merely made a sound of general assent.

'Dr Fairbairn is so looking forward to seeing you again, Bertie,' Irene said, and then added, 'Sweet dreams,' innocent of the irony in such a wish, given Dr Fairbairn's known and unhealthy interest in the dreams of others.

Irene hesitated in the doorway. Bertie hoped that Ranald would not suddenly sneeze or have a coughing fit, or do anything else that might give away his presence. He thought that he could hear Ranald breathing, and if he could, then presumably Irene could as well. To mask the sound, Bertie decided to hum a tune as loudly as he could.

'Do stop that noise, Bertie,' Irene said. 'Humming is such a mindless exercise.'

'But I feel so happy,' Bertie said. 'It makes me want to hum.'

'There are other ways of expressing a positive state of mind,' said Irene.

Bertie thought he heard a noise from under the bed. He froze, thinking it inevitable that Irene would hear, but she did not, and now the door was closed and he and Ranald were left alone.

Waking early the next morning, Bertie and Ranald were out of the house by seven. Irene had taken to sleeping in since she moved to Aberdeen, and would not be getting out of bed for another hour. When she arose, she would find the note left for her by Bertie. 'Dearest Mummy, I have had to return to Edinburgh,' he wrote. 'I am so sorry. Please say hello to Dr Fairbairn for me. Tell him I have been having lots of interesting dreams and I shall write some of them down for him so that he can think about them. Tell him not to worry. Thank you so much for having me. Love, Bertie.'

It did not take long to get to the railway station, where Ranald used more of his father's Bank of Scotland notes to purchase two tickets to Edinburgh. Then, after buying themselves a bacon roll and a bar of chocolate, they sat down on a platform bench and waited for the Edinburgh train to draw up for boarding.

In retrospect, neither boy could work out how they made the mistake. Ranald, at least, had the excuse of not being able to read; Bertie had no such excuse, but he still failed to see that the train manifestly proclaimed itself as being bound for Inverurie and not for Edinburgh. And so it was that when, after its short journey north, the train drew to halt at Inverurie Station, both Ranald and Bertie were surprised to find themselves somewhere that did not look at all like Edinburgh Waverley.

'I think we've come the wrong way,' said Bertie. 'This sign says *Inverurie*. See? That's what it says, Ranald. Inverurie is north of Aberdeen – I've always known that.'

Ranald tried to put on a brave face. 'Oh well,' he said. 'It's better than still being in Aberdeen.'

Bertie had to agree. 'We can go and look at the time-table,' he said. 'We probably won't have long to wait to get a train to Edinburgh.'

Ranald looked miserable. 'I want to go home, Bertie,' he sniffed.

Bertie put his arm round his friend's shoulders. 'You mustn't get upset, Ranald,' he said. 'We'll get home eventually.'

Ranald tried to control himself. But soon his shoulders started to heave as the full extent of their plight sank in. They were far from home, and presumably by now they would have been reported as missing. Their photographs would be on the television news, and the police would be looking for them, perhaps even using dogs to track them down. As he thought this – and shuddered – Ranald imagined he could hear the baying of a bloodhound, although it was not that at all, but the sound of a flock of geese passing overhead, squawking to one another as they dipped and wheeled across the northern sky.

## 57. Bless You

From behind the counter of her coffee bar, Big Lou watched Fat Bob in discussion with Angus and Matthew at Matthew's favourite table on the other side of the room. The three of them had taken to sharing morning coffee together and would spend an hour or so chatting before Matthew would look at his watch and remember that he had a business to run. Angus would do the same, and remind himself that not only did he have a canvas awaiting him on an easel, but he had his dog, Cyril, to exercise. Cyril, of course, was in no hurry, and was as happy to be in one place as in any other, and to remain there indefinitely. He was on dog time, which is quite different from human time, being punctuated only by meals, periods of wakefulness or sleep, and by the occasional salience that comes with the pursuit of a cat or squirrel. Apart from that, an hour is much the same thing to a dog as a day, a week, or a month – and of course there is no terminus. No dog knows that he or she must die: what we have now is what we will have forever, in the mind of a dog, just as it is in the mind of a small child.

Big Lou knew that the three of them were planning something, but she was not sure exactly what that might be. It pleased her, though, to see Angus and Matthew getting on so well with Fat Bob. They came from such different worlds, with Angus being a portrait painter, Matthew being the director of an art gallery, and Fat Bob being a professional, or semi-professional, strongman – he also had a job in a stone merchant's yard, where he cut and polished marble for kitchen surfaces. Scotland's democratic traditions, though, meant that people talked to one another as equals whatever the difference in their level of education or their station in life, and that was just how it should be, thought Big Lou. It did not matter in the least what bed you were born in: what counted was what you were inside. People in England, she suspected, sometimes just did not grasp that, and that was a pity: their society was more stratified than Scotland's; they needed to read Robert Burns' *A Man's a Man for a' That*, she felt, because that said all that had to be said on that subject. If you understood what Burns was saying in that poem, then you understood how Scotland felt – at heart.

That morning her curiosity got the better of her. 'You boys,' she called out, 'you're sitting there like a pickle of conspirators. What are you talking about?'

Angus looked at Fat Bob, expecting him to answer.

'Just a wee set of Highland Games,' Bob replied.

'In Drummond Place Garden,' added Angus.

Big Lou came over to hear more. They were planning, she was told, to have an afternoon of Highland Games the following Saturday. 'It will be in aid of charity,' Fat Bob said. 'We'll charge a pound to get in ...'

'And two pounds to get out,' said Angus. 'That was my idea.'

'And I've approached the George Watson's Pipe Band,' chipped in Matthew. 'They've agreed to come and play.'

Fat Bob ran through the events they had agreed to include.

There would be a tug-of-war, he said: lawyers against accountants, and Catholics against Protestants.

Big Lou raised an eyebrow. 'What a good idea,' she said. 'Who thought of that last one?'

'I did, actually,' said Angus. 'These things are community-building.'

Fat Bob nodded. 'And then tossing the caber and throwing the hammer, of course. And a few track events for the weans. A sack race, maybe.'

'Good,' said Big Lou. 'It should be a very good afternoon.'

Big Lou got up to attend to a customer, leaving Bob, Angus and Matthew to their planning. She looked over her shoulder at Fat Bob; she was so proud of him. Her previous men had been loners, for the most part – rather moody types who would never have sat down with people like Matthew and Angus and hatched a plot to hold Highland Games. She had known Bob for a few weeks now, and there had not been a single day, nor indeed a single moment, when she had entertained so much as a scintilla of doubt about him. He was a man of complete honesty – that was just so obvious – and he was kind and attentive too. The previous evening, he had insisted on cooking for her and had persuaded Finlay to help him prepare the meal. She had heard the two of them chuckling in the kitchen, and she had seen the look of pride on Finlay's face when he and Bob had served the meal.

And then, before Finlay went off to bed, she had seen Fat Bob down on the floor fiddling with the points on Finlay's train set, while the young boy adjusted the tiny benches and trolleys on the miniature platform.

'That should do it,' said Bob. 'There, that's working now.'

And she heard Finlay say, 'Thanks, Fat Bob. I like it when you come round to our place.'

'Aye, and I like it too,' said Bob. 'And thanks for making me so welcome, Finlay.'

Big Lou took a deep breath. She wanted to cry. The sight of a man being gentle and kind towards a child is something that moves women profoundly – it just does. And she knew that she would never find anybody like Fat Bob again, and that if he were to ask her to marry him she would give a positive reply, immediately, there and then, without waiting to consider the matter. She would say, *Yes*, and then, just in case he had not heard, she would say, *Yes*, again.

Which is exactly what happened two hours later when, with Finlay off to bed and the two of them sitting together on the sofa, Fat Bob turned to Big Lou and said, 'Lou, I have an important question to ask you.'

And she had said, rather quickly, 'Yes,' as if in answer to a question that he had not, in fact, asked. She corrected herself, saying, 'Yes?'

He said, 'Will you marry me, Big Lou? I'm not much to look at. I haven't got a lot in this world – not when you come to think of it. But I have a good job, and we'll get by on what I earn, and I'll try to make you happy – I promise you that, Lou, I promise to God.'

She gave him her answer, and he took her hand, and pressed it against his chest, where he believed his heart to be. And it was a broad heart, and a strong one too, and she felt it beat, which was such a strange thing, and so wonderful – the heart-beat of another.

She looked at him, and he at her. Their happiness required nothing else; it was complete.

'Bless you, Bob,' Big Lou whispered.

She meant it. Whatever power there was to confer a benediction, she now invoked, in the sure and certain belief that it was the right thing to do.

## 58. A Thursday Meeting

Every Thursday the Professor of Philosophical Psychiatry at the University of Edinburgh – the holder of a personal chair conferred after the publication of his groundbreaking *The Brain, Identity and the Continuity of the Self* – held a lunchtime seminar meeting with a small group of like-minded colleagues. Also invited to these meetings were several of the more academically inclined medical students, particularly those who were showing an interest in pursuing psychiatry as a speciality. These meetings took place in the Professor's room at the Royal Edinburgh Hospital, where sandwiches would be provided, along with tea, coffee, and sparkling water. People were encouraged to bring occasional items to add variety – a few sticks of celery, for example, or cheese, or, as on this occasion, some fruit. The Professor's garden had recently yielded a crop of plums, and these were now being offered round in a small basket.

'Very delicious,' said one of the students. 'I love apricots.'

'Thank you,' said the Professor. Youth should be corrected gently. 'Plums,' he whispered. 'We've had a large crop this year. It all depends on the weather.'

'Everything depends on the weather,' said one of the research fellows.

'Indeed,' said the Professor. 'You might well say that.'

There was a short silence. The Professor began. 'I may as well begin,' he said.

One of the students licked his fingers after finishing a plum. Another looked surreptitiously at her phone. She was expecting a text message from her boyfriend. She suspected that he had stopped loving her. The Senior Lecturer in Abnormal Psychology dabbed at her lips with a handkerchief. She wanted another plum, but was not sure whether she should ask for one. She decided not to.

The Professor reached for his notes. 'I thought that we might look today at the most extraordinary case,' he said. 'I have only just seen the patient and shall be seeing him again, but I thought some preliminary observations might be of interest.'

They looked at him expectantly.

'The patient is a young man in his late twenties,' said the Professor. 'I shall call him Bruce. He was referred to me by a colleague in the Royal Infirmary who asked him if he wouldn't mind a psychiatric examination after he had pre-sented with a non-psychiatric complaint.' He paused. 'He had been struck by lightning.'

The Senior Lecturer in Abnormal Psychology let out an involuntary laugh. 'I'd certainly complain if I were to be struck by lightning.'

One of the medical students smiled. 'Shocking,' he said.

The Professor looked at him with slight disapproval. 'Let us not make light of our patient's misfortunes,' he said.

The student looked apologetic, and blushed. He had merely followed on the remark made by the Senior Lecturer in Abnormal Psychology. She had made the original joke, but he was getting the blame. That was hierarchies for you, wasn't it? It was.

'Bruce was quite prepared to see me,' the Professor continued. 'Physically, he had escaped largely untouched. A small area of very superficial burns – and a rib fracture or two where he had landed on the road. He was, apparently, thrown some distance into the air by the impact of the lightning.'

'Astonishing,' said the Psychiatric Registrar. 'You'd think that . . . how many volts are there in a bolt of lightning? More than 230, I imagine.'

'As it happens,' said the Professor, 'I looked that up before I saw him. The figure is surprising. It's millions of volts, apparently. Millions. And yet I read that ninety per cent of those who are struck survive. Yes, I was surprised by that, given that we're talking about that many volts, but you're unlucky if you succumb.'

'Unlucky if you're hit in the first place, surely,' said the Psychiatric Registrar. 'What are the odds of being hit? It must be pretty unlikely. Anybody here been struck by lightning? See? Nobody.'

'Actually,' said the Professor, 'I looked at that too. There are wild variations in the estimate of the odds. I saw one in three hundred thousand being mentioned. But the *British Medical Journal* assured me that it's more like one in ten million. The Office of National Statistics, however, says that it's roughly one in a million each year. That means about sixty people are struck by lightning in the UK annually.'

There was a short silence as this information was digested. It was not a comfortable thought. It could happen. It was not all that unlikely.

'But the point,' the Professor continued, 'is that this young man was, in fact, struck by lightning in Dundas Street.'

One of the medical students thought, *I'm not going there. Not me.*

'He was walking down the street when it happened, and he was taken by ambulance to the Royal. As I said, there was little physical damage. But then, when I saw him, I realised that there was a far more interesting dimension to the case. Put simply, the lightning strike had led to what may amount to a significant personality change.'

The Senior Lecturer in Abnormal Psychology frowned. She did not like it when people bandied the term *personality* around indiscriminately, and she had particular views on any reference to *personality change*. What exactly did that mean?

The Professor caught her eye. 'All right, Alice,' he said. 'I'm aware of your views on this, but put it this way: there was a significant, not to say complete, change not only in *affect* but in *attitude*. Will you accept that?'

'So far as it goes, yes. But . . .'

The Professor raised a hand. 'Bear with me. A notable feature of this case is that the patient appeared to have a significant degree of insight into his own behaviour. There was considerable self-awareness. He went to some pains to tell me of his defects. He used terms like *narcissism* and *selfishness* and

262

painted a rather uncomfortable picture of what he had been like prior to this experience.'

The Senior Lecturer in Abnormal Psychology looked unimpressed. 'Not all that uncommon, of course,' she said. 'People often refer to what they see as a past self in disparaging terms. It happens when they have a conversion experience, for instance. Talk to a born-again Christian about what they were like beforehand, and you may get a striking degree of self-abasement. Or to a reformed drinker. This doesn't mean that there has been any fundamental change in deep-seated traits. What it may mean is that there has been a conscious reappraisal, and a strategic decision to suppress certain urges, certain behaviours, if you like. That's not the same as so-called personality change. The underlying impulses may still be there.'

The Professor looked out of the window. He felt slightly irritated. This was *his* seminar. She had been eating *his* plums. And if you couldn't talk about personality change in a case like this, then what could you say about it? Nothing, really.

He looked away from the window. 'I take your point about caution,' he said. 'But let's put that to one side for the moment and look at what happened here. This is not about theoretical positioning on taxonomy or aetiology, or anything like that.' He glanced disapprovingly at the Senior Lecturer in Abnormal Psychology. 'This is about the experience of a real young man to whom something very unusual has happened. Let's look at that for a moment or two.'

## 59. Pluscarden Abbey

'This young man,' said the Professor, 'was something of a Lothario – before he was struck by lightning, that is.'

'In Dundas Street,' muttered the Psychiatric Registrar. '*Il Lothario della via Dundas* ... Donizetti, perhaps.'

The Professor gave him a sideways look. The Registrar had a tendency to find an operatic analogy in everything, and he found it trying. *Obsessive behaviour*, he thought. *Reductio ad opera* ... If that was the correct accusative ... 'Yes,' he said. 'In Dundas Street. He told me that he had a stream of girlfriends. He said they were queuing up.'

One of the medical students, a thin young man still wearing cycle clips, closed his eyes. *Queuing up* ... For a moment he saw himself looking out from the window of his flat in Gladstone Terrace, observing the line of attractive young women that started at the door of his stair and wound all the way down to the edge of the Meadows. Bliss. And he would be preparing to interview them before choosing one, with one or two in reserve, should his choice prove not to be quite up to his exacting standards. Oh bliss, bliss. And his MB, ChB done and dusted and with no further exams until some easy membership exam at some time in the vague future, and a good job lined up somewhere ...

The Professor's voice brought him down to earth. 'There is

a range of possible explanations. One is the effect of trauma. PTSD springs to mind. That obviously has behavioural ramifications as well as implications for mood. Being struck by lightning is clearly traumatic ...'

'I would have thought so,' agreed the Psychiatric Registrar. 'Electricity, you see ... You know, by the way, that there was an opera called *The Electrification of the Soviet Union*. Nigel Osborne wrote it. The libretto was by Craig Raine – he of "The Onion, Memory' – such a memorable poem ...'

'Yes, yes,' said the Professor. 'But even if trauma in that conventional sense has a role in the aetiology, there is another possibility – that the exposure to a large jolt of electricity has had a physical effect on the brain.'

'Interesting,' said the Psychiatric Registrar. 'In the same way as ...'

The Professor, fearing another operatic reference, cut him short. 'In the same way as electro-convulsive therapy. Yes. In that way.'

They looked at one another.

'Of course, people argue about exactly how ECT works,' said the Professor, in an explanation intended for the students. *They know so little*, he thought. 'All we know is that in some cases it *does* work.'

'Changes in regional cerebral blood flow and in glucose utilisation,' said the Psychiatric Registrar. 'My money's on that.'

'Possibly,' said the Professor. 'But not everyone would agree.'

'Not everyone agrees that night follows day,' observed the Registrar.

'But they do,' said one of the medical students. 'Of course they do.'

'I'm speaking metaphorically,' snapped the Registrar.

'Just about all speech is metaphorical,' said the Professor. 'Look at a passage of prose and you'll see that the structure is almost all metaphor. Metaphor is deep in the bones of language.'

'I don't think we need explore metaphor at these lunches,' the Registrar sniffed. 'The issue is behavioural change following electrical stimulation of the brain.'

'Being struck by lightning is certainly stimulation,' observed the Professor. 'And I wonder whether this is just a further instance of the sort of result claimed by proponents of cranial electrotherapy stimulation. There are claims for the benefits of that for anxiety and depression. If it works on mood, then ...'

The Senior Lecturer in Abnormal Psychology remembered something. 'What was the name of that unfortunate man? The railway worker?'

The Professor looked impatient. This discussion was getting nowhere: metaphors, railway workers.

But the Senior Lecturer in Abnormal Psychology had recalled the name. 'Gage,' she said. 'Phineas Gage.'

One of the medical students brightened. 'Oh, I read all about that,' he said. 'This is the guy who got a great big metal spike blown through his head. Right through. An explosive charge went off and blew it out of its hole all the way through his brain. And he survived.'

'Yes,' said the Senior Lecturer in Abnormal Psychology. 'It was a well-documented case. The fact that he survived was astonishing, but what secured him a place in medical history was the personality changes that resulted. This drew attention to the physical basis of personality, which people at that point of the nineteenth century were only beginning to wrestle with. Apparently, Gage had been a reasonable, affable man before the accident and thereafter became what was described as a vulgar and aggressive.'

'Not surprising,' said the Psychiatric Registrar. 'Consider what even a slight lesion may do to behaviour and personality.' An idea had occurred to him. 'The Phineas Gage case would make a good subject for an opera, don't you think? *The Case of Phineas Gage*. Quite a title, that. Almost as arresting as *Nixon in China*.'

A medical student raised a hand. 'Are psychopaths psychopathic because of a brain abnormality?'

'Yes,' said the Professor.

'No,' said the Senior Lecturer in Abnormal Psychology. 'We don't know that. But there does appear to be a genetic link.'

'It can be inherited?' the student asked.

The Senior Lecturer in Abnormal Psychology smiled. 'It would appear that a disposition to psychopathy may be passed on. We're not certain how the genes in question function – although there are theories.'

'So you can't blame them for what they do?'

The Professor winced. 'That's *very* complicated.'

'I don't think so,' said the Senior Lecturer in Abnormal Psychology. 'Surely it's simple: the psychopath doesn't *choose* to be a psychopath. I thought that choice lay at the heart of any notion of blame, or fault, or whatever you want to call it. That's been so since the time of Aristotle, I believe.'

'Then you exculpate roughly one third of the prison

population,' said the Professor. 'That's the proportion of people in prison who are thought possibly to have psychopathic personality disorder. Am I right?'

The question was addressed to the Senior Lecturer in Abnormal Psychology, but before she could answer – and she would have agreed – the Psychiatric Registrar asked, 'What did you find when you spoke to this patient?'

The Professor was pleased to be back on the topic in hand. 'He was most impressive,' he said. 'There was good social presentation. He struck me as being modest and considerate. He was neither too self-effacing nor too assertive. He spoke cogently.'

'And yet he was – according to his own account of himself – rather different before the incident?'

'Yes. As I said earlier, he was very pleased with himself. He was aware that women found him attractive, and he made maximum use of that.'

'And you think that this self-assessment was true?'

The Professor nodded. 'I had no reason to doubt it. It sounded credible. And in my experience, if somebody mentions his faults, they exist. It's different with virtues. Those may be entirely aspirational.'

The Senior Lecturer in Abnormal Psychology looked up at the ceiling. 'I think the real test will be what he's like in, say, three months. It will be interesting to see.'

'By then,' said the Professor, 'he will be up at Pluscarden Abbey, I imagine. You know the place? It's up near Elgin. Benedictines.'

They looked at him.

'Yes,' he went on, enjoying the drama of his announcement. 'He's going up there as a lay brother in the first instance – pending his acceptance as a novice. He's been put up to it by some Italian nun he became friendly with. Extraordinary – but there we are.'

The Senior Lecturer in Abnormal Psychology raised an eyebrow. 'Hysterical over-reaction,' she muttered.

'Possibly,' said the Professor. 'But I'm not sure that we should completely discount that old-fashioned phenomenon – a change of heart.'

The Senior Lecturer in Abnormal Psychology shook her head. 'Leopards don't change their spots,' she said.

The Professor's tone was withering. 'Forgive me for saying this, but is that what twenty years of studying the intricacies of the human mind have led you to conclude?'

The Senior Lecturer in Abnormal Psychology nodded. 'More or less,' she said.

## 60. Ca' the Yowes

Ranald Braveheart Macpherson was reported missing less than thirty minutes after he walked out of Albert Terrace, bound for Waverley Station. It was not until the next day, though, that a general alert went out to the police and public throughout Scotland to be on the lookout for him. And by that time, of course, Bertie's absence was similarly made public. It required little thought thereafter to conclude that the two boys had absconded together, and the bulletins were adjusted accordingly. *Look out for this boy* became *Look out for these boys*, with a photograph below of the two friends standing together, smiling into the camera – a moment of happiness caught by Nicola when she photographed them playing *Jacobites and Hanoverians* in Drummond Place Garden.

For the adults it was a time of chilling desolation and relentless anxiety. Stuart was beside himself and had to be calmed by Nicola, who did her best to reassure him that the two boys would undoubtedly turn up before the day was out. 'Boys tend to do this sort of thing,' she said. 'They get an idea in their heads and act on it without thinking. They'll be fine.'

Stuart's state of mind was scarcely improved by a series of recriminatory phone calls from Irene. Bertie must have run away because Stuart had encouraged him to get back to Edinburgh; the blame, by this logic, was entirely his, and how did he feel about it? 'If you feel that you should reproach yourself,' she continued, 'then you are absolutely right. You should. This is your doing, Stuart.'

Stuart had struggled to control himself. He wanted to point out that Bertie had run away from Aberdeen because he did not want to be there. He could have said that this was Irene's fault, for insisting that Bertie should spend time with her, but he did not. There was no point in rubbing salt into any wounds, and part of him felt a real sympathy for Irene. So he ended up saying, 'Take a deep breath, Irene. Bertie will be all right. This is a childish escapade that will soon blow over.'

When it became apparent that this was all a joint enterprise between the two boys, Ranald Braveheart Macpherson's father, thinking that Ranald and Bertie might be wandering around Aberdeen, decided to drive there immediately and to start scouring the streets for any sign of the boys. It was better than sitting at home and fretting, he decided.

Of course, the searches that were conducted in Edinburgh and Aberdeen, including a thorough search of Drummond Place Garden, Queen Street Gardens, and the Scotland Street tunnel, were destined to reveal nothing, as Bertie and Ranald by this time were in Inverurie, north of Aberdeen, examining the timetable of train departures displayed on the main platform of the railway station.

'We're going to have to wait for hours,' said Bertie despondently. 'Hardly any of these trains go to Edinburgh, Ranald.'

Ranald looked anxiously at his friend. 'Couldn't we hitchhike, Bertie?' he asked. 'I saw people do that in a film once. They stood at the side of the road and held out their thumbs. A car stopped and took them.'

'We could try,' said Bertie.

'But then in the film the people who stopped were bank robbers,' Ranald continued. 'They were being chased by the police.'

'Maybe not then,' said Bertie.

It was while this conversation was taking place that Bertie noticed a boy walking towards them on the platform. He was a few years older than they were, Bertie thought, but his expression was friendly, and he seemed keen to speak to them.

'You seen my dad?' the boy asked.

Bertie shook his head.

'He was going to pick me up here,' the boy said. 'We're taking some yowes down to Lanark – although we're going to my auntie's place in Balerno first.'

'I haven't seen him,' said Bertie. Then he thought: *Balerno*. Balerno was just outside Edinburgh – on the edge of the city. He looked at the boy.

'Can we come with you?' he asked.

The boy frowned. 'In the back of the lorry? You wouldn't mind travelling with the yowes in the back?'

'No,' said Bertie. 'We wouldn't mind, would we Ranald?'

Ranald looked doubtful, but eventually nodded.

'Because my dad might not say yes if I ask him whether you can sit in the cab with us.'

'Of course,' said Bertie. 'But don't worry, we'll sneak in. He won't see us.'

'In that case, you can come,' said the boy. 'And that's him coming. See that lorry over there? That's him.'

Smuggled into the back of the lorry, they set off. Buffeted by the sheep, Bertie and Ranald eventually found a place to sit, and spent the next few hours in the rough warmth and odour of a herd of Scottish Blackface ewes. By the time the lorry drew up in Balerno, in the driveway of a well-set bungalow in a quiet street, Bertie and Ranald had had more than enough of their ovine travelling companions and were happy to start the walk back along the Water of Leith pathway. Signs erected for hikers obligingly showed them the way, and within a couple of hours, having said goodbye to one another under the towering arches of the Slateford aqueduct, they were standing before their respective front doors, worried about being scolded for absenting themselves, but relieved at having found their way home so easily.

Nicola opened the door to Bertie and fell upon him with shouts of inarticulate delight. Stuart appeared and picked him up bodily, hugging him so tight that Bertie struggled for breath. Similar scenes took place at Ranald Braveheart Macpherson's house, although Ranald's father was still in Aberdeen and was obliged to enthuse by telephone.

Nicola put Bertie straight into the bath and washed away the smell of sheep. 'It could have been worse,' she said. 'It could have been pigs.' Then, when he was thoroughly washed, and clad now in fresh clothing, she heard his account of his escape.

'I wasn't happy in Aberdeen,' Bertie said. 'Please don't make me go back.'

'Of course we won't,' Nicola promised.

It fell to Stuart to inform Irene of Bertie's safe return. 'And I'm afraid he won't be coming back up,' he said.

There was an ominous silence at the other end of the line. Then Irene's voice, severe and threatening, broke the silence. 'We shall see about that,' she said.

Nicola grabbed the phone from Stuart. 'You listen to me, Irene Pollock,' she said. 'Bertie has voted with his feet. Do you understand that? With his feet. And let me make this one hundred per cent clear, in case you haven't taken it in: Bertie stays here. Full stop. End of story. Here, Scotland Street.'

Bertie listened. He did not like conflict. He knew that his mother wanted the best for him. He knew that his grandmother wanted the same thing. And his father too. They all wanted the best for him. And that made him feel a whole lot better. He imagined how hard it would be to go through life without anybody at all wanting the best for you.

Bertie was composed of love – pure love. He wanted nobody to be unhappy. He wanted them to enjoy their lives. He wanted that so much – more than he could express, in fact.

He went to Nicola's side. 'Please tell Mummy something,' he whispered.

Nicola looked down at him.

'Tell Mummy that I love her – I really do. But could I please love her from Edinburgh, rather than from Aberdeen?'

Nicola caught her breath. Into the receiver she said, 'Did you hear that, Irene?'

There was silence on the line down from Aberdeen. No humming. No cackle. Just silence. Irene had heard what Bertie said.

'Tell him if that's what he wants,' she said, 'then that's all right by me. Because I *do* love him, you know.'

Nicola struggled with herself. Plato's white horse would take her chariot one way, and his dark horse another. The struggle was resolved, for now she said to Irene, 'I know that, Irene. I know that you love him a great deal.'

Later, Nicola tried to work out how Irene could have managed such a volte-face. There are roads to Damascus, she told herself. People travel on them.

## 61. How the Cyclops Felt

The return of Bertie and Ranald Braveheart Macpherson took place on a Saturday. On that Sunday, Big Lou and Bob walked to South Queensferry and back, through Dalmeny, taking Finlay with them. Finlay was a keen walker and when unobserved would practise his leaps and pirouettes, sometimes using the bough of a tree as a barre or a fallen trunk as a platform from which to cast himself briefly into space. When he did this in Bob's view, he received enthusiastic applause – a compliment that would be returned when Bob, walking through the woods at Dalmeny, stopped to pick up the occasional felled pine and tossed it casually through the air – a caber arc across the sky.

Big Lou had left James in charge of the coffee bar. He had shown himself to be completely capable of running it singlehandedly, and this had liberated her from the constant responsibility of ensuring a steady supply of cups of coffee, cheese scones, and bacon rolls. Like any owner of a small business, she had found the demands of work oppressive. Now she could take time off to spend in the company of Bob and Finlay, and she was luxuriating in the sheer pleasure of being with the two people who had come to mean everything to her.

Their plans for the Drummond Place Highland Games were now at an advanced stage. Permission had been obtained from the Gardens Committee, and several notices advertising the event had been prominently displayed in the area. Local businesses had donated prizes, and catering requirements were being met by Nicola's firm in Glasgow, Inclusive Pies, which had agreed to send over a large supply of Scotch pies at a very favourable price. James had been involved too: he had baked several trays of shortbread and obtained three kegs of ale to be served in biodegradable paper cups. Everything was ready and lined up, including the equipment needed for the events themselves – the caber, the hammers, the tug-of-war ropes, the sacks for the sack races, and bales of hay to pre-vent people from hurting themselves in the various contests planned as the afternoon's entertainment. Bob had even secured the services of a Scottish dancing team that would perform various dances on a raised platform, clad in short tartan skirts, tartan knickers, and white blouses with frills. A small pipe band, known for its enthusiasm rather than its skill, had agreed to play as the Games began, during the interval between events, and at the conclusion of proceedings. The prizes were to be awarded by Domenica's friend, Mary Davidson. Everything was in place.

As they walked through Dalmeny Estate, the Firth of Forth stretching out in front of them, Big Lou asked Bob whether he was proposing to enter any of the competitions himself. He thought about this for a while before he said, 'I'm not sure, Lou. What do you think?'

'Some folk might think it unfair,' Big Lou said. 'It would be like giving yourself a prize, don't you think?'

'I wouldn't necessarily win,' said Bob. 'Some of my friends have agreed to take part. They're pretty good.'

'Even so,' said Lou. 'Family hold back. You know that saying?'

Bob did. 'You're right, Lou. As always.'

She basked in his praise. Few people had ever said any-thing like that to Big Lou – indeed, throughout her life she had received very little praise from any quarter. She had worked hard on the farm as a child, and had received scant thanks or acknowledgement of her efforts. That was not because she had been unappreciated – it was simply because she came from a part of the world where people did not think it necessary to say too much. You said what needed to be said and left it at that. You did not waste words. And here was this man – this kind, considerate man, saying that she was right. Bless you, Bob, she said under her breath; bless you Bob, and thank you.

Over the days that followed, Angus helped Bob to install the platform, pitch the small marquee that had been hired, and generally prepare the grassy expanse in the middle of the garden, where the main events were to take place. This was an open area, rather like a glade, which allowed adequate room for the tossing of the caber and the throwing of the hammer. The track events could take place on the perimeter of this space.

Observing the preparations from her window, Domenica reflected on the tribal nature of the forthcoming gathering. The prism through which anthropology viewed the world – the prism of *otherness*, had of course been abandoned, and not before time; now it was not the differences between societies so much as the similarities that engaged the attention of members of her profession. There was no difference, she thought, between these Highland Games and the trials of strength she had observed in the remote New Guinean village in which she had spent six months in her early post-doctoral years. Human society, she felt, was much the same, whatever its external trappings. At heart we were all concerned with the same essentials: food, shelter, security, and status. All the rest was little more than the superficial complication of these eternal fundamentals. And complication, she told herself, was nothing of which to be proud. Complication was not the same as culture.

But what function, she wondered, did these trials of strength, these crude competitions to see who could throw things furthest, jump higher than others, or most effortlessly transfer heavy weights from one place to another? What was the point? Was it a form of mating selection: sorting out whose genes were the most likely to produce the fittest children, the offspring most likely to survive? Was it that simple, that sociobiologically focused?

And as for the strong men themselves – what went on in their heads? How did they see themselves? Were they concerned with strength because that was all they had?

It was not always a simple matter of being strong. She thought, rather inconsequentially, of Polyphemos, the one-eyed giant and son of Poseidon, who had trapped Odysseus and his crew in his cave. She thought of his rage and his throwing of boulders into the sea, and of his unhappiness. She thought of how he had been outwitted, because that was what such a person must fear above all – being outwitted by nimbler, more adroit opponents, who would laugh at you in your strength, would mock your ungainliness, and eventually, with impunity, evade your angry lashing out.

She felt sorry for Polyphemos. Odysseus and his men were interlopers, who stood for colonialism and intrusion. Polyphemos represented their horror of the *other*, the *indigène*, made to appear brutish when the brutishness, in reality, came from their own side – from those who would make the Cyclops creatures feel bad about themselves, feel inadequate, feel unentitled. Of course, such creatures would throw rocks into the sea in their rage. Who wouldn't?

## 62. Let the Games Begin

'Of course you're nervous,' Big Lou said to Fat Bob on the morning of the Games. 'These are the first Games you've ever organised yourself.' She paused. 'And dinnae worry, Bob – this is going to be a big success.'

'Mega,' said Finlay.

'Aye, mega,' Big Lou agreed.

'I hope so, Lou,' said Bob. 'Last night I was lying there thinking, *What if nobody comes? What then?*'

Big Lou made light of his fears. 'But of course folk are going to come. Lots have already said so: Angus, Domenica, Elspeth, Matthew; their wee boys. Matthew says he's had them all fitted with kilts for the occasion. They're all coming. Bruce. Antonia and that nun of hers. Those students who live in the flat below Angus and Domenica. You ken them, Bob? The tall one told me he was coming and that he'd bring some friends from the university who were good runners, he said. And James Holloway. He's coming. He said he was going to try throwing the hammer. He said he was already practising, but I had to tell him it wasn't an ordinary household hammer – the sort you get in toolboxes. He seemed a bit disappointed, but he's still going to try.'

Bob looked a bit more cheerful. 'That's reassuring, Lou. Having a big crowd makes a difference. Atmosphere, you know.'

'You cannae have too much atmosphere,' said Big Lou.

'There's atmosphere in the sky,' joined in Finlay, who had been listening to the exchange.

'Aye, you're right there, wee fellow,' said Fat Bob. 'We'd be gey trochled if we didnae have atmosphere.'

These predictions of a good turnout might have been optimistic, but, as eleven o'clock approached – the hour at which the Games were due to be inaugurated – a sizeable throng of people had assembled at the west gate of Drummond Place Garden.

'You see, Bob,' Big Lou said, as the pipe band wheezed into action and the first members of the public were admitted. 'It's already a big success.'

Fat Bob was still slightly on edge, but it did not show, and within a few minutes of the opening of the gates he was beaming with pleasure, giving instructions to his helpers and greeting some of the professional strongmen whom he had lured into participating. The prize money – such as it was – would normally not have attracted any of these competitors, but favours had been called in. The fact that he was the organiser also helped: Fat Bob was popular on the Highland Games circuit, and most of the professionals present would have willingly supported him in any venture he undertook.

The pipe band paraded, the notes of *I See Mull* drifting up to the windows of the surrounding buildings. Dogs barked, children squealed with delight, the crackling sound of an ancient public address system announced the first of the events; smoke drifted up from the food stall; passers-by stopped to stare and then to join in. The few clouds that had been in the sky cleared, as if dispersing on the orders of the

Chieftain of the Games. Angus, wearing his steward's badge, a Glengarry on his head, girt with his faded kilt, moved amongst the lined-up competitors, instructing one, exhorting another, pointing out on the programme where individual events would take place.

Near the judges' tent, the place from which the Games would be ring-mastered, Domenica sat with a small group of friends, enjoying the spectacle. To Dilly Emslie, one of her longest-standing friends, she pointed out Fat Bob, singing his praises as she did so.

'I've never seen Big Lou so happy,' she confided. 'And she certainly deserves it.'

Dilly agreed that Fat Bob seemed to be just the right man for Big Lou. 'It wouldn't seem right for her to marry a mousey man,' she said. 'And there are one or two of those around these days.'

They surveyed the crowd, hoping to identify an example, but there was none that stood out, which was not surprising, perhaps, as that was what mousey men, by definition, tended not to do.

'I have a feeling,' Domenica said, 'that these Games are somehow *right*. It's odd. I don't quite know how to put it, but I feel that the *energy* here is just as it should be.' She paused. 'I know that sounds a bit New Agey, but ...'

Dilly smiled. 'I know what you mean. But I think you're right. There are moments when it seems that the world is at peace with itself. It's curious. But you know them when they happen.'

'And we have had rather a difficult time, haven't we?' Domenica continued. 'It seems to me that there's been so much confrontation and conflict. Where does one look for something positive?'

'Perhaps over there,' said Dilly. She pointed towards a corner of the garden where Elspeth and Matthew were standing with their triplets, holding the hands of the boys who, although overwhelmed by the noise and the movement, were looking at the scene with expressions of wonder.

'Look at them in their little kilts,' said Domenica. 'Oh, my goodness, I'm welling up inside . . .' She pointed at Bertie and Ranald Braveheart Macpherson, both of whom had been given a role as runners, carrying results from the judges of individual events to the tent where they were recorded. They, too, were in their kilts.

The caber tossing was about to begin, and their conversation paused as they watched five extremely muscular men, clad only in kilts, singlets, and rough working boots, take their place beside a couple of heavy poles. The first competitor, a red-haired mesomorph with impossibly bulging biceps, struggled to lift the pole, managed to get it vertical, and then, with a few staggering steps, tossed it across the grass. The judges ran after it, tape measures at the ready, to record the length of the throw. A cheer arose from Domenica's student neighbours. 'Epic!' shouted one.

More cabers were tossed, and a winner was identified. This was one Rab Macreadie, from Fife, who waved a hand to his cheering supporters when his name was announced as winner. Then Billy Gilmore, from Ayrshire, won the men's long jump, and received his two-pound prize with dignity and modesty. Cookie Dunbar, from Kirkintilloch, won most of the women's running events, but generously declined to take home more than one first prize, donating it instead to the competitor who finished last. 'It's not just coming first that's important,' she said. 'Coming last is important too.'

Now it was time for the hammer throwing, and silence descended as the first of the entrants, Rab Macreadie, who had distinguished himself in the caber tossing, took to the field. Round and round he twirled before, with a grunt that could be heard throughout the garden, he let slip the hammer shaft and sent the implement on its journey: a mighty throw that stretched the judges' tape measures to their limits.

The next to step forward was Bruce. In the past he would have done so with braggadocio, savouring the attention, preening himself as he prepared to throw. Not so now; he was a picture of self-effacement as if he had been pressed to compete only in order to keep numbers up.

He picked up the hammer and began to twirl. Round and round he went, until, after he lost his grip at a critical moment, the hammer prematurely left his hand, sailing off in entirely the wrong direction. Although not as burly as Fat Bob and his friends, Bruce was powerfully built, and the hammer had considerable velocity. It crossed the road and made landfall through the window of a house on the south side of Drummond Place, landing in a shower of glass. Nobody was hurt – not even the man at whose feet it came to rest. He was playing the harpsichord at the time, and barely missed a note.

'Caroline,' he called to his wife. 'A Turner Prize event has occurred in the drawing room.'

And with that he continued his prelude by Bach.

## 63. A Hammer Hurled

The Games drew to a triumphant conclusion. The major events – the caber tossing and the hammer throwing – were dominated, as Fat Bob had expected they would be, by the professional entrants. The results of the tug of war, though, in which sixteen sides competed, were more difficult to predict. A team of Watsonians emerged victorious in the final heats, beating a side composed of Hearts supporters; the Fettesian team came last, not even managing to beat the Scottish Arts Club team, which was two members short.

The children's relay race, although supervised by Big Lou herself, was marked by blatant cheating. That was won by Olive's team, in which she, Pansy, and their friend, Arabella, elbowed, tripped up, and generally disrupted the efforts of Bertie, Ranald Braveheart Macpherson, and an unknown boy with spectacles. At the end of the race, the boy with spectacles complained vociferously to Big Lou, who unfortunately had seen none of the foul play.

'They cheated, miss,' said the boy. 'Those girls cheated like mad. They tripped me up twice and that one . . .' He pointed an accusing finger at Olive, 'That one tried to tie my laces together.'

Ranald Braveheart Macpherson nodded. 'He's right,' he protested. 'They're the biggest cheats in Scotland. Ask anyone.'

Olive bristled with indignation. 'Oh, listen to the poor losers. Sad. Tragic. Listen to them. They can't bear the thought that the girls have won. They can't bear it.'

'Male privilege,' spat out Pansy. 'It's always the same. They think they should win everything.'

Bertie put an arm around Ranald's shoulder. 'Don't worry, Ranald. We know we would have won. That's the import-ant thing.'

'But it's so unfair,' sniffed Ranald Braveheart Macpherson.

Bertie sighed. 'Lots of things are unfair, Ranald,' he said.

Big Lou felt unable to disturb the result, although she had her suspicions, and the first prize was awarded to Olive's team.

'See,' said Olive. 'That's going to give you something to think about, Bertie Pollock. The days of boys winning any-thing are over.'

'Finished,' said Pansy.

Olive was ready to rub it in. 'Yes, finished. Past tense, Bertie. You and Ranald and that stupid boy with glasses are *soo* past tense.'

At the end of the Games, after the pipe band had played its last tune and the spectators had left the garden, Domenica went back to her flat in Scotland Street to prepare for the dinner that she and Angus were hosting to mark the occasion. The menu was to be the same as it always was, as nobody really wanted anything new to happen. Why should they, when what they were used to was so perfect?

It was a slightly larger gathering than usual, though, as the students from down below came up, and Fat Bob and Big Lou had been invited too. While they were waiting for dinner to be served, Roger Collins and Judith McClure jointly proposed a toast to the newly engaged couple. 'To Big Lou and Fat Bob,' said Roger, raising his glass. 'May your happiness be complete,' added Judith.

There was a murmur of assent, but this was soon followed by spontaneous applause, led by the students. They knew neither Big Lou nor Fat Bob, of course, but they were still at that stage of life where they liked everybody – because they thought everybody was the same. And as the evening progressed, that liking became firmer and more real as they talked to the newly engaged couple. Torquil spent a good hour in conversation with Domenica and Big Lou, discussing the essays he had been writing at university. He had finished Nero and had embarked on an examination of the persistence of myth.

'Nothing is original, you know,' he said airily.

'Including that statement,' Domenica said wryly, but added, immediately, 'Sorry, I didn't mean to sound dismissive.'

Torquil laughed. 'Oh, I don't mind. I have a tutor who sits there and winces whenever any of us say anything. Now *that's* dismissive.'

'But what you say is true,' said Big Lou. 'When did you last hear anybody say anything new?'

Domenica looked thoughtful. 'Occasionally somebody questions the consensus. But it's rare: there's immense pressure to conform.'

This chimed with Big Lou. 'Aye, you're right. People are becoming afraid to think for themselves. They're definitely afraid to express their views in case they offend somebody.'

'The classics are pretty offensive,' said Torquil. 'Did you see that piece in the papers recently about removing texts that might offend students because of violence and so on?'

'Which would leave very little,' said Domenica.

'Exactly,' said Torquil. 'Nothing, in fact. Take the *Odyssey*. Look at the way Odysseus behaves when he gets home. Where's the forgiveness? Not there. Instead, there's a bloodbath. Odysseus goes and . . .'

'Goes and behaves exactly like an ancient Greek?' interjected Domenica.

Big Lou laughed. 'That's the way they were. And we were too. Scotland was red in tooth and claw until . . . well, yesterday, I suppose.'

Domenica was not sure that she would go quite that far. 'There must have been peaceful corners, surely. And relatively peaceful times, too. Isn't it thought that Macbeth's rule was benevolent and relatively untroubled? And yet he got such a bad press.'

'Shakespeare's fault,' said Torquil.

'Mind you,' said Domenica, returning to the *Odyssey*. 'I was thinking only the other day of the Cyclops. I forget why he crossed my mind, but he did.' She paused. She remembered now: it had been his strength, and she had been thinking of the strong men at the Games.

Torquil became animated. 'But there you are, you see. Polyphemos is completely pertinent to what we're talking about.'

'What are we talking about?' asked Big Lou, and laughed.

'That whole encounter,' Torquil continued, 'can be read in a way that's sympathetic to the Cyclops. There are whole papers on the issue, you know. I've been wading through them. And a fantastic book, *The Return of Ulysses*. It's by a classics professor called Edith Hall. It's about how Homer has penetrated every corner of our culture – and still does. There are films . . . every year there are films that are replays of the story of Odysseus. Again and again. Computer games. Comic strips. Fan fiction. The lot. It goes on and on. It's *the* big story.'

Domenica listened carefully. Torquil was right. 'It's because we're all yearning for home,' she said. '*Heimat*, as the Germans put it. We want to find the place we've lost. We remember it, but when we look out of our window, it's not always there. So we look for it.'

'And do we find it?' asked Torquil.

'Sometimes,' said Domenica, and then added, 'Almost.' She paused. 'Scotland,' she said simply.

Big Lou was silent. Then she said. 'Is that what you're looking for, Domenica?'

Domenica looked into the eyes of her two friends, suddenly aware, with great clarity, of their humanity.

## 64. *Love, Simpliciter*

'The only reason I can be here,' Elspeth said to Stuart, 'is because James – you know him, I think, our au pair – has taken the boys back to Nine Mile Burn. He has his driving licence now, and it takes all the pressure off.'

'I know what you mean,' said Stuart. 'The only reason I can be out is because of my mother. She looks after Bertie and Ulysses. She does the shopping. She does everything. I do my best to help, of course ...'

Elspeth assured him that she knew that he did. 'I've always known you were hands-on,' she said. 'With Irene being so ...' She stopped herself.

'Don't worry,' said Stuart. 'You can say what you like. I made a mistake. I know that.'

Elspeth waited. Then, very cautiously, she said, 'In marrying her in the first place?'

Stuart looked down at the floor. He had been loyal. For years he had said nothing, but now he felt that he could be honest. He nodded.

Elspeth reached out and touched his forearm gently. He looked up. She did not say anything.

'Yes,' Stuart continued. 'We weren't suited. She never thought much of me.'

'I don't know,' said Elspeth. 'I'm sure she appreciated you – in her way.'

Stuart smiled. 'You're being kind.'

'No, I mean it.'

'Perhaps she did,' Stuart conceded. 'Anyway, it's over now. We had a long conversation yesterday. We've agreed to go our separate ways properly now. She told me she wants to marry Dr Fairbairn.'

Elspeth hesitated. But did Dr Fairbairn want to marry Irene?

'Apparently he does,' said Stuart. 'And that makes me happy for her. I know that may sound corny, but I don't want her to be unhappy.'

'Of course you don't.' Elspeth paused. 'Will you ... Will you find somebody now?'

Stuart nodded. 'I'm going to be serious about it. I'm ready.'

'Good.'

'And you?' Stuart asked. 'How are you feeling ... about everything?'

Elspeth shrugged. 'I'm all right. I felt a bit low, I suppose, being stuck out of town with the boys, but I've thought long and hard about it, and I'm all right with that. I realised that it's going to get better. They're growing up, and I don't want to miss their being little anyway. I've reminded myself to value what I have.'

'Which is a lot,' said Stuart. 'Matthew. And the boys. And that house of yours. And the view of the hills.'

Elspeth smiled. 'I suppose we should all remind ourselves of our view. Things may get bad, and then we say to ourselves, *Remember your view.*'

'And everything looks better,' said Stuart.

Elspeth leaned forward to whisper something to him. 'Over there. Bruce. Have you heard?'

Stuart followed her gaze to the other side of the room where Bruce was sitting next to Sister Maria-Fiore dei Fiori di Montagna, deep in conversation. 'I find it hard to believe,' he said.

'Yes, it's true. He's going up to Pluscarden Abbey next week.'

'All from being struck by lightning?' Stuart looked across

the room again. 'Will one of the monks shave his hair off, do you think? What about that hair gel of his?'

Elspeth laughed. 'I read a book by Iris Murdoch in which one by one she made her characters better. At the end there was only one – a real psychopath – whom she had to work out how to redeem. So you know what she did?'

'No.'

'She had him see a UFO. He was changed completely.'

Stuart rolled his eyes. 'Novels should be credible. That sounds a bit unlikely.'

'Maybe it's life that's unlikely,' said Elspeth. 'Who would have thought that Big Lou would meet somebody called Fat Bob? And that he would toss the caber? And that they'd be blissfully happy?'

Stuart shook his head. 'I always believed that,' he said. 'Always.'

From a corner of the room, James Holloway tapped a glass for silence. 'Every year,' he said, 'Angus writes a poem for us. This has not been an easy year for many, but perhaps that makes his poem all the more important.'

'It does,' agreed Dilly.

Angus rose to his feet. 'I thought I might say something about love,' he said. 'Because love, as well all know, is at the heart of the lives of all of us – whether we know it or not.' He paused. He closed his eyes. 'So this is about love.'

> Love [he began] *is as often about what does not happen*
> *As it is about what actually occurs;*
> *Love is to be found in things unsaid*
> *When it would be easy, or tempting,*

*To say something harsh or unkind;*
*Love is a matter of silences,*
*Just as much as it is of open declaration;*
*Love is never concealed nor disguised,*
*Its face and position are always familiar,*
*Which means that it is only rarely*
*Mistaken for what it is not;*
*Love is not diminished by use –*
*That is its particular miracle; love fills*
*The entire space it is offered,*
*Never denies those who approach it,*
*Turns none away who mean what they say;*
*Love merely warns: "Make sure you choose*
*That form of my expression that is true to you."*
*Love remains on duty constantly,*
*Is never dimmed by night, nor too faint*
*To assume the demands of the day;*
*If you would say anything about love*
*To one about to embark on life's journey,*
*It might be this: There is only one guide*
*To which you should pay attention,*
*And that guide is love; only one voice*
*Whose whispers should be heeded,*
*And that voice is love; remember that, my dear,*
*I ask you to remember that.'*

Angus sat down. There was silence. But after a moment or two, they heard, from outside, the sound of one of the pipers who had entertained them at the Games playing a final tune before he went home. They waited until the last notes had drifted away. There is a particular silence at the end of a piece of pipe music. It is very moving.

THE END

(for the time being, at least)